RICHARD RUSSO'S
THE RISK POOL

ALSO BY RICHARD RUSSO,
AVAILABLE FROM VINTAGE CONTEMPORARIES

Mohawk

T H E
R I S K
P O O L

THE
RISK
POOL

RICHARD RUSSO

VINTAGE CONTEMPORARIES
VINTAGE BOOKS
A DIVISION OF RANDOM HOUSE, INC.
NEW YORK

FIRST VINTAGE CONTEMPORARIES EDITION, November 1989

A portion of this book appeared
in slightly different form in *Granta*
(Granta #19, Fall 1986).

Library of Congress Cataloging-in-Publication Data
Russo, Richard, 1949–
The risk pool/Richard Russo.—1st Vintage contemporaries ed.
p. cm.—(Vintage contemporaries)
"Originally published, in hardcover, by Random House, Inc., New
York, in 1988"—T.p. verso.
ISBN 0-679-72334-X: $8.95
I. Title.
[PS3568.U812R57 1989]   89-40075
813'.54—dc20   CIP

The town of Mohawk, like its residents,
is located only in the author's imagination.

Manufactured in the United States of America
10   9   8   7   6   5   4   3   2   1

For Jim Russo
In Memoriam

Its inhabitants are, as the man once said, "whores, pimps, gamblers, and sons of bitches," by which he meant Everybody. Had the man looked through another peephole he might have said, "Saints and angels and martyrs and holy men," and he would have meant the same thing.

—John Steinbeck, *Cannery Row*

ACKNOWLEDGMENTS

The author gratefully acknowledges support from Southern Connecticut State University and Southern Illinois University, Carbondale while he was working on this book. Special thanks also, for faith and assistance, to Nat Sobel, David Rosenthal, Gary Fisketjon, Greg Gottung, Jean Findlay and, always, my wife Barbara.

PART 1

FOURTH OF JULY

1

My father, unlike so many of the men he served with, knew just what he wanted to do when the war was over. He wanted to drink and whore and play the horses. "He'll get tired of it," my mother said confidently. She tried to keep up with him during those frantic months after the men came home, but she couldn't, because nobody had been shooting at her for the last three years and when she woke up in the morning it wasn't with a sense of surprise. For a while it was fun, the late nights, the dry martinis, the photo finishes at the track, but then she was suddenly pregnant with me and she decided it was time the war was over for real. Most everybody she knew was settling down, because you could only celebrate, even victory, so long. I don't think it occurred to her that my father wasn't celebrating victory and never had been. He was celebrating life. His. She could tag along if she felt like it, or not if she didn't, whichever suited her. "He'll get tired of it," she told my grandfather, himself recently returned, worn and riddled with malaria, to the modest house in Mohawk he had purchased with a two-hundred-dollar down payment the year after the conclusion of the earlier war he'd been too young to legally enlist for. This second time around he felt no urge to celebrate victory or anything else. His wife had died when he was in the Pacific, but they had fallen out of love anyway, which was one of the reasons he'd enlisted at age forty-two for a war he had little desire to fight. But she had not been a bad woman, and the fact that he felt no loss at her passing depressed and disappointed him. From his hospital bed in New London, Connecticut, he read books and wrote his memoirs while the younger men, all malaria convalescents, played poker and waited for weekend passes from the ward. In their condition it took little enough to get good and drunk, and by early Saturday night most of them had the shakes so bad they had to huddle in the dark corners of cheap hotel rooms to await Monday morning and readmission to the hospital. But they'd lived through worse, or thought they had. My grandfather watched them systematically destroy any chance they had for recovery and so he understood my father. He may even have tried to explain things to his daughter when she told him of the trial separation that would last only until my father could get his priorities straight again, little suspecting he already did. "Trouble with you is," my father told her, "you think you got the pussy market cornered." Unfortunately, she took this observation to be merely a reflection of the fact that in her present swollen condition, she was not herself. Perhaps she couldn't corner the market just then, but she'd cornered it once, and would again. And she must have figured too that when my father got a look at his son it would change him, change them both. *Then* the war would be over.

The night I was born my grandfather tracked him to a poker game in a dingy room above the Mohawk Grill. My father was holding a well-concealed two pair and waiting for the seventh card in a game of stud. The news that he was a father did not impress him particularly. The service revolver did. My grandfather was wheezing from the steep, narrow flight of stairs, at the top of which he stopped to catch his breath, hands on his knees. Then he took out the revolver and stuck the cold barrel in my father's ear and said, "Stand up, you son of a bitch." This from a man who'd gone two wars end to end without uttering a profanity. The men at the table could smell his malaria and they began to sweat.

"I'll just have a peek at this last card," my father said. "Then we'll go."

The dealer rifled cards around the table and everybody dropped lickety-split, including a man who had three deuces showing.

"Deal me out a couple a hands," my father said, and got up slowly because he still had a gun in his ear.

At the hospital, my mother had me on her breast and she must have looked pretty, like the girl who'd cornered the pussy market before the war. "Well?" my father said, and when she turned me over, he grinned at my little stem and said, "What do you know?" It must have been a tender moment.

Not that it changed anything. Six months later my grandfather was dead, and the day after the funeral, for which my father

arrived late and unshaven, my mother filed for divorce, thereby
losing in a matter of days the two men in her life.

They may have departed my mother's, but my father and grandfather remained the two pivotal figures in my own young life. Of
the two, the grandfather I had no recollection of was the more
vivid, thanks to my mother. By the time I was six I was full of lore
concerning him, and now, at age thirty-five, I can still quote him
chapter and verse. "There are four seasons in Mohawk," he always remarked (in my mother's voice). "Fourth of July, Mohawk
Fair, Eat the Bird, and Winter." No way around it, Mohawk winters did cling to our town tenaciously. Deep into spring, when
tulips were blooming elsewhere, brown crusted snowbanks still
rose high from the terraces along our streets, and although yellow
water ran along the curbs, forming tunnels beneath the snow, the
banks themselves shrank reluctantly, and it had been known to
snow cruelly in May. It was late June before the ground was firm
enough for baseball, and by Labor Day the sun had already lost
its conviction when the Mohawk Fair opened. Then leper-white-
skinned men, studies in congenital idiocy, hooked up the thick
black snake-cables to a rattling generator that juiced The Tilt-A-
Whirl, The Whip, and The Hammer. Down out of the hills they
came, these white-skinned men with stubbled chins, to run the
machines and leer at the taut blue faces of frightened children,
leaning heavily and more heavily still on the metal bar that hurtled us faster and faster. When the garish colored lights of the
midway, strung carelessly from one wooden pole to the next came
down that first Tuesday morning in September, you could feel
winter in the air. Fourth of July, Mohawk Fair, Eat the Bird, and
Winter. I was an adult before I realized how cynical my grandfather's observation was, his summer reduced to a single day; autumn to a third-rate mix of carnival rides, evil-smelling animals,
mud and manure; Thanksgiving reduced to an obligatory carnivo-
rous act, a "foul consumption," he termed it; the rest Winter,
capitalized. These became the seasons of my mother's life after
she realized the truth of my father's observation about the pussy
market. She worked for the telephone company and knew all
about places with better seasons. At the end of the day she told
me about the other operators she'd chatted with in places like
Tucson, Arizona; and Albuquerque, New Mexico; and San Diego,

California; where they capitalized the word Summer. "Someday
. . ." she said, allowing her voice to trail off. "Someday." Her
inability to find a verb (or a subject, for that matter: I? We?) to give
direction to her thought puzzled me then, but I've since concluded she didn't truly believe in the existence of Tucson, Arizona, or perhaps didn't believe that her personal seasons would
be significantly altered by geographical considerations. She had
inherited my grandfather's modest house, and that rooted her to
the spot. Its tiny mortgage payments were a blessing, because my
mother was not overpaid by the telephone company. But the
plumbing and electrical system were antiquated, and she was
never able to get far enough ahead to do more than fix a pipe or
individual wall socket. And of course the painters, roofers, electri-
cians, and plumbers all saw her coming. So she subscribed to
Arizona Highways and we stayed put.

Until I was six I thought of my father the way I thought of "my
heavenly father," whose existence was a matter of record, but
who was, practically speaking, absent and therefore irrelevant.
My mother had filed for divorce the day after my grandfather's
funeral, but she didn't end up getting it. When he heard what she
was up to, my father went to see her lawyer. He didn't exactly
have an appointment, but then he didn't need one out in the
parking lot where he strolled back and forth, his fists thrust deep
into his pockets, his steaming breath visible in the cold, waiting
until F. William Peterson, Attorney-At-Law, closed up. It was one
of the bleak dead days between Christmas and New Year's. I don't
think my mother specifically warned F. William there would be
serious opposition to her design and that the opposition might
conceivably be extralegal in nature. F. William Peterson had been
selected by my mother precisely because he was not a Mohawk
native and did not know my father. He had moved there just a
few months before to join as a junior partner a firm which employed his law school roommate. I imagine he had already begun
to doubt his decision to come to Mohawk even before meeting my
father in the gray half-light of late afternoon. F. William Peterson
was a soft man of some bulk, well dressed in a knee-length overcoat with a fur collar, when he finally appeared in the deserted
parking lot at quarter to five. Never an athletic man, he was
engaged in pulling on a fine new pair of gloves, a Christmas gift

from Mrs. Peterson, while trying at the same time not to lose his footing on the ice. My father never wore gloves and was not wearing any that day. For warmth, he blew into his cupped hands, steam escaping from between his fingers, as he came toward F. William Peterson, who, intent on his footing and his new gloves, hadn't what a fair-minded man would call much of a chance. Finding himself suddenly seated on the ice, warm blood salty on his lower lip, the attorney's first conclusion must have been that somehow, despite his care, he had managed to lose his balance. Just as surprisingly, there was somebody standing over him who seemed to be making rather a point of not offering him a hand up. It wasn't even a hand that dangled in F. William's peripheral vision, but a fist. A clenched fist. And it struck the lawyer in the face a second time before he could account for its being there.

F. William Peterson was not a fighting man. Indeed, he had not been in the war, and had never offered physical violence to any human. He loathed physical violence in general, and this physical violence in particular. Every time he looked up to see where the fist was, it struck him again in the face, and after this happened several times, he considered it might be better to stop looking up. The snow and ice were pink beneath him, and so were his new gloves. He thought about what his wife, an Italian woman five years his senior and recently grown very large and fierce, would say when she saw them and concluded right then and there, as if it were his most pressing problem, that he would purchase an identical pair on the way home. Had he been able to see his own face, he'd have known that the gloves were not his most pressing problem.

"You do *not* represent Jenny Hall," said the man standing in the big work boots with the metal eyelets and leather laces.

He *did* represent my mother though, and if my father thought that beating F. William Peterson up and leaving him in a snow-bank would be the end of the matter he had an imperfect understanding of F. William Peterson and, perhaps, the greater part of the legal profession. My father was arrested half an hour later at the Mohawk Grill in the middle of a hamburg steak. F. William Peterson identified the work boots with the metal eyelets and leather laces, and my father's right hand was showing the swollen effects of battering F. William Peterson's skull. None of which was the sort of identification that was sure to hold up in court, and the lawyer knew it, but getting my father tossed in jail, however briefly, seemed like a good idea. When he was released, pending trial, my father was informed that a peace bond had been sworn against him and that if he, Sam Hall, was discovered in the immediate proximity of F. William Peterson, he would be fined five hundred dollars and incarcerated. The cop who told him all this was one of my father's buddies and was very apologetic when my father wanted to know what the hell kind of free country he'd spent thirty-five months fighting for would allow such a law. It stank, the cop admitted, but if my father wanted F. William Peterson thrashed again, he'd have to get somebody else to do it. That was no major impediment, of course, but my father couldn't be talked out of the premise that in a truly free country, he'd be allowed to do it himself.

So, instead of going to see F. William Peterson, he went to see my mother. *She* hadn't sworn out any peace bond against him that he knew of. Probably she couldn't, being his wife. It might not be perfect, but it was at least some kind of free country they were living in. Here again, however, F. William Peterson was a step ahead of him, having called my mother from his room at the old Nathan Littler Hospital, so she'd be on the lookout. When my father pulled up in front of the house, she called the cops without waiting for pleasantries, of which there turned out to be none anyway. They shouted at each other through the front door she wouldn't unlock.

My mother started right out with the main point. "I don't love you!" she screamed.

"So what?" my father countered. "I don't love you either."

Surprised or not, she did not miss a beat. "I want a divorce."

"Then you can't have one," my father said.

"I don't need your permission."

"Like hell you don't," he said. "And you'll need more than a candy-ass lawyer and a cheap lock to keep me out of my own house." By way of punctuation, he put his shoulder into the door, which buckled but did not give.

"This is my father's house, Sam Hall. *You* never had anything and you never will."

"If you aren't going to open that door," he warned, "you'd better stand back out of the way."

My mother did as she was told, but just then a police cruiser pulled up and my father vaulted the porch railing and headed off through the deep snow in back of the house. One of the cops gave chase while the other circled the block in the car, cutting off my father's escape routes. It must have been quite a spectacle, the one cop chasing, until he was tuckered out, yelling, "We know who you are!" and my father shouting over his shoulder, "So what?" He knew nobody was going to shoot him for what he'd done (what *had* he done, now that he thought about it?). A man certainly had the right to enter his own house and shout at his own wife, which was exactly what she'd keep being until *he* decided to divorce *her.*

It must have looked like a game of tag. All the neighbors came out on their back porches and watched, cheering my father, who dodged and veered expertly beyond the outstretched arms of the pursuing cops, for within minutes, the backyards of our block were lousy with uniformed men who finally succeeded in forming a wide ring and then shrinking it, the neighbors' boos at this unfair tactic ringing in their ears. My mother watched from the back porch as the tough, wet, angry cops closed in on my father. She pretty much decided right there against the divorce idea.

It dawned on her much later that the best way of ensuring my father's absence was to demand he shoulder his share of the burden of raising his son. But until then, life was rich in our neighborhood. When he got out of jail, my father would make a beeline for my mother's house (she'd had his things put in storage and changed the locks, which to her mind pretty much settled the matter of ownership), where he'd be arrested again for disturbing the peace. His visits to the Mohawk County jail got progressively longer, and so each time he got out he was madder than before. Finally, one of his buddies on the Mohawk P.D. took him aside and told him to stay the hell away from Third Avenue, because the judge was all through fooling around. Next time he was run in, he'd be in the slam a good long while. Since that was the way things stood, my father promised he'd be a good boy and go home, wherever that might be. Since one place was as good as another, he rented a room across from the police station so they'd know right where to find him. He borrowed some money and got a couple things out of storage and set them in the middle of the rented room. Then he went out again.

He started drinking around three in the afternoon and by dinnertime found a poker game, a good one, as luck would have it, with all good guys and no problems. Except that by ten my father had lost what he had on him and had to leave the game in search of a soft touch. That time of night, finding somebody with a spare hundred on him was no breeze, even though everybody knew Sam Hall was good for it. He hit a couple of likely spots, then started on the unlikely ones. He got some drinks bought for him, sort of consolation, by people who wouldn't or couldn't loan him serious cash. Midnight found him in the bar of The Elms, a classy restaurant on the outskirts of town, where he tried to put the touch on Jimmy Albanese, and who should walk in but F. William Peterson, and on his arm a good-looking young woman who happened not to be his wife, but was surely someone's. The lawyer took her to a dark, corner booth and they disappeared into its shadows. When the cocktail waitress came back to the bar with their order, my father said he'd cover the round and would she tell his friends "Up the Irish." When F. William Peterson looked over and saw my grinning father with his glass raised, the blood drained from his face. He recognized his former assailant from the diner, of course, and had in fact been on the lookout for him, especially in parking lots, though lately he had relaxed his vigilance somewhat after my mother informed him of her decision to drop divorce proceedings, a decision he went on record as opposing on general principle and because it meant he'd taken a horrible beating for nothing. Had she bothered to inform her husband that she had dropped the suit? the lawyer wondered. Probably not, or what the hell would Sam Hall be doing at The Elms? It would be just like her not to tell him, and now he'd have to think of a way to avoid another beating, this time in a public place. A public place he wasn't supposed to be, in the company of a woman whose husband worked the night shift. The good news was that the bar was still pretty crowded, and he doubted Sam Hall would assault him until the place cleared out a little. He and the young woman could make a run for the parking lot, but he doubted they'd make it and he'd have to explain to the woman why they were running, and this was hardly the image of himself that he chose to cultivate. Probably the best thing, F. William Peterson concluded, would be to determine the man's intentions and try to talk him out of them. So he got up, excused himself, and went over to where my father sat talking to Jimmy Albanese.

"You understand," he said to my father, "that by sitting on that stool, you are violating the peace bond sworn against you, an offense for which you could be incarcerated?"

My father looked over at Jimmy Albanese, who happened to be

the next best thing to a lawyer, having failed the New York bar exam on three separate occasions.

"He's full of shit," was the honorable Jimmy's expert assessment. "You come in first. He's harassing *your* ass."

"I tell you what," my father said. "You let me take a hundred right now, and I forget the whole thing. You get the hundred back on Wednesday. Friday the latest."

It was a strange request, but F. William Peterson was tempted because he was very afraid of my father, who he was now convinced was certifiable. Unfortunately, he was a little short. "I can let you have fifty . . ."

My father frowned. "Fifty."

The lawyer showed him his wallet, which contained fifty-seven dollars.

"All right," my father said reluctantly, pocketing the money. It was better than nothing, and it was easier to touch somebody else for the other half a hundred. And besides, he'd just had an idea. "I guess that makes us even. Thanks."

He was in a hurry, but there was a telephone booth outside The Elms and my father could feel that his luck was changing. Everything was beginning to have that falling-into-place feeling. Before driving to my mother's, he called Mrs. F. William Peterson. Yes, she knew right where The Elms was located. And yes, if she hurried she supposed she could meet her husband there in fifteen minutes.

Now they were even.

By the time he got to Third Avenue it was late and the house was dark, but he managed to raise my mother. "Don't call the cops," he said urgently when he heard stirring inside.

My mother suspected a trick and raised the shade and window tentatively.

"Let me take fifty till tomorrow," he said.

"What?"

"Fifty. I'll pay you back tomorrow and after that I'll stay clear of here."

"Will you give me a divorce?"

"No," he said. "But I won't bother you anymore. That's the deal."

My mother knew him and knew she had him. "We have a son to raise," she said. "I can't do it alone. You'll have to give me fifty a month."

He thought about it. "Okay," he said finally. "Sure."

With matters settled thus satisfactorily out of court, my mother gave him the money and considered herself fortunate, which she was. She would never collect a dime of the informal, modest alimony settlement, but then she didn't expect to. The important thing was that she'd gotten my father to agree to it in a moment of weakness, and he'd feel guilty about not keeping his word, and he'd stay a suitable distance rather than give her the opportunity to bring the matter up. After a year or so, the debt would be considerable and he would be alert to chance meetings on the street and, in effect, she would have her divorce. She slept soundly that night, knowing the burden she had placed on him. As it turned out, her strategy worked better than she could have hoped, because in the middle of June she ran into F. William Peterson, who informed her that Sam Hall had blown town. The lawyer also wanted to know if she'd like to go out with him sometime, what with Mrs. Peterson divorcing him and all.

Mohawk didn't see my father again for nearly six years, and my mother never got over what you could buy with fifty dollars, invested wisely.

2

Even as a child, I never had much use for conventional honesty. I can't remember my first lie, but I do recall the first one I was caught at. Many years later when I was at the university, I confessed it to a young woman I was infatuated with, and she used me for a case study in her psych class, in return for which I got to use her for nonacademic advantage. Here's the story I told her. The true story, more or less, of my first imaginative untruth.

I was a first grader in McKinley Elementary School (kindergarten was optional and we hadn't opted), and word had gotten around among the other children that my father did not live with my mother and me, an unusual circumstance in 1953 and one which made me the center of attention that September, the Mohawk Fair being over, and no real freaks (like the Heroin Monster: "See her, you'll want to kill her!") to gawk at for another year. My mother instructed me to say only that it was nobody's business where my father lived, which suggests how little she understood children if she thought such a lame response would have any effect other than the inflaming of their natural, arrogant curiosity. Happily, I arrived at a more sensible solution to my problem. I informed everyone that my father was dead, and the beneficial effect of this intelligence I felt immediately. I couldn't have been more pleased with myself.

One day, not long after I began telling this lie, however, my teacher, Miss Holiday, took me by the hand and led me outside while the other children, obediently curled up on mats, had been instructed to nap. There at the curb was a lone, dirty white convertible. Inside was a man, and when he leaned across the front seat to open the passenger-side door, my heart did something funny and I stopped right where I was, Miss Holiday pressing up against me from behind. The man in the car had a gray chin, and the fingers that first encircled the steering wheel, then came toward me to release the door lock, were black and calloused. A cigarette dangled carelessly from the man's lips, and bobbed when he spoke. "Thanks, young lady," my father said.

Miss Holiday wasn't pressing against me anymore. Maybe she too was looking at his black fingers. "I don't know about this," she said. "I could lose my job."

"Nah," my father said, and perhaps his failure to elaborate why not was just the right thing, because she suddenly nudged me into the car and scurried back up the walk.

"Well?" said my father. I've often wondered whether he was as sure that I was his son as I was that he was my father. There was little enough physical resemblance at that stage. My hair was blond and curly, his wiry and black and bushy. Did he think that maybe the fool of a young woman had grabbed the wrong kid, or did he feel something when he saw me that said this is the one? "You know who I am?"

I nodded.

"Can you talk?"

I nodded again, feeling my eyes fill.

"Who am I?"

I couldn't force anything out, couldn't look at him, except for the black thumb and finger which pressed the life out of the burning cigarette and deposited the stub in the full ashtray.

"All right," he said. "Who are *you*?"

"Ned," I gulped.

"Ned Who?"

"Ned Hall."

"Right. You know where the name Hall came from?"

I shook my head. He was lighting another cigarette, and when he had done it, he tossed the still burning match into an ashtray, the flame inching down the cardboard stem, leaving it as black as my father's thumb and forefinger.

"Your mother tell you to say I was dead?"

I shook my head.

"Don't lie to me."

I began to cry, because I wasn't lying.

"She'll wish she hadn't," he said. "You can bet your ass."

He sat and smoked and couldn't think of anything else to ask me. "You want to go back to school or do you want some ice cream at the dairy?"

I reached for the door handle, which I couldn't get to move. The black fingers came over and did it. By the time I got back inside, I was shaking so badly that Miss Holiday took me to see the nurse, who examined me, and finding a low-grade fever decided to drive me home. As we turned the corner onto my street, a white convertible fishtailed away from the curb and away up the hill, just as a police car appeared at the rise coming in the opposite direction. Several neighbors were out on their porches and pointed the way of the fleeing convertible, and the patrol car did a clumsy, two-stage U-turn.

"This means war," my mother said when she finally got calmed down. Her eyes were glowing like the tip of my father's cigarette.

War it was.

My mother was game, at least in the beginning. Every time he turned up—he averaged twice a week—she called the cops. For my father's part, it was a guerrilla war, hit and run, in and out. His favorite time was three in the morning below my mother's window, drunk often as not, and ready to kick up a hell of a fuss before vanishing into the night thirty seconds before the cops pulled up. He had a drunk's radar where cops were concerned. One night during the second week of his marauding, a policeman was stationed around back after dark, so my father phoned instead of putting in a personal appearance. "How long is that fat cop planning to squat in the bushes back there?" he asked my mother. "You better draw your blinds, I know *that* son of a bitch." In fact, he knew them all, and that was the problem. Every time a policeman was assigned to us, my father knew about it. Usually, he knew which one.

Nobody seemed able to find out where he was living, though rumor had it that he was working road construction down the line in Albany. His nocturnal visits continued all summer, and by the end of August my mother was done in. At first he just accused her of instructing me to tell everybody he was dead, but he had other gripes too. He'd had a good look at me in the car that day, and he didn't like the way I was turning out. In his opinion she was turning me into a little pussy. And speaking of pussy, he heard she'd been seen around town.

This last accusation was beyond everything. In the six years he'd been gone, my mother might as well have been a nun. She could count the dates she'd had on one hand, she said. "That's not the point," he said. His long absence did not strike him as a mitigating circumstance, any more than did their mutual lack of tender feeling for each other. "You're my wife," he said. "And as long as you are, stay the hell home where you belong."

As I look back on this period in our troubled lives, what astonishes me is how little the trouble touched me. My father's nocturnal raids seldom woke me fully, and the next morning I was only vaguely aware that something had happened during the night. On such mornings my mother always questioned me about how I'd slept, and when I said fine, her expression was equal parts relief and astonishment that it was possible for anybody to sleep through what invariably woke the neighbors. Probably I willed myself to sleep through those episodes, too afraid to wake up. I remember that summer as a nervous time. I was always on the lookout for the white convertible and under explicit instructions to run inside and tell my mother if it appeared.

That year must have been a lonely one for my mother, who had to work all day at the phone company, then come home and endure the horror of being awakened in the middle of the night, sometimes out of sheer anticipation. She had no one to share her burdens with, your average six-year-old being an imperfect confidant. To make matters worse, she had scruples about the way she dealt with my father and even about the way she portrayed him to me. "No, he isn't a bad man," she responded to my surprise question one day. "He wouldn't ever do anything to hurt you. He's just careless. He wouldn't look out for you the way I do."

I thought about him a lot that winter, though the cold weather and deep snow discouraged him from beneath my mother's bedroom window. The few minutes I'd spent with him in the dirty white convertible had somehow changed everything, not that I could have explained how or why. It was as if I suddenly understood intuitively nameless things I hadn't missed before becoming aware of them. I kept seeing his black thumb and forefinger snuffing out the red cigarette tip, a gesture I practiced with candy cigarettes until my mother caught me at it and wanted to know what I was doing. I knew better than to explain.

It wasn't that I loved him, of course. But when I thought about my father, my heart did that same funny thing it had done that afternoon he leaned across the front seat of the car and threw open the passenger-side door.

In the yard behind our house was a maple that had been planted by my grandfather before the war. It was a small boy's dream. I lived to climb it. Its trunk was too thick to shinny up, but a makeshift ladder of two-by-four chunks had been nailed into it, and these brought the climber as far as the crotch, about six feet up, where the tree divided, unequally, the dwarf side rising about halfway up the house, the healthy dominant side to a much higher altitude.

I was forbidden to climb the tree after the day my mother came out onto the back porch, called my name, and my voice drifted down to her from second story level, at the very top of the tree's dwarf side. I swung down from branch to branch to show off my dexterity. My mother wasn't impressed. "If I ever catch you in that tree again . . ." she said. She either liked unfinished sentences or couldn't think of how to finish them, and I resented her unwillingness to spell out consequences. It was impossible to weigh alternatives without them. But I was an obedient boy and did as I was told whenever she was around.

After school got out at 3:30, my mother's cousin—Aunt Rose, I called her—looked after me until quarter of five when my mother got home from the phone company. Aunt Rose's little house was around the corner and up the street from where we lived, halfway between my school and home. She fed me macaroons and we laughed immoderately at Popeye the Sailor. Aunt Rose also liked professional wrestling on Saturday afternoons, though her face got red with moral indignation at what some of the contestants got away with and how blind the referees were. Weekdays, after Olive Oyl was rescued, I headed home to await my mother on the front porch. Ours was probably the only house in Mohawk that was always locked. The only one that needed to be, my mother said. I knew why, though I wasn't supposed to. It was to keep my father out.

The fifteen minutes between 4:30 and 4:45 was my time in the tree. Each day I dared a little higher, the slender upper branches bending beneath my seven-year-old weight. I was convinced that if I could make it to the top of the tree, I would be able to look out over the roof of my grandfather's house, beyond Third Avenue, across all of Mohawk. I quickly mastered the dwarf side, but I was afraid to try the other. The branch I needed in order to begin was just beyond my reach, even when I stood on tiptoe in the crotch below. Although no great leap was necessary, my knees always got weak and I was afraid. If I failed to grab hold of the limb, I would fall all the way to the ground.

Day after day I stood sorrowfully in the crotch, staring into the center of the tree, immobile, full of self-hate and terrible yearning, until my mental clock informed me that my mother's ride would deposit her on the terrace any minute. The ground felt soft as a pillow when I swung down, and I knew I was a coward.

One afternoon, as I stood there, gazing up into that dark green and speckled blue height, I was suddenly aware that I was being watched, and when I turned, he stood there on the back porch, leaning forward with his arms on the railing. I could tell he'd been there for some time, and I was even more ashamed than other days when there were no witnesses. I knew when I saw him standing there that I had never intended to jump.

"Well?" he said.

And that one word was all it took. I don't remember jumping. Suddenly, I just had a hold of the limb with both hands, then had a knee over, then with a heave, I was up. The rest of the way would be easy, I knew, and I didn't care about it. I could do it any day.

"You better come down," my father said. "Your mother catches you up there, she'll skin us both."

Even as he spoke, we heard a car pull up out front. I swung down lickety-split.

"You figure you can keep a secret?" he said.

When I said sure, he nimbly vaulted the porch railing and landed next to me, so close we could have touched. Then he was gone.

3

A week later he kidnapped me.

I had left Aunt Rose's and was on my way home when I saw the white convertible. It was coming toward me up the other side of the street, traveling fast. I didn't think it would stop, but it did. At the last moment it swerved across the street to my side and came to a rocking halt, one wheel over the curb.

"What's the matter?" my father wanted to know. I must have looked like something was the matter. He had a gray chin again and his hair looked crazy until he ran his black fingers through it, which helped only a little.

I said nothing was the matter.

"You want to go for a ride?"

I figured he must mean to the dairy for ice cream.

"Come here," he said.

I started around the car to the passenger side.

"Here," he repeated. "You know what 'here' means?"

Actually, I don't think I did. At least I couldn't figure out what good it would do me to walk over and stand next to him outside the car. I found out though, because suddenly he had me under the arms, and then I was high in the air, above the convertible's windshield, where I rotated 180 degrees and plopped into the seat beside him. My teeth clicked audibly, but other than that it was a smooth landing.

He put the convertible in gear and we thumped down off the curb and up the street past Aunt Rose's in the opposite direction from the dairy. I figured he'd turn around when we got to the intersection, but he didn't. We just kept on going, straight out of Mohawk. My father's hair was wild again, and mine was too, I could feel it.

The car smelled funny. My father didn't seem aware of it until finally he sniffed and said, "Ah, shit," and pulled over so that he was half on the road and half on the shoulder. First he flung up the hood, then the trunk. With the hood up, the funny burning smell was even worse. My father got two yellow cans out of the trunk and punched holes in them. Then he unscrewed a cap on the engine and poured in the contents of the two cans. In the gap between the dash and the hood I could see his black fingers working. I thought about my mother, who would be just about putting her key in the front door lock and wondering how come I wasn't on the front porch to greet her. I started to send her a telepathic thought, "I'm with my father," until I remembered that the message wouldn't exactly comfort her should she receive it.

My father slammed the hood and trunk and got back in the car. "Ever see one of these?" He dropped something small and heavy in my lap. A jackknife, it looked like. I knew my mother wouldn't want me to touch it. "Open it," my father said.

I did. Every time I opened something, there was something else to open. There were two knives, a large one and a small one, the can opener I'd seen him use, a pair of tiny scissors you could actually work, assuming you had something that tiny that needed scissoring, a thing you could use to clean your nails with and a file. There were other features too, but I didn't know what they were for. With all its arms opened up, the gadget looked like a lopsided spider.

"Don't lose it," he said.

We were pretty well out in the country now and when he pulled into a long dirt driveway, I was sure he just meant to turn around. Instead, he followed the road on through a clump of trees to a small, rusty trailer. A big, dark-skinned man in a shapeless hat was seated on a broken concrete block. I was immediately interested in the hat, which was full of shiny metallic objects that reflected the sun. He stood when my father jerked the car to a stop, crushed stone rattling off the trailer.

"Well?" my father said.

The man consulted his watch. "Hour late," he said. "Not bad for Sam Hall. Practically on time. Who's this?"

"My son. We'll teach him how to fish."

"Who'll teach you?" the man said. "Howdy, Sam's Kid."

He offered a big, dark-skinned hand.

"Go ahead and shake his ugly paw," my father said.

I did, and then the man gathered up the gear that was resting up against the trailer. "You want to open this trunk, or should I just rip it off the hinges?" he said when my father made no move to get out and help.

"Kind of ornery, ain't he," my father said confidentially, tossing the keys over his shoulder.

"Hey, kid," the man said. "How'd you like to ride in the back?"

"Tell him to kiss your ass," my father advised. "You got enough gear for three?"

The man reluctantly got in the back. "Enough for me and the kid anyways. Don't know about you. Can he talk or what?"

My father swatted me. "Say hello to Wussy. He's half colored, half white, and all mixed up."

Wussy leaned forward so he could see into the front seat. "He ain't exactly dressed for this." I was wearing a thin t-shirt, shorts, sneakers. "Course, you aren't either. You planning to attend a dance in those shoes?"

"I didn't have time to change," my father shrugged.

"Where the hell were you?"

My father started to answer, then looked at me. "Someplace."

"Oh," the man called Wussy said. "I been there. Hey, Sam's Kid, you know what a straight flush is?"

I shook my head.

"His name is Ned."

"Ned?"

My father nodded. "I wasn't consulted."

"How come?"

"I wasn't around might have had something to do with it."

"Where were you?"

"Someplace," my father said. "Which reminds me."

We were speeding along out in the country and there was a

small store up ahead. We pulled in next to the telephone booth. My father closed the door behind him, but I could still hear part of the conversation. My father said she could kiss his ass.

When he got back in the car, my father looked at me and shook his head as if he thought maybe *I'd* done something. "Don't lose that," he said. I was still fingering the spider gadget.

"As long as we're stopped," Wussy said, "what do you say we put the top up?"

"What for?" my father said.

Wussy tapped me on the shoulder and pointed up. The sun had disappeared behind dark clouds, and the air had gone cool.

"Your ass," my father said, jerking the car back onto the highway.

Ten minutes later the skies opened.

"Your old man is a rockhead," Wussy observed after they finally got the top up. It had stuck at first and we were all soaked. "No wonder your mother don't want nothing to do with him."

It was nearly dark when we got to the cabin. We had to leave the convertible at the end of the dirt road and hike in the last mile, the sun winking at us low in the trees. We followed the river, more or less, though there were times when it veered off to the left and disappeared. Then after a while we would hear it again and there it would be. Wussy—it turned out that his name was Norm—led the way, carrying the rods and most of the tackle, then me, then my father, complaining every step. His black dress shoes got ruined right off, which pleased Wussy, and the mosquitoes ate us. My father wanted to know who would build a cabin way the hell and gone off in the woods. It seemed to him that anybody crazy enough to go to all that trouble might better have gone to a little more and poured a sidewalk, at least, so you could get to it. Wussy didn't say anything, but every now and then he'd hold on to a wet branch and then let go so that it whistled over the top of my head and caught my father in the chin with a thwap, after which Wussy would say, "Careful."

I was all right for a while, but then the woods began to get dark and I felt tired and scared. When something we disturbed scurried off underfoot and into the bushes, I got to thinking about home and my tree and my mother, who had no idea where I was. It occurred to me that if I let myself get lost, nobody would ever

find me, and the more I thought about it, the closer I stuck to
Wussy, ready to duck whenever he sent a branch whistling over
my head.

"I hope you didn't bring me all the way out here to roll me,
Wuss," my father said. "I should have mentioned I don't have any
money."

"I want those shiny black shoes."

"You would, you black bastard."

"Nice talk, in front of the kid." A branch caught my father in
the chops.

"What color is he, bud?" my father poked me in the back.

I was embarrassed. My mother had told me about Negroes and
that it wasn't nice to accuse them of it. Wussy's skin was the color
of coffee, at least the way my mother drank it, with cream and
sugar. "I don't know," I said.

"That's all right," my father said. "He's none too sure either."

And then suddenly we were out of the trees and there was the
cabin, the river gurgling about forty yards down the slope.

Wussy tossed all the gear inside and started a fire in a circle of
rocks a few feet from the ramshackle porch. When it got going
good, he brought out a big iron grate to put over it. With the sun
down, it had gotten cool and the fire felt good. My father fidgeted
nearby until Wussy told him he could collect some dry sticks if he
felt like it. "You could have brought a pair of long pants and a
jacket for him at least," he said.

"Didn't have a chance," my father said.

"Look at him," Wussy said critically. "Knees all scraped up . . ."

"How the hell did I know we were going to blaze a trail?" my
father said. "You cold?"

"No," I lied.

Wussy snorted. "I think I saw blankets inside."

My father went to fetch them. "Your old man's a rockhead,"
Wussy observed again. "Otherwise, he's all right."

He didn't seem to need me to agree, so I didn't say anything.
He opened three cans of chili with beans into a black skillet and
set it on top of the grate. Then he chopped up two yellow onions
and added them. You couldn't see much except the dark woods
and the outline of the cabin. We heard my father banging into
things and cursing inside. After a few minutes the chili began to
form craters which swelled, then exploded. "Man-color," Wussy
said. "That's what I am."

My father finally came back with a couple rough blankets. He draped one over me and threw the other around his own shoulders.

"No thanks," Wussy said. "I don't need one."

"Good," my father said.

"And you don't need any of this chili," Wussy said, winking at me. "Me and you will have to eat it all, Sam's Kid."

My father squatted down and inspected the sputtering chili. "I hate like hell to tell you what it looks like."

It looked all right to me and it smelled better than I knew food could smell. It was way past my normal dinner time and I was hungry. Wussy ladled a good big portion onto a plate and handed it to me. Then he loaded about twice as much onto a plate for himself.

"What the hell," my father said.

"What the hell is right," Wussy said. "What the hell, eh Sam's Kid?"

My father got up and went back into the cabin for another blanket. When he returned, Wussy said no thanks, he was doing fine, but didn't my father want any chili? "You better get going," he advised. "Me and the kid are ready for seconds."

We weren't, exactly, but when he finished giving my father a pretty small portion, he ladled more onto my plate and the rest of the skillet onto his own.

"I bet there's a lot of shallow graves out here in the woods," my father speculated, pretending not to notice there was no more chili whether he hurried up or not. "You suppose anybody would miss you if you didn't come home tomorrow?"

"Women, mostly," Wussy said. "I feel pretty safe though. Mostly I worry about you. Anything happened to me, you'd starve before you ever located that worthless oil guzzler of yours."

"Your ass."

When I couldn't eat any more, I gave the rest of my chili to my father, who looked like he was thinking of licking the hot skillet. "The kid's all right," Wussy said. "I don't care *who* his old man is."

It was so black out now that we couldn't even see the cabin, just a thousand stars and each other's faces in the dying fire.

Wussy blew the loudest fart I'd ever heard. "What color's my skin?" he said, as if he hadn't done anything at all.

I had been almost asleep, until the fart. "Man-color," I said, wide awake again.

"There you go," he said.

I woke with the sun in my eyes next morning. There were no curtains on the cabin's high windows. I was still dressed from the night before. My legs, all scratched from the long walk through the woods, felt heavy and a little unsteady when I stood up. I looked around for a bathroom, but there wasn't any.

My father and his friend Wussy were face down on the other two bunks. My father's arms were coffee-colored, like Wussy's, but his legs and back were fish-white. Wussy had taken the trouble to crawl under the covers, but my father lay on top. The cabin had been warm the night before, but it was chilly now, though my father didn't seem aware of it. I was cold, and it made me really wish there was a bathroom. In the center of the small table was an empty bottle and a deck of cards fanned face up. They'd kept score in long uneven columns labeled N and S on a brown paper bag. The S columns were the longer ones, and the number 85 was circled at the top of the bag with a dollar sign in front of it. I had awakened several times during the night when one of them yelled "Gin!" or "You son of a bitch!" but I was too exhausted to stay awake. I watched the two sleepers for a while, but neither man stirred, so I went outside.

The iron skillet, alive with bright green flies, still sat on the grate. There were so many flies, and they were so furious that their bodies pinged against the metal like small pebbles. They would buzz frantically in the hardened chili for a few seconds, then do wide arcs above the skillet before diving back again. I watched with interest for a while and then went down to the river. We were so far upstream that it wasn't very deep in most spots, a river in name only. Rocks jutted up above the surface of the water and it looked like you'd be able to jump from one to the next all the way to the opposite bank. I tried it, but only got partway, because when you got out toward the middle, the rocks weren't as close together as they'd looked from the bank. One solid-looking flat rock tipped under my weight and I had to plunge one sneakered foot deep into the cool current to keep from falling in. The water ran so fast that the shoe was nearly sucked off, and I was scared enough to head back to shore on a squishy sneaker, aware that if my mother had been there, she'd have thrown a fit about my getting it wet. I doubted my father and Wussy would even notice. I found a comfortable rock on the bank and had another look at my father's knife gadget, trying to pretend I didn't have to go to the bathroom. Having the river right there made the necessity to pee hard to ignore. I wasn't sure I could hold it all day.

After a while the door of the cabin opened and Wussy appeared in his undershorts. "Hello, Sam's Kid," he said. He tiptoed over to the spot where he'd built the fire, yanked himself out of his shorts and watered the bushes for a very long time. I could hear him above the sound of the river.

When he saw me watching, he said, "Gotta go, Sam's Kid?"

I shook my head. I could hold out a while longer, and I wanted it to seem like my own idea when I went. I was very relieved to learn that peeing in the weeds was permissible, though it was one more thing I didn't think I'd mention to my mother.

"First thing every morning for me," Wussy explained. "Can't wait."

When he was finished, he went back inside for his pants and shoes. I went over to where he'd stood, as if it were an officially designated area, and released my agony.

Wussy came out with the rods and his tackle box. "Better get our ass going and catch breakfast," he said. "Your old man ain't going to be no help. I see you got your shoe wet."

"Fell in," I admitted, surprised that I had been wrong about him not being the type to notice.

"River runs pretty quick out there in the middle," he observed without looking at me, and I was suddenly sure he'd seen me out there, though he wasn't going to say anything.

At the water's edge, he attached the spinning reels to the rods and ran line through the eyelets all the way to the tips. I watched, full of interest. "Ever fish before?"

I shook my head.

"It's about the best thing there is until you're older and can do some other stuff, and it's better than most of the other stuff too."

I watched him tie on the hooks, and he did it slowly so I could see. He pointed to the little wing on each hook. "Called a barb," he said. "So the fish can't slip off once he's on. Works the same way on your finger if you aren't careful."

We walked upriver about a hundred yards so that when my

father woke up there'd be nobody around. "Serve him right," Wussy said, without explaining what for.

When we got to a spot that looked lucky to Wussy, where there was a good safe rock for me to sit on, he handed me a rod. Then he opened up a can that looked like it was full of dirt, but when he fished around with his brown index finger I could see the bottom was alive and writhing. He pulled out an astonishingly long worm and hooked him three times until he oozed yellow and twisted angrily. I must have looked a little yellow myself, because Wussy baited my hook with two bright pink salmon eggs. Then he taught me how to release the bail and let the current carry the bait downstream, and how to reel in. "How will I know when there's a fish?" I said when he started out toward the middle.

He said not to worry about it, I'd know, though that didn't strike me as a satisfactory explanation. Then I was by myself with only the sound of the running water for company. The sun was high and warm and when I saw Wussy had taken off his shirt I did the same. I watched Wussy for a while, then studied the reflected sun on the water near the drooping tip of my rod.

I couldn't have been asleep more than a few minutes when I felt the excited tugging. For some reason it was not what I had expected. The jerks came in short bursts, like a coded message to a sleepy boy: "Stay—Alert—There—Are—Fish—in—the—River." Thirty yards downstream a fish jumped, but I didn't immediately associate this phenomenon with my now frantic rod tip. Wussy had waded further upstream and did not hear when I shouted "Agh!" in his general direction.

I was not at all certain I wanted to reel in the fish. Every time I tried to, he seemed to resent it and tugged even harder. When he did this, I stopped and waited apologetically for the tugging to stop. I only reeled in when I felt the line go slack. When the fish jumped, or rather flopped onto the surface, a second time, he was much closer, and my already considerable misgivings grew. I was thinking I might just let him stay where he was until Wussy came back, whenever that might be. But then I got my courage up and reeled in a little more, all the time watching the spot on the surface where my line disappeared into the stream, beads of rainbow water dancing off it with the tension.

Then I saw the fish himself off to the side in a spot far from where I had imagined him to be. He was no longer tugging so frantically, but he darted first left, then right in the large pool of

relatively calm water beneath my rock. Then he must have got
a gander at me sitting there, because he was in full flight again.
I stopped reeling and just watched his colors in the clear water.
After a while he stopped trying to get away and just stayed even
with the current, his tail waving gently, like a flag in the breeze.
Then I looked up and Wussy was there and he had my fish out of
the water and flopping in the green netting, cold water spraying
on my knees. I examined the fish without pride as Wussy extracted him from the net and probed his gullet for the hook he'd
practically digested.

"Well, Sam's Kid," Wussy said, "you're about the most patient
fisherman I ever saw. Nobody won't ever accuse you of not giving
a trout a chance. If I was him, I'd have had about three separate
heart attacks."

Tired of the fish's uncooperative squirming, Wussy took out his
knife and brained my trout with the handle. The fish shuddered
and was still.

"There," Wussy said to the trout. "Now you won't have no more
heart attacks."

It took him a few minutes, but he finally got his hook back. Then
he handed me the jar of salmon eggs, reminding me to be careful
of the barb when I baited up. He slipped my fish onto his stringer
next to a larger trout already dangling from it. "We got us *our*
breakfast, anyhow. I guess we should catch one for the rockhead
if we can."

He watched me while I baited my hook and released the line
into the current the way he'd taught me. "You're a fisherman,"
Wussy said. "A good, patient fisherman."

We fished until the sun was directly overhead. I didn't have any
more luck, for which I was grateful, but Wussy's fat worms located
two more trout, and then we headed back downstream to the
cabin. My father was standing in the doorway, scratching his
groin. "Where's the bacon and eggs?" he wanted to know.

"Back in Mohawk," Wussy said. "Your kid caught a fish."

"That's good," my father said, studying the stringer as if mine
might be recognizable. "I could eat about three."

"So happens I got some for sale," Wussy said. "What's three into
eighty-five?"

"Your ass." Then he studied me. "What're you scratching
about?"

"Itch," I said. I'd been scratching most of the morning, first one spot and then another. For some reason one scratch just wasn't enough, no matter how hard. After a minute or so, the itching would be even worse.

"You could go wash that pan in the river," Wussy said to my father, "and keep from being *completely* worthless."

"I had *my* fish on the line last night," my father said. "Cleaned him too." But he grabbed the pan and headed for the river. I followed him.

"Well?" he said, squatting at the water's edge.

I shrugged. It was his favorite question, and I never knew what he meant by it.

"Caught a fish, huh?"

"Wussy taught me how," I said, suddenly full of pride about the fish, my throat full, as if there was a hook in it.

"Wussy's all right," he said. "I'm the only one calls him that though. You better call him Norm."

I said I thought Norm was a better name anyhow.

When the pan was clean, or clean enough so the flies weren't interested in it anymore, we returned to the cabin. Wussy was cleaning the last of the fish, tossing its string of insides off into the bushes. My father found some oil in the cabin and before long the four fish were sputtering in the big skillet. Then we ate them right down to their tiny bones and drank from the icy river. Even my father had stopped complaining.

We fished some more that afternoon. Wussy was good at it. Between pulling them in, baiting up, stringing the catch, and tending to me, he was pretty busy. My father could have used some help too, but Wussy ignored him and my father, who claimed to know how to fish, refused to ask. They were always needling each other anyway, and my father didn't want to ask the kind of stupid question about his equipment that Wussy could turn to advantage. Every time we looked at my father, he was either tying on a new hook, or rebaiting it, or trying to figure out why there was a big nest of monofilament line jamming his reel. After a while my father took his act up around the bend in the river where he could fight his gear in private. "With most fishermen," Wussy remarked, "the contest is between the man and the fish. With the rockhead, it's between him and his reel."

I caught two more trout during the afternoon and would have

been among the world's truly happy boys if I could have just
stopped itching. In addition to my legs, my stomach and shoulders
were now covered with angry red blotches. "Looks like you found
some poison ivy all right," Wussy remarked. "You'd be better off
not scratching if you could avoid it."

I couldn't though, and after another hour of watching me dig
myself, Wussy said he was going to fish his way upriver and tell
my father we'd better head back before I drew blood. I reeled in,
leaned Wussy's rod up against the cabin porch and jumped from
rock to rock along the river edge to where I found my father
seated on the bank. Wussy was standing thigh deep in the river,
about twenty yards away, calmly reeling in a trout and smiling,
no doubt at the fact that my father was engaged in extracting a
barbed hook from his thumb by swearing at it. Swearing was
about the only thing he did that didn't work the hook deeper into
his thumb. To make matters worse, there was only an inch or two
of line at the end of the rod, which kept falling off his knee, and
further setting the hook. By the time he washed the blood away
so he could see what he was doing, and balanced the rod on his
knee, the bright blood was pumping again and he'd have to stop
and wipe the sweat off his forehead. He looked like he was mad
enough to toss everything into the woods, and he probably would
have if he himself hadn't been attached to it.

When Wussy had landed, cleaned, and strung his last trout, he
came over and surveyed the situation. "Where you got all your
fish hid?" he said. "There's a little room left on this stringer." He
sat down on a rock out of striking distance, but close enough to
observe what promised to be excellent entertainment.

My father didn't bother answering him about the fish.

"Your old man looks like he could use some cheering up,"
Wussy said. "Tell him how many fish you caught, Sam's Kid."

I wasn't sure it would cheer him up, but I told him three, and
I was right, it didn't.

"Anything I can do?" Wussy said.

My father gave him a black look. "How you planning to get
home?" he said weakly.

"I figure I'll just sit right here till you pass out from loss of blood
and then take your car keys. Somebody will find you along about
Labor Day and that hook will still be right where it is now."

"You better hope so, because if I get it out it's going up your
ass."

Wussy ignored the threat. "Of course ycu know best," he said slowly, "but if that hook was in my thumb, the first thing I'd do is release my bail."

My father looked at him, not comprehending. I was close enough, so I leaned over and tripped the bail, releasing the line. My father flushed.

"Now you got room," Wussy continued, "I'd bite that line in two."

Humbled, my father did as he was told. Wussy picked up the rod and reeled in the slack.

"And?" my father said.

"And now I got the majority of my gear back," Wussy said, turning back toward the cabin. "You can just go ahead and keep that hook."

I think he would have chased Wussy, hook and all, except that he'd noticed me for the first time and it scared him so he forgot all about his thumb. I had been scratching nonstop and the patches of poison ivy skin were everywhere, including my face. "Look at you," he said. "Your mother's going to shoot us for sure."

"Shoot *you*," Wussy said over his shoulder. "Come with me, Sam's Kid. Stay a safe distance from that rockhead. He's a dangerous man."

My father got back at him by refusing to carry anything out of the woods. I helped a little, but by the time we got back to the convertible Wussy was beat and trying hard not to show it. "What's that streaming from your thumb?" he asked when we were back on the highway heading for Mohawk. The monofilament line took the breeze and fluttered like a cobweb from my father's black thumb.

About that time I noticed the car smelling funny again, and my father pulled over onto the shoulder. He took two cans of oil from the trunk and headed around to the front via the passenger side. I stopped scratching myself when he held out his hand. "Let me see that thing a minute."

I felt an awful chill. I could see the gadget in my mind's eye and it was sitting on the last rock I fished from. I pretended to look for it. "I . . ." I began.

But he already knew. "What'd I tell you when I gave it to you?"

I tried to speak, but could only stare at my patchy knees.

"Well?"

"Don't lose it," I finally croaked.

"Don't lose it," he repeated.

I was suddenly very close to tears, even though all the way home I'd been feeling as happy as I thought it possible to feel. I had caught fish and peed in the woods and not complained about my poison ivy. I had felt proud and important and good. Now, having betrayed my father's simple trust, it came home to me that I was a disappointment to him, just a worthless little boy to be taken home to his mother where he belonged. It might have helped a little if Wussy had said something in my defense, but he was silent in the backseat.

My father walked around to the driver's side and kicked the convertible hard. "Let me see that knife," he said to Wussy.

"You aren't using my good knife to punch no holes in no oil cans," Wussy said.

There was nothing to do but kick the car again, so my father did it. Then he did it five more times all down the driver's side of the car. That was all right with Wussy, in as much as it wasn't his car, but I began to cry, even though it wasn't my car either. When he was through kicking the convertible, he said, "Come on, dumbbell. Help me find a sharp rock."

Then he felt the monofilament line flapping in the breeze, wrapped it between the thumb and forefinger of his good hand, and yanked. The hook came out all right, and along with it a hunk of flesh. Fresh blood began to pour out of the wound and onto the ground. My father swore and flung the line and hook with all his might. It landed about five feet away.

We started looking along the shoulder for a jagged rock, my father kicking the round ones for not being pointed. When he was a ways up the road, Wussy came over to where I was crying. "Don't pay no attention," he advised.

Then he went back to the car and plunged his knife into the two oil cans. By the time my father got back with a jagged rock, Wussy was tossing the empty cans into the neighboring field and wiping the knife blade on his pants. My father dropped his rock and we all got back in the car.

"Hey!" he said, looking over at me before putting the convertible back on the road. "Smile. I'm the one with something to cry about."

After his walk he wasn't mad any more and he let me see his thumb. It really was an ugly-looking thumb.

When we pulled up in front of the house, my mother was sitting on one of the front porch chairs with a blanket over her lap, looking like she'd been there for days. Her face was absolutely expressionless. "Uh-oh," Wussy said, and suddenly I felt awash in guilt for having enjoyed myself. Looking at her now, I realized how long the last twenty-four hours had been for her. "Don't forget to take your fish," Wussy said when I got out, probably hoping that a couple nice trout might appease my mother.

Let me try to view through her eyes what she saw when we pulled up at the curb that afternoon. First, she saw my father at the wheel, looking a tad nervous but far from repentant. Next, she saw a large man of indeterminate breed wearing an absurd hat full of fishhooks, just the sort of companion she imagined my father would select for his son. And finally, she saw me. My rumpled shirt and shorts were filthy, my hair wild from the ride in the convertible. My arms and legs were red and raw, my eyes swollen nearly shut from digging and crying. And she saw too that under the law she was completely helpless since, as F. William Peterson had that day informed her, a father could not be guilty of kidnapping his own son.

She did not get up at first. My father got out of the car to walk me as far as the porch steps, though he looked a little pale, even before he saw my grandfather's service revolver, the same one that had already been stuck in his ear once. He stopped, his head cocked, as if listening for something as my mother stood and raised the gun. I heard Wussy say "Jesus!" and he slumped as far down into the backseat as his big body would allow. The first explosion surprised my mother so, she almost dropped the gun. After that, she did better. She shot my father's car five more times, taking out the windshield and the front tire, neither of which she was particularly aiming at.

"God damn you, Jenny!" my father exclaimed when the shooting stopped. He had scooted behind the car and was now peering tentatively over the hood. "I think you shot Wussy."

"Nope." Wussy's voice came from the floor of the rear seat. "Except for just the coronary, I'm okay. She isn't reloading, is she?"

"Look at my car," my father said. The glass from the windshield was all over the street, but for some reason he didn't look as mad as he'd been when he discovered I'd lost his gadget, though a lot more surprised.

"Look at my son," my mother said.

"Our son," my father said.

"You can't have him." She was still aiming the gun in his direction, empty now, though she didn't know it. She had just stopped shooting when it seemed she'd made her point.

My father was pretty sure she was through, but he couldn't be certain. The neighbors had all come out on their porches, and he was feeling increasingly self-conscious about being pinned down behind his own ruined car. He'd been shot at before and guessed that my mother wasn't really trying to hit him, but those were precisely the situations that got you shot. He knew from his experience overseas that if you only got shot by people aiming at you specifically, war wouldn't have been nearly such a hazardous affair. He'd have felt safer if she'd been aiming at his skull. As things stood, it was the people on the porches across the street who he judged were most vulnerable. Since there was nothing to do but test the water, he slowly stood and when she didn't shoot he got back in the car. Naturally, it wouldn't start. "Jesus," Wussy said from the floor of the backseat.

Finally the engine turned over. My father leaned over the backseat. "You want to ride up front with me?"

"I'm fine right here," Wussy said.

"Which is how come I call you Wussy," my father said.

There must be something about getting shot at that changes the way a man looks at things. According to my mother and some other people who knew him before the war, my father came home from Germany a different man. That was to be expected, of course. What was surprising was that the volley my mother aimed at the white convertible marked the beginning of a long hiatus in their personal conflict instead of escalating it. I honestly doubt he was all that scared, and when I asked him about the incident years later, I think he told me the truth when he said he was less surprised by the bullets burrowing into his car than by the fact that my mother had taken their ongoing differences so seriously. That she should so puzzled him that he even questioned his behavior, entertaining, albeit briefly, the idea that he might in some fashion be responsible for the apparition of his once loving wife, who had faithfully awaited his return from overseas, now calmly and purposefully blasting away, without visible remorse, in the general direction of his life and property.

They had always had a rather contentious, combative relationship, and a good fight had never before spoiled things. One night a few months after my father had returned from the war and they'd gone dancing, they were accosted by a drunk who kept insisting that my father must know this welterweight from Syracuse. "Hall," he kept saying. "He fights under the name of Hall." My father got a charge out of the idea. "That's the name my wife and I fight under," he said.

Back then, they had enjoyed making up, and if they'd thrown things at each other, the broken pieces could always be swept off the floor later. He never bought anything without considering its possible use as a missile, and he knew that there were few purer pleasures in the world than throwing things. During the long months of his nocturnal raids, he had considered the whole thing good fun, and he looked forward to eventual, inevitable reconciliation with my mother. They were both Catholics, at least nominally, and my mother had said till death. Even her calling the police had seemed fair enough. After all, she had few weapons to fight him with, and besides, he had enjoyed eluding cops. It did not occur to him that she might really mean the things she said about him—that she considered him a menace, that she would keep their son away from him for the same reason that she would not let him play in traffic or pet rabid dogs.

Could it be true that he was a dangerous man? He had killed men in France and Germany, but their deaths were more the result of their own stupidity or bad luck than any deadly efficiency on his part. The men who had fought beside him had never considered him careless, or at least hadn't said they did. He had been neither cowardly nor foolhardy, just dependable. How had his wife gotten the idea he was a dangerous man?

Still, when the first bullet slammed into his convertible, it punctuated a thought that had been gnawing at him all the way home from the river. He had not been much of a caretaker for me during the last twenty-four hours. He hadn't intended to do such a bad job. He hadn't thought that it would *be* a job. In fact, he had intended the kidnapping—an idea he thought of and acted upon in the same instant—to demonstrate that a boy *needed* a father. Instead, everything had turned out badly. When we were a few blocks from home, he had looked over at me and seen the unavoidable evidence of his guardianship. He had snatched a clean, happy, reasonably well-adjusted boy and was returning less than twenty-four hours later a dirty little vagabond in wet sneakers and a torn t-shirt, whose poison-ivied legs and arms were raked raw, whose eyes were nearly swollen shut with crying over the loss of a two-dollar gadget. And if all that and getting shot at weren't enough, he had to listen to a lecture from Wussy. My father still remembered it years later.

"You know where I found him when I looked out the window this morning?" Wussy wanted to know. "Standing on a rock in the middle of the river. You're pretty damn lucky we weren't bringing home a drowned corpse. I don't blame her for shooting at you."

"She came closer to you than me," my father pointed out weakly.

"People usually do. That's how come I live out in the country."

They drove the rest of the way there in silence, contemplating how different it was in a car with no windshield, dodging tiny windblown shards of glass. When they pulled up in front of the trailer, Wussy got out and unloaded the gear. "Shot one of my reels," Wussy observed, holding it up.

My father wasn't interested. "What would you do?" he said.

Wussy shrugged.

"Maybe I should stay away from him for a while."

"For a while wouldn't hurt," Wussy said. "Until he grows up a little."

"Or until I do?"

"No point waiting *that* long," Wussy said. He studied the convertible from his cinderblock step. "*First* thing I'd do is get a new car. This one's full of holes."

4

And so he went away again.

No one knew where. For a while my mother got phone calls from people he owed money. They wanted to know how come he disappeared, and when she told them she neither knew nor cared they only believed the last part. Some wanted to know if she felt like squaring his debts.

In fact, my father left town so quickly and quietly that there was considerable speculation about whether he'd really left at all, especially after the story of how my mother had shot his car got around. About two weeks after his disappearance, two policemen in street clothes rang our bell and wondered if they might ask my mother some questions. There'd been talk at the phone company, so she wasn't surprised.

They wanted to know everything. What happened the afternoon my father's car got shot, why she had done it, and had we seen my father since. By the time they got around to us, they'd already talked to the neighbors, and all the eyewitnesses had agreed, at least in the beginning, that just the car had been shot. But the more they were questioned, the less certain they became. Maybe my father *had* been shot, they conceded hopefully. Or maybe the man who had slumped down in the backseat had been. Yes, my father *had* driven the wounded automobile away, stopping a couple of blocks down the street to change the tire my mother had exploded, but they couldn't be absolutely certain nobody had been hit. Sometimes people got shot and weren't aware of it until later. Maybe my father had crawled off someplace and died. Or maybe my mother caught up with him later and finished him off.

The policeman wanted to see the gun my mother used, unaware that it had been confiscated by the patrolman who answered the call the afternoon of the shooting. And they wanted to talk to me about the kidnapping. I told them all about the three fish I'd caught and how my father had only caught his thumb. I informed them that another man called Norm—a.k.a. Wussy—had gone with us, and described the little trailer he lived in outside of Mohawk. They must have located poor Wussy, because the next morning F. William Peterson called to say that the official investigation into my father's disappearance had been concluded after a friend told the cops it was my father's intention to head out west and work on the interstates. A car answering a pretty accurate description—one side full of bullet holes—had gassed up at a Thruway station near Utica and the driver had purchased a case of oil.

"How can people think such things?" my mother said to F. William Peterson. To her mind there was a real distinction between shooting a man's car and shooting a man. She had never given anyone reason to think she was capable of the latter.

Even though it had quickly become clear that there was no connection between her assault on the convertible and my father's subsequent disappearance, the resulting gossip was the beginning of serious trouble for my mother, who began to suffer acute anxiety attacks. When they got so bad she couldn't stop shaking, the doctor prescribed librium, which calmed her way down. She mostly stared at a spot on the wall about a foot above the Victrola, and her work at the telephone company suffered. But when it came time to renew the prescription, she decided to start attending church instead. As a girl she'd always felt serene in church, a feeling not unlike a couple libriums, without the drowsy side effects.

Once she started going to church, she couldn't stop. She attended Mass the way drunks went on binges. She couldn't get enough. In church she felt safe and secure. Not even my father would dare violate its cool, dark sanctity. She took me along for company.

Our Lady of Sorrows was white, Mission style, simple and clean, without any ornate ostentation. I loved its long side aisles and rich stained-glass windows. In the early morning, the little church, never locked, would be nearly black inside, except for the thin crease of light beneath the sacristy door. The old Monsignor, our pastor, always arrived before his parishioners. As the eastern sky lightened, the windows along one side took on color, and the church would grow warm and still, except for the creaking of an occasional pew or clicking of beads. The quiet and beauty of Our Lady of Sorrows reminded me of the woods that morning I was alone on the river before my father and Wussy woke up. More than anything I wanted to investigate the sacristy, the church's inner recess where the old priest and altar boys clothed in rich vestments plotted the mass for the rest of us. I asked my mother what you needed to do to become an altar boy, and the question made her very happy, as if for the first time she believed that my father had really gone out west and the two of us were safe.

In due course I was enrolled in catechism class where I effort-lessly distinguished myself, and by 1957, when I entered the fifth grade, I was cataloging an impressive list of plagiarized venial sins every Saturday afternoon in the dark confessional. I held my hands over my ears to avoid hearing the exact same confession from whatever boy happened to occupy the opposite cubicle of our three-seater, the old Monsignor separating us two liars. I ritually confessed that which I was not guilty of in order to make up for not confessing what I *was* guilty of, about the most heinous crime I could imagine. I was ten years old, and I had discovered by accident that an older woman of twelve undressed in front of her bedroom window every night precisely at ten, ten-thirty on weekends. She was apparently very proud of her small but clearly developing breasts, because she admired them every night, al-most as much as I did, before slipping over them a pastel night-gown. I dreaded the night she would discover the error of her two-thirds-drawn window shade, and was much older when it occurred to me for the first time, a blinding revelation, that the lovely little minx probably knew perfectly well my hot ten-year-old breath was fogging the bedroom window opposite hers. When her family packed their belongings and moved to Florida a year later, I felt a sense of loss rarely paralleled in adult life, though by then her performances had grown less frequent, even as her breasts had grown more worthy of adoration.

I cannot imagine that my confessions impressed the good Mon-signor, but for one reason or another, I was made an altar boy, and thereby brought into the inner sanctum of the church behind the lighted sacristy door. It was a profound disappointment. Nothing mysterious happened there, and if any plotting was done, I wasn't privy to it. The old Monsignor dressed in silence and spoke only from the altar and to the entire congregation. I soon realized that my selection did not mean that I was more holy, more worthy, more intelligent, or more fully catechized than the twenty or so boys passed over for the honor. My initiation into the ritual of fishing had been far more satisfying, and Wussy a far more amiable teacher, his tendency toward gunshot flatulence notwithstanding, than the old Monsignor, who said scarcely two words to me, leaving matters of instruction to the older boys. I thought things would change when I started serving weekday masses, where only one altar boy attended, but by then I knew what I was doing and the old priest had even less to say to me. From out in the congregation it had seemed that the boys on the altar were busy and essential to the service, but now I saw that the old Monsignor ran the whole shebang himself. At least with Wussy I had caught a fish.

Things looked up, however, when Our Lady of Sorrows was assigned a young priest named Father Michaels to relieve some of the burden of duties from our aging and allegedly infirm pastor. Though not a large man, the new priest was a very handsome one, with longish brown hair and dark eyes. His hands and fingers were slender, like a woman's, and just as white. Otherwise, the only truly notable thing about him was that he perspired terribly in all weather. He had been with us only a few weeks when the old Monsignor ordered all new outer vestments, very costly ones that priests within a parish often share, and made a present of the old darkening ones to the embarrassed young priest. Father Michaels always carried a thick cloth handkerchief with him when he said mass, secreting it on the altar behind the Bible stand, a respectful distance from the holy tabernacle, using it several times during the course of proceedings to mop his glistening forehead and neck.

Father Michaels was very conscious of his perspiring, and on Sundays, when there were sometimes half a dozen irreverent altar boys on hand to remark the fact, he sweated even more profusely than during the week. When he distributed Communion, with me preceding him backward along the altar rail, gently inserting the gold communion paten beneath the urgent chins of the faithful in case their tongues did not accept cleanly the sacred host, the sweat actually dripped from the tip of the young priest's nose, plinking onto the gold plate, like rain into a tin gutter.

We took to each other right off. Unlike the Monsignor, who was always in the sacristy no matter how early I arrived and who managed to convey the impression that boys were undependable by nature and that he would probably have to do my work—lighting the candles, cleaning out the censer and making sure it contained a fresh lump of charcoal, toting the big red Bible up the pulpit steps—Father Michaels often blew into the sacristy through the side door ten minutes before mass was supposed to begin, blinking, tired, and mussed, as if he'd just been awakened in the middle of a nightmare.

"You're the only one?" he said nervously the first morning I served the seven for him.

I said I was.

"Aren't you a little young to be going solo?" he said, as if he hadn't counted on himself to be there with me. I was by then a seasoned one-year veteran, and had to resist the temptation to remark that he too looked a little young for a solo flight.

Before leaving the shadowy sacristy for the bright altar, he always said, "I guess we're all set then?" as if he couldn't be sure without getting my educated opinion on the matter. I doubt mass would have been said that day had I professed uncertainty. But I never did, and so he took a deep breath and put his hand on my shoulder, the way a blind man grabs hold of someone he trusts not to lead him over any open manholes. He was complimentary of my bell ringing, my handling of the water and wine cruets, my lighting of the candles. "When Ned Hall lights a candle," he often remarked, "it stays lit." That might have been said for any candle lit by an altar boy, but it made me feel good anyway. After each successful mass, when the sacristy door closed behind us, Father Michaels acted like it was all my doing. "Ned, you're a wonder. You'll be pope someday."

After we got comfortable with each other, he wanted to know about my father. The old Monsignor had probably told him a little, because the new priest already knew Sam Hall wasn't around. It had been over three years since he left Mohawk, I assumed, for good. I never talked about my father with anybody, including my mother, and at first I felt awkward, but I soon learned that talking about him didn't make me feel the way I had thought it would. After mass, Father Michaels and I often sat on the sacristy steps in the sun, and there I told him how I had lied about my father being dead, and about his nocturnal marauding, and about the fishing trip with him and Wussy, and how that ended with my mother shooting the convertible. He laughed at the part about the fishhook in my father's thumb, and I did too, though it had never seemed funny before. When I got to the shooting part, he went pale and wanted to know if I was exaggerating, as if it made him uncomfortable to think that one of his parishioners owned a gun, much less shot one. He had trouble associating the mother of my story with the quiet, pretty woman he'd seen in church who sometimes waited for me when mass was over.

Perhaps to make me feel better, he told me about his own father who had been a drunk and beaten him and his mother until his unexpected and highly unusual death. When he spoke about the man, his eyes became unfocused and distant. Apparently, when Father Michaels had been a year or two older than I, his father had had a vision which reformed him on the spot. At the time he had been on a bender for nearly two weeks, during which he had not been home, much to the relief of the boy and his mother, whose eyes he had blackened before leaving and which were still greenish yellow. When he finally returned one afternoon, his wife was prepared to leap from the third-story window if necessary, but though shaky, her husband was sober and dressed, unaccountably, in a new suit. He was shaved and combed, and he announced that he had returned to them a new man. He certainly looked like one. The boy and his mother scarcely recognized him. The bag of groceries he was carrying was welcome though, as was the news that he had a job, a good one. He then kissed his wife's yellow eyes and asked his son if he would like to go to a ball game at the Polo Grounds while his mother prepared dinner. At the ballpark they drank sodas and watched the game from high in the stands, and Father Michaels remembered it as the happiest day of his young life.

When the game was over, the older man took his son's hand and together they came down out of the stands. Father Michaels remembered the bright sun seemed to rest right on top of the opposite bleachers, and perhaps for that reason, his father thought they had reached the bottom when there was still one step to go. As a drunk, he had miraculously survived his share of dangerous falls. More than once he had missed the top step on the stairs outside their third-floor flat, unaware that he had done so until he discovered himself seated on the landing below. He had fallen off chairs, out of moving cars into gutters, off porches, off bicycles, off ice skates, off countless bar stools, even off women. But that afternoon, when he was sober and full of new life and aching love for his long-neglected boy, his leg stiffened when he thought he had reached the bottom of the stadium stairs, and though he had misjudged where he was by inches, his leg shattered like a dry twig, the separated bone driving up into his groin. He immediately went into shock and died before the doctors at the hospital to which he was finally taken could diagnose the problem.

If Father Michaels had not explained the moral of the story, I would have missed it, for it seemed to me that the man's mistake in judgment had been to sober up when his natural state was clearly an alcoholic trance. But my friend explained that God had generously given his father the opportunity to die in the state of grace, and to allow the two of them a wonderful afternoon and its memory. He went on to explain that his father's memory probably had more to do with his becoming a priest than any other single factor. Even viewed thus providentially, God's design, though unmistakable now that it was pointed out to me, appeared to me a trifle convoluted, though I was hardly an expert. It just seemed that if He wanted disciples, His method with Saint Paul on the Damascus road was cleaner since it involved just the man in question (unless you counted the horse), not the beating of the man's wife or the prolonged torture of his son, or any other innocent bystander to effect the conversion. Nevertheless, Father Michaels and I were bound by mutual sympathy, and he was of the opinion that even if my own father never showed up again, he would very likely continue to shape my life. I should be thankful for him, and for the brief time I'd spent with him, even if he didn't seem like so very much of a father.

My new friend also encouraged me to be thankful for my mother, whom he regarded as an extraordinary woman, not just as a gunfighter, but as someone of courage and endurance, who accepted what she couldn't change, who did the work of both a mother and father, who did whatever was required of her without complaint. He could tell all this from the altar, just by looking at her, though she usually sat halfway between the vestibule and the altar in the darkest section of church beneath the fifth station of the cross. She never took Communion, a fact that was much puzzled over and commented on among the sparse congregation. Neither did she go to Confession. She was a contradiction, often attending weekday morning masses, which were not required, without ever, to use the terminology of Sister Matilda Marie, who taught catechism, "partaking of the Mass, His Body, His Blood." How odd she looked, now that I think back on those days, kneeling there in the nearly empty church, first light just painting the stained-glass windows, among the dozen or so elderly women with fleshy throats and gnarled fingers tracking noisy rosary beads. But my mother, I suppose, was also a widow of sorts.

I never gave her much thought until Father Michaels said what an extraordinary woman she was. I loved her, I suppose, but the way ten-year-olds love, arrogantly, aloofly, without much urgency. She was the constant in my life; she made sure I had clean underclothes in the top drawer of my dresser, that the meat in the freezer got defrosted in time for the dinner she would have to cook when she got home from the telephone company.

Father Michaels wanted to know all about our life together, so I told him, understanding only then in the telling just how unusual that life was. When I explained our daily routine, he guessed immediately my mother's most pressing concern—the approaching summer. Something would have to be done with me when school let out. I was nearly old enough to be self-sufficient—to make my own sandwich at the noon hour—and nearly mature enough to be trusted. But not quite. Though quiet and studious and shy by nature, I was beginning to show signs that troubled my mother. I admired Elvis Presley, for instance. Especially his hair. Neither the man, his hair, nor his music seemed worthy of admiration to my mother, who forbade me to carry the slick black Ace comb in my hip pocket, the purpose of which was to subdue a stubborn un-Elvislike cowlick. No, I needed looking after. In the past we had relied on Aunt Rose for July and August, but this year she had hinted she might like to go away for the summer, explaining that she had not been out of Mohawk since the war. She'd seen pictures of the national parks out west that made her want to see them for real and find out if they could be so pretty in real life. My mother found the notion of Aunt Rose in Yellowstone ludicrous, but she knew what her cousin was trying to tell her. She didn't want the responsibility for an eleven-year-old boy for an entire summer. Forty-five minutes a day was all right, because she could feed me coconut macaroons and turn on the television, but she couldn't imagine how to keep a boy my age entertained during a whole summer. She loved children and it was the great sorrow of her life that she hadn't had any, but I wasn't really a child anymore, and I certainly wasn't *her* child.

One morning, Father Michaels suggested I introduce him to my mother. She had left immediately after mass, however, so as to be in time for her ride to work. It was only a few blocks to my school and I was used to walking them alone. So I suggested that Father Michaels come by that evening when she got home from work. He could have dinner with us if he liked.

By afternoon, of course, I had forgotten all about my unauthorized invitation, and we were just sitting down to a dinner of beans and hot dogs when a car pulled up outside. My mother feared all automobiles, because my father had one, though this was not his most effective distinguishing characteristic, since everyone we knew owned a car but us. Even Aunt Rose had a Ford. She never took it out of the garage, but she did have one. Still, not many cars pulled up in front of our house, and though no one in Mohawk had seen my father in years, my mother quickly got up from the table to make sure. She got into the living room just in time to see the young priest, his forehead glistening and a dark ring beneath each arm, getting out of the parish station wagon. He was carrying a bottle of wine.

I don't know what my mother was most confused by—the fact that a priest was coming to visit, that he was carrying a bottle of wine, or that he hadn't common sense enough to avoid dinner hour. It had been a warm day, and the heavy inner door was already open so that the house could air, so there was just the screen between them when Father Michaels mounted the porch steps. When he saw my mother staring at the bottle of wine, he raised it timidly and said, "For purely sacramental purposes."

This was a joke, but it confused my mother even more. She had made no move to open the door, but it was clear from the expectant way the man was standing there smiling at her that she was expected to. Surely this was no casual social call at such a time. Did the man intend to say mass in the living room? There was nothing to do but let him in.

My mother's hesitance finally tipped my friend that something was amiss. "I hope I'm not late," he said. "Ned didn't say what time."

They were both looking at me now. I'd started backing up when I saw who it was on the porch, but I was caught. I could feel myself flushing, but so was everybody else. My mother, no doubt

remembering the small beans-and-hot-dog casserole already
steaming in the center of the kitchen table, looked homicidal, and
I was glad the police had confiscated my grandfather's revolver.
Of the three of us, however, Father Michaels looked to be in the
worst shape. He was not only red with embarrassment, he looked
as if he might faint. Three distinct trails of perspiration disappeared into his collar.

My mother was first to rally, and she refused to hear of the
priest leaving, though he expressed a fervent and sincere desire
to. Instead, she got him to sit down on the sofa, and she left me,
as she put it, to entertain our guest. I had no idea what that might
entail. Father Michaels was too kind to say anything, but he wore
the expression of a man cruelly betrayed by a trusted ally. We
both stared at the floor and listened to the sounds emanating from
the kitchen. I heard the casserole return to the oven and the
sound of anxious, angry chopping on the drain board.

"Ned?" my mother's voice floated in, high and false from the
kitchen. "Would you ask our guest if he'd like something cool to
drink?"

I looked over at Father Michaels, who shook his head at me, as
if speech were an impossibility.

"Nope," I yelled.

"Perhaps he would like to open the bottle of wine?"

He nodded this time. He was still holding the bottle and had
read the front and back labels several times, rotating the bottle
again and again, making me wish I had something to read too. My
mother left the salad she was tossing in order to hand me the
corkscrew along with a scalding look. Working on the bottle,
Father Michaels appeared to regain his composure. He thanked
me for handing him the corkscrew and I felt like thanking him
for thanking me. "Ever see one of these in action?" he said.

I hadn't. The corkscrew's presence in the utensil drawer had
always perplexed me since it was the only item in there that was
never used. Father Michaels used the pointed tip to cut the outer
wrapping and expose the cork, which he then extracted so deftly
I was surprised. His movements on the altar and even in the
sacristy always seemed clumsy, as if he were remembering what
he was supposed to do at the last second. No matter how many
times he wore certain vestments, he could never seem to remember where the clasps were and would circle himself trying to
locate them like a dog chasing his tail. I'd never seen anybody

remove a cork from a wine bottle before, but I doubted anybody
could do it more gracefully.

He was examining the cork when my mother came in and said
"Gentlemen?" She seemed to have regained her composure too.

When Father Michaels presented her with the bottle, he said,
"I hope it doesn't clash with what you've prepared," and my
mother laughed like that was about the funniest thing she'd ever
heard.

All things considered, I thought dinner went quite well. Our small
kitchen was overheated from the oven, but with the back and
front doors open we got a breeze. My mother apologized for the
casserole, but the priest wouldn't hear of it, and pretended to read
from the back of the wine bottle that it was a perfect complement
to red meats, pasta dishes, and hot dog casseroles. He praised my
mother's oil and vinegar dressing, claiming that most people
showed neither judgment nor restraint when it came to vinegar.
I was given a small glass of wine. To everyone's surprise, Father
Michaels turned out to be a wonderful conversationalist and
when he found his stride there was no need for anybody to talk
who didn't want to. He also stopped perspiring. He told us how
he had worked as a waiter and busboy in a big New York hotel
on vacations before entering the seminary. He had many interesting stories to tell, and listening to him you had to remind yourself
that he was a priest. My mother must have had the same reaction,
because after a couple glasses of wine she relaxed and even smiled
over at me with something like her usual fondness. Before long,
the casserole dish had been scraped clean and two lonely Ber-
muda onion rings swam in the bottom of the salad bowl. And then,
as if the evening hadn't been strange enough already, Father
Michaels suggested I go outside and play ball against the side of
the house while he talked with my excellent mother about some
little matter of business. I hadn't said two words during dinner,
but I was still surprised to discover my friend considered my
presence dispensable to the social equilibrium. My mother looked
surprised too.

But I grabbed my mitt and rubber ball and went outside. The
foundation of our house was stone and perfect for throwing
grounders. There was only one more week of fifth grade, then a
whole summer of I did not know what. I doubted you could just

catch grounders for three whole months. If my father had been around, we could have gotten Wussy and gone fishing, and that would have accounted for one day. As it was, I wondered what would become of me.

From where I threw the ball against the side of the house I could see diagonally in the kitchen window, but the late afternoon light reflected off it, and only the outline of Father Michaels's back was visible. Occasionally, though, I heard my mother laugh.

5

And so the rectory became my second home, much to the satisfaction of everyone except the old Monsignor, who took no pleasure in having even such a quiet boy on the church grounds. My presence continued to surprise him when we encountered one another on the lawn between the rectory and the church, and I could tell that he would have liked to run me off the way he did the other boys who occasionally climbed the chain-link fence on a short cut to the ball field. I never caused him any trouble that I know of, but he always looked at me suspiciously, and if I happened to be carrying my rubber ball, he reminded me that stained glass windows were not cheaply replaced. It was clear that he did not think much of me, which was understandable enough, given the number of my confessions he'd heard. One of the things I liked best about Father Michaels was that after hearing people's confessions he didn't seem to think the worse of them. He heard mine a couple of times and didn't treat me any differently afterwards. I preferred confessing to the old Monsignor though. My new friend was too nice a man to lie to.

On weekday mornings, after mass, we usually had breakfast in the high-ceilinged rectory dining room. I'd never seen so much food at a morning meal. At home, my mother had neither the time nor the inclination to cook breakfast before going to work, so usually all I got was a sugar donut or buttered graham cracker. At the rectory, Mrs. Ambrosino, a widow of advancing middle age, who had cooked for the Monsignor since the death of her husband, brought on huge platters of food that filled the long rectory table. Except on Fridays, there were bacon and sausage, and sometimes ham, along with towers of toast, half a dozen eggs fried in butter, pitchers of juice and milk and bowls of fruit. You could have pancakes if you asked for them. There was so much food and so much of it went unconsumed that for a long time I was under the impression that company was anticipated which kept failing to show up. The old Monsignor, even before his health began to fail, had never been a prodigious eater, and most mornings he could be induced to eat little more than half a grapefruit, which contributed, in my opinion, to his sour disposition. That left the rest of the feast to Father Michaels and me. My friend ate like he did everything else, nervously, and I often felt that he would have eaten more and enjoyed it better if he'd felt entitled to it. But eating with genuine good appetite is no easy thing when you are seated at the opposite end of a long table from a man who makes it a point of moral significance to subsist on half a grapefruit, eaten in under a minute so that the bowl could be pushed emphatically away, another duty done. It's not nearly so hard when you're a boy seated halfway down the table, directly in front of the bacon and sausage and influenced more by aroma than moral statements. I ate like a dog.

"Ned," my friend would say, using his cloth napkin to mop his forehead before placing it in the middle of his plate, "you're a wonder."

Mrs. Ambrosino apparently thought so too, though she derived no satisfaction from the fact that *somebody* was eating the food she prepared. As far as she was concerned, nobody counted but the old pastor. Father Michaels she ignored as if he did not exist, despite his repeated compliments on her cooking. She was not cooking for the handsome young interloper any more than for the urchin he had, for reasons known only to himself, allowed to invade the sanctity of the rectory. Everything she did was for *the* father, the old Monsignor, who had officiated at every important religious ceremony in her lifetime, the last being her husband's funeral. She had not always been a religious woman, though she was one now. As a young woman she had lived with the man she eventually married while they waited for his wife to oblige them by dying, which she eventually did. Mrs. Ambrosino had been wild then, as wild as any girl in Mohawk, uncontrollable in her passion for that awful woman's husband, but when she finally got him the passion leaked away, and now her only passion was for the old priest's health, which she equated with eating. *"Mangia,"* she implored him, hemming him in with platters of food, many of them rich delicacies searched out and ordered all the way from New York City to tempt him back to health. "Keep up your spirit."

"Good Mrs. Ambrosino," the old man responded. "It is not a question of spirit but of cholesterol. Your husband died of lasagne. An avoidable fate."

As a matter of principle, however, the old priest had no objection to the overabundance of food, though he himself had no intention of eating it. A pastor for nearly forty years at Our Lady of Sorrows, he liked to keep up appearances. The rectory and church were freshly painted on alternate years, and a large part of the collection money went to upkeep. A full-time grounds-keeper was employed to tend carefully planted, cross-shaped flower beds on the main lawn, and the hedges and weeping willows were kept manicured. In the autumn, leaves were raked every day, and when people came to mass on Sundays in October they often remarked that leaves knew better than to fall where they were not allowed. The Monsignor considered himself both a good priest and a successful one, and he enjoyed the idea of a well-stocked table, in contrast to which his meager grapefruit might be fully appreciated.

After breakfast the old priest usually retired and Father Michaels often had visits to make in the community. As often as not, I was left to my own devices. The grounds within the chain-link boundaries of Our Lady of Sorrows were extensive and lovely. There were several trees that I yearned to climb, but I knew that such deviant behavior would have been frowned on by the Monsignor, whose tolerance of my mere presence seemed precarious enough. A stand of tall pines along the back fence behind the church provided cool, dark shade, and most days I sat beneath them on a blanket of pine needles reading about the wonderfully improbable adventures of two teenage boys on an island populated exclusively by the world's foremost scientists, who were given to inventing things like ray guns that first got the boys into and then out of trouble. Sometimes when he returned from his duties Father Michaels would join me and we would listen to the breeze high up in the pines and I would tell him what was new on Spindrift Island. "Ned," he would say, "you're a wonder. Who else would think to go around *back* of a church?"

In fact, my stand of pines was the coolest, prettiest part of the church grounds, and from the base of the trees you could look all the way up through the branches to the milk-white cross on the roof.

"This could be the coolest spot in all Mohawk County," my friend said, and it was true, he sweated hardly at all when we relaxed there. "Only a boy would be clever enough to find such a spot."

I didn't see where it was all that clever, but I didn't mind him saying so. I liked listening to Father Michaels talk, even though most of what he said was so odd I couldn't figure out whether he was brilliant or simpleminded, though I feared the latter.

"People forget to notice beautiful things," he said, looking up through the dark branches at the circle of blue-gray sky. "They outgrow it, I guess. A man who lives in a house on the beach forgets to look at the ocean. A man with a beautiful wife is just as likely to wander off someplace and forget her entirely. God must think we're silly people."

Then he added, "Except for you, Ned. You're a wonder." His favorite observation, the strongest evidence I had in favor of simplemindedness in my friend.

My only other companion that summer was the groundskeeper, a man called Skinny, who wasn't particularly, though he may have been once. Now he had a melon under his white t-shirt. Skinny was in his forties, his stubbled chin a mixture of gray and black. He did not take to me until he learned I would not only do his work for him but thank him for the opportunity. I had a terrible yearning to feel useful, and Skinny, who had yearnings of the opposite nature, wasn't the sort of man to let me suffer when there was something he could do about it. Of all his duties he most disliked mowing the great expanses of lawn, something the Monsignor wanted done every fifth or sixth day. To Skinny, a lawn didn't look so scraggly that a sensible person would notice unless it went untended for a good two weeks. His basic philosophy was that mowing lawns was perverse and unreasonable behavior to begin with, the proof of which lay in the fact that the grass grew right back again. He was not himself a religious man and had little good to say concerning people who saw God's will in the everyday world, but if he *had* been the sort of man to see meaning in things, he would have concluded that God had never intended grass to be mowed. At least not by Skinny.

In the beginning I just helped with the trimming in spots the mower couldn't negotiate. Especially in the cool moist shade along the sides of the church and rectory, where the grass grew thicker. Unfortunately, the hand shears I was given were designed for a full-grown hand. I made little progress and was unhappy with the task. What I really wanted was to run the big power mower. By happy coincidence, what Skinny really wanted was the shade and the hand shears, for he suffered mightily under the broiling sun, mopping sweat from his forehead with the stretched sleeves of his t-shirt until they were ribbed with brown.

"I don't know," he said dubiously, glancing at the rectory when I suggested we swap jobs. On the one hand, he didn't want to be observed shirking his duties. On the other, he didn't want to do them. This particular day he had a driving headache, and the very idea of starting the rattling engine of the power mower made him feel weak. There was a nice cool patch of ground on the far side of the church that needed his attention. It was well out of sight from the rectory and he kept a flask in the vicinity for company. He could even bring along the hand shears. "I don't know," he repeated, scratching his stubble.

We decided, predictably enough, on "just this once," a phrase Skinny found so reassuring that the next time the grass needed mowing he used it again. Each time he pulled the mower out of the shed he handed it over to me "just this once" before disappearing. I liked both the mowing and the idea that the whole thing was more or less illicit. Some morning the old Monsignor would look out the window and catch me at it, and that would be the end. It didn't happen though, and after a while I caught on to the fact that when the old priest went upstairs after breakfast it was to take a long nap that lasted until lunch. My friend Father Michaels caught me behind the mower one morning and looked startled. He began to shout something at me, but when I waved at him happily, he changed his mind. He watched me though, until he was sure I was in command of the situation, then waved

again and shouted something at me before getting in the parish
station wagon and driving off. It looked like it might have been,
"Ned, you're a wonder."

There was other work too. Though he wasn't much with lawns,
Skinny earned his keep with flowers. His rough fingers moved
expertly among the good plants, uprooting weeds with a deft,
flicking motion. He never got confused, as I sometimes did. With
a small hand spade he could turn earth without disturbing the
tender roots, as if by intuition he could sense how far out and
down they grew. He knew in advance if any growing thing was
going to turn sick and often began to administer the cure before
the first leaf turned yellow. After a while I began to learn some
of the signs.

I was surprised to discover one day that he knew my father.
"Everybody knows Sam Hall," he said.

"He's out west building roads," I said, ashamed I could offer no
other information about him.

"He is like hell," Skinny said. "He's right here in Mohawk."

Home was only a few blocks from the church, but Father Michaels liked to bring me home in the afternoon. Sometimes he
and my mother would sit on the porch and talk while I threw
grounders. The day Skinny told me about my father, I wished the
priest had just let me walk. He tried to get a conversation going,
but I clammed up.

We pulled up in front of the house as my mother was inserting
her key in the door. She turned and flashed a big smile that
encompassed me and my friend. There was nobody else on the
street. I looked.

"Patrick Donovan," said my mother, in reference to Skinny, "is
a fool and a drunk."

It was later that same night, and I'd told her what Skinny said.
She was never generous where Skinny was concerned, and my
stories about him were always greeted coolly. It was true what she
said, though. Skinny was always drinking or getting over drinking.
But even so, it seemed to me that if he said Sam Hall was in
Mohawk, it might be true. My father wasn't the sort of thing you'd
just imagine. I could tell that my mother was worried that it might
be true, though she kept saying that it wasn't and that Skinny was

a malicious little snail. "Trust me," she said. "If your father were in Mohawk, he'd be here tormenting us."

"Maybe he's afraid you'll shoot him," I ventured, realizing as I said it that I resented her for wishing him away and for shooting his car. I had always been on her side, and it surprised me to feel annoyed with her. I hadn't thought about my father or their conflict in a long time, but now, for some reason, when I recalled that afternoon over three years ago, her emptying my grandfather's revolver into the white convertible seemed a little excessive. My attitude toward my father had changed subtly too. I remembered enjoying myself fishing with him and Wussy, though I still felt guilty about it. My mother had called it kidnapping and said whether I knew it or not I had been in grave danger the whole time, as my condition upon return—beat up, cut up, swollen, diseased—made abundantly clear. I had been reduced to such a sorry state in a mere twenty-four hours, she reminded me, adding that "People who hang around your father often require hospitalization." She considered F. William Peterson a prime example, though it seemed to me that his hospital visit had more to do with teaming up with her than with my father.

It was hard to find fault with her basic thesis, though. Sam Hall, as one of his friends remarked to me many years later, should have been issued with a warning label. My mother hated Skinny for having raised his specter. "Why do you employ that horrid man?" she asked Father Michaels the next evening when he brought me home from the rectory. Often the priest lingered a few minutes on the front porch before heading back to the dark rectory dining room and one of Mrs. Ambrosino's heavy, complicated dinners.

"*I* don't," my friend explained, "though I don't see any great harm in the man."

"*You* don't see any great harm in anybody," my mother replied petulantly. "You'd probably find much to admire in my husband."

"Now Jenny . . ." he said, and for a moment I thought he was going to reach out and take her hand.

There may have been no great harm in Skinny, but the very next week I nearly got him fired. I was cutting the wide strip of grass between the church and rectory when the mower picked up a stone the size of a Ping-Pong ball. How it happened onto the sacred stretch of ground beyond the chain-link fence, I couldn't guess, but there it was, and I saw it just as it disappeared beneath the mower. Instead of stopping—and I'm not sure I could have—I gritted my teeth and listened for a bang. I had picked up pebbles before and the clatter they made dancing around among the rotating blades was horrible. This time, however, there was just one modest thunk, then the normal sound of the mower. About two seconds later, however, there was the sound of shattering glass.

At first, I did not connect the stone that disappeared beneath the mower with the hole in the stained-glass window on the second floor of the rectory. After all, the building was nearly fifty yards away, farther than I could have thrown a stone that size. I pulled the mower backward, examining the just-mowed area, hoping to discover the stone there on the ground, which would render the broken glass coincidental. No stone.

The Monsignor had it in his hand when he came out. It had violated his bedroom, and the old priest was in no mood to marvel at the accuracy and difficulty of the shot, to me the single most impressive fact of the occurrence. Under different circumstances such long odds might have appeared miraculous, evidence of something other than natural law at work in the universe, for the round stone had plinked a neat hole in the red geometric center of the small window, a feat that a hundred stone-throwing sharpshooters couldn't have duplicated given a hundred tries each. Unfortunately, this miraculous aspect of the event was lost on the Monsignor, whose horizontal matins the stone had interrupted. He was in his stocking feet, a fact I couldn't get over.

"Where is Mr. Donovan?" he wanted to know.

That was a troublesome question. I didn't doubt but that Skinny was asleep in the shade around the other side of the church. He had disappeared around the corner an hour earlier and one recent sweep of the mower had taken me close enough to see his work shoes, forming a V, pointed heavenward, jutting out from behind a bush. So I looked around, as if I expected to see the groundskeeper at my elbow and was surprised to discover him missing. "He was just here," I said.

The old priest squelched the still rattling motor, and the resulting silence was accusatory, like that of the confessional.

"Kindly locate Mr. Donovan and ask him if I might have a moment of his time."

With that, he turned in his stocking feet and padded back to the rectory still clutching the stone.

I found Skinny right where I had seen his shoes and he was in them, rubbing his eyes, awakened when the mower was turned off. "What's going on?" he said suspiciously. He knew, of course, that the day would come when I would be discovered and he would have to explain why a boy was doing his work. He was prepared for that. He would shrug his shoulders and say, "How's a kid supposed to learn?"

"Monsignor wants to see you," I told him.

"Sure," he said, blinking, trying to look wide awake. "What the hell. Why not." He would bring the hand shears along as a prop.

"I didn't see the stone in time," I said when we rounded the corner of the church and the rectory came into view.

"Stone?"

I wished I had it to show him. The window was still too far away and the hole too small to see from where we stood, and Skinny had stopped in his tracks when it became clear the situation was more complicated than he had imagined. It took me several minutes to make him understand what had happened, because he could see where the mower was sitting and he doubted it was possible. (At least somebody had a proper appreciation of the miraculous.) "What would a stone be doing there?" he kept asking, probably to waste time. He did not want to face the Monsignor.

He not only did not want to, he flat refused to do it. For a while he paced up and down in the shade, then gave up and went back to where he had been sleeping and began to clip the border with the hand shears. He stayed right there until it was time for lunch, and then he made me fetch his lunch pail.

Mrs. Ambrosino met me on the back porch. Clearly, she had been sent to see if the groundskeeper was in sight. She approved of Skinny even less than she approved of me, refusing even to let him into the kitchen for a glass of water. She'd known Skinny Donovan forever and he'd known her, too. As far as Mrs. Ambrosino was concerned, Skinny wasn't too good to drink out of the hose if he got thirsty. "Where's he hiding?" she said.

I pretended ignorance.

At the table in the dark dining room, the two priests were already seated. The younger was saying grace, though he looked up when I came in. The Monsignor always studied his own folded hands until they made the sign of the cross. I slipped quietly into my chair, hoping that when the prayer was concluded the Monsignor would not notice I was there. Most days he didn't.

The table was full, as usual. In the center was a large white soup tureen in the shape of a dove, leaking steam. Nearby, a large platter of cold cuts, including rare roast beef, spiced ham and salami, was surrounded by bowls of salads, condiments and two loaves of bread, one light, one dark, on separate silver platters. The Monsignor lifted the lid from the tureen and peered inside suspiciously. Mrs. Ambrosino hovered nearby, anxious to assist. "What is that floating?" he wanted to know.

"It is a wedding soup," the good woman explained, without precisely answering his question. Having discovered that "The Father" often ate little more than a shallow bowl of broth at the noon meal, she had taken recently to serving "heartier" soups. "The meatballs are made with the finest veal," she added.

The Monsignor frowned when the ladle came up full of meatballs, pasta, assorted vegetables. "No one at this table is contemplating matrimony that I am aware of," he said, and proceeded to ladle carefully just the stock into his bowl until a shallow puddle formed there. When a meatball plopped in by mistake he speared it with the outside tine of his fork and plunked it back into the tureen before sending the whole apparatus to the younger priest, who at that moment looked unusually pale and failed to notice its approach. The Monsignor accepted a single slice of dark bread from near the heel and massaged a small dab of butter into it methodically.

"Mr. Donovan is unavailable for consultation?" he said without looking up.

Mrs. Ambrosino was staring at me maliciously, as if she would have liked to prevent the soup tureen's arrival until the matter of my worthiness to receive it had been decided. Where soup was concerned, my method was the Monsignor's in geometric reverse. I would shamelessly search out her finest veal meatballs like rare jewels. Or at least I would have on a normal day. At the moment I was a little too nervous to conduct my customary feed.

"He might be clipping over on the other side of the church," I said. It was sort of a compromise statement, true but phrased without the conviction that would initiate an immediate search.

"He no doubt imagines that his services cannot be terminated if he himself cannot be found," said the Monsignor, which struck me as pretty sharp. It was Skinny's flawed plan in a nutshell.

"I doubt your mother would approve of your operating heavy machinery," the old priest continued, still not looking at me. "After all, you are only a boy, and not a very large boy at that. If you happened to be injured, we could be held legally liable. We could be sued. As it is, the rectory has sustained damage, though that is not the issue."

He then discussed the price of stained glass so thoroughly that I thought perhaps it might be the issue after all.

"Operating a powerful mower is a hazardous occupation, as Mr. Donovan is well aware," he went on. "A paperboy in Poughkeepsie was killed last summer when a stone flew across the street and knocked him off his bicycle. You can appreciate how your mother would feel if I had to inform her this evening that you had been killed while in our care. Knowing the sort of man your father is I doubt any of us would be safe, assuming *he* could be located and informed."

Had it been anyone but the Monsignor I might have taken up one or two issues. Though hardly a skilled debater or thinker, I remember wanting to point out that the dead paperboy would still be alive had he been pushing the mower instead of delivering papers across the street. Indeed, the present circumstance, viewed objectively, suggested that the Monsignor himself, indoors and nearly fifty yards away, had run a greater risk than I. If one insisted on drawing a moral from the stained glass window and the dead paperboy, it might have been that life was quirky at best and that being careful wasn't much of a guarantee.

I don't know what Father Michaels thought of the Monsignor's logic, but when he heard the remark about my father, he colored and quickly came to my defense. "I think Ned just wanted to help. He's not the sort of young man who just accepts hospitality without giving something back," he said quietly. He didn't look up either, and the conversation, one of the longest ever conducted at table that summer, was made the more bizarre by the fact that nobody looked at anybody else. "His mother was pleased when I told her how much he was helping out around the rectory. Ned and his mother are fine people."

"Then you were aware the boy was operating machinery?"

"The mower? Yes. I thought you were as well. He passed right in front of the library window last week when we were discussing consubstantiation."

The Monsignor stopped spooning broth. "I assure you I did *not*

know. It would have been good of you to bring it to my attention.
You bring other unpleasant matters to my attention."

Father Michaels folded his napkin carefully. "Your wedding
soup was splendid, Mrs. A," he said. And then he did a thoroughly
unexpected thing. With the Monsignor still seated and soaking up
the last of his puddle with black bread, and before grace could
conclude the meal, the young priest got up and left the room.

6

I had mixed feelings about the possibility that my father had
returned to Mohawk. I doubted he was quite as dangerous as my
mother said. Or maybe I just concluded he wouldn't be dangerous
to me. As with the mower, it was largely a matter of positioning.
Still, life had become comfortable and happy without him. My
mother was clearly happier than ever before, and she seldom
even complained about the phone company. I enjoyed my long
days at the rectory. They started with the early morning mass,
and most of the time my mother accompanied me. We liked the
walk together past the bakery, which at that hour was awash in
lovely aromas. In church, my mother sat closer to the altar now,
but still off to one side, between the first and second stations of
the cross. She still did not receive communion, and most mornings she was the only person in Our Lady of Sorrows who did not.

After mass, Father Michaels and I would sometimes give her a
lift home in the parish station wagon before returning to the
rectory for breakfast, and then the day would stretch out before
me. Part of it I would spend on Spindrift Island, part helping
Skinny tend the grounds. Once the storm of indignation over the
stained glass window blew over, I even started mowing again, this
time with the Monsignor's blessing, which was secured indirectly
through Father Michaels. He called it interceding, like what the
Virgin did with her Son, and he interceded for Skinny too, so he
could come out of hiding and do *some* work at least.

In short, life seemed pretty much the way it should be, and while I sometimes felt a strange yearning to see my father again, I didn't want him turning up and upsetting things. I kept imagining that late some afternoon, when my mother and Father Michaels and I were all sitting on the front porch before she went in to fix dinner, my father would careen around the corner in the same old bullet-riddled white convertible and come to a rocking halt, one wheel over the curb, his blackened thumb tapping time on the steering wheel. For some reason I feared this scenario even more than a second kidnapping or the resumption of his nightly marauding when my mother and I would be alone. Not that Father Michaels wasn't prepared for the sort of man my father was. I just didn't want them to meet. The young priest might have had the courage to stand up to the old Monsignor, but I doubted he'd be a match for my father.

One morning after breakfast I found Skinny in the shed sharpening the long-handled cutting spade he used to trim the terrace along the street. The Monsignor did not believe in allowing grass to grow over the edge of the sidewalk, so every third week or so we dug a small two-inch trench along the border of the walk. Skinny enjoyed the job about as much as he enjoyed mowing. Early morning often found him in a bad mood anyway, and he was sometimes sharp with me then. I knew he felt insulted that I should be invited to the feast each morning when he himself wasn't allowed in the back door for a drink of water. He didn't blame me exactly, but the whole thing didn't sit well. Today, he seemed in a better mood than usual. "Your old man says hi," he said.

I stopped still and didn't say anything. I'd been wanting to pin him down on the business of having seen my father, but I was a little afraid and a little ashamed to admit how little I knew about his whereabouts.

"Said to tell you he'd be around to see you one of these days."

I didn't tell my mother. It would just get her started on Skinny again. She wasn't a great person to bring bad news to. Father Michaels may have guessed that something was wrong on the way home, but he didn't try to make me talk and did not join us on the porch as usual. He got out of the station wagon and stood there in the street until my mother appeared at the screen door to let me in.

That night our dinner was so silent I began to suspect she already knew. Probably someone had seen him and called her, she was so thoughtful and nervous. After dinner she did the dishes hurriedly, checking the clock every few minutes, and when I didn't get to listen to my usual Friday night radio shows I was almost grateful. "Go to sleep," my mother instructed me when I was tucked in, but it wasn't completely dark yet and she seemed so agitated I didn't think I'd be able to. Alone in bed, I tried to gear myself up for the future. Sam Hall was back in town, and that meant things would change. There was no telling how. Maybe I would be swiped again. Maybe they would just yell at each other. Maybe my mother would shoot him and go to jail. She didn't have a gun anymore, as far as I knew, but then I hadn't known about the first one. I lay awake for a long time thinking about the possibilities and how they would change things.

I wasn't aware of having fallen asleep, but when I awoke from the vivid dream, my room was dark and it felt late. In the dream the old Monsignor, my mother and I were all seated around the long table in the rectory waiting for Mrs. Ambrosino and her steaming tureen of wedding soup. My father was there too, where Father Michaels usually sat. He had a fishhook in his black thumb.

"Honestly, Sam," my mother said when she saw the monofilament line dangling there. The Monsignor was to marry them all over again, as soon as we finished lunch. But now she had spotted the line, and I could tell by the look on her face that she didn't want to marry anybody with a fishhook stuck in his black thumb. For my father's part, he didn't seem to care. "Kiss my ass, Jenny," he said, and yanked out the hook so that blood spurted out onto the white table cloth. "The finest veal meatballs," Mrs. Ambrosino said, apropos of nothing. The Monsignor ladled broth as he spoke. "I would appreciate a word with both of you on the subject of this boy . . ."

From my open bedroom window I could see out across the dark backyards where the cops had chased my father that winter so long ago. The night was quiet and sleepy, but I was wide awake now. A dog down the block barked sharply twice and shook his chain. I got up and looked out the window, but it was too dark to see much. In the quarter moonlight only dark outlines—of garages, fences, trees, and houses—were visible against the night. The maple I had been climbing the last time my father was in Mohawk had grown too; fully mature, its highest branches now far above the peak of our house. He had stood there, silently, on the porch below and watched me. I had been too afraid to jump even so short a distance, and it had seemed to me that no one understood me so completely as my father must have at that moment. And when I heard a soft footfall on the porch below, followed by the creaking hinge on the screen door, I knew he had come for me. Again the dog shook his chain, but this time he did not bark.

Positioning myself at the bedroom door, I listened. My mother always kept the downstairs doors locked, not that that would keep my father out. Down the hall I saw a thin crease of light below her door, enough to make the top of the stair gray instead of black. A stair creaked before I could decide whether or not to warn her.

It was all happening too fast, as if he had somehow walked right *through* the locked door below, as if inserting, turning, withdrawing a key were mere formalities to be dispensed with since no one was present to witness them. The footfalls on the stair were not anxious, though. They came, softly and heavily, stopping on the landing, as if to listen for my breathing. I counted the stairs and before he reached the top, scrambled back into bed. Sleep, I thought. If I could just get to sleep, it would not be happening. If he thought I was asleep, maybe he would not take me. I waited.

Surprisingly, there were no more footfalls, and the dog outside was quiet. I thought I heard low voices, and listened intently until I heard them again. Had they come from the street outside? I waited for the dog to bark again.

When he didn't, I crept to the door and opened it a crack. The pale ribbon of light was still visible beneath my mother's bedroom door, and I heard her voice, soft and low, before the light went out.

Then I went back to bed, my heart pounding. He had not come to steal me. My father had simply come home.

I woke up early, still excited, to the sound of voices in the kitchen below. The sun was shining brilliantly and I stopped dressing long enough to locate my friend the dog, who was vigorously shaking his chain, three backyards away. Good dog, I thought.

I took the stairs three to a stride, pulling my t-shirt over my head at the same time. I stopped at the landing. My mother was at the table, sitting in my chair, her back to the stairs. She turned when she heard me coming and smiled. Father Michaels was at the table too. He was not wearing his collar.

"Look who's come for breakfast," my mother said.

My friend, who had been studying his hands, smiled at me weakly.

"So what's the matter?" she said. "Are you going to just stand there?"

When I did precisely that, she broke into song:

> 'Cause when you're up, you're up.
> And when you're down you're down.
> And when you're only halfway up,
> You're neither up nor down.

"Can I go outside and play ball?" I said.

"Okay," she agreed. It was an unheard-of privilege before breakfast, but she was in about the best mood ever. "Don't wander off though. I'm going to fix us all a *stunning* breakfast."

Outside, I checked the street for any car that might conceivably belong to my father, but there wasn't a convertible in sight. And nothing with bullet holes. Inside, they were talking, but their voices were low. I heard my mother say, "Don't worry." Then she resumed humming, "When you're up, you're up."

I fielded hard, angry grounders, and when I was called for breakfast, I said I wasn't hungry.

"Be that way, sourpuss," my mother said, and went back inside. Then Father Michaels said something, and she told him again not to worry. Horrid Patrick Donovan just had me all worked up over my father.

"I'll go talk to him," he said.

"No," she said. "You'll talk to me."

It was nearly lunch time when I heard him leave. My mother came out onto the back porch and called, but I was out of sight around back of the small storage shed and I didn't answer. I heard her say, "I don't know where he's disappeared to."

Our house was next to the corner, and when the priest turned up the block toward Our Lady of Sorrows, he got a good view of the backyards all down the block. He spied me sitting up against the back wall of the shed and stopped. There was a fence between us, so he couldn't come over. We looked at each other for a minute, and he raised his hand in a half wave. I made him wait before raising mine. And I only gave in because he looked like the saddest man in the world.

My mother and I went to the nine o'clock mass on Sunday, and I hoped, for the first time ever, that it would be the Monsignor's service. We got there early and the church was practically empty, like a weekday mass, except that the sun was high and the light from the stained glass windows illuminated the whole church without the aid of the overheads. My mother looked a little like one of the stained glass windows, radiant and colorful in a summery dress. She wouldn't have been able to hide in the shadows even if there had been any. Her mood was irrepressibly good, just like Saturday's. I had tried to damage that mood both days, and I knew it couldn't be done. "When will Dad come see us?" I had asked her.

"Hard to say," she admitted. "We've been lucky so far."

But having said that, she relented a little and took my hand. "I know you can't forget him," she said. "He *is* your father. But you shouldn't take everything to heart so. I know you want to think he loves you, and maybe he will someday. When someone loves you," she went on, "you don't have to wish for it to be so. You just know it is."

"Well, I know," I told her.

"No, you wish. You have to be careful of wishing. It can hurt. It's better to wait until you know. Waiting for your father to turn up won't make him do it."

I didn't care for that answer, so I withdrew my hand.

"You needn't take it out on me, in any case," she said. "If you wanted *me*, it *would* help. I'd know, and you wouldn't have to tell me. That's the way it is between people who love each other."

Then her eyes got a faraway look and it was like talking to somebody who wasn't there.

I figured I'd be the first one in the sacristy, but Father Michaels was already there, and if that wasn't strange enough, he was already fully vested and praying at the kneeler beneath the window, which nobody ever used except to stack things on. He didn't appear to notice when I came in, which was fine with me. I got my cassock and surplice on, lit the low mass candles, carried the red Bible to the pulpit, turned on the correct overheads. All this took ten minutes or so, and when I got back to the sacristy, he was still at the kneeler staring off into space. I wondered if the minds of priests wandered when they were praying the way mine did. Sometimes, if I was just an extra on the altar, without any specific duties to stay alert for, I'd drift away and miss just about the whole thing.

He noticed me this time and got up quickly. "Ned," he said with satisfaction, and he smiled at me so warmly I decided not to be mad at him anymore. He couldn't help not being my father and he hadn't meant to disappoint me by being at the breakfast table when I had in mind a different sort of man entirely. Right then, when he smiled at me, I decided it would be better if I had dreamed the dog barking and the footsteps on the stair and the light beneath my mother's door. All day Saturday I had thought about whether or not I had dreamed it, and now I decided I had. He offered a hand, and I took it.

"Are we ready?" he said.

"Sure," I said, "but we've still got ten minutes."

"You're right," he said, glancing at the clock. "I suppose we have to wait."

With five minutes to go, the sacristy door blew open and three other altar boys came in, laughing and shoving each other, then making a point of desisting.

"Ned will serve," Father Michaels said, much to everyone's surprise, when we were all assembled. Of the four, I had the least seniority, and normally I would have been assigned to guarding the sacristy door. Though considered competent to serve at week-day mass, boys of my age and limited credentials were thought unequal to the same task on Sunday before a packed house, which had been known to give even the steadiest hand the shakes at bell-ringing time. I flushed at the breach of decorum, and the looks on the faces of the older boys spoke plainly that no such travesty would have been tolerated by the Monsignor.

But no one dared protest, and when we lined up Father Michaels put me before him and rested his slender hand on my shoulder. Then, solemnly, we approached the altar of God, the Holy Tabernacle, to celebrate the great mystery of faith.

The first hint that something was wrong came after the gospel, when Father Michaels closed the book, retreated from the pulpit to the altar and began the offertory. I could not remember another instance of a Sunday mass without a sermon, and I could tell that the other boys were equally astonished and grateful. I tried to think what the reason might be, but there just wasn't any. Father Michaels usually did not talk as long as the Monsignor, and his sermons were generally less interesting than his casual conversation, but he always said *something*. Now, as he read from the ordinary of the mass, it seemed to me that his voice had become terribly thin.

When I took him the cruets, he was pale and perspiring, and it occurred to me he had not been sweating so profusely of late, which was odd, since the early August heat was the worst of the summer. I wanted to ask if he was all right, but as he poured the wine into the chalice, his Latin, though halting, was unbroken. And besides, during this portion of the proceedings all conversation was, by convention, taboo. When he placed the cruets back on the tray, there was nothing to do but return to my station at the foot of the altar. On my way, I glanced out into the congregation where my mother's bright dress stood out, and she smiled at me, apparently aware that my serving a Sunday mass was an honor. On my padded kneeler, I touched the cool handle of the gold-plated bell, though it wasn't yet time.

I removed the gold communion paten from its cloth sheath when the four long lines of communicants approached the railing. We began as always on St. Joseph's side and inched our way toward the statue of the Virgin, which presided over the other side altar. Those kneeling waited a few moments after receiving the host, then made the sign of the cross and stood, their places immediately filled by other communicants. I was proud of the job I was doing, smoothly inserting the communion plate beneath each expectant chin without chopping any throats. There was a rhythm that took over after a while, and it became easier to follow my friend's hand from chalice to tongue.

I was so intent on my job that I almost did not notice when one of the vacated places along the rail was taken by my mother. Seeing her kneeling there made me wonder if all the strange things in the world were going to happen in this one mass. During the years that we had been attending mass, she had never received Communion, and when I asked her why, all she had said was that she would when she felt like she was in the state of grace.

Catechism class had taught me the answer to that one, but when
I suggested she just go to Confession and wipe the slate clean, she
only smiled. But now there she was, and if ever a woman *looked*
like she was in the state of grace, my mother did then. She looked
as radiant as the virgin who stood above her, as different as could
be from the woman who had shot out the windshield and front
tire of my father's convertible and then eaten Librium for two
months to calm down. She had become softer, lovelier, almost
younger, in her bright, sleeveless summer dress. Everyone in the
church seemed to be looking at her.

As we receded from her along the Communion rail, her eyes
followed us, and Father Michaels stumbled, then righted himself.
His eyes no longer appeared focused and he began to have difficulty locating the tongues of the faithful. He looked like a blind
man going on sound and touch, though I think I was the only one
who suspected he was in serious trouble.

When we reached the far end of the communion rail, we
started working our way back, Father Michaels doing the backing
now, I following, toward where my mother knelt. The communion plate was spattered with his perspiration, and when he
missed the tongue of an elderly woman I was ready and caught
the sacred host. The old woman looked surprised, for I had
brushed her chin. Then she saw the host, her host, soaking up
perspiration like a sponge in the middle of the communion plate.

"Corpus Domini Nostri Jesu Christi," I heard Father Michaels
murmur, as if the host were still between his thumb and forefinger. But the look on his face was terrible. The old woman before
us waited patiently, but the priest could only stare down at his
own hand as if it had betrayed him. Finally, as if convinced that
she was the one holding things up, the old woman made the sign
of the cross and arose uncertainly, turning away from the rail.

Father Michaels took one step toward the retreating communi-
cant and held out his own offending hand, as if to invite her
return, but the communion rail was between them. He watched
the old woman all the way down the center aisle. Then he met
my mother's half-lovely, half-alarmed stare, which shifted from
him to me and back again, and for a moment it was as if we three
were the only ones in the church, perhaps in the world.

When the spell broke, the priest turned back toward the high
altar. I stayed where I was. It occasionally happened that there
were not enough hosts in the chalice to serve all the parishioners,

and the altar boy was expected to remain at the rail to mark the celebrant's place. And so I did, but not without misgiving, because I had seen the chalice and it was still half full. Father Michaels placed it in the center of the open tabernacle and then, for some reason, disappeared into the sacristy.

At the Communion rail we all awaited his return, and when the organ stopped, the church was still, except for some nervous rustling. There's no telling how long I would have remained there at the rail if one of the other boys had not retrieved me. The back door of the sacristy was flung wide open, and the other altar boys were clustered just inside, framed in the light, looking out across Skinny's well-tended floral cross, past the rectory, past the bakery, past the boundaries of our collective imaginations, for we never dreamed anything like this could happen.

7

The most famous man in the history of Mohawk County was Nathan Littler, the town father. The junior high school, the hospital, and the city hall were all named after him, and there were statues erected to his memory on the long sloping lawn in front of the junior high and the terrace of the Mohawk Free Library. Nathan Littler never exactly did anything, he just had money. A lot of it he left to the city. About the only thing in Mohawk that wasn't named after him was Myrtle Park, and that was named after his sister.

A considerable body of myth surrounded Myrtle Littler when I was growing up. Local legend had it that she had been very beautiful and very unhappy. She died when still a young woman without revealing the great secret of that unhappiness. Now, over a hundred years later, her ghost haunted the great park at the center of Mohawk, searching for someone to share her terrible secret with. Those she told died. No one knew why.

Her park was large and rambling, and the town had grown around its steep slopes on three sides, the new highway forming its northern boundary on the fourth. Its thick woods were allowed to go untended, and its macadam paths allowed to conform to the terrain, winding and turning back upon themselves. Two streets entered the park—one from the east, one from the west—but each dead-ended less than a hundred yards from the stone pillars that marked the entrance. Sometimes people in Mohawk grumbled about the park, which cut the town off from itself. Some places were less than a half mile apart, but with the park in between they could be reached only by going around. Every time there was trouble in the park the city council debated whether to cut down a swath of trees and blast a tunnel through the rock, but it was just talk and everybody knew it. The tanneries—the town's lifeblood—conceded to be in temporary decline before the war, began to close down after its completion, victims of foreign competition and local greed. While the men who worked in the shops waited for them to reopen, the owners, those who hadn't moved to Florida with their profits and the faith of Mohawk's men and women, were working diligently to keep other industry out of the county, thereby ensuring that Mohawk would remain destitute even in the midst of postwar prosperity. There certainly was no money to squander on dynamiting the hillsides.

The summer of 1959, the year I turned twelve, I loved to lose myself in Myrtle Park's dark winding paths. Even on the sunniest days, the park was cool and shady, the macadam trails and dirt paths just right for biking. In the daytime, patches of sunlight revealed isolated gazebos back among the trees, and at night these were reportedly used as lovers' hideaways. I wasn't allowed in the park at night though. In fact, my mother wasn't keen on the idea of my being there anytime, but the big twenty-six-inch bicycle that mysteriously appeared on our porch liberated me. When I waved goodbye to my mother and promised not to go too far (how far was that?), she could only wave back and hope. Since Father Michaels had walked out the sacristy door and down the street nearly two years before, my mother had scarcely left the house. Rumor had it he had been gathered up and sent somewhere, to Phoenix, or Santa Fe, or one of the other places my mother talked long distance with and dreamed of moving to. Now, except for work, she stayed put. We ordered our groceries from the only market in town that delivered and quit church cold turkey, both of us.

The bicycle was just sitting there one morning, and we figured it had to be from my father because there wasn't anybody else. Aunt Rose had gone out to visit the national parks and not returned, authorizing a local real estate company to sell her property and send the money to an address in Aspen, Colorado. After the bicycle arrived, I kept expecting a convertible to pull up in front of the house any day, but none did. Once two men in a black car came and knocked on the door, wanting to know how they could get in touch with my father. They said he'd come into some money. My mother offered to hold on to it for them, but they said they had to give it to him personally.

One day when I was downtown I heard somebody yell, "Hey! Sam's Kid!" and I recognized Wussy standing out in front of the pool hall. I was glad to see him, and he looked just like I remembered. He was even wearing the same kind of shapeless hat, though this one wasn't decorated with fishhooks. We shook hands. His was large and brown. Man-colored.

"Good-lookin' bike," he said.

"My father gave it to me," I said, hoping fervently that it was true, or that if it wasn't, Wussy wouldn't know.

"You look a little better than the last time I saw you," he said, as if it had been only a few days and not five years. "Your old lady still shooting at people?"

I told him that he and my father had been the last, that she didn't even own a gun anymore. He looked relieved, as if he'd been on the lookout for her all along and was glad he could give it up. I wanted to ask him about my father, but I couldn't think of a way. Having dropped his name in connection with the bike, I didn't want to admit I wasn't even sure if he was in Mohawk.

"Some men came by last week," I told him, explaining about the money they had for my father.

Wussy was interested. "Big guys? Black car?"

I said yes.

"If they come by again, tell them he went up to Alaska to work road construction."

"Alaska?" I said, my heart falling.

"Right," Wussy said, but he must have noticed how disappointed I was. "He'll be back pretty quick," he said. "You'll look up some day and there he'll be. That's the way with Sammy. It don't do no good to wait."

We said goodbye and I climbed back on my bike.

"You ever go fishing?" he called after me.

I shook my head no.

"Too bad," he said. "You were an alright fisherman. Patient, too."

So, I took Wussy's advice and stopped waiting. One day I'd look up and there he'd be, I told myself. As it turned out, the direction was the only thing Wussy got wrong.

Most of the labyrinthian dirt trails in Myrtle Park ended up in somebody's backyard if you followed them far enough, but there were so many and they were so complex that you could get all turned around, and by the time you came down out of the maze you'd be on the opposite side of town from where you thought you were. One of my favorite trails wound through the densest part of the park ending at the edge of a steep dirt embankment, at the foot of which was a shack with a sheet metal roof that gleamed in the sun. In the clearing around the shack were high mounds of junk. There were stacks of bald tires, car bodies without hoods, rusted hubcaps, foaming car batteries, splintered wooden ladders, broken sheets of fiberglass, brown bed springs. It was interesting to look down from the top of the embankment at all that junk, because a lot of it you couldn't even identify and it was fun to see if you could figure out what it had once been used for. Sometimes stray dogs found their way into that clearing and sniffed among the mounds, looking for the right place to lift a leg. When you tossed pebbles down from the embankment, they believed in God.

One afternoon, not long after I ran into Wussy, I stopped along the embankment and leaned my bike up against a tree. There weren't any dogs to convert, so I just sat. It was quiet and cool, and you could barely hear the cars that whizzed by on the invisible highway beyond the trees. Still further, about a mile away on a hill of its own, a white jewel of a house sparkled in the sun. Green lawns sloped down into the trees on each side. There had to be a road to get up there, but you couldn't see it. Sometimes I wondered what the view must be like from there. I was willing to bet you could see all the way to the river.

I collected pebbles until I had a small pile. When there weren't any dogs, I selected at random some target below and tested my marksmanship. Today, I selected the open window of a rusted-out DeSoto. The angle made it a challenge. Most of the pebbles just plinked off the roof. After a while I ran out of pebbles and started to unearth a rock at my feet. It had looked tossable until I started to uncover it and saw that the rock was about the size of a softball and far too heavy to throw with accuracy. I doubted I'd even be able to hit the roof of the shack directly below, a target I had always spurned as unchallenging.

The rock hit near the peak of the corrugated roof like a gunshot, then banged down into the rain gutter. The reverberation had not even died when the door of the shack blew open and a man came out on a dead run. He didn't look up into the park or anywhere. He just ran, and if he hadn't been headed in the opposite direction, I'd have been running too, because the last thing I expected was for somebody to be inside that shack. At first I thought the man was trying to catch whoever threw the stone and was confused about the direction the attack had been launched from. But as I watched him tack left, then right among the mounds, head down, even as he hurtled fenders and sharp, ragged fiberglass, I realized he wasn't chasing. He was running away. He looked back over his shoulder just once before he disappeared into the trees.

It did not matter that I had not seen him in over five years. The surprise was replaced almost immediately with the same tightness in my chest that I'd felt the afternoon outside school when he'd leaned across the seat of the white convertible to open the passenger-side door. Sam Hall wasn't in Alaska. He was in Mohawk. I didn't care what anybody said. I knew my own father.

Off and on for the rest of the summer I returned to the embankment in Myrtle Park, but the shack remained uninhabited, and when I rattled stones off the sheet metal roof, nobody bolted. Occasionally, shabby men appeared in the clearing below to root around in the trash mounds, removing a door handle from a rusted-out car body perhaps, then disappearing back into the trees in the general direction of the highway. I continued to mystify dogs until one day a mangy yellow cur caught sight of me, and the look on his face clearly said, "Aha!" as if my visible pres-

ence resolved an issue that had troubled him for a long time. He
would spread the word.

In contrast to the scene below was the white jewel of a house
on the other side of the highway. It occupied the whole top of the
hill, and on sunny days its whiteness reflected the sun like a tiny
mirror directed precisely into my eyes. What would it be like to
live in such a house? Though it looked very small in the distance,
I knew up close it had to be huge. It drew the sun like a magnet,
and I would have liked to see it up close, though I doubted you
could get there from where I sat. There were two hundred yards
of thick woods between me and the busy highway, then another
quarter mile or so of the same before you even got to the vast
sloping lawn. There had to be a road, probably on the other side
of the hill, and, anyway, I wasn't permitted to cross the highway
on my bicycle.

It occurred to me that summer, from my perch in Myrtle Park,
that there might be any number of corrugated shacks in my
personal future, but no jeweled houses. I could think of no good
reason for my father to be living in such a place, if that's what he
had been doing there, any more than I could think why he had
run away. But if my father had ended up in such a place, mightn't
the same happen to me? Until recently, I would have scoffed at
such a notion. After all, I was my mother's son, not his. He drifted
into and out of our lives without influencing them unduly. We
lived in a clean house on a nice street and we had what we
needed. But things were changing, and I knew that they were,
even though I could only guess why. Since that Sunday when
Father Michaels left church by the side door, my mother had lost
ground an inch at a time. When she was finally let go by the
telephone company, she appeared almost relieved, and we lived
for months on her modest savings account before she even began
to look for work. When she came home from interviews, her
hands shook so badly she had to sit on them, and there were days
when she would not come out of her bedroom until midafternoon. She refused to go back to the doctor for more Librium, and
without church to calm her down, she didn't know where to turn.

When the savings account money was gone and she'd quit making a pretense of looking for work, she telephoned F. William
Peterson, who came to see us. His big gray car took up most of
the curb outside our house. Before he actually came inside, he
walked all around the place, studied the house and shed, the little

yard. When he finally came in, I was sent out and they talked for a long time.

"You're making a big mistake," I heard him tell my mother later when they came out on the porch. I was fielding grounders along the side of the house.

"I just need some time," I heard her say.

"You need help, Jenny," F. William Peterson said. He had only a few strands of baby-fine hair left on top, and these required constant smoothing.

Then for a while there was money again; I did not fully understand how. There wasn't a lot, though, and my mother watched what there was carefully, cutting back on the amount we ate and the extras we purchased. Every other week she called the bank with instructions to cash a check I would be bearing within the half hour. She herself never left the house.

8

That same summer I made a dubious friend. Compared to some of the other dubious friends who followed, Claude was harmless enough. By an odd coincidence, his family had bought Aunt Rose's old house, and Claude hadn't had time to make many friends, not that time was the issue. Mohawk was far from friendly to outsiders, and whatever it took to break into clique-riddled Mohawk High Claude didn't possess, and he gave up after about a week. I was having similar difficulties in my first year at Nathan Littler Junior High. Claude was a big kid, but pear-shaped and soft-looking like his father, whose Connecticut employer had punished him with a transfer to Mohawk, where he supervised the manufacture of small, plastic, lime-green swimming pools in the shape of turtles. Claude's mother badgered her son about his weight, but Claude Sr. always took the boy's part. "He's built like his father," he told her proudly, not sensing that it was precisely this that his wife would have prevented if she could. "Going to be a big man." Then he tousled, or tried to, the close-cropped hair on the boy's small head. He might as well have tousled a volleyball.

Aunt Rose's little house had always been one of the prettiest on the block, with bright green shutters and window boxes, and a small white fence, the sort you can easily step over, bordering the front and back yards. Claude's parents immediately set about improving the property, even as their neighbors looked on malevolently. The two-story addition nearly doubled the size of Aunt Rose's modest little dwelling, making it the biggest house on the block. But when the heavy machinery arrived a second time and began to scoop out large hunks of earth for what could be nothing but an in-ground swimming pool of immodest proportion, the neighbors circulated a petition to prevent its completion, claiming that it would be a hazard to the neighborhood children, who often cut cross-lots when they played. The real reason was that such ostentation had never been permitted in our neighborhood. The only pools in Mohawk were over on Kings Road by the golf course, and the wealthy Jewish section on the northwestern slope of Myrtle Park.

Claude's parents were Jews, as I later discovered, though so thoroughly reformed as not to practice their religion at all. Indeed, Claude's father had expressed thoroughgoing distaste for Judaism's more orthodox adherents, a sentiment he had hoped in vain might circumvent the covenants and restrictions of the Kings Road neighborhood. Anyone could have told him that wasn't likely, but he didn't ask anyone. The new in-ground pool was combined recreation and revenge, and the neighborhood petition lost momentum when in place of Aunt Rose's little picket fence a five-foot-high chain-link fence went up around the entire property, undercutting the sole rational basis for objection, and refocusing the object of resentment from the big hole in the ground to the fence that surrounded it. There would be no cross-cutting this particular lot. "Good fences make good neighbors," Claude Sr. often remarked with satisfaction and without attribution. It certainly was a fine fence, and when completed, the pool was fine too, along with the ramada and gas grill, all firsts in our neighborhood and all regarded with distaste.

I was Claude Jr.'s only friend, perhaps the only friend of the family. And never was the term friend more qualified. As I remember it, I can honestly say that back then there was never an ounce of honest affection between myself and any of the Claudes (their name was Schwartz, but I always thought of them as the Claudes after discovering that the mother's name was, incredibly, Claudine). Mrs. Claude and Claude Sr. were clearly disappointed that I was the best their son could do. After all, I was two years younger than he, and undistinguished to boot, though I overheard Claude Sr. once remark that at least I wasn't "typical Mohawk," which I took to be a compliment. And while they treated me well enough—I was practically a fixture at their dinner table (they ate abundantly, wonderfully) that summer the pool went in, I cared for the Claudes no more than they cared for me. Claude Sr.'s sarcastic and condescending manner made me feel ridiculed, and his wife's constant lament about Mohawk's not being able to support a single top-notch hairdresser I took to be somehow my fault.

My relationship with Claude Jr. was strangest of all, predicated entirely on competition, or, more precisely, the lack of it that I could provide. Claude insisted that everything we did be a contest. Swimming, throwing, running, eating—it did not matter. He loved to win at anything, and the two years he had on me pretty nearly always ensured success. I have since heard of psychological profiles done on children that illuminate, to some degree, Claude's character. A child is given a beanbag and invited to toss it into a circle. From close up, the task is easy enough, but as the child, on succeeding tosses, is backed farther and farther from the circle he inevitably encounters more difficulty. From across the room, the circle is pretty tough to hit and the child's chances of success are diminished. When the child has tossed the beanbag from each varying distance, he is told he can have one more toss from anywhere he likes. Relatively few will grasp that success from the nearest stripe is a rather qualified affair and these will go directly to the farthest. Others, caring only for the assurance of success, no matter how qualified, indeed never suspecting that success could *be* qualified, will stand at the lip of the circle, plink the bag down, and be enamored of themselves for so doing.

Claude Jr. was just such a boy. His appetite for victory was insatiable. If he beat me ten times in a row swimming freestyle laps in the pool, he'd immediately lobby for an eleventh race under the pretext of giving me another chance. If I demurred, he would lecture me that I'd never get anywhere if I was just going to give up.

One September day after lunch, he emerged from the house with three large bags of Oreos. He carefully arranged the cookies in three equal columns, one group before me, the other before himself. I was extraordinarily fond of Oreos, but the long phalanxes—eight cookies deep, three high—were discouraging to look at, as was Claude, whose greedy eyes had already begun to devour his. His thick stomach hung out over his bathing suit, and his chest looked vaguely feminine. It did not take a genius to figure out what he had in mind.

We ate Oreos.

I scarfed the first half dozen or so happily, the second six without serious misgivings, except when I contemplated how many remained. Before long, however, it became obvious I wasn't going to win, though Claude was slowing down too. He kept a comfortable half-dozen lead at all times, and at the end of my second dozen I attempted to concede. I could tell he was gravely disappointed in me. "Come on," he said. "You can do it."

When I refused, he ate one more and proclaimed that under no circumstances could he eat another Oreo. This was an opportunity to show what I was made of, he said. I was six (count 'em) cookies away from victory. He separated them from my phalanx and returned all but the remaining six to the package. Suddenly I felt like I was all throat, throbbing and full, but I was even more full of defeat than cookies, and awash in black, desperate determination. Incapable of swallowing normal mouthfuls, I nibbled, birdlike at the dry crust of the cookies. It took me half an hour to dispatch four more. Another would give me a tie, and I realized as I stared at it that a tie would have to do. I didn't need to say I won, provided Claude couldn't either.

It is difficult to describe the quality of Claude's excitement as I approached the final cookie. I was terribly ill and my head was pounding savagely from the chocolate. I don't think I could have stood. But strangest of all, and I remember this quite vividly, was the feeling I had that Claude was feeling what I felt—that each new wave of nausea somehow registered in his being as well as my own. He was pulling for me. He wanted us to be equals. Perhaps that was what he had wanted all along, I thought. He was giving me a chance.

I picked up the last Oreo.

I don't know how long it stayed in my cheeks before I swallowed, but when I did I kept my hand up to see what would happen. My stomach churned, but to my surprise did not immediately rise. I was afraid to breathe, except through my nose, and then not deeply.

Claude was grinning at me. I did not notice at first that he was holding another cookie. He held the Oreo elevated with two hands, thumb and forefinger each, like a priest at high mass, but instead of offering it to me (I recall sliding away from him on the bench), he placed it on his own tongue, and I watched with horror as the cookie disappeared, whole, into his mouth. His heavy jaws worked methodically, and soon his Adam's apple bobbed.

As the winning Oreo descended into Claude, the losing one began to rise in me, along with all its brothers. They surged upward angrily, and the black, impotent self-contempt that accompanied them made a pretty awful mess of the Claudes' redwood picnic table.

The following weekend we had a heat wave, the intensity of which took everyone by surprise, coming as it did in the first week of October. On Friday when the temperature hit 90, the windows of the Nathan Littler Junior High were flung open, but even then a tiny rivulet of perspiration disappeared down the open neck of Miss Devlin, the new English teacher, whose breasts were the subject of considerable admiration among us seventh-grade boys. We envied the perspiration. At night, things cooled off, but Saturday morning dawned with a low, white-gray sky and the sun, a magnified white ball, burned through by nine and an hour later the tar on the streets was shimmering. The Russians were using Sputnik to screw around with the weather, people said. Russians weren't too popular in Mohawk anyway, and we certainly didn't appreciate their mucking up autumn.

Around midmorning on Saturday the telephone rang and it was Claude. He wondered if I'd like to go to the beach. I had not seen the Claudes since messing up their redwood picnic table. I consulted my mother through her bedroom door—it would be hours before she emerged for the day—and she seemed relieved at the prospect of not being required to deal with me until dinner time. The Claudes picked me up in their brand-new Pontiac station wagon (according to Claude, they'd had a Jaguar sedan when they lived in Connecticut), the backseat of which I shared with young

Claude and several bags of groceries. I must have gone very pale
when I saw the big package of Oreos sticking out of one.

Only the Claudes would have thought of the beach in October.
After the Mohawk Fair, convention strictly forbade summer
amusements until the following Memorial Day, at which time
swimming would be permissible, though far too cold to be enjoyed. When we pulled into the state park, the large parking lot
was virtually abandoned and the man in the guard shack who was
supposed to be collecting the parking fee was sleeping far too
blissfully to disturb, at least in the opinion of Claude Sr., who was
in rare good spirits. During the summer he would not have
dreamed of packing off to the beach, which would have been
"littered with Mohawk County." Even the tattooed men who
pressed his concave plastic turtles would be there with their
swarming families, perhaps at the very next picnic table, an
egalitarian circumstance to be avoided. There would be no such
problem today. The long, sloping beach stretched before us,
white and empty, not one in fifty picnic tables occupied.

I helped Mrs. Claude carry the bags of food, while Claudes Sr.
and Jr. unloaded the trunkful of paraphernalia. Young Claude had
a set of large black fins, and a mask and snorkel I knew I wouldn't
get to try even when he was done with them. I wouldn't ask to,
of course. He'd volunteer the refusal, saying, "It's expensive
stuff," an explanation apparently preferable to more generous
alternatives like "The fins wouldn't fit," or "Dad would feel responsible if you got hurt." Claude was *such* a shit.

As soon as we were unloaded, Claude Sr. said that the last one
in was a rotten egg and immediately bolted for the water, his
flabby middle jiggling. It was the same strategy his son often used
to ensure victory against me. Running was the only contest
Claude Jr. feared, since his size and weight were no great advantage. He knew that unless he took me by surprise I would beat
him. For this reason there was never any "ready-set-go" nonsense. Rather, he'd wait until I was carrying something or heading
in the opposite direction. He also liked to determine the finish
line, and having crossed its invisible barrier to his own satisfaction, he would stop, catch me as I flew by and after explaining
"No, not that tree, *this* one," he'd raise my hand in the air and
proclaim, "The LOOZAH!" It's difficult to say for certain whether
there was any bottom to the abyss of my humility with regard to
Claude.

That day I was more than content to watch father and son as they hurtled down the beach toward the water, their pear shapes generating little speed but a terrible momentum. It looked for a second like Claude Jr. might win, but they were running close together, and when the boy came abreast of his father, the older man gave him a big hip that sent him sprawling into the moist sand at the water's edge, plowing it with his chin, as Claude Sr. parted the water of the green lake, his arms upraised in victory.

Other than just that single defeat, Claude Jr. had a winning day, though beating me at stone skipping, kickball, hamburger eating, and sudden foot races did not engender in him the usual satisfaction. His raw chin was bubbly, and he behaved a little as if he regretted inviting me. After lunch we tossed the football around listlessly in knee-deep brackish water. The only other people on the beach were a group of teens roughly Claude's age. They were fifty yards or so down the beach, and he eyed them sadly, as if they were much further. I myself wouldn't have minded strolling down the beach in that direction to have a look at the girls in their bikinis, but Claude said he wasn't up for it.

"Go on," Claude Sr. said to his son. "Nedley's got the right idea, and he possesses a mere fraction of your age and native intelligence."

Claude Sr. always called me Nedley. I never knew why. He also liked to make comparisons between his son and me. They were supposed to be jokes.

"And quit feeling your chin," he went on. "It's just a little scrape."

I wouldn't have characterized it as "just" a scrape. Claude had a lot of chin, and all of it was raw and oozing, like a burn.

"Don't be a baby always," Claude Sr. concluded.

After a while I became aware of somebody besides us and the teenagers. There was a solitary man at the crest of the hill where the trees had been cleared to form a path to another section of the campsite. The man just stood there, a silhouette, with the sun at his back, watching Claude and me toss the football.

"I'm tired of this," Claude Jr. said. "Besides, you stink."

Mrs. Claude was stretched out on the beach towel nearby, her nose, eyes, and forehead beneath a ribbed hand towel. "I don't think *that's* a very nice way to address your friend," she said vaguely.

"I don't mind," I said. If you objected to being told that you

stank, Claude wasn't the person to chum around with. Besides, I
wasn't paying any attention.

"Who the hell's that?" Claude said, following my line of vision
and apparently a little unnerved by the man's just standing there.

"My father," I said, though I don't remember being certain.
With the sun at his back it was impossible to tell.

"Sure," Claude Jr. said sarcastically.

I happened at that moment to be holding the football, so I gave
it a good heave straight out into the lake.

"Now you can go get it," Claude said.

But I was already headed up the beach in the opposite direction.

"Hey!" Claude said, looking alternately at me and the bobbing
football, which had caught the current and was floating down the
beach in the direction of the teenagers. "Hey, goddamn it!"

"I don't think *that's* such a very nice way to talk," I heard Mrs.
Claude say.

"Hello, Bud," my father said when I'd made the long trek up
the beach. "Who's your fat friend?"

I told him Claude Schwartz. We stood there looking down the
sloping beach at the Claudes and the tiny bobbing football, now
a good hundred yards out in the current and still on the move. Big
Claude and Little Claude were staring at us openly, while Mrs.
Claude peeked from beneath her towel.

"How'd you get hooked up with them?"

That was what he wanted to know after all that time—how I
had managed to get hooked up with the Claudes. I shrugged.

"You're still talkative, I see."

He was right. I wasn't much of a conversationalist, especially
around him. For a while there I'd gotten to like talking, but only
around certain people, like Father Michaels. Since he'd gone, I
had pretty much given it up again. Part of the problem, with my
father anyway, was that the things he said didn't exactly lend
themselves to response.

"Well?" he said.

A case in point.

"I missed you," I said. It sort of came out of left field, not at all
naturally, but it was the only thing I could think of.

Apparently it was all right with him, because he said, "I missed
you, too." That settled, we just stood there for a while until the
Claudes' football bobbed out of sight around the point.

When I went back down to gather my stuff, Mrs. Claude wanted to know if it really was my father, and I said it was. "You're sure?" she said, obviously a little apprehensive about letting me go off with him. Why didn't he come down and introduce himself, or at least let somebody get a look at him? After all, the Claudes were in all probability legally responsible for my safe return to Mohawk. The poor woman looked like she would have liked to consult her husband on these matters, but the other two Claudes had rounded the point in pursuit of the football.

I pulled on my shirt and scuffed into my tennis shoes. "Sorry about the ball," I said. "It's just that Claude can be a real turd."

I half expected her to be angry with me for saying that, but she just looked sad, as if I'd voiced a sentiment she herself had been trying to find the right words to express. "I hope you'll keep being his friend," she said when I started back up the beach to where my father waited.

I turned and gave her a smile, surprised to discover that just then I liked her. "Sure," I said. Why not.

9

We headed up the dirt road toward the guard shack at the entrance to the park. There were just a few cars parked in the shade along the way and none of them looked like the sort that would belong to my father. I did not mind walking, or even not knowing where we were headed. He seemed content too, not all that interested in catching up on things. I was grateful for that. I don't know how I would have summarized such a long time. He did want to know if my mother was all right, and when I said I guessed so he didn't press me.

At the entrance to the park, the attendant was still asleep inside the shack, his chair tilted up against the inner wall, his legs alone protruding out the front door. Spying them, my father put a hand on my shoulder and motioned for me to be quiet. There was a tiny open window on the side wall of the shack and my father peeked in before unfastening the screen door from its outside hook. The door moaned on its hinges a little, but the sleeper did not stir.

When the screen hit the side of the shack like a pistol shot, the feet resting on the legs of the tilting chair went straight up in the air. Things were still crashing inside the shack when my father disappeared around back. A taut face appeared for just an instant in the tiny window and looked directly at me. Then its owner came out, rubbing the back of his head. He looked pretty mad.

Having circled around the other side, my father came at him from behind. The man must have seen where I was looking, but too late, and he found himself in a double nelson, his arms extended outward and dangling, like a big awkward bird. When he struggled, my father put a knee on his spine and lifted him off the ground. The man gurgled, but could not speak.

My father rotated him so that the man's right hip was toward me. "Take his gun and shoot him," my father said.

"It's not l-l-loaded," the man squeaked.

"Well, *that's* good," said my father, releasing his victim. "I'd hate to think anybody'd give live ammunition to a blockhead like you."

"God d-d-damn you, Sammy," the man said. "You're gonna go too f-f-fucking far some day." He shook my father's hand reluctantly.

"I wish you'd watch your l-l-language around my son," my father said.

"Screw you," the man said, fingering the back of his head. "Is it bleeding?"

My father examined the man's head. "Not bad," he said.

"I oughta let you have one," the man said. It didn't sound like much of a threat.

"Nah," my father said. "I'm just trying to keep you sharp, Tree. What if there was a real evildoer around here?"

The man called Tree went over and examined the screen door, which angled crazily now on its bent hinges. "You're about as close to an evildoer as we get around here. By the w-way, somebody said you w-w-weren't around, if anybody was to ask."

"That's all straightened out," my father said, glancing at me. "Just a couple of fellows I met out in Nevada."

"Too bad they didn't work on your kneecaps. What's the kid's name?"

My father told him.

Tree looked me over and shook his head. "Never adm-m-mit he's your old man," he advised, "and m-maybe you got a chance."

"You hurt my f-f-fucking back, Sammy," he added.

My father told him to come with us. There was a little, dusty-looking tavern called The Lookout just outside the park entrance. There were a couple cars out front. One was a cream-colored Mercury convertible that looked like somebody had ridden hard, though there weren't any bullet holes that I could see. "We'll get Alice to rub your back," my father said.

"I'm w-working," Tree said, nodding first at the shack, then at his uniform, as if these constituted proof. "Besides. Alice and I aren't getting along."

"Since when?"

"Since lately." He stared down the dirt road at The Lookout with a mixture of longing and fear.

"Suit yourself, Tree."

"I c-c-could drink a beer," the man admitted, then considered everything for about two seconds. "Let me lock up, at least."

Inside the guard shack, he took some money out of a shoe box and put the thick wheel of red tickets in a drawer and locked it. Then he locked the inside door and did the best he could with the screen, throwing my father another malicious glance. "Park closes day after tomorrow anyways," he said. "W-w-wouldn't be much point in canning me, I guess."

He counted the money as we walked, then put a rubber band around it. "Took in f-f-fourteen dollars," he said. "They gotta pay me twenty."

"That's about right," my father said. "Mayor of Mohawk works things the same way."

Tree shrugged. "July, we do two, three hundred a day. More on weekends."

"What'll happen to that big roll of tickets when the park closes tomorrow?"

"Disappear, p-p-probably."

My father nodded. "You're all right, Tree."

The Lookout was dark and cool inside. When the screen door clapped shut behind us, I couldn't make out anything but the flickering lights above the shuffleboard machine and the scripted fluorescent beer signs. Tree and my father went straight for the long bar at the other end of the room. They either knew where it was or were used to night soundings. They took stools at the opposite end of the bar from The Lookout's two other patrons. I figured my father had forgotten me completely until he checked the stool next to his and I wasn't there.

"Well?" he said when I finally arrived. I climbed onto the vacant stool at the end of the bar, pleased that for once I seemed to understand the significance of his favorite question.

A huge woman seated behind the bar was talking to the other customers. You couldn't exactly see the stool she was sitting on, but there had to be one. All along the bar were lighted candles in red goblets that reminded me of the stained glass in Our Lady of Sorrows, and my father used one to rap on the bar. The huge woman was already looking at us and shaking her head.

"You got a little exercise, you wouldn't be so fat," my father observed good-naturedly.

"Or I could have more customers like you, in which case I could just sit still and starve," the woman said, making no move to get up. "What's this? Your first visit in three years?"

"It wasn't me that told you to put this place way the hell and gone out in the woods."

That was apparently an adequate explanation, because the woman got off her stool with surprising lightness and came over. "And look what you drag in with you when you finally show up."

My father nudged me. "You don't have to take that, you know."

That confused me, because I could have sworn she was referring to Tree, whom she was glaring at maliciously. For his part, Tree looked like he would have liked to run away.

"Hello, Tree," the woman said, so loud he jumped. I jumped too, just to keep him company.

"H-h-hi, Alice," Tree managed.

"Well, what do you know," Alice said. She'd lowered her voice, but was still glowering at him. "He *can* talk. Every day for a month, he sits over there in his little shit-house, but he's too busy to stop and say hello. I thought somebody ripped his voicebox out."

"I never knew you'd treat me so n-nice or I'd of c-c-come in before."

"You want to talk about the way to treat people, is that it?"

"Hell, Alice," Tree said. He was clearly suffering, and that, at least, seemed to cheer Alice up a little.

"Hell, Tree," she said.

"When you two are all done, could I get a beer?" my father said.

Alice looked over at me for the first time. She had nice eyes, but she sure was a big woman. "And he's eighteen, right?"

"Eleven," my father admitted.

"Twelve," I said, because I was.

"What?" my father said.

I told him I was twelve.

He thought about it, counted on his fingers, then shrugged. "Say hello to Alice. She's not as bad as she looks."

"Or sounds," Tree added, though it got him another murderous glance.

Alice drew beers for my father and Tree and put a 7-Up in front of me. "Too good-looking to be yours," she remarked.

"He is though, just the same," my father said.

"Somebody said you were having problems," she said, her voice confidential.

"Who, me?"

"Who, you."

"Nothing I couldn't handle."

"You should have come by."

"I thought about it."

"And?"

"And it wasn't your problem."

They both looked at me then as if it were my turn to say something and I'd missed my cue.

"Anyhow, it's all straightened out now," my father said.

Tree had slid off his stool. "So where are *you* going?" Alice said.

"To pee," Tree said, with an injured expression.

"You gotta watch him," Alice said. "He's a great one for sneaking off."

"Hell, Alice."

"Hell, Tree."

Alice and my father talked softly for a few minutes and when Tree came back, he sat in the middle of the bar instead of with us. After a while Alice went over and they talked, quietly, not yelling. Then Tree surprised me by putting a hand on hers and she surprised me by letting him.

"So," my father said, turning to me for the first time. "What's this I hear about your mother?"

* * *

I tried not to tell him, at first, because I knew she wouldn't want me talking about her, especially with my father. So I tried to play dumb, like I didn't know what he meant.

He put out the cigarette he was smoking between his thumb and forefinger and sat the stub on its filter. I watched the procedure with more interest than I felt, not wanting to meet his eye. After all those bogus confessions at Our Lady of Sorrows I counted myself about as good a liar as Catholics ever got, which was good. But I hadn't much confidence a lie would work on my father. He'd always known what was going on at our house better than if he'd lived there. But I heard myself say, "She's fine," in a voice that wouldn't even have convinced somebody like Father Michaels, who believed whatever you told him.

Surprisingly, my father did not contradict me. At least not exactly. "Glad to hear it," he said. "Somebody said she was sick."

When I didn't say anything, he got up and went over to the cigarette machine, stopping on the way back at the other end of the bar where the two men who were there when we came in still sat. Tree and Alice were still holding hands midway down the rail. I couldn't hear what they were saying, but Tree kept shrugging his shoulders and looking hangdog.

On the wall above where I sat was a conical beer sign, and rather than think about my mother or the implications of lying to my father right after not seeing him for so long, I devoted myself to figuring out how it worked. A small bead of light traversed the cylinder in waves, elongating all the way up the crest and down the other side, but shrinking to bead size again in the trough, its color always changing, first red, then blue, then green, then yellow, then white. Somehow they got the bead of light to move, change shape and color, but I was stumped.

I drank the rest of my soda, ate the cherry, and was still puzzling over the beer sign when my father came back and tossed the pack of Marlboros on the bar. "Don't ever smoke," he said, lighting up.

"I saw Wussy," I said, for something to say.

"So he said."

I thought about mentioning the bike, but if it wasn't my father who bought it, I didn't want to know.

"I'm surprised you remembered him."

I said I remembered all about the fishing trip—the gadget he'd given me, getting caught in the rain with the top down, our dinner in the woods, the fishhook he'd gotten stuck in his thumb. He'd forgotten most of it, all except that part about my mother shooting at him when we got home. It felt funny to remember it all so clearly when he didn't—like maybe I should have forgotten it too, since it wasn't that important.

He finished his beer and squeezed the life out of another cigarette, standing the gray butt up next to the other one, exhaling the last of the smoke through his nose.

I looked at his black thumb and forefinger. "Doesn't that hurt?" I said. It was something I'd always wanted to ask him.

"Nah," he said, placing his hand palm up on the bar so I could examine the hard, yellow-black skin that extended all the way down the inside of his thumb and forefinger. "You just have to do it all the time."

"Didn't it hurt at first?"

He shrugged. "So?"

I tried to think of a so, but couldn't come up with anything good.

"So?" he repeated, cuffing me in the head to indicate that the subject wasn't closed yet, and wouldn't be until I offered at least a feeble argument against self-mutilation.

I took a deep breath, and when the yellow comet's tail of light became a pure white bead, I said, "I think there's something wrong with her. She quit her job."

He nodded. "So I heard."

When the two men at the other end of the bar got up and left, Tree and Alice slid further away from us, and then I told him all of it. How she'd borrowed money on the house; how she never went out, even onto the porch anymore; how we telephoned for groceries; how I cashed checks at the bank, how she stayed in her room more and more, how I suspected that she was getting more scared every day; how her world was shrinking; how the ringing of the telephone caused her hands to shake uncontrollably; how sometimes she even seemed frightened of me. The only thing I left out was the business with Father Michaels. In the roughly two years since it had happened, I'd come to understand, gradually, what had happened, and what the consequences had been. The only thing I didn't know was whether anyone else knew.

In response to what I did tell him, my father just rapped the bar with his dead thumb. Somebody else would have asked all kinds of questions, but not him. It made me realize that I hadn't wanted to tell him or anybody else because I doubted they'd believe me. And when my father did, I felt a sudden, almost overwhelming love for him, as if the five long intervening years amounted to nothing.

At the other end of the bar, Tree leaned forward and kissed Alice. "Hey. Go get a room, why don't you," my father suggested, not that they paid any attention. Turning back to me he said, "Maybe you better come stay with me for a while. Unless you don't want to . . ."

I remember thinking at the time that it was dumb even to consider it, that I was not really my father's son, that it wouldn't work. But there were Alice and Tree, and I remember thinking that life was full of things you couldn't figure. How could you be sure something wouldn't work until it didn't? And even if my father wasn't exactly enthusiastic about the prospect (he'd said "you better" as if only in a terribly imperfect world would it be preferable that I live with him "for a while"), so what? Maybe it would work anyway. "Maybe," I said. "For a while."

10

Downtown Mohawk had never been much to look at and was never exactly prosperous, but it had once been whole, at least. No more. The old hotel, the most elegant of the structures along Main, had come down when I was eight, leaving a large gap in the center of the block. The rubble had been quickly removed, the space graded and blacktopped, parking meters installed. But the effect was unsettling. There was no longer an unbroken corridor of three-story buildings, and the vista now offered by the new parking lot was like a glimpse behind a painted stage backdrop in a theater, all rusted pulleys and frayed ropes and dark, smoky windows. With the demolition of the Mohawk Grand, the illusion of a thriving downtown was forever shattered, and within the next few years three more buildings were vacated, condemned, and summarily razed, all on the same side of the street. Disturbed by the implications of this trend, the city council had commissioned a huge sign to be painted on the now visible side of one of the adjacent buildings. SHOP DOWNTOWN MOHAWK it began, in big block letters ten feet tall, "Where There's Always Plenty Of Parking."

And then still other buildings came down, giving the street a gap-toothed appearance further emphasized when smaller, one-story, strangely temporary-looking buildings were erected as an alternative to the parking lots that were fast becoming the town's long suit. The remaining three-story buildings all exhibited narrow fissures from their stone crowns, down brick faces, all the way to the street. It was in front of one of these—Klein's Department Store—that my father parked his cream-colored Mercury convertible that afternoon. There was a big empty lot next door, but my father pulled up, one wheel over the curb, right beneath a no parking sign. I thought at first that he was planning to go into the A&P up the street, probably to get something for our dinner.

"Well?" he said. He had gotten out of the car and was standing on the sidewalk. "Grab something."

On the backseat of the convertible amid the usual Sam Hall clutter—greasy tools, rags, an old hooded sweatshirt, junk mail—were the two cardboard boxes we'd filled with the contents of my dresser and closet.

He raised the hood of the trunk, pulled out the bike, and headed for a dark doorway beneath an unlit brick arch. I looked up at the black third-story windows, my heart sinking. I grabbed the smaller box with my underwear and socks, leaving on the seat the larger box containing my shirts, pants, sweaters, and jackets.

The door he had disappeared through had "Rose's Beauty Salon" stenciled on the window, several letters flaked or missing. Inside, the narrow flight of stairs was dark, with no handrail on either side. A bare bulb dangled from the ceiling at the second-floor landing. At the third there was a foyer and two doors. One said, ROS 'S BE TY S LON. Inexplicably, the same letters were missing on the upstairs and downstairs doors. As my father inserted the key into the other door, which had the words AC-COUNTING DEPT stenciled in big black letters, a woman with a large beehive of bright red hair emerged from the beauty parlor.

"Jesus Christ, you scared me, Sammy," she said, staring quizzically at the bike he was carrying, as if it presented a riddle my own presence did little to solve.

"What are you scared of, rape?" my father said.

"I wish," she told my father. "Who's the kid?"

"Meet Rose," my father said. "She's all right for a red-headed Polack."

"Polack and proud of it," Rose said. She offered me a hand full of nails painted the same shade as the beehive. I balanced my cardboard box and shook. "Rape I could handle," she said, looking right at me, as if I had been contemplating it. "It's the goddamn robbers that scare me. This used to be a nice town."

"When?" my father said.

"Way back."

"I don't go as far back as you, Rose."

"Like hell you don't," Rose said. "I seem to recollect graduating with a kid named Sam Hall."

"Not me."

"Not you." She nodded, still looking at me. "Your kid like to work?"

"Ask him."

"I'll give you fifteen bucks to clean the salon on Sundays. Wash the sinks. Vacuum. Empty the trash."

"Sure," I said. Fifteen dollars was a lot of money. My mother had only made eighty-three a week at the phone company.

She looked over at my father. "I been trying to talk your old man into doing it, but he's too good. I never knew he had such a handsome son."

I was confused again. The woman never seemed to look where she was talking. When she took a bright key off her pink rabbit's foot key chain, I wasn't sure whether I was supposed to keep it or give it to my father. The key seemed to be mine, but I wasn't sure it was a good idea to trust me with something like a key. I'd never even had one to my mother's house, and until today I had belonged there.

But Rose seemed confident she'd done the right thing. "You look responsible. Not like your old man."

"There you go," my father said when she disappeared around the corner at the landing below. "Now you're employed."

My father's apartment had clearly once been part of the department store below. The inner walls which separated the various large rooms were of different construction than the outer ones and did not go all the way up to the ceiling, which was very high and peeling green paint. The living room was huge, its dimensions further emphasized by the fact that my father appeared to have next to nothing to put in it. He leaned my bike up against the wall near the door as if he were grateful for the additional furniture. An old sofa floated in the middle of the room a good fifteen feet from the nearest wall, placed there, apparently, to be within shouting distance of the television in the corner, a monstrous piece of pale cabinetry for such a small screen. For some reason it was already on when we walked in. A television was one of the things I'd often yearned for and which my mother and I did without, though she insisted that it was a question of preference. She'd just rather listen to music on my grandfather's old Victrola. My mother wasn't the sort of person who needed a point of comparative reference to know what she preferred. In general she preferred not to have what we couldn't afford. Still, even I wasn't sure this TV of my father's represented much of an improvement over our antiquated radio at home. The screen was so full of snow that the difference between Huntley and Brinkley was purely auditory, and the events they reported were all played out against a backdrop of intense blizzard. Along the wall opposite the television was a sink, a small refrigerator and a two-chair Formica dinette. That was it.

"Well?" said my father, when he discovered me still in the doorway with my box of underwear and socks.

The bedroom looked even more absurd. Containing just a small set of drawers and a single bed, it was the same size as the living room, and our steps echoed off the walls when we entered. "Drop that someplace," my father said.

I looked around for the right place. There was room for about five hundred boxes. Finally, he took it out of my hands and dropped the box where we stood. "There," he said. "Easy."

"You gotta go to the bathroom?" he said, as if I looked like I might.

I said I didn't.

"You probably will eventually," he said. "It's in there."

I nodded. I could see the commode from where we stood, and part of the tub. It looked like we had one normal-sized room, anyway.

"You can sleep in here." He motioned to the bed. "I usually fall asleep on the couch anyhow. You sure you don't have to go to the bathroom?"

I didn't, but I went in anyway and closed the door behind me. I sat on the commode with the top down and wondered if I would be able to hold back the tears. On the small sink sat a cluster of my father's toiletries. His toothbrush lay on the spotted porcelain next to his razor and cologne. A white puff had hardened at the end of the can of shaving cream. The narrow gray bowl had just enough flat surface to accommodate what was already there. I sat, waiting for the minutes to pass so I could flush the john and go back outside. Looking up, I noticed that even the bathroom walls did not go all the way to the ceiling. It was not an ideal place to pretend to relieve yourself.

I flushed before leaving, but it was a wasted gesture, my father already having gone back to the living room where he was parked in front of the snowy television. I stood in the doorway between the two monstrous rooms, unsure what was expected of me. "You want something to drink?" he said.

I said no.

When I headed for the door, he wanted to know where I was going. I said, to get my other box of clothes.

"Come sit down. We can get it after the news."

I did as I was told. When the news was over, he asked if I was hungry.

"There's no stove," I said, because there wasn't.

"The diner's right across the street."

I wasn't sure how that rendered a stove superfluous, but to my father's thinking it apparently did. He was looking at me as if he found me about as odd as I did him.

"It's not nice like your mother's," he admitted.

I again felt tears beginning to well up and I didn't trust my voice to say it was fine, it was all fine.

"I'm not like your mother," he went on. "That's what you'll have to get used to."

When I didn't say anything, he looked over and cuffed me in the ear. "Don't worry about her. She'll be all right. Don't go through life crying about things."

"All right," I croaked, disobeying.

Eventually he remembered the other box of clothes and went down after it. He was too late though; the backseat of the convertible was empty, and I could hear him cursing in the street below.

"Don't worry about it," he said when he returned. "Don't cry over what you can't help."

I wasn't crying anymore anyway, so I took his advice, though it seemed to me that letting my clothes get stolen fell under the heading of things that *could* have been helped. And there were probably other things, too. My mother, for instance.

He insisted that I take the bed. In the morning we would "get things straightened out," whatever that meant.

I undressed quietly and got into bed. On the other side of the unshaded window, Mohawk stretched outward, from the blank face of the building opposite, dusky above the streetlamps, then further up into the darkness of Myrtle Park, finally into the blackness of the night sky itself. I hadn't much faith that the kind of straightening out my father had in mind would be all that beneficial to anybody, not after the way things had been straightened out with my mother that afternoon. We had driven there straight from The Lookout, and when we pulled up to the curb he told me to stay put. His plan was to tell her that this would just be temporary, that she could get over whatever was wrong with her better if she didn't have any headaches for a while. Meaning me.

So I sat out there in the convertible, half expecting either gunshots or a police car to come careening around the corner to carry him off. Instead, in a very few minutes, he returned and said I'd better go in and get what I needed. He looked shaken and I felt suddenly chilled. Never before in the history of our family had there ever been an amicable settlement. Could it be that my mother had actually agreed to let me live with him? If so, she was even sicker than I had imagined, and it came home to me then that the only reason I had agreed to live with my father was that I knew she would never go along with it.

Up and down the street the leaves on the maples had begun to turn, and suddenly I did not want to leave. The modest neighborhood houses all contained whole families, it seemed to me. Ours had always been different, containing just my mother and me. That my father had learned to live without us was a fact I had become accustomed to. Us. My mother and me. Now it appeared that she had decided things would be better without any headaches, as my father put it, and it occurred to me there in the car, and later that night in my father's bed, that maybe the problem was me. Maybe it had always been me. She had taken all she could, and now I was being handed over. It wasn't a question of me deciding who I would live with. All that had been settled, and my life, in that instant, was changed. It was agreed that I would visit her on Saturday mornings, go to the bank for her like always so she would have money for the grocer's delivery boy. That was all she needed.

She had retreated to her room when my father and I went back to fill up the two cardboard boxes from my dresser drawers. We worked quietly and quickly, like burglars, walking on tiptoe past her closed door.

After we had deposited the boxes in the backseat of the convertible, my father, to my surprise, said I had better go back in and say goodbye.

"Let's just go," I said. I didn't want to see her, didn't want to hear whatever it was that she would say to me, didn't want any explanations. Maybe, in a week or so, after I'd digested it. But not now. Not with my clothes piled in cardboard boxes in the backseat of my father's car. Not in front of all the whole houses on our tree-lined block. I imagined the neighbors watching from behind darkened windows.

My father shrugged. "Do what you want," he said. "If it was me, I'd go say something."

I just sat until he cuffed me on the side of the head, his signal that I should look at him. I didn't want to. He cuffed me again though, so I did. "You want to take your bike?"

It was leaning against the back porch beneath the maple tree. I went to get it while he opened the trunk and rearranged the clutter. I could have put it in myself, but he took it from me and nodded toward the house. Telling myself it was to avoid the back of his hand, I went.

Her door was still shut, and there was no response when I knocked. "Mom?" I said to the door. "We're going."

There was a moment's silence, a gathering up, then a formal voice. "All right, dear," she said, as if she hadn't spent the last twelve years trying to prevent this very event. And so I just stood there, the door between us, studying the tiny bubbles in the varnish, as if their design would tell me what to do. Finally, I pushed the door open a crack.

She lay in the fetal position, her back to me. The squeak of the hinge had no visible effect, but when I put my hand on her shoulder, she began to shake, so I took it away. She tried to tell me something then, but she got stuck on the first-person pronoun, repeating it again and again. Everything but sorrow drained out of me as I listened to her. My knees became liquid. "It'll be all right," I told her.

And then I left.

Pulling away from the curb, my father said, "How the hell did she *get* like that?"

I said I didn't know.

"Stuff like that doesn't just happen," he said, almost accusatorily. There was something like fear in his voice, too, as if he suspected that whatever was wrong with her might be viral, contagious. He looked at me as if I might be a carrier. "Well?" he said.

That night, he waited until he figured I was asleep, then left. I heard his footsteps echoing down the stairs. I got out of bed and went over to the window in time to see him emerge directly below and drive off in the Mercury. It was after midnight by then, but sleep seemed a long way off and I wished I'd had the foresight to bring a book to read. Spindrift Island suddenly seemed an improbable place though, and I doubted its power to comfort now.

In the living room my father had left the television on, but the station had gone off the air. I flipped around the dial, but managed only to locate the last few bars of "The Star-Spangled Banner," then more snow. I was about to turn off the set when I noticed a small framed picture hiding behind the dusty rabbit ears. I held the photograph to the snowy screen for light and found myself studying a grinning, six-year-old me, all ears and teeth.

It was an odd discovery. All you had to do was look around the room to see that my father didn't have much. I wondered how he came to have me. It wasn't a picture I recognized. Who had taken it? Had my mother sent it to him? Had Aunt Rose? And how had it found its way into a frame and onto his TV? I fell asleep soon after without having figured any of it out.

11

When you lived on the top floor of the tallest building in Mohawk, you didn't really need curtains, or at least that's what my father's thinking must have been, because when the sun cleared the summit of Myrtle Park, it streamed right in our tall windows, warming the big apartment and making sleep next to impossible. I woke with the feeling that I had recently been cold, and vaguely aware that there was something strange about my surroundings, but not strange enough to be alarming. I dozed for awhile, until I remembered where I was and sat up.

The vast, nearly empty bedroom seemed even larger in the daylight. The bathroom was a very long way off across the cold, uncarpeted floor, and my slippers were safely at the foot of the bed in my mother's house. I dashed, wishing I'd done more than pretend to pee the night before. When I was done, I stood on tiptoe to check myself out in the mirror. The face that looked back at me seemed less desperate than last night's.

I found my father stretched out on the living room sofa in his undershorts, his mouth wide open, snoring loudly. I watched him for a few minutes, amazed. If it weren't for the noise, you would have sworn he was dead. I put index fingers in my ears and watched with the sound off, but only for a minute, because it was too spooky. His eyelids were not completely closed, and the liquid eyeballs appeared to move beneath them. I wondered if maybe he was just pretending to be asleep so he could watch me watch him, a possibility that made me too self-conscious to stay in the same room with him.

Back in the bedroom, on top of the box that contained my socks and underwear, was a large brown bag that hadn't been there the night before. Inside were an assortment of shirts, a couple pairs of pants, and a lemon-yellow windbreaker, all in plastic wrappers. I piled the clothing on the bed and studied it nervously to the

rhythm of my father's snoring in the next room. Around him—
never mind whether he was awake or asleep—I always felt a little
slow, unequal to situations that should have been clear. Here was
another. The clothing was my size and the bag that contained it
had been sitting on top of the box containing my underwear.
Surely these clothes were meant as replacements for what had
been stolen the night before. A working hypothesis. I picked up
each package and examined it in the plastic, less interested in the
contents than the possibility that my father had rushed right out
to buy me these things. If he had, the gesture might be interpreted as representing some affection for me, or a feeling of
responsibility, at least.

But where had the clothes come *from*? There were no tags and
he had left the apartment long after the stores closed. It was now
barely seven in the morning, two hours before they would open
again. He simply *couldn't* have purchased them in the interval.
But if that was true, if they had been purchased earlier, then it
was far from certain that the clothes were intended for me, since
he could not have known that I would need them. Perhaps they
were for someone else, coincidentally my size.

One thing was certain, as it nearly always was where my father
was concerned. There was a good chance that whatever conclusion I came to would be wrong and I would later be shown the
stupidity of my reasoning, assuming I could even remember it
when called upon. Still, it seemed to me that in the past I'd been
more guilty of *not* jumping to obvious conclusions than jumping
to erroneous ones. I had the impression that of the many character flaws my father privately noted in observing me, the most
egregious was sluggish passivity. "Well?" I could imagine him
saying, that one word containing a multitude of possible questions: How long do you intend to stand there in your undershorts?
Can you figure this out, or do you need a blueprint? How many
size-twelve sons do I have?

I thought about putting on the same clothes I'd worn yesterday
and pretending I hadn't seen the others, but there were inferences to be drawn from this course of action as well. (So, I've got
a blind kid?) The other alternative was to just stand there and wait
for a nervous breakdown.

In the end, I carefully unwrapped the package that contained
a plaid shirt and removed the pins, saving them in a neat pile on
the window ledge just in case. Then I did the same with the

army-green chinos, which were a little long. I felt so nervous standing there in the new clothes that I decided I'd go for a ride and come back after he'd had a chance to wake up. The heat wave had broken during the night and the air coming in the bedroom window was chilly, so I put on the yellow windbreaker, grabbed my bike, and slipped out. My father's snoring followed me all the way down to the sidewalk.

The street was deserted, except for a few cars outside the Mohawk Grill. I pedaled slowly up Hospital Hill, and from there past the stone pillars and into Myrtle Park. I was glad for the yellow windbreaker, the air was so full of autumn. Up in the park, the sun only found its way among the pines in splotches. Since I had the place to myself, I raced along the winding paths until the chill in the air felt good, then rode over to my favorite vista and leaned my bike against a tree.

Far out across the highway, the white jewel house I always admired gleamed in the clean morning light atop its own hill, and as usual I wondered what sort of people lived there, and what it must be like to wake up in such a big house, and what they thought about when they looked out from their vast privacy across the highway into the wild green of Myrtle Park. But maybe they didn't look in my direction at all. Maybe way off beyond them was another gleaming house on another hill with an even better view, and maybe they looked at that. Or it could be that they just drew the blinds and didn't go gazing off anywhere. Whoever they were, they had to be pretty happy about things.

Directly below me, among the mounds of junk, a yellow mutt appeared and sniffed around for a good place. I tossed a pebble, which rattled off a car fender. I studied the shack with the corregated iron roof apprehensively. I knew my father was back downtown, snoring on the sofa, yet right then I felt him there below me too, as if there were no contradiction to his being two places at once. It was such a scary idea that I got on my bike and pedaled back downtown.

I got spooked again when I dismounted in front of Klein's Department Store. In one of the windows stood a boy mannequin wearing the same plaid shirt and green chinos I had on. His arms were extended outward from his sides, frozen in expectation, as if there were someone nearby he meant to embrace. But he had the small window all to himself and there was nothing much on his side of the glass.

* * *

My father was in the bathroom when I got upstairs, and Dave Garroway, Chet Huntley's identical twin, was on the snowy television. I leaned my bike against the wall near the door and tried to think if there was something I should be doing. If I'd been in my mother's house, there would have been something, but here it was different. Making the bed seemed like a good idea, so I did that. I was finishing up when the bathroom door opened and he came out in his shorts, smelling of lime, his cheeks smooth, his hair wet and shiny.

He seemed to have taken waking up and finding me gone pretty much in stride, though he looked me over carefully, in as much as I was back again and he had a minute. "The pants are a little long," he observed. "How come you're a runt?"

That didn't seem to require an answer, so I didn't say anything. He stood there waiting though, and it seemed an awfully big room for two people with so little to say to each other.

"Well?" he said.

"Well what?"

"How come you're a runt?"

"I don't know," I said.

That seemed to satisfy him. He nodded meaningfully, as if maybe *he* had an idea why I was a runt. "Let's go get some breakfast."

He scratched himself, and for a minute, I thought he meant right then. I envisioned the two of us crossing Main Street, me in my new yellow windbreaker, him in his undershorts.

In the living room he pulled on the same pants he'd draped over the sofa the night before. "You eat?"

Like most of his questions, this one caused me to hesitate. *Did* I eat? *Had* I eaten? Did he want to know if I was hungry? Whether I usually ate breakfast? Whether eating was customary with me, as with other mortals? I took a stab.

"Sure," I said.

"What?"

I blinked. "What?"

"What did you eat?"

"Nothing. I meant I'm hungry," I said.

He tucked his shirt in, and zipped his fly, the television having for the moment caught his attention. He placed each black-shoed foot on the arm of the sofa to tie his shoelaces, then pocketed his keys and brushed the cigarette ashes off the coffee table and onto the floor. "Well?"

We went down to the street. I walked right past the convertible, figuring he meant to go to the diner across the street. Instead, he got in the car. I retraced my steps and got in too, just in time to get cuffed in the head. "Pay attention," he said.

"All right," I said.

"Smile."

I did my best.

We pulled away from the curb and rode silently toward the outskirts of town. For some reason, my spirits began to dip again. I was wearing new clothes and didn't have much to complain about, but I couldn't dispel the feeling that somehow my personal fortunes had taken an unmistakable turn for the worse. Everywhere, the leaves had begun to turn, but their brilliant oranges and yellows failed to cheer me. I thought about my grandfather. Fourth of July. Mohawk Fair. Eat the Bird, and Winter.

Out near the highway my father pulled into a steep driveway and cut the engine. A curtain in the small brown house at the end of the drive twitched, then was still. My father got out, so I did too, confused as usual. There was a front door, but we went around back where there was a large, unshaded concrete patio. A blond-haired boy in a thin t-shirt, who looked three or four years older than I, was working on a dismantled motorcycle, parts of which were strewn all over the patio.

"Hello, Knucklehead," my father said when the boy looked up. I recognized the boy as being from Mohawk High, but didn't know his name. He was big and good-looking enough to notice on the street, even if the girls he let hang on him were ordinary to ugly. He stood straight, studied my father for a second, then pointed at his own dick with both index fingers.

"Don't say it," my father advised.

"She's inside," the boy said, bending to pick up a greasy wrench.

"Say hello to Zero," my father said, nudging me. "He thinks he's tough."

"Hey," the boy nodded at me for a split second before returning to my father. "I *am* tough."

"You just think so," my father said.

"Someday we'll find out," the boy said, tossing the wrench into the air, catching it nimbly by the handle.

"Careful," my father said. "Don't hurt yourself."

"Leave him alone!" came a voice from one of the windows directly above us. I jumped, but my father seemed to be half expecting it.

"You dressed?" my father said, mounting the concrete steps to the back door.

"It's almost nine-thirty. What do you think?"

My father held the screen door for me and we went in. There was a woman my mother's age at the kitchen sink doing dishes, about a week's worth, it looked like. Soapy to the elbows, she studied my father critically, as if she suspected him of bringing her some more.

"Just wanted to make sure," he said. "I got a weak ticker."

"I hate to be the one to tell you, but it's not your heart that's weak." She dried her hands and forearms and stood looking at him. She was a gangly woman, sort of pretty and not pretty at the same time, with lively eyes that conveyed both amusement and irritation.

My father touched the coffee pot with the back of his hand and, finding it warm, opened an empty cupboard, looking for a cup. The woman tossed him a wet plastic one from the mound on the drainboard.

"I'm Eileen," she said, offering a red hand, "since nobody's going to introduce us."

My father ignored her, pouring himself a cup of coffee. "Didn't work last night?"

"Yes, I worked last night," she said angrily. "Some people have to."

"I dropped by," he said. "You weren't there."

"Then you dropped by after eleven. I was early waitress. For once."

"Mike lose his head?"

"Must have. You could have called. My phone still works."

"I got tied up."

"Mmm," she said.

I had drifted off during the conversation. As usual, everybody seemed to know my father better than I did, and I always ended up feeling like an outsider. It had been the same when I was a kid. My father and Wussy had talked between themselves for ten or twenty minutes at a stretch, and when I was finally spoken to I'd be surprised to discover myself still present, a palpable if relatively unimportant part of the scene. Now, for some reason, my father and the woman called Eileen were suddenly looking at me, and I felt myself flush. "What?" I said.

"What do you mean, what?" my father said. "Try and stay awake."

"Tell him to take a long walk off a short dock," Eileen suggested to me.

"If you don't start being nice to me, I'm not going to take you out for breakfast," he said.

Eileen snorted. "Breakfast! Look at this mess."

My father shrugged. "Let Worthless do the dishes."

"That'll be the day he ever does a dish," Eileen said, glancing out the window to where her son knelt beside the motorcycle, her expression half affection, half exasperation.

"He will if I ask him," my father said.

"You never ask him anything. The only thing you know how to do is threaten and call names."

"He pays attention, anyhow."

"That's not the sort of attention I want."

"It would be a start."

Eileen grabbed a light coat from a wooden rack near the door. "Don't go telling me about my kid."

"All he needs is his ass kicked," my father smiled.

"We won't discuss it," she said. "Shut up and take me out to breakfast."

We went outside, single file—Eileen, then me, then my father. "Don't talk to him," Eileen said. "Don't say a word."

The boy looked up, saw us, nodded knowingly.

"Sam," Eileen warned.

But my father had already moved past her. He put his hand on the boy's shoulder. "Zero," he said. "I got a job for you."

The boy held up a greasy bolt for inspection. "Good. I get five bucks an hour."

My father snorted. "You'll never get five bucks an hour if you live to be a hundred. Unless it's to go away and not come back. In the meantime, there's a big stack of dirty dishes in on the sink, and your mother's worked every night this week."

"So?"

"So when we get back from breakfast, it'd be nice to see them done."

"Ignore him," Eileen said.

"Don't worry," the boy said, his voice even more pointedly contemptuous of her than of my father.

"Who buys your food?" my father said. "Who gives you a place to stay? Who bought you this motorcycle you couldn't live without?"

"Not you."

"No," my father admitted. "But I'm the one that's going to pound the snot out of you some day if you don't start remembering."

There was a flicker of fear in the boy's eyes, though he covered it quickly. "Someday, right Sammy?" he said.

"That's right."

Eileen had gotten in the car and she laid on the horn until my father turned his back on the boy. "The soap's under the sink, in case you forgot," he said.

"I'll think about it," the boy said, and his eyes met mine before I could avoid them. His were sullen and dull now, as if he'd already had the snot pounded out of him and had never gotten over it.

"The dishes will be done by the time we get back," my father said quietly when he slid in behind the wheel.

"I want you . . . to leave him . . . alone," Eileen said, her voice a knife edge.

"*I* want some breakfast," my father said.

I'd gotten in the backseat, and when he turned around so he could see to back out of the driveway, I instinctively turned around too, so I didn't see the cuff coming. It caught me right on the cowlick. "Don't grow up thinking you're tough," he said.

"Like your father," Eileen added.

12

Until my father told me not to, I worried about Rose not being able to afford fifteen dollars a week to have me clean the salon. It was a lot of money, enough to make a wealthy man of me, even if I only banked ten a week. "Don't lose sleep over Rose," my father advised. "She needs a wheelbarrow to cart all her money around."

I didn't see how that could be. How much business could she attract up those three flights of narrow, unlit stairs over Klein's Department Store? The only people who ever seemed to use them were my father and Rose and me. I understood only when I actually saw the salon that first Sunday. Rose's business came up by elevator from the store below. Her ladies, most of them elderly, did their shopping and their hair in one trip. At closing time, an accordionlike mesh gate was closed and locked, preventing entry from the elevator. Similar grids were used in the department store on the two floors below.

And my father was right. Rose had about the best business in town. That first Sunday he accompanied me to make sure I did the job right. It turned out he'd done the job himself when he was laid off. He showed me where the big vacuum and the cleaning supplies were. Then he showed me Rose's big black ledger, which she kept in a poorly fastened drawer at the receptionist's station at the elevator door. Along the left margin were the hours and half hours of the workdays—Monday through Saturday—and six columns across the pages which corresponded to the six chairs spaced evenly before the long wall mirror and individual sinks. For every hour and every chair at least one appointment was scheduled and dollar amounts recorded, sometimes in ink, sometimes lightly in pencil. We totaled up one day and multiplied by six to arrive at a figure for the week. I was so stunned by it that I went back over our calculations to find out where we'd goofed. We hadn't though.

"You should see the house she's got up on Kings Road," my father said, making himself comfortable with the racing form in one of Rose's six reclining chairs.

I doubted it could be as grand as the jeweled house on the hill across the highway from Myrtle Park.

"Jack Ward's place?" my father said when I described it.

I doubted there could be more than one, so I said that was it. "What does he do?" I said, figuring he must have a pretty good business, like Rose's.

"Not a goddamn thing, that I know of," my father said, not particularly interested. When he studied the racing form, he was hard to engage in idle chatter.

"Where does it come from?" I said. "The money, I mean."

"Doesn't come from anywhere. It's just there. *Been* there for a hell of a while. You couldn't spend it all if you tried."

I frowned at what seemed a silly observation. Of *course* you could *spend* it, I thought, and I said as much, too.

My father shook his head. "You couldn't do it," he said.

"Why not?"

"You just couldn't," he elaborated. "Jack's trying like hell, and even he can't. Which means it can't be done."

It turned out that Jack Ward was an old army buddy of my father's who had married into about the wealthiest family in the county and become a rich man. Since then, according to my father, he was trying to become a poor one again by throwing away money with both fists. But every time he thought he was making headway he discovered there was even more money than he'd thought. "Like shoveling shit against the tide," my father concluded pessimistically.

It struck me as an interesting problem to have, nevertheless. It shed new light on the forty dollars my mother had had me bring from the bank every week for us to live on. It had seemed a large sum, and I'd always wished I could be master of it for just one week, because I was convinced I could make it go a lot farther than she did. In fact, with forty dollars to live on every week, I had always considered us pretty well-to-do. Maybe there wasn't money for everything we wanted, but I had figured that was a pretty universal condition. Other people couldn't be all that much better off. Admittedly, there were people with cars, new ones even, but my mother had given me to believe that the people who owned them made extraordinary sacrifices to afford this single luxury. The fact that we never owned a car was, I believed, a matter of choice. We did not *need* a car, and by not owning one, we were able to enjoy whatever it might be that other people who *did* own them sacrificed. My mother had never been specific about what other people sacrificed, but she insisted they did, and I believed her. When I brought up the Claudes, she just smiled knowingly, and I thought long and hard trying to discover just what secret sacrifices they must have made to maintain a car *and* a swimming pool. About the only other extravagant wealth I'd ever personally encountered was at the dining table in the rectory of Our Lady of Sorrows, but my mother said the church didn't count. She was talking about *people*.

The idea of having more money than you could spend took

adjusting to, and I considered it for a long time as I vacuumed brittle black hair off Rose's red pile carpet, my father having fallen asleep in the chair with the racing form over his face. I tried to understand, but there were just too many holes in the theory.

When I was finished, I turned off the noisy vacuum and my father started awake. "He could just *give* some away," I ventured.

"What?" my father rubbed his eyes.

"The money," I said. "If you couldn't spend it all, you could give some to people who didn't have any and let *them* spend some."

I could tell by the look on his face that it was a dumb suggestion, so I started on the sinks, sponging the circles of hair toward the drain until the porcelain glistened white. Then, together, we dusted the tables and rearranged the magazines and emptied the dozen or so small trash buckets. It was a long job, but with two of us working it went faster and, besides, I was getting paid. Not the sort of sum Jack Ward would have trouble spending, but a good-sized chunk by my own standards.

"Take that trash down to the basement and you're all done," my father said.

When I shouldered the big bag and headed for the back door, he stopped me and said not to be a dummy. I should use the elevator like a white man. When I pointed out that the grid was locked, he said I had a key, didn't I? Well? And sure enough, the key I'd been given for the back door fit the lock on the gate, which lunged open when released as if on a well-greased, downhill track. I got on the elevator and pressed "B."

The doors opened again on a long, dark room with a low ceiling and glistening walls. A row of tall metal garbage cans lined the far wall, and in the largest of these I deposited my plastic bag full of hair and nail-polished tissues. When the elevator doors closed, I was left in total darkness and when I got back to the elevator I discovered I could not locate the button that would reopen them. I ran my hands up and down the adjacent walls, trying not to panic, but feeling fear rise in my throat anyway. It was terribly quiet there in the dark and when the big furnace clanged on a few feet away, I nearly cried out.

There was no use banging on the doors, because my father was four floors up and, besides, I was nearly as frightened of needing to be rescued as of being trapped in the dark. After a while he would begin to wonder what had become of me and investigate. The elevator doors would open and the light from inside would clearly illuminate the button I could not find in the dark. It would be in plain sight, right where it should be, right where any dummy but me could find it.

I knew it had to there, but I could not locate the button. I ran my fingers up and down the doors and walls, like a blind man reading Braille, but all they encountered was smooth, damp brick and steel. I went over the whole area around the doors several times, cursing inwardly, then finally crying tears of exasperation. Find it, dummy, I said aloud. It's *right* here. It has to be.

Finally, I decided on another tack. Feeling further along the wall, I started searching for a light switch, telling myself there had to be one in a basement with no windows. What I found instead, about ten feet from the elevator, was a wooden door that opened on a stairwell with a handrail, just barely visible. A faint light was coming from somewhere above, so I started slowly up the narrow stair, using the handrail as a guide. At the top there was a landing, then a right turn, then another flight. At the top of the stairs my heart plummeted when I saw that the passage ended at a single door, beneath which was a slender ribbon of light. Surely, it would be locked.

But when I tried the knob, the door creaked inward and I found myself on the threshold of Klein's Department Store, ground floor. Aisle upon symmetrical aisle stretched before me. The store was unlit except for the sunlight streaming in the long showcase windows a few feet away. In the nearest stood the boy mannequin wearing my clothes, his arms still extended outward, as if to embrace passersby on the street. From behind, he appeared awkward, paralytic, as if he were about to pitch forward through the glass. I let the door swing shut, the darkness suddenly welcome.

There in the dark stairwell I remembered the conversation I'd had with my father in the convertible on the way home from The Lookout. We had left Tree and Alice inside, and I'd asked my father about something that had been puzzling me. "What will he *do* with them?" I said, referring to the roll of admission tickets Tree had said would disappear from the guard shack at the end of the season.

"Keep them," my father explained. "Then next summer when it gets good and busy, he'll bring in eight or ten a day. People expect a ticket when they pay, so he'll give them one. Not from the new season's roll. They're numbered. The boss counts how many are given out every day. The money for those goes right in

the drawer where it's supposed to. The money from the old tickets will go into Tree's pocket."

He let me think about it for a while. "Well?" he said.

"It's dishonest," I said finally.

"Uh huh," he admitted. "And?"

When I didn't know what he meant by the question, he clarified
it. "So what?"

I made my way back down the stairs to the basement and
emerged from the stairwell just as the elevator doors opened. My
father was framed by the interior light, his black finger on the
button that held the door open. "Well?" he said. "You decide to
stay down here?"

He was grinning, and I saw there *was* no button outside the
elevator. The wall was as blank and featureless as it had felt in the
dark. For reasons beyond my comprehension, the elevator could
not be summoned from below.

I got in.

"What's the matter?" my father said.

"Nothing," I said angrily.

The elevator strained upward.

"You wanted me to leave you down there in the dark, is that
it?"

"Yes," I said through my teeth, staring straight ahead at the
stupid control panel on the elevator wall, hating it blackly, hating
the way it worked, hating him too. "Yes."

13

We got along all right, most of the time. During the week my
father worked on a new road up in Speculator, and he was usually
gone in the morning before I got up for school. He returned
around seven, having stopped for a couple of quick ones on the
way down the mountain. Then we'd eat hamburg steak dinners

across the street at the Mohawk Grill where there were plenty of people my father knew to keep us company. He was held in high esteem by just about everybody there because he had a good-paying job outside of Mohawk, unlike the rest of the men, who worked, when they could get work, in the few remaining tanneries and glove shops. They also liked him because he was an easy touch and had a lousy memory. Seldom did our dinner go uninterrupted by some hangdog supplicant, hands shoved deep into baggy trouser pockets, hovering over our Formica table, making obligatory small talk before wondering if maybe, Sammy, you could spare ten, because things weren't so hot and there wasn't any food in the house for the kids and, Jesus, was this any way for an able-bodied man to have to live . . . in Mohawk . . . in fucking Mohawk, excuse the language in front of your boy, but is this any way for a man to live? Then my father, who did not own a wallet, would fish in the pocket of his work pants for the folded wad of bills he kept in no particular sequence—tens, ones, fives—and peel off a couple, sliding them across the table unobtrusively so that the other men in the diner didn't have to know that it was a touch taking place and not just talk about the Giants, though they must have had a pretty good idea and some were probably thinking about their own prospects. Then the supplicant, always slightly more erect in posture for the infusion of cash, would tell my father to look for him come Friday, and my father would say sure, all right, Friday. He would often run into the same man later that night in Greenie's or The Glove or one of the countless other twelve-stool bars where a ten-dollar bill bought a man-sized share of camaraderie and oblivion at fifteen cents a draft, forty-five cents a shot.

If my father didn't turn up by seven or so, I usually made myself a sandwich out of the small refrigerator and prepared for an evening alone. On such nights he would not careen in until after the bars closed. Then he would piss for about five minutes in the general vicinity of the commode before falling asleep on the sofa with his mouth wide open. He had traded in the ragged old couch for an equally suspect model with just as many miles, but which converted, by a tricky, complicated process, into a double bed. On late nights, however, he was unequal to a task requiring so much dexterity, and since comfort wasn't the issue he usually decided the hell with it. Four hours or so later, the alarm having wound down to a feeble tinkle, he would jolt awake with a loud

"Ah!" and go pee again, with even greater urgency and, blessedly, accuracy. Finding himself still dressed from the night before, there would be nothing to do but stumble down to the Mercury, trusting the cold wind to air him out and sober him up. It was asking a lot, even with the top down.

On still other evenings we drove over to Eileen's. Usually, we'd stop at a market and buy a big package of pork chops and a couple cans of creamed corn to take with us, and Eileen Littler would fry the chops in butter and oregano and mash a half dozen potatoes into huge white mounds. Eileen, it turned out, was a direct lineal descendant of Nathan Littler, the town father, and his fabled sister Myrtle, whose park Eileen's small brown house sat at the edge of. The decline of the Littler family more or less paralleled that of Mohawk itself. Eileen excepted, the two dozen or so Littlers remaining in the county now lived, albeit marginally, on public assistance, which permitted them lives as full of leisure as their privileged ancestors. According to Eileen, who always held down at least two jobs and hadn't much use for her relatives, they'd all inherited a lazy gene. Her own industry, however, did not prevent her from being equated with the rest of the Littlers, and she herself was viewed as an object lesson in moral decline.

Right before the war, Eileen was said to have gone a little wild, and half a dozen surprised local boys claimed she was sending them into battle with at least one thing to be grateful for. When she disappeared from Mohawk, rumor had it that she'd followed one of these boys to an army camp in Savannah. But she was gone a long time, and when she reappeared she had a baby on her hip. Some maintained that she had married down south, others that her timing had been bad, and that she would have to await the end of the war to marry the child's father. And there were those who said that her timing was pretty good, that she'd had the war years to decide who she wanted the father to be, to see who made it back and in what condition. When the news of the surrender reached Mohawk, people remarked that Eileen Littler was as full of anticipation as any of the town's young wives-in-good-standing, but for her these exciting months passed uneventfully, and no young soldier came to claim Eileen or her son. When she enrolled the boy in grade school, he had his mother's name, Littler, now thoroughly and finally besmirched. In place of the lazy gene, Eileen had inherited a stubborn, circumspect one, and if the matter of the boy's paternity remained an open question for the curious, they knew better than to raise that question to her face. This new degenerate breed of Littlers all died penniless, and were buried in the county section of the cemetery, far from the huge black marble obelisk that marked the grave of their distant ancestor. My father told her not to worry. As soon as she died he'd have her cremated, have the ashes put in a mason jar, which he'd bury in a little hole under the black obelisk. "Right on top of old Nathan," he promised, "so you'll have someone to talk to."

"As long as I don't end up next to you," said Eileen, who claimed that hell would be having to talk to Sam Hall throughout eternity.

"Don't get me riled," he threatened, "or I'll put Zero in there with you, too."

"You plan to outlive *everybody*?" she said.

"Yes, I do," he said, nudging me.

About the time the three of us sat down, the motorcycle would roar up the driveway and Drew—that was the boy's name— would saunter in, plant his helmet on the table next to the bowl of creamed corn, and spoon about half the mashed potatoes onto his plate by way of hello. If he made conversation at all, it was with me. He'd taken, at least once, most of the classes I was now in, and he considered himself an authority on every teacher in Nathan Littler Junior High. "*That* asshole," he'd say, not without affection. Having finally made it to Mohawk High, he was nostalgic about my school, where he'd enjoyed himself immensely. Most afternoons, when the junior high let out, Drew would be out front astraddle his motorcycle, in the shadow of the big statue of Nathan Littler, his own distant relative.

A meal at the Littlers' was a feast of tension which always seemed to me on the verge of erupting into open hostility. When the motorcycle roared up the drive, Eileen always warned my father to be good for once, but his promise seldom amounted to much. Having watched Drew fill his plate with potatoes, my father would nudge me and nod across the table. "Not a bad life," he'd say. "Ride around on your motorcycle all the while. Take money for gas from your mother. Show up for a free dinner when you're hungry. Eat without bothering to wash your hands. Then say, 'So long, Ma,' and off you go. Ma can do the dishes, wash the clothes, work all night while you ride around and pretend you're a big shot. Not a bad life, if you can swing it."

"You my father?" Drew would say.

"I wouldn't admit it if I were."

"Don't blame you. Be embarrassing to have a kid that could kick your ass."

"Any time you want to try," my father would say, carefully cutting a chop. It was part of the way they talked to each other at such times that neither would look up from his plate. I often thought that if either had made eye contact with the other, blood would have been shed. The expressions on their faces were terrifying, and I was glad they concentrated on their food.

"Let's all mind our own business, shall we?" Eileen would suggest. "I like Ned better than either of you. At least he doesn't go around flexing his muscles all the time."

"Hasn't got any," Drew pointed out, not untruthfully.

I would flush twice over, once because Eileen had remembered I was there and said something nice, and again for lack of musculature. I liked Eileen a great deal. I liked the way she didn't get bent out of shape about things. My mother could have learned all sorts of things from her if she'd felt like it.

Actually, Drew and I got along fine too. After dinner I'd go out to the garage with him and act as spotter while he bench pressed. He was only five-ten, three inches shorter than my father, and he had a fleshy midriff, but his arms and shoulders were massive. I very much admired his strength. When he lay on his back on the narrow bench, his blond hair hung straight down and a single blue vein on his broad forehead pulsed when he held his breath before exploding into the lift. The weight of the bar was something he seemed to take personally, as if in his imagination he had infused the cold metal with life and personality. He shoved the steel up and out of his way with savage contempt, as if its mere presence offended him. On those occasions when he misjudged his strength and needed me to help guide the wobbling bar back to its resting place, his expression darkened and he would give up, refusing to take weight off the bar, refusing to try a second lift. He had failed, and that was all there was to it. He would then turn his attention to the cycle, pulling it all apart, as if while lying on his back beneath the great weight of the bar, he'd suddenly remembered something wrong with the way it was running. He'd spend the rest of the evening cursing the machine.

But Drew was seldom defeated by the bar, and when his first lift was successful, he would continue his workout until exhaustion finally overtook him. Then he would get up from the bench—the only lifting he seemed interested in was from flat on his back—his chest swelling with accomplishment, his blond hair wet with perspiration, the blue vein on his forehead still throbbing intensely, as if its angry excited pulsing contained the very center of his being. Then he would fling one leg over the bike, kick back the stand, and roar down the steep drive. You could hear him changing gears all the way to the highway, and by the time he returned half an hour later his pale hair would be dry again and the blue vein gone from his forehead.

Sometimes, depending on his mood, he would take me for a ride. The first time scared me good, because he took off before I could locate the pegs to rest my feet on, and when we took sharp turns my feet went straight out like wings. Leaning into the turns seemed foolhardy, and for a long time I refused to do it. Often I leaned in the opposite direction to make up for what Drew was doing in front of me, so that our bodies formed a V, Drew leaning into the danger, I away from it. Eventually I got better, but seeing the pavement whiz by a few inches beneath my kneecap was something I never did get used to.

In the beginning we just circumnavigated a few blocks, but our rides got progressively longer. One night in late October, instead of just disturbing a few peaceful streets, Drew took us out to the highway and let the bike full out. On our right, the dark expanse of Myrtle Park, rising abruptly against the dusk, flew by. On the left, off in the distance, was the radio tower, its twin red lights pulsing. I hadn't as much hair as Drew, but what I did have stood straight up and I felt the exhilaration of raw speed so strongly that I had all I could do not to howl in animal pleasure. Drew was rock solid as the bike itself, and together we leaned into the turns.

About a mile beyond Myrtle Park we left the highway and followed a narrow, winding road until we came to a clearing at the top of a steep crest, and there before us, suddenly, was my white jewel house, the one I always wondered about from my perch in Myrtle Park. It looked different now, but I knew it had to be the same house. There could be no other like it in Mohawk, or in the entire county, or in the whole world. Drew pulled the bike over, let the engine die, and we just sat there looking at it, a mere hundred yards away.

Up close, it did not glisten the way it appeared to from across the highway, but the house was even more vast and impressive than I had imagined. Its tall TV antenna caught the last ray of sunlight from behind the park, but everything else—the house itself and the surrounding lawn and woods were deepening purple, the highway below almost black.

"Gotta be twenty rooms in there," Drew said, his voice unexpectedly loud. The only other sound was the faint whirr of the cars on the highway below, their headlights flickering in and out of the trees.

I couldn't get over how strange it felt to be looking at the house up close, and even stranger to be in the company of Drew Littler. It was like learning that the girl you had a secret crush on for a very long time was also the object of somebody else's affections. Somebody you doubted was worthy of her. "Let's go," I said. "We shouldn't be up here. The sign said private road."

My companion shrugged. "It's a free country. Besides. This house is going to be mine someday."

I must have made a sound, because he looked over his shoulder at me.

"You wait and see if it don't."

I shrugged.

It didn't matter much if I wanted to go. Drew didn't. So we sat there and stared at the house and the long sloping lawn. If I'd been there alone, it would have been okay, but I could not enjoy the house from the back of Drew Littler's motorcycle. I felt like telling him that he was nuts to think he'd ever own a house like this one, any more than I would. It was dumb to kid himself. I didn't say it, of course, but I was surprised to discover myself so blackly angry at his presumption. Did he imagine he was going to come into a fortune just because he could bench-press more than anybody in Mohawk, assuming he *could* bench more than anybody? The dancing blue vein on his broad forehead embodied his only skill as far as I could see. Did he actually see himself seated at the head of the long mahogany table (I imagined one like that in the rectory of Our Lady of Sorrows) in the rectangular dining room, shoveling mounds of white mashed potatoes onto the gleaming china?

"Come on," I said. "They'll be wondering where we are."

"Your ass," he said quietly. "They'll be glad. Your old man is probably banging her right now."

He was still staring at the house, but his expression had gone bad, as if he'd seen something nasty through one of the windows.

My own face must have borne a similar expression, because when Drew looked at me he said, "You didn't know they go upstairs so he can crawl on top and put it to her?"

His voice was so full of contempt (for me, it seemed then) that I had to lie. "Sure," I said.

He started up the engine. "Your ass, you did."

A man came out of the jewel house and stood on the patio, his hands shoved deep in his pockets. If I hadn't been thinking about my father and Eileen Littler, I might have been able to take pleasure in the fact that I knew the man's name. He was Jack Ward, and he was standing there trying to figure out more ways to spend money. When Drew revved the engine, the man looked up and saw us, but I doubted the angry revving bothered him much.

Drew circled the bike once, then threw us back down toward the darkness of the highway below. "Fuck him!" he bellowed over the roar of the bike. "Fuck them all!"

On Saturday mornings I went to see my mother, and the few hours I spent at our old house were always the strangest of my week, which is saying a good deal when you lived with Sam Hall the rest of the time. To begin with, the house itself had changed, a fact I attributed to so little of it being lived in. The air downstairs seemed full of dust, millions of particles suspended in midair. No doubt this was largely the effect of the heavy curtains remaining closed, only one of two windows leaking a narrow slant of light in which the universe of atoms played. The kitchen was in the back of the house, and the maple darkened and obscured the yard with its lush foliage and allowed only late afternoon light to filter through the kitchen windows. I suspected, though I could not be certain, that the gray kitchen now represented the outer extremity of my mother's world, and that she ventured down into it no more than once a day.

For a while I tried to convince myself that our arrangement was working and that, as she herself continued to insist, all she needed was a little time alone to draw things back together. She had waged her solitary war with the outside world too long. Only time would heal her wounds, restore her health. But I was gone only a month or so before I began to notice her face hollowing and the flesh along her upper arms growing slack. Like a cave-dweller,

her skin became sallow, then almost translucent, and when I
mentioned that I didn't think she was looking well, she responded
that she didn't think it would work out (my visiting on Saturday
mornings) unless "we" could refrain from comments of that nature. It was hard enough for her to get well without somebody
offering personal comments. It wasn't much of a threat, of course.
I don't know who else would have cashed her meager checks,
straightened out the mistakes made by her grocer, and purchased
anything that required leaving the house.

As it turned out, my mother's gradual physical decline was not
the only proscribed subject between us. Since she never responded to any information I chose to impart about my father or
our lives together, I gradually understood that I was not to communicate anything of that sort. Of course I knew enough not to
tell her anything troubling. Even when she was in perfect health,
she never had been the sort of person to whom you confessed
riding motorcycles. But I soon discovered that even carefully
selected anecdotes about my father, ones calculated (even fab-
ricated) to suggest that our life together was normal and healthy,
were deeply disturbing to her, and it took me a long time to
realize that among the myriad torments my mother suffered
alone in her room, having given me over to the dubious care of
my father was the keenest and the most deeply rooted. Any re-
minder of his existence caused her eyes to go dull and dead, and
she would look away, at the wall, at the drawn window shade, at
nothing at all. I think that for the purposes of her day-to-day
reality she had constructed some sort of fable to account for my
absence. Probably I was supposed to be away at some posh private
school, and therefore able to visit only on weekends. Whatever.
I know she particularly liked hearing about my triumphs at
school, and these I began to manufacture with some ingenuity.
Rigid slavishness to the truth had never been one of my particular
vices, and it was during this period that my mother's and my
relationship was entirely rewritten, grounded firmly in kind false-
hoods. It would never change again. For the rest of our lives I
would lie and she would believe me.

Once I got the hang of the fact that only lies gave her any
measure of peace, I never told her the truth about anything again.
I became a perfect son, creating what amounted to an alter ego
for our own private edification, for I may as well confess that my
lies were not completely altruistic, whether or not they had a

salubrious effect on my mother. The worse my actual performances at school, the more glorious the academic achievements I reported to her. The more arrogant and aloof I became with regard to everything that happened at Nathan Littler Junior High, the greater stature I accepted in the totally fraudulent renderings I concocted for her. First, I became a member of the eighth grade council, then class president. I also became a case study in morality, returning examinations to my instructors who, out of understandable force of habit, had given me a perfect score when in fact I had achieved a mere 98.

I was telling my poor mother all of this during the same period that I began to make weekly raids into Klein's Department Store, using my key to Rose's salon, then the elevator down into the dark basement, where I pressed the hold button and took the stairwell up into the store. The store itself was nearly as black as the basement I emerged from, the only illumination that which streamed in at odd angles from the streetlamps outside. Sometimes I did not even know what I was stealing until I got it upstairs.

All that autumn, a Saturday morning at a time, I joined my mother in her murky bedroom and watched her decline, unable in any way to prevent it. By Thanksgiving, I was sure she was going to die.

In the beginning I never went into the Mohawk Grill except in the company of my father. It was one of a dozen or so places (along with the pool hall and Clausen's Cigar Store, where magazines with bare-breasted women were displayed in plain sight), that had been on my mother's list of proscribed places. I remember that when I was a small child we had always crossed the street rather than pass directly in front of these dubious establishments. They were located on opposite sides of Main, and we must have looked pretty funny tacking and veering, as if to avoid invisible obstacles. My mother disliked the sort of men that congregated in these doorways, though they spoke well of her, and loud enough so we could both hear, even as we were in full retreat. These men were fickle though, and they said much the same things to all passing women.

One of my father's favorite anecdotes concerned a man called Waxy—I was introduced to him one Saturday afternoon in the Mohawk Grill—who had a fine eye for shapes. His favorite roost was the doorway of the pool hall on South Main, from which vantage point he could keep an eye on the action inside and out. "Get a load of *this*," he would say out of the corner of his mouth when something worthwhile appeared on the horizon. He could isolate an exceptional set of knockers on a crowded street, then hone in and track them like radar. "Scope *this*," he said one evening just as my father emerged from the pool hall. It took a minute, but my father located the object of Waxy's fixed stare beneath the traffic light at The Four Corners. "It's your wife, Wax," my father said. "What the fuck's wrong with you?" Waxy shook his head, gravely disappointed. "Too bad," he said. "It had potential."

After a few visits to the Mohawk Grill, I much preferred it to the lunch counter at the shabby Mohawk Woolworth's which, it then occurred to me, wasn't such a great deal. The food at the dime store looked all right in the bright pictures on the wall, but it was invariably disappointing on the plate. Usually, I contented myself with a hamburger and Coke, sixty cents total, but I yearned for one of the "Fabulous Woolworth Triple-Decker Club Sandwiches" depicted in Technicolor above the milk machine. These were extravagantly expensive—a dollar ten—and I never saw anybody order one. I wondered if such a sandwich could be eaten by one person. Lettuce, bacon, red tomato, cheese, and turkey spilled out everywhere. The sandwich was so full that toothpicks were required to hold it together.

After the second Sunday I cleaned for Rose, I brought a crisp five the next day to the Woolworth's counter. The waitress regarded it suspiciously, feeling it carefully with her thumb and forefinger, before going over to the sandwich board. "What's the matter?" she wanted to know when she set the club sandwich in front of me. I was staring alternately at the plate in front of me and the picture above the milk machine, trying to discover a discrepancy that would hold up. There *was* a fragmented bacon strip, a thin slice of greenish tomato, a thick, spotted spine of lettuce, even some gray turkey. "Toothpicks!" I said angrily. "I *want* my toothpicks!"

At the Mohawk Grill, Harry Saunders, the big ornery-looking cook, didn't gyp you. In fact, for twenty-five cents he would fill a plate with hot, glistening french fries, and even ladle brown gravy over them if you asked him. They were a meal. People who ate at Harry's didn't go away starved. What's more, it was a lively place, especially in the winter, when work in the mills slowed and half of Mohawk was on unemployment. My father usually quit construction in November when it got too cold to work comfortably out of doors. Some afternoons and most evenings there was a poker game up above the grill, and when I lost track of my father for a while I'd know where to find him. If he wasn't at the Mohawk Grill there was usually somebody there who had seen him within the last few hours and knew where he was. If I needed to get in touch with him, I'd just go across the street and tell Harry, and then a couple hours later he'd turn up.

Lest it seem that I was neglected, I should point out that once I became known to the Mohawk Grill crowd, it was like having about two dozen more or less negligent fathers whose slender attentions and vague goodwill nevertheless added up. Tree was usually around when he wasn't out visiting Alice, and my old friend Skinny Donovan, who had few duties at the rectory during the winter months, divided his time about equally between the pool hall, Greenie's Tavern and the Mohawk Grill. He seemed pleased that I had fallen from grace at Our Lady of Sorrows, and I got the impression that life had become more tolerable there now that I wasn't seated at the right hand of the fathers. There was a new assistant priest, apparently. An alright Irishman who wasn't too good to share a belt from the flask. The Monsignor was still sick and dying, but strictly at his own pace.

The Mohawk Grill was also an educational place, and it was here that I learned to handicap horses. There was always a racing form lying around, and usually somebody willing to explain its intricacies to a novice. Around noon, Untemeyer, the bookie, came in and sat on the last stool at the counter and took whatever action there was, writing out small slips that disappeared into the baggy pockets of his black alpaca suit. "Don't mean a goddamn thing," he said of the racing form and its statistics. According to

Untemeyer, the other factors that didn't mean a goddamn thing
were the jockeys, the track conditions, and the horse's lineage.
"What *does* mean something?" I innocently asked one day.
"Nothing," he grumbled. "Nothing means anything."
I thought about that. "There's *no* way to predict?"
He snorted. "There's all kinds of ways. That's the trouble. None
of them work. How old do you think I am?"
I couldn't tell how old Untemeyer was, but I knew he was
pretty old. I said fifty and he snorted again. "Try sixty-six. Guess
how much I've lost on the horses."
"A lot?" I said. If he was that old, it had to be.
"Not a goddamn dime," he said. "Guess how much I've bet."
I was on to him. "Not a goddamn dime?"
"You're smarter than your old man," he said. "Course, you're
younger, too. You got all your dumb years ahead of you."
Actually, when it came to the horses, my father was nobody's
fool, and he'd made Untemeyer uncomfortable more than once.
Untemeyer was a poor man's bookie who never took any really
heavy action. In fact, most of the book he wrote was under the
traditional two-dollar minimum wager. My father, who made
good money working on the road, had nailed him with ten-dollar
daily doubles on more than one occasion. This made the old
bookie grumble pitifully, though my father's long suit wasn't sympathy for bookies. "I guess this means you'll have to go out in the
garden and dig up that strongbox," he said.
"Footlocker, you mean," somebody added.
"Footlocker, your ass. We're talking about my retirement."
"Retire from what?" my father said. "You haven't worked a day
in forty years."
"As long as there's Sam Halls around I don't figure I'll ever need
to," Untemeyer said. "And there's another coming right behind
you."
That meant me. I was off in a corner studying the form, and
suddenly everybody in the place was looking at me, including my
father, who nodded knowingly.
Sometimes we studied the racing form together, and he'd tell
me why my selection was wrong. "Class will tell," was his favorite
reason. He had a hell of a time convincing me that the fastest
horse wouldn't necessarily be the winner. In the beginning I just
scanned the columns looking for the fastest six-furlong times.
"Forget that," my father advised. "For one thing, this isn't a

six-furlong race. And for another. . . ." There were about half a dozen "for anothers." He taught me how to look at how much the horse cost, his sire, and whether he was moving up, and perhaps out, of his class. My father wasn't a big believer in betting jockeys, because the horses were carrying them, not the other way around. He liked fast, well-bred, expensive horses with a fondness for the rail.

Betting the horses is not something I advocate, but there is a great deal to be said in defense of handicapping, and I have often thought, and occasionally argued with people who considered themselves educators, that courses in handicapping should be required, like composition and Western civilization, in our universities. For sheer complexity, there's nothing like a horse race, excepting life itself, and keeping the myriad factors in balanced consideration is fine mental training, provided the student understands that even if he does this perfectly there is no guarantee of success. The scientific handicapper will never beat the horses (Untemeyer was correct, of course), but he *will* learn to be alert for subtleties that escape the less trained eye. To weigh and evaluate a vast grid of information, much of it meaningless, and to arrive at sensible, if erroneous, conclusions, is a skill not to be sneezed at. Since my days in the Mohawk Grill, I have known many great handicappers, and not one has ever preceded an Ayatollah into battle or become a Born Again anything. The handicapper is a man of genuine faith and conviction: There *will* be another race in twenty minutes.

My father would have been a great handicapper but for one fatal weakness. Where many failed as a result of missing some important nuance, my father erred by making things more complex than they already were. When he was on a streak—and it was not all that unusual for him to hit three or even four races in a row—things would invariably go very bad, usually all at once. The problem was that after hitting three or four in a row, my father began to suspect that the true determining factor in the next race's outcome was himself. Destiny was awaiting his wager. Yes, he was a skilled handicapper, but I think he sometimes believed that this skill merely opened some door to an inner sphere of far greater influence. He began to suspect that the race was being run for his exclusive entertainment and benefit, that an act of faith on his part—say a hundred-dollar wager—was all that was needed to rig the race.

At such times his expression became both fierce and distant. Neither I nor anyone else existed. And when he lost, finally and inevitably, he looked like a man turned away at the threshold, as if some fine promise had been made, then without explanation, welshed on. Sometimes, too, he appeared almost relieved, as if he wouldn't have known what to do if the promise had been kept. Having been taken advantage of, he was reassured of his purpose, and he'd grin at me weakly then, as if to say he hoped I'd been paying attention.

15

The Sunday before Christmas I went next door to clean Rose's as usual. My father, after that first time, never accompanied me. Rose made me a list of things that needed doing, and I checked each one off methodically. I also went through her black ledger to find out how she was doing. Between Thanksgiving and Christmas she set new records every week, though many of the entries were made in light pencil, others on slips stuffed carelessly into the crease of the binding.

On Mondays, usually late in the afternoon, Rose knocked on our door and handed me my pay. "Your father leaves you alone too much," she often observed, as she craned her neck to see inside.

I shrugged. As a rule I didn't mind being alone. I'd taken up reading with even more of a vengeance in the months since moving in with my father, making at least two trips to the library every week. I'd grown fond of being the only one in the vast, high-ceilinged apartment, and sometimes I pretended I was its sole proprietor, an illusion not all that difficult to sustain, given my father's unpredictable comings and goings. Once he learned that I would not starve if he didn't show up at mealtimes, he felt better about not showing up. He set up an account at the Mohawk Grill and told me to eat there when I didn't have cash. Sometimes, he would disappear entirely for a day or two and then come back looking sheepish, though he never offered any explanation. I never worried much, because there was always somebody at the Mohawk Grill who knew where to find him if I needed him, and usually I forgot to need him. I had plenty of ready cash and a growing savings account, the existence of which nobody knew.

"Boys your age need guidance," Rose went on. "Before long you'll have some girl knocked up, and then where will you be?"

I felt like explaining to her that it wasn't so simple. But she wasn't the only one to worry mistakenly about my unsupervised life in the big apartment. The guys at the grill were always wanting to know if I was getting any, and saying that I better had be. "At your age I'd have gotten myself laid every night if I'd had a place," Skinny was fond of observing. I had trouble imagining Skinny at twelve, much less his getting laid.

"You know how to protect yourself?" Rose wanted to know.

I nodded. Wild Bill Gaffney, the town derelict, who spoke gibberish, had on more than one occasion pressed me to accept a small package, the contents and purpose of which I divined only after removing the prophylactic and unrolling its unnecessarily long sleeve. At the moment I had three still in their sealed packages. Protection was my strong suit. I needed something to be protected from.

I was thinking about this very problem that Sunday morning before Christmas in Rose's when I heard the heavy step on the stair outside. I'd left my father asleep on the sofa next door, and when whoever it was on the stair stopped and pounded on our apartment door I heard him snort awake. Through the frosted glass of Rose's rear door, I watched the dark shadow of our apartment door yawn inward and the figure before it disappear inside.

It was a little early on a Sunday morning for visitors. We had few enough in any season, and I wondered if this might be one of the men from the black sedan who had once been looking for my father. I shut down the vacuum cleaner and listened. The walls were flimsy and I could hear voices across the hall, but they were vague, like voices in a cave. I thought I heard my father say, "He's next door," but I couldn't be sure. They were there for five minutes before the door opened and my father limped out into the hall in nothing but his shorts.

"Let that alone for now," he said when he poked his mussed head in.

"I'm almost done," I objected, certain now that the man was a policeman, that the items I had stolen from Klein's Department Store had been missed, the unlocked door discovered, the correct inferences drawn. I must have gone very white.

"You can finish later. We gotta take a ride."

To the police station, I thought, illogically, since that was only half a block away. I pulled the vacuum cleaner plug out of the wall and studied the floor, unwilling to move.

"It's your mother," I heard him explain, as if from a long way away. "She's in the hospital."

It was F. William Peterson who had come to find me, though I never did find out how he himself learned of my mother's breakdown and hospitalization. Of course, news in Mohawk traveled fast, and it would have been more of a mystery if he had *not* heard, eventually. In fact, my father had heard part of the story the night before at The Elms, where Eileen worked as a waitress, but he hadn't believed it. She had finished her shift and they were having a drink when Darryl somebody—my father couldn't remember his last name—came in drunk and walked right over to the table where they were sitting.

"You hear about your wife?" Darryl Somebody said.

"Don't *you* have nice manners," Eileen observed.

"Okay, forget it," the man said. "Screw it, in fact." Then he went over and sat at the bar beneath the inverted cocktail glasses.

My father had wanted to get up, but Eileen didn't like trouble, especially where she worked.

"Where does he get off . . . ?" my father wanted to know.

"He's drunk," Eileen said.

But Darryl Somebody had Mike the bartender by the sleeve and was telling him a story. From time to time they glanced over at the table where my father and Eileen Littler were sitting.

"Let's go," Eileen said. "I've had enough of this place for one night."

My father motioned for Mike to come over. Sam Hall was personal friends with about half the bartenders in the county.

"What's *his* problem?" my father said, indicating Darryl Somebody, who was studying his beer, now that he had no one to talk to.

"No problem."

"What."

"Forget it, Sammy."

"Ask him if he'd like to tell me all about it outside."

"He claims he saw your wife wandering around downtown in her robe and slippers. Kept stopping people in the street and said she was looking for 'him.' When they asked who, she just smiled."

My father nodded. Darryl Somebody was watching them now, smiling vaguely.

"You must be confused with your own wife," my father suggested across the room.

"I haven't got no wife," Darryl Somebody said.

"Surprise, surprise," Eileen said.

The two of them left then, though my father insisted they wait a few minutes in case Darryl Somebody came out. But either Mike advised against it or my father's reputation as a skilled bushwhacker had preceded him, because Darryl stayed right where he was.

The reason I relate all this is that my father did, right there in the front seat of F. William Peterson's big Olds on the way to the hospital. Eileen he didn't mention by name, but I knew it had to be her. F. William Peterson listened to the whole tale politely, concealing his irritation. No doubt he too felt the absurdity of my father's detailed rendering, as if Sam Hall's reasons for refusing to believe what turned out to be true were more important than the reality of my mother's pitiful condition. That's the way he'll tell it, even if she dies, I remember thinking. It will always be *his* story, about how he hadn't believed it could be true, about how nobody who knew my mother *could* have believed it.

When we got to the hospital, my father ran into someone he knew in the lobby, someone who wanted to know if he'd heard, and when he launched into the whole thing again, F. William Peterson took me aside.

"Your mother is sedated," he said, placing his pale, almost hairless hand on my shoulder. "You know what that means?"

I nodded, growing increasingly apprehensive about whatever the man thought I needed to be prepared for. "You saw her?"

He shook his head. "I'm sure though. She's had what's called a nervous collapse. I doubt she'll be the person you recognize. And they'll probably only let you stay a few minutes." He paused briefly. "Your father won't be permitted in at all."

Something about the way he said this gave me the idea that he himself had seen to it.

"They'll probably take her to Albany this afternoon. There's nobody here that knows much about stuff like this. Not many people around here are smart enough to have a nervous breakdown."

He half smiled at his own observation and ran his pale fingers through the few tenacious strands of blond hair on top of his head. "You ready?"

My father had his back to us and didn't notice when we turned the corner by the elevator. The second floor looked deserted. There weren't even any nurses in the corridors. Each room we passed was the same dull shade of green. Some of the occupants of the beds made small insignificant mounds beneath the sheets, while others sat upright, their mottled backs to the open door, as if contemplating flight through the transparent curtained windows. I didn't see anybody who looked like he could pass a pop quiz on what day of the week it was.

There were two beds in the room that contained my mother, but she was alone there, the other bed tightly made, its blanket and crisp white sheet tucked between mattress and metal frame. She lay on her back in the bed near the window, her thin wrists restrained by leather straps attached to the rails of the bed, though she appeared unaware of this hindrance. Her eyes had the same faraway look they once had when she thought about Tucson, Arizona, or San Diego, California. We went around to the other side of the bed, F. William Peterson hanging back several paces so that I alone would come between her and the white window. Whoever had put on her hospital gown hadn't done much of a job, because part of her right breast was exposed, along with her rib cage, now clearly defined. F. William Peterson may have noticed too, because he retreated to the middle of the room.

My mother did not appear to see me at first, but then her eyes began to focus and something like a smile of recognition formed. "Sam?" she said. "Sam?"

Suddenly I was choking back tears and my throat was as thick as it had been that afternoon I'd eaten Oreos with Claude. "It's me," I said. "Ned."

Her smile changed, first becoming perplexed, then troubled, then inexpressibly sad, as if she'd been informed of my death. Her own tears welled up, but before they could be shed, she lost her focus. A bird had landed on the window ledge behind me and pecked at the glass with its tough beak before flying off with her attention into the white sky.

That night, after my father got in the convertible and drove off, I let myself back into Rose's and took the elevator down into Klein's Department Store and filled a paper bag with the most expensive items I could find in the dark. I stayed there a full hour, shopping carefully, angrily. And when I was finished, I took it all over to our house on Third Avenue. F. William Peterson had arranged for the house to be locked up and I had no key so I climbed the maple tree up to the roof, then lowered myself onto my bedroom window dormer. The storm windows had not been put on, nor would they be that winter. Neither the screen nor inner window offered resistance.

Once inside, I went back downstairs, unlocked the rear door and fetched what I had stolen. There was a pewter ashtray inscribed with something in Latin for the coffee table, along with a fancy cut-glass nut dish. On her dresser I placed the ornate jewelry box. The other stuff I scattered after removing the price tags and flushing them down the toilet. I mentally totaled what I had taken, and it came close to three hundred dollars, but I was neither satisfied nor ashamed. Until that night, I'd stolen only insignificant items: a cheap, imitation-leather wallet, a package of undershorts and socks, an athletic supporter for gym class (these were kept in a special place behind the counter in the sporting goods department, never on display). I had told myself that the store would never be aware of such trivial losses, that the truest test of my ethics was that I had the perfect opportunity to steal a great deal, yet took only the cheapest items. But try as I might to absolve myself, the petty thefts ate at me, especially at night when I recollected how much money I had in my account at the bank.

But tonight I had stolen big. My only criteria had been price and size. I had stolen out of pure malice and I felt not the slightest remorse, regretting only that I could not have carried more. If I could, I would have taken it all. What pure pleasure it would have been on Monday morning to see the store's owner gape at the bare shelves, the astonished voices of the employees echoing off the walls and high ceilings in the emptiness I had left them.

And so, after locking the house again from the inside, I went back to our apartment and waited for my father to return, not caring much whether he did or didn't. Finally, I went to sleep and did not dream. During the night it snowed and the tall windows froze white and brittle. Winter. With a capital W.

PART 2

MOHAWK FAIR

16

In February of that same year my father started talking about heading west for a while. There were lots of jobs on the interstates, and it was warm enough to work in your shirtsleeves.

"In your imagination," Untemeyer grumbled from his end of the Formica lunch counter in the Mohawk Grill.

My father took that as an invitation to the sort of dispute that might earn him a dollar or two without leaving the warmth of the diner, or even getting up off the stool.

"Phoenix," my father said. "I bet it's fifty degrees there right now. In fact, I'll give you a fin for every degree under fifty. You give me one for every degree over."

"You got that kind of dough, how about paying your tab," Harry said, without turning around from the grill. We'd been eating Harry's food on credit for the last couple weeks while my father figured his next move. I gathered that things worked this way pretty much every year. My father was a seasonal kind of guy. May through November he was flush, but along about Thanksgiving when the road construction dwindled, he'd get himself laid off and collect unemployment until late spring. The unemployment was meager though, compared to his normal summer earnings.

"If you didn't piss money away, you wouldn't be in this fix every year," Untemeyer offered, ignoring my father's proposed wager. "You ever hear of banks? They'll take your money and hold it for you till you need it. Pay you interest on it too, you chowderhead."

"Five bucks for every degree under fifty," my father reiterated.

"Take a hike," said the bookie.

My father nudged me. I was seated comfortably on the stool next to him, absorbing the heat from Harry's grill, thinking about nothing at all. "You can't get to Unc," my father said. His favorite nickname for Untemeyer was Uncle Willie. "He knows I'm right, the bastard. Hell, I bet it's *sixty* in Phoenix."

That was what he would do now—sweeten the pot until there was no way he could win the bet. In another half hour he'd be giving five to one it was a hundred and ten in Phoenix in February, so worked up was he over the fabled heat in the desert Southwest. The only thing that would save him in the present instance was that, except for Harry and the bookie, we had the diner to ourselves, and neither of those two worthies was dumb enough to bet with a man who'd been bellyaching for a month that he couldn't even afford to pay attention. Another time they might anyway, just to teach him a lesson, but not today.

"*I* bet it's not sixty," I said. It was so cold outside the Mohawk Grill that I couldn't imagine it being sixty anywhere.

"Are you shitting me?" my father said, as if this finally settled it. I was God's own fool, a militantly unteachable dimwit.

"So *go* to fucking Phoenix," Harry growled. "Give us all a break. Give my customers a break. Look at this place. Untemeyer's the only one who's not scared to come in here."

It was true. Come February, my father was bad for business. Summers he loaned money indiscriminately and generally forgot how much and to whom. But the higher the snowbanks grew along Main Street the more these foolish loans began to weigh on him and he became more than a little insistent about being paid back. True, he didn't know who owed him what, but he thought he did, and the more broke he got, the more clearly his memory functioned. Virtually everyone triggered some vague recollection, and whoever appeared in the doorway to Harry's diner would be greeted with a "Look at *this* deadbeat!" And, likely as not, the accused would in fact *be* a deadbeat, but a deadbeat who understood that my father's memory was of the most shadowy and elusive character. Having escaped payment for six months, they refused to pay up now and were deeply indignant when my father recollected a debt far larger than was actually incurred. Many of Harry's regular customers had taken to sidling along the front wall of the diner and peeking in to make sure that my father was someplace else before entering.

"Give your goddamn *kid* a break, too," Untemeyer said. His own business generally tailed off when Harry's did. "How the hell do you put up with him twenty-four hours a day? Tell me that."

I shrugged. In truth, I probably saw less of him than Untemeyer himself. There was school, of course, until the middle of the afternoon, and after dinner he'd usually disappear, sometimes to play poker, sometimes to visit The Elms to see Eileen and talk to Mike, the bartender. About the only time I saw him was in the late afternoon, like now. I could usually figure on finding him at Harry's when I got off school. Sometimes, we'd eat dinner there. Other times at Eileen's. If he wasn't around, I'd eat dinner by myself in the apartment overlooking the gray, deserted Main Street below.

Of the three, I most hated those dinners at Eileen's because they were like sitting atop a powderkeg. When my father had money, we'd stop at the market and buy groceries to bring with us. Lately, though, he'd been taking a beating at the poker table and the bookmakers', which meant that when we turned up, it would be empty-handed. That wouldn't have bothered him so much if it didn't rob my father of his trump card with Eileen's son Drew, whom my father rode hard about freeloading off his mother. "It must be supper time," my father would say when we'd hear the motorcycle, usually still a couple blocks down the street.

"Lay off of him," Eileen would warn.

Lately, my father didn't have much to say, though that, it seemed to me, actually increased the tension, because Drew Littler sensed that for the moment, anyway, he had the upper hand. The last time we'd gone over to the Littlers' for dinner, the cycle had been parked in the garage and Drew had lifted his blond head from a comic book when we came in and called out, "Must be supper time," to his mother.

That had been over a week ago, and we hadn't been back since.

My father dug into his pocket and came up with two folded bills, tossing one on the table in front of me. "Well?" he said.

I picked up the dollar bill and studied it. "Liars" was one of our favorite pastimes. Played with the serial numbers of dollar bills, the game developed some of the same intellectual rigors as handicapping horses. If you said four fives and there were only two fives on *your* dollar bill, then there had better be two more on the bill your opponent was holding. If there weren't, and you were called upon to produce the four fives you'd claimed the existence of, you lost your bill. The idea was to trick your opponent into making a claim he'd have to support entirely on his own. If you could convince him that your bill contained, say, threes, and it was in reality devoid of threes, you could challenge him later if he claimed to have an inordinate number of them. It was a wicked little game that placed a premium on confident bluffing, misdirection and rapid analysis of probability.

"What am I going to do with you if I go someplace for a while?" I shrugged and called three deuces.

He studied his bill disinterestedly. "Three fives."

"Three eights," I said, holding my breath. There wasn't a single eight on my bill; I was hoping to trap him into coming back to eights later on. I did have three fives, but fives were what he'd just called and he might be using the same strategy on me.

"Four fives," he said.

"Four eights," I said, a little too quickly, trying to sound casual.

"Your ass, four eights," he said, but we always played strict rules. You had to say "liar." "I know you're not telling the truth, but I'll let you skate this once because I've got five fives."

He had me and I knew it. I had three fives myself. No way he'd believe five eights. My only hope was that he too had three fives. That would make six between us.

"Six fives," I said.

He was nodding and flicking his tubed-up bill with his black thumb and forefinger. "You better have five of them, you liar."

He unrolled his bill and showed it to me. One measly five. "If I could chain you in the basement and play you for a living, I wouldn't have to worry about working." That was one of his favorite lines, and he used it whenever we played Liars. When I won, which was seldom, he always accused me of having a no-brainer bill, the kind that had maybe four deuces on it and you couldn't lose with it.

"I'd be all right," I said, though I hoped he wouldn't go anywhere.

He ran his hands through his hair. "Well, don't worry about it," he said. "We'll make out, somehow. White people don't starve in America."

I wasn't worried about starving. I'd been banking practically all of the money I made cleaning Rose's and could have loaned my father a couple hundred dollars if there had been a good enough reason to. But then we really would be broke, and I preferred to let him just think we were. I'd save us if I had to, but not until I became convinced there was no other way. Right now we were only a hundred or so into Harry and two months behind on rent. The situation was far from desperate.

Before we left, my father boxed a number with Untemeyer (he

always had a dollar for that purpose) and then we crossed the street to our apartment, climbing the two dark flights of stairs. The local news was on when we came in. I watched while my father read the sports in the morning paper that Harry let him take with us. When the weatherman came on, he talked about how cold it was everywhere, even the desert Southwest, which was recording its lowest temperatures on record. They showed pictures of Phoenix, Arizona.

"Look at the goddamn snow," my father said seriously, as if snow were not a permanent condition on our television set. I was mentally adding up how much he would have lost if anybody had taken his wager.

He must have been doing the same, because he shook his head and said, "Some fucking thing's gotta give here. And quick, too."

A few days later my father's personal fortunes took a turn for the better. Suddenly, there was money. Harry eyed him suspiciously as my father peeled bills off a sizable roll, but he took the money and that squared us at the Mohawk Grill. He also paid our back rent, along with the next month's, thus guaranteeing that we'd be all right until he started work in the spring. The only other thing was to pay his bar tabs, especially the one at The Elms. He'd stopped going there when it got too steep, not wanting to embarrass Eileen. "Not that Mike gives a shit," he told me. "Mike's all right."

Mike was my favorite bartender. Whenever my father and I came in on a Saturday or Sunday afternoon, he rang up No Sale and slapped a couple quarters on the bar for the jukebox so I could play Elvis and my own personal favorite, Duane Eddy. He let me sit at the bar, too, which I didn't always get to do in some of the lesser dives my father brought me to. My father explained that in the better joints you didn't have to worry because the cops stayed away unless they were called. In places like Greenie's, where the men from the mills drank, the bartenders had to be careful, but Mike said never mind cops, as if he weren't convinced of their existence. Sit at the bar. Eat peanuts. Watch the ball game. Anybody doesn't like it, tough. Mike had the shiniest black hair I'd ever seen. His fingers were pink and elegant, his nails scrubbed white. He always ignored my father, speaking first to me. "So," he would say. "How's he treating you?"

When I said good, he'd remind me that I didn't have to live with such a stiff if I didn't want to. I could come live with him and his wife upstairs over the restaurant. Today, though, he put his hand over his heart and pretended to stagger when he saw us.

My father nodded knowingly. "If I had all your money, I'd have a weak ticker too. I'd be scared somebody else might get a dollar or two."

We took stools near the end of the empty bar. Mike put a quarter in front of me.

"Take it," my father said. "It's his one good deed. When was the last time you bought a drink?"

"VJ Day," Mike said.

My father tossed three twenties on the bar.

"Sweet rollickin' Jesus," Mike said. "Go back out and come in again."

"Our friend working tonight?"

"She's off Thursdays. You know that."

"I forget."

Mike held one of the twenties up to the light, fingering it with his thumb and forefinger. "I heard somebody'd knocked over a Brink's car yesterday. I never made the connection."

"We got time for a quick one, I guess," my father said. Mike drew my father a tall glass of beer and poured a 7-Up for me while I was busy punching three songs into the jukebox.

"So who's this?" my father said when Duane Eddy came on. He always wanted to know who Duane Eddy was.

Mike broke one of my father's twenties, put the change on the bar. My father pushed it back at him, along with the other two twenties. "Let's settle up," he said.

Mike took twenty-five, left the rest.

"What?" My father frowned.

"That's it," Mike said. "We're square."

"Not close," my father said. "Let me see."

"Trust me," Mike insisted, but his eyes looked nervous to me.

"Let me see," my father said.

Mike rang another No Sale and lifted the register drawer. Beneath it were a couple dozen tabs. Mike went through them till he found the one with my father's name on it.

My father surveyed the tab. The largest number, about midway down the column, was fifty-five, but it had been crossed out, along with each of the numbers beneath it, except for the last, which was twenty-five. Mike was red-faced.

"So what the hell's going on?" my father asked.

"Take it up with your benefactor."

"You took money from her?"

"She tells me it's from you. How the hell do I know? You disappeared off the face of the earth."

"Drink your soda," my father told me.

"Don't go getting sore for Christ's sake," Mike pleaded.

"Did you ask her for money?"

"Jesus, Sammy."

"If I find out you did . . ."

Mike threw up his hands. "She says it's from you. What do I know? Your old man's a knothead," he said to me.

"Bullshit," my father said, his eyes still narrow slits. I sucked the last of my 7-Up through the straw.

"Have some dinner," Mike said when he saw we were really going to leave. "You and the boy. I'll spring."

My father left the twenty-five on the bar. "*You* give it back to her. And tell her you had no business taking it to begin with."

"Sure, Sammy. Whatever you say. Suit yourself."

"I will," my father said. "I do."

We stopped at the market on the way to Eileen's. My father wasn't saying anything, and I knew what that meant. At the store he slung expensive roasts into the cart, causing people to stop and look at us suspiciously. By the time we got to the checkout though, the purple had begun to drain from his face, and he stacked the meat in a careful pyramid on the counter.

"How are you, young lady," he said to the girl at the register, who was too bored to answer.

My father nudged me, his favorite conspiratorial gesture. My part in such conspiracies was always the same. To get nudged. I'd come to the conclusion it was all he thought I could handle. "Whatever became of the child labor laws in this state?" he said.

The girl did not seem to think that this remark applied to her. I didn't see how it could myself. She was small-boned, but hardly a kid.

He nudged me again. "I'll give you a dollar for every year over sixteen," he said.

"Okay," I said.

The girl rang the total, just over sixty dollars worth of standing rib, rolled pork roasts, hams, family-sized packages of ground beef, all bleeding profusely. The girl made a face, said "yecch," and dried her hands before bagging. "I'm twenty-five," she told us.

"You're just saying that so my son won't ask you out," he said, nudging me again.

Actually, she looked more apprehensive that *he* would. By the time she was done bagging, she had bloody hands again, and she reiterated her "yecch," as if her condition were our fault.

"It *will* wash off, you know," my father said.

She might have believed that if she hadn't spied his black thumb and forefinger, which may have looked to her like the natural result of bagging too many bloody sirloin tip roasts.

My father wheeled the convertible out of the parking lot and up First toward Myrtle Park. "She's a pretty good girl," he said. "You ever get a chance to do her a favor, you do it."

For a moment I thought he was referring, inexplicably, to the checkout girl back at the market. Then I realized it was Eileen he was thinking about and probably had been thinking about since we left The Elms.

"She's not pretty, like your mother," he conceded, as if he imagined I'd found his preference in the matter puzzling. I turned and stared out the window, my eyes filling. We'd stopped speaking of my mother by mutual unspoken agreement. My father had brought me to visit her in the Albany hospital only once. I'd wished he hadn't. There'd been even less of her than the Sunday morning at the Old Nathan Littler Hospital when she'd been little more than a ripple of flesh and bone beneath the otherwise placid sea of sheets and blanket. The afternoon we visited her in Albany she had looked like a child, her long hair chopped at the nape of her neck, her arms bruised where she had been hooked up to the machines that monitored her vital signs. A nurse had explained it to me, assuring me that the crisis had passed, unaware that I knew nothing of any crisis, was unaware that her heart had stopped beating briefly during the week and that she'd been revived. Unaware that our turning up that particular weekend had been pure coincidence.

My father had waited in the lobby, and I was too frightened by what I saw to say anything to him. When he asked me how she was I told him good and made up a small conversation about how she'd said she would be coming home soon and that we'd live together again. It was a week later when I learned the details of my mother's brush with death. I was summoned to the principal's office during home room. When I saw F. William Peterson there and the principal said why didn't we use his office, my throat got tight and I could feel my eyes filling, until the lawyer made me understand that it wasn't what I thought, that he had come to tell me she was out of immediate danger now and was being transferred to a nursing home in Schenectady, where I could go see her whenever I wanted. I didn't tell my father about this either.

"She's a good girl, though," my father was saying. I didn't have to turn my head to know that he was looking at me. When we pulled up into the driveway, he let me look up into the dark woods of Myrtle Park for a minute before delivering the cuff to the back of my head that I was waiting for.

"Stop crying," he said.

I did. I wasn't, really, to begin with. Just scared I might start.

"What's the matter?"

I said nothing was the matter.

"I'm not going to marry her, if that's what's eating you."

It always amazed me how little he understood what I was feeling. It meant, among other things, that my understanding of him probably wasn't much better.

"You can if you want," I said.

"Thanks," he said.

In the distance we heard the sound of a motorcycle approaching, and my father shook his head. "I'd cry too, if I thought I'd end up with Zero for a brother."

We got out of the car.

"Smile," he said. "And smooth your hair down." It always stood up where he cuffed me. "You look like the village idiot."

There wasn't much danger of my being mistaken for the village idiot with Drew Littler around. When the motorcycle fishtailed into the drive, its rider was so bundled against the cold that it could have been anybody. Anybody crazy enough to ride a bike in February with the temperature in the twenties. It hadn't snowed in several days and the streets were dry, but the sloping dirt drive was spotted with patches of ice that had been a problem even for our car, which was now blocking the open garage, tall snowbanks close on both sides.

The boy throttled down and waited on the rumbling cycle. My

father made no move to get back in the car. Instead, he began to
unload the groceries from the backseat, balancing the first bag
precariously on the slanted hood. Drew Littler gunned the engine once for emphasis, then raised his goggles. "You want to
move that trash heap?"

My father ignored him, handing me one of the bags of groceries. We went around and in through the back, leaving him at the
foot of the drive, gunning his engine.

Eileen was waiting for us inside. "Move your car," she told my
father. Her voice had a sharp blade on the end of it.

"Okay," my father said. "Mind if I set these down first? You
figure His Royal Highness can wait that long?"

We put the bags of groceries on the dinette. Just in time, in my
case, because the blood had weakened the paper and the roasts
were threatening to plunge through. My hand and wrist were red
and dripping.

My father started to unload meat.

"The car, Sam," Eileen said, elbowing him out of the way.
"You're dripping blood on my floor. I just mopped it."

"Sorry," my father said, as if he wasn't, particularly.

Outside, the motorcycle's engine roared to life, and I heard a
patch of rubber being laid on the street below. At first, I thought
Drew had decided to ride off someplace, but then I saw his head
flash by the dining room window heading up the drive. Immediately following, there was a dull thud; the engine coughed once
and died.

My father dried his hands on a paper towel and peered out the
kitchen window, shaking his head in disbelief.

I followed Eileen outside. The motorcycle was angled crazily,
deep in the snowbank next to our car, its front wheel unaccountably up in the air. Drew had apparently tried to blast through the
snow. The hard-packed part at the edge of the pavement had
accepted the weight of the bike, but then the cycle had sunk
seat-deep. Drew was still on it, looking like an astronaut awaiting
launch. He got off reluctantly, himself sinking thigh-deep in the
snow.

"Terrific," Eileen said.

"Tell your friend," her son said.

My father came out, still drying his hands on the towel. "I never
would have thought to park it there, Zero."

"Kiss my ass."

"Let me get this out of your way," my father said, indicating our car.

"Screw that rust bucket. Give me a hand with the chopper."

"What," my father said. "A big strong guy like you? Just lift it right out."

"You think *you* could?"

"Not me," my father admitted. "But then I wouldn't have put it there to begin with."

"Quit acting like children, the two of you," Eileen said. "Help him, will you."

But my father was having too good a time. He might help, eventually. But not yet. "What good is it to lift weights all day if you can't pick your own bike out of a snowbank?" he wanted to know.

"Screw yourself then," Drew said. "I'll settle with you later."

"Wait about twenty years is my advice. And even then I'd be careful."

Then he nudged me in the shoulder hard enough to make me take one step forward. "Go help Dumbbell," he said. "Take the heavy end."

Drew snorted at the suggestion that I might be able to help, and even Eileen smiled, as if the one thing the three of them could agree on was that I was the weakling of the group. I flushed angrily at that and without thinking climbed the snowbank and positioned myself next to the bike. Grabbing the seat with both hands, I pulled hard, actually imagining the cycle would come free of the snow, which had already begun to freeze around the back wheel. Instead, I found myself seated in the snow, my feet having gone out from under me, which everybody thought was pretty funny.

When I followed Eileen and my father back into the house, leaving Drew to shovel the snow away from his half-buried bike, I was full of hatred so black that I can still taste it now, almost twenty-five years later. When I had fallen, one leg had gone under the bike and my groin had come in violent contact with the rear tire, sending waves of nausea over me like surf. At that moment, I hated them all blackly—my father, Eileen and Drew Littler, everybody. Even my poor mother, who lay wasting toward oblivion in a big strange bed in Schenectady. In the cold agony of surging pain and humiliation, I would have been content to consign them all to everlasting perdition. I'd have watched the flames licking them with perfect equanimity.

"Do a roast," my father suggested.

It was Eileen's turn to sling the unoffending meat this time, and that's what she was doing, bouncing packages off the sides of her freezer. Altercations between my father and Drew always infuriated her, but my guess was that there was more to it in this instance. She'd been ready to take my father on when he walked in the door. The episode with the cycle had distracted her, but now she had remembered whatever it was that had angered her before. My father looked like he knew what was on her mind and wished he didn't. He probably figured that getting her to cook a roast would have a calming effect. You couldn't cook a roast and stay mad at the person who bought it, may have been his thinking. And that's probably why she wasn't having any part of our carnivore peace offering. The set of her jaw had my father looking like a scolded dog, an effect my mother had never been able to achieve. He had always fought with her the way you would with a man, stopping only at the very brink of physical violence. He never treated her with the sort of care you use with something you considered fragile. And that's what struck me at the time, because Eileen was the one who looked sturdy. In fact, when I saw that dark look on her face as she slung roasts against the back wall of the freezer, it scared me, and I remember wondering if maybe it didn't scare my father too.

But I don't think so. I think he saw something I couldn't see back then, and his expression was a little like the one he'd worn the afternoon we'd gone in to tell my mother I was going to live with him. It was as if when he looked at Eileen, he saw my mother the way she'd been that day, so broken inside that she couldn't stop shaking.

"A roast would take two hours," Eileen said.

"So?"

"So it's six now. So I don't feel like doing dishes at ten o'clock. So."

"So don't. I'll do them."

"My house. My dishes," she said. The freezer was full now, and when she tried to slam the door by way of punctuation, it just swung back at her. The second time she put her weight behind it until the whole refrigerator rose up an inch or two off the linoleum.

"You want to go out someplace?"

"Sure," she said. "Why not? You're done baiting my son. Let's go out to eat someplace nice. Like where I work, maybe. While we're there, you can threaten my boss, maybe."

"I wasn't baiting him," my father said. Only the first part of her complaint had registered. "He could have waited until we unloaded the groceries, in as much as he's the one who's going to eat them."

"Somehow I got the idea *you* were here for dinner."

"Not if you don't want us," he said, looking even more hangdog.

The "us" made my presence official, and they both looked at me for arbitration. I would have flushed if the recent blow to my groin hadn't drained all the blood from my face.

"Ned can stay," she said. "At least he's no troublemaker."

"Neither am I. I just brought you some groceries. If I'd known that would upset you . . ."

The television was on in the next room, so I went in there and sat down on the sofa, glad to be alone. Eileen always kept the room dark—because it was so ugly, she said—the only light emanating from the television screen. In this relative privacy I slipped a hand into my trousers to check myself out. The year before, a boy in my class who had been picking his nose on third base had taken a line drive in the crotch and he had swelled up sufficiently to require special underwear. I hadn't actually seen him in this swollen condition, but I'd heard the matter discussed in the locker room before gym and a boy had lifted his own member to remind us of the size of a normal testicle, this compared to the big fist he put next to it. Going strictly on feel, mine still seemed about their usual size, but I couldn't be sure.

By cracking the blinds, I could watch Drew from the sofa, though it had grown dark outside. He too seemed to have lost the edge of his anger. He had shoveled all around the bike, leaving it a shiny island. He was now engaged in carving out some of the snow beneath the cycle so that he could plant his feet and gain some purchase. After a few minutes the bike was mostly free, though still magically reared up, frozen in place. Tossing the shovel aside, he stood before it, blowing on his hands, seemingly lost in thought.

I'd spotted for him enough when he benched in the garage to know what he was doing. He was collecting himself, preparing. Breathing. Swelling his muscles, as if in a mirror. Studying his own steamy breath, feeling the power surging in his body until he was certain it was equal to the weight of the bike. I watched with genuine anticipation when he finally bent to the task, knowing that he intended more than simply dislodging the bike and rolling it forward into the garage. My father's taunts were eating at him, and I didn't need to see his broad forehead to know that the blue vein was pulsing there. I could visualize his expression, too, his contempt for whatever he was up against. He put one red hand under the seat, the other in the crotch beneath the frame and above the wheel, holding his squat position perfectly for a second before throwing himself back and up, his knees and arms straightening without quite locking. The bike stayed stuck for a second, then gave with an audible crack.

He nearly lost his balance then, but somehow righted himself, still refusing to set the bike down. For a moment I thought he actually intended to clean and jerk it, but instead he turned with it, still held chest-high, 180 degrees and stepped with it over the snowbank. The rear wheel of the cycle caught the antenna of my father's car and snapped it like a twig.

A moment later he emerged from the dark garage and came toward the house. On the way he stopped and picked up the busted antenna, used the palm of his hand to reduce its length, then his thumb and forefinger to stretch it full again, whereupon he cocked his arm and whistled the antenna out over the top of the garage, deep into the black trees.

In relating what follows I must confess to a certain chronological vagueness. The events themselves I can see in sharp focus, and I want to think they happened that same evening, and there are good reasons to suppose they did. In a narrative sense they present a nice neat package, effect dutifully tripping along at the heels of cause. Perhaps it is the attraction of such simplicity that makes me suspicious; that along with the conviction that real life seldom works this way.

The events which follow may have been the culmination of many meals eaten in the Littler kitchen, the four of us cramped into the nook where their dinette was stationed, walled in on three sides. Eileen herself always insisted on the seat at the free end so she could get up and grab the coffee pot or pour drinks. Drew, my father, and I would all be penned in once the meal began, unable to push our chairs back more than an inch or two. I think I was the only one who felt the terrible restriction, since Drew had no intention of getting up as long as he had his mother to fetch for him. My father seemed to enjoy tight places, always spurning the empty end of the counter at the Mohawk Grill in favor of the end jammed with people and stacks of dirty dishes.

Once we were seated around Eileen's table it was impossible to stand up without pushing the table forward and pinioning whoever was opposite against the wall, and I think Eileen took solace from the fact that if she could just get my father and her son seated they could rise in anger only with supreme difficulty. Nobody needed worry about me rising in anger, but I couldn't have, regardless. Being the smallest by several degrees I got the narrowest seat, opposite Eileen herself, hemmed in by a wall behind, my father and Drew on either side, the table in front. I always relieved myself before dinner began.

The little dinette itself was always crowded beyond belief. Condiments that did not require refrigeration were always left in the center of the table and these were joined, half an hour before mealtime, by cold jars of every description. Drew devoured pickles—sweet, dill, bread and butter, kosher—while my father ate olives—green ones, bulbous purples, shriveled blacks. Their tall, slender jars he would probe thoughtfully with his black forefinger, extracting the fruit expertly, even from the bottom of the tallest jars without the aid of a utensil. To this day, I cannot contemplate an olive, even when attractively displayed, say, on a silver relish dish, without seeing my father's finger worming around the jar in search of the last elusive marble afloat in its own murky juices. Drew was equally disgusting in his personal search for pickles, which I too was inordinately fond of. But unless I could spear the first slice out of a fresh jar, before the contents became polluted, I abstained.

I freely confess that my fastidiousness about the condiment jars was unwarranted. I was myself a grubby boy who had to be reminded about washing my hands before coming to the table, and it was my father who reminded me. I had been far cleaner when I had lived with my mother and eaten at the long table of the old Monsignor, but since coming to live with my father I had backslid

badly in the area of personal hygiene. Since I ate alone much of
the time, or with people it was pretty hard to offend at the Mohawk Grill, I had become a social liability. In our apartment I had
indulged many bad habits that my mother would have blanched
at. I drank milk from the carton, ate pepperoni in bed and fell
asleep sticky. My father never objected to these practices at
home, but if he happened to notice anything particularly foul
about me in public, he would hold it up to considerable humor
and ridicule, blaming my condition on lax maternal training.
More than once the clients of the Mohawk Grill were invited to
inspect my caked fingernails. And while comparisons to most of
Harry's regulars weren't necessarily invidious, my father was
right. I was frequently revolting.

Which makes my squeamishness about his finger in the olive jar
that much more absurd, my father being himself a brutal hand
scrubber. He bought coarse, gravelly Lava soap for the apartment
and required Eileen to have a bar on hand for him at her house
as well, though I don't believe he advocated it for her personal
use. Sometimes, in addition to sandpapering his own knuckles and
palms, he'd do mine as well so I'd "know what it felt like to be
clean, for once." By "clean" he apparently meant "raw." No
doubt the Lava got his hands clean, but it made no difference in
the appearance of his thumb and forefinger, and try as I might,
I couldn't shake the idea that once his black digit invaded an olive
jar, the juices therein were tinged a subtle shade darker.

By the time Eileen began to bring hot food to the table it
seemed to me that breakage was inevitable. The jars of pickles
and olives were never cleared away, seldom even consolidated
sensibly. To the center of the tiny table were added each night,
first, a huge bowl of mashed potatoes and an oblong platter of
meat, then, at the outer edges of the table a bowl of vegetables
and basket of rolls, a dish of fruit or applesauce. By the time
Eileen was finished bringing food, it was possible for me to knock
something off her end of the table by nudging something at my
end by slender centimeters. To make matters worse, we passed
things, setting off chain reactions. Lifting the platter of roast pork
would upset the bowl of green beans, which someone would try
to save, his elbow sending the big bottle of Thousand Island dressing to the floor. In this way, the person who appeared to have
made the mess seldom actually *caused* it, but was rather trying
to prevent another calamity altogether, the threat of which he

alone perceived. My father and I ate dinner with the Littlers at least once a week, and I can remember no single meal free of casualties, though what got shattered varied from an old, nearly empty bottle of maraschino cherries (what could *it* have been doing there amid the roast pork, mashed potatoes, canned asparagus, and Parker House rolls?) to a valued fancy casserole dish said to have come down to Eileen all the way from the venerable Myrtle Littler herself.

Though I was just a kid, it was obvious to me that our attempts to wedge ourselves into Eileen's little house were not working and that, to borrow my father's phrase, some fucking thing had to give, but I was the only one who saw it that way. I remember Eileen as a better than average cook, and I'm confident when I say I was the only one unable to enjoy a single morsel at that table.

So. What follows may have happened that same evening when Drew lifted his cycle out of the snowbank and whistled my father's broken antenna out into the woods. Or it may have been a month later, with several such meals as the one depicted above intervening. Since neither Drew nor my father ever forgot a single grievance, it probably doesn't matter. What my father had done and what Drew had done would have been as fresh to them a month later as if it had happened moments before. In any case, the episode begins in my memory with Drew spearing a roast with his mother's silver serving fork.

God help me, I had to watch him.

I didn't want to, because that's what my father was doing. I tried to appear occupied by taking some mashed potatoes, arranging them in one corner of the plate, flattening them out with the back of my fork, depressing a cavity in the center for gravy, then spooning some green beans next to them. All of this to mark time while Drew, who was first, as usual, at the meat platter, built a huge mound, one slice at a time while the rest of us waited for him to finish.

At the time I thought he must be oblivious to us, or at least to my father, who was watching him with an air of quiet homicidal menace, but I've since changed my mind. The opposite hypothesis makes far more sense—that Drew Littler was perfectly aware of my father and of himself. With such a large fork, he could easily have removed half the meat from the platter with one forceful thrust. Instead, he made a point of his hoggishness, taking each slice singly so there could be no mistaking his intent, by arranging each slice artfully, by not surrendering the silver fork until he was good and ready. When he finally did surrender it, he turned his attention to the gravy boat, which he emptied over the mound of gray beef.

"Mind your own business," Eileen said to my father, who looked ready to spontaneously combust. "There's plenty more."

She pushed back her chair and took the empty gravy boat with her. I could tell that she too was miffed with her son's behavior, but she never publicly took my father's side in matters of conflict.

My father helped Eileen to some of what little remained of the roast, then me, then himself, leaving one thin slice in the center of the big platter. For a vigorous man, my father hadn't a large appetite, and the portion he took for himself was comically small, a pointed contrast to Drew's heaped plate.

Eileen returned with the gravy boat and we ate. My stomach had shrunk to pellet size and I'd have given a lot to be able to return to the platter some of the roast my father had given me, because I could see where we were headed with that one remaining slice of beef. Each mouthful was a struggle.

Drew had no such difficulty. With his steak knife he sliced through several layers of meat at a time and raised them, dripping gravy, to his mouth. He never changed hands with his fork or set his knife down. He seemed almost not to chew. His Adam's apple bobbed once and the food was gone. We all watched, my father openly, Eileen and I surreptitiously, engaging each other in small talk, trying in vain to draw my father into it, to disturb his focus, but all the while adopting that focus ourselves. There was no point in trying to draw Drew into any conversation while there was food around, and in the end the talk died.

Drew ate.

In steady, workmanlike fashion he devoured what was before him without looking up from his plate, exhibiting the same concentration he used under the weighted bar in the garage. My father ate much more slowly and I knew why. It was a matter of timing. He did not want to be finished before the boy. He was working it so the two of them would swallow that last bite of roast at exactly the same time, with just the one remaining slice of meat between them in the center of the table. I doubt Eileen saw the strategy of it or she'd have either taken the slice of meat herself or gone to carve more, but I'm quite sure Drew knew where they

were headed, knew it without having to look up, just as he knew
my father was trying to shame him.

He must have understood all this, because Drew Littler
couldn't have *wanted* that last slice of beef. He just had to have
it. I was sure of that as I watched the blue vein in his forehead
work over that last mouthful of food. And when he reached, I saw
that my father was holding his own fork like an ice-pick, tines
down. At first, I thought he intended to stab the back of the boy's
hand. Instead the fork pierced the meat, pinning it to the platter
so that Drew's came away clean. Then, suddenly, it was on my
father's plate.

I thought for a second I would wet my pants.

"There," Eileen said. "Are you happy now, you two children?"

My father kneed me under the table. "You gonna let her call
you names?"

"Sure," I said.

"That's where you're smart, unlike some people," my father
said.

"Some people are smarter than you think," Drew said.

"I doubt it," my father said. He relit a cigarette he'd extin-
guished at the start of the meal. Then, after a thoughtful drag, he
put it out again in the center of the still untouched slice of beef.

"You think it's smart to waste good food," Eileen said, getting
up to clear away the dishes. "That's your idea of smart?"

My father ignored her. "You enjoy your dinner?" he asked me.

I said I did.

"How about you?" he asked Drew.

"It was all right," the boy said.

"Just all right."

"The potatoes were lumpy," he said.

"Just all right," my father repeated. "I thought it was a very
good dinner, myself. Of course, that's just me. But it was the best
meal I've had in a long time. Maybe if you had to work for a meal,
you'd appreciate it more."

"Potatoes either got lumps or they don't."

"Stop it, the two of you," Eileen warned, and she looked to me
like she meant business.

"I tell you what," my father said. "Just to be nice to your mother
and show a little appreciation, you and I will do the dishes. Your
mother can go in and watch TV. Relax."

"Get *him* to help," Drew said, indicating me.

"He can help too."

"I'll help," I agreed. I would have stood up and started right in if I could.

"I got someplace to go," Drew said.

"I tell you what. Go later," my father said. "People won't mind if you're late. Trust me."

"I'll tell *you* what," the boy said. Then he cleared a place in the center of the dinette large enough to plant his big elbow. "Loser washes."

"Enough," Eileen said. "In a minute everything's going to be broken, and guess who'll get to clean up the mess."

My father put his elbow next to Drew's, but they didn't lock hands immediately. "You better move those bottles," my father said. "I don't want to hurt you."

Where I was sitting, I figured to get the worst of it. Drew had an arm like a leg, and when he slammed my father's into the table, I'd get the gravy boat and the dregs of the green beans for sure. It took me a split second to prepare for this and even less for my father to slam the back of Drew Littler's hand onto his mother's plate, flipping it into the air like a Tiddly-Wink. The boy let out a sharp howl as the chair went out from under him and he disappeared onto his back beneath the table. He never hit the floor though, because my father never let go of his hand, which stayed pinned right where it had been slammed. Drew looked to me liked he'd have given a good deal to just fall, but he couldn't. Like a big, excited bug, he tried desperately to right himself. His feet had become entangled in the capsized chair and his free hand frantically climbed the smooth wall in search of something to grab on to. With all that weight on his pinned forearm, it was a miracle it didn't snap, especially the way the boy continued to thrash, kicking the fallen chair violently, but ineffectually, since with every blow it rebounded off the wall and back on top of his feet to be kicked again.

"You let go, Sammy, you fucker!" Drew bellowed, the blue vein in his forehead wriggling frantically. "So help me, I'll break it!"

It took me a moment to realize the unusual nature of this threat—that it was his own arm he was threatening to break. And while its obvious sincerity scared the hell out of me, its comic aspect did not escape my father, who looked willing to risk it. I think it was the knowledge that if the arm broke he'd eaten his last dinner at Eileen's that finally caused him to let her son drop. And from the frozen expression on her face, I'd have sworn his decision came too late.

Drew no sooner hit the floor than he was back on his feet again, and I thought there would be blood now for sure, but here again I was mistaken. Drew looked like he was going to attack, but my father did not get to his feet, and something about the way he just sat there so calmly prevented the boy, and when he saw my father lean back against the wall it was suddenly all over. He grabbed the arm my father had pinned to the table top and sank to his knees. "I wasn't ready, Sammy, you cheating son of a bitch, you cocksucker," he wailed.

"No," my father admitted, "and twenty years from now you still won't be. That's your problem."

Drew was sobbing now, but his fury had leaked away almost instantly. "I'm getting stronger every day, Sammy. I am. Every day. My day's coming, Sammy, you shithead."

My father snorted at the idea, but the boy neither heard, nor reacted. I could tell from the lack of focus in his eyes that he was talking inwardly, trying to pump himself up again, not allowing himself to hit bottom, like a boxer talking rematch before his handlers could even stop the bleeding.

"Be *my* day then. My day," he said. "All you sons of bitches. *My* day."

He was on his knees now, rocking, his wounded arm tucked in to his middle, rocking there in the middle of the broken glass and pickle juice.

"Good," my father said, winking at me, his unwilling accomplice. "We'll call it Dummy Day. We'll crown you king, Zero."

17

At his worst, no human being is attractive, and that day we'd all
seen Drew at his worst, raging out of control, bent on destruction,
even self-destruction. But most times he was not a bad sort, and
he wasn't nearly as dumb as my father and his teachers down
through the years had concluded.

He had, in fact, something rather like a personal philosophy of
life, and unless I am mistaken, I am the only person he ever
discussed it with, including his mother. In fact, he recruited me,
along with another dubious fellow named Willie Heinz, to become members of an organization to implement his philosophy,
an organization whose membership never did exceed three,
though we had great hopes of expanding into a worldwide net-
work. The only goal of our organization was to abuse rich people,
all of whom Drew Littler hated with a white-hot passion. The
"Money People" he called them, the people who thought they
were too good, who considered themselves above the rest. According to Drew, who explained all this one afternoon as I spotted
for him in the garage, it was the fault of the people who had
money that those who hadn't any lived difficult lives, a notion he
considered original to himself. Though five years older than I,
Drew was only two grades ahead of me just then, having been
held back, once due to a prolonged childhood illness, the other
two times as the result of academic failure. When he turned
eighteen that May, he intended to drop out and go to work in a
garage that serviced motorcycles.

Trust me when I say he had neither read nor heard of Karl
Marx. In fact, my guess is that nobody in Mohawk had actually
read him, and in my later studies at Mohawk High, which I attended to sporadically, I can recall no more than a passing deroga-
tory reference to Marx in social studies class. It was many years
later, after I had taken a degree at the university and was thinking

about Drew Littler, which I often did and still do, that it occurred to me that he was a Marxist au naturel, perhaps the only one ever produced in the entire county.

His brand of Marxism was simple and in several respects unorthodox. He never, at least in my hearing, extolled the worker. In fact, he was openly contemptuous of people like his mother, who worked for wages, for the simple reason that the work didn't seem to get them much of anywhere, and he intended to work only until he could get enough money to take his bike onto the open road. In the meantime he meant to wage war on those who had enough money to look askance at those who didn't. People had been looking askance at him for as long as he could remember, and he thought it was about time to put a stop to that. To this end he had a plan.

The first part of the plan was to lift weights, because he had observed that since his taking on physical dimension fewer people looked askance at him, at least while he was looking at them. And, too, I think he held great abstract admiration for physical strength. I could tell that when he lifted, the iron bar became a metaphor—that it represented something to him, a problem, a dilemma. When he shoved the bar up and away from him, he won a personal victory over whatever obstacle it represented, and when the bar defeated him, he took that defeat blackly, morosely, personally. It deflated him instantly, just as my father had when he slammed the boy's wrist to the table.

When Drew Littler first started giving me rides on the back of his motorcycle, we'd cruise the neighborhoods where the Money People lived, and it was surprising how thorough was his information on who lived where. When we leaned into the turn onto some tree-lined street, he'd slow so his voice could be heard above the roar of the engine, and he'd tell me who lived in the better homes and whether they were doctors or lawyers or just rich. It troubled him when he did not know or could not remember who lived in a particularly well-groomed house set back from the street, a late-model car in the drive. Then he looked for all the world like a kid who's studied hard for a test, devised an elaborate way to recall disparate facts, then forgotten the key association. It's a terrible thing to have a long list of enemies.

The most amusing part of all this—at least it's amusing now—is that there were so few people in Mohawk with any real money. Since the tanneries had begun closing down, the county had got-

ten progressively poorer, and most of the men who had made
their money in leather had taken it with them to Florida. There
was still some relative wealth on Kings Road and all along the east
edge of the country club, and in the Jewish enclave near one
entrance to Myrtle Park. Otherwise, houses that evidenced any
genuine signs of material wealth were relatively scarce, and most
of the once grand older homes had fallen into neglect, shrinking
behind weed jungles and unpruned trees. But for Drew Littler
you could qualify as one of the Money People if you had a picture
window in the living room or a Doughboy pool in the backyard.
It was from Drew that I learned the ultimate relativity of
wealth—that wealthy people are those who have a dollar more
than you do.

How odd we must have looked, Drew Littler and I, cruising
those neighborhoods we had no business in, slowing down on the
quiet streets, looking the houses over with a cool appraiser's eye,
Drew pointing at them like a Beverly Hills tour bus director.
Drew with his shaggy hair sticking out like straw beneath his
Brando motorcycle hat, always wearing black, rhinestone-stud-
ded, impossibly pointed boots, dusty black jeans. And me, his little
pilot fish and understudy, trying not to look like too much of a
doofus. Up and down the streets of Mohawk we cruised, just the
sort of people my mother would have been tempted to report to
the police had she seen us slow down in front of her house, looking
it all over, as if for means of nocturnal entry.

But there was only one house we visited regularly. Up that long,
winding drive through the woods we would climb until we burst
out into the sunlight, the whole county stretched out below us, all
the way to the black trees that bordered the river to the south.
Then Drew would turn off the engine and dismount just outside
the stone pillars that marked the entrance to the jewel-house
property, and light a cigarette there, just looking, his face a dark
contrast to its gleaming white facade. He never repeated what
he'd said that first evening about the house being his someday, but
I could see him thinking it and I'd remember my father's nickname for him—Zero—and smile at his rippling back, as I too
smoked under the cool trees.

Sometimes, the man we'd seen that first evening would come
out by the double garage, no doubt having seen us loitering, just
outside his entryway, a mere hundred yards from his front door.

I always expected to meet a police cruiser on our way back down the private road to the highway, but we never did.

It was on one of these motorcycle excursions during the spring of 1960, that first year that I lived with my father, that we turned down Third Avenue and I saw the sign in front of our old empty house. I had not even been by since refurnishing the place with my plunder from Klein's. The house looked different, smaller somehow, no doubt the result of my recent travels among the affluent, whose gabled Tudors and big split-level ranches had given me a new sense of the appropriate dimensions for a human dwelling. The house now seemed almost a miniature, as if people of normal height might be required to stoop in the doorways. Winter had taken its toll on the place too, and I've often wondered since how it is that the elements invariably do greater damage to houses that are not lived in than the inhabited houses on either side, as if granted some strange cosmic license for destruction. The house looked dingy and gray, its paint peeling badly under the eaves and beneath the arched peak. I couldn't remember it ever looking so shabby before, and its sad condition, together with the For Sale sign on the lawn, combined to force a sudden, terrible realization—that my mother had died during the winter and no one had told me.

"What's the matter with you?" my father wanted to know when we returned. He and Drew were not feuding just then, my father having loaned him the money for new tires for the bike, but he still razzed Drew unmercifully, telling him, among other things, that if he ever had an accident with me aboard, he'd better just get back on the bike and keep riding, as far away from Mohawk as he could get.

I said nothing was the matter.

His eyes narrowed.

"Don't look at me," Drew said, himself surprised when he looked over his shoulder at me and saw my dark expression. "I can't be to blame for *every* fucking thing."

As soon as I'd seen the For Sale sign and realized what it meant, I'd concluded that my father must know. Maybe they all did. Eileen, surely. Drew, perhaps. Why else would he be bothering with me, giving me rides on the cycle when he could just as easily have been acting as chauffeur to one or more of his slightly overweight, dirty-haired girlfriends, all of whom nuzzled into the small of his back with large breasts. Maybe the men at the diner knew too. I tried to remember which of them had shown me special kindness recently, and the more I thought about it, the more evidence I came up with. Some of it was several months old, but there was no telling how long that sign had been on the terrace. Perhaps my mother's death was old news. Maybe they'd already forgotten the secret they'd been sworn to keep from me. Many of them were men who forgot their own families without even being asked to. By now they'd probably forgotten my mother had ever existed.

That night, when we were alone in the apartment, watching the eleven o'clock news, my father in his shorts, scratching himself thoughtfully, I told him I wanted to visit my mother on Sunday. My voice must have sounded odd, because he looked at me before answering.

"Why not," he said.

"I mean it," I said.

I watched for a reaction, but there wasn't any. Not that I should have expected one. In Liars my father could call six deuces without a single one in his hand for comfort and his expression would remain distant, abstracted, almost bored. Was it possible, though, that he didn't know? Was it possible that my mother was so insignificant that she had died in Schenectady and no one had taken the trouble to inform us? After all, we had no telephone in the apartment, and I wasn't sure the nursing home even had our address. Our mailbox inside the dark hallway below didn't even have the name Hall on it and the mailman didn't even bother to stuff it with junk mail. Anybody who wanted to contact my father left a message at Harry's or Greenie's or at the Littlers' or one of his other haunts. Probably legal wheels were turning, my mother's estate being settled by some downstate law office where no one knew of my father and me, or, if they'd heard rumors of our existence, could find no listing, no official record of it. If so, we deserved it, my father and I. No doubt some dark-suited man had appeared at the nursing home with a notepad, ready to take down information. Had my mother any relatives? Visitors? Surely *some*one came to see her? Leaned forward to kiss her hollow cheek? No, the good nurse would have been forced to admit. She had been alone. Died alone.

"You better get a haircut then," my father said, looking me over

again, vaguely dissatisfied with what he saw, but unable to identify whatever else might be required to make me presentable to
a woman who, assuming he thought her to be alive, he had no
reason to believe would be other than diminished, withdrawn,
sedated, or comatose, but whom he preferred to remember as
beautiful, easily angered, possibly armed, and bearing a grudge.

As I look back upon this period of my life from something like
objective distance, what strikes me as strange and more than a
little horrifying is the ease with which I had managed to banish
my mother, to push her into some far recess of my consciousness.
Most of the time I simply did not think of her.

The only case I can make in my own defense is that I don't think
I was being extraordinarily cavalier or unfeeling. I know I loved
her and feared for her. I banished her from the forefront of my
mind for the same reason and by the same mechanism by which
I willed myself to sleep through my father's nightly assaults on our
house when I was a little boy, at which time I simply could not
afford to consider them. Any more than I could now afford to
consider my mother's horrible condition in the nursing home, or
of what in the end would happen to her. At least I could not think
of these things on a daily basis.

There were times, however, during the long months between
visits, that she would sweep over me in waves of memory, and I
would feel terrible guilt, guilt so intense that I wished not to be
alive. But after a while I'd succeed in filing her safely away again.
Seeing the For Sale sign had sent me plummeting into the worst
depression I'd ever experienced and my emotional state must
have been apparent even to my father, who decided that Saturday afternoon, the day before the promised visit, that we'd go out
to dinner someplace nice to cheer me up, or, failing that, be
around other people who might be willing to share the burden of
my moroseness. When he told me we were going out to The Elms
it all made sense. When Eileen got off work, the two of them were
going to sit me down and break the news. There wouldn't be any
trip to Schenectady on Sunday. There wasn't anyone to visit anymore.

As soon as we were on the road he started doing all the stuff I
wished he'd do before turning the key in the ignition. Found his
cigarettes wedged down in the seat, located a match, lit up,

turned on the radio full blast, each station shouting at us angrily for a split second before disappearing. Finally he settled on the original station, cuffed me in the back of the head, told me to smile, watched me and not the road until I did.

In short, he was a menace. As usual. The old rusty Merc pulled naturally to the right, a tendency he always failed to notice or correct until we'd drifted within inches of a curb of parked cars. Then he'd swerve suddenly, dangerously, back out to the center line and sometimes beyond. Whenever he saw somebody he knew, he always stopped. Right where he was. Beneath a traffic light, blocking a busy driveway. On a bridge. On the sidewalk. The kind of behavior my mother had always called selfish. His idea was that if people couldn't get around him they weren't trying very hard.

"That new?" he said, eyeing me.

I said yes, it was a new shirt. In fact I'd swiped it from Klein's the night before, the first thing I'd stolen since furnishing my mother's now abandoned house.

He nodded, glanced at the road to make sure it was still there, then went back to studying me. "You don't have to spend your own money," he said. "You need a shirt, you tell me you need a shirt. That's all."

I told him I would in the future, but right now I just needed the one. I knew what he was up to. I was supposed to get the idea that I would be coming to him for things now. That I could.

"You just say, I could use a shirt . . . right?" he shrugged. "That's all. That's not so tough."

I said fine. I would.

"How come your mother's on your mind all of a sudden?"

"She's not," I said.

"You wouldn't shit a shitter . . ."

I said I wouldn't, but he knew I would, and did, and was. "I just feel like seeing her. It's been a long time."

We were out in the country now, the sky darkening in the west. Dark trees flew by and I just watched them to keep from having to look at him.

"Fine," he said. "But that doesn't mean I can't buy you a shirt. I'm not your mother, but I can buy you a shirt."

Back to the shirt.

"You need anything else?"

I told him no. I hadn't even really needed the shirt. I told him I couldn't think of anything I needed.

"Nothing?" he said.

Nothing.

The parking lot was packed and my father had to park over a tree stump. Eileen saw us when we came in and gave my father a thumbs down. The bar was crowded too, every stool at the horseshoe bar occupied, each of the small cocktail tables surrounded, the booths packed and virtually invisible in the thick cigarette smoke. One of my father's real social skills, however, was carving out space in a crowded bar. Someone would pivot slightly and there he'd be, one elbow on the mahogany, clearing somebody's highball glass out of the way with a sophisticated slight of hand, a twenty-dollar bill materializing in its place. Given this small opening he then managed somehow to look for all the world as if he'd been right in that spot since the building was erected. The illusion was so overpowering that those he displaced often apologized when they discovered him there.

Mike and a new bartender were both pouring drinks, two-fisted, behind the bar, and it took the former a minute to gravitate to our end with about a dozen dirty glasses, which he bunched on the metal drainboard with another two or three dozen already sitting there.

"So," my father said. "What's the story."

"Once upon a time there was a man who wished he was somewhere else," Mike said. He had a quarter in his soapy hand, which he plunked in front of me for the jukebox, which was right behind the stool my father slipped onto when the woman who was there stood to search out the ladies' room. There was already a song on, but only the thumping bass was audible above the noise in the bar.

"One of my girls never showed," Mike moaned.

"Tough life," my father said, surveying the room. "You bury your money out back?"

"It's in the bank," Mike said. "In Vegas. In somebody else's account. What's the matter with him?"

Him was me. I was pretending to read song titles on the jukebox.

"Some damn thing," my father said. "He won't talk till he's ready."

"I wonder where he gets that from."

"Not his mother. She'd talk whenever."

Eileen came over.

"Don't look at me like that," she told my father after rattling off a long order.

"Like what."

"Like it's my fault. What's wrong with him?"

Silence. Shrugging, probably. All three of them staring at me now. I read song titles.

"Anybody ask him?" Eileen said.

"I'm fine," I said, a little too loud, still not turning around.

"You could say hi, after you get that jukebox memorized," Eileen said.

I punched in "You Ain't Nothin' but a Hound Dog," a song I knew she hated, but Eileen was gone with a trayful of cocktails high over her head before it could come on.

"Sit here," my father told me, indicating the bar stool he'd laid claim to. Rolling up his sleeves, he went around to the other side of the bar. "We'll see if we can't get a free meal off this tight son of a bitch."

By nine the place was even more crowded than when we came in. My father washed glasses and sliced fruit for the frozen daiquiris while Mike and the other bartender poured and rang the register.

A woman I couldn't see, seated somewhere on the far side of the room, kept cackling, "I *love* it, Jesus, I LOVE it!" her voice somehow clear and distinct above the din.

Eileen came in from the dining room, saw my father and grinned, then told Mike she thought she might have to take somebody named Karen into the girls' room and break her face. Mike said he'd give her a raise if she did. Irma, Mike's wife and the restaurant's hostess, appeared in the doorway a moment later, and pointed a dangerous-looking finger at him. My father saw this and advised Mike to just run away. "I LOVE it," the woman in the far corner howled.

"What do you figure she loves, Sammy?" Mike said.

My father started to answer, then remembered me and didn't.

Around ten, a well-dressed party of a dozen or so came in and I recognized F. William Peterson among them. He didn't notice me, but started visibly when he saw my father, who was rolling his sleeves back down now that Mike and the other bartender had things under control again. Eileen came in and said she'd arranged for a table in her section.

"You see your buddy?" she said.

"Yep," my father said.

"Kindly remember I work here."

"So do I," my father said, showing her his wrinkled hands; even the blackened thumb and forefinger looked soft and porous. "We'll sit a minute. We've waited this long. Irma's gotta let you off eventually."

My father took out some one-dollar bills and handed me a few for Liars. We'd played only a couple when a drink arrived and Mike said guess who. "Shall I say thank you?"

"If you want to," my father said.

In a few minutes F. William Peterson came over. He looked quite relieved when he saw me, probably figuring that meant my father wouldn't start trouble. "Sam," he said. "Ned."

"Well?" my father said.

"So," said the lawyer. "What do you think?"

"What do *I* think?" my father said. "I think there are four threes."

"Have you talked to Ned?" the lawyer said.

"Every day. He lives with me."

So, I thought. This is how it will come out. I will be officially informed of my mother's death in a noisy bar. Then we will go in and eat dinner. My father will explain that he'd been meaning to tell me, that he was waiting for the right moment, that it was just like F. William Peterson to mess things up, like he'd been doing for how many years now? How old was I? Right. For damn near thirteen years he'd been messing things up.

F. William Peterson's face was red. "I guess I don't understand your objection."

"It's like I told you before," my father said. "You tell me what you're going to do with the money and it's all yours. Just don't give me that crap about it being her wishes. You may have bullshitted her into giving you power of attorney, but you aren't bullshitting me. You can *have* the money, like I said. I just want to know what you and your doctor buddies are going to spend it on, that's all. You're all going to the Bahamas? Fine. Just don't try and bullshit me."

By the time my father finished, F. William Peterson was so angry he'd forgotten to be scared, but he kept his voice low. I

could barely hear him over the bar noise, but I'd never seen him
so animated. "How'd you *get* so smart, Sam?" he said. "How'd you
figure it all out like that? How'd you know I needed that little
run-down piece of shit worth all of ten grand so I can retire in the
tropics. You're too smart for guys like me, Sam. I should have
known better than to think I could pull something over on a sharp
cookie like you."

"Well, Attorney Peterson," my father said. "I may not be the
smartest guy in Mohawk County. I may not even be as smart as
you. But let's see how smart *you* are. See if you can figure out the
only reason you aren't flat on your ass."

Mike was now looking over at us and trying to pretend he
wasn't.

My father nudged me. "Tell him 'you're welcome.' Tell him if
it wasn't for you he'd be right on his ass. And while you're at it,
ask him how much longer he figures it'll be before he ends up
there anyhow."

Eileen came in on the fly, nodding at Mike behind my father's
back. "We're all set up," she said. "You want to eat or what."

When my father stood, F. William Peterson moved back a step,
though he still looked determined and flushed.

"You want some dinner?" my father said to me.

I stood up, turned toward the dining room.

"You want some dinner?" he repeated.

"Yes," I said.

"TALK, for Jesus Christ's sake!" he said.

"That's great," F. William Peterson said. "Take it out on him."

I think F. William Peterson knew he'd finally pushed the wrong
button even before my father hit him. Either he had the slowest
reflexes of any man I ever saw, or he was a fatalist. The punch my
father threw was short and hard, and F. William Peterson's lip
seemed to burst like a grape upon impact. Suddenly his whole
chin was red, and he wobbled uncertainly before righting himself.
If the bar hadn't been so crowded, he might have gone down.
Instead, he blinked twice and said, "Agh!" quite loudly.

Mike's other bartender, who had made his way around the bar
but arrived too late, grabbed my father and pinned his elbows
behind his back and Eileen stepped in front of him to prevent my
father from kicking F. William Peterson, who was still within
range.

"Agh!" F. William Peterson said again, even more loudly, as if he'd been hit again with some phantom blow. Everybody looked at him, puzzled, including my father. Then F. William Peterson did something nobody expected. He sneezed. Apparently my father's punch had glanced off the lawyer's nose, causing an uncontrollable, undignified sneeze, the force of which sprayed blood from his split lip all over everybody in the area. Eileen's white uniform was suddenly speckled, and a man in a light blue, summer sport coat, who had not seen the punch my father threw, but who had the misfortune to turn just when F. William Peterson sneezed, looked down at the shoulder of his jacket and said, "Hey! Have a fuckin' heart, Mac!"

Suddenly, Irma, Mike's wife, looking mean as a snake, was in the middle of it and Mike himself was heard trying to soothe things, saying that it was all over and just a misunderstanding. Eileen finally succeeded in turning my father in the general direction of the dining room, a sensible plan made difficult by the fact that the big bartender seemed reluctant to let go. The lawyer sneezed violently several more times into his own bloody hand, apologizing fervently between onslaughts. Nobody noticed me, for which I was grateful, because I was crying and I couldn't stop.

A few minutes later, somehow, my father and I were seated in the dining room with everybody staring at us. I was choking back sobs, and my father was telling me not to worry about it. We were both looking at menus. "You got any business of your own, lady?" my father said to a woman at a table near ours.

"Why, yes. Thank you so much," she said.

"Good," my father said. "Good for you."

After a while, people did go back to their meals.

"You gonna cry all through dinner or what," my father said, not looking up from his menu.

I didn't say anything. In the lounge, things had quieted down. Mike came in and said he'd got it all fixed, adding that there wasn't much that a round of free drinks wouldn't take care of, but he looked angry just the same, and Irma stayed away from us entirely. "What's the matter with him?" Mike said before returning to the bar.

"Nothing," my father said. "And if he doesn't stop it in about two seconds . . ."

"Forget it, buddy," Mike said to me. "Your father's all right. Everything's all right."

18

"There," my father said the next afternoon. "You feel better now?"

The answer to that was yes and no, but I said yes and it appeared to satisfy him, that and cuffing me alongside the head. He put the convertible in gear and headed us back toward Mohawk.

"I still don't get it," he said.

I had blurted out, finally, there in the restaurant, when Eileen joined us, that I knew my mother was dead, that I just wished somebody would say it. They looked at each other in disbelief so authentic that I considered them the best pair of liars I'd ever run across. They worked on me for about ten minutes, but I wouldn't budge. I was that sure. To unconvince me (and to show that there were no hard feelings) my father went back into the bar and fetched F. William Peterson. He looked pretty awful with his lip swollen up three times its normal size, even before my father explained the misconception I was laboring under, and then the poor fellow looked like he was going to cry. If he was lying too, he made my father and Eileen look like pikers. Which meant they weren't liars, at least not on this occasion. Which meant I had some explaining to do. I started out with the For Sale sign and how it had made me think she was dead. Otherwise, why was our house being sold? And what was this talk about power of attorney and following her wishes? I explained how just about everything people had said during the last week or so had confirmed my suspicion, though now that I thought back over the various conversations, the evidence had been far from conclusive. It seemed to fit because I was convinced that my mother's death was part of what I saw as my own downward spiral into neglect and ignominy. Naturally, since I saw both my father and Eileen as symptoms of that decline, I didn't mention that more abstract fear to them.

Now, of course, in the bright sunshine of a spring afternoon, I saw all of my hasty and erroneous conclusions concerning my mother in pretty much the same light as my father did—as bird-brained. The worst of it was that I had not trusted my own father. I had virtually accused him of withholding from me my own mother's death. Blessedly, the stupidity angle bothered him more than any demonstrated lack of faith in him as a good, trustworthy father. Every time he thought of some other reason why my mother couldn't be dead—like how come it wasn't in the paper? Why didn't anybody stop me on the street and say they were sorry to hear?—he trotted it out and examined my faulty logic further, as if he planned not to let the matter rest until I'd been officially entered in some sort of fool's compendium.

"There," he said, pointing to a For Sale sign on the front lawn of a small brick house set back a ways from the wide Schenectady street, then to another house on his side of the road. "Look at all the dead people's houses."

I didn't say anything. Another few residential blocks and we'd be coming up on the Thruway entrance. Then there wouldn't be any more real estate signs until we got back to Mohawk. Not that he would forget in the interim. The next sign he saw would put him right back on the same track, and it was easy to foresee that real estate signs were destined to be a reliable source of ridicule in the future. For Sam Hall there was no statute of limitations on other people's idiocy. He may even have felt that there'd been a kind of unwitting justice in the whole circumstance. After all, as a kid I'd told people *he* was dead; now I'd unwittingly done the same thing with my mother.

"Well?" he said, pointing out one last sign.

What he was after, of course, was a smile, and I was holding out, as usual. Once he decided you owed him a smile, he just kept after you until you paid up. Normally, I would have given in, but I didn't feel like smiling at him today. As soon as I gave him what he wanted, he'd stop razzing me and want to know about her, how she'd looked, whether we'd talked, what we'd said. I preferred the razzing.

I knew it was cruel of me to want to withhold information about her condition from him, but I did. It wasn't that I was particularly angry with him anymore. And it certainly wasn't that I wanted to protect him from any guilt he might be feeling concerning her, since I wasn't sure he felt any, unless you count as guilt a vague, general regret at the way things sometimes worked out. Rather, I didn't want to open the subject of my mother's condition because I knew I'd start lying to him. I couldn't tell him that my visit had lasted all of five minutes; that after he'd let me out in front of the home at one, promising to return at three, I had discovered her frail and alone in the large communal dining room next to the long window that overlooked the rambling, shadowy grounds out back, where tall pine trees prevented the sun from melting the still deep snow; that I had not been permitted to just walk up to her like a son, but had to wait while she was "prepared" for me, her mind given the opportunity to adjust; that a nurse had been dispatched to tell her, startling my mother out of her meditation on the reluctant, wintry grounds beyond the protective glass; how she had listened for the longest time, not appearing to comprehend, then finally looked slowly around the large room until her gaze fell upon me beneath the tall archway, seeing there someone she was not sure she recognized.

And who could blame her? I hardly recognized myself, having grown a couple inches in the seven months since she'd seen me last and become even more angular and birdlike as a result. Since going to live with my father, I wasn't the same boy. I felt certain that I carried myself differently now, that my gait was altered, my mannerisms different. Had I swung my arms before, when I had been her son, the way I did now? Did I have, back then, my current habit of standing on one foot? Had I that sullen expression that sometimes surprised me in the cloudy bathroom mirror of my father's apartment? I wanted to be her son again, if only for the afternoon, but I'd forgotten how and did not know where to begin.

When the nurse finally motioned to me, I went toward them slowly. When I reached the table where my mother was sitting, the nurse took her hand and then mine, so that we could touch. "Jenny," she said. "This is your son Ned. Do you know him?"

"Why, yes," my mother said. She had watched me all the way across the room, but the other woman's question distracted her now and she looked away from me and up at the nurse. "This is my son Ned."

"And a very fine-looking young man," the nurse said. "You must be very proud."

My eyes were already full, but the nurse took no notice. Instead she pulled up a chair from a nearby table and sat me down next to my mother. "Now I know how happy you are to see Ned," the nurse said. "But you mustn't forget to eat your lunch."

My mother was looking at me again and did not appear to hear.

"Jenny?" the woman repeated, and this time my mother heard and looked down at her plate, which clearly had not been touched, a small square of something under a coating of tomato sauce, alongside some washed-out-looking peas and a tiny roll, all of it cold and unappetizing. "Would you like me to stay?"

Only when my mother lifted her fork and slid it beneath the triangle of peas did the nurse leave us alone. I watched my mother chew the peas, her attention again drawn to the scene outside her window. "The snow won't go away," she said, as if this were a matter for concern.

"It has, most places," I told her.

"Fourth of July, Mohawk Fair, Eat the Bird, and Winter," she said, then turned to me, smiling. "Good Ned."

Almost unbelievably, we stopped in at The Elms on the way home. Over the years one of the points I've debated about my father is whether he was in those days impossible or just very difficult to embarrass. Here it was less than twenty-four hours after he'd started a fight there; a normal human being would have taken at least a temporary leave of absence from its vicinity, especially since it wasn't one of his regular in-town haunts anyway. True, Eileen worked there, assuming Irma hadn't fired her for consorting with undesirables, and sometimes my father stopped in for a quick one before she got off her shift, but he had already demonstrated during the long months when he was broke that he could live without The Elms, where Mike got "some kind of a price for a lousy bottle of beer." So, it seemed to me the easiest and (considering Eileen) the kindest thing in the world to give Mike and Irma wide berth for a few penitential weeks, at least until the sharp edges of their current and completely understandable resentment were worn smooth by other concerns.

But no. Back we went, like iron filings to a magnet. I could feel myself glowing scarlet with shame when we pulled into the nearly empty parking lot. It was late afternoon, in between the big after-church wave and the smaller early evening one. I could tell by my father's gait that he saw no reason we shouldn't be a welcome antidote to the late Sunday afternoon boredom that was sure to have gripped the place, especially if the basketball game was one-sided and the previous evening's exhaustion imperfectly banished. To his mind, we were just what the joint needed. If Mike and Irma wanted to remember something about the night before, let them recall how he'd washed glasses and sliced fruit. He'd bailed them out, and maybe it was time they showed a little gratitude.

Pretty clearly though, gratitude was not Irma's first emotion when we appeared in the doorway of the dark lounge. She was seated at one end of the horseshoe bar next to her husband, who was hanging dripping cocktail glasses upside down from the over-head rack.

"You're gone," she said, looking first at my father, then at Mike. "You hear me? He's all done here."

She was sucking on a maraschino cherry, its stem rotating in the gap between her large front teeth. Mike shrugged like it might be true. He didn't even give me the usual quarter for the jukebox. Eileen appeared in the doorway to the dining room, shook her head in amazement, and disappeared again. The dining room was practically empty, except for two busboys clearing and prepping tables for the dinner crowd.

My father winked at Mike and put an arm around Irma's big shoulders. "Let's you and me ditch this stiff," he stage-whispered. "We'll go throw down a blanket in the walk-in cooler. Like the old days." Then he took the maraschino cherry stem and pulled.

"Git!" she elbowed him hard in the ribs, though not as hard as she might have. He held his ground.

"Your trouble is you just need a little of the old innee-outee," he said. "Relax you a little, so you aren't so mean all the while."

"How the hell would you know what I need?" she said, but even I could see she was loosening up under his outrageous onslaught.

"I'm the expert," he said.

"You're the eighty-sixed expert. Go be expert someplace else. Kill somebody else's business." She took a toothpick from the glassful on the bar and jabbed the back of my father's hand with it, slipping neatly out of his embrace. "He's history," she warned Mike again.

When she was gone, Mike slipped me a quarter for Duane Eddy and my father went around the bar and got himself a bottle of beer so Mike wouldn't get in trouble.

"You better watch out," Mike warned him. "She ever takes you up on one of your offers you'll be one sorry son of a bitch."

My father shivered at the thought. "I don't know how you do it," he admitted, his voice full of genuine admiration.

"What," Mike said. "I haven't been as close to her as you just were in a month. I never come out from behind here you know."

"I don't blame you."

"How did she get that way is what I always wonder."

My father shrugged. "It could have something to do with the fact that every time you get a couple grand ahead you take it to Vegas and come home without it."

"Think so?"

"Yes, I do. Take her with you sometime. She works hard too."

"I always have more fun with you."

"I can't help that."

Mike studied me, then returned to my father. "He looks better today, anyway."

"Took him to see his mother. We just got back."

"How is she?"

"Better, according to my source. I'm the only one not allowed in."

"She should have been so smart fifteen years ago."

"She's not so smart now. It's our buddy with the fat lip that had it fixed. I so much as walk in the front door and I'm in the caboose."

"You figure he could fix it so I'm not allowed to see Irma?"

"Probably."

"You cost me a round of ten drinks and two complete dinners, you know."

"You want some money?" my father offered.

Mike waved goodbye to the idea. "The guy comes in once in a blue moon. Everybody else enjoyed it. I always said you were better than a floor show. Don't offer Irma though, unless you want her to take it."

"All right, I won't."

Eileen came in and sat down next to me. "How's your mother?" she said.

"Good," I said, grateful to be spoken to.

"Really? She's getting better?"

I nodded. Maybe it was true. When I'd left, the nurse told me that her eating in the dining room was a new thing, and that the dosage of her medicines was being gradually reduced. "She'll be coming home one day," the nurse had promised.

Strangely enough, that was the last thing my mother had said.

For the longest time she had stared quietly out into the deep snowy trees, so long that I had concluded that she forgot I was there. But then she had turned and taken my hand and said, "Be brave. Before long we'll be home again."

By home she no doubt meant the house with the For Sale sign out front, the one that would be devoured by the cost of her care, whether or not my father signed on F. William Peterson's dotted line.

Some people came in and then some others. The Elms dining room began to fill. We were getting ready to leave when the door opened and the man from the white jewel house who sometimes came out and stared at Drew and me at the end of his long drive appeared. With him was the most beautiful girl I had ever seen, and she looked about my age.

"Hey, *look* out," Jack Ward said, squinting in our general direction. He was dressed wonderfully, like somebody from another part of the world who'd come to a modest party expecting an extravagant one. He was wearing a cream-colored, lightweight sport coat over a light blue shirt and peach-colored sweater and slacks. His shoes were white mesh. He was tanned, somehow (so was the beautiful girl), and his longish, light brown hair swept back from his high forehead and settled behind his ears as if each strand had been cut to a precise length and trained. "I think we've stumbled into the wrong place," he said to the girl. "Look at *this* crew."

At the moment the whole crew consisted of Mike, my father, and me, and we were unsavory only in comparison to himself and the girl, it seemed to me.

My father looked Jack Ward over critically. "Must be tops to be loaded."

"Sam," the other man said as they shook hands, "it is. I recommend it to everybody. You remember my daughter Tria."

"I remember the little thing that used to bounce on my knee."

Tria Ward frowned and looked up at her father as if to inquire whether this could be true. But she did allow my father to put an arm around her. "Hi, dolly. Are you married?"

Jack Ward had stepped away from his daughter's side and made a circular motion to Mike with an elegant index finger. "And for yourself," he added quietly. Magically, there was a crisp fifty between his middle and ring finger and he slid it across the mahogany as if he were proposing to Mike some secret transaction. "We can do this without fanfare, you and I," the gesture seemed to imply. "It will be so quiet that no one will know that it's been done, and that will be its beauty." Almost as deftly, Mike spirited the money into the register before going to work, confident that Jack Ward did not intend for the money to sit there on the bar attracting attention to itself.

What was most amazing is that I noticed any of this, because I swear I had not once taken my eyes off Tria Ward. I think I contemplated homicide against my father for putting his arm around her. Couldn't he see how shy she was and how embarrassed to be hugged by an adult stranger in a dark lounge? How close to panic she was now that her father was no longer at her side? I was suddenly burning with indignation that my father thought he had the right to touch this lovely girl, herself as perfectly clean and fresh as her father.

No, she told my father, she was not married.

"That's good," my father gave her shoulder a squeeze. "You know, I happen to be available."

"You're also just the sort of old goat she's been warned about," Jack Ward said, his grin displaying two rows of perfectly white teeth.

"I tell you what," my father said. "How about I introduce you to somebody your own age. He's not as good-looking as his father, but you can't have everything."

Suddenly, everyone was looking at me, as luck would have it, just as a song ended on the jukebox. Tria Ward gave me a weak smile, as if to acknowledge my reality, or perhaps the fact that I wasn't *too* bad-looking, or that, yes, it was true, I wasn't as good-looking as my father.

And in response to her beautiful smile, I bleated.

I remember the horror of it even now. The sound I made resembled no word. It didn't even sound human. My father blinked, probably in disbelief, and for long terrible seconds nobody said anything. I flushed so deeply that my skin burned.

During that first year with my father, I often had the feeling of having disgraced myself, but the moment I bleated at Tria Ward, I knew that if I were to become a murderer, a traitor to my country, and an abject coward in the face of battle, I would never feel lower or more worthy of universal disdain than I felt at that moment, a prediction, I am happy to say, that has been borne out.

Fortunately, my humiliation was of major significance to me alone. I eventually discovered something like my normal voice, and I think Tria Ward and I had something like a conversation. We must have, because I came away from it knowing that she presently went to school at St. Francis, though she had attended a private school in Schenectady before that, both of which circumstances explained why I had never seen her around. Like me, she was entering the eighth grade in the fall, and she said she was trying to talk her mother into letting her go to Mohawk High the following year, though she thought she'd probably end up at Bishop McGuin in Amsterdam, or maybe this school in Connecticut.

I think we were both more than a little conscious of the adult conversation that was going on next to us. Listening in on adults was a habit I'd picked up very young, and I remember suspecting that Tria Ward was the same way, that she was eavesdropping on her father even more intently than I on mine, as if she hoped to learn the answer to some urgent question, one she'd have just asked if she hadn't known she wasn't supposed to.

My father was still needling Jack Ward about leading the good life.

"We both know what the good life is, Sam," Jack Ward said, his voice low and confidential. "The good life is not being shot at. Money. The rest of it. All fine and dandy. But not waking up in the Hürtgen Forest, hemorrhoids all adangle, no feeling in your feet—that's the good life."

"They didn't kill us, anyway," my father said.

"No, but they tried like bloody hell, and I got awful tired of it."

"We were trying, too."

"Not me," Jack Ward said. "I honestly couldn't say for sure I killed anybody. I just ducked, got off a round or two, tried not to hit any of our guys, prayed like a schoolgirl. You never prayed, did you."

"Never once," my father said.

"You wouldn't shit me," Jack Ward said.

"We all prayed," Mike said.

"Never once," my father insisted.

Jack Ward smiled. "I never stopped till we passed Staten Island."

"You stopped then though, I bet."

"I did," he admitted. "I made about a hundred deals with God over there and never honored one."

My father shrugged. "If he's half as smart as the preachers say, he knew you wouldn't."

"We never shook on them, is the way I look at it."

Mike was looking pale and nervous, as if he expected lightning. "You shouldn't talk like that," he said. "Don't let Irma hear you."

"I got God covered anyhow," Jack Ward said. "This one claims she's going to be a nun, and her mother's practically one already. I get prayed for all the time."

"For all the good it does," Mike observed.

That reminded my father of a joke, which he told at excruciating length. It was about a guy who was constipated and went to half a dozen doctors. Nobody could help. Finally, the last doctor prescribed a powerful enema, which the man took home with him, but he was back the next day complaining of even greater discomfort. When the doctor expressed surprise that the enema had had no effect, the patient snorted, saying he might as well have shoved them up his ass for all the good they did. In place of the word "ass," my father substituted a humming sound, turning his back on Tria and me for the finale. I already knew the punch line (it was one of the eight or ten jokes my father told regularly) and so I watched for Tria's Ward's reaction to it, expecting disgust. Instead, her expression registered something like fear, as if somebody had once warned her that the world was a foul, vulgar place, though this was the first concrete evidence that it might be true. I felt very sorry for her, and if I could have thought of a way, I would have tried to convince her that the world was neither foul nor vulgar, the painful erection in my chinos notwithstanding.

All that night I thought about Tria Ward. After her father took her away, into the dining room, my father and I left for a dinner of hamburg steaks at the Mohawk Grill, and there he finally got me to talk a little about my mother. What the hell, he said, he'd even sign F. William Peterson's papers if I wanted him to. He just hated like hell to be taken for a ride, that's all. Then he launched into a familiar diatribe about lawyers in general and F. William Peterson in particular, concluding that F. Willie was no prize, far from it, but he wasn't as bad as most.

As I listened to him talk and looked around the diner, which we had to ourselves this late on a Sunday evening, except for Harry and Wild Bill Gaffney, the town idiot, whom Harry looked after sometimes. Everything looked shabby, somehow. Shabbier than usual. And when Wild Bill used his index finger to scour the last drop of dirty coffee from the bottom of his cup, I wanted to cry.

I was sensible enough to be embarrassed about feeling this way, for here I was, warm and decently dressed, with a plate full of fries dripping brown gravy in front of me, with over three hundred dollars in the bank that nobody knew anything about. My mother was not dead, as I had imagined twenty-four hours earlier, and for all I knew she might even draw her mind back out of the dark woods that attracted her and come home. In general, things were looking up, but for some reason I'd never felt lower, and when my father said he thought maybe he'd go out for a while, I was glad to have the rest of the night to myself.

We ambled across the deserted Main Street, hands in our pockets, and up the stairs to our dark flat. I got undressed right away and pretended to read, so my father wouldn't stay around the apartment any longer than he wanted to, about five minutes, as it turned out. Then he was gone, the convertible jerking away from the curb below, back toward The Elms to torment Irma and wait for Eileen to get off work. Harry came out of the diner below, Wild Bill shuffling behind him, and locked the front door, officially surrendering downtown Mohawk to ghosts. The Mohawk Theater, three doors down from the grill, had closed after Christmas, its dark marquee still insisting IT'S A WONDERFUL LIFE, A CLASSIC. The theater was the fourth business on Main to fail that year, though two of the others had reopened on the new highway that skirted town. Looming up behind Main Street was the dark top floor of the junior high, and behind it the yellow windows of the hospital perched atop the treacherous Hospital Hill. Beyond it, the vast expanse of Myrtle Park, its unlit winding trails too spooky to visit at night. I'd read about a place in Arizona called the Superstition Mountains where people had a habit of disappearing without a trace, and it occurred to me that you could disappear without a trace right here in Mohawk and that I probably would, eventually.

On the other side of the park and the new highway, out beyond the city limits, was Tria Ward, and I thought about her and the scared look on her face when my father told the joke about the constipated man. Had her father recognized me as one of the boys who sat on the motorcycle at the end of his drive? Probably not. Probably it didn't matter. The Wards were all safe inside the white jewel house. Safe from the lunatic Drew Littlers of Mohawk County, safe from boys like me who might be tempted to fall in love with their dark-eyed, convent-bound girl child.

Somewhere in the gray consciousness of half sleep, though, my mind skittered away from beautiful Tria Ward and resolved a riddle that had been in the back of my mind all day. At the nursing home, I'd been asked to sign a big visitor's ledger. There had been a page for each resident, and I had expected my mother's to be clean. Instead, one illegible scrawl was entered there again and again, at least fifteen or twenty times. I had given it little thought, because it looked like the kind of scratching a doctor might be guilty of. Who else was there?

When I started awake, though, that signature seemed written in the air above my bed, and before the scrawl could disappear I was able to decipher it: F. William Peterson, it said.

When school got out for the summer, I had a lot more time on my hands, what with my father working on the road every day. Mornings I liked to spend at the Mohawk Free Library, an old stone building with a nice circular dome you could stand beneath and look up into. In the big archways just above the second floor were stained glass windows, and in the mornings the sun streamed through the eastern ones giving the stacks below a churchlike atmosphere, though the tall narrow windows along the first floor reduced the effect with a more natural light. All of the books were on the first floor, which also housed the loan desk, the children's room, and the general reading room, where a few white-haired men gathered to talk loudly every morning over the *Schenectady Gazette*, which filled them in on events ignored by the *Mohawk Republican*. These were fierce, belligerent old men who wouldn't stand for any shushing, and the librarians ignored the occasional complaint lodged against them, though an identical QUIET PLEASE sign posted in the children's room was strictly enforced.

The library itself was oddly shaped, as if the architect had followed the curve of the land, ducking around boulders and trees
rather than removing them. Even the rows of shelves inside
meandered, each a different length and height, sometimes stopping abruptly to accommodate a floor register or green pipe jutting out of the wall. My favorite place was a tiny, out-of-the-way
alcove where a small oak desk and chair had been placed, one of
half a dozen such scattered throughout the stacks. There I could
take off my shoes and rest my bare feet on the cool slate floor and
read for hours, uninterrupted by the low, confidential whispers
of the librarians at the nearby circulation desk, the whirring of
the large rotating fan near the front door, the distant barking
of the old men in the reading room. If there was a new librarian,
she might come check on me, suspicious of a disappearing teen-
ager (I'd proudly turned thirteen that May and was worthy of the
accolade), but the rest of the staff knew me, expected me, ignored
me.

They never even minded when I opened the little unscreened
window in the alcove, which provided a nice breeze until midday,
just enough to lift the pages of whatever I happened to be reading. Until noon, even on the hottest days, my alcove was the
coolest place in town. After that, the whole library became close
and hot, and by midafternoon even the rotating fan did little to
disturb the dead, heavy air. Both I and the bickering old men
were gone by then, leaving one or two librarians there all by
themselves until six when the library closed.

I read some good books that summer, along with a great many
bad ones, and I liked them all. Off in my own retreat and my own
world, I learned some important things. Sometimes I would take
any book off any shelf and start reading, as much as twenty or
thirty pages without understanding so much as a word, or imagining I didn't, only to discover that if I came back to the same book
and passage a few weeks later what it said would make sense and
I'd realize I'd understood more than I thought. If I was feeling
energetic, I'd look up words I didn't know, but more often I'd be
content to wait for the word to crop up again in another context,
and by its second or third appearance I'd know what it meant. I
began to develop a firm conviction that most efforts to teach
people things were wasted. All they needed was to go off some
place quiet and read.

Around noon, or shortly thereafter, I'd hop on my bike and

head over to the diner, where lots of times there would be something going on. The place would get busy and Harry would let me wash dishes for an hour or so, then feed me. On Friday he'd slip me a five or ten, depending on how much I'd worked and eaten. He had a good mind for figuring out what I had coming. I saw lots of people I knew. Untemeyer was in between two-thirty and three, a dead time when Harry didn't mind him sitting at the end of the counter and taking some action. Having him was good for business then, because the men who wandered in off the street to get a number down probably wouldn't have otherwise, and sometimes they'd stay for coffee or a piece of pie if they thought it hadn't been sitting in the case too long. Tree came in all the time too, though he never spoke to me unless I was with my father. My guess was he didn't recognize me otherwise. According to my father, Tree still had the two biggest, ugliest women in Mohawk County on the line, and when I asked him if he was counting Irma, Mike's wife, he said he was counting everybody. "You should see *Tree's* wife," my father said, but he wouldn't go into detail. Less frequently, my old friend Wussy would amble in wearing the same formless fishing hat, alight with colorful, hand-tied flies, which he would detach and let me examine, especially if my father was around. He always made a big deal about not letting my father touch his tackle, claiming he couldn't afford to waste hours tying a fly if all it was going to hook was Sam Hall's ugly black thumb. Wussy must have done something besides fish, but I never knew what it was. During the spring and summer he sold trout he caught to the Holiday Inn out on the highway, along with one or two other local restaurants. Sometimes, if he had a good catch, he'd have a half a dozen smaller ones left over and give them to Harry, who'd grill them if you asked. "Five-fifty up at the Holiday," Harry grumbled every time he served one of Wussy's trout. For some reason Harry always viewed the Holiday Inn as his chief competition for the Mohawk restaurant dollar, and he could never see why people would spend the extra to go there. When they'd opened a year ago, he'd given them six months to go belly up. "Same friggin' trout," he insisted.

"They got backs on the chairs there," my father explained from his stool at the counter. "You can lean back without falling on your ass."

Harry snorted. "Give me the extra three bucks and I'll stand behind you."

"I could never be sure you wouldn't let me go right to the deck."

"That's true," Harry admitted.

"You ever think your business might improve if you worked on your personality?" said a man named John, one of the regulars I didn't like.

"I do all right," Harry barked. "I do all fuckin' right."

"And you only work eighty hours a week," John said.

"What would I do in this fuckin' town if I wasn't working?" Harry wanted to know. "Go to the track. Chase married women. Fall off bar stools?"

"There you go," somebody said.

"I wish somebody'd chase my wife," John said. "I'd throw in a color TV if he caught her."

"What's wrong with her?"

"She's a bum lay."

"I didn't think so," my father said.

"Me either," Wussy agreed.

It got pretty quiet then. John stirred his coffee thoughtfully. Under normal circumstances he would not have felt compelled to defend his wife's honor, but he wasn't used to having her reputation assailed by a mulatto. "In Mississippi a guy could get lynched for talking that way," he said.

"This ain't Mississippi?" Wussy said. "You coulda fooled me."

Wussy, I learned years later, had something of a reputation as a back door man, though I have no idea if he ever did anything to earn it. "Somebody's gonna whack his big black dick off one of these days," John said when Wussy was gone.

"How do you know how big his dick is?" my father said. Everybody thought that was funny but John.

Sometimes, early in the morning, Skinny Donovan would be pacing outside the diner in the gray predawn light waiting for Harry to open. I'd see him from my bedroom window in the Accounting Department. The sound of my father peeing with the door open before he left for work always woke me. That summer he was working in Albany, an hour's drive, and he always eased his bladder last thing before leaving. I kept my watch by the side of the bed to time him, because peeing was one of my father's amazing talents. For quite a while forty-two seconds was the record, forty-two honest seconds from the instant his stream first hit the water full force (he never used the side of the bowl), until the noise ceased. I never counted the incidental plinks that resulted from shaking. Then one heroic morning he suddenly shattered his previous mark with a startling 55-second pee. I thought at first that I must have calculated wrong, but that's what it was and I stand by it. At various times in my life—in restaurant and airport rest rooms—I've unobtrusively timed perfect strangers and have concluded that my father in his day was the stuff of legend.

I'd see Skinny always pacing in the deserted street below as if he had to do the same thing, but it was Harry's strong black coffee he needed to face his day at Our Lady of Sorrows, where he continued to plant and tend floral crosses under the watchful eye of the old Monsignor, who was dying even more surely now than before, though no more rapidly. Mrs. Ambrosino still adamantly refused to allow Skinny inside the rectory, and he now looked upon those old days when we'd worked together as a golden age, and would grow quite nostalgic over their memory, having forgotten completely his deep resentment at my being accepted into the inner sanctum. Or maybe it was that he had forgiven me, quietly confident that I was unlikely to be accepted there any longer.

I had the long summer afternoons to myself. The library, the Accounting Department, and the Mohawk Grill were all too hot, so I usually spent the afternoon exploring on my bicycle. I biked everywhere—up to the Sacandaga Reservoir beaches, public and private, as well as to the marina, where I would stroll around like I owned the place, evaluating the speed boats and bikini-clad girls who greased themselves and lay on boat decks under the hot sun, oblivious to it and to my own hot orbs; free now of maternal restraints, I rode down to the Mohawk River, which rolled lazily east toward the Hudson, full of slow, murky sludge, a dead river back then, its banks encrusted with discarded cellophane and rusty pop cans.

I also explored the winding cart paths of the Mohawk Country Club, where the long rolling fairways, most of them, were broad, funnel-shaped and forgiving. Racing along the edge of the woods, I would occasionally jump a foursome of silver-haired women on some remote tee, flushing them almost into perpendicular flight, like aged quail left behind by the flock in the general migration to Florida. Yes, I was perfectly ubiquitous that summer, present everywhere I had no business, mildly annoying as a breach of

security, without giving any particular offense, or at least sufficient offense to warrant mobilizing the authorities, whoever *they*
might have been. It struck me even back then how ill-equipped
the Money People, as Drew Littler called them, were to keep
away intruders (admirers, in my case). The more you had, it
seemed to me, the larger your border that needed defending. At
the country club, for instance, they could effectively keep inter-
lopers off the first, ninth, tenth and eighteenth holes, but I owned
the rest.

My favorite afternoon haunt was still Myrtle Park, and most
afternoons I would stop there on my way home. From the embankment overlooking the abandoned shack and mounds of discarded Mohawk trash, I would stare across the treetops to the
blue-green hilltop a mile away on the other side of the highway
where Tria Ward lived with her father, a man who had so much
money he couldn't spend it all, no matter how hard he tried, and
who was still glad, after so many years, not to be shot at. I thought
about Jack Ward a lot, and the way he had slipped Mike that fifty
so smooth that nobody had noticed but me, and I compared him
to my own father, who always carried what money he had deep
in his front trouser pocket, an unorganized wad of mixed denomi-
nations from which he peeled bills to slap on the bar when he sat
down. He always left the money right where it was when he went
to the men's room, its duty to carve out a small personal space
there, establish beyond question his right to return.

It seemed strange that he and Jack Ward had known each other
as younger men, that they had awakened cold and wet in the
same German forest, clutching machine guns, thinking about Mohawk and what their lives would be like in the unlikely event they
made it home. Had they planned it all there in that dark forest?
Had Jack Ward planned to marry the jewel house on the hill, the
shiny Lincoln in the circular drive, the money he couldn't spend?
Had he planned to engender the dark-eyed, frightened-looking
girl I wanted to teach how not to be afraid, a lesson I felt confident
to convey, despite not having mastered it myself? And my own
father. Had he planned things too? The long, bitter wars with my
mother? The big, hollow third-floor Main Street apartment? The
long days working on the road? A life where the principal diver-
sions were endless parades to the post and daily number draw-
ings? And what about me? He couldn't have planned on me, I
thought.

Having awakened in the Hürtgen Forest remained a bond between the two men even now, something with the power to draw
them together for five quick minutes in a dark bar for the swift
exchange of secrets, the quick acknowledgment of present realities (this is my daughter, this is my son), of past realities (are we
lucky bastards or are we lucky bastards? what the hell were the
odds we'd be in Mohawk sharing a beer in 1960?).

It was doubly odd that I spent so much time thinking about Jack
Ward, because I always went up into Myrtle Park to think about
Tria, with whom I now counted myself in love. The trouble I had
was coming up with fantasy scenarios. How would I ever see her
again? Where? Was it possible to infiltrate the private and paro-
chial schools that were her future? Would my father and I be
eating dinner at The Elms some night and, seeing Jack Ward and
his lovely child in the doorway, wave them over to our table? And
would they condescend to make a happy foursome, the Halls and
the Wards, Jack and Sam to exchange war stories, Tria and Ned
left to play footsie beneath the table?

The above story line was so rickety that I couldn't hold its lovely
focus, and as the summer progressed, I discovered that I couldn't
even remember exactly what Tria Ward had looked like—only
that she had been more beautiful than any girl I had ever seen.
Most annoying was the cruelty of my perversely selective memory. What kind of sense did it make for me to remember every
expression and gesture of the *father* of the girl I loved, when her
own beloved face became daily more vague, little more than an
ill-defined value judgment? It didn't matter. The white jewel
house, shimmering magically in the afternoon sun, contained
them both, and it was a long way away.

When he didn't get waylaid, my father usually wheeled up in
front of the Mohawk Grill around four-thirty in the afternoon. I
tried to be there myself about that time, so I'd get some kind of
idea what was on tap for the evening, whether he'd be around or
not, always assuming he knew himself. Usually there would be
somebody, or a couple of somebodies who'd intercept him between the curb and the door of the Mohawk Grill, sometimes to
let him know about a game upstairs, or a sure thing at Aqueduct,
or touch him for a quick five. But eventually he'd make it in, cuff
me in the back of the head and say, "Well?" Then he'd want to
get a number down and off we'd go in search of Untemeyer, after
promising Harry we'd be back for dinner.

"You know that Schwartz kid?" he asked me one afternoon after our ritual greeting.

"Claude?" I said. I'd neither seen nor thought of him since school got out.

"His old man runs the factory out in Meco?"

I said that was the one.

"Tried to commit suicide this afternoon," he said. "Hung himself, the crazy son of a bitch."

A lunatic discussion ensued. Several people in the diner had heard of the event, or overheard somebody talking about it, just as they'd overheard my father's mention of it to me.

"Schwartz," somebody said. "Bernie Schwartz?"

"Bernie Schwartz is older than *you*. This was some kid."

"Maybe it was Bernie's kid," the original speaker suggested.

"Bernie never had no kids and he never run no factory in Meco. Other than that, it could have been Bernie."

Everybody laughed.

"It was Clyde Schwartz," my father said, getting it wrong, but close. "Third Avenue they live, somewhere."

"There's no Jews on Third Avenue. My wife lives up on Third Avenue."

"It's Clyde Schwartz," my father insisted. "And they live on Third Avenue, I'm telling you."

"What's he want to kill himself for if he owns a factory?"

"It's not him, it's his kid. Clean your ears."

"The Schwartzes live on Division Street, all of them. Right by the west entrance to the park. Except for Randy over on Mill."

The door opened and Skinny shuffled in, filthy and smelling of fertilizer from an afternoon in the Monsignor's flower beds.

"Hey, Skineet," my father hailed him. "Where does Clyde Schwartz live?"

"Third Avenue," Skinny said, happy to be deferred to in this local matter. "He damn near cooked his own goose today."

"Not him," my father said. "His kid."

"No, him is what I heard. Tried to string himself up from the ramada in his backyard."

"From the what?"

"I heard it was the kid," my father said, unsure of himself now.

"Couldn't be," Skinny said. "He tied a rope to the roof and

jumped off the picnic table. Neighbor looked out the window and saw him standing there on his tiptoes, eyes all bugged out. When he didn't wave back, she got suspicious. Old Lady Agajanian."

"There's no Agajanian on Third Avenue," said the man whose wife lived there.

"Old Goddamn Lady Agajanian," Skinny shouted, "you simple shit! On Third Avenue. Next to Claude Goddamn Schwartz."

"Besides," somebody said. "Your wife lives on Second Avenue."

The man had to admit this was true. He'd forgot. His wife did live on Second Avenue.

"I heard it was the kid," my father said.

"All right," Skinny said. "You tell me how a kid's gonna bend down the crossbeam on that ramada."

"I'm just telling you what I heard," my father said, throwing up his hands. "Some kid named Clyde Schwartz tried to kill himself is what I heard. Sue me."

"I don't want to sue you. But I'll buy your dinner if you're right."

"I didn't know there was any Jews living on Third Avenue," said the man whose wife didn't live there either.

"Hey," my father shouted after me. "Where are you off to?"

The hospital was right around the corner and up the hill, but I pedaled over to Third Avenue instead. The neighborhood was so quiet that I thought at first that the whole thing had to be a mistake. The Claudes' house looked deserted and their station wagon wasn't in the drive, but on the other hand there were no police cars, no neighbors clustered on porches, no indication of anything amiss. But instead of turning around and heading back I got off my bike and walked it up the drive. I was staring at the bent, mangled crossbeam and the tipped-over barbecue, when a voice behind me said, "I remember you. The friend."

There was an elderly woman standing in the shadows of her screened-in porch, her white face and hair close to the dark metal webbing. I'd seen her before, when I was a regular visitor at the Claudes. About the only thing I could remember about her was that in the middle of summer she always wore a fur coat when she came outside. She was looking past me at the bent, tilted ramada, as if she could still see the ghastly spectacle there, as if she might see nothing else for a long time. I felt sorry for her, because she was pretty old and she shouldn't have had to see Claude Jr. staring at her the rest of her days.

That night my father and I stayed home and watched television. He didn't try to make me talk, but I could feel him looking at me, frowning, puzzled, not that this was unusual. When he noticed me at all perplexity was the predictable result. Finally, when he couldn't stand it any more, he cuffed me a good one.

"What," I said.

"You ever try anything like that and I'll kick your ass," he said.

I didn't know whether the threat of an ass-kicking was much of a deterrent to anyone contemplating suicide, but I appreciated the thought. Mostly, he was still pissed at Skinny, who had refused to pay up when it was confirmed that it wasn't the father who'd tried to croak himself. "You was just as wrong," Skinny claimed. "*Clyde* Schwartz, you said. There's no such goddamn person even."

20

About this same time, I joined a gang. Or rather, a commando strike force. Its other two members were its leader, Drew Littler, and a friend of his named Willie Heinz. Our purpose, according to Drew, was to right wrongs wherever we found them. Do what needed doing. Do what nobody else had the balls to do.

I found this rhetoric, which Drew had borrowed from an old comic book, most appealing, especially in its unspecificity. It did not seem to me that we'd discover any of the world's major wrongs here in Mohawk, but it was fun to imagine that evildoers contemplating nefarious activities would have to deal with us. We could count ourselves a deterrent, sort of like the magic powder that warded off elephants in the old joke. Basically, we roamed the streets at night in search of injustice. I was able to join the gang only when my father was out, but that was most of the time, what with poker games, trips to the harness track, and bars he sometimes couldn't get past on the way home. Drew only bothered with the gang when his motorcycle was disabled, a day or two out of the average week. Then we'd meet out in back of the Littlers' house sometime before sundown and head up into the park to train, where nobody would see our paramilitary drills and suspect our existence. Indeed, we spent an inordinate amount of time making sure there was no breach in our security. Drew was particularly worried about Willie Heinz, who was not very bright and who lived for our commando raids. In fact, Drew so completely distrusted Willie's ability to keep a secret that he refused to give our gang a name for fear that Willie would spill the beans bragging about us.

Once up in the woods we'd do calisthenics and practice the chain of command, which required that Willie Heinz do, without question, whatever Drew told him, and that I do whatever Willie told me. This arrangement was entirely satisfactory, since Willie never could think of anything to tell me to do. Drew himself was every inch a soldier. He wore thin t-shirts that had their short sleeves torn away so that his huge shoulder muscles were visible when we worked out. Willie Heinz and I had a tough time concealing our admiration for his big, tan torso and rippling biceps. He was exactly the sort of fellow to inspire confidence in his troops, and I was only occasionally discomfited to recall that my father had slammed one of his huge arms onto the dinner table with such force that the boy's feet had gone straight into the air.

I think Willie Heinz was even more envious of Drew Littler's musculature than I, probably because Willie was tall, with a sprinter's build that shamed him when he wasn't in full flight. That, however, is what I will always associate Willie Heinz with: flight. He was the most unabashed coward I ever met, so cowardly, in fact, that his cowardice was impossible to hold against him, since you knew in advance what to expect. Running away with Willie always reduced the most serious of situations to comedy. His long, loping strides and churning elbows always seemed a preface to literal flight. You expected him to be airborne momentarily, and when he remained grounded he resembled nothing so much as a badly designed bird.

Strangely, it was Willie Heinz who usually made flight necessary, and I've since come to the conclusion that he simply delighted in the sensation of fear. No night of roving the streets of

Mohawk was ever complete until Willie Heinz had put an impressive mound of dogshit on someone's porch and rung the doorbell. His terrorist attacks often came as a surprise even to Drew and me. We'd be walking peacefully down the middle of the street and without warning Willie would become possessed. "Arghh . . ." he would begin to moan, barely audibly at first, but rapidly getting louder. Then he'd pretend that something invisible had grabbed him by the elbow and was dragging him off toward somebody's dark porch. If we knew what was good for us, we hightailed it. I'd get a good lead, but within a block or so Willie, his fists flashing high in the air, would blow by me, shouting, "Motherfucker, motherfucker, motherfucker, motherfucker," about one motherfucker per stride.

Such behavior always embarrassed Drew, who hated, I suspect, to see our high purpose trivialized by mere pranks and silly minor vandalism. He not only hated to run, he refused to. Nobody who got a good look at Drew ever wanted to chase him. Even when the police pursued us, it didn't rattle our leader, who knew all the Mohawk cops and made small talk with them when they pulled over to the curb where he was strolling, alone by then, Willie Heinz and I having beaten a hasty retreat. Sometimes he sent them off in the opposite direction looking for us, once nearly causing our capture after we'd cut across lots and doubled back toward home, a maneuver much favored by Willie Heinz, who considered it the height of deception and who hated to run more than a block or two in a direction other than the one he ultimately intended to pursue.

These were exciting times, but I worried about Drew Littler, who seemed never to derive much enjoyment out of our sneak attacks, even though our targets were invariably those who qualified as "Money People." Often he seemed abstracted, vaguely annoyed with us for being younger, though Willie was only a year Drew's junior. His opinion of Willie and me was none too high, and I knew he doubted he'd be able to count on us in a pinch. What troubled me most was that I could sense a pinch on the not-too-distant horizon. He had something in mind for us, some reason for hanging out with us, captaining our band. I watched him carefully when he thought I wasn't looking, watched the purple worm tunneling beneath the skin of his forehead when he became immersed in thought. What, I continually wondered, could he want with us?

As the summer progressed Drew Littler became more deeply moody and sullen, often not inviting me to ride on the back of his motorcycle on those evenings my father and I came over for dinner. Sometimes, he didn't even want me spotting for him when he bench-pressed, once remarking that he was better off depending on himself. That hurt my feelings a little, but it was also a relief not to be around him when he was so morose.

One sweltering evening toward the end of July, the phone rang just as Eileen and my father were finishing up the dinner dishes. Drew had roared down the drive a half hour earlier, and when she set the phone down, all the blood had drained from her face. She spoke through her wet fingers which had worked their way over her nose and mouth, prayer-fashion. "He's done it," she said. "He's had an accident."

We all piled into the Mercury and my father backed it down the drive fast, scraping the rear bumper hard. When we came to the intersection, he started to turn left, toward the hospital, but Eileen said no, the trooper had told her the accident was out on the highway.

My father was still for meeting the ambulance at the hospital, but Eileen was adamant and my father turned right for the highway.

"Which way?" he said when we got to the stoplight at the intersection of Park and the highway. When Eileen realized she didn't know, I heard myself say "Right" with such conviction that my father, who normally paid no attention to my opinion in such matters, did as he was told. The orange sun was down behind the dark trees which formed a corridor on both sides of the highway, peeking through in brief blinding flashes as we hurtled through the curves. It was the same time of day as when Drew had given me that first ride on the bike, and about a half mile from the entrance to the road that wound up toward Jack Ward's house, I told my father to slow down. I'd hardly spoken when we came around a curve and saw the cluster of cars and people and flashing lights. Eileen was out of the car even before the convertible came to a halt.

There were two police cars and an ambulance, but it was a middle-aged fellow in a red plaid hunting cap who was directing traffic around the flares that had been set up in the middle of the road. In the ditch across the highway a blue Impala sat, its rear door and hood caved in where the motorcycle had struck, its rear

wheel collapsed in upon itself like a weak-ankled ice skater.
Thirty feet up the embankment the mangled cycle had come to
rest, an almost unrecognizable hunk of twisted black metal. Drew
Littler stood over it, holding the detached handle bars in one
hand. The fifty or so people who had gathered were staring at
him, but no one was closer than twenty yards. Even from the
other side of the road I could see that his jeans and t-shirt were
covered with blood.

My father followed Eileen across the highway. "You the
mother?" I heard one of the troopers say to Eileen, who had
slowed as she drew nearer her son, who was surrounded on three
sides by police officers and ambulance attendants, all of whom
were keeping their distance.

Apparently Drew had been just catching his breath, because a
moment after we arrived, he raised the twisted handlebars of the
ruined bike over his head and began to pound the cycle, shouting
something I couldn't make out.

"There he goes again," I heard somebody say.

Several people laughed nervously.

"I never see anybody so mad at a dead motorcycle," another
commented, "have you?"

"It wudn't the motorcycle," said a huge woman. "It was the nut
behind the wheel." Everybody thought this was funny too,
though as an old automobile joke it worked imperfectly with
respect to motorcycles.

A middle-aged woman in a yellow dress, who had been sitting
on the ground next to the blue Impala and sobbing, quietly got
to her feet to watch Drew go at the bike. There was a ragged tear
along her forehead and the white towel in her hand was splotchy
red. Each time Drew wailed the motorcycle with the handlebars,
she covered her ears, though the sound he was making wasn't
particularly loud now. "Can't somebody make him stop!" the
woman screamed. "Can't somebody just make him stop?"

Nobody looked all that anxious to, and they must have figured
that from the look of Drew Littler he couldn't keep it up much
longer. Each blow was increasingly feeble.

"Look at my beautiful car!" the woman cried, as if noticing its
condition for the first time. "Can't somebody just make him
stop?"

My father and Eileen were talking to a tall trooper, while two
others, their backs to Drew Littler, seemed to have been ordered

to prevent anyone from approaching the boy until he'd spent himself.

Near where I stood, a big red-haired man, full of momentary self-importance, was giving an eyewitness account of the accident, so I moved closer to listen.

"At big kid aire . . . he come down from up aire" (pointing to the winding road that led to the Ward house) "goan like I never see. Like he forgot the highway was aire, till the last second. He sorta wakes up then and seen where he wuz, and then you know what that kid done?"

Everybody wanted to know.

"He just raised hisself up and steps off that murtercycle like he was parked along of the curb, and off that sonofagun went without him. Went over on its side, then bounced right back up like it was rid by a ghost, hit that aire blue car in the door and stuck like a arrow. That aire blue car went right up sideways on its wheels and flung that murtercycle off into the weeds up aire where 'at crazyboy's beatin' on her now. You never see nothin' like it for weird."

There was a murmur of appreciation among the red-haired man's listeners, but the man wasn't finished.

"And that aire crazyboy . . . summer-saultering along the road after that murtercycle like he can't wait to catch up, screaming at it all the time. You never see nothin' like it. Never even stopped to look at hisself afore he tuck off after that murtercycle to kill it. Beat on it with his hands until he come across 'em handlebars, yelling 'I'm gonna kill the sonofabitch.' Like 'at murtercycle was a person. He's a crazyboy is what he is."

Down in the ditch the tall trooper talking to Eileen shrugged and my father started up the weedy bank. Drew looked over his shoulder once, then went back to beating the cycle with renewed purpose. I couldn't watch.

When I looked away, I saw Tria Ward standing on the other side of the road with a small woman an inch shorter than she. The girl had the same frightened expression she'd worn that afternoon at The Elms when we'd eavesdropped on our fathers' conversation. She looked like she was straining to hear now, though I couldn't imagine why. I looked around for Jack Ward, but I didn't see him anywhere. The small woman with her looked to be in her fifties, but she was mummified, somehow, her skin shrunken tight over her tiny bones, like parchment. The spooky part was that she looked enough like Tria Ward for me to be sure that she was the girl's mother, this despite the fact that Tria seemed, just then, to be even more beautiful than I remembered her, her long dark hair lush, a wonderful contrast to her pale white, almost translucent skin. When she saw me, I flushed, half hoping she wouldn't recognize me, half praying she would.

She smiled immediately, though somewhat fearfully, as if I was just the sort of person she expected to find in the middle of such a terrible scene. And, because of this, I felt the same insane urge I'd felt when we had been introduced in the restaurant—to apologize. For what, I couldn't imagine. Her mother noticed me then and looked up at her daughter, then back at me, suspiciously, I thought, as if validating my need to apologize.

"Hi," Tria Ward mouthed, a silent, lovely syllable that gave me sufficient courage to join them. "Isn't it terrible?" she said when I arrived. Traffic was now halted in both directions.

This time I managed something better than a bleat, something to the effect that, yes, it certainly *was* terrible, though I wasn't sure precisely what she was referring to—the wrecked Impala, the woman with the sliced forehead, the bloodied specter of Drew Littler, his awful yelping as he bludgeoned the bike, or the fact that so many people were gathered around in ghoulish enjoyment, hoping the show wouldn't end just yet. I figured she meant all of the above.

"Do you *know* him?" Tria Ward said, as if she suspected I must.

"No," I said, fearful of guilt by association. But my answer was a split second off in its timing, slowed, somewhat surprisingly, by real guilt. "My father does," I added, and a fresh tide of guilt washed in. I hadn't meant to implicate him, but it did seem wise to explain his presence on the opposite embankment where he had now arrived at the twisted pile of metal and the bloody, still raving boy.

Drew had turned to face my father when he got close, and they each stood their ground now, my father just outside the reach of the ragged metal handlebar. We couldn't hear anything, but I saw my father gesture in the general direction of the crowd; Eileen remained with the troopers and ambulance attendants. Drew studied the gallery for a second, as if this were the first time he'd noticed he wasn't alone, but did not seem particularly impressed with the assembled mass. When my father held out his hand, Drew cocked the handlebar in response. I saw one of the troopers unsnap the strap on his holster.

Silence descended on the crowd. Even the red-haired man had interrupted his umpteenth account of the accident. The only sound was the faraway rumble of an approaching dump truck still two hundred yards up the highway.

And then suddenly it was over. Drew Littler dropped the metal bar and went to his knees, my father catching him as he pitched forward. Quickly, the troopers and ambulance attendants were scrambling up the hill, and I saw Eileen sit down on the asphalt. "He's a crazyboy is what he is," I heard the red-haired man say. "Thinks that murtercycle is a person."

"The nut behind the wheel," the big woman said, but the crowd had changed and the reference become elliptical. This time nobody laughed, and the big woman looked confused and hurt. She remembered how it was to be funny.

21

Only when the ambulances disappeared around the curve heading back toward Mohawk did I realize I'd been forgotten. The attendants had rolled Drew onto a stretcher and struggled with his dead weight down the incline to the waiting ambulances. I thought they did a pretty good job, dropping him just the once, and then not very hard. Drew was about as big as the two attendants put together. They placed him in the second ambulance, which had just that minute pulled in behind the first. Eileen rode in the back with her son and an attendant, my father up front with the driver. The woman who'd been driving the Impala had the other ambulance all to herself.

"Mother," Tria Ward said, when the crowd began to disperse. "This is Ned Hall."

I don't know what surprised me more—that Tria Ward remembered my name or that she thought me worthy of introducing to her mother. Introductions were not part of my father's normal

social routine. When we went someplace, he more or less assumed
that people would know who we were, or if they didn't, they
ought to. When pressed on the subject, he'd admit that, yes, I was
his, but there were a lot of people I knew pretty well who had no
idea what my name was. Some others, like Wussy, got too much
of a kick out of calling me Sam's Kid to use my name anyway.
Now, being introduced by my correct name to someone like Tria
Ward's mother had an odd effect on me. On the one hand it was
flattering, like suddenly being granted personhood, but also a
little unnerving, because I wasn't certain I'd prove worthy.
Would she divine after a few exchanges that I didn't merit so
specific an identity and ask her daughter, à la Mike at The Elms,
what's wrong with *him*?

"Hall," Mrs. Ward repeated. "That is a common name, but not
a local one."

I did not know what to say to that. I had counted eleven Halls
in the Mohawk directory once, but I felt this might be the wrong
time to volunteer that information.

"That looked rather like a young man I used to know," she said,
pointing across the highway to the empty embankment where
my father and Drew Littler had stood, as if she could still see them
there. "His name was Samuel Hall, I believe."

I admitted that someone named Samuel Hall was my father.

"He has not aged particularly well, has he?" Mrs. Ward said, as
if she imagined that I might confirm her opinion by comparing
the way I saw him now with her recollection of him as a younger
man. "Of course, people live hard lives, don't they."

Clearly, from the tone of her voice, she counted herself among
those who lived hard lives.

"Perhaps your young friend would like something cool to drink,
dear," Mrs. Ward speculated, settling on a phrase midway between an indefinite pronoun and a specific identity. The traffic
had resumed on the highway now, the cars on the shoulder inching back into the stream, an occasional horn blaring.

There was nothing I would have liked better than "something
cool" with Tria Ward, but her mother was giving me the willies,
as did the fact that Tria herself had not uttered a syllable after
saying my name. I thought perhaps this silence might be indica-
tive of something. Perhaps good breeding required me to admit
frankly at this juncture that I was not Tria Ward's young friend,
we'd met only once and then very briefly, that "something cool"

might better be saved for those who could lay better claim to the title of "young friend." On the other hand, if I declined the invitation, I would have to admit to being stranded there on the highway. In a moment, my father's would be the only car left on the shoulder, and for some reason I did not want to admit to either Tria Ward or her mother that I had been abandoned. Trotting on home would not have been such a big thing, of course, but I wasn't sure I could pull it off with them watching. Surely, Mrs. Ward would say, in her strange, formal manner of speech, you don't intend to *walk* all that way into town, along that fearfully busy highway. I accepted.

"Why don't you have your young friend sit in the front with us, dear," Mrs. Ward said. Jack Ward's white Lincoln was sitting at the edge of the trees, and when Tria went around to the driver's side, I followed her, failing to comprehend that she, not her mother, was going to drive. I think I may even have concluded, momentarily, that on extra-expensive big cars like this one, the steering mechanism was on the right.

"Tria is learning to drive, you see," her mother said from the other side of the Lincoln, only the top half of her head visible above the roof. Her daughter, a slender inch taller, climbed up on top of two large pillows that allowed her to see over the dash. Then Mrs. Ward also got into the car.

That left me outside. I knew I had been invited to sit in the front seat, but it now appeared that all access to that front seat had been blocked. My problem, of course, was that I had mentally pictured the scene—Tria behind the wheel, I in the middle, close enough to admire the light brown hair along her slender arms, and the mother, since she insisted on intruding, riding shotgun. But with both of them already in the car, I didn't see how it would be possible for me to assume my rightful station without crawling over one of them. Until Tria closed her door I believe I actually contemplated squeezing myself between her lovely self and the wheel, all the while muttering, excuse me, excuse me, just a moment, there we are. The fact that her mother's door remained open finally clued me to the alternate seating arrangement I hadn't imagined, and by the time I trotted around to the other side, Mrs. Ward had slid over next to her daughter, leaving me red-faced and despondent.

"I myself do not drive," Tria's mother was saying when I

ducked in and pulled the door shut. "So I am far from an ideal instructor. Her father is doing the real teaching, you see."

I nodded, crestfallen. If Tria Ward was old enough for a learner's permit, then she was probably two years older than I, though she did not look any fifteen. But hadn't she told me that she too was entering the eighth grade? Had I misunderstood?

"I myself have never comprehended this nation's ongoing fascination with the automobile. In this day and age, learning to drive is considered as necessary as learning to swim, though it certainly wasn't in my day."

"You don't swim either, Mother," Tria Ward observed. She held the big Lincoln in the very center of the narrow road and we inched up the incline at no more than ten miles an hour, a hazard, it seemed to me, to anyone coming down the road from the house, or up from the highway at a reasonable speed, since they would come upon us virtually parked there in the center of the pavement. Had a yellow line divided the road, we would have been impartially astraddle it. Tria gripped the steering wheel hard, seeming to pull it toward her, like the column of an airplane, as if attempting with all her strength to get the big Lincoln airborne while still in first gear.

"Water and your mother do not agree," Mrs. Ward was saying, without explaining what the bone of contention between them might be.

Up through the trees we crept, all of us straining to see in the deepening dusk.

"My father drives a convertible," I said, apropos of nothing other than a sudden need to plunge into the conversation and a vague desire to demonstrate my own familiarity with things automotive.

"A convertible automobile," Mrs. Ward said, as if the concept required analysis. "I think, my dear, that headlights just might be the order of the day."

This was true, of course, it being very dark among the tall trees, but I immediately wished the old woman had not suggested it, seeing the startled effect that this complication had on Tria. In order to turn on the headlights, she would have to remove one hand from the wheel, something she was apparently loath to do. Had she glanced at the dash she would have been able to locate the lights in half a second, but taking her eyes off the road at our current breakneck speed was unthinkable. So she was reduced to fumbling for the lights with her left hand. To make matters worse, when her left hand came off the wheel, her right foot, for some reason, came off the accelerator, as if the two opposite limbs were controlled by the same invisible string. She discovered the lights at the same instant the strangling Lincoln gave a violent lurch forward, coughed once, and died.

"Oh dear," said Mrs. Ward, as if she could imagine no way out of this unforeseen circumstance and suspected that they would now have to purchase a new car.

Suddenly, it was very quiet. The air-conditioning had gone off, and with it the radio, which had been playing softly. In their place we now had lights, and we all three watched the trees unaccountably climbing the hill before us. So were the ones out my side window. It was so quiet we could hear the sound of pebbles being ground beneath our wheels. We were adrift, backing down toward the highway at roughly the same speed we had climbed.

With neither power steering nor brakes, the car was suddenly foreign to Tria. She tried everything she could think of, but nothing worked. She gave the Lincoln more gas, naturally, to no effect. The key in the ignition was frozen, the steering wheel locked, and her legs too short to press down hard on the brakes. With a look of pure terror, she turned to her mother and said something that surprised me more than anything that had happened so far—"I love you, Mother!" she said.

Mrs. Ward turned to face her daughter with an expression that bespoke astonishment, fear, and sincerity in equal parts, as if both mother and daughter had been signaled unambiguously that the end of the world was near. "Why, I love you too, dear," she said.

We left the Lincoln right there, its rear end well off the pavement, its long front sticking way out onto the roadway. God, it was a big car.

Tears tracked down Tria Ward's cheeks as the three of us made our way up through the corridor of dark trees. She made no sound though. There was nothing wrong with the car, except that the engine was flooded from her attempts to accelerate up the hill after it had stalled.

Unfortunately, my own driving skills were limited to what I had already done. You couldn't very well be Sam Hall's kid without knowing what to do about a rolling car. About once a month my father would park on an incline, put the car in neutral, and get out to talk to somebody. If I happened to be in the car, I'd just lean over and throw it into park when it started to roll. If not, he'd usually catch up to the convertible before it got too far. We changed the convertible's broken rear reflectors every few weeks and drove blithely away from the fender benders and cracked headlights of unlucky adjacent automobiles. So, when I saw that Jack Ward's big white Lincoln was about to bear us back into the trees, I knew what to do.

What I didn't know was whether I was permitted to do it. I mean, I wasn't driving, and it wasn't my car, and I hardly knew these people. I could imagine Tria and her mother deeply resentful of my impertinence if I were to just ignore the chain of command by leaning across and slamming the Lincoln to a rocking halt without permission. And, too, there was something a little unnerving about the two of them turning to each other and professing their love at that precise moment, as if doing so might have some sort of incantatory effect on the vehicle. So I didn't do anything until we got up a pretty decent head of silent steam and I heard the back wheels on the soft shoulder. By that time, putting the car in park had about the same effect as slamming into a tree, which we would have done in another three feet. For a moment we all just sat there, our back wheels well below the road, the front ones on the outer edge of the shoulder in launch position, looking at patches of dusky blue through the treetops.

"We'd made it *very* near the top, you see," Mrs. Ward said to her quietly weeping daughter, as if reasonable people hadn't any right to anticipate a better result, really, since very few automobiles ever made it the entire way. She pointed toward the house, just now visible through the trees ahead, to illustrate her point. "And we were *very* fortunate to have your quick-thinking young friend in our midst."

Somehow I didn't feel like I was "in their midst," though I was certainly tagging along all right, and quite happily too, thoroughly full of myself, utterly content to consider that I *had* saved the day, and only vaguely troubled to recollect that when I had finally lunged across the big Lincoln's front seat to throw the car in park, I had planted my left hand, for leverage, squarely in Mrs. Ward's crotch.

"And the car is totally without damage, you see, so there is no reason for concern or alarm on the part of anyone."

I was unclear whether this last was to reassure her daughter or to anticipate an unfair response on the part of Jack Ward, who, at that precise moment, appeared on the patio and discovered us, three abreast, entering between the stone pillars at the far end of the oblong drive. He came toward us at a strange gait, as if he wanted to run, but knew he wasn't supposed to. With all due respect to Mrs. Ward's confidently uninformed opinion, I doubted the Lincoln was undamaged, at least if the grinding, then thunking noise it made when forced into park was any indication, but it *had* come to rest without hitting anything, and that, anyway, was a blessing.

"What's wrong? Where's the car?" Jack Ward wanted to know when he was close enough to inquire. He looked at us each in turn, spending a little more time with me, since my presence posed a second riddle he plainly hoped was unrelated to the first. Surely his wife and daughter hadn't traded in a new car on a used boy?

"In the woods, you see," said Hilda Ward. "Be a dear and fetch it."

"What's it doing in the woods? Who's this?"

"Resting," said his wife. "This young man happens to be our savior, if you want to know . . . if you can forget your beloved car for the moment."

"Saved you from what?" Jack Ward said. He stood before us now, hands on his hips, clearly frustrated at not getting the kind of information that genuinely illuminated.

"From Lord knows what," said Mrs. Ward. "Injury. Disfigurement. Death. Do you care?"

"Of course I bloody care. What do you think?"

"Well, then. That's gratifying. Do run along and get the car and let us catch our breath. Then, perhaps we'll tell you about it, since you care."

The woman's tone was halfway between mirth and malice, but Jack Ward seemed less puzzled by it than I. "Sweetheart?" he said to his daughter, and the lovely child buried her head in his shirt front. "Oh, Daddy!" she said.

"You run along with your father, dear. Show him where to find his beloved. He mightn't be able to locate it otherwise, you know. In the meantime, I'll entertain our savior."

And with that she took me by the hand—with her own cool and ever-so-dry hand—and led me toward the white jewel house.

* * *

"Something cool" turned out to be a layered green parfait in a glass shaped like a tulip. Mrs. Ward took me into a huge kitchen, where a short, heavyset woman was whaling away at an innocent piece of pale pink meat with a wooden hammer. She did not look happy to see us.

"This is Mrs. Petrie," Tria's mother told me with a wave of her hand in that woman's general direction. "Mrs. P., meet the young man who just saved our lives."

Mrs. P. looked like, if this happened by some strange chance to be true, she would have had me summarily strangled by way of reward.

"Do you imagine," Mrs. Ward went on, apparently unmoved by the other woman's murderous expression, "that something cool might be given him? Something ice cream, you know, or something soda? He could sit right here, I think, don't you?"

There was a large wooden island right in the center of the kitchen, and it was ringed on three sides by tall stools. Overhead, suspended from the ceiling, hung a wrought iron circle from which a dozen or so gleaming copper pots and pans in a variety of sizes hung. Mrs. Ward had directed me to a stool directly beneath a still dripping one.

"Quite a harrowing experience, actually," she told Mrs. Petrie, without the slightest intention, apparently, of going into detail. Which was probably just as well, since the other woman gave no evidence of the slightest curiosity. "But we have excellent cause to congratulate ourselves that no one was . . . you know. Such terrible things sometimes happen to people."

Mrs. Ward appeared to be searching her memory for an illustration, but apparently Drew Littler, who might have qualified, it seemed to me, had already vanished from her consciousness. When, after a fleeting moment, she couldn't think of anything terrible that ever happened to anyone, she gave up the project and remembered me. "Well now," she said, "enjoy your . . . you know, and. . . ."

And then she was gone, leaving me in the big kitchen with Mrs. Petrie, whose expression softened only slightly when the other woman disappeared. I got my parfait and a long-handled spoon to negotiate the tulip glass. Mrs. Petrie watched me eat the first mouthful, probably to see if I'd make a face, so I didn't. Actually, it tasted pretty good, especially the green minty part. While I ate, she whacked away at the meat until it was thin, then divided it into squares and placed these in a puddle of what smelled like vinegar. After wrapping the bowl in cellophane the whole thing went into the refrigerator.

"I hope she didn't expect me to stay here till you finish that," she said, though in truth I was only a spoonful from the bottom. "I was supposed to be home half an hour ago. I don't suppose it would ever occur to her that I might have a family of my own to cook for or that they get hungry about the same time as other people."

From where I was sitting, I had a view of the drive and I saw the Lincoln emerge from the trees and pass between the stone pillars. Jack Ward was at the wheel, Tria, white-faced, beside him.

Mrs. Petrie disappeared into a small room off the kitchen, then reappeared struggling into a lightweight raincoat. Her handbag she grabbed from atop the refrigerator. "I spect they'll be in in a minute," she said, "less they forget about you, which they might. There's a half dozen more of those in the freezer and nobody around here ever counts a blessed thing. Eat them all if you want. Keep the glasses. Take home anything you like."

I studied her in vain for signs of levity. Did she possess some bizarre second sight that had allowed her to size me up as a thief right off? I hoped not, because I had no intention of stealing anything from the Wards. In fact, I'd given up thieving forever, right there in the Ward kitchen. Life had taken a miraculous turn. Just a few short days before I hadn't been able to imagine ever seeing Tria Ward again, yet here I was eating out of a tulip glass *inside* the very house I'd studied from Myrtle Park and the rear end of Drew Littler's motorcycle. And I was a savior no less. Tria Ward's own personal savior. And she would be *my* savior, as well. She would reform me. Once we had professed our love for one another, I would confess how I had sneaked down into Klein's Department Store back when I was shiftless. She would want to pay it all back, of course, out of her own money, but I'd nix that. I myself would sneak down into the store once a week, slipping ten or twenty into the register until I was an honest man again. By then I would be of marriageable age. I formulated this whole scenario as I sat there beneath the dripping pot.

Outside I saw Jack Ward and his daughter emerge from the garage and from where I sat in the kitchen I got just a glimpse of Tria as she darted down the hall, where I heard a door open and close.

When her father spied me, he looked puzzled, as if he'd forgotten about me entirely. I stood up. "Sam Hall's boy, right?" he said.

I admitted it.

"Left you all alone, did they?" he looked around the kitchen.

I shrugged, as if to suggest that this did not matter.

"It happens around here," he said.

How strange I must have appeared to him, standing there at parade rest in the middle of his big kitchen, waiting for I knew not what. Something.

"There's a ball game on, probably," Jack Ward said, though there was no television in sight. "We could watch that."

I followed him out through the dining room into a smaller one that was walled with bookcases that rose right to the ceiling. Most of them were full of books, though some held expensive-looking knickknacks like the ones I'd stolen to spruce up our old house. I even recognized a piece or two, and I thought it strange that anybody would actually buy pewter goblets and cut glass owls and green bottles wrapped in leather.

There was a television in the corner of the room and Jack Ward turned it on, ripping through channels impatiently. When he didn't find a ball game, he turned it off again, though I'd have been happy to watch just about anything on a TV with no snow.

"You like to read?" he said.

I said I did. Very much.

He looked around the room with distaste. "Well," he said, letting the thought trail off. It was my father's word, but with Jack Ward, you could guess what direction his thought was headed. "Somebody'll be in in a minute," he said, without much confidence. And then he too was gone.

Maybe Jack Ward didn't care for it, but I was never more impressed with a room than I was with that one. I wasn't even sorry to be left alone in it for a while. It was tight and quiet and good smelling, a contrast to the big, drafty, echoing rooms I lived in with my father. Here each sound had only a moment's life before it disappeared into the carpet or the tall shelves full of heavy books. There was a stone fireplace along one wall, its polished wooden mantel lined with photographs. The majority of them were pictures of a young Mrs. Ward with a very slender older man who reminded me a little of the photographs of my grandfather my mother was always showing me when I was a little boy. I have examined these since, and the two men could not have looked more dissimilar, except for their exaggerated slenderness and a rather peculiarly erect carriage. But there was an uncanny resemblance between the young Mrs. Ward of the photographs and her daughter Tria, and I examined each photo for clues to the mother's transformation from young woman to mummy. There appeared to be no transition, however. In girlhood Mrs. Ward had been light, small, lovely, like Tria, though more pale; then suddenly she was a woman standing there beside the same man, who had appeared not to have aged at all, though his daughter had shrunken in upon herself. There were also pictures of Tria as a little girl, with those same anxious eyes, perched uncomfortably on her grandfather's lap. Jack Ward himself wasn't pictured anywhere.

Next to the stone fireplace was a bookcase unlike the others in that one whole shelf was empty except for a thick, leather-bound volume on a stand, opened to the middle, like the big dictionary in the Mohawk Free Library. At the top of each manuscript page was typed, in gray fading letters, "The History of Mohawk County," just to the right of the author's name—William Henry Smythe. Since there was nobody to tell me I shouldn't, I leafed through the brittle pages, discovering that there were nearly seven hundred, all in the same fading gray type. The manuscript was flanked by two red candles in squat gold holders, and the whole arrangement reminded me of the Monsignor's altar at Our Lady of Sorrows.

As I took all of this in, I became vaguely aware of voices in a remote part of the house. I had been alone in the room for quite some time, and when I opened the door and poked my head out into the dining room to see if anyone was around, the voices were louder. I recognized them as belonging to Mr. and Mrs. Ward, and they were coming from the bedroom farthest down the long corridor. Nearer me, halfway down the hall, the door Tria had disappeared behind was partially ajar, and it moved almost imperceptibly as I watched. When the voices stopped, it closed.

It took me a while to make it back down the road through the pitch-black trees, arms out in front of me like a blind man, with just the sound of the highway below and the feel of the blacktop

to go by. I emerged from the trees just as a car pulled up and let
my father out by the convertible. "What a crazy son of a bitch,"
he said when I got in. He was referring to Drew Littler, of course,
but for a moment I thought maybe he meant me for still being
right where he'd left me.

22

Among my entrepreneurial activities that summer, I salvaged
golf balls from the narrow pond that served as a hazard on the
thirteenth and fourteenth holes of the Mohawk Country Club. To
judge from its location, you wouldn't have thought it would come
into play on either hole, since each offered a wide fairway and
every opportunity to go around the water, but I doubted it could
have attracted more balls had it been twice as large and right in
front of the green. The more people faced away from the water,
stared off into the friendly fairway, the more surely their ball
would be destined for the pond. One afternoon before it had
occurred to me that I might retrieve the balls that were down
there, I sat on my bike for three hours and charted in my mind
where the tee shots dropped, growing more and more amazed at
the dense concentration of shots that ended up in the small strip
of water. It was enough to make you reconsider the wisdom of
deciding, on the outset of any human endeavor, that there was
this one thing you didn't want to do.

The country club raked the pond on Tuesday nights, reselling
the dredged-up balls as "used" the following week, priced according to the size and ugliness of the sneers cut into their dimpled
skins. Many were aerodynamically suspect, but perfectly acceptable as "water balls." People stocked up on them at fifteen cents
apiece and seemed almost happy to give them back to the pond.
It was easy to bid farewell to a yellowed ball that smiled up at you
from the tee.

Since the club conducted its weekly salvage on Tuesdays, I did mine on Mondays, sneaking onto the course around sundown, my gym bag stuffed with mask, snorkel, and flippers, all borrowed from the sporting goods department at Klein's. I also had a fishing net on a long pole, courtesy of Wussy, who'd jumped to the understandable conclusion that I'd be fishing for fish.

Dusk was not the ideal time of day to snorkel for golf balls, the low slanting rays of the sun producing only vague, ghostly light in the murky pond. Few balls on the weedy bottom showed up until I was right on top of them. Often they would not look like golf balls at all, but rather like brown boils in the sand. They hit the bottom with the force of a small explosion, burrowing out for themselves a small cavity in the silt, which would rise, then filter back down, covering the ball with a thin brown skin. I actually observed the process one evening when an errant tee shot narrowly missed me. As a rule I wouldn't ease myself into the pond until I was reasonably sure I wouldn't be interrupted. Mondays were usually slow, and I never started work until the fading light made golf impractical. I always checked out the two preceding holes before stripping down to my trunks and donning my snorkel.

On a good night I'd retrieve enough balls to fill Wussy's net at least once, though I was careful not to overfish the pond. I always left enough for the club's Tuesday night raking to avoid undue suspicion, though there must have been some anyway, especially when I set up shop just outside the club's main gate on Saturday mornings, underselling the pro shop markedly. My most expensive balls—unblemished Top-Flites and Titleists—I sold for thirty-five cents. Others I took what I could get for, learning the fine art of haggling with the drivers of shiny new cars who would pull off to the side and inspect my carefully arranged assortment, often grumbling over the quality of my eight-for-a-dollar specials and intimating that they might report my activities to the club management if I didn't throw in this or that sliced one as a gesture of goodwill, in as much as the buyer recognized it as his own to begin with, lost the previous week. I always gave in, often pretending that I was being cruelly taken advantage of, confident that come Monday evening the grinning Ben Hogan number 7 would be mine once more, and once again for sale.

Within a few weeks I was doing so well with this new enterprise that I could afford to cut in an associate, though I wouldn't have

done this had I not been scared into it. The bottom of the pond
was spooky enough, even under normal circumstances. Skim-
ming among the weeds, my mask mere inches from the inky
bottom, my fins stirring up black muck behind me, I didn't de-
pend on sight that much because experience taught me where
the balls congregated, the result of trajectory and the subtleties
of underwater physics. A blind kid could have gathered them,
which was good, because that was what I was in the parts of the
pond nearest the bank where the grass grew tall and the long
shadows of the trees bordering the fairways darkened the surface.
I quickly became a proficient snorkeler, able to stay down over
a minute at a time, then rising gently, just the snorkel itself breaking the smooth surface of the pond, releasing the rubber ball to
let the air in. Inevitably, some of the pond's brackish water got
into the tube, but I learned to expel it without swallowing too
much. Its taste was vile all the same and the duration of my
scavenging was determined as much by my ability to endure that
sour taste as by false or fading light or fear of discovery.

One evening, my net heavy with my dimpled catch, I became
conscious of having stayed in the pond longer than usual. One of
the things I worried about was forgetting about the time and
coming up out of the pond to pitch darkness, disoriented and
unable to locate my bike, which I always hid in the woods. Twice
I had nearly lingered too long and had located my gear by pure
chance in the darkness. The days were getting shorter now, and
I was suddenly certain that I had stayed in the pond too long and
that when I broke the surface it would be into an even darker
darkness. When I pushed hard toward the surface, my snorkel was
suddenly jammed down and wrenched out of my mouth, as if by
a large hand. Almost simultaneously my head rammed something
so hard and unyielding that it sent shivers of pain to the base of
my neck and shoulders. The shock drove the air from my straining lungs in an explosion of frantic bubbles.

My first conclusion was that I had somehow become confused
about which direction was up, that I had propelled myself into the
bank of the pond. This did not square with the direction my
escaping air bubbles were taking, however, which was the same
direction I had tried to go. Surely *they* knew which direction was
up. How was it, then, that the ground came to be above me?
There could be no doubt that it was the ground, especially after

my second desperate lunge, this time with my arms extended before me, my hands encountering a solid wall of dense clay. At that moment it seemed that there was only one certainty in the entire world—that I was about to die. Somehow, I had become the victim of the cruelest hoax ever played on mortal man. Each direction I turned I encountered that smooth hard clay which became for me that instant "down." There simply was no "up," and up was the only direction that would do me any good. And though it seems odd now that it should have occurred to me at the time, I remember distinctly the terrible feeling that I had been in precisely the same situation before, that first week after going to live with my father when I'd been trapped in the basement beneath Klein's. Then too my first reaction had been surprise, then panic, then an attempt at calm rationality. There had to be a button that would open the elevator door. To admit that maybe there wasn't was to admit the possibility of an irrational universe.

But in the basement of Klein's I had been able to breathe and with each terrified breath assure myself that though I could see no way out, in time I would be rescued. Now I had neither time nor air, and so of course I would die. And it would be my fault. Because even though everything had suddenly become irrational, there was a dark shape, a message even, to its insanity. I was about to die because I had not learned my lesson. I had gotten myself into another dark place, and this time no door would open, my father would not appear, no hand would yank me into light and air for the simple reason that there *was no up*. At least not for me.

And the truth is that if I'd had to figure it out in order to survive, I would have died there in that narrow black cave beneath the bank of the pond. I hadn't the presence of mind to solve the riddle, to see that if I'd swum into a situation where there was no up that the only solution was to *back* out. When forward, right, left, up, and down all yielded the same result, I simply gave up, shoving in blind rage against the earth before me, furious with it even as I surrendered to it. I stopped kicking with my fins, accepted the brackish water into my lungs and felt gentle sleep coming.

Then, miraculously, I was on the surface, my arms thrashing in the air, clawing, without any instruction from me, at the grassy bank. My last angry shove against mother earth, combined with my surrender and the end to my frantic webb-footed kicking, had floated me back out of the cave and into the world.

I was alive.

Willie Heinz was the first person I tapped to act as sentinel, though he didn't work out. For one thing, he was easily abstracted, and for another he was extremely stupid. Once I disappeared beneath the surface of the water, he forgot about me as completely as if I had never existed. While I was under, he amused himself by stoning jays that screamed obscenities down at us from the innermost branches of the dark fairway trees. Sometimes when I surfaced I'd see him tearing ass down the cart path throwing stones up into the dark limbs as fast as he could pick them up. He took all feathered insults with vicious good cheer, like a taunt from a friend on the other side of the school-yard fence, and bore down on the offending chatterers with murderous, though wildly inaccurate, intent. The other obvious problem with Willie Heinz as a lookout was that he couldn't swim, which meant that if I managed to get myself in trouble I was still on my own.

His uselessness notwithstanding, I'd have been happy enough for his vague, distant company if he'd done no worse than stone jays. In the end though, we couldn't agree on how to run the business. Willie Heinz was of the opinion that swimming in muck after lost golf balls was foolish when there were so many perfectly good ones right out there in the middle of the fairway. They sat right up in the dry grass and the people they belonged to were often two hundred yards away. Willie advocated allowing a four-some to hit, then collecting their drives while the players were still bagging their drivers and ribbing each other on the tee. There were several holes with doglegs and hills that provided excellent cover. You could dash out in the middle of the fairway, collect all four balls, and be back in the trees before a single pale blue golf hat appeared on the horizon. It was astonishing how long people would search up and down a wide open fairway, how willing they were to believe that all four shots had simply disappeared.

I tried my best to reason with him, to explain that this outright theft was ultimately bad for business, that the men in the shiny cars who pulled over to buy water balls from us on Saturday

mornings would not hesitate to turn us in if they ever suspected
that they were buying fairway balls hit straight and true, but I
could never get him to see it. What it came down to was my
personal belief that the men in the pale blue hats should pay for
their failures, whereas Willie Heinz perversely expected them to
pay for their successes, a more radical philosophical position, the
ramifications of which were scary to anybody who hadn't entirely
given up on the possibility of the odd success in life.

So, much as I hated to, I had to let Willie go. And just in time,
as it turned out. He was in business for himself only a few days
when he fell victim to a classic error in judgment. Spying a party
on the distant tee, he had positioned himself on the far side of a
hill that all the players had to drive past and awaited their offer-
ings. The first three hitters whistled shots out into the middle of
the fairway within thirty or forty yards of each other. Patiently,
Willie awaited the fourth crack of the driver, his signal to gather.
When it didn't come immediately, he did not alarm himself. The
worst player in any foursome would be hitting last and often these
took forever addressing the ball. He should have taken alarm
though, because the party on the tee had just become a three-
some after one of their number had proven too drunk to continue
after a long lunch in the clubhouse at the end of the front nine.
The remaining members of the foursome came over the hill not
on foot but in two carts, both barreling flat-out in a race. When
they cleared the rim of the hill the driver of the lead cart saw
Willie Heinz in time to swerve, but the second, in the wake of the
first and a tad slower for carrying two men, ran right over the boy
as he struggled to his feet. The impact propelled one rider out of
the cart. He inscribed a clean perfect arc and landed unhurt on
his haunches in the fairway. The driver of the second cart was also
pitched clear, leaving Willie alone with the vehicle, or rather
pinioned underneath it. The paper bag he'd been using to collect
balls had ruptured on impact and they now lay fanned out over
the hill. "Motherfucker!" Willie Heinz bellowed from beneath the
golf cart. "Motherfucker, motherfucker, motherfucker!"

Claude wasn't much of an improvement, though he was as
faithful to me as any mutt you'd ever save from starvation. At his
mother's insistence, he wore turtleneck sweaters to hide the
white scars left by the rope. Not that Claude wasn't amenable.
Since the afternoon he'd strung himself up from the ramada, he'd
become amenable to everything. Mostly he just sat in front of the

television, staring at it blankly, except for Ben Cartwright and
Bonanza, which struck some kind of chord within him and sometimes made him cry. Otherwise, he did whatever his mother told
him. If I came over to visit, he'd follow me out the door and down
the street. In the old days, the first thing he would have done was
trip me, or shove me in a snowbank, or declare a race after getting
a good four-step running lead. Now he just heeled to my command, abstracted, vague about whatever was on our (my) agenda.

The only thing that ever attracted his attention was a blue
Thunderbird. Whenever he saw one, Claude would want to follow or, if it was parked, wait beside it. His father had bought a new
one to replace the Pontiac station wagon just before his son's
attempted suicide and taken it with him when he abandoned
them a week or so after the doctors assured him and Mrs.
Schwartz that their son would live. It was a terrible irony that
blue Thunderbirds were popular that year. I knew of at least
three owned by people in Mohawk, and I always had a devil of
a time convincing Claude when he spotted one parked that he
shouldn't wait there by the curb for his father to come out.

Actually, Claude wasn't that bad a sentinel. He stationed himself on the fairway edge of the pond where he could see well in
both directions. When anyone approached the tee, he clapped
two flat rocks together underwater, an unmistakable, sometimes
earsplitting signal. Now and then he'd give the signal if he just got
lonesome for me, or lost track of my bubbles, or thought I'd been
down too long. He always looked enormously relieved when I
surfaced, as if he suspected that I had been visiting the same dark
place he had visited at the end of his rope. I think I may have been
the only person he told about it, what it had felt like. It was spooky
listening to him explain in half a dozen words with that hoarse
whisper his voice had become. For some reason, I had not imagined that he had gone blind there, but he said he had, almost
immediately, with his eyes wide open. Other than suffocation,
he'd felt no sensation, except in his toes, as if, even in his semicon-
scious state, something in him remembered that his life depended
on them. We never talked about why he had done it. I figured
he'd say, if he felt like it, without provocation, the way he'd rolled
down his turtleneck one day to show me. But he never did say
anything about his reasons, as if these might be even more hid-
eous than the livid white flesh.

To say that he was a changed boy would be less accurate than to suggest that the Claude who'd got me to barf Oreos died at the end of the rope that afternoon, leaving behind another person entirely, this one without defenses. He no longer cared to compete with me or anyone. There were no more arm wrestling contests, sprints or eating tournaments, no more sarcastic remarks about my being a wimp. When pretty girls were around he stared at them forlornly, his hands in his pockets, working there but somehow without conviction, as if he'd lost the capacity to imagine pleasure.

All in all, I preferred the old Claude, asshole though he had been. I doubt if I'd have befriended the new Claude if it hadn't been for his mother, who seemed to take my visits as personal favors, medicinal in their effect. In fact, she looked about as forlorn as her son, and she never asked questions about where we were going or where we'd been when we returned after dark. She either trusted me completely or had concluded that I was the least of the dangers her son faced. I don't think she ever discussed with anyone his attempted suicide or the sudden disappearance of Claude Sr. I'm not sure they even talked to each other. Whenever I visited, I never seemed to be interrupting anything, and I often got the feeling that there no longer *was* anything in that house to interrupt except silence. They often gave the appearance of having been watching each other for hours.

It finally dawned on me that Claude's mother was waiting for him to try it again, and that part of her gratitude to me for taking the boy away for a few hours was that the time he spent with me was the only time she could relax her vigilance, at least until school started in the fall. Often when we returned home, we'd find her deeply asleep in the big armchair that had been her husband's. It faced the kitchen door and she would not wake up if we entered quietly. Then Claude would take a seat and watch his mother sleep and breathe, though this was too spooky for me, and I'd have to leave. I always wanted to get away before she woke up and saw her son sitting there looking at her from across the dark room, across the wide chasm of his experience and her imagination.

23

My savings account continued to swell. Between the money I got from cleaning Rose's and the cash Harry slipped me on Fridays and the golf balls I sold on weekends, I was loaded. Life was good. After dinner at the Mohawk Grill, my father would shoot a rack of pool with me at the pool hall before heading out to The Elms or tracking down a poker game. I had an immediate passion for the game and before long I could shoot pretty well. Not well enough to beat my father, but pretty well. I'd have stayed there in the pool hall all night if I'd been allowed to. Around eight o'clock, however, the place would begin to get jammed and the crowd would get rougher and my father would put up our cues before things really got cooking and the sticks got used to settle disagreements. It was a rare night that did not generate at least one fight in the pool room, and while most of the combatants were either too drunk or too inept to hurt each other much, bystanders were sometimes mangled hideously. My father said if it was just him, he'd let me stay and shoot to my heart's content, but there was one thing he never wanted to do, and that was report to my mother that I'd been killed in the pool hall. I couldn't blame him for that.

He understood my passion though, and one Saturday afternoon when I returned from selling golf balls there was a pool table sitting in the middle of the apartment. My father was on his back, swearing up at its underbelly, trying to level the table through the sheer force of his obscenity. Wussy was there too, stretched out on the couch with a beer, clearly enjoying himself.

"Howdy, Sam's Kid," he said. "Come over here and watch this."

A wrench appeared, airborne, missing Wussy by a fair margin, but not the rabbit ears on the television, which clattered to the floor.

Wussy drained the rest of his beer, crushed the can, and

belched significantly. "When you finish with that," he said, "you can fix the TV."

"What's wrong with the TV?" came my father's voice from under the table.

"Nothing a master fixer like you couldn't handle," Wussy said.

"Get your black ass over here a minute. Lift this table."

Wussy ignored him. "Well, Sam's Kid, how's the golf ball business?"

That he knew about it was only mildly surprising. Wussy found out about most of what went on in Mohawk.

"I hear they nailed your associate," he said.

I decided to play dumb. "Who?"

"Who," Wussy said. "Willie Heinz, who. Ankle fractured in about nine places. Totaled a brand new golf cart. Who."

I poured myself a soda and handed Wussy another beer.

"You never heard of Willie Heinz, right?"

"If I have to come out from under this table—" my father said.

Wussy got up and lifted the big pool table effortlessly.

"Don't drop it, either," my father said.

"I should," Wussy said. "Solve all *your* problems, right Sam's Kid?"

"Cocksucker," my father muttered, apparently at the table. The legs were supposed to be adjustable.

"Tells me not to drop it and then calls me names," Wussy said.

After a minute, my father crawled out from underneath and Wussy set the table down. Anybody could see it was cockeyed, but my father refused to believe it. Wussy set a ball in the center of the table and it rolled right into the corner pocket. "Perfect," he said. "Shoot everything into that one."

"Cocksucker," my father said. Then he looked at me as if the whole thing was my fault. I could tell they'd been at it a while. "Every time I fix it, it's worse," my father admitted.

"Give up, why don't you," Wussy suggested. "Saw all four legs off, set the bastard on the floor. If the building don't slope, you're in business."

"Cocksucker," my father said.

"Lift it up a minute," Wussy said. He never would have suggested this an hour ago. He always let my father go ahead with whatever he was trying to do until there was something in the tone of his "cocksucker" that suggested he was ready for help. When Wussy disappeared under the table, my father winked at me. "Don't worry about a thing," he said. "I got a pretty fair grip on this thing. If it starts to go, I'll shout."

But Wussy was through already and when my father set the table down, it looked about right. Wussy took a ball from one of the leather pouches and set it in the middle of the table, where it stayed. Then my father rolled it slow and we all bent to watch its miraculously straight path to the green bumper.

"There," my father said, cuffing me. "You got a pool table. Don't tell your mother."

If ever there was an ideal place for a pool table, the Accounting Department was that place. The central cavernous room we lived in was far too large for us, the sofa and television taking up only a small portion, leaving the rest bare and conducive to lonely echoes. The table was a big tournament-sized one, but there was still plenty of room on all sides to circle and brandish a cue. The problem with pool tables outside of pool halls is that there's never really enough room to play. There's usually some basement post that makes one part of the table inaccessible, or a wall that's too close, requiring a short cue wielded at a sixty-degree angle. But our bowling alley of a flat was perfect.

The table itself was old, but in wonderful condition. I learned later that my father had had his eye on it for some time, ever since he learned that the man who owned it had gone into the hospital. The fellow's wife had always hated having the table in her home and was contemplating its disposal when my father, having read the obituary column in the *Mohawk Republican,* appeared in their long drive with a pickup truck offering to cart it off for free. The widow, who was on her way to the funeral, agreed to let my father take it, provided he could get it out of the house before she returned from the cemetery. She and her husband had argued over the table for years and he'd told her flatly that she'd get rid of it over his dead body. It was going to stay right the hell where it was until he was in the ground, he'd boasted, and it occurred to her now that if my father carted it off right away, it would rankle her husband in the afterlife.

That night, when we finished eating hamburg steaks at Harry's, my father pushed his plate away, studied me shrewdly and said, "Well?"

"It's a great table," I said, guessing wrong, as usual. "Thanks."

"Don't change the subject," he said. "What's this about you selling golf balls?"

Confronted so directly, there wasn't anything to do but tell him, so I did. I told him that during the week I scoured the woods that lined the fairways, that if I worked hard I could usually find a couple dozen balls there, that I didn't figure they belonged to anybody since their owners had stopped looking for them, that I was providing a public service by reselling them so cheap. What I told him had just the right amount of truth to it, enough to sound plausible, not enough to worry him. I didn't see where the woods were so different from the pond, or why the pro shop had any more right to sell other people's lost golf balls than I did. Not telling the truth about precisely how I came to have the balls actually clarified the legal and ethical issues, it seemed to me, and therefore it wasn't what a reasonable person would call lying. I knew I was vulnerable on the issue of being on the private golf course in the first place, but I didn't think my father would raise it. He was a born trespasser who believed he had a right to go anywhere he pleased in a free country. In his opinion, signs that warned people to keep out did their job by keeping *most* people out, and the owners of the said property hadn't a right to expect much more. Anybody that wanted *him* to stay out would have to tell him so personally.

Anyway, my fabric of lies and half-truths had the desired effect, though I made a mental note, after telling my father that I found the golf balls in the woods, to leave my snorkel and fins over at Claude's. He never asked me how much money I was making or what I did with it, so I was left to conclude that it didn't matter to him that I was becoming a wealthy man. I charged most of my lunches at Harry's and my father settled up each week, letting me keep whatever Harry slipped me for bussing and washing dishes during the rush. When he was working, Sam Hall cared nothing for money, or when it was likely to run out, or how much he'd spent the night before, or where. He paid his bills when he thought about it, then forgot and paid them again, or remembered paying them when he hadn't and offered to settle the matter outside. He kept no records.

All in all, I preferred his attitude toward money to my mother's. She had always watched it carefully, as if money possessed magical qualities, chief among them the ability to vanish. She had always planned her paychecks from the phone company a month in advance and she never forgot a bill or when it was due. She even had a category in her ledger for "unexpected"—the run nylon stocking, the school trip to the Albany museum, the frozen water pipe in February. When nothing unexpected happened in September, she assumed two unexpected things would crop up in October, and over the course of a calendar year, she had "unexpected" pegged to within a few small dollars. She always congratulated herself on the fact that she had nothing to worry about, and wouldn't have, as long as she continued to worry all the time.

Though I admired my father's nonchalance, his innocent faith that some fucking thing would give when it had to, I had to admit that I myself was more like my mother. I knew exactly what was in my savings account and I couldn't understand my father's unnatural lack of curiosity about my growing fortune. I had little faith in his "something's gotta give" philosophy about bad times, and I delighted as I watched my money accumulate, not out of any abstract fondness for wealth, but rather from the conviction that the day was approaching when my father and I would be very glad to have it, and from the fear that no matter how much I saved, when that dark day arrived, we were unlikely to have as much as we needed. Not one fucking thing would give, whether it had to or not.

So, when my father offered no objection, I continued to sell golf balls and even expanded my operation a little. Lying about finding balls in the woods gave me the idea that there might actually be some there, and it turned out that there were, though the pickings were slim in comparison with the pond. Still, come Saturday morning I always had between a hundred and two hundred balls for sale, and by Sunday noon I'd have another thirty or forty dollars for deposit. Plus the money from Rose's. Plus the money from Harry. I was a money-making machine.

Among my customers most Saturday mornings was Jack Ward, who always pulled the Lincoln over and got out, looking like an ad in a fashion magazine. When he was by himself, he seldom bought more than one or two of the best balls, which I took to be evidence of penury until I discovered he was one of the best golfers at the club. Sometimes, though, he had a young, blond-haired woman with him who talked him into buying her a half dozen or more. She was very pretty, with breasts that strained against the fabric of her shirt, but I didn't like her because she acted like a schoolgirl, talking what sounded like baby talk in a paper-thin voice. Right in front of Claude and me she'd slip her hand into Jack Ward's pocket and coo, "Buy me . . . , okaaay?" The "buy me" routine was a regular feature until one morning she noticed Claude off to the side, admiring her absently and playing with himself, his face more suggestive of infinite sadness than lust. The sight of him unhinged her and she stepped back quickly as if from a snake. "That's revolting," she said in her natural voice, which put her at about thirty, as opposed to the seventeen she'd been aping. I think she would have bolted for the safety of the Lincoln if her hand hadn't been caught in Jack Ward's pocket.

The second or third time he stopped, Jack Ward recognized me as someone he knew, someone who'd been in his house, though he seemed puzzled as to how that might have come about. I reminded him that it was I who had saved the day when his daughter had lost control of the car. He nodded then. "And only three hundred dollars worth of damage to the transmission, too."

"That's good," I replied seriously, imagining that this extravagant amount might actually constitute a good deal for repairs to a car as expensive as the Ward Lincoln, and not wanting to appear unworldly. Then I asked him whether they'd decided if Tria would be going to Mohawk High.

"She would be if it was up to me," he said in a way that suggested it wasn't up to him and that a lot of other things weren't up to him either. "Call her sometime," he suggested.

I did. That very afternoon. We didn't have a phone, so I had to do it from the Mohawk Grill. Mrs. Ward answered on the first ring, and when I identified myself she did not seem surprised. "She's gone, you see," Tria's mother informed me. "School starts early in Connecticut. In August, you see."

"Get fuckin' lucky, you jitbag!" Wussy bellowed from a few feet away, where he and my father were playing gin on the Formica counter.

For some reason, I was unable to hang up the phone. I talked and I refused to stop talking. I mentioned having run into Mrs. Ward's husband at the country club, intimated that our paths crossed there frequently, told her that he himself had suggested that I call. I asked after her own health and told her I was glad the Lincoln was all right now. I believe I even inquired after Mrs. Petrie, the cook, and asked to be remembered to her. All this I

said, my back to the counter and the card players, my hand partially cupped over the mouthpiece. I don't know what I was thinking. I'm not sure I believed that Tria was gone. Wouldn't her own
father have known? But maybe he did. Maybe that was why he'd
urged me to call, like telling someone to call you on Monday when
you know you'll be out of town. I think what I wanted from Mrs.
Ward was for her to consider me worthy. Hadn't I once been
thought worthy? Hadn't she referred to me as their savior? Was
it possible that I had slipped so far, so suddenly, in her estimation?
Would I ever get another invitation to join them for something
cool?

"There!" Wussy said. "Gin, you bastard."

"It must be Dummy Day," I heard my father say.

I have heard expressed more than once a theory that claims a
direct relationship between skill at pocket billiards and a corre-
sponding lack of skill in matters sexual. I lean toward the theory,
especially if you happen to be talking about adolescents. In Mohawk, all the best pool shooters had reputations as ladies' men, but
I could never see where these reputations were earned or deserved. There was the general sense that guys who hung around
the pool hall were men of the world, and stories of conquest travel
even better over green felt than calm water. But I never knew
back then, nor do I know now, a real stud with a pool cue who
could carry on a normal conversation with a woman.

I'm not talking about the sort of player who shoots well enough
not to embarrass himself, who can make the occasional bank shot
and still leave himself in position for the eight. I mean the guys
who can do real magic, the ones who can't find a game without
leaving town and who leave town, often as not, in a hurry, their
underwear still in a drawer at the Y.M.C.A., custom pool cue in

its case tucked neatly under one arm. And I'm talking about that lower echelon of players who aspire to such an existence.

The ignorance of such men concerning women is peculiar, many of them having participated greedily in numerous obscenities, and feeling no compunction about dropping their trousers in the dark room above the pool hall for some toothless old woman hired off the street at a flat hourly rate who has no idea how long the line outside in the hallway is growing. Such men are sometimes adept at slipping quietly up the back stairs to a dingy third-floor flat where graveyard husbands dwell with bored young wives. But this is the extent of their experience.

I called Tria Ward just that once from the Mohawk Grill, and then I took up pool, a magic, hypnotic sport, a Freudian playground of balls, stiff rods, a variety of holes to approach from a variety of angles, all promissory, all destined to be filled, eventually, regardless of the shooters' skill. Don't take my word for it. Watch a foursome of thirteen-year-olds around a pool table in somebody's basement. See how long it takes one of them to see the cue as a makeshift prick, placed proudly between the legs and waved around to the detriment of lamps and wall hangings. No thirteen-year-old sharpie is ever content to just sink a shot, he's got to ram it into the pocket manfully. He'd rather miss altogether, sending the ball skittering along the concrete floor, than have it roll harmlessly up to the precipice, quiver there a moment before giving in to gravity.

No thirteen-year-old but me, that is. For this is precisely the game I learned to play on the table my father and Wussy set up in our living room. After the Mohawk Fair in September, the chill winds my grandfather had known so well made a memory of the summer of 1960. It was then too cold to dive for golf balls or hang out at the Sacandaga Marine. I entered eighth grade, my last at Nathan Littler Junior High. When school got out I went home and shot rack after rack of pool feeling peaceful and glad. Sometimes I let Claude come with me because he had become even more of an object of ridicule after it became widely known why he always wore turtlenecks and talked in a hoarse whisper. He shot pool like he did everything else now, listlessly, expecting defeat, ensuring it by not concentrating or missing on purpose (no one could really have been so bad) on those rare occasions when he found himself in a position to win. Not only was I far too good for Claude, I was becoming too good for almost everybody, including my father, an indifferent pool shooter who could never keep his mind on the game, sometimes could not remember whose turn it was, having been lured into a nearby conversation at the bar. He was a little better when he played for money, but not much. After a while I could beat him easily, though I seldom did, afraid that he would intuit from my growing mastery that I was neglecting my studies, which I was. I continued to read voraciously, almost everything except that which had been assigned, and years later I was told that I occasioned many an argument among my teachers, some of whom claimed I was a brilliant underachiever, others that I was just another homegrown militant moron. I don't remember coming to any conclusion about my teachers at all.

Pool I thought about constantly, seeing in my mind's eye during civics class the brightly colored balls rolling straight and true over green felt. I played hundreds of imaginary games, mapping strategies, examining contingencies, discovering character flaws and weaknesses in my imaginary competitors. I stopped playing in public, not wanting anybody to know how good I was getting, but playing sometimes into the early morning hours when my father stayed out, bolting for bed only when I heard him coming on the stairs below. I had no goal in mind, no plan to check my progress by playing local studs, no need to boast. Playing was enough, and the table drew me like a beautiful woman, satisfying me, I'm ashamed to admit, completely.

When the old woman who had let my father and Wussy cart off the table died a few short months after her husband and the beneficiaries to her estate discovered the table missing, they tried to force my father to give it back, claiming he had duped a senile old woman into believing the table worthless. They believed it to be worth upwards of a thousand dollars. My father told them they could go fuck themselves, then hired F. William Peterson to tell them the same thing, later refusing to pay the lawyer's fee. I don't know what I would have done if I'd had to surrender the table. Tria Ward, away at a private girl's school in New England, I thought about seldom, and as the long gray Mohawk winter settled in, my world was lit by the hot bare bulb that dangled from the high ceiling directly above the table's smooth green lawn and buffed mahogany.

That winter promised to be nip and tuck, like all my father's winters. He got himself laid off, as was his custom, around Thanks-

giving and signed up for unemployment the next day. After a few
weeks the checks started coming and it looked like we'd be all
right until spring. I *knew* I would, but my father was always a
question mark because his habits never changed, even when his
income did. If anything, not working was the double whammy
where Sam Hall was concerned, because he not only didn't have
as much money, but even more time to discover uses for it. Once
the leather shops started laying off after the holidays he didn't
have to go looking for a poker game. They were everywhere, the
only visible sign of a fluid economy in town, if you didn't count
the half-dozen downtown gin mills and the Mohawk Grill, where
Harry sold little but coffee, though he sold a great deal of that at
a dime-a-cup clear profit. Most of the stores along Main closed at
two or three in the afternoon on weekdays to conserve heat, and
the snowbanks grew so high that only the heads of people on the
opposite side of the street were visible. My father's convertible,
its rag top up for the season, he refused to park anywhere except
in front of Klein's, and he left it at increasingly crazy angles, the
passenger-side wheels two or three feet higher up the bank than
those on the driver's side. One night in January there was a thaw
and when we came down to the street in the morning a crowd
was gathered around my father's car, which was balanced precariously atop a fire hydrant that had been invisible beneath the
snowbank the night before when my father had come home. It
was barely visible even now, its yellow top wedged in behind the
convertible's right front wheel. By that night we were famous, a
picture of the car gracing the front page of the *Mohawk Republican.* My father had me stand next to the convertible with my arm
extended, so that it looked for all the world like I was holding the
car up with one hand.

For a while he tended bar at The Elms on weekends and Mike's
night off, but then he stopped doing that and we didn't go out
there for a while. During the winter Mike's business tailed off
because people hated getting stranded way the hell and gone out
there, two whole miles from Mohawk, when they could just as
easily get stranded at Greenie's or some other place in town. I
suspected, however, that the real reason was that my father and
Eileen were on the outs. The only thing he would say about it was
that he couldn't take being around Numb Nuts. There had to be
more to it, though, because Drew Littler was seldom home. Since
wrecking his bike, he'd turned eighteen and dropped out of
school and become even more morose, hanging out at the pool

hall all hours where he bragged about knowing how to hot-wire cars whenever he needed transportation. He was theoretically saving up for a new bike by shoveling snow and doing odd jobs that, according to my father, even a dummy couldn't fuck up. He didn't have much luck though, even with foolproof employment. When my father got him a job shoveling out the parking lot of a hardware store over on Union, Drew threw a shovelful of hard-packed snow through the second-story window and got canned.

That night Eileen met the three of us (Wussy was along) at the back door on our way in. Drew was at the small kitchen table eating a long Italian roll he'd stuffed with ham and cheese and everything else he could find in the refrigerator.

"Don't start on him," Eileen warned my father.

But my father had been steaming ever since he'd heard, and there was no stopping him, at least not right away. "Put that sandwich down a minute," he said. "I want to talk to you."

Drew kept eating.

"First-floor window I can see," my father said, standing over the boy. "A mistake. A dumb mistake, but . . . a mistake. Dumb for anybody else, normal for you. But how the fuck could you throw a block of ice through the second-floor window and sit there and tell me it was a mistake?"

"I didn't say nothin' to you," Drew said.

This was true. My father had been anticipating the exchange all the way over in the car, figured that Drew would claim it was an accident, but had forgotten to wait for the boy to say it.

"You're telling me you did it on purpose? You threw a block of ice through a window on purpose?"

"I ain't telling you shit," Drew said.

"I wouldn't either," Wussy said. "I wouldn't explain to nobody who parks on top of fire hydrants."

"Bullshit," my father said, surprised by Wussy's disloyalty, despite its predictability.

"Bullshit yourself," Wussy said. "Anybody didn't know better would swear he was your kid brother."

My father looked at each of them, saw that he was clearly outnumbered, shook his head and went back outside. In a minute we heard him shout, so we all crowded at the window to see what was up. He was standing in the middle of the drive and he had a shovelful of snow, which I thought for a minute he was going to toss at us. Instead he flipped it gently to the top of the snowbank. "I'll do it once more, Zero," he said. "Watch carefully. Even you can master this."

One afternoon in early March, when the snow had turned as gray as the low sky and the weathered buildings along Main, I came home from school and was surprised to find the apartment empty. My father's Mercury, more rust than metal after the severe winter, was parked at the curb out front. Lately, my father had taken to falling asleep on the sofa in the afternoons after long nights at the poker table, snorting guiltily awake when I came in, professing surprise to have drifted off, even though it was pretty obvious that he had "drifted" off several hours earlier. Today, though, I had the place to myself. I shot a few racks of pool waiting for him to show up, pretty sure he would because the car was down there in the street.

Shortly after five Rose stuck her head in and regarded me suspiciously. She left the salon the same time every day, her red hair a wine-colored cloud through the frozen glass of the door. Her stopping was unusual. She usually slid an envelope with my pay under the door sometime on Monday; otherwise, I rarely saw her.

She looked the pool table over as if it confirmed her worst suspicions. "You okay?" she said.

I said I was, trying to think if there was some reason I wasn't supposed to be.

"Can you lock this door?" she said, twisting the knob.

"I guess," I said. "If anybody wanted to."

She studied me, reluctant, for some reason, to leave. I didn't think she was waiting for an invitation to shoot a rack of pool or I'd have asked her. "You ever see your mother?" she said finally.

"Sometimes," I said. In truth, it hadn't been since Christmas. I hated for people to ask that question because it always felt like an accusation. "She's in Schenectady."

"Where would you live if you didn't live here?"

"With him, I guess," I told her. "With my father. Wherever."

"You could live with me," she said. "I suppose. For a while."

It was clear that she had so little appetite for this prospect that I wondered why she'd bothered to give it voice. I told her thanks.

She was no sooner gone than I heard Wussy's lumbering approach on the stairs outside. "I suppose we should all be thankful this ain't no ten-story building," he said, kicking his boots off in the hall and leaving his down vest on the floor next to them. "How's things here in the Accounting Department?"

I said fine. My father had never bothered to scrape off the black letters stenciled on the door. It didn't bother either of us, or even seem strange anymore.

We shot a couple of racks of pool. Wussy was a pretty fair shooter, but I stayed right with him, winning more than I lost, a fact that did not appear to impress him particularly.

"Let's you and me go eat a hamburg steak, Sam's Kid."

It was dinner time all right and I was pretty hungry, but I said maybe I'd better wait for my father.

"We'll just be across the street," Wussy said. "Even Sam Hall could find us there without no trouble."

That was true, so I went along, still wondering where my father could be. The convertible hadn't moved and he wasn't in it asleep or anything because I checked. I half expected to see him at the counter in the Mohawk Grill, but he wasn't. Harry had a pretty good crowd and a waitress on the floor, but he came over to take our order personally.

"So?" he said.

"So," Wussy agreed.

Skinny Donovan was there, two stools down, snoring peacefully, his head on the counter, cowlick astir.

Wussy and I ordered hamburg steaks. People looked at us, went back to private conversations, their heads a little closer together. I began to feel spooked. I didn't mind eating dinner with Wussy, it wasn't that. Maybe it was just that the usually noisy diner was so quiet. We could hear Skinny's bottom lip flapping when he exhaled.

"You might not see your old man till later in the week," Wussy said when the food came, as if he hadn't wanted to open a conversation until he had a pretext for abandoning it. "He said for you to go out and stay with Eileen for a few days if you want."

"Do I have to?" I said, not wanting to ask the obvious question, not with the convertible sitting at the curb right across the street. I didn't have anything against staying with Eileen, but I didn't really want to. There had been other nights when my father hadn't come home, or came home so late that it didn't count as coming home, and I didn't mind staying alone in the apartment. I was going on fourteen, after all.

Wussy shrugged as if he wasn't sure whether or not I had to do something I didn't want to. "You got money?"

I said I did.

"Take this anyhow," he said, a folded twenty materializing from his flannel shirt pocket.

I said I was fine, really.

"Now you're finer," he said, stuffing the bill in my own shirt pocket. "Nothing could be finer. Than to be in Caroliner."

If things weren't strange enough, who should walk in right then but Eileen herself. She came right over and slipped onto the stool between me and Skinny Donovan, who gurgled but did not budge.

"So," she said. "You want to stay with me for a couple days?"

"Why?" I said. "I'm all right."

"Just till your father gets back?"

"Why?" I repeated.

"Why not?" Eileen said, trying to sound jovial.

I didn't feel jovial. There were too many people who knew something I didn't, and it was all too clear that they weren't going to tell me. It wasn't me, this time, either. Before, I had jumped to the wrong conclusion in the matter of my mother, but this was different. Then I had marveled at what great liars they all were, how well they'd concealed the truth. Now it turned out they were pretty pitiful at trying to pretend nothing was up.

"Do you have money?" Eileen wanted to know, bending down for her purse. If Wussy hadn't been there, I'd have said no. I was suddenly angry enough to take a hundred and spend it. There was my father's convertible sitting out there in the street, and here we all were talking about him as if he'd left town for the weekend. All I could think about was what must have happened. I saw the poker table, my father leaning forward to draw in the pot, somebody pushing a chair back and standing up, like in westerns. Or somebody else raking in the pot and my father standing up. Somebody pulling a gun.

Of course there were all sorts of places he could be. He could be in Las Vegas with Mike. They had gone before, gotten good and drunk and driven to the Albany airport. That made as much sense as anything, and it accounted for the car being out front. They would've taken Mike's, and he wouldn't have wanted me to know where he was going, either. I tried to picture him and Mike shooting craps in a big casino, but my imagination refused to conjure the scene. Instead I kept seeing him in a hospital bed, tubes everywhere, beneath an oxygen tent.

Wussy paid for dinner and the three of us went outside, leaving Skinny where he was, with his head on the counter. The cold March wind tunneled up Main Street, and we hunched our shoulders against it. There was a light on in the living room of the Accounting Department. I remembered distinctly turning it off before we left. A shadow passed before the shaded window, then disappeared.

Neither Eileen nor Wussy appeared to notice. Eileen was still talking to me, trying to convince me to come stay with her. I didn't want to appear too anxious to get away from them, so I played it cool and just shrugged and waited for Eileen to get tired of talking to a blockhead. I saw the shadow three more times before Eileen observed that I couldn't be anybody's kid but Sam Hall's, and Wussy said, "So long, Sam's Kid. You know how to find me," which I did, more or less. Finally, I said I thought I'd just do some homework and go to bed, and they gave up and drove off.

About half a block up the street was a black Cadillac with big tail fins I'd never seen before, and I remembered the men who had come to Mohawk looking for my father years ago, and how he had hidden out until they left. I walked by the street entrance to our apartment and glanced in, then headed up the street, then back again, this time going in, quietly, so as not to rattle the glass. The shadow I'd seen in our apartment hadn't looked like my father's. It hadn't moved right, but I couldn't be sure. At the first landing I leaned over the rail and peered up into the darkness between the banisters. I didn't see any movement and the stairs were quiet except for the creaking that registered my own weight.

I fingered the keys in my pocket, recalling that I had one to Rose's. If I was quiet, I could slip in there, open the door a crack and wait to see who came out. Whoever it was couldn't stay in there forever. The more I thought about it, the more it seemed like a good plan.

I could tell her key by feel. The first thing Rose had done when she signed the lease was change all the locks, and her keys were different from the big, old-fashioned one that fit the door of the Accounting Department. On the other side of the frozen glass, whoever had let himself into our apartment was pacing, curiously unconcerned, it seemed to me, about the sound of his footfalls.

When I turned the key in Rose's door and the lock thunked audibly, the shadow in our apartment stopped pacing, but made no move toward the door. After a minute, it resumed again.

I don't know why I didn't duck into the salon. Maybe, in the back of my mind I was wondering why whoever was in our apartment had the light on. Somebody wanting to surprise my father would have left it off. And maybe the more I watched the figure pace, the more I listened to its impatient heavy footfalls, the more certain I was that I recognized it. (Lord knows I should have.) Leaving the door to Rose's ajar so that I could beat a retreat in there if I had to, I faced the door to our apartment and turned the brass knob.

Inside stood F. William Peterson.

25

Naturally, I blamed him. F. William Peterson was just the sort of person you took things out on if he happened to be handy. I remember understanding, when I saw him standing there in the middle of the room, why my father had beaten him up in the parking lot so many years ago. You'd kick him for the same reason you'd kick a faithful dog that didn't know any better than to keep its cold, wet nose out of your crotch when you'd had the kind of day that diminishes a human being's capacity for fundamental decency.

He had come to tell me what nobody else would, and I hated him even more blackly than the liars. Hated him for the way he sat me down as if I were a little boy and told me not to think badly of my father just because maybe he'd done something wrong, just because he was in jail. I hated him for making the news bearable, for reminding me that even good people sometimes did bad things. It didn't mean they didn't love us. That I shouldn't worry too much anyway, because if F. William Peterson was right, and he thought he was, things were going to start looking up for me very soon, and I didn't want to waste my time being depressed when I should be preparing for the good times. I could tell that he would have liked to put his arm around my shoulder like I was *his* son, though he must have guessed that I would have none of that. When he was finally finished, when there wasn't anything else he could think of to say and we were facing each other, I drove my hands deep into my pockets to prevent him from offering one of his.

"He'll tell you about it," F. William Peterson said. "He should be the one, not me. I don't think they'll be able to hold him more than forty-eight hours."

The card he left me, with his office and home phone numbers on it, I tore to shreds as soon as the door closed behind him. It reached the snowy sidewalk below before he did. A block and a half up Main Street was City Hall, which contained the jail where my father was. From the front windows of the Accounting Department you could just see it if you turned out the lights and put your nose to the dark, cold glass. In fact, because of the angle and the thickness of the glass, it looked right next door, close enough to touch.

If F. William Peterson imagined that my father was going to have a rough time explaining to me about why he'd been thrown in jail, he still had a lot to learn about my father. Much to everybody's surprise he was out the next day. I'd skipped school and spent the day here and there, imagining that strangers I passed on the street could tell by the look of me that my father was locked up. I came home about the same time I normally did and noticed that the Mercury wasn't sitting at the same angle in the snowbank, which meant that it had been driven and returned. Which meant that my father was a free man again. I found him right across the street drinking coffee at Harry's.

"Hello, Buster," he said when he looked up and saw me there. "You gonna sit down or what?"

I took the stool next to his. Tree was on the other side of him, looking hangdog. If he noticed me come in, or noticed my father notice, he made no sign. "I don't know," he kept saying. "I just w-w-wisht I knew what to do."

"Say hello to Tree," my father said. As I've mentioned, Sam

Hall wasn't much on introductions, but there were certain people he introduced me to all the time and could never be convinced, even when both parties protested, that we'd ever laid eyes on each other. I said hello to Tree because it was easier to go along and because Tree was just as likely to have forgotten me, in which case I'd be all alone in claiming prior acquaintance.

"I w-w-wisht I knew, Sammy. Honest to . . . Christ I do."

"I wish you did too, you pain in the ass," my father said. "I got a problem or two myself right this minute."

Tree began to cry. "Jesus," he said. "I know you do, Sammy. How do you think I feel asking. At a time like this, when you're up sh . . . it crick yourself. I just w-w-wisht I knew what else to do."

My father slipped him twenty.

"Jesus, Sammy," he said, crying harder now. "I don't know how to thank you."

"You could go away and let me talk to my kid a minute."

It was just the sort of suggestion that Tree was looking for, now that he had the money. You could tell. It was something he could do by way of repayment. "Y-you got it," he choked. "Anything. Y-you got it."

He got halfway to the door and remembered something and came back. "I just w-wisht I knew what to do," he told my father. "If I knew w-what to do, I'd be all right."

"I know, Tree," my father said. "You and everybody."

Finally, the door closed behind him.

"Wisht he knew what to do," Harry grumbled from way down the counter. "Anybody with half a nut could tell him what to do. Go home to his wife and kids and bring his paycheck with him. Once in a fuckin' while, anyhow."

"Love," my father said. "When he's got the bug, he's not himself."

"Bullshit," Harry said. "It's the only time he *is* himself. Problem is, he's got a shitty self."

"And no taste, to boot," my father said.

"Argh!" Harry concluded, spitting onto the surface of the hot grill, where the wet spot crackled, jumped, and disappeared. It was late afternoon and he'd be cleaning it in a few minutes anyway before the small dinner crowd came in wanting grilled rib steaks, on special today because they'd been in the cooler a while and were beginning to look as gray as the surface of the grill.

"So," my father said. "I guess you heard about my little prob-lem."

He ran his hand over the stubble on his chin as if the little problem he was going to tell me about was the loss of his razor.

"It'll get straightened out here pretty quick," he predicted. Since we had the place to ourselves, he got Harry to change a ten so we could play Liars.

"How do you know?" I said.

"Got to," he said. " 'Cause if I get screwed, some other people get it even worse. In another day or two they'll figure that out, if they haven't already. Once they do"—he lip-farted—"the whole thing disappears. It never happened even. That's all. Sim-ple."

"Simple," I said.

"You don't think so?"

"Sure," I said.

He had me down to my last bill already and wondering if I'd ever learn to play the game. I wondered if I'd be any better playing with my own money instead of his. Maybe not. Maybe I'd be worse.

"Wussy come by?"

I said he had. "We had hamburg steaks."

"He pay?"

I said he had.

"You could look all over hell and gone and never find a better one," he said absently. My father didn't object to the word "nig-ger," but he wouldn't use it on Wussy except when Wussy was there to hear it.

"Eileen came by too," I said, and before I thought, "and Mr. Peterson."

"And he told you where I was, right?"

I could have kicked myself. "He wanted to know if I needed anything, mostly. Eileen wanted me to stay with her," I added, hoping that this new subject would take.

"Funny the way he turns up," my father said, as if he consid-ered it genuinely curious.

I won two quick rounds while he thought about it.

"I like him," I said, though I hadn't the night before.

"You do," he said.

I shrugged.

"You know what?" he said.

"What?"

"I don't."

There was no point in asking him why, because if I did, he'd tell me and get himself all worked up in the process. Eventually he'd get around to his lawyer speech and it was a long one, absolutely to be avoided if possible.

"Let me tell you something about all these guys," my father said.

"Four sixes," I said, and settled in.

Blessedly, Eileen stopped in for a minute on the way to work, interrupting our Liars game and the lawyer speech. When she left, we ate some dinner and tried to get the Liars going again, though it was clear that neither of us felt much like it. Sitting there in Harry's for so long gave me the idea that maybe we were waiting for somebody, though I couldn't think who. Eventually, we left.

Out in the street a thaw had begun, the temperature having actually risen since late afternoon, and water was running beneath the gray snowbanks along the gutter.

"I wish I could have done it some other way," my father said, "but I had to let you help out."

"Help out how," I said, unaware that I'd done anything.

I had though.

"We'll get you straightened around, don't worry."

"Sure," I said. "Okay."

"I had that figured for your college," he said. "So you won't go through life a dummy."

The next day, on the noon hour, I cut lunch at school and ran downtown to the bank to find out how bad it was. My favorite teller got to break the news, and he looked pretty guilty explaining the bank's policy with regard to minors. I was wiped out.

In the end, things turned out pretty much the way he predicted, though it was years later, when I came back to Mohawk from the university, after a six-year absence, that I heard the story, overheard it in a bar actually, where my father was. I was the only one in the bar who'd never heard the story before.

"Simple. Anybody coulda done it. My son was all of twelve," he said, getting my age wrong, as usual (I was nearly fourteen), "and he coulda done it. The car's out back of City Hall, right there in the parking lot. Somebody gives you a set of keys and a map. Then you drive the car is all. You get to where you're going, you park the car, go sit in a bar and wait for your ride home."

Simple. You didn't know what was in the trunk and you didn't want to know. All you knew was that it was worth a couple hundred to somebody to have you drive it. If it was something really bad, it would have been worth a couple hundred more, so you're not that worried.

Simple, except that it had to snow like a bastard and he'd run into a roadblock at the entrance to the Thruway. Nobody was being let on without chains. My father had no idea whether there were chains in the trunk and wasn't about to open it and find out. Never mind, he told the trooper. I'll make the trip tomorrow.

It wasn't easy getting out of line at the Thruway entrance, but he'd have made it if not for the standard transmission, which he knew how to drive, but wasn't used to. Trying to pull away in third instead of first, he'd stalled, then couldn't get the engine to turn over. There was nothing to do then but sit there a few minutes and listen to the drivers behind him blow their horns. Nothing but roll down the window and give them all the finger. By the time he got the car started again, some of the drivers behind him had started to go around, and when he popped the car into gear it lurched forward just in time to clip the rear end of one of the passing cars, separating from its body the rear fender, which folded neatly and drove with an eerie screech up into the radiator fan of the car my father was driving, stalling him again. Even then, things might have been all right if the driver of yet another car, also trying to pass, hadn't seen the collision, braked himself into a skid and sluiced sideways through the fresh snow until he came to rest with a barely audible thump against the rear of my father's car. The impact was so slight that my father was not even sure he'd been hit, and the snow on the back window prevented him from seeing that the impact had popped his trunk open as cleanly as if a key had been inserted.

It had taken ten minutes to get everything straightened out. My father exchanged license numbers with the two other drivers, got the fender extracted from the radiator, chatted with a helpful young trooper and even offered to get him Giant football tickets. My father was about to drive off when the trooper said, "Not like that," and went over to close the trunk that my father, during the entire conversation, had not noticed yawning open like an invitation to the penitentiary. "Goodnight, Irene," my father said to the man he was swapping stories with, the irony, the tragedy of the whole escapade still fresh after a decade. So much for simple.

The good news was that my father knew enough about the whole deal to implicate a cop and suggest a thing or two about a couple of city councilmen. F. William Peterson handled the out-of-court negotiations skillfully and in the end my father was convicted of a misdemeanor and given a suspended sentence. Charges of transporting stolen property were dropped, and it was entered into the record that the contraband had been placed in the trunk of the car my father was driving by unknown, mysterious forces. He was even slipped a little something by the prosecuting attorney to help with the fine, and the men my father had protected slipped him a little something more for being a sport about spending the night in jail.

"I been there before," he shrugged, but admitted that the money would come in handy, since he was already mired in the lowest depths of the insurance risk pool and the accident was going to play hell with his rates. "I don't give a shit about me," he explained, "but I got a kid to support."

Losing my savings served me right, I had to admit. Having myself stolen, I considered myself, with some justification, a thief. And if there was some sort of cosmic accounting (did we not live in the Accounting Department?) at work in the universe, then I wasn't square yet, for while I had never totaled up all that I'd copped from Klein's I knew it had to be more than the four hundred dollars my father used to extricate himself from his "little problem" and never gotten around to paying back. Not only that, I knew I didn't have much cause to be miffed at him, because he paid for a lot of things, like my tab over at Harry's.

What got me thinking and worrying, though, was that he had apparently known about my savings account all along. I wondered if he was surprised when he got out of jail and found out how much I had, or if he'd been monitoring my progress all along. One thing was clear—he had been way ahead of me, like always. He'd known and he'd not let on that he knew.

And it wasn't like I'd never been warned. According to my

mother, Sam Hall had always been slippery with money. After the war, during that first frantic year when they were going to the track all summer long, she'd leave him in line at the two-dollar window and visit the ladies' room. When she came out, he'd be just finishing up and he'd hand her the tickets to keep warm when they got back to their seats. When the race was over and the two or three tickets my mother held were officially worthless, he'd say not to worry, he'd held on to the winning ticket himself. And there between his thumb and forefinger would be a ten-dollar winner.

The way such tickets occasionally materialized did not have the reassuring effect on my mother that he might have hoped, however, because she was smart enough to realize that the ticket's existence had broader, unsettling implications. Somehow, she realized, my father had slipped out of the two-dollar line in favor of the always shorter ten-dollar one, then returned to where she'd left him so she wouldn't be suspicious. She discovered that in addition to the pocket that held the tickets he admitted to, my father had other pockets, and these sometimes contained larger wagers she was kept ignorant of, which meant that she never knew where they stood. On a night when they appeared to be winning, according to the tickets he let her cash, my father's other pockets might be bulging with losing tickets.

She tried to regulate how much money they brought to the track so that she'd know when it was gone, but often he would have more than he admitted when they left the house and he sometimes borrowed from friends once there. Putting the touch on people was something he was so adept at that the transaction was sometimes accomplished right under her nose without her suspecting a thing until later when she made him explain how they'd lost so much. The more she tried to keep tabs, the more sneaky my father became until, in the end, the track lost its appeal for her and she stopped accompanying him, which disappointed my father greatly. She wasn't able to make him understand that she never knew which horse to root for, because she never knew where their real money rode. "I want you to tell me everything," she insisted. "If you keep things from me, I'm lost. *We're* lost."

I don't know what his response to that was, but I can guess what his solution would have been. He would have wanted her to join him in the game—to have something secreted away in the inside pocket of her own blazer, something to surprise *him* with. You see, what I worried about most after he'd wiped me out was, ironically, what he must have thought of me for keeping my money a secret from him, or trying to. At the very least, he must have concluded that I did not trust his judgment, which of course was true, though hardly the inference I would have wished him to draw. But now I don't think that ever occurred to him, or if it did, I don't think he minded my reluctance to confide. And I don't think it would have pleased him for me to be so foolish as to trust him completely.

I had the good sense not to dwell on my misfortune or consider myself unlucky. The A&P, along with one of the seven remaining glove shops, had closed permanently that winter, putting another fifty or so men out of work and making the Mohawk Grill even more crowded with dejected coffee drinkers. My father would be going back to work on the road soon, and I was still employed. I kept my old savings account and continued to add to it. Ten dollars a week. The rest I put in a new savings account in a small bank way out by the marina and made sure they sent us no monthly statement.

When the weather started warming up and the streets began to run wet with water from the still high snowbanks, there was nobody to tell me not to get my bike out and ride around Mohawk, so I did. Riding the bike felt both good and bad. Good, because it made me the envy of all the younger kids who upon seeing me went home to beg their sensible parents to haul their bikes up out of the cellar, to no avail, for another month or so. Good also because there are few things better than riding a bike after a long winter. A bicycle promises spring as surely as the hollowing out of melting snowbanks, the return of song birds, the first bright tulip bud. Still, there was something wrong with the bike that year. During the winter months it had occurred to me that a car was more suitable transportation for someone like myself, who'd be entering Mohawk High in September, and it occurred to me well after the fact that the money my father took was money I had been saving for a car. My father wasn't just a thief, he was a car thief.

So was Drew Littler, I discovered. The only reason I knew was that he asked me if I wanted to be one too. The idea was to sneak over to Kings Road where the expensive houses were, hot-wire somebody's Cadillac, take it for a joy ride, and then park it in the Mohawk River. It was part of a new, intensified, comprehensive "Screw the Money People" campaign he had in mind. Swiping and/or destroying their transportation was a form of vengeance that particularly appealed to Drew since losing his motorcycle, and he bragged to me one day that he and Willie Heinz had already driven half a dozen cars into the Mohawk and watched them float off toward Albany.

He had in mind to get himself another bike, a Harley he had all picked out, as soon as he could convince his mother to sign for it. The owners were willing to let it go for a song, too, their own son having been thrown from it and killed, and his memory still fresh in their minds. Once Drew had convinced them that the bike wasn't right after the wreck and probably never would be, they'd settled on a figure and he'd gone home to find the down payment. The first hundred he found in the top drawer of his mother's bureau. Then he went looking for my father.

"Sure," my father said when Drew Littler slid onto a stool next to him at the Mohawk Grill, interrupting our supper. "I'd love to loan three hundred dollars to somebody dumb enough to throw a shovelful of ice through a second-story window."

"Come on, Sammy, I'm asking you."

"Not really," my father said. "Because you're not stupid enough to think I'd give it to you. And even if I *was* stupid enough, your mother'd never go for it. You just *think* you're asking me."

Drew fished in his jeans pocket. "If she don't want me to have it, how come she just gave me a hundred dollars for a down payment."

My father never even stopped eating. Neither did he look at the money. "Let me get this straight," he said, carving a fatty piece of rib steak away from the bone. "You want me to believe your mother gave you a hundred dollars toward a motorcycle?"

"You want to bet she didn't?" he said. He put a pretty good face on, too. I don't think I'd have called him. But my father apparently saw the lie even in his peripheral vision, and before the boy could stuff the money back in his pocket he grabbed the bills and handed the wad to Untemeyer, who was seated two stools down, his customary spot at the end of the lunch counter.

"Hey!" Drew Littler said, looking at the bookie so ferociously that the blood drained from the old man's face.

"Hey, your ass," my father said, getting the boy's attention back. "If your mother gave you that hundred dollars, I'll give you another five hundred. In fact, if you even came by that money honestly, I'll give you another five. We find out you didn't, I put the money in my pocket. We can call your mother right now."

"She's at work," the boy said, so feebly that even I knew he'd been lying now. It was all over his face.

"I know the number. Meyer here can call. I won't even say a word."

"I got a better idea," Drew Littler said. "I give you ten seconds to give me back that hundred or I break your face."

"Whose?" Untemeyer said, handing over the money. "His or mine?"

"Nobody's," Harry said without turning around. "Go down to the pool room if you gotta fight. Kill each other, for all I care. Just not here."

26

With Claude at Mohawk High and me in the junior high, I seldom saw him that winter. All things considered, he wasn't treated that badly. True, some kids made choking noises when they passed the table that he had all to himself in the cafeteria, but they seldom got much closer or became truly abusive. No one wanted the responsibility of being personally acquainted with someone who'd tried to kill himself. About the cruelest thing was done by the principal of Mohawk High who, without being petitioned, excused Claude from his gym class requirement, an exemption granted only in cases of severe handicap. Not taking gym pretty much completed Claude's ostracism.

Not that he minded so very much. He'd taken to drawing elaborate, baroque dinosaurs in his spiral notebooks, and these appeared to satisfy him. No one, including his teachers, bothered to discuss his dinosaurs or anything else with him and he told me he didn't mind school at all now that he was never called upon in class.

Sometimes, if my father wasn't around and nothing was doing at the diner and I was bored with shooting pool by myself in the Accounting Department, I'd get on my bike and head over to Claude's and spend an uncomfortable hour with him and his mother. Their property was beginning to show the effects of the weather and Claude Sr.'s desertion. The rusted gas barbecue in the backyard tilted crazily, snow having been plowed up against it. Nobody had bothered to straighten the bowed crossbeam of the ramada after Claude hanged himself from it, and a fissure now ran the length of the empty in-ground pool. The house itself, though I couldn't put my finger on anything wrong with it, also seemed different. It smelled like no one lived there, the way my mother's house had smelled the day I'd broken in to furnish it with knickknacks from Klein's.

Whenever I turned up, Claude would have something he wanted me to examine, something he thought was pretty cool. Usually, he'd just hand me whatever it was without preface, as if he didn't want to bias my judgment by alerting me to whatever I was supposed to appreciate. Sometimes it would be a comic strip, or a magazine article, a weird marble from his father's collection, or one of his better dinosaurs. He liked watching me as I examined whatever it was. Claude had a wonderful eye for typos, the most amusing of which he always cut out and saved for me. Our favorite was from the *Mohawk Republican*, which reported the conviction of an Amsterdam man for "Rape," it said. "Three cunts."

Most of the curiosities Claude showed me did contain something pretty interesting, if you looked long enough, but it was Claude's facility at spotting them that was fascinating. Once he showed me a full-page color ad for Kentucky bourbon he'd torn from a magazine, handing me a magnifying glass, as if to suggest that, of course, I would want to examine it closely. The ad pictured a country road bordered on both sides by tall dark trees and just inside them a white fence, the kind used to border horse pastures. There was a pheasant in the foreground, and way down the road where the dark line of trees converged, was an oncoming car, an old Model T it looked like, though I couldn't tell for sure, even with the magnifying glass. But that wasn't what he'd wanted me to look at anyway. Finally, he moved my hand and the magnifying glass to a large bush in the left foreground, partially obscured by the pheasant. But beneath the bush was what looked like a child's lifeless hand, palm up. The density of the bush made it impossible to make out anything else, but the more I looked at it, the more certain I became that the hand was real, not some doll's hand.

It was Claude who finally folded the page carefully and put it away in a drawer.

"How?" I heard myself ask, and even now I'm not sure what I meant by the question. How had a dead child happened into a bourbon ad? How was it that nobody had noticed the hand and prevented the picture's publication? How had Claude himself first noticed, something virtually undetectable with the naked eye? How had he known to look with a magnifying glass?

One afternoon when I went to visit him and his mother, I had leaned my bike against the house and started inside when I heard an urgent tapping on glass. It was coming, I discovered, from the window of the house next door, where the dark curtains had parted sufficiently to accommodate Claude's round white face. Come around, he was motioning, to the back of the house.

He let me in through the screened porch and the kitchen, into a dark sitting room where the old woman I'd spoken to on the afternoon of Claude's attempted suicide was bent over a large stack of 78 rpm records that teetered against the biggest cherry Victrola I'd ever seen. Its turntable, which folded up into the rich cabinet's innards when not in use, now lay flat on a hinged door and was spinning noisily, awaiting a record. The speakers crackled and buzzed horribly, as if the idle needle were picking up energy and sound from the atmosphere.

Around the room stood several other equally massive pieces of furniture—a credenza, a library table, and an oak secretary—along with a sofa, love seat, and chair, each sporting an identically faded pink floral pattern. With the curtains drawn, the only light was from an old lamp with an opaque shade. Claude was beaming, as if to say, *Pretty interesting, huh?*

"The friend!" the old woman, whose name I later remembered was Agajanian, exclaimed when she noticed me. Arising lightly, as if she were filled with feathers, she was apparently delighted to see me, as if my arrival were long awaited. The old woman's hair, as faded as the furniture, was wild, clamped down here and there by black bobby pins to ghastly effect, as if her hairdresser were a cruel child. The old woman was terribly thin, and her gray housedress was cinched at a waist not much larger than one of Claude's thighs. "Please!" she cried, gesticulating wildly. "Have a seat. Do!"

The love seat was right there, so I sat, but it was the wrong thing. "There!" she gasped. "Now you've sat right on top of Ralph, and he's been cleaning those disgusting fish all day!"

I looked over at Claude, who was beside himself with delight.

"Baking soda!" Mrs. Agajanian said. "Tell your mother as soon as you get home. Nothing like baking soda to get out fish stink."

I promised I would, but she kept right on glaring at me until I slid over onto the other cushion and off the lap of the invisible Ralph. She found the record she'd been looking for and slipped it onto the turntable, which hissed even more ferociously now. I braced myself for the inevitable blast, but when the needle touched the surface of the spinning record, the terrible background noise vanished utterly. The music that replaced it was an instrumental arrangement of "September." Mrs. Agajanian listened to a strain, then did a fluid waltz move that culminated with the old woman landing gracefully in the center of her armchair.

"This was my husband's personal favorite," she said. "His name was Byron and he was a terrible queer, though he never told me until just before he died. Out of consideration for my feelings, he said. Anybody can believe that that wants to."

The old woman glared at me to see if I wanted to.

"I'm a Christian woman, of course, and not the sort to abide faggotry of any description. He kept his secret until he was ready to die and there wasn't anything I could do to him. He was clever about things."

She had a glass of something on the end table beside her and she took a sip from it.

"God's got him now, so it doesn't matter."

When "September" finished she put on another record. "Saber Dance," she said. "The S.O.B. liked this one, too."

We listened to the whole thing, the old woman tapping her foot to the increasingly frenzied beat, her hair even wilder now. I kept expecting the bobby pins to come loose and ping across the room at me and Ralph, whom I remained conscious of now, invisible or not. Ralph was her son, I discovered, and his refusal to quit cleaning fish when they had company his mother considered unreasonable. "I don't see why everyone should be made uncomfortable just so you can show off," she said to the cushion next to me.

I was pretty relieved to learn there were only the four of us in the room, because I had feared there might be more. There weren't, so I began to relax a bit. After all, Ralph was occupied with his fish and no trouble at all except for the smell. She read him the riot act about that and the fact that they were always knee-deep in scales, then went back to her husband, Byron. "I was always a sucker for tall men," she admitted, and Byron had been tall and always neatly dressed in dark pinstriped suits. His dark beady eyes should have tipped her off, but they didn't. She hadn't discovered he wore a toupee until after his death. "Don't ask me how I found out," she said.

When I asked her how come she played all his favorite records if she hated him so much, she explained that never once in their thirty-odd years together had he ever let her buy a record *she* wanted, which meant that if she felt like music, well this was it. She didn't mind the music so much, she just hated the memories.

"So," she said. "Tell me about your girlfriends."

I was willing to let Claude go first, or even Ralph for that matter, but the old woman was glaring right at me. I didn't want to admit the truth—that I hadn't a girlfriend—for fear that the admission would be seen as evidence that I was destined for a life of faggotry like Byron. "There's this one girl . . ." I began, thinking about Tria Ward and getting ready to describe her if need be.

"Good!" the old woman thundered, looking over at Claude now, as if to suggest that he listen up, that mine was an example worth following. She seemed completely satisfied with my flat statement that there was a girl, as if she were quite capable of filling in the details. And indeed she slipped right into a reverie, a snockered smile spreading across her face, as she rocked gently, back and forth, in a chair that didn't. In a few short moments she was fast asleep, leaving Claude and me alone with Ralph.

When the old woman began to snore, Claude went over and covered her with a heavy quilt that lay over one arm of the sofa. In back of the chair he found a bottle and held it up so I could see. It was bourbon, the same brand as the one in the magazine ad. His eyes were alive with significance.

For a minute the two of us stood there, watching Mrs. Agajanian's narrow chest rise and fall gently beneath the quilt. I think we both feared that her breathing would stop right then with the two of us standing over her ghoulishly.

We slipped quietly out the back and went over to Claude's house. According to Claude's mother, Mrs. Agajanian was all alone in the world and was subject to "spells." She had no son named Ralph, never a husband, homosexual or otherwise. She was living in the house she'd grown up in, visited by her doctor, who wrote her prescriptions for the spells.

Mrs. Agajanian's nap must have been pretty short, because half an hour later, when I was ready to head back to the diner for my five o'clock rendezvous with my father, I heard a light rapping on the window, and there she was, her white face right up against the glass, faded hair ringing it like a thundercloud. It sounded like she had the Victrola on again, and she did the waltz move, the heavy curtains coming together as she spun away.

27

My father liked to wait until he was sure winter was finished before he went back to work on the road. That meant May, even when spring came in April. This year, though, he went back to work at the end of March. The reason he gave was that he owed me money, and for a while I thought I might get it back, or part of it. But, like the previous winter, we'd gotten behind a couple months rent and we owed Harry, too. Then Drew Littler got himself in a jam and my father loaned Eileen some money. My father's ideas about debt were vague, cosmic. He figured if you had money and somebody needed some, you gave it to him, at least if the guy was all right and would do the same for you. Later on, if you needed it and he had it you could call on him. In the meantime, if you didn't need it, you left him alone.

My situation was this. I'd loaned him money, sort of. Because he needed it and was good for it, sort of. But I didn't need it back, which meant I had no business worrying about it. Later on, if I needed it and if he had it, he was supposed to give the money back. If he didn't have it, he'd regret the fact and wish there was something he could do. But right now, Eileen needed the money and I didn't, so he gave it to her. The reason she needed it was that Drew had landed himself in jail after beating some Negroes half to death outside the pool hall. I hadn't been there, but the event was recounted at the Mohawk Grill in several versions, each apocryphal after its own fashion. After listening to all of them, I did a composite sketch based on my knowledge of Drew Littler and those details common to the several versions of the event, tossing out variants that seemed out of character or attributable to the character and prejudice of the speaker. Having seen Drew Littler shoot pool, I absolutely believed certain aspects of the story that other people doubted. Drew believed that pool operated on much the same principles as weightlifting. He never could be made to understand that a cue ball could not be blasted through a dense cluster of balls and come out the other side with its original trajectory intact, like a fullback plowing through the line of scrimmage. It never paid to daydream when he was shooting either, because balls had a way of becoming airborne in multicolored blurs, rattling off walls and cracking along the floor at shin level. He attacked even the side pockets viciously.

One afternoon, Drew and I had shot a few racks up in my father's apartment. I didn't like playing with him because he couldn't win but hated to lose. I'd sandbag like a son of a bitch, but there was just no way to keep him in the game. The only time he ever made a shot was by mistake, after the cue ball had rebounded off seven or eight rails. He was that lousy. We'd been playing for about an hour, Drew's face darkening with each successive loss. Wussy came in and drank a beer, watched us for about thirty seconds, said we both stunk, and lay down on the sofa. I purposely left the cue ball about three inches from the seven, which in turn was no more than three inches from the side pocket. Drew always approached easy shots hungrily, and when he lined this one up, I looked around the room for a safe place. What happened was something I'd never seen before and have never seen since. Drew Littler drove into the cue ball with such force that the felt tip of the cue stuck at the base of the side pocket, snapping the stick in three like a twig. The thick butt remained in Drew Littler's hand, the slender tip vibrated in the side pocket like an arrow, and the long middle section, razor sharp on both ends, impaled itself in the back of the sofa where Wussy had fallen asleep.

So I wasn't the least bit surprised to learn that the whole incident in the pool hall had its origins in Drew Littler's inability to keep his game separate from the others. According to one eyewitness, Drew Littler had launched the cue ball with such velocity that it cleared the three adjacent tables and hit the skinny Negro kid at the base of the skull so neatly that everybody who hadn't seen it happen concluded that the ball must have been thrown.

"Cocksucker!" the kid said, rubbing the base of his neck.

The significance of this expression was much discussed in the diner. Everybody agreed that the word was used, some claiming that it represented a personal observation, others suggesting that it betokened only the speaker's general dissatisfaction with the turn of events. In either case, the fateful word was uttered, and several people heard it. The funny part was that Drew himself was not among those who heard. In fact, according to several eyewitnesses, when he approached the Negroes' table, he was after nothing but the errant cue ball without which his own game could not continue. The Negro kid with the knot swelling on the back of his head had picked it up, and was inspecting the nearest tables, figuring one of them was minus a white ball. When Drew came up and demanded it, the kid handed it over, along with a dark look, and Drew returned to his own table without having offered an apology. He later claimed not to have known that the ball had actually hit anyone, and this may have been true.

When Drew had returned to his own table, the Negro kids huddled together at one end of their table, their brows knit suspiciously, but too badly outnumbered to be more than indignant. The boy Drew hit let the others examine the base of his skull. All four were about sixteen, and after a few minutes they went back to shooting pool, though more carefully now, three watching the room in anticipation of another attack, while the fourth shot. Negroes, at least Negroes in groups, had never been welcome in the pool hall, but these boys apparently were determined to finish their rack so they could leave without the appearance of running away.

By the time they were ready to go, at least two or three of the idle men who had been lounging around the snack bar had gone over to where Drew Littler was slapping balls around the table and had a word with him. When the Negroes left, Drew Littler said nothing, but watched them go. According to some, he had been drinking, but few picked up on a far more important detail. When the Negroes left the pool hall, they had the misfortune to be parked right out front. They were in a shiny, late-model car that one of the boys had borrowed from his father. And, when they got into the car, they made another mistake; they did not drive away. Rather, they held a caucus of some sort, allowing Drew Littler to pay for his table time and follow them outside. For some reason they did not drive away even when they saw him emerge from the pool hall with a cue stick in his hand. Perhaps it was because he came out alone and because there were four of them, and maybe because they thought they knew him. One of the boys turned out to be Wussy's nephew, and he later said from his hospital bed that they all thought Drew Littler was coming over to say he was sorry.

They were wrong. Without stopping for pleasantries, Drew Littler smashed one of the new car's headlights with the cue stick and kicked a dent in the front door on the passenger side. Then he asked if anybody wanted to call him a cocksucker to his face. All four of the boys got out of the car and crowded around the dent, staring at it in disbelief. The boy who had borrowed the car from his father looked like he might cry. Staring at the damage, he said, "Cocksucker," before he could think.

The word was no sooner out than Drew hit the boy in the ribs with the cue, sending him to the sidewalk gasping for breath. By the time the fat cop on duty up the street at the Four Corners arrived on the scene, Drew had beaten all four boys so badly that each had to be taken to the emergency room. He had used one boy as a battering ram until he'd gone limp and then he'd taken the pool cue to the shiny car again. He was bashing the windshield when the cop arrived on the scene and told Drew Littler he'd better quit it right now before he got into serious trouble. Whereupon Drew told the cop to go fuck himself. This had the effect of subtly shifting the cop's allegiances, and when Drew came around the car to have at the other side and made the mistake of turning his back, the cop coldcocked him with his nightstick and that was that.

When Drew woke up, he was in jail and he had no idea that he was only part of that afternoon's excitement in Mohawk. For at approximately the same time that he was administering a savage beating to the four Negro boys and their shiny car, Jack Ward was having a heart attack on the sixteenth hole of the Mohawk Country Club. Both ambulances had already been dispatched to the pool hall, where the attendants had their work cut out for them. By the time one of the two made it back across town to the country club, Jack Ward had been dead for twenty minutes.

The best thing about my being something of a fixture at the Mohawk Grill was that my presence in the establishment lacked significance. To the men who gathered there in the late afternoon, I was at once ubiquitous and invisible, and they seldom took special care not to talk in front of me. Only the word "fuck" (and it had to be shouted) had the effect of making me real to them. They were the sort of men who said the word, then looked around to see who was there. "You didn't hear that, Sam's Kid," they joked. (Only a few even remembered my name, and even they had picked up on Wussy's nomenclature.) Sometimes Harry would grumble about the diner being "no place for a fuckin' kid," whereupon my father always wanted to know whose fault that was.

Actually, since my father had cleaned me out, Harry was giving me more hours. My father had told him it was all right if I wanted them, and knowing my father, he probably figured he was in this fashion paying me back. Anyway, I worked Saturday mornings and early afternoons now, in addition to the hour and a half or so after school on days when enough dirty jobs had piled up. It wasn't that long before I was back in the dough, and with the warmer weather coming I'd soon be starting up my golf ball business again. My father gave no indication of having located my new savings account, though I had to admit that this didn't mean much, since he'd given no sign of locating the first one.

At any rate, when Jack Ward had his heart attack, I was privy to the considerable discussion that the event occasioned. With the exception of my father, none of the men who frequented the Mohawk Grill had known Jack Ward personally, but they'd all seen him around and knew who he was and how much money he had, and so of course they were interested. In fact, Jack Ward's death made religious mystics of them. The *idea* of it. If a guy that young and handsome and rich could just up and die like that, what the hell were any of them doing alive? After all, he hadn't smoked, and they all did. Out at the Holiday Inn Jack Ward would order a Campari and soda and nurse it most of the night, while

Harry's crew was over at Greenie's slamming down boilermakers. Jesus, Jack Ward never even gambled, and that was the official town vice, all the others being unofficial ones. So what in holy hell was he doing dead?

Though he tried not to let on, I could tell that Jack Ward's death did rattle my father. The two of them had gone ashore on Utah Beach and surprised the hell out of themselves by living through the war. You'd have had to know my father pretty well to guess just how rattled he was though, because he played Jack Ward's death like he played Liars—flawlessly, boldly, arrogantly. When the circumstances of the tragedy became known, nobody got more mileage out of his former friend's death than my father. For Jack Ward, it seemed, had had a busy day.

He'd arrived at the Mohawk Country Club around eleven and teed off with a foursome who played for a buck a hole, allowed pushes on the odd-numbered holes, an arrangement that established a new bet, double in value, from that point forward. By the end of the front nine Jack Ward had won enough to pay for lunch at the clubhouse, which he did. It was early in the season and the May air had been damp, so there were no takers for the back nine. In fact, Jack Ward had pretty much decided to forgo them himself until he ran into the pretty fiancée of the club pro who wanted to play and had nobody to play with. Jack Ward thought that a shame.

They teed off on number ten around two-thirty, just as the sun came out from behind the clouds, quickly drying the short fairway grass and making the two golfers glad to be alive. They had the course to themselves. On the elevated tee of the fifteenth hole, which overlooked the preceding three, they must have seen just how alone they were. The sixteenth hole contained a sharp dogleg, and there they stopped near the edge of the trees.

"That's the w-w-way I want to go, all right," Tree said, standing up on the rungs of his stool so he could demonstrate proper hip movement. "In the s-s-saddle."

As sad as I was for Jack Ward, the one I couldn't stop thinking about was the girl. Not Tria, though I thought about her too, fatherless now in the big white house. But rather the girl Jack Ward had been with there at the edge of the woods. I kept wondering what I'd have done in her place, and how she must have felt. She would have had to go for help, of course, but even that couldn't have been easy. Apparently, she'd started off in the

wrong direction, disoriented by the winding fairways, surrounded by trees. She imagined she was heading for the clubhouse, only to discover when she emerged from the woods that
she wasn't. Disoriented, she decided to do the sensible thing.
Instead of guessing where the clubhouse was, she followed the
fairways—first fifteen, then sixteen, then seventeen, then eighteen, the green of which lay some twenty yards from the canopied terrace of the clubhouse. The first person to see her puffing
up the long approach was her fiancé, who had just finished giving
the lesson that had prevented him from playing with her to begin
with. He hopped in a cart and headed out to meet her. By now
the young woman was completely awash in guilt and utterly inar-
ticulate, and the two of them headed back in the cart the way she
had come. By the time they arrived back on the scene, Jack Ward,
now in the fetal position, his splendid white trousers still down
around his ankles, was struggling with his last breaths, his face
gray, but remarkably calm, his longish hair in rakish disarray.

Together, his two rescuers did the best they could with his
pants and loaded him onto the golf cart. Then, since there was
room for only two, the club pro again headed for the clubhouse,
Jack Ward slumped up against him, leaving the girl to follow with
Jack's clubs over one shoulder, her own over the other. The full
force of the tragedy, along with its attendant embarrassment,
must have come home to the young woman somewhere along the
long fairway of the par-five seventeenth, because the two sets of
bags were later discovered leaning up against the ball washer on
the eighteenth tee. From there she must have been able to see
the assembled crowd on the clubhouse terrace and the tardy
ambulance pulling in, and the whole sordid mess must have
seemed more than she could contemplate.

In all the excitement it was nearly forty-five minutes before her
fiancé realized that she had not returned to the clubhouse, and
even longer before he discovered that her car was no longer in
the parking lot. And by the time things calmed down enough so
that he could go over to her apartment and ask her just what the
hell . . . she had thrown her clothes into the back of her Dodge
Dart and departed Mohawk only three months after moving
there. She was never seen again.

Now, so many years after the fact, it is possible for me to see the
dark comedy of these events, but at the time I saw nothing amus-

ing about Jack Ward's tragic end. True, he had been little enough to me. I'd been in the man's company only briefly and had spoken no more than a dozen words to him. Still, the fact that the details of his death should be the subject of lewd conversation at the Mohawk Grill and Greenie's Tavern and the pool hall, not to mention the Mohawk Country Club, The Elms, and virtually every other public place, seemed to me criminal. When the men of the Mohawk Grill joked about Jack Ward dying in the saddle, I felt a strong homicidal impulse and I'd have erased the lot of them from the face of the earth had it been within my power.

More than anything, though, the news of Jack Ward's death made me want to find some dark and solitary place as far from my father and the men of the Mohawk Grill as I could get to reconsider the shape of things. For some reason, I settled on Our Lady of Sorrows, whose precincts I had not visited in several years. The church had not changed, though it was smaller than I remembered. My sign of the cross at the holy water font still felt natural, though I had not made one since moving in with my father, and anyone who saw my genuflection before slipping into one of the back pews wouldn't have guessed how long it had been since my last. There was no one to see it though. Inside the church, it was just me and the late afternoon sun, barely strong enough to color the stained glass window along the upper story of the church. Everything below was lost in the general murk.

Up on the main altar, Jesus was visible, thanks to the glow of the two red EXIT signs, which marked the sacristy side entrances and which stayed on even when electricity was cut to the lamps and chandeliers. The long low altar rail reminded me that once I had served at mass and that nobody had questioned my exhalted status, the appropriateness of my attendance upon the holiest rites, my bearing witness to the mysteries of the tabernacle.

But surely the tabernacle had contained no mystery as profound as the death of Jack Ward. After all, you didn't need a crystal ball to predict what was going to happen to Jesus. The way he'd gone about things it would have been a miracle if he *hadn't* been crucified, it seemed to me. The empty tomb? Was that a mystery? The empty tabernacle I'd so often glimpsed over the shoulder of the old Monsignor? Its contents a mystery? Maybe, but not nearly so curious as the mystery of how anybody could be Jack Ward and not live happily ever after. His death made me realize that despite living through the war, marrying a rich woman, fathering a beautiful daughter, living in the white jewel house, driving the big Lincoln, and dying in the saddle, Jack Ward had not been happy. I was suddenly positive of it, despite the equal certainty of my father's cronies that his final moments had been, like the rest of his existence, bliss. I remembered the afternoon he took me into the library of the Ward house, the way he looked around as if he'd forgotten what all was in there, if he'd ever known. How little pleasure he had derived from taking inventory. It hadn't occurred to me then, but when I thought back on it, the way he'd come into the house from the outside, hesitating in the foyer, the crossroads of his own house, his daughter having disappeared down one long corridor, his wife out of sight somewhere, a strange boy peering out at him from the kitchen, he'd looked like a man returning to a place he'd visited long ago, having in the meantime forgotten the floor plan, the location of the room he'd once slept in, occupied now, surely, by somebody else. Not one of the books in that library had been his, nor had he ever turned down a page of one of them to mark his place.

And now he was dead, his legacy the lewd account circulating about his last living act and how it had taken three men to unbend him sufficiently to get his shorts and grass-stained trousers back over his narrow hips before his wife arrived at the country club. Now *that*, all of it, was a mystery worth pondering, and I thought about it for an hour or so in the sweet darkness of Our Lady of Sorrows without coming to any conclusions, but feeling a little better anyhow. By the time I decided I'd better go home, what little color there had been was now drained out of the stained-glass windows, and if it hadn't been for the red EXIT sign above the vestibule door, I doubt I would have been able to find my way.

Outside, it was only slightly less dark, but from the church steps I was able to make out a figure coming down the middle of the street full tilt. It was Willie Heinz, and when he saw me he grinned and waved before I had a chance to step back into the shadows beneath the arched doorway. I thought about trying to catch him so I could ask if it was true about him and Drew Littler stealing cars and parking them in the river. But Willie was too fleet to catch once he had a running start, and he'd no sooner blown by me and made a sharp turn down an alley than a police car, tires squealing, flew down the street in pursuit, missing the turn Willie had made. They didn't know he always doubled back. I waited a few minutes before emerging from the shadows and heading home on my bike.

I had come to a conclusion after all. Life was a crapshoot, and it didn't pay to be mistaken for Willie Heinz.

Late the next afternoon the busiest stretch of road in the county was the small winding one that led from the highway up through the trees to the Ward house. We crawled up the incline even slower than Tria had done on the afternoon Drew totaled his motorcycle. My father swore every time the brake lights on the car in front of us flashed red. To make matters worse, Eileen was with us and it looked now like she would be late for work at The Elms.

"What the hell difference does it make," my father said. "Everybody in Mohawk County is right here. If Irma's got more than three tables I'll eat your—" he'd crept up on the bumper of the car in front of him, then had to brake hard and blare the horn.

"Eat my what," Eileen said, offering her first half-smile of the day. She'd been in an uncharacteristically black mood all day, and we'd talked her into coming at the last minute to take her mind off things. Drew had been released from jail earlier that afternoon. Eileen had been waiting for him to turn up so she could read him the riot act, lay down a whole new set of ground rules for as long as he lived under her roof. But he'd apparently seen that coming, and now she feared he'd be in trouble all over again before she could even lay down the law. Since that was a distinct possibility, she'd dispatched my father to look for him in the dives he was known to frequent, the only consequence of which was that by five o'clock my father was half loaded and no longer anxious to find Drew Littler, if indeed he ever had been.

I had surprised my father by asking if I could go along to the viewing. That morning I'd awakened feeling better about things and I spit-shined my cordovan shoes and even ironed one of my white dress-up shirts. We always had our dirty clothes washed and folded at the laundry around the corner, but we did our own ironing when being wrinkled wasn't acceptable. For me that was practically never. Today was different, though. After I bathed, I tried half a dozen new styles while my hair was soaking wet and would go where the comb said. Once dry of course it would do what it wanted, but it was fun to imagine having hair like James Dean or Elvis. They wouldn't have worn a white shirt with gold cufflinks and matching tie clasp, but I had to admit I didn't look too bad all spiffed up, my big ears not withstanding. The only problem was my blue blazer, which I hadn't worn in many months and which turned out to be too tight. When she'd purchased it a little over two years ago, my mother was insistent that there be "room to grow," and she wasn't content until she found one that hung limp, its sleeves down over the second knuckle. Now, no matter how I tugged at them, those same sleeves were up over my wrist and my shoulders strained the seam down the back. Still, I concluded, as I sat impatiently in the backseat of the convertible, my fingernails were clean and I looked good enough to court a girl at her father's wake.

"Anyway," Eileen said to my father, "you finally got around to wearing the cologne I got you for Christmas." He was inching toward the center of the narrow road, apparently contemplating passing the long line of cars that snaked around a blind curve in the woods.

"What?" he said, after thinking better of it and drifting back. Then they both turned around and looked at me.

I shrugged.

"At least it's not going to waste," she sighed.

"Stay downwind of the casket," my father said. "You don't want to start Jack sneezing."

By the time we got within sight of the Ward house, night had fallen. Cars lined the long circular drive on both sides and were parked all over the lawn both inside and outside the stone pillars, which were themselves nearly a hundred yards from the house. In fact, cars were parked all the way down to the edge of the trees where Drew and I had parked the motorcycle and watched the house until Jack Ward came out on the patio to watch us.

I was reminded again of Drew's strange vow to one day own the white jewel house, and it gave me a chill to realize that even so small an obstacle to his doing so had now been removed. After all, if Jack Ward, who had everything, could lose it all, including his life, on the back nine of the Mohawk Country Club, then wasn't it possible that the wheel of fortune could spin in the other direction? What if when we got inside we discovered Drew Littler all dressed up and standing next to Tria Ward in the receiving line, holding her hand by way of comfort? For a dreadful instant it seemed plausible. The Ward house was one of the few places my father hadn't looked for him.

The more I thought about it, I had to smile, even though my

own chances of ingratiating myself into the affections of Tria Ward and her mother were not appreciably better. I was a little smarter than Drew Littler, maybe, and a little less of a social liability, a lot less belligerent and aggressive. I could say I knew who my father was, the advantage of which was not clear-cut, it seemed to me. If pure luck—indeed some rather extravagant manifestation of it—did not intervene, Drew Littler and I would probably share a common, very common, destiny. But I feared fortune just the same, even if it was more likely to intervene on my humble behalf than Drew Littler's.

"I wouldn't park here," Eileen said when my father turned off the lights and the ignition. We were half on the shoulder, half on the pavement.

"That's interesting," my father said, getting out.

One of the reasons Eileen wouldn't have parked there was that the car was right up against a bush, which made it impossible to get out the passenger side.

"Come on, Slick," my father said to me, letting his own door swing shut.

Once I was out, there was nothing for Eileen to do but slide across the seat and get out on my father's side. "The trouble with my life," she said, "is that it's too goddamn full of gallantry."

There was a bottleneck of about fifty people at the front door, patiently waiting to get in. It occurred to me then, perhaps for the first time, that what the white jewel house had meant to me as I looked at it from the hill across the highway in Myrtle Park it also meant to most of Mohawk County. And when the modest obituary in the *Mohawk Republican* announced that friends of the deceased would be received at the Ward home, it had been seen as an invitation to the entire county to tour the house they'd seen from the highway and wondered about for decades. They couldn't have been more delighted for the opportunity without having been informed that the event was to be catered, which in fact it turned out to be.

"I've got to find a phone," Eileen said, consulting her watch when we joined the throng on the patio awaiting admittance. "I was supposed to be at work fifteen minutes ago."

But nobody was coming out of the Ward house, and those on the patio looked like they were settling in for a long siege. Every-

one was in excellent spirits, however, and these were not the least
dampened at the prospect of having to cool their heels or by the
general solemnity of the occasion. Rumors circulated that there
was food inside, which seemed only right. Jack Ward had been
Irish, and many took that to mean there'd be booze as well.

"You might have worn a jacket at least," Eileen said to my
father, who was in fact the only man on the patio not wearing one.
Something about the way she said it made me notice the way she
herself was dressed. Normally I wouldn't have paid any attention
to the floral print dress she was wearing, except that she was
standing among women more quietly and expensively dressed.
My mother, even on her limited budget, had always dressed well,
and I discovered that I could tell the difference between good
taste and bad, at least when they conveniently rubbed shoulders
for the sake of comparison. Eileen was looking at the other
women too, I could tell, and the regret in her eyes, which seemed
to encompass more than just the cheap dress she was wearing,
made me feel sorry for her. "I wish I hadn't let you talk me into
this," she told my father. "Do you cry at funerals?" she asked me,
as if she thought she might cry herself and would have appreciated the company.

"The way everybody's standing around," my father remarked,
apparently oblivious to Eileen, "you'd think this place had only
one door."

I followed, but refused to believe he actually intended to slip
in the back. As we weaved our way through the swelling crowd,
I overheard one man say, "There. At least *some*body's leaving."
Blessedly, nobody followed us. Around back we found the caterer's truck parked by the open kitchen door. We went in.

Mrs. Petrie, the Ward cook, who had once pegged me for a thief
and encouraged me to swipe parfaits from the freezer, was there,
dressed in a light blue uniform that might have fit her once but
didn't any more. The kitchen looked like a battlefield, and she was
sitting contentedly amid the casualties, smoking a cigarette. It
was the biggest kitchen I'd ever seen, but every inch of counter
space was stacked with dirty plates and large oval serving trays.
From outside the kitchen came the din of conversation, and it was
clear that Mrs. Petrie had retired from it. There were half a dozen
serving trays on the island loaded with hors d'oeuvres and ready
to go, but you could see from the woman's posture that they were
going to stay right where they were. She had not seen us come
in, and it would not have mattered if she had.

My father went up behind Mrs. Petrie and began massaging her shoulders. "Sam Hall," she said, looking straight up at him. "I was just wondering how things could get worse."

"Be nice, Tilly," my father said.

"I *am* nice," Mrs. Petrie said, blowing smoke up at him. "I'm the nicest person you know. I'm fifty-three and I never shot anybody yet, including my husband, who deserves it. Including her, too," she added, gesturing toward the noise outside. "It would never occur to her that I might be having a hard time serving five hundred freeloaders all by myself."

"This hasn't exactly been the best day of her life either," my father pointed out.

"You sure?"

"It's her husband . . ." my father began.

"And now she's rid of him," Mrs. Petrie said.

"Tilly . . ."

"Sam . . ."

She saw me then, and Eileen, too. "I got a ratchet jaw, don't I," she mumbled.

"Mind if we use the phone?" my father said. There was one hanging on the wall.

"Not a bit. Dial 0 for the Philippines."

While Eileen called The Elms, my father sampled something brown on a cracker off one of the serving trays and handed an identical one to me. I made the mistake of stuffing the whole thing in my mouth before tasting it. My father was grinning at me. "You want people to go away, I'd trot these right out there, Tilly."

"Don't blame me. It's catered all the way from Schenectady. Too important a shindig to trust to me."

In as much as I still hadn't swallowed, my father handed me a cocktail napkin. I used it, too.

"There," Eileen said, hanging up the phone. "I got the night off."

Then, to everyone's surprise, she shouldered one of the serving trays full of hors d'oeuvres and disappeared out into the noisy foyer. My father and I looked at each other.

"Where's the caterer?" my father said to Mrs. Petrie, who remained parked and unshamed.

"Stretched out drunk in the front seat of his truck," Mrs. Petrie said, stubbing out her cigarette. "I may join him."

"Well," my father said, taking a deep breath and cuffing me one in the back of the head. "Let's go see my old buddy Jack."

*   *   *

It was a while before we saw him, though. The casket stood along
one wall of the long living room and the line of people waiting to
pass before it snaked around like the welfare line down at the
unemployment building on the first of the month. The first person
we ran into was Wussy, who I discovered, to my surprise, was half
bald. I'd never seen him without his fishing hat before, and he
looked like he wished he had it on now, along with his old chinos
and flannel shirt, instead of the plaid sport coat and tie. The coat
fit him about as well as mine fit me. "Pretty spiffy, Sam's Kid," he
said to me. Then to my father. "Nice turnout."

"Jack had friends, all right," my father said. "I didn't know you
were one."

There was something a little wrong with the way my father said
it, but if Wussy noticed, he didn't let on. "What's with Eileen?"
he said, having spotted her across the room, returning to the
kitchen now with the empty tray.

"Reflex," my father said. "Or something." It was clear he didn't
think much of this particular reflex, if that's what it was. Not that
there was anything he could do about it. "You seen Zero today?"

"Nope," Wussy said. "Heard they cut him loose. No reason to
keep him. Wasn't no white boys he put in the hospital."

"You know how it goes," my father said.

"That's right."

"There were four of them, you know."

"And they were where they weren't supposed to be to begin
with, right?"

My father raised his eyebrows and shrugged, as if to say, *You tell
me.*

Tree was there too and he came over and joined us. He'd been
standing next to a woman so big that at first I'd thought it was
Alice from The Lookout, but when she turned around I saw it
wasn't. "Nice crowd," Tree said, then to Wussy, "Y-y-you a friend
of Jack's?"

Wussy didn't say anything. After a minute he drifted away.

"Nice going," my father said.

"W-what," Tree said.

"Nice going, that's all."

"W-what's he doing here?"

"What're *you* doing here?"

"Don't get t-t-touchy, Sammy."

"R-r-right," my father said.

Eileen came by and Tree took an assortment of hors d'oeuvres, balancing them halfway up his arm. My father and I watched the expression on his face as he chewed the first one.

"Now what're you going to do with the others?" my father said.

Tree looked around desperately for a place.

My father took a couple, popped one in his mouth. "You never had pâté, you rube?"

"I should've known. If it looks like sh . . . it and smells like sh . . . it, it must be—"

"Right," my father said, munching the other.

"I'll just give this last one to M-marge," Tree said, obviously pleased to have remembered her.

"She looks hungry," my father admitted.

We watched him return to where the huge woman was standing all by herself, elbow to elbow with strangers, nobody to talk to. She looked pleased and relieved by Tree's return, as if she'd half expected to be ignored the rest of the evening. She accepted the cracker and chewed on it daintily, not at all offended. Tree shrugged at us across the room.

I could not take my eyes off the big woman, who continued to eat the cracker as if she doubted it would be her lot in life ever again to eat anything so delicious.

After a while I slipped away. As usual, my father knew everybody. Eventually he would notice I was gone, but we had an understanding about that. I could be gone all I wanted, provided I was back by the time he was ready to go someplace else. And gauging when that might be ready wasn't as tough as you might think. He had a rhythm to him. In bars I could tell, within a minute or two, when he'd get up to go to the men's room, when he'd figure it was time to beat me in a game of shufflebowl. Now, I could tell just by looking at him that he'd be pretty content for a while.

Somebody had opened the door to the library, where Jack Ward had left me on my previous visit, and people had spilled in there to escape the crush. Only now that room was crowded too, if not quite as noisy as the big foyer. A large man knelt in front of the big console television, as if he were contemplating turning the set on so he could compare its picture with his own. Nearby, a frizzy-haired woman removed a leatherbound volume from one of the tall oak bookcases, glanced around the room, and slipped it into her big bag. Then she noticed me, and when I didn't look away, she checked again to make sure nobody was watching, and replaced the book. When the man kneeling in front of the TV straightened up, he and the frizzy-haired woman left the room together, though not before she located me again and narrowed her eyes at me murderously. Out of curiosity I went over to the bookcase to find out what she'd wanted so badly, because I'd never seen anybody steal a book before. This one was a fancy movie edition of *Gone with the Wind,* which explained it.

I wandered. There were other people I knew in the crowd. Rose, her orange hair in a shockingly tall beehive, looked right at me and away again. She'd never seen me all spit-shined before, so I couldn't blame her for not recognizing me. Just inside the living room doorway, the old Monsignor sat in a high-backed throne-shaped chair, Mrs. Ambrosino, soberly resplendent in a billowy dress, in attendance at his side, rather pointedly refusing hors d'oeuvres on his behalf, well in advance of the old man's actually seeing a single offering. I steered clear.

Then F. William Peterson materialized at my elbow and drew me aside like a conspirator, looking excited and flushed. "You'll be home in the morning?" he wanted to know. I said probably, and that seemed to please him. He had just a thin tuft of baby-fine hair on top now, and it stood on end. "Great things," he whispered. "You wait."

After a while I joined the line filing slowly toward and past Jack Ward's casket. He was dressed the way I remembered him, in a white suit with a pale pink sweater, slender and graceful even in death. I refused to think of him as a comic figure on the terrace of the Mohawk Country Club, his trousers down around his knees. I promised myself I would never laugh at the story when it was recounted at the diner, for it surely would be, for a long time to come. Maybe, I thought, even if I never amounted to anything, it would be enough not to be the sort of man who'd tell the story of Jack Ward's final round for laughs.

There was no way to tell by looking at Hilda Ward whether she'd been spared the details of her husband's death. Even smaller than I remembered, the tiny woman gave no hint of grief or loss, and I thought of what Mrs. Petrie had said in the kitchen about her being rid of him. I also remembered the way she'd treated him the afternoon Tria had backed his Lincoln into the woods. Tria stood next to her mother now, her dark eyes full, and she was so lovely I felt a dull ache in my chest. Her face was the color of her father's fine suit, and she could not take her eyes off him, even to receive condolences. Suddenly, I knew I could not face her, could not present myself to her. I left the line and the living room.

My father was still talking to some people in the foyer, so I went back into the library, which had emptied out. For some reason, the first thing I saw was the small gap on one of the shelves across the room. I ran my fingers along the spines of the books, stopping at the space where the fancy *Gone with the Wind* had been. The horrible woman had come back for it.

We dropped Eileen off and drove home.

"What'd our friend want?" my father said when we were alone.

"Who?"

He looked over at me. "Who. Your ass, who."

Pretending ignorance never got me anywhere with him, somehow, though he never questioned legitimate dumbness.

"Nothing," I said, which wasn't exactly a lie, since he certainly hadn't said anything specific. But it wasn't exactly the truth either.

"Nothing," my father repeated.

When we pulled up in front of the apartment, a pair of big legs were sticking out of the dark entryway and onto the sidewalk. They didn't move, but when my father turned off the ignition an empty bottle landed on the canvas top of the convertible and broke in the middle of the street. "Speaking of nothing—" my father said.

When we got out, Drew Littler tried to stand, lost his balance and crashed backward through the fogged glass door and into the unlit hall at the foot of the staircase.

"Get back in the car," my father said.

There was just enough light from the street to see Drew Littler trying again to struggle to his feet. I had half a mind to do what I was told for once, but I stayed where I was.

"Come on, Sammy," Drew Littler said. "Let's do it. You and me."

"Do what, Zero?"

"Don't call me that. I'll have to kill anybody calls me that," he

said seriously, as if the need to kill my father were to him a matter
of infinite regret.

"All right," my father said, stepping through the door frame
and into the broken glass. "What should I call you?"

"Let's fight," Drew said, as if the proposal required my father's
permission.

"Nah," my father said.

"Come *on,*" said Drew, disappointed. "Let's fuckin' fight. Kick
my ass, Sammy. You're supposed to be some kind of ass kicker.
Kick my fuckin' ass, Sammy."

"I got a better idea," my father said. "We go upstairs, get a good
night's sleep, and fight in the morning when we're fresh."

"No sleep," Drew said. "Kick ass."

He didn't look like he'd be doing any ass kicking to me. I'd got
close enough to see pretty well. He was leaning up against the
banister, a jagged piece of opaque glass sticking out of the top of
his blond head. He seem unaware of both the glass and the ribbon
of black blood that snaked down his neck and into his shirt.

"Aw, Sammy," he said, slumping onto the stairs. He was crying
now. He ran his fingers through his hair where they encountered
the shard of glass. Lowering his head between his knees, he shook
his head like a wet dog until the fragment fell out. Then he began
to moan. I missed what he said the first couple of times, then
finally understood. "He's dead, Sammy," Drew Littler cried.
"He's dead."

He was way too big, and we had to get Wussy to help us. My father
went looking for him while I stayed with Drew in the hallway. He
was bleeding quite a lot, but my father said head wounds always
did, and not to worry. Remember whose head it is, he said.

Drew slept peacefully, slumped up against the wall. He smelled
something awful, a mixture of sweet odors—whiskey and body
odor and blood. And my guess was that he'd wet his pants too. I
stayed with him as long as I could, then went outside to keep from
throwing up. After a while my father returned with Skinny Donovan in tow.

"Jesus H. Christ on a crutch," Skinny said when he saw. "You
sure he's alive?"

Drew groaned, as if in answer, then was still again.

"Wha'd you do, Sammy? Knock his ass through the door?"

"Didn't have to," my father said. "He fell through it."

"You need somebody to swear to it?"

My father said he didn't think so, though it was good of Skinny to offer.

"He sure did show those coons where the bear shit in the buckwheat," Skinny observed, as if he hated to see someone of demonstrated worth so cruelly reduced. "You want to drag him upstairs?"

"Let's wait for Wuss," my father said. "It's three flights up and he weighs a ton. We're liable to get halfway up and lose him."

"You and me and the kid could manage," Skinny said, insulted.

"Probably, but let's wait."

Skinny shrugged. "Let's wait outside then. It's like a toilet in here."

In a few minutes Wussy pulled up and parked across the street. He'd changed back into his regular clothes, including his fishing hat. He shook his head at me. "More foolishness, eh Sam's Kid?"

We went inside and stared at Drew.

"Which end do you want?" my father said, ignoring Skinny.

"I don't want either end," Wussy said, but he positioned himself at the sleeping boy's feet. "This one's not quite so ugly, though . . . anybody check to see if he's alive?"

"He's alive," my father said, trying to get some kind of grip under Drew's armpits.

"Be just like you to have me lug a two-hundred-and-fifty-pound retard up three flights of stairs and then find out he's dead."

Every time my father tried to lift, Drew's arms went limp over his head. "You picked the right end, asshole," my father said to Wussy, who had his hands locked under the boy's knees. "I suppose you want me to back up the stairs, too."

"Only if you want him up there," Wussy said. "I'm all for leaving him right where he is."

It took them fifteen minutes. Finally my father had to take one arm, Skinny the other, going shoulder to shoulder up the narrow stairs, cursing each other's clumsiness every step. "Don't fight, girls," Wussy said, his hands still locked under Drew Littler's tree-trunk legs. Somebody farted silently, gruesomely, and the three of them argued over who it was, finally settling on me, though I was both downstairs and downwind. Wussy complained about the fact that the boy smelled like bait, and Skinny said he

must have pissed not only in his pants but his shirt as well, because
that was clammy and wet, too.

"Where?" Wussy said when they got him into the apartment.

"Bathtub," my father gasped.

It took some maneuvering, but they finally got him in. Skinny
sat down on the commode, deathly white and breathing hard. All
three men were sweating.

"You could stand a shower your own self," Wussy said, glaring
at Skinny Donovan.

"It's not me that stinks," Skinny said defensively. "It's him."

Drew's blond head was still slumped forward on his chest, and
the spot where the glass fragment had stuck in his skull was now
black and matted, though the bleeding had pretty much quit.
Wussy put a finger on the boy's throat. "Well, you're right for
once," he said. "He's alive. Anybody call his mother?"

"Run over to the diner," my father said to me. "Take your time.
Try not to scare her to death. Maybe we can get him cleaned up
by the time she gets here."

They didn't though. I took my time, like he said, and I didn't
tell Eileen anything except that he was with us. She must have
heard something in my voice though because she pulled up behind my father's car about a minute later and got out of her little
car just in time to hear a billiard ball come crashing through the
window above and land on the hood of Wussy's truck across the
street. During the minute or so I had waited for her, the deserted
street had filled with Drew Littler's howls, and they were more
animallike than human.

By the time Eileen and I got upstairs, my father and Wussy had
succeeded in pinning Drew to the floor while Skinny Donovan,
in a strictly unauthorized maneuver, kicked the boy in the head
until he stopped trying to get up. Wussy had a big knot on his
forehead, and my father's little finger was bent back at an absurd
angle. There were billiard balls everywhere.

Thanks to Skinny's pointed-toed attacks, the wound in Drew
Littler's head had opened up again and the boy's face was ghastly
with blood. He lay there on the floor beneath the two men, pant-
ing and crying and howling like a dog. Then, finally, he passed out
again. This time they didn't put him in the tub. Turning on the
shower was what had revived him. Instead, Skinny Donovan was

instructed to go across the street and call a doctor my father knew. I offered to go, but they wanted Skinny out. Eileen had immediately fallen to kicking him in the shins for kicking her son, and she was now glaring at him as if she might start up again without provocation. When the doctor came, he found a blue vein in Drew's arm on the first try. The boy never even twitched.

The doctor recommended getting him out of his wet clothes and letting him sleep where he was—on my bed—until morning, warning that in Drew's condition, his morning was likely to be midafternoon. Then we were to bring him to the hospital. The gash on his head, though not life-threatening, would probably require stitches and a tetanus shot.

"You better go over to the emergency room your own self," the doctor told my father, who, now that he had the leisure to do so, was studying his little finger and cursing it for refusing to go back into place.

"Don't worry about me," he said.

"I'm not," the doctor said. "The only one I'm really worried about is him."

I didn't recognize this as a reference to me until I saw everybody staring at me. I guess I must have looked pretty pale. The sight of all the blood had me weak in the knees, and for about the last ten minutes everything in the apartment had taken on a vague, otherworldly quality. I didn't think I would faint, but I was in the minority. Eileen, who didn't look so hot herself, got a washcloth and put it to my forehead. The last thing I remember was that the washcloth came away red.

When I awoke, Wussy and I were alone in the apartment, if you didn't count Drew Littler (and there was no reason to). Eileen had gone with my father over to the emergency room. Skinny, who claimed a twisted ankle, had begged a lift home, but Eileen wouldn't give him one, so he'd limped a couple blocks over to Greenie's Tavern for rye whiskey and sympathy and the opportunity to tell the tale.

All of this according to Wussy, who was in the bathroom examining the purple knot above his left eye. "You all right, Sam's Kid?" he said when he spied me in the mirror.

I said I was.

"Me too," he said, though the knot in the mirror continued to hold his attention. Nobody had troubled much about him when it came time to assess damages. They'd fussed about my father's finger and Drew's head and Skinny's ankle, and even about me for getting bled on. Wussy, everybody just assumed, was okay, and that didn't seem right to me, even though it turned out to be true.

Drew Littler had taken the worst of it, that was for sure. He was sleeping fitfully now, one whole side of his face swollen hideously from ear to chin, his eye nothing but a narrow slit. The pillow beneath his head was pink.

I knew what the doctor had said, but I couldn't get it out of my head that he might rise up out of bed and go on the rampage again. I watched him nervously until Wussy came out of the bathroom.

"What should we do it he wakes up?" I said.

Wussy started picking up billiard balls, which lay scattered underfoot around the apartment. "Run like hell," he said, but when he saw that wasn't the answer I'd been hoping for, he relented. "He won't be in the mood for no more fighting for a while. If you were about a quart and a half low and had a broken jaw and only one eye to see out of, you wouldn't feel like it either. The only thing that kept him going as long as he did was stupidity."

That was only partly reassuring. I was sure Drew Littler wasn't out of stupidity.

I helped Wussy tape a piece of cardboard over the hole in the window, and together we picked the place up, at least some of it. "We've lost the twelve ball someplace," he said when there was a space left in the rack. I didn't have the heart to tell him where it was. He was about the unluckiest man that ever was when it came to crossfires, and now his truck's assortment of dings and dents was richer by one.

It was late now and there was just one snowy station on the television. Wussy stretched out on the sofa and watched it for almost five minutes before he started snoring loudly.

It was nearly two hours until my father and Eileen returned, and that gave me time to think. I was groggy, but too nervous to sleep. Drew Littler, it occurred to me suddenly, was dangerously insane. Maybe he had been all along. The meaning of those trips on the motorcycle up the hill to the white jewel house, where we'd stopped outside the stone pillars and just watched, until Jack Ward came out on the patio and stared us away—all of it made sense now. I hadn't been able to comprehend Drew Littler's insistence that the Ward house would be his one day.

He'd expected to inherit it.

* * *

It was nearly daybreak before everybody got to sleep. Wussy woke up when my father and Eileen returned from the hospital, then fell asleep again almost immediately. My father tried to get Eileen to go home and come back midmorning, but she wouldn't. She finally fell asleep curled up next to her son on the bed. I glanced at her there when I went to the bathroom, and felt bad for thinking then that she really was a homely woman. There were times when she was almost pretty, like when she waitressed at The Elms, all fluid, efficient motion. But when the motion stopped, it was like what had made her almost pretty drained or settled somewhere out of sight.

My father, who was spreading a sheet on the pool table when I returned from the john, read my mind. "She's not the prettiest girl you ever saw," he said, "but she's one of the best."

I said I thought so too, and he showed me his pinky, though there wasn't much to see, taped as it was to the two fingers next to it. "Does it hurt?" I said.

"Not much," he said, flexing the fingers that would. "Did when he set it, but what are you gonna do?"

I climbed up on the makeshift bed. "Where are you going to sleep?"

"In there," he said. "Just in case. Aren't you going to put pajamas on?"

I said I wasn't. I didn't plan to take my shoes off either. Just in case.

"Don't worry about him," my father said, running the fingers of his good hand through his hair. "Some day, huh?"

I said it was some day, all right.

"You okay?"

"Sure," I said.

"Need anything?"

I could have used a pillow, but that was the only thing. I didn't want Drew's (my) pink one.

"Things get bad sometimes," my father said, as if he thought that needed saying. "It's nothing to worry about. It doesn't mean a thing."

I said sure, I understood.

"If it meant something, it'd be different," he said. "But it's just how things are."

I finally fell asleep to the tune of Wussy's whistling snore, the sky outside our Main Street apartment turning gray. Maybe the bad things didn't mean anything, as my father said, but in my head they kept trying to. For a while I was back at the Ward house, part of a long circular procession of perfect strangers filing endlessly past Jack Ward's casket. I must have done that funeral loop a dozen times before I fell into a deeper, dreamless sleep.

I never heard the footsteps on the stair outside, and the banging on the fogged glass door of the Accounting Department seemed at first a part of some new dream just getting under way. It must have gone on for some time before I struggled half-awake. F. William Peterson had just tried the door and found it to be unlocked. His face was white and he looked like he expected to find an apartment full of dead people, which, given the condition of the entryway below—broken glass everywhere, dried blood on the wall and a trail of it leading all the way up to our door—was a reasonable, if incorrect hypothesis. Behind him in the dark hallway was a small woman, and just as I became aware of her, I heard Wussy say, "Oh, shit!" and duck behind the sofa back he'd been peering over. My father was in the bedroom doorway in his undershorts. "Who is it?" came Eileen's sleepy voice from the bedroom.

I wanted to know, too. I sat up on the pool table for a better view, and until she stepped forward from the gray hallway into the full morning light, I did not recognize my own mother.

28

And so began the final stage of my boyhood in Mohawk. Later, as an adult, I would return from time to time. As a visitor, though, never again as a true resident. But then I wouldn't be a true resident of any other place either, joining instead the great multitude of wandering Americans, so many of whom have a Mohawk

in their past, the memory of which propels us we know not precisely where, so long as it's away. Return we do, but only to gain
momentum for our next outward arc, each further than the last,
until there is no elasticity left, nothing to draw us home.

F. William Peterson had managed it all. He had found my
mother a nice flat on the second floor of a stone house on Greenwood Drive. The owner was an elderly woman whose husband
had recently died, and she charged my mother less than the going
rate for rentals in that area. I was part of the deal. I would mow
the lawn with her rickety old mower in summer, rake leaves and
incinerate them in the big rusted drum in autumn, shovel the
sidewalk and the long drive that led from the street to the empty
two-car garage in winter. (Neither we nor our landlady would
own a car until 1965, the second half of my senior year in high
school, when I bought a 1959 battleship-gray Galaxie to take me
west to the university.)

There was no way F. William Peterson could have saved the
old house, and most of its profits had been eaten up, but we were
far from destitute. The furniture was still ours and a few thousand
dollars besides. And my mother, who had to continue her medica-
tion and was thus certified disabled, received a small Social Security benefit. From my new cozy bedroom window, I had a nice
view of our quiet, tree-lined street, one of the ones Drew Littler
and I had cased on his motorcycle.

I think F. William Peterson had pretty much made up his mind
to marry my mother once the matter of her still being married
to my father could be resolved. I don't think she had done anything to give him the impression that she would marry him, but
she hadn't exactly told him she wouldn't either. At thirty-eight,
she'd gone almost completely gray, a metamorphosis that had
taken only a few short months once the process had begun. In
other respects, however, she looked more youthful than she had
in years. The terrible frailty that had laid waste to her girlishness
in the year before her nervous breakdown was reversed, and she
had put on some weight. The thin breast that F. William Peterson
had caught a glimpse of inside the pale green hospital gown was
ample again, and he couldn't have admired my mother more had
he made her himself from his own design, which in a sense he had.

In the beginning, he was our frequent, our only, visitor for
dinner, though he never stayed the night.

Incredible though it may seem, my other life simply ceased to exist. I didn't see my father anymore, seldom saw any of his friends, never went into the Mohawk Grill. At my mother's insistence I quit my job cleaning Rose's and I had to give up my golf ball business, too; in return for these considerations I again got used to clean sheets, freshly pressed shirts, dinners eaten at a table in the house where I lived. I saw Wussy once and he told me that Drew Littler was in the state mental facility in Utica. After I'd gone back to live with my mother he'd gotten himself arrested three times for trespassing at the Ward house, and each time he was thrown in jail, where he entertained the drunks and the duty officer by beating his own forehead bloody against the bars of his cell until he passed out.

One day, about a month after we moved into the new flat, the doorbell rang and it was two policemen who wanted to talk to me about the disappearance of Willie Heinz. My mother informed them that she knew the family in question, and she was certain that her son had no more than a passing acquaintance with such a boy. I followed the cops down to their car and told them about the afternoon I'd come out of Our Lady of Sorrows and seen Willie race by, a police car in hot pursuit. They wanted to fix the exact date and time, and it turned out I was able to because of Jack Ward's death. Nobody they'd questioned, it turned out, remembered seeing him after me, which was pretty spooky. Did he ever talk about running away? they wanted to know. Did he ever discuss his home life? I told them no. I wanted to add that he seemed incapable of running more than a few blocks without doubling back, but I didn't know how to explain without implicating myself in about a year's worth of petty vandalism.

All in all, we were not unhappy, my mother and I. Greenwood Drive was not a bad place to live and the flat became home soon enough. "So many lovely things," my mother mused one day, with her now familiar vague smile. She was examining one of the items I'd stolen from Klein's Department Store. "So many lovely things, and I cannot remember owning them."

But in the hospital and then the nursing home, she had stared at a great many mysteries and had learned to accept what was.

What she and F. William Peterson feared was another war. It was Sam Hall they were dealing with, after all, and they both had good cause to remember what that could mean. The lawyer had pur-

posely taken a second-floor apartment for my mother and he'd
installed new locks, front and back, at considerable expense, just
in case things took an ugly turn. He also arranged for certain
preparations at City Hall. Nobody asked me what I thought, but
I wouldn't have gone to the trouble. Even with my mother eating
Libriums, it wouldn't have taken more than a phone call or two
of the sort my father was a past master at to send her back to the
nursing home, deadbolt locks or no deadbolt locks.

Anyway, the attack never came.

One afternoon, a week before summer vacation was to start, I
came home from school and Wussy's pickup was parked out front
with the tailgate down, looking pretty thoroughly out of place on
our green street. He and my father were coming out of the garage
when I pulled my bike into the driveway.

"Hello, stranger," my father said, and a wave of guilt washed
over me so powerfully that my knees went liquid. "You forget
where downtown is?"

"No," I said.

"Then you must be invisible," Wussy said.

"We got it set up pretty good," my father said. "It should go
inside, really, but your mother wouldn't hear of that."

I looked up at the row of windows along the second floor. A
curtain twitched in one.

When Wussy went back to the pickup, my father and I didn't
say anything for a minute. In the two years I'd lived with him
we'd gotten to the point where, on a good day, we might actually
converse, at least a sentence or two. But in the few weeks since
I'd returned to live with my mother, we'd already lost the knack.

"You gonna be all right here?" he said finally.

I said sure. I'd be all right. I could feel my throat tightening. He
and Wussy hadn't fought the pool table down three flights of stairs
just because he wanted me to have it.

"She looks good," he said. "She actually let me in. Showed me
around and everything. I about dropped my teeth. She wouldn't
let Wussy in, of course, but . . ." he let the thought trail off. "She's
got it done up nice, though."

"Where are you going?" I said finally.

"Away. For a while. I'll be back, I imagine."

"When?"

He took out a couple of dollar bills and handed me one.
I said three threes.

"Liar," he said. He was right, too. There wasn't a three on it, and I'm not sure I could have seen one if there had been.

We walked down the drive to where the pickup stood. My father slammed the tailgate up. "That table's worth seven, eight hundred dollars," he said. "If she can't stand to have it around, sell it. I don't care. As long as you don't get stiffed."

I said I wouldn't sell it.

"I didn't fight very hard to hold on to you, did I?" he said, in reference to the fact that all he'd said to my mother that morning when she'd stepped into his apartment and announced her intention was, "All right, take him."

"It's not what you probably thought," he went on. "You're better off here, that's all. Away from the mess."

There was nothing left to do but cuff me in the back of the head, so he did. "We had *some* fun, at least, didn't we?"

I said we did, and it was true.

After we shook, he got in next to Wussy and rolled the window down and grinned at me. "You don't know it yet, but you loaned me a couple a hundred. I'll mail it to you in a week or so."

"That's all right," I told him, "I don't want it."

"You must," he said, "or you wouldn't have made me look all over for it."

And then he was gone.

I didn't see him again for ten years, nor did I ever hear a word concerning his whereabouts. Not a letter, not a Christmas card.

I must have known I wouldn't, too, because when they drove off, I went into the garage and shot rack after rack of pool beneath the bare lightbulb that dangled from the ceiling, just me and a cloud of silent, circling moths.

PART 3

EAT THE BIRD

29

Robert Crane followed me out onto the bright patio, shading his eyes from the glare of the desert sun. From the foothills, the Catalina Mountains looked blue and close. Their very existence was surprising. Somewhere during the night I'd lost track of time and space. I couldn't have passed the simplest reality quiz.

Things can get that way when you're playing losing poker in somebody's basement—no windows, no clocks, nobody interested in windows or clocks. Finally somebody taps out, says piss on it, I'm going home. Home. A difficult concept, too long obscured by thick cigarette smoke and warm scotch.

"What time is it, do you figure?" said Robert Crane, plopping down next to me on the other chaise lounge at the edge of the kidney-shaped pool. Neither of us owned watches, at least at the moment.

"Spring," I said.

The sun was high above the Catalinas. Nine-thirty, I might have bet, if I hadn't been betting and losing all night, all week, all month. Dog track, pro basketball, poker games.

"Well," Robert said. "You won their sympathy, anyway."

"That's important to have," I said.

As a rule there was pocket money to be made playing poker with university professors who gambled nickles, dimes, and quarters once a month to maintain the relatively inexpensive illusion that they were normal people, real guys. It had taken real talent to lose so grandly—nearly seventy dollars—in such a piss-ant enterprise. "Anybody nervous about my paper?" I said.

"Not really," he said. "Though it's beginning to dawn on them that they don't know you."

"This will happen."

"You okay till Monday?"

"Fine," I lied. "Great, in fact. I could use a lift back into town though."

We went back inside. Ben Slater, the fiftyish English professor whose house it was, was just coming up out of the basement carrying a tray full of dirty glasses, ashtrays, and other dregs of the long night. "Sorry about the beating," he said, as if he wasn't, particularly. "Think of it as part of your education."

We shook hands all around, and Slater told Robert Crane any time he wanted to introduce any more new blood into the game, he could go right ahead. There was a grandfather clock in the hallway and it said 8:00, not 9:30.

"Nice fellow," I said when Robert had backed out of the gravel drive and onto the pavement.

"Actually, he's not so bad," Robert said. "He's got his own problems."

I stared out the window at the desert, hoping to communicate through pointed silence that whatever problems Ben Slater might have, I wasn't interested in them. Disliking him was the only purely pleasurable thing about the morning. Counting last night, I'd lost nearly a thousand dollars in six weeks, wiping out my savings account, which had contained the student loan money that was supposed to last me through the end of May, almost two months away. On Monday I'd sold my pool cue, and yesterday morning I'd given blood to get table stakes in Ben Slater's poker game. My rationale was that by playing poker with Ben Slater and the boys I'd be *saving* money, a line of reasoning I'd borrowed from Robert Crane, who used it whenever he needed a night off from the dogs and away from his wife.

For some reason I thought of Lanny Aguilar, my roommate, who'd accused me of being lucky. He and I had been sharing a three-bedroom apartment with another guy, all of us finishing degrees at the university, each planning to enter graduate programs the following year. And so we'd gathered round the stereo receiver that December afternoon in 1969 to listen to the new draft lottery and find out whether the government would insist we continue our educations in Southeast Asia. There'd been a bunch of us, I remember, all with vested interests. Lanny's birthday had been first, his number nineteen.

"Well," he said, standing up, "that's over."

Nobody said anything. There wasn't anything to say.

"In fact," he went on, looking at each of us individually, "just about everything's over. If nobody minds, I think I'll go over to the library and write my will or something."

My own number had been 348 and when Lanny returned from the library later that evening, he'd lifted me right out of the chair I was sitting in and pinned me against the wall with his big forearm up under my chin. "Three forty-eight?" he said. "Three-fucking-forty-eight?"

As we wound down out of the foothills, Tucson lay below us on the left, shimmering in the already considerable heat. At First Avenue we passed the horsetrack, recently abandoned and already reclaimed by desert weeds. The quarterhorses had run there for a short season until about two years ago, but it had been a hot, low-budget, dusty experience. I tried to think if I'd ever heard of any place that offered pari-mutuel wagering going under before. I couldn't. In fact, it seemed a violation of natural law, the sort of thing that if it became common knowledge could seriously undermine the way things were done in America.

"What was your draft number?" I asked Robert.

He looked at me suspiciously. "Why?"

"No reason," I said. "Curiosity."

"I don't remember," he said. "I ended up Four-F anyway."

I frowned at him. Robert was a big man. Fit-looking. "Flat feet?"

"Acne."

"What?"

"Really. If you had bad acne, they wouldn't take you. Said the gas masks wouldn't fit snug. I ate about a dozen Hershey bars a day for two weeks before the physical. Stayed up late, watched dirty movies, quit beating off, wouldn't wash my face. You should've seen me."

"Pretty smart," I said, though I wasn't sure I believed him.

"Yes and no," he said. "Took me about a year to get rid of the rash. Couldn't get laid. Couldn't quit the chocolate. Got to be a vicious circle, kind of."

I looked over at him. He was absolutely deadpan. I examined his face for signs of acne. "Bullshit," I said finally.

"Good for you," he grinned. "Most people believe that story. The acne was my fall-back plan actually. I've always wondered if it would have worked."

I didn't say anything, unsure whether acne could be induced.

"So what *was* your number?" I said when I remembered he'd dodged the issue.

Robert flushed deeply. "Three sixty-six," he admitted.

"Come on."

"Really," he said. "They had to account for February twenty-ninth, remember? Leap years between '44 and '50."

I laughed out loud.

"I know," he said. "I'm a lucky prick. Watch where I walk. Step in my footprints."

"That's what I've *been* doing, if you think about it," I reminded him. It was true, too. I'd met Robert and his wife Anita at a party six months earlier. Everybody had been pretty stoned and Robert, who was also pretty stoned, had confessed to me that he preferred less trendy vices. "You ever go to the dog track?" he wanted to know.

We went the next night and I could tell right away he was compulsive. The funny part was that Anita was just as bad. They were finishing up M.A.s—Robert in psychology, Anita in English—and living in a dingy married student housing facility. By pooling their meager teaching assistant stipends and eating boxed macaroni and cheese dinners they were able to finance their evenings at the dog track. Anita was as savvy about the dogs as anybody I knew, and if Robert had left things to her, they probably would have been rich. But, of course, there were times when the dogs wouldn't run for either of them, and then she would resort to writing freshman compositions for football players. She had a knack for writing a genuine C+ paper on just about any topic. She knew just the words to misspell, how to mess up the sentences without messing them up *too* much, how to miss the point of the assignment narrowly and do the whole thing in language that never aroused the suspicion of the instructor. Robert said he'd tried it a couple of times, but he'd fucked up and written a solid B+ essay for a borderline illiterate and the kid had gotten caught. According to Robert, he'd been the biggest, dumbest, nicest kid you ever met, and he hadn't given Robert up, even when threatened with suspension. Now Robert stuck to the dogs and poker, and left the freshman essays on *Heart of Darkness* to Anita. When they were hitting at the track, their bank account swelled up to around five grand and they ate out a lot. When the right dogs ran out of the money they ate at home and bickered about whose fault it was until their luck changed. What they both feared most was the day they'd be so broke they couldn't afford admission to the clubhouse.

"So," Robert Crane said, when we pulled up in front of my apartment and I'd finished telling him how Lanny had tossed me into the wall for having a 348 draft number. How he'd lasted two months in Vietnam. Robert was looking at me intently, a little cross-eyed, like when he concentrated on the racing form. "You figure if you keep losing long enough you'll prove you're just as unlucky as him, is that it?"

I laughed at him. "Not even close."

"Okay," he said. "My other theory is you're just the dumbest gambler ever."

"You're getting warmer," I said, sliding out of his car.

"Sure you don't need a couple bucks till Monday?"

"If I did, I'd say so."

"You don't have to get pissed."

"I'm not," I told him. "You've never heard of a losing streak, right?"

"Your telephone's ringing," he said.

It was. We could both hear it, all the way out there by the curb.

"The pups run tonight," he said.

"The pups run every night," I reminded him. "I think I'll take a break, if it's all right with you. Losing is bad enough without having to listen to people tell you why it's happening."

He put the car in gear. "You're missing an opportunity. Monday you'll have to lose twice as much to make up."

He was grinning at me, still cross-eyed.

"And you are a butthole," I grinned back.

"A lucky butthole," he corrected. "And proud of it."

By the time I got inside the telephone had stopped ringing, for which I was thankful. It was Sunday, my mother's day to call, though she usually waited until evening. She was about the last person in the world I wanted to talk to.

Portraying yourself as triumphant is no easy task when you're in a tailspin. It requires energy, for one thing, imagination for another. And if you had sufficient amounts of those, chances are you wouldn't be *in* a tailspin. Telling my mother the truth, unfortunately, was not an option. Ever since her nervous breakdown, she had an impossibly low truth threshold, as I had occasion to learn

and relearn during those interminable years of high school when
only lies contained the power to soothe. She was prone to upset.
Doubts, minor failures, inconveniences, disappointments, quirks
of fate—all flung her first into a tizzy, then into the bathroom for
a librium to calm her nerves. She had left the hospital addicted,
of course, though I hadn't realized it at the time. But for the pills,
she would not have returned at all. She took four a day, as a rule,
but if I managed to upset her she'd take a couple extra. As many
as it took. Then she'd smile at me, puppy-faced.

Mostly, though, our days had fit nicely, end to end, and I was
satisfied. The two years I'd spent with my father weighed upon
me, more heavily than they had in the living. That first night in
my mother's new flat, when I slid between the crisp, cold sheets
in my fresh pajamas, it occurred to me that I was lucky to be alive.
Wussy had been right all those years ago when he'd warned me
to keep a safe distance from the rockhead—he was a dangerous
man. Living under Sam Hall's roof, I had become a thief and a liar.
I'd made dangerous friends and knew too damn much of the
world for my own good. All of this was directly attributable to my
father's influence, it seemed to me, and I was thankful to have
escaped it. In our new flat, there was wallpaper on the walls and
rugs on the floors and a real kitchen and we ate dinner in the
dining room. When I opened my closet, there were clean clothes
hanging inside, and I bathed daily to be worthy of them, instead
of waiting until I offended myself. I had a haircut every other
week by a barber whose morals my mother approved of.

If I missed my father, I did not miss his world. It felt good to
know that I would not have to suffer another meal in Eileen
Littler's tiny kitchen. I didn't have to see Drew Littler any more,
or serve as reluctant witness to his violent lunacy. I considered
myself well rid of the lot of them—Drew, Eileen, Skinny Donovan, Tree, even Harry and Wussy, both of whom I had actually
imagined I liked, back when I was under my father's dubious
spell. I now lumped them all together as somehow responsible for
my own degeneracy. But mostly I blamed my father, and blamed
him most for not looking after me, for not seeing how low I was
sinking or for not caring, for not seeing that I deserved better—
that I was, if not a wonder, as my old friend Father Michaels had
thought, at least a good boy.

So I put him behind me. The only vestige of my father's world that I allowed myself during those endless high school years in my mother's cheerful flat was the pool table. My passion for the game took a long time to dissipate. For the first year I played just about every day, even in the cold of winter. Sometimes, down there in the garage, I would catch a glimpse of her white face framed by the small kitchen window upstairs, where she would watch and worry, as if she imagined he was down there with me, just out of sight along the blind wall, giving me quiet instructions.

If I was seldom truthful with my mother, it must be said that she was seldom truthful with me either, though back then our most blatant lies took the shape of silences. It had not taken us long to intuit the rules of our new relationship. She would tell me nothing about what it had been like in the hospital or the nursing home, or that private inner place she lived for so long where no one could reach her. And in return, I would refrain from any reference to my life with my father—our routines, our habits, our activities. Those two years, she often suggested, were simply lost. Tragically lost. It had been a dark time for both of us, and now it was best forgotten. There was certainly no need to invoke it.

She was all for pretending the chronological gap did not exist. Often, at night, when we were about ready to turn in and my mother had taken her final pill, she'd smile and take my hand. "It's like we were never apart," she'd say. "That's the way it always is when people truly care about each other." Her eyes would go dreamy and distant then, as if she weren't talking to me, but some imaginary person. "No amount of time, no amount of distance . . . nothing matters when two people . . ."

I always felt horrible when she said such things, though I knew that thinking them made her feel good and helped her get to sleep. Trouble was, after listening, *I* couldn't get to sleep, because what she insisted on was so *un*true it was frightening. The more she harped on what good friends we were, and how we knew each other's thoughts so completely that speaking was unnecessary, the longer I stayed awake wondering what was wrong with her, what kind of blindness it was that kept her from seeing that the two years I'd lived with my father had changed everything. I wasn't even *a* boy anymore, much less *her* boy. Every time she smiled and said we must take care never to lose that special thing we had, that rare ability to be completely honest with each other, it made me want to cry, because of course our rapport—that was one of her favorite words, rapport—was purely a figment of her imagination. I hadn't the slightest intention of telling her anything but the most soothing lies I could invent.

Most of the time we had nothing to say to each other at all. The long nights I'd spent alone in my father's apartment had made me introspective, the world's worst company, and there must have been times when she wondered what had become of the kid whose mouth had run nonstop from the moment she walked in the door from the telephone company, in need of a little peace. It probably would have charmed and eased her mind to hear me chatter again, and I think I would have if I could have thought of something to say.

What seemed inevitable to me was that one day, probably one day soon, she would suffer another collapse and return to the hospital. By being a model son and avoiding truth and other natural upsets, I hoped only to delay that return as long as possible. In the beginning, I hoped for a year. When at the end of that period she was not only still intact but had actually gained some ground, I was glad but unconvinced, even though by then she had reduced her daily ration of libriums from four or five to three or four. She had also put on more weight and begun to look womanly again. Her hair, which had been cut short when she was in the home, grew out again, and she spent a long time each night, just before bed, brushing it out before the mirror in her bedroom. Sometimes, when the light was right, and she tilted her head a certain way, she looked more like a girl of nineteen than a woman sneaking up on forty.

For her rejuvenation F. William Peterson deserved all the credit. Something about my mother had touched him long ago, maybe even that first afternoon she had come to see him, to get him to help with her divorce. At some juncture he must have realized that she was trouble, but he stuck with her. I don't know how much of his own money and professional time he spent in the hospital and later in Schenectady. I've asked him about it more than once, but never gotten a straight answer, and I know now that I probably never will. That he visited her regularly I know. That he spent his own money I deeply suspect. By no means the worst lawyer in Mohawk, he seemed to profit as little as any of them. I know he paid dearly and dutifully to the wronged Mrs. Peterson until that good woman finally relented and married real money in the shape of a plumber from Amsterdam, but I think when the money from the sale of my mother's little house began to evaporate he helped with the arrangements. As far as I've been able to ascertain, the night that my father caught him with a woman at The Elms must have been an anomaly in his behavior, symptomatic of the decline of his marriage, because from the moment my mother became the woman in his life, I've never known him to show the slightest interest in any other.

In fact, F. William Peterson's devotion to my mother bordered on the pitiful, especially given the trouble she'd caused him. Thanks to her he had been administered a thorough beating by my father, who seldom, over the years, missed an opportunity to promise another thrashing should the opportunity arise or the lawyer's behavior warrant. I once counted nine separate public humiliations that Will, as my mother referred to him, suffered at the hands of my father.

Though he remained undeterred from his objective, he must have considered giving up, especially that first year after my mother's return from Schenectady. Three nights a week he dined with us, and afterward, when my mother would allow him, he would mingle his soapy hands with hers beneath the suds of the yellow dishtub she placed in the sink. His own flat was a few short blocks away and not nearly as nice as the one he rented for us. When he wasn't visiting us, he was calling to make sure we were okay. Like me, he was afraid my mother would suffer a relapse, and he watched her carefully for the signs of the withdrawal that had signaled her previous breakdown, aware that this time, things would happen more swiftly and completely. Fearing this result, he was preternaturally patient in courting her affections, drawn to her ever more urgently as her health improved, but frightened that stepping up the pace of his courtship was as likely to result in disaster as euphoria.

I don't think he suspected, as I did, that my mother's feelings for him were restricted to gratitude for his great kindness. She was fond of him, of course. Only a monster wouldn't have been, given all he'd done. She may even have felt that it was her duty, now, to love him. That she did not was so obvious that even he should have seen it, and for all I know maybe he did. Maybe, the fact that she did not love him half as much as he deserved was balanced by the fact that he loved her twice as much as she deserved. In any case, he was there for the long haul.

I'm glad he never asked my opinion, because I'd have had to

tell him he had no chance. Night after night my mother played "Moon River" on our tinny portable record player, her eyes glazing over in the dark, until the record bupp-bupp-bupped against the center label. One thing was for sure. It wasn't F. William Peterson she was thinking about when she got like that, though I began to doubt it was anyone. My guess was that it was some imaginary person she'd met in the deep recess of her breakdown, the result of staring so long and hard out that nursing home window deep into the dark, bare woods outside her room. One afternoon when I came home from school I caught her looking at an old photograph of my father in his army uniform taken just before he went overseas, and she had the same faraway look in her eyes then. It wasn't that she was still in love with Sam Hall, of course. The photograph probably just reminded her of the boy she'd been in love with before the war, the boy who had returned changed, who may never have existed, at least as she now imagined him.

This is only a theory. I've never pretended to understand my mother.

In the end she relented, and I'm glad, too, because I think F. William Peterson himself would have had a nervous breakdown eventually if she hadn't let him into her bedroom. I don't know exactly when it happened, but I do remember being suddenly certain, absolutely certain, that it had happened. "Will" seemed suddenly calm and content, like a research scientist whose theories had finally been proved correct after years of collegial scoffing. The down side—and he would have many years to consider this—was that my mother, after holding him at bay for so long, apparently realized now that it had been a mistake to do so, that letting him into her bed was not such a big thing. If it made him happy, there wasn't a reason in the world he shouldn't *be* happy, or at least as happy as he could be in the knowledge that he was not, and never would be, the man of my mother's dreams.

The fact that F. William Peterson and my mother had become lovers was one of any number of truths my mother refused to confide in me, this despite her insistence that our relationship was built on trust and that we could tell each other anything. The result was grand comedy. When "Will" left, at around ten in the evening, I was supposed to believe that he was gone for good, never mind that the back stairs groaned under his considerable bulk when he returned a short hour later. I wasn't supposed to know that the signal for his return was the lowering, then raising, then lowering again of her bedroom shade, though this maneuver was nearly as noisy as the stairs.

Theirs was about the dumbest signal ever, and not just because it reduced the life expectancy of window shades (she went through three during my high school years), but because it required such extraordinary vigilance on the part of the person awaiting the signal. Poor F. William Peterson couldn't just drive by the house every half hour. He had to be out there in the street and watching until the signal was given. If he got distracted, or nodded off, he was likely to find the light in my mother's bedroom gone off entirely, and that was another signal. Usually, what he'd do was back out of the driveway, go around the block, and park a few houses down. From my bedroom window I could usually spot his car by the red spot where his cigarette glowed in the front seat as he waited.

Not that this was an every-night occurrence. She let him come to her this way no more than three nights a month, and afterwards he usually creaked back down the stairs around one in the morning to sleep in his own flat. Only rarely did he stay the night, and I always figured that was because they forgot and fell asleep. Then I'd wake to whispers in the kitchen and I'd have to wait until he tramped down the back stairs in the gray half-light of dawn before I could get up and use the bathroom.

The weirdest part of all this was that things had to be played this way solely for my mother's benefit. I knew what was going on. F. William Peterson knew that I knew. Without trying to, we would sometimes run into each other on the stairs or in the doorway to the bathroom at a time when he wasn't supposed to be in the house, and then I'd have to duck back into my room before she saw that I saw and thereby avoid a long, utterly bizarre explanation about how the heat had gone out in Will's flat and so he'd slept on our sofa (which sat pristine and unrumpled, devoid of blankets and pillow or other evidence of recent occupancy, in our collective peripheral vision). I always nodded soberly at these accounts, desiring only that she stop talking, stop piling up absurdities, so that I could stop pretending abject stupidity, for stupid I would have had to be to believe a word of her nonsense. I hadn't any great objection to her not telling me the truth, but if I couldn't have lied any better than that I'd have told the truth and faced the devil.

I think it was the weight of living with her, the dreadful thinness of our lies to each other, that got me thinking about going to college, and one sufficiently distant that I would not be expected to come home for holidays. I did not dislike my mother, and I certainly did not dislike F. William Peterson. It was just too nuts, like being forced to play Liars day after day with an opponent who had transparent bills. As profoundly as it had rankled me to lose to my father all the time, this slightly different version of the game I acted out with my mother was far worse. It was like playing with a kid.

So, in my junior year in high school, I started collecting college catalogues, and finally stumbled on just what I was looking for—an anthropology major with a specialty in archaeology. The best affordable schools were all in the western United States, a perfect excuse to go far, far away. My mother put up little fuss when I made applications. Colorado, Arizona, New Mexico, California. The very places she'd spoken long distance to and dreamed of. She understood me. Perfectly.

I slept until 6:30 when the telephone woke me. I counted seventeen rings before it stopped. It was dusk outside and the Sunday street was quiet. The Ford Galaxie I'd bought to come west with over six years ago sat at the curb. I'd have to sell it in the morning, unless I could get F. William Peterson to float me a loan when my mother called back, as she surely would. He'd send the money, no questions asked, which was why I knew I wouldn't ask him.

There was nothing in the refrigerator but an old jar of sweet pickles I couldn't remember buying. I ate the three or four that remained, dumped the empty jar. In the morning, after I'd sold the car, I'd see about a part-time job, one that didn't require a car, formally withdraw from the classes I'd stopped attending anyway, rethink, start over. That left just tonight. I thought about the loan Robert Crane had offered and regretted not taking him up on it. I should have agreed to meet him and Anita at the track. I could have told him I was sorry for getting steamed at him for explaining my losing streak and let them buy me dinner to show there were no hard feelings. The pickles had made me hungry.

It was such a pleasant scenario I hated myself for nixing the idea earlier. I consulted my watch and realized that they'd probably already left for the track. They both liked to arrive early, have a beer, pore over the program one last time. Lacking the price of admission to the clubhouse, there was no way I could drop in on them, and there was nothing to do but sit in my own dingy living room and listen to the telephone ring.

As I sat there on the sofa feeling sorry for myself, I realized I was staring at money. My makeshift coffee table was a tree stump from the front yard, the top of which I had leveled and shaved. A girl I'd dated briefly had hammered quarters, dimes, and nickles into the soft wood surface and laminated them there, creating an illusion so real that the few visitors I had were always trying to pick them up or brush them aside so they could set their beer cans down. I don't know how long I'd stared at them now before realizing that I wasn't broke, not as long as I had a good claw hammer.

An hour later I was on the road, four dollars and eighty cents in my pocket, only vaguely concerned that I had crossed an invisible line that prevented other men from mutilating tree stumps. I parked on a dark side street in South Tucson, several blocks from the fluorescent green dome of the dog track so I wouldn't have to pay for parking. It cost extra to get into the clubhouse, but that's where Robert and Anita would be, so I paid. I had enough left over for a beer by way of dinner.

I drank it, leaning against the small bar where the dark men who would spring for the clubhouse, but not the extra three bucks for table seating, always congregated. I tipped the bartender my last quarter, which he rubbed, then sniffed, just as he had the slick coins I'd used to pay for my draft.

The beer was cold and it immediately made me light-headed. In the last forty-eight hours I'd eaten nothing more substantial than Ben Slater's pretzels. It was already the third race and too late to get a bet down even if I'd had the money, so I glanced through my program quickly, deciding that the first race I really wanted to bet on was the fifth, where a dog called Blue Piniella looked like he couldn't lose. The funny part was that two of the three handicappers had him out of the money, which meant the mutt might even pay a fair price. The third handicapper, Jester, had him first, right where he should be, but Jester was acknowledged to be a flake, and this too could help.

As the third race was being run, I watched the people at the tables along the mezzanine. The same faces every night, most of them. The old hands stayed seated and watched the race on the ceiling and wall-mounted monitors. Newcomers got up and went over to the brass railing which separated the section they were in from the one immediately below. For some reason, they wanted to see the real race under the lurid yellow lights. Only after the dogs flashed by the finish line did they return to their tables.

When I spotted Robert and Anita Crane on the other side of the clubhouse, I went over and said hello. I liked talking to Anita, and I hoped Robert would intuit my situation and beg me to take the money he'd offered earlier. "Fuck me," he said when I walked up, tearing several tickets in half and tossing them over his big shoulder. Not a good sign.

Anita's attention was divided between Robert, the big tote board on the track's center island, and the legal pad attached to her clipboard. A Marlboro dangled from her pale lips. "I really hate it when he does that," she said, referring to Robert's torn tickets. "*Un*official it says up there big as life, and he's got the tickets torn up already."

"He's a jerk," I agreed, though I shared Robert's habit.

"Only four f'ing dogs would have to be disqualified for those tickets to be winners," Robert Crane said. "F'ing" was his one concession to Anita's tenderness and breeding.

"What do you know about Hawthorne?" Anita said to me.

"The Unpardonable Sin," I said. "You can screw up all your life and still get saved, provided you don't think you're better or worse than everybody else. English 102."

"Too clear," she said. "How about this: 'Nathaniel Hawthorne thought the unpardonable sin was one you couldn't forgive. The important thing was don't put people down, like in Goodman Brown.' "

"There you go," I said.

"That's the Hawthorne I knew and loved," Robert agreed, then to me, "She speaks the language, doesn't she?"

"She does indeed."

"Bad night, amigo," Robert said. "These particular dogs don't seem to know who's supposed to win."

"Blue Piniella," I said.

"Keep your voice down, for God's sake," Anita said.

We watched the handlers parade the dogs to the post for the fourth race, and I took Robert's chair when he went to get a bet down.

"I hear you're in the middle of a pretty amazing tailspin," Anita said, not looking up from her legal pad.

"These things happen," I said, trying to affect world-weariness.

"How bad is it?"

I ran my fingers through my hair. "Something's gotta give pretty soon, let's put it that way."

I'd no sooner spoken the words than I felt a chill. It took me a minute to place them, to realize that I had summoned them from across a gulf of over a decade. It was that long since I'd seen my father. According to my mother he'd moved back to Mohawk, but she hadn't seen him and didn't know if it was true.

"Robert says you're trying to lose," Anita said over the top of her reading glasses, and for some reason it pissed me off that she should say so. She herself looked like a cave dweller, her skin sallow, almost transparent, like a dusty moth's wing. "He says you're a classic case. He's going to do a paper on you." She raised her eyebrow significantly.

Her husband came back then, so I surrendered his chair. "Who you got here?" he said.

I told him I was letting this one alone.

"Let them all alone and then you might have something, right?" he said.

Anita made a face at him. "*Do* tell. What would *you* have?"

"I have you," Robert said, and I realized I had in fact stumbled into the middle of a marital spat. The subtlety of these things always surprised me. My father and mother had fought openly, their disagreements spilling out into the street or backyard. When married couples concealed their animosities in public, or tried to, it always threw me for a loop, and when the fourth race went off I was glad. I didn't want to hear their next coded, civilized exchange.

I also didn't want to be the subject of Robert Crane's thesis, so I strolled back to the little bar to mingle with the other desperate men who were waiting for some fucking thing to give. On my way I passed a table occupied by an affluent young couple who had gotten up and gone over to the rail to watch the race below under the yellow lights. It was probably their first time at the track and they'd left a twenty-dollar bill on the table. In all the commotion it would have been the easiest thing in a difficult world to lift it, put it down again on Blue Piniella's sleak nose in the fifth, and slip the twenty back later in the evening after the dog won and paid off. The next easiest would be to wait for Robert Crane to get up from the table to place his bets and put the touch on him. I'd pay him back tomorrow after I sold the Galaxie if Blue Piniella found a way to lose.

But I didn't do any of those things. Despite having slept all afternoon I was suddenly exhausted. Too tired to steal, to borrow, to cheer a long shot, to care much whether some fucking thing gave or whether it didn't. So I just stood there and watched the small monitor above the bar as Blue Piniella broke from the gate a head in front of the pack and ran like the wind, wire to wire. He was beautiful, and I thought about his pure need to run, all the way back to my car.

When I got home, sure enough, the telephone was ringing. It was just like my mother to call and call, to stay up all night calling if need be. I decided to tell her I'd been home the whole time and working too intently to bother answering. Make her feel guilty about interrupting. "Yes, what is it, for heaven's sake?" I said into the receiver.

"Ned?" the voice was female, distant and unrecognizable on the fuzzy long distance line. A Mohawk voice, but not my mother's. "Ned Hall?"

"Who is this?" I said.

"This *is* Ned, isn't it?" A pause. "I wouldn't have called except it's important," Eileen Littler assured me. "It's about Sam . . . your father."

30

I tried my best, all the way across country, but it was hard to imagine my father a drunk. But then it was hard to imagine my father.

Ten years was a long time. I hadn't seen him since the late spring afternoon he and Wussy had delivered the pool table. I'd been fourteen then, and I wasn't even sure I'd recognize him. My first night on the bus—we must have been somewhere in New Mexico—I dreamed that when I arrived in Mohawk, a toothless, feeble old man with a cloud of gray hair was there to meet me at the Four Corners. When I stepped off the bus, he croaked, "Ned? Ned my boy?" and I pushed him away angrily, my own father. The dream had been so spooky it got me trying to calculate how old he was, so I wouldn't be surprised. I figured he had to be between forty-five and fifty. That was as close as I could get.

Eileen hadn't gone into detail. She said she'd called because she was wondering whether I had any plans to visit my mother once school was out (How had she known that I was *in* school and where?), because if I was, I should look my father up, because his life wasn't so hot right now and because maybe a visit from his college graduate son would buck him up. "You don't have long hair, do you?" she added.

"Not very," I said.

"Good," she said. "Long hair's one of the things that's got him bent out of whack, or so I'm told."

They themselves were on the outs, at least from what I could gather. I was to forget this call, in fact. There wasn't much she could do with him anymore, not that she ever had been able to do that much. Hadn't my mother written about him?

I said no, not a word, which struck her as odd and me as normal. According to Eileen, he'd been arrested no fewer than five times in the last two years, his drunken exploits fully chronicled in the *Mohawk Republican,* a newspaper that she seemed surprised to discover was not routinely for sale at newsstands in Tucson, Arizona. Was I sure I hadn't heard a thing?

For some reason, again according to Eileen, in the most advanced stages of his drunkenness he would recall that he had a son who was a college graduate and then he'd start talking about me to anybody who'd listen. People were getting tired of it. I said I could understand that.

We left it that I'd think about paying a visit in a couple of months, but by the time I hung up I'd decided to leave for Mohawk in the morning. There was nothing keeping me in Tucson, I realized. Certainly not the doctoral degree I'd begun to lose interest in the moment the draft lottery had freed me to pursue it. My landlord would be pissed if I bolted midterm, but he'd keep my deposit and sell my few sticks of furniture to make himself feel better. And he'd long coveted my tree stump. So, I threw my clothes into my grandfather's old navy duffel bag, and in the morning I drove the Galaxie down to a used car lot across from the Greyhound terminal. I told a man wearing a sport coat that was shinier than any of the cars on his tiny lot that I could let him have the Ford for three hundred dollars. We settled on eighty-five, with which I purchased a See America special fare ticket. There was almost twenty dollars left over, which meant that I'd be able to eat during the three-day trip, at least occasionally.

In Albany, I had to change buses for the short trip further upstate to Mohawk. I had a few fellow passengers to begin with, but the last of them got off in Amsterdam, leaving the big bus to its driver and me. I stayed where I was, halfway down the aisle, and watched the cold spring rain through the dirty window. The countryside was already lush and everywhere green, except where tilting rusted billboards interrupted the landscape, last season's advertisements for bankrupt businesses peeling down in strips. The constant sunshine of the Southwest, so full of false optimism, had often depressed me, and it occurred to me, as I sat there in the straining bus as it lumbered up Fonda Hill toward Mohawk, that I had solved the problem of excess optimism, anyway. It was the kind of gray late afternoon that promised dusk within minutes, but wouldn't make good for three hours. That was fine with me. I was in no hurry.

When the bus pulled up in front of the cigar store on the Four Corners and I was handed my duffel bag, I realized I didn't know what to do next. Main Street was virtually deserted after business hours, and sad-looking too, the emptiness of it, compared to the downtown of my childhood. From the Four Corners I could see that several more buildings had come down, including the movie theater and the old City Hall where my father had on numerous occasions spent the night. With so many gray buildings gone, the town resembled a Hollywood back lot. In the gaps between buildings you could see things that weren't supposed to be visible from the street—dirty side entrances to shops that kept up halfway decent appearances out front, full garbage dumpsters awaiting trash collection, a car or two on blocks—things that would have been secrets had the buildings along Main formed an unbroken line. No doubt the back alleys of every town were more or less the same, but it seemed a shame the town should be so transparent. Like people, communities deserved a facade, however flimsy. The old SHOP DOWNTOWN MOHAWK, Where There's Always Plenty of Parking sign had faded into the bricks of the wall it had been painted on, and people must have seen the irony and just let it go. Since I didn't know where my father was living, it made sense to go see my mother, who would surely take it as a betrayal if she discovered I'd gone someplace else first. Trouble was, I didn't feel up to confronting her quite yet and besides, just walking in on her without warning with my longish hair and four-day beard might knock her for a hell of a loop.

There was a phone booth in front of the Mohawk Trust, so I shouldered my duffel bag and made for that. It didn't take me long to realize it would be useless. There was no listing for Sam Hall or Eileen Littler. My father had never had a phone. Eileen had always kept her number unlisted. I started to check on Wussy until, after a few moments of vague, dazed leafing, I remembered I didn't know his last name. I had more or less the same problem with Skinny Donovan. There were about a dozen Donovans listed but, not surprisingly, no "Skinny." (His real name—Patrick—I'd somehow forgotten.) It occurred to me as I stood outside the phone booth in the persistent drizzle that my knowledge of these people was incomplete, though this peculiar way of knowing— these nicknames, partial identities, aliases—represented standard commerce in Mohawk. Sign here, Tree.

There was nothing to do but readjust my thinking, get back to local time and place. The clock above the Mohawk Trust flashed the former, and I synchronized my watch, which made me feel a little better. After all, I was a tough, worldly, steely-eyed twenty-four now, and college educated to boot. If I couldn't locate my father in his own hometown, there was something wrong with me. The place to start was the Mohawk Grill.

I never got there though. I hadn't gone more than a dozen steps toward its buzzing neon sign, clearly audible in the late afternoon stillness, when a door opened between the Rooker Pharmacy and Lauria's Men's Wear and a large, well-dressed man stepped into the street, his back to me. He was in the act of struggling on with a new pair of leather gloves and I knew who it was before he even looked up.

The door that locked shut behind him confirmed it: F. William Peterson, Attorney-at-Law, was one of the names listed there.

When he looked up and saw me smiling at him, he gave me a curt nod and headed down the street in the direction I'd just come from. He got halfway to the bank before he stopped dead, stalled there for a second, then wheeled around. I'd stayed right where I was, duffel bag over my shoulder. "Ned?" he said.

"Will?" I said.

"Ned *Hall?*" He was coming toward me now, still tentatively, as if when he got there, he meant to touch my cheek to make sure I was real.

"Pop?" I said, since the situation couldn't have been much more absurd.

He stopped right in front of me, his red face beaming. "Look at *you,*" he said, offering a gloved hand.

"I can't," I said. "I'm looking at you."

Poor F. William Peterson never did have much of a handshake, and he still didn't. Always soft, he was even softer now, a boneless roast of a man. He looked genuinely glad to see me as we shook, but then he stopped in midpump, his brow darkening. "You haven't been home yet?"

I told him I'd just that minute stepped off the bus.

He looked up and down the deserted street then, as if to be sure we hadn't been spotted. "Thank God," he said. "Come with me."

A moment later we were upstairs in his second-floor office. We had the place to ourselves, half an hour past closing. Like the offices of many small-town lawyers, F. William Peterson's could have passed for that of an insurance agent, with its cheap wood paneling and big metal desk.

"I'd better call her," he said, picking up the phone, motioning me to a chair by the window overlooking Main, one story lower and fifty yards closer to the Four Corners, but otherwise quite similar to the view I'd had from the Accounting Department. It occurred to me that if I wanted to find my father, the best plan might be to stay right were I was. He was almost sure to come strolling out of the pool hall or the Mohawk Grill or The Glove Tavern some time in the next twenty-four hours, his hands plunged deep into his pockets, rolling gently at the knees as he surveyed his domain.

After he dialed, F. William Peterson swiveled in his chair so his back was to me. When my mother answered, he spoke softly, as if anticipating embarrassment. "Hi," he said. That must have been all she let him get out, because he started to say something else, stopped abruptly, and just listened. "I know," he said. "I know. Half an hour."

He swiveled around to make a face at me. His free hand went yap-yap-yap.

"You know Fridays," he said, when he sensed an opening. "Half an hour, the latest."

She must have hung up without saying goodbye, because he looked at the receiver as if they'd been disconnected. "What a woman," he said, with red-faced cheer, and then, as if the two ideas were related, "Am I glad to see *you*!"

"How is she?" I said. "Really."

I had spoken with him once or twice on the phone in the past few years, but my mother had always been there in the room with him, and of course her own protestations on the subject of her health I considered completely worthless.

"Better!" he said. "Almost better! Almost completely better!"

"That's good," I said, studying his performance.

"Down to one pill a day," he went on. "You won't know her. Sometimes, she even skips the one. Those are rough days, but . . ."

Something about the way he said this last suggested that the rough days were rougher on him than her. "Remember how she couldn't do anything at first? Couldn't decide ketchup or mustard? You should see her go now."

"I'll bet it's something," I said.

"What you'll want to do," he said, "is call her. Tonight. Tell her you're in Buffalo or someplace like that. Give her the night to get used to it. Then come by tomorrow. She's a trooper about day-to-day stuff, but surprises throw her."

"All right," I said, relieved.

His expression darkened. "Seen your father?"

Suddenly, something made sense that had been nagging at me. "*You* gave Eileen my number—"

He nodded, reluctantly. "If I'd called and your mother'd found out—" he drew his index finger across his throat. "I didn't want you to leave in the middle of the term though. Did that foolish woman tell you to come right away?"

"No," I said. "It sounded serious though."

"What did she tell you?" he was watching me carefully.

"That he's a drunk."

He rolled his eyes. "Charming woman, Eileen Littler. The soul of delicacy."

"Is it true?"

F. William Peterson leaned back in his chair, exhaled through his nostrils. "His most pressing problem is more immediate. He was in an accident last fall on the lake road. A young girl in the other car ended up in the hospital. Damn near died. A goddamn miracle everybody wasn't killed, including Sam. It was a head-on collision. The good news is the girl was driving illegally, at night, on a learner's permit and probably speeding. Her boyfriend lied to the cops, said he was driving, but we know better. The bad news is Sam was legally DWI. We'll push the hell out of mitigating circumstances, but—"

"He'll go to jail?"

"Almost certainly."

"For long?"

"Probably not. And probably not for a while. The insurance companies are wrangling and the medical people are involved. It's been six months already and it may be another year before it comes to trial. The other bad thing is that he's been arrested twice in the meantime, the last time two nights ago. I just got him out on bail yesterday."

This didn't make sense. "Why haven't they taken his license?"

"They did," F. William Peterson said. "This is your father we're talking about, remember?"

Unfortunately, that did make sense. In fact, I had forgotten the way he operated. To take Sam Hall's license proved only one thing—that you didn't know him. If you didn't want him to drive, you had to take his *car*, not his license. And while you were at it, you'd have to take his friends' cars, too. And even then, you'd only be making it more inconvenient for him. He had a lot of friends.

"All of this is off the record, by the way. A young colleague of mine is the attorney of record. Your mother ever found out I was involved . . ."

I drew my index finger across my throat. He shuddered.

We just sat and looked at each other for a minute, and suddenly we were grinning like a couple of conspirators who shared important inside knowledge, or perhaps even affection.

Finally, we stood and shook again. "Damn, it *is* fine to see you, Ned."

I said it was good to see him, too. "You better get on over there," I told him.

Outside in the street, we shook hands a third incredible time, and suddenly he said, "How you fixed for money?"

I was very glad he asked. "Actually . . ."

"Right," he said, and handed me a twenty.

"I don't know when I'll be able to give it back," I warned him.

"What difference," he said. "You're here. That's the main thing."

I shoved my hands in my pockets, because he looked for all the world like he wanted to shake on that too.

"You better call by ten-thirty. That's when she goes to bed," he said, flushing red in the gathering darkness.

I said I'd remember. "Any idea where I can find him?"

"Try right around the corner on Glenn. The Night Owl. If not there, Greenie's. If not there . . ."

"Right," I said.

"By ten-thirty," he said. "You'll . . . shave, of course."

I shouldered my duffel bag and we parted. At the Four Corners I stopped and looked back up the street and saw that he'd stopped too and was waving. I waved back.

The Night Owl had been called something else the last time I was in Mohawk. I tried to remember what, and couldn't. But I was pretty sure it was one of the few bars my father hadn't frequented. Standing outside, I suddenly felt weak, partly from not having eaten in a while, but mostly from being spooked. The possibility that I might not recognize my own father swept over me again, and along with it a wave of nausea. I propped my duffel bag up against the wall of the tavern and sat on it for a minute or two until the low dusky sky turned honest black. From inside came the clack of billiard balls and the occasional volley of deep-throated male laughter. He probably wasn't even in there, I told myself. In fact, I probably had a long night ahead of me. I not only wouldn't find him here, but I'd have to hit Greenie's and the High Life and The Glove, and the Outside Inn, and he wouldn't be at any of them. He would be someplace like The Elms on the outskirts of town, too far to walk with a duffel bag in the dark. Or maybe he was even farther off than that, in some new favorite place in Johnstown or Mayfield or Perth, or someplace on the

Saratoga road where bars grew out of the surrounding woods like native flora. Maybe he would be out at The Lookout, the first of the bars he took me to with Tree, that afternoon in October when I'd gone to the beach with the Claudes. He could be anywhere, and it was doubtful that F. William Peterson, of all people, would know his precise whereabouts.

I was just getting to my feet when a blue pickup with a tiny camper balanced on the back pulled up at the curb and Wussy got out. He looked exactly the same, a little heavier maybe, and wearing what could well have been the same shapeless fishing hat, still full of bright hooks. "Sam's Kid," he said right off, as if he'd left me in this precise spot an hour ago with instructions to stay put till he got back.

We shook hands. "The rockhead inside?" he said.

I told him I'd been just about to go inside and find out.

He held the door for me. "That's his car, so. . . ." He was pointing to an ancient battleship of a gray Cadillac convertible across the street, one wheel up on the curb. For some reason it had a white hood. I don't know how I could have failed to notice and draw the necessary inference, but I had. No doubt about it, I'd lost the rhythm of Mohawk life, forgotten what to look for, how to see.

"Not that that means anything," Wussy was saying. "He could have left it there two days ago, forgot all about it and reported it stolen by now."

Just inside, I hesitated, grabbing the sleeve of Wussy's blue flannel shirt. "I hear he's in rough shape," I said.

"Sam Hall was born in rough shape," Wussy said, apparently unconcerned. "Or did you forget."

We were standing in an entryway, between the inner and outer doors, the noise from inside louder now. "You better come in and say hello anyhow, before he spots you."

We went in, Wussy making an immediate detour into the men's room. "First thing I gotta do is pee, Sam's Kid. Tell your old man it's his round and I'll be right there."

I heard him before I saw him. There were only a dozen or so men at the long smoky bar, a few others around the pool table, off to the side. My father's voice, the unmistakable pitch and texture of it seemed to come not so much from the far end of the room as from some prememory, filtered through amniotic fluid.

My heart fluttered in the old way, and when I located him through the smoke on the last stool before the bar cornered, I stopped and watched for a second. He was talking to a young fellow about my own age. The only vacant stool at the bar happened to be right next to him, so I slid onto it quietly, jostling him only when I stuffed my duffel bag in between our stools.

When he turned to see who'd nudged him, his eyes were red and slightly unfocused, but only for a second.

"Son," he said.

31

It was almost two in the morning when I remembered I was supposed to call my mother. We'd closed the Mohawk bars and were on the lake road, climbing into the dark Adirondacks, Wussy at the wheel of my father's convertible. For some inexplicable reason we had the top down and it was cold as hell. I was in the backseat, leaning forward between my father and Wussy, trying to take advantage of what little protection the windshield offered against the brittle wind. The dark trees extended out over the narrow road, their top branches forming a canopy, the full moon darting among them, racing us all the way.

"Shit," I said.

What, my father wanted to know. He'd been half asleep, and didn't know where he was.

"I was supposed to call my mother," I said.

"You can call her from up here," he said.

"It's too late," I said. "She'll be asleep."

"I'll call her if you're scared to," he offered. "She's used to being disappointed in me."

"Let the kid call her," Wussy advised. "You'll get her all worked up and then she'll shoot me by accident."

"I'll call in the morning," I said.

"It is the morning. Before you know it, it'll be this time *tomorrow* morning."

In fact, the night had just that deliciously out-of-control feel to it, enhanced by the fact that I had no idea where we were headed, though my father and Wussy claimed to. The proceedings had begun innocently enough. I'd told my father that I meant to have just the one beer with him, that I was exhausted and smelly from the long trip, that I needed to flop. He was already pretty bleary-eyed and it was my intention to drag him home with me, wherever the hell home might be. Wussy said he was going home himself, after just the one, but then somebody they knew came in and said who's this, and my father had told him, and then the somebody bought a round to celebrate. This happened several times. Before I knew it, I had three sweating bottles of beer lined up in front of me. They hit me like a shot of adrenalin from a cardiac needle and the next thing I knew I was shooting pool and quarters were lined up in challenge from hell to breakfast. I hadn't played in a long time, but my first two opponents were my father and Wussy, and by the time they'd beaten themselves I was beginning to get my stroke back. Wussy said so long, he was going home, and so, after traveling nearly three thousand miles, ostensibly to rescue my father from alcoholism, I discovered myself partners with him, the two of us winning beers faster than we could drink them, my father seldom even getting the opportunity to shoot. It took us two hours to leave.

"Let's stop in here and say hello to somebody you know," my father said when I wheeled his big convertible onto North Main. I had expected him to argue when I asked if I could drive, but he didn't. The place he wanted me to stop at was another gin mill that had been something else before I left Mohawk. It was called Mike's Place now. The first person we saw when we came in was Wussy, who bought a round in the time it took to walk from the front door to the near end of the bar.

"What can I say," he said before my father or I had a chance to comment. "Anymore, this is home."

The bartender turned out to be my old friend Mike, from The Elms, which he'd lost two years earlier in Vegas. He seemed in pretty good spirits, considering. The first thing he did was slap a quarter in front of me and tell me to play the jukebox.

"Fucking Duane Eddy," he winked at my father. "The kid must

have played a hundred dollars worth of Duane Eddy, in quarters."

"Who's Duane Eddy?" my father said. I don't think he ever heard music, no matter what kind it was or how loud you played it.

"So," my father said when Wussy was in the john and Mike had gone off to pour drinks. "What's up?"

"What do you mean?" I said, though I knew what he meant, all right. He meant I hadn't been in Mohawk in seven years and now here I was, and he was curious about the timing. Not so curious that the question couldn't wait three hours to get asked, but curious.

"A little bird's been whispering in your ear, I imagine," he said.

"Not really," I replied lamely.

"Nobody's mentioned my little problems, right?" he said, looking at me the way he used to when we played Liars, or when he wanted to know what the hell was wrong with me.

"I just got here," I said. "I haven't seen anybody yet."

He nodded. "They don't have telephones out there in New Mexico, right?"

"Arizona," I said.

"No telephones in Arizona, right?"

"Right," I said. "If there were, you'd have called me sometime, right?"

"Or you'd have called me, since you knew where *I* lived."

"Or you'd have called my mother to find out my number," I said. Then it occurred to me that something he'd said wasn't true. "Besides, how was I supposed to know you were back in Mohawk."

He answered the part he was comfortable about. "I don't talk to your mother. You know that."

"Bullshit," said Wussy, fresh from the men's room and trailing the unmistakable scent of urinal cakes. "We saw her last year when we went over there to get the pool table. Take it back to New Mexico with you when you go. I've busted my balls on it for the last time."

"Arizona."

"I don't care where," Wussy said. "Just take it. Every time the rockhead gets evicted, I get to have my back fucked up all over again. Wouldn't be so bad if he'd get a first-floor apartment every now and then."

My father nudged me. "Everybody should work once in a while, don't you think? Just for a change of pace?"

"I'm just glad there aren't no ten-story buildings in Mohawk," Wussy said.

"They got the high rise going up," Mike said, having drifted back from the other end of the bar.

Wussy shook his head. "The good news is you gotta be sixty-five to get in there. Sam Hall won't live to *be* no sixty-five. There's less of him every year."

"I'll piss on *your* grave," my father said. "After that, I don't care."

"You show the kid your finger?" Wussy wanted to know.

"What finger?" my father said. His left hand was on the bar, fingers surrounding the tapered stem of his beer glass. His right hand was tucked under his left armpit as he hunched forward, elbows on the bar. It occurred to me that he'd been sitting that way pretty much all night.

"What finger?" I said.

" 'What finger' is right," Wussy said.

"You mean this one?" my father said, putting his right hand on the bar where I could see it. All that was left of his once blackened thumb was a stub, which stopped just short of where the knuckle would have been. I stared at it stupidly, unwilling to accept the testimony of my senses. Was it possible I had played pool with him for two hours and not noticed? It wasn't his bridge hand, but still.

"Could have been worse. It wasn't his pussy finger, anyhow," Wussy said.

"Nope," my father said, showing Wussy his middle finger.

"Put that away before you lose it too," Wussy advised. "Pretty soon you'll be left-handed."

I was still looking at the mangled thumb. "Jesus," I said, feeling suddenly woozy.

"No big thing," my father said, flexing the other fingers on the right hand, the thumb stub bowing forward in awkward concert with the others. "Little accident last summer is all. Some dumb Polack forgot to hold on to a four-hundred-pound pipe."

"Jesus," I said again.

My father shrugged. "You don't really think you could beat me at eight-ball if I had all my fingers, do you?"

"I'm going home," Wussy said.

"So go," my father said. "You're always promising, but every-place I go, you're there."

"Take care of him, Sam's Kid," Wussy said, pocketing his change from the bar. "He's a dangerous man."

"Are you still here?" my father wanted to know.

"Not me," Wussy blew him a kiss. "I'm history."

When he was, in fact, gone, my father ordered us yet another beer. Our agreement to have just one was a couple six packs defunct, not even worthwhile as a pretense anymore. "So," he said. "You figure on staying around for a while, or what?"

"I guess," I said. "First thing is to find a job."

"That's easy," my father said and called to Mike, who rejoined us. "I got your new day bartender," he said.

Mike looked me over. "I could use one," he admitted. "A good, clean-shaven, short-haired bartender is something I could use come Monday."

"There you go," my father said. "You know how to make a Manhattan?"

"Not really," I said.

He shrugged. "You got till Wednesday to learn. Otherwise it's just drawing beer from a tap and pouring shots. Stuff a hotshot college graduate should be able to figure out."

He cuffed me then, pretty hard, too. Which made it official. I was home.

"You're telling me I don't know where the Big Bend is," my father said in feigned disbelief.

Wussy paid him no attention. He handled my father's convertible with the kind of ease that suggested that this was not the first time the driving had been relegated to him.

I was not only drunk, but lost. I'd been okay until Wussy turned off the lake road, then turned again. Two turns was all it had taken to disorient me completely.

"All I'm telling you," Wussy said to my father, "is that if I stopped the car and let you out right here you couldn't find your way back home in two days with a map."

"Your ass," my father insisted. "You missed your turn, I'm telling you."

"Right," Wussy said. "I missed my turn." He kept right on the way he was going, though.

"How come you never go home when you say you're going to?" my father wanted to know. It was puzzling, I had to admit. We'd gone to two more bars after Mike's Place, and at the second one, there was Wussy again at the end of the bar, big as life.

"It's a good thing for you I don't," Wussy said. "Be just like you to take your kid up into the mountains his first night back and the two of you never heard from again."

"Can you get something to eat in this place?" I said, suddenly ravenous in the cold night air. My eyes were streaming now. It felt cold enough to snow, April or no April.

Wussy looked over at my father. "If you aren't too particular, I guess."

My father was still convinced we were going the wrong way. "Lake George has all kinds of food," he said. "That's where we're going to end up if we stay on *this* road. We'll be there just about in time for a late breakfast."

"What's this up here?" Wussy said, slowing down, pointing to a building set back off the road in a clearing. At the dirt road turnoff, our headlights swept across a carved wooden sign nailed to a tree. "BIG BEND HUNTING LODGE" it said.

"Son of a bitch," my father said, running his fingers through his hair, which was standing straight up from the wind.

"I never heard you," Wussy said. "What's this place? Lake George?"

My father shrugged. "What can I tell you? It's not the way I go to get to the Big Bend, that's all."

"The fact that we got here proves that," Wussy said, pulling into the large lot. There were only three or four other cars besides ours, and the place was dark except for a "Carling Black Label" in one window. "Welcome to the Happy Hunting Grounds, Sam's Kid," Wussy chuckled.

We all got out and felt our way in the dark toward the big porch, the lodge itself nothing but a vague outline against the dark trees, which moaned high up in the wind. On the steps it occurred to my father to ask me something. "You aren't married are you," he said.

I told him I wasn't.

From inside we heard faint music, distant, as if it were coming from deep in the surrounding woods. It was louder when Wussy opened the door and yellow light spilled out onto the porch. A woman, naked from the waist up, was sitting cross-legged on a bar stool across the room, talking to the woman bartender, who was also topless.

"This is on me by the way," my father said. "I missed your graduation."

"You gonna wike up, Honey-bun, or just sleep through the best part?"

The young woman was roughly my age, a better-looking girl than you might expect to find in a hunting lodge, though not much better. She was right, too. I'd gone right to sleep while she was in the little closet bathroom doing I couldn't imagine what. She was astraddle me now, though, having pulled my jeans down around my knees.

"I don't mind jump-startin' you, but I want you awike enough to know you got what you got."

That sounded reasonable to me. I watched her work for a minute, then asked her what was most on my mind. "Where are you from?" I said.

"Marion."

"All right. Where are you from, Marion." It wasn't a Mohawk accent.

"No, I mean I'm *from* Marion. Illinois. Where the penitentiary is. My boyfriend is in there, or was. They said they weren't ever gonna let him out, but I was scared they might anyway. Which is how come I de-parted. He was trouble with a capital tee. How we doin'?"

"Fine," I said, though we weren't. She had large, fine breasts, but watching them roll was making me seasick.

"Good," she said. "You know you feel just like a ace cube?"

"I'm warming up though," I said.

"I can feel it," she said, continuing her workmanlike assault on what ailed me. "I come up here, 'cause it's a place he won't think to look."

"It's true," I said. "It would take a stroke of luck to find you here."

It had taken a stroke of luck for me to find her, and I deeply regretted it. After a while she stopped. "I don't thank you're near as fond of me as you should be b'now."

"Marion," I said. "Forgive me."

She must have, because I don't remember any more struggles. When I woke up again, I was alone, gray light filtering in through the small window above the bed. It was incredibly still except for a hissing sound on the other side of the wall I'd been sleeping

against. My jeans were still down around my knees, so I pulled
them up, buttoned the fly, all the while listening to the hissing.
When I pulled back the curtain and glanced outside, I saw it was
Wussy pissing in an isolated patch of snow. He looked up and saw
me.

"First thing every morning," he said, his voice flat and distant
on the other side of the glass. "Can't wait."

I checked the little room that Marion had disappeared into and
discovered that it was nothing but a tiny dressing room, not a
bathroom. There was nothing to do but join Wussy, so I did. By
the time I got out there, he was finished, but he kept me company.

"Snowing," he said, and sure enough it was. When you looked
up, you could see the flakes coming down through the trees,
melting before they reached the ground. "Looks like you're
gonna have a good effect on him," Wussy said. "Behaved himself
last night for the first time in a hell of a while."

I looked at him in disbelief. If last night constituted good behavior, I didn't want to know about the bad.

"I wonder where he is," I said, afraid he might be awake and
listening on the other side of the wall.

We found him snoring on the sofa, his mouth wide open, the
way he'd always slept when we lived together. He snorted awake
when Wussy kicked his foot. "It's about time," he said, sitting up,
consulting his watch. He studied Wussy first, then me. "Well?" he
said.

"Well enough," I told him.

"Good," he said.

We went outside to where the convertible sat, all by itself now.
"How'd the top get down?" my father said.

Wussy and I looked at each other.

"It was down last night?"

"Right on the first try," Wussy said.

My father shrugged. "We must've froze, didn't we?" he said,
looking to me for confirmation. When I nodded, he grinned and
said, "Let's go see your mother."

On the way back to Mohawk, it occurred to me that sometime
during the long night I'd gotten separated from my duffel bag. I
was pretty sure I hadn't had it with me when we got to the Big

Bend Hunting Lodge, and Wussy was even more sure than I was, and my father was positive. Which meant it might be back there anyway, but probably not. If I'd had to lay odds, I'd have put it at the Night Owl or Mike's Place.

"I hope it's the Owl," my father said. "Mike'll be asleep, and I can't face Irma this early in the morning."

He was half sobered up and he insisted on driving home, license or no license. He didn't care. Fuck 'em.

"You tell 'em, Rockhead," Wussy said. He was slumped down in the front seat, trying to sleep, but every time my father caught his eyes closing he'd swerve the car.

"I'm on my way to work," my father said. The way things stood, he wasn't allowed to drive, except to and from his place of employment. Of which there was none, right now, because he wouldn't be going back on the road for another week or two, depending.

"What you're on your way to is Canada," Wussy said. "You missed your turn back there."

My father ignored him.

"That asshole Angelo thought he had me last week, the prick," my father said to me over his shoulder. "I'm in Mike's. It's about closing time. All revved up. I figure if I'm smart, I'll walk, but it's cold, so I say fuck 'em. I go around the corner where I'm parked. I look up and down the street. Nobody. Just me."

"Right," Wussy said.

"I get into the car. Pull away from the curb. Look in my rear view and—blip—here comes Angelo in the cruiser. You son of a bitch!"

"You see that sign, Sam's Kid?" Wussy said, pointing out the window.

In fact, I had. It said we were five miles from Speculator, twenty miles from Indian Lake. There hadn't been any mention of Mohawk.

"So I whip around the corner, throw the car into park and slide over in the passenger seat. Angelo, he barrels right by. The dumb son of a bitch gets all the way down the block to the dead end, and he sits there. Where the hell did Sammy go, he's thinking. He's gotta be."

I could tell that Wussy was just waiting for my father to finish his story before pressing his point about the way we're headed.

"Finally his backup lights come on, and here he comes, backing

all the way down the street, flashing his spot light into the drive-
ways on both sides of the street. I don't move. I stay right where
I am in the passenger seat. Pretty soon he's right alongside of me
and he's got the light in my eyes. *There* you are, you bastard, he
says. I say, Angelo. What's up. I got your ass, that's what's up, he
says. I tell him, Angelo, shit is what you got. He says are you gonna
sit there and tell me you weren't just driving this car? Right on
the first try, I say. Then who the hell was, he says."

My father stopped talking long enough to light a cigarette. We
were climbing further up into the mountains, no doubt about it.
Wussy was shaking his head.

"I'm about to say some fucking thing when I look up, and who's
shuffling toward us, not even from here to that tree?"

My father pointed, but as we were in the middle of the woods,
it was impossible to know which tree he had in mind.

"Untemeyer," he said, when neither Wussy nor I offered to
solve the riddle. "I say, Meyer, where the hell'd you go? He comes
right around and gets in behind the wheel. To pee, he says, not
that it's any of *your* fucking business. What's Angelo want? He
wants to get me for driving drunk, I say. How can you be driving
when I'm driving, Meyer says. We can't see Angelo because of the
light, but we can tell he's fuming.

"That's pretty funny," I said, hoping to put an end to the story.

"That's not the funny part," my father insisted.

"No," Wussy agreed. "It isn't."

"The funny part is Meyer's never owned a car in his life and he
doesn't have a license either. Everybody in town knows that but
Angelo, and Angelo knows it too if he could think of it."

We came to a "T" intersection and my father stopped to dry his
tears on his shirt sleeve. "Ah, shit," he concluded. "Life, right?"

"Life. Right," Wussy said, grinning over at him.

My father looked left, then right. "All right, Wuss." He grinned
back at his old friend. "Where the hell are we?"

It took us a little over an hour to get back to Mohawk. Just outside
the city limits, my father pulled over and let me take us in. When
I parked behind Wussy's pickup, which was right where he'd left
it in front of the Night Owl, Wussy said, "So long, girls. I'm not
going to be party to no breaking and entering."

In fact, my father had opened the trunk and located his tire iron.

"I'm glad you finally come home, Sam's Kid," Wussy said. "Time somebody else was the Rockhead's lookout. I'll come visit you both in jail."

"You never did yet," my father said before disappearing into the alley alongside the bar. When Wussy drove off, there was nothing to do but follow my father.

He had the window open by the time I caught up. Unbelievably, he had his hands cupped to offer me a leg up. Even more unbelievably, I put my foot in the stirrup.

It was pitch dark inside, but I knew right where I was. The smell of the urinal would have been unmistakable from across the room. When you're snaking head first down a wall and you've got nothing to grab onto except wet porcelain, that same urinal is not only unmistakable, it's real, especially when its last visitor the night before had not taken the notion of brotherhood seriously. I found the handle and flushed.

"You pissing upside down?" my father wanted to know.

I told him to just let go of my ankles, and when he did, I cartwheeled to the floor.

"There's a light switch somewhere," he advised.

Actually, I could see fine once my eyes had adjusted. I went out into the bar, half expecting to meet somebody with a mop and broom, or maybe a shotgun, but I had the place to myself. The brown light from the pitted smoky windows along the front was ghostly. I went along the bar to where my father and I had been sitting, but there was no sign of my bag. Nor was it out in the entryway. "Check behind the bar, dumbbell," my father called from the men's room window, and that's where it was, too, wedged in tight beneath the sink in a pool of water. I tried to remember what I'd packed on the bottom.

When I got back to the men's room, I heard my father talking to somebody and concluded that Wussy, who could be counted on to break any promise to go home, had returned. So I shoved my duffel bag out the window, climbed up on the urinal, and poked my head out into the alley. The person my father was talking to was the tiniest cop I'd ever seen. "Here's our burglar now," he said.

"Yup," my father said. "Get your cuffs ready."

I climbed through the window and dropped to the ground where they were standing.

"Meet Andy Winkler," my father said. "The only cop in Mohawk that wouldn't have shot you in the head coming out that window and asked questions later."

I shook hands with the tiny cop, who grinned up at me good-naturedly.

"This is my son, and he's all right," my father explained, "just like his old man."

"Ned, right?" Andy Winkler said. "We graduated together. Class of '65? Good old Mohawk High."

That was when I'd graduated, all right, but I was damned if I could remember Andy Winkler. It didn't seem to bother him though. "You was college entrance," he said. "I was voc-ed."

"What's that?" my father said. "Shop?"

"You got that right," Andy said, then gestured with both thumbs to his uniform. "Turned out I done better than they expected."

"Want to look through that bag," my father suggested, "just so you know?"

"Hell, Sammy, I wouldn't insult you. Ned either."

"You're the jewel of the force," my father said. "Go slow."

"I will," he promised.

I was sure of it.

"Too bad they aren't all like him," my father said when we got back in the car. I couldn't tell if he was serious. "His only trouble is that people keep beating him up."

"He's awfully small to be a cop," I said.

"Not really." My father turned the key in the ignition and the big convertible roared to life again. "Just too good-natured. When guys figure out he won't shoot them, they take advantage. I keep telling him all he'd have to do is shoot just one and then he wouldn't get his ass kicked all the while. But he won't listen."

"Why not let me drive," I said. I didn't know what part of town he lived in and the storied Angelo could be anywhere.

"Nah," he said, doing a U-turn in the middle of the street and heading toward the traffic light. We'd gone all of twenty yards when he pulled over to the curb and got out.

"Forget something?" I said.

"Nope," he said, pointing to the dark line of windows above the jewelry store. "We're here."

32

At my father's suggestion, I called my mother from the pay phone at the cigar store and told her I was in Fultonville. I'd see her in half an hour.

"Pretty excited, I bet," my father said, as we climbed the stairs to his flat.

In fact, she had squealed like a pig. She just couldn't wait to tell Will, that old clairvoyant, who'd predicted the night before that something nice was going to happen to her soon, he'd *felt* it. By the time I got there she'd have bells on.

"She says she'll have bells on," I told him.

"That's her all right," he said. "Ding-a-ling."

Where the old apartment above Klein's had borne a distinct resemblance to a bowling alley, my father's present flat was much smaller, one room, really, plus a small bath that featured a sink, a commode, and a jerry-rigged shower stall. The living room itself was just long enough to accommodate the old sofa when it was folded out into a bed, which it happened to be at the moment. The television at its foot was new, but it sported the same old bent rabbit ears which pulled in the same old snow.

"You don't have to stay with her if you don't want to," my father said. "Wussy's got a roll-away someplace."

The only place I could see to put it was on top of the pool table, which was wedged into the remaining corner and covered with a sheet of plastic.

"I should though," I said.

"You'll be kicking our mutual friend out of the spare room," he said. "Or didn't you know about that?"

One of my very few rules in dealing with my parents had always been an adamant refusal to discuss each with the other. My silence had been known to infuriate both, but it kept my sanity and allowed me to pretend equal loyalty and affection. "I did, actually," I admitted, without elaborating.

"We had a little discussion about the arrangement one night," my father said. "Right on Main Street across from the diner. He got lippy when I mentioned a couple of little things I didn't like. Had to pick himself up off the seat of his pants."

"What do you care what they do?" I said.

"That's not the point," he said.

"Oh," I said, since it seemed like the point to me.

He shrugged. "I figure let it go. Being around your mother is punishment enough."

I rooted around my duffel bag until I found my razor and stripped off my shirt. The way I smelled, it was a terrible temptation to shower first, but the bathroom mirror looked like the only one in the flat and it was already cloudy. I lathered while he talked behind me.

"Funny part is, he's helped me out of one or two little scrapes. He's not a half-bad lawyer, for around here anyways. Stands right up and talks to the judge and the judge listens. I just hope he doesn't try that with your mother."

He came over and leaned in the doorway so he could watch me shave.

"Last time I saw you, you weren't shaving, were you?"

I said that was true. I could tell he was trying to remember how old I was that last time.

"You could have got luckier in the father department," he said.

"Or unluckier," I said.

"Not likely." In the distorted, cloudy mirror, his face looked long, his eyes disproportionately large.

When I'd showered and put on clean clothes, I felt very nearly human again. My hair was pretty shaggy, but I didn't look bad enough to give my mother serious misgivings. We drove directly there, stopping just once when the Cadillac smelled hot, so my father fetched a couple bright yellow cans of oil from the spare case he kept in the trunk. He punctured these and turned them upside down into a plastic funnel, tossing them a great distance into an empty lot when he was finished.

"What's so funny?" he said when he caught me grinning.

"Nothing," I said. "I was just thinking of something."

The morning had turned bright and warm. My mother was sitting in the sun on the second-floor front porch. She jumped up when the car pulled into the drive and came down at a dead run before either my father or I could get out of the car. She paused, questioning, only when she saw my father.

"Look who I found getting off a bus downtown," my father said, the lie more smooth and natural than the truest thing he'd ever learned.

That night, to celebrate my return, we went out to dinner at The Elms, the restaurant Mike had lost in Vegas. My mother asked if it was all right if Will joined us, and I said sure, grateful for his company after the long afternoon. Besides, it was clear that "Will" pretty much had to come along if *we* were going to go, since it was his car that would transport us, his credit card that would eventually find its way under the check when that was presented. In return for these considerations, my mother consented to choose the restaurant, against F. William Peterson's recommendation.

She looked quite wonderful, actually, very much like the girl who had done battle with my father twenty years earlier. She had on a black dress with a simple string of pearls, and she took a pill right before we left. That, in concert with a martini she termed "indifferent," made her confident and loudly talkative in the dining room. From the moment we entered the restaurant, nothing escaped her notice and comment, from the rather cool reception of the hostess to the colloquial friendliness of our young waitress, who had smiled as if she were actually delighted to see us and squeaked, "Hi, folks!"

"Folks," my mother stage-whispered when the girl was gone. "Honestly."

"She seems a pleasant enough girl," F. William Peterson ventured. He had warned my mother earlier that The Elms had gone downhill since the new ownership, but seemed now intent on making the best of the situation.

"You know what you are?" my mother said.

F. William Peterson winked at me with more good humor than I could have mustered in the face of such a direct and potentially malicious question.

"A midwesterner," she said. "And a midwesterner you will be until the day you die."

Actually, F. William Peterson was from Pennsylvania, but this fact did not, to her mind, invalidate my mother's point. He was from the western half of Pennsylvania, "practically Ohio," and you couldn't grow up that close to Ohio without *being* Ohio. Ohio was that pervasive. Next to Iowa, she couldn't think of a worse influence. And only a midwesterner wouldn't object to the term "folks" so loosely applied.

"Do you think we can trust this midwesterner with our secret?" my mother said.

"Yes, certainly," I said, trying to imagine what this secret might be. I'd been telling her lies all afternoon and there was no way to know which one she'd fastened on as "our secret." Whichever; it was clearly her intention to use "our secret" to make certain that F. William Peterson understood his role as official outsider at our table. We were confidants, conspirators, she and I, and we might bring him partly up to speed if he behaved himself.

"With all the important research he's involved with at the university, you must be wondering what Ned is *doing* here in Mohawk," she said. "Even midwesterners have curiosities."

In fact, F. William Peterson *did* look curious to discover what absurdity I had concocted to explain my sudden appearance in the middle of the spring term. So, there was nothing to do but repeat what I'd told her—that I was doing research in the concept of social hierarchy among primitive societies for my postthesis in cultural anthropology. For this reason I had arranged to become a bartender in backwater upstate New York, where I would take notes and interview the denizens of local gin mills without their knowledge. Later, the whole thing would be written up and published by a university press. I hadn't decided which, yet, but we were leaning toward Stanford, where my major professor had friends. Actually, I only began this absurd story. After a few sentences my mother took it up, embellished its already pure fantasy, embraced it as purest truth. The designation of Mohawk as a primitive society she accepted without hesitation, having always believed this to be the case.

F. William Peterson nodded seriously. I think he may even have appreciated that the tale was not more absurd than it needed to be to explain my sudden appearance, my new employment, come Monday. When she was finished, F. William Peterson said, "Jesus," almost reverentially.

When it came time to order, my mother said, "I know what *we're* having," as if to suggest that tradition, telepathy, and geography had put us in perfect synch, our nearly seven-year separation no reason to presume changes in taste. "A filet mignon," she told our young waitress. "Need I say, medium rare?"

Not being telepathic, the girl looked grateful for this intelligence and even wrote it down. Then, mistaking our pecking order, she went the wrong way around and stood at the elbow of F. William Peterson. When he ordered the crab legs, my mother said, "Really?," her voice rich with astonishment, as if he'd ordered a diet plate of cottage cheese and peaches. "Well, I suppose," she went on, "if you actually *like* frozen fish."

"I like crab legs," F. William Peterson said.

Then the girl made her third mistake. "They're frozen by law, ma'am," she said.

My mother pointedly ignored her. "Oh, why not get something *good*," she urged F. William Peterson. "This is a *special* evening. Don't spoil it by trying to save a dollar."

"I hadn't meant to," F. William Peterson said, and he then changed his order. A filet mignon, medium rare would be fine.

It made my mother happy. She took his hand and said, "There, Mr. Ohio, you'll have a good dinner despite yourself."

"Sir?" said the waitress, at my elbow now.

"Crab legs," I told her. "I'll have the frozen crab legs." Then I added, to a mortified F. William Peterson, "We can share."

My mother's face registered nothing at first. Then it came apart, and the hand holding her second martini began to shake perceptibly. Finally, she too became aware of it. "If you two fine gentlemen will excuse me," she said, pushing her chair back.

F. William Peterson jumped up to aid her, but she would have none of it. "Sit *down*, for heaven's sake. You'd think we were at the Ritz," she said, all too audibly. Then she spun on her heel.

She got halfway to the bar, then stopped in the geometric center of the dining room, where it must have occurred to her that she did not know where the ladies' room was, that it could be anywhere, that she hadn't a clue.

"Wouldn't it be just scrumptious if tonight could last forever?" she said, less than forty-five minutes later.

We were drinking liqueurs and coffee. She had ordered an Amaretto and I'd said that sounded good to me, and F. William Peterson said him too, and we were a loving trio again. I'd ended up sharing my crabs legs with both F. William Peterson and my mother when her steak came well done. Normally, she'd have sent it back, but in the ladies' room she'd rearranged things in her

mind and returned defiantly good-natured, claiming that the
company of two such charming gentlemen was far more important than the way some old dead cow was prepared. She'd even
admitted that she'd never eaten crab legs, that they had always
seemed a lot of trouble, and that they tasted wonderful. Her
newly discovered goodwill did not extend to our waitress, however, and she refused to believe there was such a thing as a law
governing crab legs.

Sitting there sipping Amaretto, I remembered something I'd
forgotten out in the desert—that things always worked better
when my mother got her way. After all, there was nothing wrong
with filet mignon. And there was nothing wrong with Amaretto.
And if you thought you were going to enjoy something else even
more, you were wrong, because she'd see to it that you didn't. I
hadn't even tasted the crab legs. "There's only one thing in life
your mother wants," my father had often remarked, "her own
way." And somehow now, I realized, I'd suddenly come to share
his perverse unwillingness to *give* her her own way if it could
possibly be avoided. I'd probably been doing it in little ways since
I could remember, thwarting the will of this woman who derived
so little pleasure out of life and seldom wanted more than the
occasional public demonstration of loyalty and love, a small
enough gift, since the gallery she was playing to was primarily in
her own imagination.

And you had to admire her resiliency. Somewhere, probably in
a private stall in the ladies' room, she'd not only composed herself,
convinced herself that things were not as bad as they'd seemed,
refused my betrayal tragic significance, but actually talked herself
into believing that the evening was everything she'd hoped it
would be. Because by the time she told F. William Peterson that
she wished our special evening would never end, she was telling
simple, literal truth, her eyes so glazed over with emotion that it
was impossible for her to see our slack-jawed amazement. The
whole bloody mess could not have concluded soon enough to suit
either of her charming male companions, but my mother had
found peace, and she didn't even object when F. William Peterson tipped the waitress as if he had recognized in her nervous
demeanor his own long-lost illegitimate child.

My mother, who seldom left the house, and never drank at
home, was none too steady by the time we returned to the flat,
but she seemed to think that with my help she could negotiate the

back stairs, and she dismissed F. William Peterson at the curb with a vague promise of brunch the following morning. At the landing, she gave me her keys, all two of them, so that I could open the door. I was hoping she'd opt for bed right away, but instead she slipped into one of the dinette chairs in the kitchen and began to cry, her head on the table. When she finally looked up at me, her eyes were red and swollen. "Look at me," she sniffled, "crying all over you your first night back."

Actually, she wasn't crying anywhere near me. I had pulled up the chair opposite her and waited.

"He's such a good man," my mother said. "How I *wish* I loved him."

"He's certainly crazy about you," I said, trying to make carefully chosen words sound casual.

"I know," she admitted. "It's horrible."

"It's horrible that someone loves you?"

"Yes," she said, looking off somewhere. "I want . . . my own true love."

Her own true love. The outrageous simplicity, modesty, and arrogance of it took my breath away. It seemed to me, then and now, a wish that everyone had a right to, but that only the very foolish or the terminally naïve trouble themselves over.

"Don't worry," she said. "I'm not like this most of the time. Thank God for your grandfather."

The remark took me off guard, though I should have seen what was coming.

"You don't remember?" she said, her smile crooked, her eyes narrowing, as if at something nasty.

"No," I said, but I had an idea.

"Mohawk Fair, Eat the Bird, and Winter," she grinned.

"You forgot Fourth of July," I said.

"No," she said. "It's just gone. Long, long gone."

She got up then and went into her room, allowing the door to swing shut behind her. My guess was she'd be asleep in five minutes. I knew I wouldn't.

33

Mike's Place did a surprising daytime business. When I opened up at 7:30 in the morning, there were always several men waiting outside with the shakes and if I knew what was good for me I opened at 7:30 and not 7:31. They streamed in through the open doorway like ghosts in the early morning light, compromising my attempts to give the place a good airing out. Most of them were on their way to the shops and would be gone by eight, and only then would the stale beer and cigarette smoke and the smell of urinal cakes from the small rest rooms begin to dissipate in the crosscurrents. The fresher air brought talkative liquor salesmen and truck drivers making deliveries, bullshitters one and all, who drank coffee with a little pick-me-up in it and wanted to know about my love life. I could have told them about Marion, but I didn't. I used the slack midmorning to swab down the bar and the dark, high-backed booths that lined one long wall from the front door to the end of the bar. At least once a week I took down all the bottles off the back bar and dusted, replacing the two dozen or so brands of whiskey that were seldom called, along with expensive vodkas, gins and liqueurs on top of the rings they'd left on the dark wood surface.

It took me a while to understand why I was not embraced enthusiastically by the salesmen and delivery men and the regular day crowd at Mike's Place. I knew they'd been used to Satch, my predecessor, who had been unceremoniously canned to make room for me. Eventually, however, I discovered that the reason Satch was so much loved and missed was that he was the sort of fellow who hated to take money from guys he knew. The trouble was that Mike's was the sort of place where after a week or two you knew everybody. Satch not only let the salesmen drink coffee for free, but he laced that coffee freely, and generally dispensed spirits as if he were heading up a nonprofit organization. According to my father, whole hours would drift by with the place half full, its peaceful atmosphere never interrupted by the raucous ringing of the old cash register. And when it did ring, chances were it said "No Sale." Satch and my father had pretty nearly got into it one afternoon when my father suggested the bartender use the drawer for something besides making change. Just what the hell was that supposed to mean, Satch wanted to know. He did pretty goddamn well by Mike. He treated Mike's business like it was his own. Right, my father said. You put the money in your pocket. There must have been some truth to my father's allegations because my first week behind the bar saw half as many customers and about twice as much profit.

Mike usually came in about the time the salesmen started arriving and left as soon as he'd signed what needed signing, just about the time his wife Irma arrived to cook for the lunch crowd. They passed each other silently, Mike giving her plenty of room. Rumor had it that they'd not spoken meaningfully since he'd lost the other restaurant, even though this more modest establishment, according to my father, did just about as well without half the aggravation. Be that as it may, Irma looked even meaner than I remembered her from The Elms. You could hear her muttering furiously and slinging pans in the tiny kitchen, and as the steam rose up from the big cauldrons she used to cook spaghetti, the sweat poured down her broad expanse of forehead from the roots of her now white hair, disappearing eventually into the stiff uniform she always wore to remind Mike how cruelly she was reduced since losing The Elms.

I gave Irma plenty of room until I discovered that she liked me. I could tell this from the occasional gestures of intimacy she offered me and no one else. Two or three times a day she emerged from her steam-bath kitchen for a soda, which I'd draw her in a larger tumbler full of ice. This she would accept, drain on the spot, and wait for me to refill it. This second glass she would take back into the kitchen with her, but not before looking around the place, nodding, nudging me with one of her big elbows, and saying, "Assholes!"

Though she took little enough pleasure in it, Irma made the best spaghetti sauce in town, and between twelve and one-thirty we jammed the place with the downtown lunch crowd that could afford a buck a plate more than Harry got for a hamburger and thick gravy-drenched fries. And, while nobody thought of tipping at the Mohawk Grill, it was generally understood that you had to save at least a quarter for the girls who waited on the booths at Mike's Place, one of whom turned out to be Eileen Littler. She worked three lunches a week for Mike, four or five evenings at a restaurant in the valley.

"A little bird told me you were back," she said accusatorily, the first shift we worked together.

"A little bird?" I said, surprised, curious.

"A little blackbird," she said, "who was up at the hospital this morning looking for a shot of penicillin. I hear it's nice up at the lakes this time of year."

Most days the waitresses could go home by two, at which time the regular drinkers would start wandering in. Three-thirty to four-thirty was Untemeyer territory. Mike's was the bookie's next-to-last stop of the afternoon, after Harry's and before Greenie's, where he did most of his business when the shops let out. Necessity made me something of a bookie myself, taking the action of the lunch crowd who had to get back to work. I was also expected to be knowledgeable, serving up a tip with a boilermaker, in return for which I got good-natured insults when the nags didn't run.

On Wednesday afternoon of my first week, my father wandered in ten minutes after Eileen left, looked around the place at my customers and said thank God he was going back to work soon.

"Thank God is r-r-right," said Tree, who had been in several times that week and not recognized in me anybody he'd ever seen before. I'd wanted to ask him about Alice, the big woman he'd smooched with at The Lookout so long ago, and about the even bigger woman who'd eaten the pâté at Jack Ward's wake, but I didn't. My father informed me later that Tree had divorced the pâté woman and married Alice shortly after I'd gone west. They were living up above the bar, and Tree only came into town once or twice a week, at which times he dropped in on his ex-wife, with whom he now had a little something going on the side. My father couldn't make up his mind which woman was bigger and razzed Tree about it pretty unmercifully, demanding to know.

"It varies," Tree always responded. "W-w-week to week."

"Stay on top if you can," my father urged.

"I'm the m-m-man, ain't I?"

"You sure are, Tree," my father said, clapping his hand on the little man's back. "You sure are."

I drew my father a beer and set it in front of him. He was usually

all right when he drank beer, so I got him started that way before
he had a chance to think about it. According to Mike, it was the
hard liquor that was doing him in, but he'd been pretty sober
since my return, and I figured if he could stay that way until he
went back to work, he might be okay.

"You learn how to make a Manhattan yet?" he said.

I said no.

My father consulted his watch. "You got about ten minutes to
learn."

He was right, too, because very shortly thereafter, the heavy
front door to Mike's Place grunted open about six inches, fell back
shut, then grunted open a second time, a wooden cane thrust in
this time, to prevent the door from closing.

"You better go help her," my father said.

I did as I was told, nearly screwing up bad, because when I
pulled the door open, the old woman on the other side, having
braced her thin shoulder against the wood, tumbled in. I caught
her just in time. The fat taxi driver who had apparently just
dropped her at the curb hadn't bothered to get out, but had
leaned across the seat to watch and now looked disappointed that
I'd broken the old woman's fall.

"Why thank you, young man," the old woman said when I had
her upright and the door had swung shut again. "I think I'll have
a Manhattan."

So I got her settled in the booth nearest the door, made her a
Manhattan under my father's supervision, and brought it to her.
For some reason, she looked familiar to me, though I didn't see
how she could be. She made no move to take off her old fur coat,
though she did remove her hat, which had been knocked cockeyed by her assault on the door. Her gray hair was thin, but
utterly wild, despite the half-dozen bobby pins arranged, as far as
I could tell, randomly.

"You're him," she said, staring up at me intently, "aren't you."

"Why, yes," I said. "I suppose I am."

"Well," she said. "He's still alive, though I'm sure I never would
have expected it."

"I'm very glad to hear it," I told her, still not making the connection. "Excuse me."

I went back to the bar.

"Give her about twenty minutes," my father said, "then make
her another one. Did she have money on the table?"

I said yes.

"Sometimes she forgets," he said.

In a few minutes I went back to see how she was doing. "I think I'll have another Manhattan," she said, as if the idea had just occurred to her. She handed me the empty glass.

Twice more this happened, and when I served her fourth, she instructed me to call a taxi. The dispatcher seemed to be expecting the call. "Aw, fuck," he said.

A few minutes later the same driver pulled up out front and tooted. I got the old woman on my arm and together we negotiated the single step down to the sidewalk and then the curb. Again, the driver didn't bother to get out. It took a minute, but eventually I got her situated comfortably enough in the backseat.

"Make sure the towel's under her," the driver said.

Oddly enough, there happened to be a ragged, dirty towel on the seat and the old woman was squarely in the center. It had begun to drizzle out and I was getting wet, but I took a moment for a word with the driver.

"When you get her home," I said quietly, "why not get off your fat lazy ass and give her a hand into the house."

He started to say something, but I held up a finger and wagged it, trying to look like a dangerous man. I must have, at least a little, because the words died in his mouth.

Back inside, I was greeted by a powerful odor that I'd been only vaguely aware of when I'd helped the old woman out of her booth. My father and the other men at the bar were all grinning at me.

"There's plenty of t-towels in the back," Tree said.

In fact, the old woman had peed all over the booth and floor, just as she apparently did every Wednesday afternoon upon finishing her fourth Manhattan.

But it was later that night, at home, when I sat straight up in bed. I'd been thinking about the cab driver I'd been too hard on, and the old woman's good-natured way of letting other people clean up her mess, when I suddenly imagined a younger Mrs. Agajanian, standing on her screened-in back porch, watching my old friend Claude dangle, red-faced, from the bent crossbeam of the ramada.

One Saturday afternoon in early May I ran into another old woman I'd known a decade before, and this one—Tria Ward's mother—I recognized right away. The amazing thing was that she also recognized me.

I didn't work Saturdays, and I had agreed to meet my father at some unspecified time and place later that afternoon, whenever and wherever I managed to track him down. At the moment I was putting it off by picking up my mother's anxiety pills (valium now) and a six-pack of Rolaids from a downtown pharmacy.

I knew what was in store for me once I located my father. In the space of an hour I'd have three or four sweating beers lined up on the bar awaiting my attention. I'd have left home with every intention of being home for dinner with my mother, and for the first hour or two I'd consult my watch dutifully and warn my father that I'd have to leave soon, to which he'd reply, sure, absolutely, why not? But when the actual time approached, he'd say what's the hurry, and by then that would seem to me a valid question. I'd try to figure out what my hurry was and not be able to. What had been *my* idea, to go home and not disappoint my mother, would suddenly seem like *her* idea, and I would resent her attempts to control my life. As soon as I finished this one beer I was on, I'd call and tell her the score, and if she didn't like it, tough. But by the time I thought of calling again, there wouldn't be much point, because afternoon would have merged with evening, and she would not only have eaten, but cleared the dishes and stacked them in the small cupboard above the sink.

By the time my father and I thought of eating it would be late, just about the time Irma would have the kitchen closed up in Mike's Place. Probably she'd have her coat on and be ready to leave when we shambled in, my father demanding veal and peppers, the Saturday special. She'd tell my father to go screw himself, and my father would say, Irma, Irma, let's sneak back in the kitchen, get away from your husband. When he emerged five or ten minutes later he'd have two steaming plates full of veal and peppers that we'd perhaps pay for, perhaps not, depending on whether anybody remembered to ask us to and whether we remembered ourselves. And then we'd be ready for the rest of the night.

This was the inevitable scenario I was trying to postpone by doing errands for my mother when I ran into Mrs. Ward at the prescription window at the drugstore.

"Forgive me," she said, after our eyes had met and I had looked away, not wanting to force the issue of our having been just about half acquainted so long ago. "But aren't you my daughter Tria's young friend?"

The answer to that seemed more no than yes, but I decided to go along. "Mrs. Ward?" I smiled. "It's nice to see you."

"I'm told you're a graduate of the university," she said, as if there were only one university in the country.

I admitted it was true, adding that I was taking a break from graduate school and wondering vaguely how she would have heard any report concerning me.

"And you are studying what?" she said, with the kind of forthright, almost insulting directness, you sometimes encounter in persons who are not merely curious but, for some reason, believe they have a right to know all about you. And, as is usually the case with such people, you gratify their curiosity and only regret doing so later. I told her I was studying anthropology.

"Why, that's practically the same thing, you know," she said, looking up at me.

I said I supposed it was, then asked what it was the same as.

"Why history, of course," she said.

"Of course." I blinked.

"Why don't you join us for brunch in the morning?" she said suddenly. "Say about one?"

"One in the morning?"

"In the afternoon, of course."

"Of course," I said. One in the afternoon, tomorrow morning. I'd be there.

"Say hello to Tria, won't you?" Mrs. Ward said, when we'd both paid for our prescriptions.

I looked around. Except for ourselves and the pharmacist and the young cashier, the store was empty. I didn't know who the cashier was, but I knew she wasn't Tria Ward. I wondered if Tria had become invisible, like Mrs. Agajanian's son, the fish cleaner.

"And she is . . ."

"In the car, of course. Out front," Mrs. Ward said. "I don't drive, you see. The driving of automobiles has never been among my skills."

I had forgotten this, and I think I would have asked her, had I been the sort of person who believed I had a right to know, precisely what the tiny woman considered her skills to be. Instead, I followed her outside to where a canary-yellow Chevette sat in a tow zone right in front of the pharmacy. Mrs. Ward started speaking even before she had the door open, which meant that the first few words had to have been lost on her daughter. *"Look who I have just discovered!"*

Tria—she was still quite beautiful, long dark hair halfway down her back—leaned forward over the steering wheel to look, first at me, then to see if there was someone else.

"You don't recognize your old compatriot, Mr. . . ."

"Hall," I supplied.

"Mr. Hall," Mrs. Ward verified.

"Oh . . . yes," Tria said and smiled almost charmingly enough to mask the fact that she had not the slightest recollection of me.

"I've invited Mr. Hall to brunch with us in the morning," she said, getting into the small front seat with some difficulty. "Mr. Hall is an historian."

"Actually—" I began.

"And a graduate of the university," she continued. "What *we* need is some informed opinion . . . some light on the subject . . . some illumination, you see."

Tria didn't look like she had much faith in the concept, or perhaps in my ability to deliver.

"Tomorrow morning then, Mr. . . . ?

"Right," I said. "Around one."

I was pleased to see, when Tria pulled away from the curb, that driving was now among *her* skills. It certainly hadn't been the last time I'd seen her. She yanked the Chevette into traffic and turned at the corner with such authority that her mother grabbed the top of her head, as if to prevent an invisible hat from flying out the window. It seemed to me that Tria Ward might be angry at something. Maybe even something to do with me.

The next day I was pretty glad that morning did not arrive at the Wards' house until afternoon. F. William Peterson came over to the flat around eleven, and I heard him and my mother talking in subdued tones in the living room. My mother was of the opinion that I had spent the previous evening dazzling the dull local beauties. I never told her when I was planning to hook up with my father, of course. He always offered to come by and pick me up, but I said no, that I'd find him, and he understood well enough.

"Well hello there, Mr. Debonair," my mother said, when I finally dragged myself out of bed. She and F. William Peterson were drinking coffee on the same end of the sofa. "Do you know what momentous decision we've just arrived at?"

"No, I don't," I said.

"Brunch," she said. "Corn bread muffins and sausage links."

"Sounds good," I said, wondering what momentous decision they'd have arrived at if F. William Peterson had been allowed a say. "I hope you won't mind me taking a rain check."

She gave me the tragic wounded look I expected, but, to my surprise, her face lit up when I said I'd been invited to brunch at the Wards'. "Ah!" she said. "Old line!"

I frowned.

"Well, not *Jack* Ward, of course. He was as plebeian as the next fellow, but his wife was a Smythe, one of the first families of Mohawk County," she said. "Strictly old line."

"It's a wonderful opportunity," I said.

"And Jack Ward cut quite a figure when he came back from overseas," she remembered. "You should have seen him and your father in uniform. . . ."

She stared off dreamily.

"Take my car if you like," F. William Peterson suggested.

I had intended to take my father's, since I knew where he kept the spare key to the Cadillac and since he probably wouldn't be wanting it until midafternoon anyway. He and Wussy had dropped me off when the bars closed and said they were going home. I'm sure they did, eventually. The convertible was probably out in front of my father's, but then again, it might be in one of half a dozen other places. So I closed the bathroom door on my mother's frying sausage, shaved and showered, put on the only decent sweater I owned over a pair of khakis and drove F. William Peterson's New Yorker out to the highway and up the narrow road that wound up through the trees to the Ward house.

Seeing it again was a shock, so much so that I stopped the New Yorker just outside the stone pillars that marked the entrance to the circular drive and just sat. The white jewel house was little more than a big, fancy ranch of the sort that sat side by side, awaiting mature foliage, in the better Tucson housing developments. It was not nearly as nice as the house of the English professor whose house I'd played poker in the night before I left the city. And in the decade since I'd laid eyes on it, the Ward house had taken on a grayish tinge, as if it had suddenly begun to absorb the sunlight it had once so brilliantly reflected. The only improvement I could see was that the place was now surrounded by flowers—bright tulips and mums, along with some other exotic blooms I didn't recognize. I'd no sooner pulled up and turned off the ignition when the explanation came slinking into view from around the corner of the house in a pair of gray work pants with dirty knees.

"Hello, Skinny," I said, stopping him in his tracks. Somebody had told me that the old Monsignor had finally died, like he'd been promising to do for so many years, and that the new pastor had had no more use for flowers than alcoholic gardeners. I'm sure I never expected him to turn up here though.

It was pretty clear he hadn't been expecting me either, because he glowered at me suspiciously, as if he'd already divined the truth of the matter—that for the second time in a life that was far too short, I had been invited *into* a house that was strictly off limits to himself. To make matters worse, he suspected that I was to be fed.

"Nice car," he said, eyeing the New Yorker and looking as if he wasn't sure he was permitted to touch its exterior. When I got out, he looked inside. Then he stood erect and looked around. "Where's Sammy?"

"In the trunk," I said.

He looked at the trunk. It was big enough to contain my father. "Bullshit," he said finally.

"You got me," I admitted. "Nice tulips."

He looked at them suspiciously, as if he suspected sarcasm. "You wouldn't have a cigarette?"

I didn't, but F. William Peterson had left a pack on the front seat, so I offered him one of those.

"Salems," he said, and spit. He took one though, and lit up, his yellow hands shaking badly. His face was jaundiced too, now that I looked.

"Take a puff," I said. "It's springtime."

"It's already fuckin' springtime," he said. "Where *you* been?"

I shrugged, as if to suggest I didn't know quite where. I didn't know how to summarize ten years, at least not for Skinny Donovan. Besides, I wasn't quite sure he'd noticed that I'd been away. "I'm tending bar at Mike's Place right now."

"How come your father don't get you on the road with him?
Damn good pay, is what I hear."

"You have to be in the union," I told him. "Besides, it's ball-
breaking work."

"*I* could do it," he said angrily. "I work three jobs right now."

"Really," I said.

"Bet your ass. All three don't pay what Sammy makes."

I said I was sorry to hear it.

"And I could use the money," he repeated, as if this were the
principal consideration. He'd never needed the money before
and now he did, so it followed that something would just have to
be worked out.

"I know what you mean," I said. "This isn't my car by the way."

He looked relieved to learn it.

"I might say something to your old man," he said, eyeing me
still.

"Couldn't hurt," I said.

"Sammy's the best," he said. "He'd do it for me if I asked him.
He'd give me his *own* job if I asked him. We're like this." He held
up crossed fingers.

The front door opened then and Tria appeared. I waved.

Skinny looked in the general direction of the girl, but appeared
not to see her. "I might not even ask him," he said. "But he'd do
it."

The Salem was down to its filter, but Skinny sucked away at it,
as if it were not smoke entering his yellow lungs, but myriad
possibilities. "I might ask him," he said. "I might."

We ate outdoors on a small patio off the back of the house. It had
a southeastern exposure, and the early May sun had some real
summer warmth to it for the first time. The gentle wooded foothills of the Adirondacks fell away to the south all the way to the
Mohawk River, which was invisible but hinted at by the weaving
black ribbon of distant trees. Or maybe it wasn't the river at all,
but something else that threaded its way, shadowlike, across the
gentle landscape.

"Mother will join us shortly," Tria Ward said when we were
seated at the white canopied table, which sported a pitcher of
orange juice and a sweating bottle of chilled champagne. Tria
looked almost too lovely in a fresh, summery dress tied at pale

bare shoulders by spaghetti-thin straps. It made me wonder why she'd want to look so splendid to entertain a virtual stranger, one invited by her mother, no less. I decided her closet was full of equally enchanting dresses, and that she was wearing, in all probability, her least favorite. I was grateful for her beauty anyway, and when she leaned over to pour champagne and orange juice into my goblet I was more grateful still.

"Do the mimosas, dear," Mrs. Ward's voice sang from the open kitchen window. "I do hope Mr. . . . likes mimosas."

Mr. . . . had never had a mimosa before, but he discovered he liked them quite a lot. The first few sips did what the handful of aspirin he'd swallowed before leaving his mother's had failed to do.

"I'm so sorry I didn't remember you yesterday," Tria Ward said. "I did by the time we got home."

"I was pretty crushed," I admitted. "After all, you did promise to marry me."

Her eyes got very large, and I could tell she was struggling with the possibility that this absurdity might be true. "What?" she said, clearly ready to apologize for having forgotten this too.

I smiled to let her off the hook.

"You're joking," she said.

"Actually, yes," I said. "I think we've only met on three occasions. Name all three and win a prize."

"One is easy. The afternoon I backed my father's car into the woods and we all had to walk up here. I wanted to die."

"Okay, that's one."

"And at a restaurant, somewhere. You were with your father and he told a dirty joke."

"And *I* wanted to die," I said.

"I can't remember the third time," she finally admitted, her faint resemblance to her mother growing more pronounced when she frowned.

Since the third was her father's funeral, and since it didn't count because we'd not actually spoken, I said I didn't remember either.

"Then how do you know there were three?"

"I don't," I said. "Maybe it was just two."

"Then there's no way I can win the prize. You don't play fair."

"I'm a scoundrel," I conceded, mildly surprised that the "prize" concept had interested her.

"Who's a scoundrel?" said Mrs. Ward, who had materialized at my shoulder carrying three more goblets, these full of fresh fruits, half of them new to me, all diced into bite-sized chunks. "Nobody is capable of being a scoundrel on such a glorious day as this," Mrs. Ward said. "Simply glorious."

I agreed. It was glorious.

"The first day of the rest of our lives," Mrs. Ward continued, seating herself in the third chair. "I heard that somewhere and it stuck in my mind. That's the way to look at this old life."

"It certainly is," I said.

"See?" Mrs. Ward said to her daughter. "You're the only gloomy-gus at the table."

"I'm not gloomy, Mother," Tria said. "I'm simply a realist."

"A *gloomy* realist. Thank heavens Mr. . . . is not a gloomy realist, or we wouldn't be able to enjoy our brunch."

We ate reverentially until Tria, as if to dispel the notion that she was gloomy, said that the kiwi was wonderful.

"It certainly is," I said, making a mental note not to use this phrase again for at least half an hour, and wondering which of the fruits I was eating might be the kiwi.

There was a long moment then when we suddenly all seemed to realize that we might not be able to recapture the rhythm of normal conversation. We were on stage and somebody had missed a cue and now nobody knew whose turn it was to speak. Maybe the whole thing had been a bad idea, we all seemed to be thinking, as we dipped with renewed interest into our goblets, as if it were in the nature of kiwi and passion fruit to save us.

"A glorious day to be alive," Mrs. Ward finally offered.

"It certainly is," I said.

There was much more to eat, Mrs. Ward assured us. No, she didn't need any help to fetch it. Tria and I watched her patter into the house, and I wondered what had become of their ill-tempered cook.

"How are you at saying no," Tria said in a lowered voice, once we had the patio to ourselves.

I said it depended on who I was saying no to, almost adding that I didn't think I'd have much luck saying no to her.

"Well, be prepared," Tria said. "Because she's working up to something."

"What?" I said, genuinely curious as to what I possessed that Mrs. Ward could possibly want.

"I think I know, but I'm hoping I'm wrong," she said. Then she reached across the table and touched my hand lightly, and only for a second. "Please don't laugh at her though."

Actually, thanks to the mimosas, I was feeling extraordinarily tolerant. Exactly one month earlier I'd hit bottom in Tucson, making a complete mess of my graduate studies, gambling compulsively, suicidally. And I had simply walked away from the mess. Now, sitting pleasantly on the Wards' charmed little patio, with just enough breeze to flutter the umbrella overhead, surrounded by Skinny Donovan's fragrant flowers, and in the company of a young woman every bit as fresh and fragrant as the surrounding bloom, it seemed to me that life was extraordinarily forgiving. I felt lucky again and there was no Lanny Aguilar around to be pissed off by my good fortune. Vietnam itself seemed relegated to the television, without local ramification, as if a town that never got to participate in the good fortune of the fifties felt no need to suffer the tragedy of the seventies. I decided that as far as I was concerned, walking away was an underrated talent, probably genetic in origin. My father had written the book on walking away from things before I ever came along. Perhaps luck was his gift to me. If so, I was grateful. After all, I could just as easily have taken after my mother, who had never walked away from anything, who paid and paid, compound interest, the principal always outstanding. This legacy she herself had inherited from her own father, who had considered himself lucky to come home from the war riddled with malaria, to break even in the cold earth of Mohawk.

I wondered what my grandfather, who had made his peace with ill fortune, who had accepted winter with a capital W as the essence of human existence, would have thought about me, with my 348, with the even luckier temperament that might well have allowed me to walk north into Canada or south into Mexico if I had failed in the luck of the draw. Maybe he'd have been happy for my disposition. I'd been told often enough that he had little use for my father, and it was reasonable to assume that he'd have had a fair number of reservations about me. But his life and thought had come to me filtered through my mother, so there was no way to tell for sure. Any more than there was a way to tell whether he had ever spent an enchanted afternoon such as this under a sun that promised summer with a capital *S*.

It was not truly summer though, and when a white cloud obscured the sun, the air was suddenly chill and we were forced inside, leaving behind the petrified remains of our eggs in hollandaise sauce. The room we adjourned to was the small, booklined study where Jack Ward had deposited me and from which the horrible frizzy-haired woman had stolen *Gone with the Wind*. The room was exactly as I remembered it, the large mantel and many of the shelves sporting photographs, including the one of a young Hilda Ward in the company of the distinguished-looking man with thinning hair, another of Tria, I presumed, balancing uncomfortably on this same man's knee. There had been no photographic evidence of Jack Ward's existence in the room ten years ago and there wasn't any now.

Tria watched me intently as her mother took down from the place of honor on the mantel the leatherbound volume that had attracted my attention as a boy. Mrs. Ward hesitated there at the altar before turning back to us, book in hand, and when she did her expression could only be described as religious. I half expected her to open the volume and begin to read aloud. Instead, she cleared her voice and said, "Mr. Hall. I wonder if you would be so good as to give us your professional opinion of this work. As an historian."

"Like I said—" I began.

"And as a graduate of the university." The book was between us now, occupying space that was neither the old woman's nor mine. There was nothing I could do but reach out and take the book, and so when Tria nodded, I did. Even so, there was a moment when we both had a hold of the damned thing, and when I drew it toward me, as I imagined I was supposed to, I encountered resistance in the fierce old fingers that did not want to surrender it. They did though, eventually, causing us both a momentary loss of equilibrium.

Once I had the volume—*The History of Mohawk County from the Earliest Times to the Present*, by William Henry Smythe—it occurred to me that I hadn't any idea what I was supposed to do with it. The way we were all facing each other in the middle of the small room gave the impression that I was expected to read it standing up, beginning to end, and render a judgment as soon as I'd finished. It seemed Mrs. Ward's clear intention was to stand

there and watch me read it, gauging my opinion from the movement of my eyebrows. For this reason I was reluctant to open the
volume, fearful of setting this chain of events in motion.

"The author of this work of history is Tria's grandfather on her
mother's side, you see. And my own father," Mrs. Ward added, as
if these two were not the same person, but rather collaborators.
"What we are in urgent need of is an informed and objective
opinion. I am convinced that what you hold in your hands is a
work of historical significance, intelligence, and refinement, but,
as my daughter has pointed out to me, I am hardly objective in
this matter, you see."

"Certainly," I said. "I mean, that's entirely understandable."

"I could never allow the volume to leave this room, of course,
but you could examine it here, at your leisure."

Tria was looking away now, flushed and beautiful.

"I'm not really an historian," I said again. "Of course I'd be very
interested to have a look, but—"

"Wonderful," Mrs. Ward said. "You see dear? Help has arrived.
I told you Mr. . . . was just the young man for us."

"I work days—" I began.

"There is no deadline, you see," Mrs. Ward said. "None. You
would be welcome to visit us any evening. I have a project in
mind, you see, but there are bridges to cross, and I am aware of
each one, you see."

"Well—"

"You will of course be compensated. We would not expect to
engage the services of a graduate of the university without providing remuneration."

This last had the ring of a line too long practiced, too desperate.
"I couldn't take money—"

"But you will read and give us your opinion. . . ." Mrs. Ward now
held out her palms for the volume, as if it had already rested too
long in the hands of a stranger, and I returned it to her, still
unopened, her thin fingers closing around it like tiny vises.

"Of course I will," I reassured her, all the while thinking, I must
confess, of the sweet promise of long evenings in conference with
her dark-haired daughter. "Of course I will."

It was that dark-haired daughter who walked me out to F. William
Peterson's shiny New Yorker less than fifteen minutes later, the
afternoon suddenly far shorter than I'd expected. The air had lost

its warmth, and so had my companion, it seemed to me. I couldn't make up my mind whether Tria Ward was irritated with me or simply abstracted.

"I hope I didn't mess up," I said when we were out of earshot. She allowed herself a half smile. "No," she said. "It isn't that. With Mother, things are never easy. Encouraging and discouraging her can be equally hazardous. I warned you not to laugh. I should have also warned you not to take her too seriously."

"Right," I said. "Then I'd have known just what to do."

She shrugged. "It's my fault anyway. I've seen this coming and didn't do anything about it. Now she's all wound up and there will be no dealing with her. You may have to be honest before you're through, and that will earn you an enemy."

"As long as it's just the one," I said, and she looked at me strangely, as if my remark would not permit interpretation. The blankness of her expression gave me a chill. It occurred to me for the first time in my long but slender acquaintance with Tria Ward that she might be slow. But I decided, as I stood there, completely charmed by the subtle flecks of color in her dark eyes, that it wasn't true, and that it wouldn't necessarily matter if it were. In the space of a few short hours, it occurred to me, I had fallen half in love with her again.

At least half.

My father said little about the legal difficulties that were closing in on him. In fact, he maintained that the lawsuit pending against him would never come to trial. The insurance companies would settle out of court, and the criminal negligence charge resulting from the DWI would be dropped. Beyond the mandated insurance coverage he had from the assigned risk pool, he himself had nothing, and to his mind that rendered him judgment-proof.

"What the hell do I have?" he kept insisting whenever anyone suggested he might be in trouble.

He was willing to concede that the accident would plunge him even further into the very deepest, darkest recesses of the risk pool, making his already exorbitant insurance rates astronomical, but beyond that he couldn't see where he had anything to lose. When I asked him whether there was a chance he might go to jail, he just shrugged. He'd been there before. And it couldn't be for too long. He'd just have to make sure he served his time during the winter, which was his bad season anyhow. "I'm all right when I'm working," he said. "If it wasn't for winters I'd be governor."

In fact, he did seem to do better once he went back on the road. He'd usually wander into Mike's Place about the time I got off and we'd have a beer before I headed home to dinner with my mother. Some nights he'd eat a hamburg steak at the Mohawk Grill or a plate of spaghetti at Mike's, and then say he was going home. He almost never did, but I could tell he was too tired after the long day of road construction to get into much trouble. Occasionally he'd go home with the intention of showering and going out again, only to fall asleep on the sofa for a few hours, long enough to make the shortened night less dangerous. And when he stuck to beer he was okay. Shortly after my return, he started up with Eileen again, too, which I considered a good sign. "She's a good girl," he said. "She's not the best-*looking* girl you ever saw, but she's all right, just the same. We stay off the subject of her asshole kid . . . we do okay."

"What's he up to these days?" I asked, feeling little more than obligatory curiosity, thankful that since my return to Mohawk our paths hadn't crossed and a little fearful that inquiring after his health might have the unintended effect of producing Drew Littler in the flesh. My first week at Mike's Place, I kept expecting him to turn up, especially when it turned out that Eileen was working lunches, but he never did. I'd often thought about asking her about him, but I knew he'd been in and out of trouble and a variety of institutions, so I thought I'd spare her. Now I was glad.

"Oh, he's up to about here," my father said, putting his maimed hand about a foot over his own head. "Like always. At the moment he's the guest of the state. They caught him trying to break into some joint down the line about three in the morning, the dumb son of a bitch. He couldn't work for a living, naturally."

"How long is he in for?"

"Not near long enough," my father said. "I got him a couple jobs myself, but things always wound up missing. It was never him, of course. Steal? Not him."

It didn't take my father much to get revved up on the subject of Drew Littler, and when he recalled conversations they'd had, he always rendered these dramatically, playing both parts, capturing the rhythms of the original discussion.

"Then how come as soon as you get hired things always start disappearing, I said to him one day. He'd just been fired, as usual. How the hell should I know, he says. Right. How the hell should you know anything, Zero. Things just vanish. They get up and walk away. As soon as you get hired, all this shit just up and walks off. It never did *before* you started working there, but now it just can't stay put."

"You know what he says to me, the big dumb son of a bitch? He says, that's right, Sammy. That's fuckin' right."

By this time my father was usually purple. One incident would remind him of another, and before long the veins in his neck would be pulsing. "We got into it about a year ago. He doesn't say shit to me anymore. He's that smart anyway, the dumb bastard."

"You can't tell his mother he's no good, either." I could tell he was unable to stop himself now. "She knows. She's got to. But do you think she'd listen when anybody tries to tell her? Not a chance. If he's not stealing money out of her purse, she's giving it to him so he won't have to. Can you imagine stealing from your own mother?"

I said no, but he wasn't really talking to me. Drew Littler stories consumed him, and once he got started a listener wasn't strictly necessary. He'd been through them all with Wussy and Mike and everybody else, and they never let him even get started anymore, cutting him off before he could get up a head of steam, for which he thanked them. Don't get me started on *that* dumb son of a bitch.

But I was a fresh listener, and I had to hear these stories several times during the course of the summer. It didn't take me long to realize that Drew Littler had become almost larger than life (no small matter) with my father, representing to him all that was wrong with things. It did little good to steer him away from the subject, because almost anything that went wrong would remind him of Eileen's son and set him in motion. And it always ended the same way, with my father shaking his head, his eyes having narrowed to the point that they were more inward-looking than outward, as if for the first time in his life he'd come across something he couldn't understand. "You should see him now," he'd tell me. "He's as big as a house."

And even though his eyes were little more than slits by the time he finished his rant, I could see something strange in them, something I'd never seen before.

It took me months to piece together what had happened between them. It wasn't the sort of thing you could just ask him about. My father had already told me all he was going to tell about how they'd "gotten into it." If I asked, all he'd do was go through the whole thing again and I wouldn't know any more than I had to begin with. You couldn't focus my father's stories, get him to clarify and expand portions. He'd start all over for you, but that was about it. So I had to make do with oblique references to the incident until I could get Wussy to fill me in. I still don't know all the details, but the outline is pretty clear, the conflict and its outcome predictable.

My father must have realized that he couldn't keep Drew Littler buffaloed forever. Even that second year that I'd lived with my father, the boy had been far bigger and stronger, and he'd known he was, at some level that was not quite belief. But his knowledge was marching steadily in the direction of belief, and he must have awakened each morning with an iota less superstitious fear of the man who appeared to have his number. He must have felt that belief coming like a wave, must have known that the day was not far distant when none of my father's tricks would work anymore, that there would be no way Sam Hall could get the drop on him. Or that even if he did get the drop, it wouldn't do him any good. That afternoon they finally got into it, Drew Littler must have known, perhaps had known for some time, that he could spot my father just about any advantage and still come out on top.

Apparently my father and Wussy had been working all afternoon in the hot sun, repairing the roof on Eileen Littler's little house. Drew, naturally, hadn't been around to help. Probably his mother had warned him to stay away, knowing that there was no way her son and my father could work on the same roof without one hurling the other off. And no doubt Drew had stayed away until he figured the job was done. He was every bit as lazy as my father accused him of being, and he wouldn't have wanted to risk being taunted up onto the roof where he'd get tar on his hands and clothes and in his blond hair.

And part of their getting it on that day wouldn't have anything to do with Drew Littler at all, but rather the lingering effects of my father's having had to work all day in the hot sun with Wussy. No doubt my father had talked Wussy into helping because Wussy knew a little bit about roofing the way he knew a little bit about everything. Unless I miss my guess, Wussy also knew a little bit more about it than did my father, whose opinion about such matters was always, "How fucking hard can it be?" It must have been some afternoon up there, the two of them finding out how hard it could be, the hot sun on their shoulders and reflecting up into their faces off the hot tar they hauled up to the roof in buckets. No doubt my father bulled his way through tasks that required finesse, Wussy shaking his head, concentrating fiercely on damage control, trying to kid my father out of the worst kinds of dumbness and getting called "you crazy black bastard" for his trouble. Eileen probably came out every half hour or so to stand in the middle of the driveway where she could see the two of them, listen to their tug of war, ask how it was going, to which Wussy would reply that the whole job would have been finished an hour ago if only he didn't have no help. Then my father would call him variations on the black bastard theme, Eileen, safe on the ground below, pointing out the literal truth that—covered with tar as they were—anyone would have taken them for brothers.

Sometime after she went inside the last time, Drew must have roared up on his new motorcycle, the first he'd owned since wrecking the other at the base of Jack Ward's private road. I doubt he would have said anything to my father or Wussy, but he probably gave them a long arrogant smirk before going into the house. At the time he had some sort of job and a cheap third-floor flat on the west end, but he still showed up two or three times a day, mealtimes, according to my father, since he couldn't cook and couldn't afford to eat out. Usually his first stop, before saying hello to anybody, was at the refrigerator, where he'd grab the plastic gallon jug of milk and tip it upright over his mouth. According to my father he could down two quarts that way, his Adam's apple bobbing rhythmically, machinelike.

"Don't be going down there," Wussy would have warned when he saw my father heading for the ladder.

"Who died and left you job foreman?"

"All right, *go* down there, rockhead."

"There's a six-pack of beer in the refrigerator and it's for us. I know because I put it there. If he's into it, I'm kicking his ass."

By the time my father got to the foot of the ladder, Drew had emerged from the house and gone into the garage, where my father found him sucking on a beer.

Probably my father gave him the opportunity to put it back. Probably Drew Littler didn't see much point in returning a half-guzzled beer. My father would have explained that this wasn't the point. The point was it was *his* beer. The point was he'd been up on the roof all afternoon in the hot sun. The point was they could have used some help. The point was Drew Littler was a worthless cocksucker who didn't know how to do anything except sponge off his mother and get into trouble. This last point I'm sure he explained to Drew Littler, because he always explained it thoroughly to me when he got going on the subject of Eileen's son. According to Wussy, Eileen came out and tried to keep them apart, but she didn't get there soon enough, and Wussy apparently didn't even come down off the roof. He told me all he could see was my father's legs dangling about eight inches off the garage floor, going like crazy, as if they were pedaling an invisible bicycle. Drew apparently had him by the throat with one big paw and was squeezing as if he intended to burst my father's purple face like a grape. Instead, he bashed him in the skull with the half-drunk can of beer and dropped him onto the cold floor. Then Drew Littler got on his motorcycle and roared off.

If my father thought he'd had it rough with Drew Littler, if he thought that sitting there on the cool garage floor, dazed and covered with beer and tar and sweat and blood from his nose, was as bad as things were going to get, he was mistaken, and he would have known that he was mistaken had he been able to focus on Eileen Littler's face. Wussy had by then started down the ladder, but he caught a glimpse of her standing over my father and went right back up again. She stood there for a hell of a while; then he heard her mutter, "Good! Sit there!" before storming back into the house.

Only when she was inside did Wussy climb down off the roof and sit down next to my father up against the wall of the garage.

My father looked at him. "You didn't get hurt up there on the roof did you?"

"No, I'm the nuts," Wussy said.

"I'm glad," my father said, fingering his nose to see if it felt broken.

"I heard all the noise and figured you were kicking ass. I just come down to keep Eileen off of you."

"From now on, she can kiss my ass," my father said, trying to get to his feet. In the process he kicked the still leaking aluminum can under the car. "At least he didn't get to drink our beer, anyhow."

"What kind of beer'd you buy?" Wussy said.

"What difference?" my father said, then bent at the waist to look under the car.

"Don't be looking under there, just tell me what you bought."

"How the hell do I know," my father said, but his expression had changed.

"You usually buy Genesee," Wussy said. "You just got brained with a Budweiser."

"So I bought Budweiser, so what?"

"So when Eileen came back from the store an hour ago she had a six-pack of Budweiser. That's so what."

My father wiped his face on his sleeve. "The principle's the same. When was the last time *he* ever brought a six-pack of beer over here? When was the last time he bought a loaf of bread? A *slice* of bread?"

Wussy was grinning at him now, watching him get worked up all over again, even more righteously now that he suspected he'd fucked up.

"So," my father said. "It's *my* fault, I suppose. All afternoon in the sun fixing her fucking roof, and I'm not supposed to tell him to stay out of the fucking beer. Right?"

He honked some blood onto the floor of the garage, used his sleeve. "Right? It's my fault. That's how come she sides with him. And that's not crazy enough, you're on *her* side."

"Nope," Wussy said. "I'm on your side. But I'm going back up on the roof anyways."

"Good," my father said. "Go."

According to Wussy he could hear them going at it down there right through the roof. Then a pot or something hit the wall and the back door slammed and my father climbed up the ladder, blasting away at the rate of about three curses per rung. When he arrived he started flinging everything he could lay a hand to off the roof, a few shingles and scraps of tar paper at first, but those were hardly satisfying the way the breeze took them. Then he threw hammers and other tools. Finally, he grabbed the tar bucket by the handle and flung it as hard as he could. Wussy figured it was his intention to throw it clean over the roof of the garage, but it only traveled ten feet before hitting a telephone wire and dropping straight down onto the hood of his convertible. My father walked over to the edge of the gently sloped roof and looked.

"Go ahead," Wussy said. "Jump."

Instead, my father turned his attention to the remaining rolls of tar paper, which he tossed down into the open car. These were followed by cartons of shingles and a box of black tacks. Then both mops and assorted little shit that had accumulated during the long afternoon—plastic glasses, the lemonade pitcher, a couple of shirts. He threw all of these down into the convertible, and stopped when there was nothing left to throw off except Wussy. Eileen came back out just in time to see him kick the ladder, which hit the convertible at the steering wheel and ended up balancing perfectly, four to five feet on either side of the car. Wings.

Eileen went back in the house.

"Fuck it," my father said.

It took him a while, but he finally calmed down, and when he did, Wussy said his first words since the tirade began. "One of us is going to have to jump down off this roof," he suggested. "It's not so far in the back, and it's a grassy landing."

"Shit," my father said, peering over. "How come you never stop me when I get like that?"

Wussy just looked at him.

"Right," my father said, disappearing over the side with a thud and a grunt.

It took them half an hour to get going again, set the ladder back up, shoulder the tar paper back and shingles back topside. Another forty-five minutes to finish.

Then they drove off without a word to Eileen and my father hadn't been back in the year and a half before my return to Mohawk, even though later that same week Drew Littler was arrested for breaking and entering and sent to jail. "She'll kiss my

ass before I ever set foot in that house again," he predicted on
their way to the junkyard for a new hood. They had to settle for
a white one, which was okay by my father. More annoying was the
fact that a year later he and Wussy were still finding roofing tacks.
Finding them the hard way.

I think I was the only one concerned about my father that summer. Eileen, who had been worried enough to call me in Tucson,
seemed to think he was doing better now. So did Mike, who had
seen him at his worst and just about given up on him. But now
he was back at work and not worrying about money, and somebody had said that the parents of the girl who'd been hurt in the
accident were talking about putting it all behind them and settling out of court. They lived in a ratty trailer on the lake road and
the idea of a lump sum right now as opposed to a much larger
lump at some indefinite point in the future was growing on them.
Thus my father's prediction that the case would never go to court,
which I had taken for bravado, seemed less farfetched. Even F.
William Peterson, who refused to discuss the case at all in my
mother's presence, and only vaguely when we had a rare moment
alone, seemed optimistic, claiming that other factors had come to
light and these were in my father's favor also. Whatever they
were, he didn't want them getting out, and I'm sure he had
communicated nothing to my father. Of course my father's
driver's license was going to stay good and suspended, except for
his drive-to-work privileges, but he'd already adjusted to that by
tightening his social circle to the in-town gin mills—Mike's and
the Night Owl and Greenie's and the VFW and one or two other
spots, each only a few blocks from the others and from his flat and
thus not very far to drive. You couldn't really even call it driving,
he maintained. If he came out and smelled Angelo, he'd walk.
   He still had the same built-in radar where cops were concerned
that had allowed him to torment my mother when I was a little
boy, then disappear mere seconds before the cruiser careened
around the corner. That radar occasionally failed him now, especially beyond a certain point of drunkenness. Otherwise, he was
astonishing. "If I was a cop," he would sometimes say as we were
barreling along, "I'd park my ass right over there." If I was driving, I'd slow down and look where he was pointing, and sure
enough, there underneath the overpass, or behind a stand of

trees, or in an alley there'd be a black-and-white, radar gun poised. If there was nobody behind us, he'd instruct me to slow down to about twenty so we could wave to the cop. If the top was up, he'd yell, "Hello, cocksucker!", convinced that all cops were lip-readers but that lip-read testimony was inadmissible in court. They couldn't do shit, the pricks, whether they wanted to or not.

I'd just look at him.

"You don't believe me?" he'd say.

"Nobody believes you."

"I'm right, anyhow."

It was undeniable that my father was in better spirits since going back to work. Maybe there was no reason to worry, but I did. Most everybody in Mohawk lived pretty near the edge—of unemployment, of lunacy, of bankruptcy, of potentially hazardous ignorance, of despair—and hence the local custom was that you only worried about people nearest the brink. Otherwise you'd worry *yourself* over the edge in short order, what with so many candidates for concern around. My father had taken a step or two back from the precipice and thereby removed himself from the official "at risk" roster. A month earlier you might have legitimately worried about him, but not anymore. Still, conventional wisdom aside, he didn't seem quite right to me. He'd become oddly religious, at times quite certain that there was a God, and that this God had it in for Sam Hall. Always a gambler, he'd become obsessed with the laws of probability and was convinced that God was toying with him via the daily number.

"Two-four-seven," he'd say to Mike. "How long did I play two-four-seven?"

"Who the fuck knows?" Mike would say. "Don't start with this shit again."

If Wussy was seated on the next barstool, my father would nudge him. "How long did I play two-four-seven?"

Wussy would shrug. "Thirty years. How should I know."

"Pretty goddamn near," my father would say seriously. "Day after day after day. Two-four-seven. Two-four-seven."

"Right," Mike said. "And it should have come up every day you played it."

My father was immune to sarcasm when on the trail of cosmic injustice. "Four-two-seven. Four-seven-two. Seven-two-four. Seven-four-two. Every combination but two-four-seven. No two-four-seven. Fuck me. I play it forever. Until I can't take it any-

more. I play three-seven-nine. Second week of three-seven-nine
and guess what pops?"

I had considered this a rhetorical question, but my father
nudged me. "Guess," he said.

"I forget," I told him. "What was your number?"

"Two-four-seven."

"All right," I said. "Two-four-seven."

"Right the first time," he said, satisfied. "I bet it wasn't ten days
after I came off it. I bet it wasn't a *week.*"

"That's one more bet you'd lose," Mike said.

"Your ass," my father said. "Some guys get special treatment.
Always have."

"God hates you?" I said in disbelief, the first time I heard this
routine.

"If he's half as smart as they say, he'd damn near have to,"
Wussy observed.

"How would *you* explain it?" my father wanted to know. He
was willing to defer to my opinion in such matters. I was a college
graduate. If God wasn't fucking him, I should be able to explain
things.

I said I didn't have an explanation.

He'd become something of a Calvinist, my father, contending
that God had his mind pretty much made up from the beginning.
Some people had it all right. Others? He lip-farted.

"Take me and Jack Ward," he said. "We both go into the service
the same month, not a pot to piss in, neither one of us, we both
go ashore at Utah Beach, we both end up in Berlin, we get home
the same week. A year later he's driving a new Lincoln Continen-
tal, loaded like a Greek, nothing to do but play golf every day.
Now you tell me."

"Jack Ward's dead," I observed.

He looked at me as if I might have an undetected brain tumor.
"So?"

I was embarrassed to state the obvious. "So his luck didn't
hold."

"You're full of shit," he said. "It held right to the end."

"Died in the saddle is what I heard," somebody down the bar
said.

"You're goddamn right," my father said, standing up to demonstrate the proper rhythm for the saddle. A canter, I judged it to
be. "He went right from the saddle into the loving arms of his
maker. Nonstop."

"Probably d-driving around in a L-l-lincoln up there in heaven," said Tree, who was much inclined toward my father's theory of an Elect and a Damned.

"Nah," said the man down the bar. "He's probably got a driver. He's in the backseat getting you know what." The speaker checked around the bar to see if there were any women.

This led to a discussion of whether you-know-what was better in heaven. Somewhere in the proceedings, my father, who had instigated the whole thing, lost interest. As the voices rose in mock anger and comic disagreement over what it had to feel like to get balled in heaven, my father, as I had noticed him do repeatedly that summer when he thought no one was looking, stared at the crooked stump of his thumb, as if the black, callused digit he'd lost contained some magic he despaired of finding anywhere else beneath the sky.

35

A few days after I served Manhattans to Mrs. Agajanian, Claude's old neighbor, who should come in off the street but Claude himself. It took me a minute to recognize him because his hair had receded and he'd become an adult instead of the soft, pudgy boy I remembered. In fact, it was worse than not recognizing him. I thought he was his father, for there was a striking resemblance between the man who stood before me and the pear-shaped Claude Sr., who'd blown town after his son's attempted suicide. And when I blinked and said, "Claude Schwartz?" it was the father I thought I was speaking to. But then I saw the turtleneck and the strange mischief of expression, the same look that had been there as a boy when he had some believe-it-or-not item he wanted to share with me from his own personal Ripley's. We shook as enthusiastically as we could with the bar between us, his large hand doughy, but warm and full of kindness. His grin was good-natured and wounded, suggesting that finding me here had

made his day, even if I *had* been around for a month and a half
and failed to look him up. Never mind, all was forgiven.

"Claude," I said, trying not to mimic his grin, but finding it
impossible to resist, "what can I get you?" The place was pretty
crowded for that time in the afternoon, for which I was grateful.
There was no guarantee Claude would speak.

He waved in the general direction of the taps, as if to say it
didn't matter to him which one I pulled. I drew him a beer and
wouldn't take his money for it.

Untemeyer came in and I told Claude I'd be right back. I had
half a dozen small wagers for the bookie, who set up shop at his
usual place at the end of the bar near the kitchen. Irma came out,
her hair in a net, dark perspiration stains under her arms from the
steamy kitchen, and tossed two dollars on the bar for her usual
daily double.

"Irma La Deuce," Untemeyer said, writing out a slip.

Irma winked at me, her face humorless. Untemeyer always took
her action first, so she could go back in the kitchen.

"You never should have took up gambling," the bookie said.
"You're an unlucky woman."

"Tell me."

"Besides," Untemeyer said, "one loser per marriage is enough."

"Not in mine," Irma said.

"Right," Untemeyer said. "Not in Mohawk."

I read him what I had while he wrote. When we finished, he
made me read it all again to make sure there was no mistake.
Then he took the money. "How come you never bet?" Untemeyer said.

It was true. I'd quit. Left the whole thing back in Tucson. "I'm
just looking for the right horse," I said.

"Me too," he agreed. "Fifty some years and I haven't found him
yet." He looked over his thick glasses down the bar to where
Claude Schwartz was sitting. "Seven-one-seven," he said, nodding. "July seventeenth. Half of Mohawk played seven-one-seven
that day."

Skinny Donovan was there with us at the end of the bar. He was
drinking Vichy water trying to dry out before Monday. My father
had gotten him on as a flagman on a nonunion road job in Speculator on the condition that he wouldn't be drunk and shaking come
Monday when he started. He looked like he wasn't going to be
drunk, but he still had the shivers pretty bad and everybody was

kidding him. Wussy had been in, looked him over and shaken his head, glad Skinny wouldn't be landing no airplanes with those flags.

"Seven-one-seven," Skinny nodded. "I played it for about a week myself, even though I should've knew better. It only works for suicides if they die."

"It popped just last week," Untemeyer observed. "You should have stuck with it."

"For ten years?" Skinny said.

"How many numbers you had in ten years?"

"Never one," Skinny admitted sadly.

"There you go," Untemeyer said. "You hadn't been fickle, you'd have had the one, anyway."

Skinny drank his Vichy and considered this seriously. "I could use the money," he said, as if he harbored a secret hope that Untemeyer might give him credit for *wanting* to bet seven-one-seven all those years and pay off on the intention.

Things always picked up when Untemeyer came in and it took me fifteen minutes or so to get back down to Claude at the other end of the bar. When I finally did, his glass was empty and he'd written me a message on his damp cocktail napkin. It contained his address and the following: "My wife's name is Lisa. Come see us. My mother lives with us, too."

"I will, Claude," I said, folding the napkin and pocketing it.

We shook again, then, and Claude climbed down off his bar stool. I didn't really expect him to speak, and when he did, it surprised me so, I made him repeat what he'd said, though I'd heard his soft voice clearly. The rasping that had characterized his speech for so long after he'd tried to hang himself was gone now, but he still spoke, out of desire or necessity, at little more than a whisper. Even so, I'd heard him clearly answer the question I'd been wanting to ask ever since I'd recognized him as his father.

"He never came back," Claude Schwartz said, as if this fact too belonged in his private *Guinness Book of World Records*.

By the time I got off work, went home, and discovered the napkin in my pocket, the ink had smeared so badly that the address was unreadable. Fortunately, Claude's mother was listed in the Mohawk directory and I was pretty sure the address was the same Claude had written on the napkin. When I called, it was his

mother who answered and said, yes of course it was Ned Hall, and
that I was to come right over. I was expected for pizza. When I
said I'd have to take a rain check until the following evening, she
said that would be fine and did I like pizza? I said I did. Very
much.

The next afternoon I had Mike let me go home half an hour
early so I could go home and shower off some of the beer smell.
It also happened to be Wednesday, which meant that I carried
about my person the odor of urine. Mrs. Agajanian had again
come to visit just long enough to toss back four murderous Manhattans and pee in her booth. And, just as in the case of the
previous Wednesdays, she was steadier on her way out than in,
her knotted, dry old bones lubricated somewhat, her face frozen
into a savage, determined grin, her stockings dripping. Any right-
minded person who hadn't the responsibility of sponging down
her booth afterward would have admired her.

Every Wednesday after that first one, she demanded more and
more of my time, and she was militantly heedless of whatever else
happened to be going on in the bar. I never sat down, but this did
not stop her from telling me a long story each time I delivered
a Manhattan. Ten years had not diminished by a jot her resentment against Byron, her homosexual and utterly fictional husband, who, I was informed, was now living somewhere in Puerto
Rico, having "sunk his faggot ass in butter." She had stories about
half a dozen other eccentric relatives too and she always told
anecdotes about them as if they were famous people who needed
no introduction. She only once mentioned the invisible son I'd sat
on ten years earlier when he was cleaning fish, remarking with
genuine regret that he was not the kind of boy you could take
places.

She much preferred me to Satch, the previous bartender at
Mike's, who had been slow to lend an arm and whose overall
intelligence she had considered suspect. His slender, hairy chest
had reminded her of Byron's. He'd not only made an indifferent
Manhattan, he was very slow about it, leaving her to shout and
bang on the back of the booth in frustration until her hands
throbbed. She showed me her clawlike hands as evidence, and it
was easy to believe that they throbbed all right, each finger going
in several different arthritic directions. She had been overjoyed
when Satch was canned, she said, indeed could not have been
happier without having been informed that he had died and gone

to hell, even though my own Manhattans were not such a great improvement, truth be told. But I wasn't to worry about it, because I was a good young fellow. She approved of me, as she could not approve of Satch and the hateful gorilla of a taxicab driver they always sent for her. As I balanced Mrs. Agajanian on my arm, out of the bar and into the gorilla's waiting taxi, I always wondered how the old woman reconciled her fondness for me with the soaked booth she always left as a token of her affection.

The Schwartz flat was located in a section of town I was not particularly well acquainted with although, according to my mother, my grandfather had once owned a house there and sold it in order to buy the one I'd grown up in. The streets west of Main were older and less symmetrical than those east. They turned around and in upon themselves, as if they'd been laid out by a drunk and then paved by a man who understood him perfectly. Small leather shops, many now closed and empty, rose up on street corners above long rows of two-family houses built much too close to one another, the broken concrete walkways between them so narrow that a broad-shouldered man would have to go sideways, tripping over the rusted tricycles and old inner tubes that inevitably collected there. Most of the houses themselves were sturdy and well built, among the oldest in the city, but they were run-down and neglected now, like the shops and green-fronted, dark neighborhood groceries, abandoned when those who had patronized them moved to newer sections of the city and did their shopping along the highway. Only the occasional tan brick church survived the general exodus, indeed benefited, to some extent, by the razing of a shabby house or two nearby, so that the church parking lot could be expanded, or some ambitious rector's plan for a church hall, named in his own honor, be implemented. Thus on Sundays the very people who had long before left the neighborhood to welfare renters returned to shake their perplexed heads at the old neighborhood and wonder how they'd ever managed to live in each other's laps like that. When they went inside the church, they locked their cars.

The Schwartz flat was on Becker Street at the bottom of a dangerous hill that claimed the life of about one child a year, usually in a sledding accident. There were steeper hills around, but Becker Street's was a long quarter-mile slope with but a single intersection at the bottom, ideal for sledding, that activity's strict illegality notwithstanding. As a boy, I had not been allowed to cross Main with my sled, and my mother had shown me newspaper clippings in defense of her intractability. These had often contained grainy *Mohawk Republican* photos, snowy because *Republican* photos were always snowy, and because these happened actually to picture snow. If you looked at these pictures long and closely enough, and read the captions and stories that accompanied them, you might be able to ascertain that the dark mass in the center was a crazily angled automobile and that the dark something jutting up from under its wheels was a child's sled. In a way, these vague white photographs did frighten me, leaving totally to the imagination as they did the condition, even the whereabouts, of the victim.

Coming down the same hill in my father's convertible, I guessed that there were still all sorts of tragedies on Becker Street. The fact that the Claudes were now reduced to living there was perhaps among them, because these second-story flats were a far cry from the house they'd owned on Third Avenue. The hallway that led up to the Schwartz apartment was dank and airless. At the landing, I stopped to wipe the sweat from my forehead and consider whether it might be possible to retreat and drive away unnoticed. There were voices on the other side of the door, but not close—they seemed to come from the back of the flat, the kitchen probably. I was about to knock when the door opened and Claude, who must have seen me pull up in the street below and traced my progress up the stairs, was grinning at me as if to ask what I thought of all *this*. We shook hands there in the entry.

His mother peered in from the kitchen and caught us at it. "Honestly, Claude," she hollered. "Don't make your friend stand out there in the horrid hall. Have him come in where it's cool!"

Claude rolled his eyes at me and stepped out of the way, so that I could come in where it was cool. Or at least so that I could come in, because I couldn't see that it was a degree cooler inside than in the horrid hall. That it was cooler must have been deliberate fiction designed to make life bearable during the summer months. In fact, the apartment was stifling. For some reason all the windows were clamped shut, their dark shades three-quarters drawn. I recognized a few pieces of furniture from the house on Third Avenue, old and faded now. I wondered how on earth they'd managed to get some of the larger pieces up the narrow staircase and into the cramped flat. Unless there was a rear entrance that was more accessible, it looked to me a geometric impossibility.

"Why don't you run along and get the pizza, dear?" Mrs. Schwartz sang from the kitchen. "And Mr. Hall can have a seat."

She reappeared in the doorway before the sound of her voice had stopped reverberating. "Scoot," she told her son. "Scoot, scoot, scoot."

"If you'd like some company," I began, already anxious to be out of the apartment.

"*I'm* the one in dire need of company," Claudine Schwartz said emphatically. "My son has a wife and the post office, too. What I have is walls."

By way of punctuation, a door slammed in the extreme rear of the flat. Mrs. Schwartz made a face in the direction of the noise.

"Scoot," she repeated to her son, whose banishment had been momentarily halted by the sound. He did as he was told though, and his mother and I listened to the sound of his footsteps in retreat down the stairs. I listened for the sound of a car starting up in the street, but there wasn't any, and I couldn't tell whether with the windows closed I'd missed it or, more likely, that Claude had set out on foot. The nearest pizza place was Al's, several blocks away, which meant that I was going to have a good twenty minutes in stir with Claudine.

Actually, Claude's mother had not aged significantly. Never an attractive woman, she looked to me like her low-slung anatomy might still be accommodated by the same dress size, and her hair was dyed the same cheerful blond it had been when Claude and I were boys. Her skin was more sallow now, perhaps from staying indoors with the shades drawn, but then the sun had never made much of an impression on it. I remembered that afternoon in October when we'd all gone to the lake and she'd beached herself in the sand, covering her eyes with a towel, defying the weak October sun to color her pale limbs. She had asked me to remain a friend to her son that day, and I thought she must be pretty dissatisfied with my performance. But then everyone seemed to have pretty modest expectations where Claude was concerned.

"So," I said. "Claude works for the post office?"

"For the last six and a half years," she said. "Since he took the civil service."

I smiled at the expression.

"He works strictly in the mailroom," she explained, as if otherwise the idea of Claude as a postal worker might strain credulity. "He's left alone to do his job and that's the way he likes it. He reads all the magazines that come in and brings home the ones that can't be delivered."

Now that she'd mentioned it, there were a startling number and variety of magazines in the room. There were teetering piles of them up against every vacant wall space.

"You wouldn't believe some of the gutter filth that comes through the United States mail," Mrs. Schwartz said, glancing around apprehensively, lest an example might be in plain view. "It's enough to make you ill. Physically ill."

I said I bet it was.

"That's why we can't open our windows," she explained, motioning to the drawn shades and drapes.

I did not want to appear stupid, but I couldn't help blinking. Clearly, Claude's mother did not consider her remark a non sequitur, but I did. Maybe it was the heat, but I was very close to asking her to experiment by opening the window directly behind me a few inches to see if any pornographic pamphlets flew through with the breeze.

"Filth," Claude's mother repeated. "You should hear what streams in. Both sides. The way they treat each other. The things they say. You know what it makes me want to do?"

I thought I did, but I said I didn't.

"Bathe," she said, surprising me. "I'd rather swelter than listen to filth. Close the windows, *I* say. Pray for winter. Then at least they have to close *their* windows."

In fact, I was hearing noises, but they sounded like they were coming from the rear of the apartment. Another door slammed.

Mrs. Schwartz started to get up, then sat down again. "Actually, we're having something of a domestic crisis of our own today," she admitted.

I said I was sorry to hear it, that perhaps I shouldn't have come, a possibility Claude's mother appeared too abstracted to protest.

"It's been suggested that there are other places where I might be content . . ." Mrs. Schwartz said, though it was clear that she considered this radical notion malicious nonsense, her own recent protestations of discontent notwithstanding. "As if the very bed she's lying on in there were not my own. Given freely, you understand, I'm no Indian giver. After all, what do *I* need with a king-size?"

Claudine Schwartz appeared to give the question much consideration.

"You men," she continued. "How I envy you. The way you can just pack a suitcase when things go wrong. Walk, as they say. Imagine." She looked around the dark flat as if for an exit sign. "Do you know what my husband took with him when he abandoned us?"

I said I didn't.

"Nothing," she said. "Underwear. Socks. A few shirts. His shaving kit."

That sounded a lot like my own hasty departure from Tucson, and it made me feel guilty, as if I'd left a girl there, one I hadn't known about.

"Do you know what I took from our house on Third Avenue when we moved to this . . . this . . . place?" she said, and waited long enough for me to raise my eyebrows. "Everything. I took every living thing. Furniture. Dishes. All of it. Half is in storage. What I kept it all for I couldn't tell you, I'm sure. But I have it, and I'll keep it."

She nodded, taking inventory of the room, her expression saddening. "We had such nice things, didn't we? For the longest time I thought after a while he'd remember all our nice things and get lonesome for them. But I guess men don't."

"I doubt he's very happy," I said, trying to cheer her up. In fact, I'd occasionally thought of Claude Sr. and wondered what might have become of him. There were two or three scenarios I'd toyed with. In one he was a guilt-ridden, grief-stricken wanderer, tormented by recurring dreams from which he would scream awake. In another he'd changed his name, found himself a long stretch of warm beach, and forgotten all about his previous life. But the one I leaned toward had him managing a small factory in a nearby state, married again, his new wife cheerfully bearing him sons through wide, good-natured hips. Big, slow boys he'd engage in foot races until they were old enough to beat him, or until they despaired and withdrew into defeat.

I continued to think about him even after Claude's mother got on to more pleasant topics, until we heard Claude's hurried feet on the stair and he burst, out of breath, into the room with a huge, hot cardboard box. It was just what we needed. Steam.

* * *

Somehow, we got through it.

I was far too uncomfortable to be hungry, but I ate two slices anyway—no toppings, double cheese—each bite pulling long sheets of swaying mozzarella toward vulnerable chins. In the center of the table was a sweating pitcher of cherry Kool-Aid, which made me wonder whether the Claudes customarily drank Kool-Aid with their meals or if this was a special occasion, a nostalgic gesture designed to remind Claude and me of the good old days when we'd drunk pitchersful on the big redwood picnic table in the backyard of their old house. Maybe it was a matter of money. Claude couldn't have been getting rich at the post office, and there were three mouths to feed. I tried to imagine Claude asking for a raise and couldn't. Tried to imagine him being given one without asking, and couldn't swing that either. The fact that they were all living together in a cheap flat suggested at least a degree of desperation. The more I thought about it, the more convinced I became that inviting me for even such modest hospitality had probably required a sacrifice, and I tried my best not to in any way reveal my most profound wish that they'd reconsidered the project and risked hurting my feelings. God, did we sweat over that pizza.

Claude's wife did not appear until after dinner when I started making excuses about having to leave. Then Claude disappeared for a few minutes, and when he returned he had a young woman in tow. Given the circumstances, I was surprised by my reaction to Claude's wife. If ever anybody deserved to be cut some slack, granted a fistful of allowances, Lisa Schwartz certainly did. Here she was, clearly in the advanced stages of pregnancy, stuck in a close, shabby, sweltering apartment, with her husband's mother for company, and with a husband whose prospects for improving their situation were, realistically, slim. And yet, I took an instant and extraordinarily intense dislike to her. So powerfully negative was my first impression that I was at a loss to in any way account for it or even, I fear, to conceal it.

The young woman Claude had married was short, with dark hair and skin. Her center of gravity seemed actually *below* her sizable hips. Perhaps in deference to the heat, she was wearing a light jumper that was designed to be worn with a shirt underneath. She was not wearing one though, and the deep arm holes revealed the sides of her moist, swollen, purplish breasts, along with tufts of matted black hair. Every detail of her perfectly dreadful appearance, it seemed to me, was a conscious and pointed indictment of the smiling husband at her side. I had all I could do to shake her hand when it was offered.

"Lisa," I said, deciding on levity. "For some reason I half expected your name to be Claudia."

"Why?" the girl said, her dark eyebrows joining when she frowned.

"I don't know," I said, regretting the attempt immediately.

"There any pizza left," she asked her mother-in-law. "I don't feel so shitty now."

I did though, and when Claude walked with me down the narrow stairs and out into the street, I sat down on the porch steps, still tasting the cherry Kool-Aid. Claude joined me. The sun was down behind the houses now, but it was still light and would be for another hour. Some grubby kids were playing kickball up the block, kicking uphill so the ball would come back to them if it didn't get stuck under curb-parked cars. It was still hot and muggy, but a tremendous relief from the deadness of the Schwartz flat. I ran my fingers through my hair and said, "Jesus, Claude," before I could stop myself. Strangely, he didn't seem to take the least offense, attributing my remark, perhaps, to the sweltering heat.

For the first time in a long while I felt rotten about not having any money. If I'd had a spare five hundred, I'd have written Claude a check right there, though I don't know what good it would have done them. It was an unholy trinity they made and I doubted all the money in the world would have made much difference, but it would have been worthwhile to introduce an air conditioner into their flat, if only to dry the glistening perspiration from Lisa Schwartz's purple breasts.

Clearly, though, I was more upset about my friend's circumstances than Claude himself, who just grinned at me and said, "Life, huh?" as if his own was sufficiently awful to be wonderfully interesting. I think it was the first thing he'd said all evening, and it pretty much killed further discussion.

After shaking hands, I left him there on the steps and pulled my father's convertible away from the curb slowly, did a U-turn and interrupted the game of kickball. I was in a hell of a mood and when one of the kids made a wise-ass remark as I crept up through their center field, I think, if I hadn't caught a glimpse of Claude in the rear view, I'd have gotten out and taken great pleasure in

bloodying the little shit's nose. Even when I was safely out of the
horrible neighborhood, my murderous mood refused to dissipate,
so I drove out of town to a spot where the old two-lane blacktop
ran straight and true for several hundred yards. I stopped there
for a second, listening to the chorus of insects brought to life by
the setting sun and the stillness of the air. Then I hit the accelerator hard and felt a rush of air as the Cadillac strained forward. I
kept my foot right on the floor, burning toward a dark spot on the
horizon where the two lanes merged in a constant, ever receding
fixed point, all speed, all focus, all illusion.

On the way back to town I had to pull over. The convertible
had done what I asked, but it was thirsty now. It took three quarts
of oil before anything registered on the dipstick.

By midsummer Tria Ward and I had become lovers.

Proximity was partly responsible. I visited the Ward house several nights a week to work on *The History of Mohawk County*,
and to my surprise, Mrs. Ward left me alone in the den she'd set
up as a shrine to her father. I told her I'd need a large table and
a typewriter, and these appeared the next night, the recliner
having been moved out to create space. There were limits to her
trust, of course, and when I told Mrs. Ward that I'd need to make
a copy of the manuscript, she insisted on doing that herself, fuss-
ing terribly about the necessity of laying the individual pages flat
on the surface of the photocopy machine. She feared cracking the
pristine leather binding. She got over it, though, and was very
pleased to discover that I no longer needed to consult the original
typescript. This she returned to its hallowed place on the mantel,
where it stayed for about a week, and where her nervous glance
would locate it as soon as she entered the room, as if she expected
it to speak to her in her father's recollected tones. Then one day

the book was gone and Mrs. Ward explained that she'd begun to be concerned for its safety in the event of fire or burglary and had placed it in a safety deposit box in the bank. That burglary was a seriously considered scenario should have alerted me to the dangerous fantasies that Tria's mother was indulging concerning her father's tome, but I didn't and wouldn't for another six weeks, and by then it would be too late.

More embarrassing to relate is the fact that I myself began to indulge a fantasy or two concerning *The History of Mohawk County*. Originally, I had intended to follow Tria's advice by reading the manuscript, telling Tria's mother that I thought it quite wonderful, but that local histories had seldom generated any interest outside their locales, and that in any case, I knew nothing about how she should go about getting it published. I'd be happy to write a letter on her behalf to a local or university press, but beyond that. . . .

This was the plan, and I no doubt should have stuck to it. But when I began to study the manuscript, I could not help but engage in the theoretical problem posed by its condition. The book was as dry and lifeless as only the worst history can be, but its most pressing problems were stylistic. The writing, though mechanically sound, was stiff, awkward, dull, repetitious, obscure. There were other problems too; the book was not truly history, at least in the best sense, because it arrived at no conclusions and lacked unity of vision. It was nothing more than a compilation of disparate facts. Here's how the Iroquois stitched their moccasins. At the very least, the book needed a long introductory or concluding essay to tie together the myriad threads the author had not seen fit to weave, and to suggest what possible significance such information might have.

But it seemed to me that *The History of Mohawk County* might be rendered readable, perhaps even marginally interesting. And I thought it might be fun to try. Working in the Ward library, so small and dark and cool, reminded me of my wonderful mornings in the Mohawk Free Library during the two years I'd lived with my father. There I had read helter-skelter, allowing the wide world to open up to me at random. The sense of wonder I felt there had been all but stifled by my subsequent education, and the huge, well-lit stacks, adjacent to sterile, modern university reading rooms had proven a poor substitute for my crooked little alcove in the town library. And too, after listening all day to the

assorted bullshitters and outright liars who frequented Mike's
Place, I was ready for an evening of quiet, cerebral pursuit, if only
I could convince myself of the worthiness of the project.

At first, Tria was all for sticking to our original plan. She was
pretty sure I had no legitimate business futzing around with her
grandfather's manuscript. But when I asked her to give me a
week she reluctantly agreed, and I went to work in earnest. Each
night I carefully reread about ten pages of typescript, then went
back and edited five of them on the theory that I'd always be far
enough ahead to catch significant repetitions of style and sub-
stance and be able to reorganize details where needed. Then I
retyped the edited pages and made further cosmetic revisions. I
was at best a mediocre typist though, and that slowed my progress, until Tria, who typed like the wind, volunteered to do the
edited text while I worked in pencil on the copy of the typescript.

We were a strange pair. Most evenings she'd join me about
forty-five minutes into my labors so I'd have something to give
her, and then we'd be together in that small room, so close that
I could smell her perfume, neither of us uttering a word. Sometimes, I'd be conscious that she had stopped typing, and when I
looked up she'd be studying me with an expression that was more
suggestive of perplexity and suspicion than the affection I would
have preferred. And she always looked quickly away, before I
could smile, as if she were conscious of having betrayed her innermost thoughts.

Paradoxically, even though I doubted that Tria Ward felt much
attraction, I began to be uncharacteristically certain that before
long she would extend me the invitation. Such arrogance, I hasten
to add, was far from customary. In my relations with other young
women to this point in my life, I had always been rather pessimistic about my prospects, a circumstance born of experience. I'd
been told that I struck most girls as gloomy, and at the university
one honest sorority girl I had badgered about going out said that
she had nothing against me personally, except that when she
went out with a guy, like, she preferred to have a good time, you
know? I knew. Perhaps I was confident about Tria because I was
beginning to suspect that she was *not* the sort of girl who preferred to have a good time.

Once we entered the library, Mrs. Ward left us so thoroughly
alone that I began to suspect the older woman's motives. An early
riser, she retired, or claimed to, shortly after nine o'clock, and

once her bedroom door closed softly behind her, it never opened again, almost as if she were observing the conditions of a contract. She even announced her retirement each evening by knocking quietly on the door of the library and advising us not to work too hard or too late. Each night Tria would say, "I love you, Mother," to which Mrs. Ward would reply, "And I you, Dear," all of this rendered even more bizarre by the fact that the library door remained closed, their protestations of affection thus required to penetrate wood.

One late July evening, after we'd been working together for several weeks, I couldn't get in gear. I'd been struggling with the same passage for over half an hour under flickering lights. A dry electrical storm was approaching and we could hear the wind coming up outside, even though the library was windowless. Mrs. Ward had already retired, and when I handed Tria the still flawed page I'd been working on, I pretended to begin another, but watched her type instead. She carried herself the same way she had when she was fourteen and I'd fallen in love with her, as if she hadn't revised her opinion of herself significantly in the intervening decade, a notion that I found quite charming, I don't remember why. She seemed to be keeping something at bay, and the result was beautiful, mildly disconcerting only if one recalled the photographs of her mother, who appeared to have done the same thing. I couldn't help wondering if, like Mrs. Ward, Tria would be transformed, almost overnight, from a young woman to an old one.

From where I sat that evening, the question was academic. Much more to the point was the smell of her perfume in the close room, the extraordinarily pale white skin of her throat, the enticing silhouette created by the table lamp which backlit the loose, peasant-style Mexican blouse she was wearing. Then the lights went out entirely, and along with them the hum of the electric typewriter.

"Great," I heard her mutter in the dark, then, "where are you?"

"Right here," I said, not having moved.

"I've always hated the dark."

I found her by smell and took her hand. "Let's go out on the patio and watch the storm," I suggested.

"Why?"

"No reason," I admitted.

"Mother has candles somewhere."

"To hell with them," I said.

The rest of the house was not so dark. Each of the long picture windows of the living room let in enough gray light for us to locate the sliding glass door that led out onto the patio. Heat lightning glowed yellow and orange in the night sky, each charge powerful enough to illuminate one quadrant of low clouds.

"It's just us," Tria said, pointing to the other side of the highway below where there were still lights from streetlamps and houses.

"What was it like to grow up here?" I said. I was still holding her cool hand, grateful that she had made no effort to withdraw it.

"What do you mean?"

I could feel her studying me and felt the strangeness of my own question. "I don't know exactly what I mean," I admitted. "Being up here, above it all, I guess. Having money, in a place like Mohawk."

When she said nothing, I decided to take a chance, and pointed to a dark place in what was the uppermost reaches of Myrtle Park. "I used to wonder about this house when I was a kid. You can see it from up there in the park. I thought of it as the white jewel house because of the way the sun reflected off it. I wondered what sort of people lived here, what they might be like. I must have been about ten."

"It wasn't anything like you imagined," she said slowly, as if choosing her words with care. "Like you imagine."

She pressured my hand lightly. It might have been a signal to let go, or an invitation. I decided it meant the latter and drew her to me. She neither returned my kiss nor drew away.

"And you've wanted to do that since you were ten?"

"I didn't know you then."

"But you were already in love with the house."

The possibility that this might be true stopped me dead, and the hot wind rattled the patio furniture urgently. For the first time I smelled rain. "Maybe we should go back in," I admitted. "We may be in for it."

"No," she said with surprising conviction. "It's not going to rain. The wind is going to howl and howl and nothing is going to come of it."

There seemed to me another invitation somewhere in this, and I was right, because this time she kissed me back, allowed herself to melt toward me, and we stayed there under the heat lightning until the low, fast-moving clouds that came at us from behind the park were blown over our heads toward the southeast and the invisible black band of trees that marked the river.

I dozed, for an hour perhaps, and awakened to soft drumming on the roof. Or maybe it was Tria stirring that had awakened me. I could tell that she was awake now and that she may have been since we made love. She lay with her back to me facing the window, its blinds three quarters drawn. When I drew her toward me at the waist, she turned and burrowed into me as if she couldn't get close or warm enough. It took me a minute to realize that she was crying. I let her, not saying anything for quite a while, just stroking her hair.

When she finally stopped, I said, "I guess this wasn't such a hot idea."

"It's . . . not . . . you," she whispered. "Please believe that. It's just . . ."

"I know," I told her, though I hadn't the slightest idea what it was. I was just glad it wasn't me.

"It's strange to be a woman in the same room where you were a child," she said, after she'd had a chance to think. "My father used to come in here and tuck me in and say that someday there'd be boys in my life, and I'd say no, never—"

"I liked your father," I told her.

She wiped her eyes and raised up on one elbow, charmingly, breathtakingly immodest. "Really? Why?"

I had to think about it. "He was different," I said finally. "I didn't know anyone like him. I was pretty impressed."

"And your own father?"

"He's different too," I said.

"You love him?"

"Sure," I said. "I mean yes, very much. I'm trying to decide if he has any feelings for me, though."

"I bet he does."

"Maybe," I admitted. "He gets along so well without me that I can never be sure. I don't think he's ever had a bad night worrying about me, for instance."

"I wish I could remember my father better," Tria said. "According to my mother, he was an empty man. All charm and style and looks and nothing inside."

"You should talk to my father about him someday. They were together a lot in the war. Anyway," I said, "I doubt he was empty. There was something that kept those guys going, the ones who made it all the way to Berlin."

"Sometimes," Tria said, rolling over onto her back again and staring up at the ceiling, "I think that Mother is right about him being empty because I feel so empty myself." She looked over at me in the semidark with the same scared look she'd had as a girl learning to drive. "Do you ever feel like you're nobody at all?"

"No," I admitted. "There are times when I feel like I'm somebody I don't like very much."

"But always somebody," she said sadly, then added, "I never dislike myself. When I was younger and first began to understand that my father was doing something behind Mother's back, I thought that if I could make him love me more, he'd love her too. I even told her that once, and she smiled at me like I didn't understand a thing in the whole wide world. You don't count, was what she said. Later that night when she heard me crying, she came in and explained what she'd meant. That Daddy was an adult, and that even though he loved me as a little girl, I didn't count as a big girl because I wasn't one. But it was too late. I'd already understood it the other way, and it had made the whole world make sense. All I had to do was understand that I didn't count and then everything fell into place. When he died, that's all I could think of."

It had stopped raining out, and somewhere below, on the highway, we heard a hot rod downshifting gears.

"I was here that night, with my father," I heard myself tell her. "The night half the town came out. I never felt so sorry for anybody. I couldn't face you I felt so bad."

She covered her face with both hands, remembering. "It was awful. I'll never forget it. All those people. They wouldn't go home. My mother was glad they were there, so she could say look, he's done it for the last time. How I hated her that night. How I hated everybody."

"Me too," I said, remembering the woman who'd stolen the book from the Ward library.

For some reason, I told Tria about it, though it did not surprise her. "All sorts of things disappeared that night. You wouldn't believe the things they took."

"Yes I would," I said, thinking that it hadn't been just Drew

Littler who resented the Money People. Most people who stole weren't taking what they believed to be others' property. They were taking what they themselves deserved, all the things they'd been cheated out of. That, now that I thought about it, was why I'd raided Klein's. It had been an act of revenge, not avarice.

"The car was the one that got us," she said.

I blinked. "What?"

"Somebody swiped Daddy's Lincoln," she said. "That afternoon. When we got back from the funeral home it was gone."

She was looking at me so strangely—as if she thought it might be within my power to explain such maliciousness—that I felt a sudden, inexplicable wave of guilt so powerful that I imagined for a brief moment that maybe I *had* stolen the Lincoln and willed myself to forget the deed. This bizarre conviction was so real that I had to force myself to reason it out, that it could not be true. I'd been thirteen when Jack Ward died. I hadn't taken driver ed until two years later in Mohawk High.

The more I tried to shake the feeling of responsibility, the more guilty I felt about my present posture. Was I not at this moment a thief in the Ward house? Hadn't I insinuated my way into their midst, misrepresented myself, stolen into Tria's bedroom, taken . . . what? Nothing that hadn't been freely given, surely. And maybe it had done some good. Maybe confiding in me about that horrible day was something Tria needed to do. I realized that her breathing had become regular and that she was asleep. I stayed awake watching the patterns made on her bedroom wall by the sliver of moon darting in and out of the clouds outside. At one point, what my imagination took to be a human form passed outside the window, but I did not dare disturb Tria, whose head lay on my shoulder, her gentle breathing providing a rhythm that I tried, without much success, to match.

Tria woke me early. Her bedside clock said it was a few minutes before six and the clear sky outside the bedroom window was not quite blue yet.

"I just heard Mother in the bathroom," she said, up on one elbow to smooth hair away from my forehead, a gentle, wonderful intimacy that took my breath away.

"You don't make it easy for a guy to break camp," I said.

She covered herself, or tried to, with the sheet. "You better had, though, unless you want to meet her in the hall."

I could hear water running in another part of the house. "Let me take you to dinner tonight," I said.

"No," she said. "But call me later."

"She's liable to hear me drive away," I said.

"She's probably seen the car out there anyway," Tria said. "Don't worry, though. She'll pretend she doesn't know. Things are always normal here, no matter how abnormal."

I got dressed and out the door quickly. My father's Cadillac gave me a bad moment when it refused to turn over or even acknowledge that a key had turned in the ignition, but then the engine coughed to life with a plume of purple smoke from the exhaust. It hung there, intact, utterly refusing to dissipate, when I drove away, between the stone pillars and down the hill.

The first thing to do was return the car. It was Saturday morning though, and there was no hurry. I'd left my father at Greenie's with half a load on around 7:30 the night before, which meant that Saturday wouldn't get under way for him much before noon. I didn't want the car for anything, though, so I left it at the curb across the street from his flat where he couldn't miss it. Then I walked to the corner and left on Main toward the Mohawk Grill. Out of habit I peeked in on my way by, and there was my father sitting at the counter eating eggs. The only other person was Harry, who was nursing his ritual Saturday morning hangover, the very apparent pain of which changed his personality not one jot.

"Here's the car thief now," my father said when I slid onto the stool next to him. "How about some eggs?"

"Sure," I said. "What's up?"

"Not a thing," he said. "Just sitting here wishing I had a car is all. I walked all the way over to your mother's and it wasn't there either."

"You didn't wake her up, I hope."

"You shitting me?" he said, as if to suggest that perhaps I'd forgotten that he was acquainted with her. "What'd you do, wreck it?"

"It's sitting right out in front of your place," I told him.

"Like hell. I walked all around the block. Two blocks."

I shrugged. "I've got twenty bucks says it's right out front."

"Then you just put it there."

Harry set my eggs in front of me and went back to frying bacon and sausage, which he had sputtering in long even rows on the grill. My father finished his breakfast and amused himself by watching me eat mine, nodding as if he knew something worth knowing.

"So," he said. "You finally found a better place to park my car at night than your mother's."

"Who, me?" I said. I liked those rare occasions when he didn't know what was up. It was pure pleasure not helping him figure it out. "I'd check the battery cables," I told him. "It wouldn't start, at first. I think you got a loose connection."

"He *is* a loose connection," Harry offered without turning around.

My father ignored him. "Does that in the morning sometimes. When it's damp. Rain out where you were?"

"Yup," I said.

He nodded. "Guess who came home yesterday."

"Drew Littler," I said. The name was out before I could call it back or figure out where it came from.

"That's a hell of a guess," he said. "You run into him?"

I said I hadn't and hoped I wouldn't.

"Got his mother all in a tizzy already. Couldn't call ahead, naturally, and say he was coming. Got to show up and give her a heart attack."

"How is he?" I said, trusting my father to intuit that I was not inquiring after Drew Littler's health so much as his mood.

"You should see him," my father said. "He's big as a house. Bigger. Moved his shit right back into the spare bedroom. Never mind waiting to be invited. Not Zero."

"Maybe you shouldn't call him that," I suggested.

My father lip-farted. "That's what he is."

"That's why you shouldn't," I said. "He probably resents the hell out of it, and he's not sixteen anymore."

"Big isn't everything," my father said, catching my drift. "Smart counts too, you know."

"Where do *you* fit in?" Harry wanted to know.

"I'm smart," my father said, grinning at him. "Smart enough to outwit that big ox, anyhow."

Then he launched into the story of how he'd got Drew a job shoveling snow and he'd tossed an icy block of it through a second-story window and then claimed it was an accident. This story led to another.

I'd heard them all, so I didn't listen. I knew what he was doing, of course. He was getting himself all pumped up for what he considered to be an inevitable confrontation. He may even have started up with Eileen again to make sure there'd be no avoiding it. So I let him rant. There was no point in trying to slow him when he got rolling down this particular memory lane. I just grunted now and then to show I was still there, and thought instead about Tria, up on one elbow, her slender fingers trying to make sense of my own ragged curls. The idea of waking up next to her for the rest of my life was tempting. I couldn't think of many drawbacks, if I didn't count the fact that, despite our successful lovemaking, I couldn't shake the feeling that Tria Ward's feelings for me did not run very deep. Her last remark—that things out there were always normal, no matter how abnormal—had stayed with me though. She'd delivered the observation like a punch line, but there'd been an edge to it, and I wondered if it was a warning I'd be foolish to ignore.

I put it out of my mind anyway. When Wussy came in, I was glad to shake free of my reverie. He looked kind of in between. I couldn't tell whether he was finishing up Friday night or starting Saturday. He slid onto the stool next to me, as he frequently did when the three of us were out together, a safe distance from the rockhead. "Guess who I just saw," he said.

My father got it right, the first guess.

Wussy ordered breakfast, and we kept him company. Harry still didn't have any other customers. I liked the diner early in the morning before it got crowded. In fact, I considered it almost worth getting up for. In another half hour, you wouldn't be able to talk in a normal voice and be heard over the din of rattling dishes, but at this hour you could use your library voice and be heard. Neither my father nor Wussy possessed a library voice, but if they had, they could have used them.

"You're looking pretty pleased with yourself this morning, Sam's Kid," Wussy observed.

I shrugged. Three guys came in from the poker game upstairs and joined us at the counter.

"He's just getting back with the car, I know that," my father said. "I asked him where he parked it all night, but he's not saying."

"Somebody smell his pussy finger," one of the newcomers suggested.

"You think you'd remember what it smelled like?" asked another.

"Better than you," said the first. "At least my finger isn't up my ass always."

"Nope," Harry said. "Not always."

I stood to leave, showing them all the finger in question.

"Where you going?" my father said. "Stick around. We'll go out to lunch later."

"I'll see you tonight," I promised. I knew what he had in mind, which was to sit around and get himself worked up, then go over to Eileen's, ostensibly to invite her out to lunch. If I was with him, it would be worse than if he went by himself. Wussy was on to him too, I was pretty sure, and when the time came he'd find something else to do. If my father was alone, Eileen would probably be able to head off trouble, but not if he had an audience.

It was a nice morning now, and I was deliciously tired. My mother's flat was a fifteen-minute walk and I was nearly there when a horn tooted and F. William Peterson pulled over. "Seen your old man?" he said.

"Why?" I said.

"Got some good news for him."

Since that was the case, I told him.

"I tried to find him last night, actually," Peterson said.

"Strangely enough, he might have been home," I said. My father had been clean-shaven and rested-looking at the diner, curious for a Saturday morning.

"I never thought to check there," the lawyer admitted. "Anyway, we got our break. One of the kids came forward and admitted they'd all been drinking and drag racing. We knew from the tire marks that there'd been a third car, but now it's sewed up. All of a sudden everybody wants to settle. Looks like Sam may walk on this one."

"How's the girl?"

"Still in a wheelchair. That's the bad part. Still, to be fair, I don't think that's your father's fault. Not entirely, anyway."

"I'm glad," I said.

When he asked me if I wanted to go along and help spread the good news, I said no, I was tired.

"Mom worried about me?"

He shook his head. "Not too bad. She can't make up her mind whether you were out all night or whether you got up early. It wouldn't hurt to spend some time with her today. You're always gone. Talk to her a little."

"I'll try."

"She loves you," he said, then added sadly, "More than anybody."

"I know," I admitted, suddenly feeling the terrible weight of her love, threatening to rip through the thin fabric of lies and deception that it rested on. "I wish to God she didn't."

"No use," F. William Peterson said. "She can't help herself."

37

The telephone half woke me. My mother's lowering her voice did the rest. With the shades drawn, it could have been night, but my watch said four-thirty and there was a ball game on TV in the living room. "Well, honestly," I heard my mother say into the telephone, "that's hardly my son's fault."

Groggy, I sat up in bed, vaguely aware that I had been dreaming unpleasantly and that the dream's interruption was likely to be even more unpleasant. I had fallen asleep thinking about the night before and Tria's perfume, but sleep had turned it all bad. Now, groggy and in between worlds, I was convinced that it was Mrs. Ward on the phone, calling to report that I had violated the sanctity of her home and hospitality, gotten her daughter pregnant. I had nearly convinced myself that this was the only plausible scenario when my mother hung up the phone. "Honestly!" she said again.

I listened to her pace, clearly trying to make up her mind

whether to wake me. We'd spent most of the morning together and I'd tried to take F. William Peterson's advice about talking to her. Nothing came out but words though, and most of them were hers. After a while I just listened, nodding and muttering an occasional yes, until finally she took my hand and said wasn't it amazing. All those years apart and we could still see into each other's hearts. She could read me like an open book, she said. Like it or not, we were *simpatico.* She held up two intertwined fingers to show me what simpatico meant. I said I thought I'd take a nap. She said she knew I was exhausted. She could tell. We were simpatico.

There was a knock and my mother poked her head in. I was still sitting on the bed, still groggy. "Who was on the phone?" I said.

"Eileen somebody. A friend of your father's. Apparently she thought that a recommendation."

"Silly her."

"What gets into people?" my mother said. I could see she really wanted to know. She'd upset herself trying to figure it out. "It's as if it's our responsibility to . . ." she let the thought trail off. "Your father has apparently had one too many. You are requested to go get him."

"Okay," I said, getting to my feet.

"I'd let them call a cab," she said. "Why encourage such behavior?"

"I'll go get him."

"Sure," she said, her upper lip curling with sarcasm. "And when you're gone, guess who'll be here to answer the calls? Guess who all the Eileens in Mohawk will call to report your father's activities?"

"If you don't want to answer it, don't answer it."

"This is *my* home."

Her hands were shaking now. "Take it easy," I said. "This is not such a big deal."

"My health may not be a big deal to your father, but it is to me. I've fought too hard for it to let him destroy it. Too hard. Too too hard. I'll not have my home invaded."

I made a dramatic gesture of looking around the room, even under the bed. "Is he here? Who has invaded your home? Me?"

"How do you think it makes me feel to see you at his beck and call? As if he ever cared about you. Don't you think I know why you came back to Mohawk? Do you imagine I'm a complete fool?

Do you imagine I think you came back out of any concern for *me* or *my* welfare?"

She was still frozen in the doorway, and there was nothing to do but wait for her to move so I could pass. I'd seen her swiftly unravel like this before, sudden, unexpected lucidity pushing her toward the brink, before she could pull herself back again. It was always awful to watch, and the worst part was that I never felt the slightest softening toward her. I knew from experience—mine and F. William Peterson's—that people who surrendered territory to my mother seldom won it back. I'd often wondered whether my stubbornness in refusing her demands was inherited from Sam Hall or an instinctive male response to emotional blackmail. Either way, I knew I could count on an almost unlimited reserve of stony resistance. I also suspected that this current confrontation had been brought on by the morning's congeniality, an action that demanded an equal and opposite reaction. Thirty days out of every month she reassured herself that things were fine. On the thirty-first, she needed to consider an equally distorted negative reality, plunge herself into despair and fury, to the outermost inconsequential limits of her own continuing dream.

She stood before me now, a full head shorter than I, an angry, self-pitying child full of terrible adult knowledge. "Why do you do it?" she said. "Why must you play Sam Hall's fool?"

"I guess he and I are just simpatico," I said, holding up two fingers, wondering at my own cruelty, its ability to surface so quickly, so powerfully, so intelligently focused on the existing scar, already red and inflamed.

Knowing right where to plant the dagger is a special gift.

Since Eileen was the one who had called, I figured my father was probably at Mike's Place, but I was wrong. Mike hadn't seen him. Somebody else said they'd seen him down at Greenie's with half a load on. At Greenie's, the bartender said he'd been there, tried to pick a fight and then left, thank Christ. That had been half an hour earlier. I thought about calling my mother to see if she knew where Eileen had been calling from, but even if she had, the trail was certain to be cold by now. Instead, I called Tria to see if she'd changed her mind about letting me take her to dinner. If so, it'd have to be a late one. Her voice sounded a million miles away.

"Is anything wrong?" I said.

"With me or you?"

"With us."

"We have something of a situation out here, actually," she said.

"That makes two of us," I said, instinctively not liking the sound of her "situation," glad for one of my own. I also had the odd feeling that someone was in the room with her, maybe even listening in on the conversation. "How about we exchange stories later?"

"Maybe," she said.

I tried a couple more likely spots without any luck, but I found his car right where I'd left it that morning, which meant that either he was in town or he'd recruited Wussy to drive him. I didn't mind not finding him right away, but I hoped Eileen hadn't got frustrated waiting for me and called my mother again. After forty-five minutes or so I circled back and stopped into Mike's again on the off chance, and there he was at the far end of the bar, big as life. Eileen wasn't around, which meant that calling me was her last official act of intervention.

Mike came over when he saw me. "He just come in," he said, guiltily, as if I suspected he'd hid my father in the back room the first time I was there. Sam Hall had all the moves of a small-town alcoholic whose wife knows all of his haunts but, due to the complicity of bartenders, still can't find him.

"Son!" my father thundered when he spied me. In front of him he had an empty shot glass and a half-gone beer chaser. He himself was completely gone.

I slid onto an empty stool next to him. A guy I didn't know and who looked even drunker than my father leaned forward to see if he could bring me into meaningful focus.

"Say hello to Roy," my father said, leaning back on his stool so Roy and I could shake, nearly losing his balance in the process. "Roy's a no-good drunk," he explained. "Like me."

"Bullshit," Roy said. "Your old man's the best."

"Right," I said, and Roy gave my father a hug.

"You know how come?" Roy wanted to know, and he waited politely for me to ask how come.

"How come?" I said.

"He'll buy a goddamn drink, that's how come. He ain't tight. You come in . . . Sam Hall's at the bar . . . you don't even have to put your hand in your pocket. There's already a drink in front of you. What's this, you say. Sam Hall, the bartender says. Am I right, Mike?"

Roy and my father looked around for Mike, who had been right there, and recently too, though he wasn't there now.

"You want to know who's really the best?" my father said.

"You tell me," Roy said. "And I'll believe you too. You know how come? 'Cause Sam Hall always tells the fuckin' truth, that's how fuckin' come."

"Then shut up and let me tell you, you drunk," my father said.

"Tell me," Roy said. "Go ahead. I'll believe you, too. I am a drunk. I can't fuckin' help it."

"Shut up before I punch you," my father said.

"It's be a fuckin' honor to be sucker-punched by Sam Hall."

My father looked at me and grinned. "What a drunk. I ever get like him, shoot me."

"Shoot me too," Roy said, and he began to cry.

"Hey!" my father shouted at him, scaring Roy half off his stool. "Answer me. You want to know who's really the best?"

"Who, Sammy?" Roy whimpered. "Who?"

"My son," my father answered, then promptly put me in a rancid headlock. "You're looking at the only thing I ever did right in my whole life. Right here."

When my father released me, Mike came over and surveyed the situation. "Roy!" he said. "No crying in the bar."

No crying in the bar was one of Mike's few rules and he was adamant about it. Roy wiped his nose and eyes on his sleeve.

"Buck up!" Mike said.

"Every man should have a son like mine," my father said to Roy, as if Mike's appearance had made exactly no impression on him. "I don't deserve him."

"I had a son once," Roy said. "But I lost him."

"He's the best," my father said to Roy, but all the while looking bleary-eyed at me. "It's just too bad his old man's a no-good drunk."

"I can't help it," Roy repeated, crying harder now.

"Can't help what," my father swung around to glare at him. "I'm not talking about you. I'm talking about me."

Mike came back over. "Buck up, Roy," he warned. "Don't make me run you."

"I had a boy," Roy wailed. "I did."

My father noticed I didn't have anything in front of me and

threw up his hands. "Can we get a drink around here or what?"

Mike ignored him, fixing Roy intently and ferociously. "No crying in the goddamn bar!" he bellowed.

"I gotta wee," Roy said, as if this sudden necessity were what he'd been crying about.

"So go," my father said.

Roy headed for the men's room. "What an asshole," Mike said. "You watch. He'll be in there for about five minutes. Then he'll try to sneak out on his tab."

"Take it out of here," my father said, pushing the money he had on the bar toward Mike.

"What for? He pulls the same shit every week."

"He probably hasn't got it," my father said.

"I can't stand that crying shit," Mike said.

"Shut up and get my kid a drink," my father said. Then to me, "You had dinner?"

I said I hadn't.

"Me neither," he said. "Or lunch, or breakfast."

"We had breakfast together, if you remember."

He stared at me. "That was yesterday."

"That was today. Yesterday was yesterday."

The door to the men's room opened a crack.

"Watch this," Mike said, pretending to go about his business.

After a minute the door opened wider, a liquid eye in the crack. Then Roy appeared. He was a little guy anyway, and pretty nimble for a drunk. All the way to the front door he scooted along, facing the wall, perhaps on the ostrich principle that if you didn't see anybody, then nobody could see you. When he got to the door, Mike yelled, "So long, Roy!"

"What's the damage?" my father said.

"Couple a bucks," Mike said.

"So why the big deal?"

"Fine," Mike said, taking them from my father's pile. "Spend your money."

"Let's eat something," I said, fearing my father had forgotten and wouldn't remember again.

"Why not," he said.

He was wobbly, but we made it to a booth.

"Eileen off tonight?" I said, for something to say, and because I wondered what had become of her after calling me.

My father shook his head. "I don't even feel sorry for her any-

more. I try to tell her a little bit. Prepare her. . . . What for? You
can't talk to people who won't listen."

"That's true," I said.

"She's a good girl. The best. It's not that. She's pretty smart, too.
Except about Numb Nuts. Then she's dumb as . . ." He looked
around the table for something that Eileen could be dumb as.

"You should stay out of it," I said.

"I should," he surprised me by saying. "I know I should. I just
can't stand the sight of him. He's no good. Hell, *I'm* no good, but
he's completely worthless, that son of a bitch."

"Ignore him."

"He's home all of twelve hours. What's the first thing he does?"

"I don't know."

"Guess."

"Forget him. Fuck him."

My father shrugs as if to suggest that fuck him is the right idea,
but he can't just now because he's too busy remembering him.
"He's home all of twelve hours and two hundred dollars disappears from his mother's dresser drawer. Do you believe that shit?
Nobody there but him and his mother. We're not supposed to
suspect him, right? It's been sitting right there in the drawer for
a month, but the minute he comes home it's suddenly gone. And
nobody's supposed to suspect him, the rotten son of a bitch. It's
not bad enough he's got to rip her off. On top of it, we're not
supposed to suspect him. How come you suspect me, he asks her.
How come you don't ask Sammy where it went?" My father shook
his head. "That's not even the bad part. The bad part is all he's
got to do is ask her and she'll give it to him. He'd rather steal it.
Take it from her. Just take it. Never mind how hard she worked
for it. Fuck you, Ma. I'm taking it. You know what he had the balls
to say to me today?"

I said I didn't.

"He says, Sammy, all I want is what's mine. What's *yours,* I ask
him. I want to know what the hell he figures is his. Just what the
hell do you figure you got a right to, I say. What's mine is mine,
he says. He keeps saying it over and over. What's mine is mine.
What's mine is mine."

Mike came over with two plates of spaghetti and put them in
front of us. My father pushed his away. "Jesus," he said, running
his hands through his hair. "I don't think I can eat."

"Eat a little," Mike said. "You'll feel better."

"I can't drink the hard stuff," my father said. "I know I can't, but I do anyhow."

"You all right?" I said. He'd suddenly gone absolutely gray.

"All I can see is that big dumb face. What's mine is mine."

My father drew his plate toward him, twirled strands of spaghetti absentmindedly. "It's not just him. Everything's fucked up all of a sudden."

"Not everything," I said. "You aren't being sued, for instance."

"I never was," he said. "Just my insurance company. Fuck them."

"You have," I said. "Over the years."

"Good," he said. "I'm glad. They only want to insure people like you who don't have accidents. It's up to people like me to make sure the bastards don't keep every last dollar for themselves."

"Thanks," I told him. "I guess the rest of us owe you one."

He surrendered half a smile. "Yeah," he said. "You and Skinny. Great favor I did him, huh? Or didn't you hear."

I said I hadn't heard anything.

"I bought him breakfast. He left just before you came in yesterday morning."

"This morning?"

"Whenever. Told me they were going like hell on the road. Pouring half a mile a day, pretty near. Saturdays overtime. I say great, Skinny, that means money, right? He's got the shakes, but off he goes. He gets up there, gets out of the car, grabs his flag, steps out from behind the trunk and gets run over by the first cement mixer of the day."

"Jesus Christ," I said. "Is he in the hospital?"

"They don't put dead people in the hospital. They need the beds."

"Jesus," I said. "Skinny?"

"They ran right over him," he said. "Him and his red flag. First fuckin' thing they did today. Then they poured concrete until five, or so they tell me."

It refused to sink in. Not Skinny Donovan, I kept thinking. In my mind's eye I kept picturing the dusty road, the stalled truck, the silent men gathered into a semicircle, Skinny's legs and feet visible, the way I'd see them when I rounded the corner out back of Our Lady of Sorrows where he liked to sleep, his back up against the cool stucco. Who'd have guessed Skinny would die working, I asked my father.

Wussy came in then and slid into the booth next to me. "Word of advice, Sam's Kid," he said. "Don't let Sam Hall pay for dinner. He's bad luck."

"That's what I was just telling him," my father said. "He should go back to Arizona. As far as he can get from his old man."

"You're a menace all right," Wussy agreed. "You don't scare me though. In fact, I'll eat your own goddamn spaghetti, since you aren't going to do nothing but stare at it."

"Good." My father pushed the plate toward him. "Eat it. I keep seeing Skinny and Numb Nuts."

"You look better than you did an hour ago," Wussy observed.

"I feel worse."

"Good."

My father winked at me halfheartedly. "Eats my spaghetti and insults me."

"Sorry to walk out on you," Wussy said. "But I can't be around Roy Heinz."

"He always speaks well of you," my father said.

Wussy nodded. "He go to the bathroom on you again?"

"Sort of," my father said. "Not *on* me exactly."

Suddenly something clicked. "Heinz," I said.

"You knew his kid," Wussy said. "You was in the golf ball business together. Willie Heinz his name was."

My father came back from the men's room looking a little better.

Wussy finished my father's spaghetti and pushed the plate away. "I got this," he said when my father took out some money.

"It's only fair," my father agreed.

"I'd let the kid pay for it except I figure he's almost as bad luck as you."

"Not really," my father said, looking me over, rather fondly it seemed to me, though more sensibly than his earlier drunken ecstasy.

"How could he come from you and not be trouble?"

"I don't know," my father admitted.

"I think I'll go home anyhow," Wussy said. "When you start whistling into the bottom of whiskey bottles—"

"No more," my father promised. "Beer only."

"Not me," Wussy said. "You drink with him, Sam's Kid."

My father bought a round before he could leave though, and

then I bought one, and we all settled in. Wussy said there must be a full moon out—Sam's Kid actually bought a round.

"It's his last, too," said my father, who always embarrassed me by refusing to let me be part of the rotation. Sometimes, I could sneak a round in, if he hadn't told the bartender not to take my money, but mostly I drank for free, paying only in good-natured insults received. The men my father drank with had all been told I was a college kid saving for tuition, which exempted me from everything but humiliation. Busting my balls about being a cheapskate was considered good sport. "We gotta get him back to school before he turns into one of us for good," my father warned, "and his mother blames me."

"Every time I think of her," Wussy said, "I pray that after she shoots you she'll be satisfied. Speaking of shooting, the table's open."

Nights like these, it was a very real possibility that I *would* become one of them, permanently, irrevocably. Here I was, twenty-four years old, and less than twenty hours earlier I had become the lover of the very girl who had haunted my imagination off and on for at least a dozen years. And somehow, without even thinking about it, I had reneged on my promise to call her back, take her out to dinner, preferring instead to be sucked into the maelstrom of another drunken evening with two middle-aged, beat-up tomcats. My father and Wussy were Mohawk men, which meant that somewhere along the line each had turned his back on a woman. Many had turned their back on more than one. Most now realized that in doing so they'd fucked up. Some would even admit it when they were drunk enough. A few, like Skinny Donovan, would try to return thirty years after the fact, to women who didn't even exist anymore, who had gone evil or horny or crazy with waiting and raising kids, or had just dried up from working two hard jobs. Other guys, like Tree, succumbed to confusion, never sure whether he'd got his most recent case of the clap from his wife or his mistress. Since each had been the other, and might be again, it probably didn't matter. Somehow he'd got them both to love him, but on Saturday nights he preferred to drink beer and shoot pool and play cards with men who had similar stories to tell.

What we shared—yes, I would be one of them tonight—was something not to be underestimated. We could all boast, this night, anyway, that no matter how messed up we were, at least our lives were not being dictated by women. Offered tender breasts and warm pussies, by God we showed them we could not be so easily bought. Never mind that in some cases the offer was twenty years old and nineteen rescinded, we were still making a point regarding the female population. A declaration of independence. We could do without them, because they were only women, after all.

And we were men. We had business. And with a blue baseball game tilting down from the corner above the bar, we tended to the business of being men, brown sweating bottles of beer lined up in phalanxes, bought not as needed, but in rounds, the real drinkers setting a pace, like the lead runners in a road race, finding a stride, feeling instinctively the race's length, its rhythms. Our collective composition always changing, as somebody heard somebody was somewhere and went there to find him, get that ten-spot he was owed, somebody else slipping into the vacated space at the bar, ensuring welcome by buying a round or promising to get the next one. Sometimes loud—all of us shouting at once, pointing at the replay on the blue screen—sometimes hushed, conspiratorial, can I take twenty till Monday, I wouldn't ask, but . . .

It was all rhythm and stride and knowing when to move, what it would take to get you from where you were to another spot just like it a hundred yards down the street where they had two pool tables instead of the one. You had to know how many quarters were lined up under the bumpers and whose they were, who was in the middle of something, who was waiting for somebody to show up. You began to sense when the forces that could cause you to pick your money up off the bar would become greater than those that kept you rooted to a particular stool. When you understood the rhythms, the subtleties made sense. You could predict that when somebody in your party got up to take a leak, it would set in motion a string of small causes and effects that would have you out the door and in the street in, say, five minutes, which meant that if you had a full bottle of beer in front of you, you either got to work or you left it.

It had always been the rhythms of my father's life that most mystified me. There had been no predicting whether he'd turn left or right. You didn't know where he was headed because he hadn't told you, and he hadn't told you because he thought you knew, or should have known, or could have figured it out if you'd been paying attention. But now, evenings with my father and Wussy and whoever else we managed to pull into our loose circle made perfect sense, and when we all headed out Greenie's front door at eleven I knew whether we'd be turning left for The Glove or right for Mike's Place. Spookier still, when my father swung around on his barstool and said, "Well?" I knew what he meant, even when he was harkening back to some earlier conversation left unresolved two hours earlier. I can only say that such moments were magic for me and they made me grin at him so stupidly, so drunkenly, so affectionately, that I had all I could do not to tell him that we were becoming simpatico.

"Simpatico," I told him later that night. We were on our third bar after Mike's Place. Wussy had left us to go home twice and managed to find us again. We'd run into Tree and Roy Heinz and half a dozen other minions, all of whom had fallen away for the moment—to the men's room, the pool table, the cigarette machine—leaving my father and me alone together. "That's what Mom says we are, she and I."

He shook his head. "Sounds like one of her words all right. She used to come up with shit like that all the while we were married. You should try coming home after a couple years of shooting people on the other side of the world and then have to listen to your mother talk. About a month and you're ready to go back. Simpatico."

We discussed simpatico for a while, to my mother's detriment.

"I never should have done what I did, though," he said. "She's wacky. Always was, but I should've stuck it out anyhow."

"Why?" I said.

"Because I should've, that's all. I just made all of it worse. Then you came along and I didn't care about that either. I couldn't believe it, for one thing. One day she tells me she's pregnant and the next day, practically, you're here. France and Germany were forever and a fuckin' day, and your mother has you in about a week . . . that's what it felt like. All the while she's saying we gotta settle down."

He looked at me, bleary-eyed. "I should've, too. Nuts as she was, I should've stuck it out. I should've gone right to the grave with your mother."

He thought this over for a while, clearly attracted to the idea of such fidelity. "Or Eileen," he went on. "You may not like her, but she saved my ass more than once."

"I *do* like her," I said, wondering where he'd gotten the idea that I didn't.

"You should," he said. "She's the best. Nothing against your mother. But Eileen's the best. I should go right to the grave with Eileen. That's what I *would* do, too, if I was any fucking good. Which I'm not."

We looked at each other, and I realized that after sobering up some when he stopped with the whiskey, the quantitative effect of the beer was catching up with him. I was pretty far gone myself, and he had about an eight-hour lead.

"You could contradict me once, if you felt like it," he said.

"You don't want me to," I said. "You're feeling sorry for yourself."

"Right," he said. "This is no life. Believe me. Don't get caught up in this shit. I got nothing. And when I die, that's what you'll inherit. It'd been better all around if I'd got mine in France."

"Thanks," I said.

He shrugged, not catching my meaning, or not acknowledging it. "Everybody would have been proud of me. They'd have argued about how great I'd have turned out if I hadn't got shot."

"You can still do what you want," I said. "You're what, forty-five?"

"Forty-seven. And anything I was going to do, I did already."

"That's bullshit," I said cheerfully.

"What'm I gonna do now?"

"How do I know?" I said. "I don't know what *I'm* going to do."

"You won't either," he said. "You'll just wake up one day and it'll all be done. All fuckin' done."

His eyes looked past me then, and they suddenly became so focused and narrow that the bloodshot whites disappeared altogether, leaving just the gray iris and black pupils. I turned around to see what had focused him. At first I thought it was the pool game, where a little guy in a thin t-shirt was lining up the eight. Everybody else was watching to see if it would drop and you could tell from the interest that there was a lot of side action. Except for my father and me, the only other person in the place who didn't seem to care what happened to the eight ball was Drew Littler, who'd slipped into a dark booth on the other side of the smoky room. The green felt table and bright light above it were an island of illumination separating him from us. My father was right. He was big as a house.

"I take it back," I heard my father say. "I might do a good deed yet, if I could get my hands on a shotgun."

The skinny kid in the thin t-shirt dropped the eight, and Wussy, who had been his opponent, handed him a five-dollar bill before coming back over to where we were sitting.

"I'm getting old, Sam's Kid," he said. "Another year or two and I'll be as over the hill as the rockhead."

A guy I didn't know came over and handed my father two fives. Wussy shook his head. "I'm glad to see somebody's making a profit on my misfortune."

"It's a living," my father said. "It'd be a good one if I could find people who'd bet on you more regular."

"You see your buddy over there?"

"Yup."

"Good. Let's go someplace else. So far this ain't been your day. There's no reason to invite total annihilation."

"Too late," my father said. "Here he comes."

"I wisht I'd kept that pool cue," Wussy said.

"I wish you had too. Why don't you go back and get it."

"If I thought you could hold your own for thirty seconds, I would."

"Hold his own what," Drew Littler said, coming in on the last part of the conversation. "Hell, Sammy's an expert on holding his own."

He nodded at me, offered a big paw, which I shook. *Christ*, he had gotten big. He wasn't so good-looking anymore though, and it occurred to me that maybe he never had been. I'd just been impressed. He looked like he'd given up on the weights, his once hard, muscular body had gone to flesh now, though it still looked enormously powerful. His hair was long, almost shoulder length, and darker now, blond only near the ends. It covered his forehead completely, and I couldn't see whether the big blue vein that used to writhe angrily when he lifted was still there.

"I hear you went to college," he said to me. "How'd that turn out?"

"Pretty good for a while," I said. "And then badly."

"It's all different around here, huh?"

I tried to imagine what he might be thinking of. I couldn't think of a single thing that had changed in Mohawk. "It sure is," I agreed.

"Look at us," he said, supplying the example I was missing.

"Zero just got out of college too," my father said.

"Right," Drew Littler said. "I got a degree in whaddycallit . . . rehabilitation."

"So what's the first thing he does when he gets home? He goes to visit his mother's dresser drawer."

"You suppose we could stop this, girls," Wussy said, "before it starts?"

"Stop what?" my father said.

"I just came over to say hello to Ned and buy him a beer," Drew Littler said. "Not mouth with you."

"Buy us all a beer," my father suggested. "You got about two hundred bucks, right?"

"I spent some of it," Drew Littler said, meeting my father's gaze squarely.

"Naturally," my father said.

"What I've been trying to figure out for twenty years," Drew Littler said, "is why it's any of *your* fucking business."

"Well," my father said slowly, "Zero, I'm not the smartest guy that ever was. But if I thought about something that simple for twenty years and still came up empty I'd be ashamed to admit it. Of course that's just me. You could be different. In fact, you are different."

Just then somebody across the room called my father's name, and when he didn't answer a chorus went up. "Your goddamn quarter, Sammy. You want to play or not?"

"It's not *my* quarter," my father said, reluctant to break away from his grinning and staring contest with Drew Littler.

"Bullshit," Wussy called. "You put yours down same time I did. Go play."

"Come on over," Drew Littler nodded toward the dark booth across the room. "I'll introduce you to this girl I'm with."

For a terrible moment I imagined that when I arrived I'd find that it was Tria with him. "Good," I said. "I'll be right there."

I watched all three of them cross the room, Drew Littler to a booth, my father and Wussy to the pool table. Then I went into the men's room and sat on the closed toilet seat inside the single stall. Somebody in ankle-high work boots followed me in, saw the stall was occupied and walked out again. Before the door closed

I heard the billiard balls crack and my father bellow, outraged at
the idea that the kid in the T-shirt had made two balls off the
break. Normally my father never bet more than a drink, at least
on himself, when it came to pool. But this was a sure-lose situation,
the kind that would tempt him. The skinny kid in the thin T-shirt
would say something that would rub my father the wrong way
and he'd decide to teach the kid a lesson. He had the fresh ten
he'd just won off Wussy's game and it would be on the table before
he even thought about it. With luck, losing it would engross him
for a few minutes.

You couldn't do him any real good, of course. Wussy, who
played my father like a drum, knew that. You could slow him
down some, but you couldn't change his direction for long. My
return to Mohawk had slowed him a pace or two, and by appearing tonight I had postponed, perhaps, the savage bender he would
still go on tomorrow or next week or next month. If I played all
my cards right, went over and talked friendly with Drew Littler,
I might even prevent hostilities between them tonight. But not
forever. Probably not even for very long. The strange part was
that my sympathies were, for the most part, with Drew. After all,
whatever happened at the Littler house was none of Sam Hall's
business. For as long as I could remember my father had caused
trouble over there, sticking his nose where it didn't belong, offering advice when none was called for, giving orders where he had
no authority. For twenty years he'd called Drew Littler "Zero"
and half a dozen other derisive nicknames. If the boy had had
enough, who could blame him?

But when push came to shove, as it had more than once and
would again, I would side with my father. Not because he was
right about Drew Littler. Not because Drew had always been
lazy, sullen, stupid, and untrustworthy. I would side with my
father because I too wanted Drew Littler brought down. Though
we never discussed it, I'd often suspected that my father felt the
same physical loathing that came over me in waves whenever the
boy was around. Even that first afternoon when I had ridden on
the back of his motorcycle up on the winding tree-lined drive and
we two had gazed at the Wards' white jewel house, I had felt it.
An intense loathing that went far beyond rationality. The moment Drew Littler admitted me into his dream by telling me that
the white jewel house would be his one day, said it with such dull,
dogged conviction that he almost made me believe it, I would

have annihilated him right there to prevent the long odds, had it been in my power. Surely it was this same animal loathing that gripped my father so powerfully, made him homicidal whenever he had to eat a meal at the same table as Drew Littler, or listen to his sullen, irrational insistence—"What's mine is mine." The boy had nothing save that dogged insistence, but even that was too much to allow him.

When the guy in the work boots came in a second time and left again, I flushed the john for show and scrubbed my hands in the dirty sink before returning to the bar. My father was still hanging on, though the skinny kid had just one stripe and the eight left. My father had five solids on the table, four of them more or less blocking separate pockets, leaving his opponent only two clear ones to shoot at. The kid looked like he didn't know whether to shit or go blind.

I had the bartender send a round over to the booth where Drew Littler was talking to a girl who, even from the rear, looked vaguely familiar. When she turned and smiled, I saw it was Marion from the Big Bend Hunting Lodge.

"You the one done this?" she said in reference to the fresh Seven and Seven.

I stole a chair and planted it at the end of the booth so I wouldn't get trapped on the bench with either of them.

"You're from around here too, I suppose," the girl said. "Everybody around here's from around here."

I couldn't tell whether she didn't remember me or just wasn't letting on.

"Originally," I admitted, "but not lately."

"Old Drew here's from around here," she said. "I bet you were buddies when you was kids."

"He was a couple years older," I said. "He gave me rides on the back of his motorcycle."

"You had a bike?" she said, pronouncing it "baak."

"Till I totaled it," Drew Littler said.

"Lucky it wadn't *you* that was totaled," the girl said. "My little brother had one and they had to spry him off the road with a far hose."

A roar went up behind us, and I turned in time to see the skinny kid whistle the cue he was using across the room where it hit a post and shattered. "That's dirty fuckin' pool," the kid said to my father. "You never even tried to win. I'd rather fuckin' lose than win that fuckin' way."

"Good," my father said. "I'd rather have you."

"What happened?" Marion wanted to know.

"Sammy just got the little shit to scratch off the eight ball," Drew explained to her. When he said my father's name there was something of the old respect and awe in his voice. "That means the end of the game."

"I don't thank it's very nice to throw the stick like that. Coulda put a eye out."

"It's a local tradition," I said. "At the end of the game the loser is supposed to throw his cue."

"How come the guy before this one didn't do that?" Marion wanted to know.

"He was black," I explained seriously. "Black people aren't allowed to throw things."

"That don't seem fair," Marion frowned. "I thank you're pulling my laig."

"Maybe a little," I said. "Actually, the black guy was supposed to throw his cue too."

"Well I should thank so," she said, clearly relieved. "This *is* America, after all."

During my entire conversation with Marion, I was aware of Drew Littler studying me through narrowed eyes, as if, despite the physical resemblance, he couldn't quite believe that I was the kid he'd known. "I hear you're tending bar down to Mike's," he said, rather pointedly putting an end to our banter. "How come you got that job?"

I shrugged, unsure whether he was asking why I'd taken it or how I'd got so lucky to be offered. I decided maybe it was the latter. "Things just worked out," I said.

"Sammy got it for you, I bet."

"He and Mike are friends," I admitted. "Why? You looking for work?"

"I don't know," he said. "Maybe. Right kind of job comes along. . . ."

"I'll keep an eye out," I said, vaguely wondering what Drew Littler would consider the right job.

Nobody said anything for a minute. My father broke a new rack of balls. The skinny kid had disappeared before it occurred to anybody to ask him to pay for the broken cue. As far as I could tell, my father hadn't so much as glanced in our direction since I'd joined Drew and Marion.

"Don't you want to know what I do?" Drew said finally.

"Sure," I said.

He drained his beer, watching me all the while, traces of a smirk playing around the corners of his mouth. Marion looked from Drew to me, then back again, probably wondering how she'd managed to disappear so completely when she'd been in the center of things a few seconds earlier.

"No you don't," Drew Littler said. "You don't need to ask me what I'm looking for because you don't plan to put in no good word anyhow. Hell, you'd warn 'em about me."

"I think I'm gonna go find the little girl's room," Marion said.

"You do that," Drew Littler said, without bothering to look at her.

I pushed my chair out of the way so Marion could slide out of the booth. Then Drew and I both watched her angle through the crowded bar, a few of the men turning to watch her with mild interest and losing most of it when they saw her wide hips straining against the fabric of her jeans.

"She's a whore," Drew said matter-of-factly when the door to the rest room swung shut behind her.

I didn't say anything. He was right. Unkind, but right. Marion was a whore. Right too that I wouldn't be recommending him for any jobs. And he was right about why I hadn't asked him what he was looking for.

"We need us another beer," he said, suddenly friendly again.

"Listen," I said. "I gotta go."

"One more," he said, putting a big hand on my shoulder in case I was of a mind to stand up. "Be right back."

My father came over when he was at the bar. "How you doing?" he wanted to know.

"Fine," I said.

"Glad to hear it," he said, returning to the table in time to see his new opponent drop the eight ball.

Drew Littler set a fresh beer down next to the one that was still three-quarters full. Marion had drained her Seven and Seven, but he'd just bought beers for the two of us. "You know who stole that two hundred from my old lady?"

"Who?" I said.

"Me," he replied. "Who'd you think?"

I took a swig of beer. "At least you're honest."

He nodded. "At least I'm honest. Your old man thinks I'm no good."

There was little point in denying that, so I didn't. "Don't let it worry you," I said. "He was telling me earlier that he was no good himself."

He studied me for a minute, as if considering all of the ramifications of this intelligence. But when he finally spoke, I couldn't be sure he'd even heard. "The only person in the whole world who thinks I'm good for something is my mother. Maybe this'll teach her."

I said I didn't think so.

"Me either," he said. "Women are dumb. Speaking of which."

"Hi." Marion slid back into the booth. "You two decide not to argue?"

"We sure did," I told her.

"Good," she said, then to me, "You're a bad boy. I watched the whole end of that game and nobody threw their stick."

"Cue," I said.

"You know what I hear?" Drew Littler said to Marion, who had noticed our fresh beers and her own empty Seven and Seven. "Old Nedley here's been slipping it to my little sister."

Again, nobody said anything for a second.

"Well, that does it," Marion said, sliding back out of the booth again. "Here I thought I was going to have a fun night off for once." When neither Drew nor I offered an explanation for why her modest expectation hadn't materialized, she said, "I just don't see why people have to act so mean." And then she headed for the door, hips and breasts all astir.

"Hey," Drew Littler said, suddenly confidential now that we were alone. "Remember how we'd go up there on the Harley and sit outside the gate?"

"And you said it would all be yours one day."

"I never figured on him dying like that," he said. "What a hell of a night that was. You remember that night?"

I said I did.

"I never knew for sure until then," he said. "When your own father dies, you know . . . in here." He thumped his massive chest. "That's how I knew for sure."

"You went out there today," I said, remembering the strange

sound of Tria's voice on the phone when she said they had a "situation."

"What a night," he nodded. "What a goddamn night. More than anybody knew."

I couldn't tell, either from looking at him or listening to the sound of his voice, whether he was in the present or back ten years ago on the night it had taken my father and Wussy and Skinny Donovan and his mother and, finally, a doctor with a horse tranquilizer to fell him into welcome oblivion. And he'd been smaller then. Now he was bigger than my father and Wussy put together, and there was no Skinny Donovan to kick him in the head if they were lucky enough to get him down, and no doctor handy with a long needle.

My father was right. He was big as a house.

All the lights were out in the Ward house when I drove up and parked in the circular drive. Mohawk, or a small part of it, glittered below and I cut the engine to listen to the quiet, hoping that Tria wouldn't be asleep, that she'd peek out the window and see me sitting there in my father's convertible. And not call the cops.

Not that I'd have blamed her much if she did. It was after midnight, which made me about six hours late, by conservative estimate. Six hours during which she would have had time to consider what, if anything, our becoming lovers the night before had meant to me. I was about to drive back down the hill and into town when a lawn chair shifted on the small enclosed patio a few feet away and a cigarette glowed red and died. In the dark I couldn't tell from the silhouette whether it was Tria or her mother. I didn't want to be wrong.

"I didn't know you smoked," I said.

"There's a lot you don't know about me."

I climbed up and sat on the back of the front seat, unsure of my current status. "And a lot I do."

"I've regretted that about a dozen times today." Her voice was silky in the dark and I suddenly had a different regret of my own.

"I'm sorry," I told her. "I'm sorry you feel that way. Because I don't."

"It hasn't occurred to you to wonder if I was on the pill?"

"I *did* actually, once or twice."

"Well, I am, so you don't have to worry. Or run away."

"Listen," I said. "Can I join you? I feel like an idiot all the way over here."

"Stay there, then. Feel like an idiot."

I did. Both.

"I'm the idiot," she said after a minute. "We're all crazy in this family."

Her use of the word "all" spooked me. After all, there was just herself and her mother, unless she was including her father in the equation. Or unless Drew Littler had convinced her to think of him as family.

My eyes had adjusted to the dark now and I could see her better. She was barefoot and wearing a thin robe that reached only to the knees. Her dark hair was down around her shoulders the way I liked it.

"Did I tell you why I left Swarthmore?" she said.

"No," I admitted.

"I was on academic probation," she said. "Valedictorian of St. Mary's, class of '67. Academic probation, '68. Guess how much I studied."

"Don't feel bad," I said. "I never studied much the first couple years."

"*I* studied every night. Every minute."

If she'd planned to surprise me, she had. My own experience had been that even the appearance of industry could sucker a B out of most professors. Academic probation was strictly for alcoholics, scholarship athletes, fraternity men, and those who hadn't discovered the college of education. "There are big differences between colleges," I said, for something to say. "I didn't go to Swarthmore, or anywhere close."

"You're smart though," she said. "I'm just smart enough to know when other people are smart. Daddy was smart. I remember that about him. Mother thinks she is, but she isn't."

"Does it matter so much?"

"Yes," she said. "When people tell you that you are, and you believe them, and it turns out that you're not, it's important. It makes you wonder what else you've been wrong about. Maybe everything. I was told today that I had a brother I didn't even know about."

"If you believe anything Drew Littler tells you then you're right about not being too smart."

"I do believe him," she said stubbornly, happy to have tricked me into admitting her stupidity. "So does my mother."

"No she doesn't," I heard myself say. "She just hates your father. It suits her to think of him as a continuing embarrassment. Now she's got another cross to bear."

"That's a terrible thing to say."

"Believe it," I told her. "I'm smart, remember?"

"Anyway," she said. "It's too terrible not to be true."

"You're wrong," I said, not caring much about the truth of it. "He just wants it to be true. He doesn't know. His mother may not even know."

"He knows," Tria said.

"He believes," I said.

"So do I, then," she said, even more stubbornly than before.

"I'm going home," I said after a long silence. "It'll probably look different in the morning. If you imagine Drew Littler's related to you, it's because you haven't seen him in natural light."

"He's a horrible person, isn't he?"

I took a deep breath. "Yes," I said, feeling immediately a deep twinge of conscience without knowing exactly why. Perhaps it was because this wisdom on the subject of Drew Littler was so conventional, universal even, that my contribution was unnecessary, even cruel. Perhaps it was because I had known him as a boy, before the verdict was in. Or that the part of me where wishful thinking held sway wasn't sure the verdict *was* in.

I slid down behind the wheel of my father's convertible, my hand on the ignition key.

"He mentioned you today," Tria said.

"Really?" I didn't want to know what he'd said.

"He said you were sweet."

"Sweet?" I tried to imagine Drew Littler saying that.

"He said you hate choosing sides in things."

"He remembers the way I was when we were boys."

"Last night, I thought you were sweet," she said.

"And now?"

"I think you've chosen sides."

I dropped the convertible off in front of the jewelry store, right where my father could find it in the morning. I'd started home on foot when the door to the tavern across the street was flung open and my father came out and weaved across the street. He never noticed the car and wouldn't have noticed me either if I hadn't called out to him.

"Hello, son," he said seriously, his legs waffling.

"I brought the car back," I said, nodding to it.

"There it is," he said, apparently surprised to discover it so close. "Take it home. Bring it back tomorrow. The next day. Whenever."

"I'm going to walk," I said.

"Take it," he insisted.

I told him I really wanted to walk, and he shrugged. "You want to come up a minute? Crash here if you want."

"Nah," I said.

"Suit yourself."

"Listen," I said. "This thing with Drew. You can walk away from it. He doesn't want any trouble. He likes you."

"I know it," my father said. "That's the weird part."

"It's *all* weird," I said.

"Don't worry about it," he said. "Tell your dolly not to worry. I'll take care of him."

"You know what he wants then?"

"*Oh* yeah."

"Can't you just get Eileen to tell him Jack Ward wasn't his father?"

"Kinda tough," my father said.

"Why?" I said stupidly.

"Because he was. Probably."

Probably.

In the end it was a mere word that sent me packing, in high moral indignation and fear, before the summer was over. In fact, I nearly left that night. I had a few hundred dollars saved, enough to get me a fair distance if I didn't care how I traveled and didn't mind ending up broke when I got there. And I didn't care, not that night.

It seemed to me, as I headed home along the dark quiet streets of Mohawk, that the whole world suffered from an epic lack of understanding, an epic surplus of probablies. Nobody knew what they needed to know, and because of it, things were slipping away. Inside the black houses that lined the streets, people were

sleeping blissfully, the hot day having finally surrendered to reassuring breezes in the tops of the trees, but in a few hours tomorrow would dawn hot and, it seemed to me, tragic. Probably. After
all, today had begun with Skinny Donovan's death and ended
with a series of reverberations, aftershocks from twenty-five years
in the past. This time the night before, Tria Ward and I had sat
together on the closed-in patio overlooking the city and watched
the gathering storm. It will blow and blow and not amount to
anything, Tria had said, but it did amount to something just the
same, as she may have feared it would.

A day later, I had not found the courage to go to her until it was
too late, and now, as I headed toward my mother's house along
a sleepy street under a clear night sky, I was more than anything
relieved. It was as if she herself had given me the antidote to
loving her, allowed me the privileged glimpse of the beginnings
of the transformation I'd long feared would someday take place.
There in the dark, until she'd spoken, I'd not been able to tell her
from her mother, and even when she did speak I'd heard a bitter
inflection in the tone of her voice that was directly traceable to
Hilda Ward. Tomorrow, a month from now, a year, I'd wake up
and find my Tria—and Jack Ward's Tria—gone, the transformation complete. It would take no longer than it took for the young
Hilda Smythe of the library photographs to go from young woman
to mummy. Perhaps Tria herself could see it coming. Perhaps that
was what she'd been trying to warn me about when she said that
things at the Ward house were always normal. She bore the legacy
of a superficially charming and opportunistic father, of a mother
shrunken and ruined for life and love by the father she idealized,
a third-rate chronicler of arcane history and, apparently, a first-
rate deceiver of worshipful children. And, to my shame, there was
one other person I held against her. As she herself had remarked,
it was too terrible not to be true.

My beloved was what she came from. After a few blessed years,
sustained by some conjurer's trick, I would not be able to tell
mother and daughter apart in a well-lit room. And then what
would I probably do? Probably what her father did, or what my
father did, or some unimaginative synthesis of these two Mohawk
paradigms. For if Tria was her mother, then what on earth was
I? Wasn't I the same shabby conjurer's trick? Had Tria come
looking for me earlier in the evening, gone from dim smoky bar
to dim smoky bar, surveying from the entryways the shadowy

figures down the long bars, spying my father and me on adjacent stools, hunched over sweating beer bottles, wouldn't she too have been granted a glimpse of the future? And as she came toward us through the smoke, would she not fear for a brief instant that she had my father and me confused, and known in that moment what the future held—herself alone in her mother's house, except for the old woman, truly old and sick now, shrunken doll-size in her king-size bed, while I sported with Marion and Mohawk's other sporting men at the Big Bend Hunting Lodge?

And somewhere in this awful mix, a monster, slouching among our separate existences. Made terrible because, unlike Tria and myself, he had no blueprint to follow, nothing clear in his mind to become. Nothing. Zero. But nothing grown huge, as big as a house, with one simple crazy philosophy—"What's mine is mine"—and imagining he could wring it free, whatever was desired, by brute force, by will.

These were the alcoholic phantoms that pursued me along the narrow Mohawk avenues until finally, the third time I arrived in front of the house that contained my mother's flat, I climbed the back stairs and found her sitting quietly puffy-eyed at the kitchen table, as patiently despairing and hopeful as she had been the afternoon my father had returned me, scratched and swollen and riddled with poison ivy, to her doorstep for repair. Her eyes now contained that same terrible sadness, submerged deep and quiet. And for a brief moment I felt I was her son again, the son of this strange woman who had tried her best to save me from probably.

38

The following Monday afternoon, Tree came in after his shift out at the campsite where during the summer he still sat in the same little shack and sold parking tickets to bathers. The arm he dangled out the window was berry-brown, the other fish-white, like the rest of him. I drew him a beer and he nodded to Irma, Mike's wife, when she emerged from the steamy kitchen and glowered at him for no particular reason. Tree was scared of women in general and very frightened of Irma. For as long as he could remember, he'd always had at least one big woman mad at him, and over the years he'd come to the conclusion that there must be something about his looks that did it to them, especially the big ones. Irma was a sizable woman, though not nearly as big as the two women he'd married. He gave her wide berth, just the same, as if he feared he might fall in love with Irma and marry her too. Her glowering at him all the time struck Tree as a dare. She glowered the same way at everybody, but her genuine ill humor had special meaning for Tree, who mistook it for foreplay. When he spoke, it was to a neutral spot on the wall that neither included nor excluded Irma. "Some r-r-ruckus over to The Bachelors last night."

The Bachelors was a nightspot on the lake road that catered to phony ID's. Anybody who couldn't start a fight at the pool hall went out there.

"Assholes," Irma said. It was her standard comment.

"I'm with y-you, Irma," Tree said, still fixed on the same point on the wall. "You couldn't p-pay me to go out there. You know what they get for a draw?"

Nobody knew.

"Ninety-five cents," Tree said indignantly. "No b-bigger'n what you get right here. Hell, I'd stay home before I'd p-pay that for a g-goddamn draw."

"You should go out to the Holiday Inn," somebody said. "It's a buck fifteen."

"For a *shot* and beer, right?" Tree said.

"Shit no. Just the draw."

"Shot and a b-beer'd be different," Tree said.

"You should go to New York City," somebody else offered.

"What the hell for?"

"What's a shot'n'beer go for there?"

The guy who said we should go to New York hadn't been there himself, but he'd heard about it and said you couldn't get drunk on less than a week's pay.

"What happened at The Bachelors?" I said, so Tree's original observation would not be lost entirely.

"Hell of a ruckus is what," said the guy who told us we should go to New York.

Tree looked at him blackly. He hadn't brought up the business at The Bachelors to surrender the tale to an interloper. "B-bouncer b-busted up a couple kids around midnight. Tossed 'em out in the p-parking lot. They come back with some friends around closing and b-beat the bejesus out of him with two-b'fours. Left him in the dumpster."

"Killed him?" the man wanted to know.

"Damn near," Tree said.

"Their own fault for hiring nigger bouncers out there."

"B-bullshit," Tree said. "It was Dick Krause's kid."

"Benny?"

"How do I know?" Tree said. There were limits to what a man could know, and he had reached his with regard to what had happened out at The Bachelors.

"You're thinking of Benny Raite," somebody explained to the man who'd wanted to know if it was Benny.

"They hire big coon kids from Amsterdam to be bouncers out there," said the man Tree had tried to silence.

Tree stared at him again. "This was Dick Krause's kid, I'm telling you."

"Benny," somebody said. "Benny Krause."

"Bullshit," somebody else said. "I seen Benny Krause this morning."

"Benny Raite's a bouncer," said a third. "I bet you're thinking of him."

They were still working on it when I got off at five-thirty. My father's car was in front of the Mohawk Grill, so I stopped in. He didn't look good. He was dirty from the road and his eyes were still red from the weekend. He was staring at two skinny grilled pork chops.

"I meant to stop in," he said apologetically. He usually did when he got home from work, before going home to clean up. "I was afraid I'd get started all over again."

"Good thinking," I said.

"Even I can't be a dummy all the while," he said.

"Right," Harry mumbled.

"Want a pork chop?" my father said, ignoring Harry's sarcasm.

"Not really," I said.

"Want two pork chops?"

We both grinned. He really did look sick.

"Tonight I go home," he said.

"Mind if I use the car?"

"Go ahead. Leave it someplace I can find it is all."

I said I would. When I got up to go, he said, "You want to come work on the road with me?"

At that moment, Untemeyer ambled by, his day done, the pockets of his black alpaca suit bulging with slips, heading for home, a destination he kept strictly secret to keep from being badgered. "They need a new flagman, right?" he said.

"Meyer," my father said. "Somebody's gonna follow you home one of these nights and his financial problems will all be over."

"Not if he chooses tonight," the bookie grumbled. "Besides, I get mugged every day by the OTB. I should have gone into prostitution."

"Who'd want to fuck you, Meyer?" my father said.

"Any number of women," Untemeyer said. "I got that certain something."

"You too?" my father said.

"I get it occasionally myself," Harry said.

"The good part is he grows the penicillin to cure it with right here on the premises," Untemeyer said, letting the door swing shut behind him.

"Actually," I said, "I may head back out west come September. Besides, I couldn't do that to Mike."

"You'd make a lot more on the road is all," my father said. "Work until it gets cold like I do. Would they let you start school in January?"

"Sure."

"Do that."

"Two nights ago you were advising me to get out."

He shrugged, cut a small wedge of pork chop and put it in his mouth. "I wouldn't let Numb Nuts run me off, is all. She's a cute little shit, that Ward girl."

"That's not it," I assured him, not very convincingly, I thought, though it was true.

"Okay," he said cheerfully. "You're sure you don't want a pork chop?"

On the way out to the Ward house I stopped at Eileen's. She'd taken on a job cocktailing at the Holiday Inn, cutting way back at Mike's, so I didn't expect her to be home. She was though. By the time I turned off the ignition, she'd come out on the little concrete slab of a back porch where she stood drying her hands on a dish towel. She was wearing an old pair of corduroy slacks and a ratty sweater. Never a pretty woman, she had always possessed an athletic quality, and there was still a little of that left, though she looked more tired now, and in the good evening light I noticed for the first time, even at a distance, that she was coloring her hair.

"Well, that explains it." She grinned. "I knew it was Sam Hall's car coming from a block away, but it didn't sound like him."

"How does he sound?" I said, grinning back at her.

"Louder," she said. "Rougher. Faster."

I got out. "I'll work on it," I promised.

"Also dumber. Sorry I upset your mother the other night."

"She gets over things," I said. "It's her specialty, in fact."

"I've often wondered whether she ever got over your father."

I snorted. "Years ago. Decades."

"I'm pretty damn near over him myself these days," she said.

Somewhere out back of the garage I heard a motorcycle cough to life and rev. I hated to think what that meant. The noise was so deafening we had to wait for the engine to die before we could continue.

"Don't ask me where he got the money," she said, staring at and clean through the garage, as if she could see her son through solid wood.

"I heard about a job," I said. "That's why I dropped by."

"You can mention it if you want," she said, as if she hadn't much faith that it would do any good. "He says he's waiting for his ship to come in."

I looked around. "We're a long way from the ocean." And Drew Littler was a lot farther than the rest of us.

I didn't say that last, but Eileen Littler looked like she heard me think it.

"Some people got thick skulls," she said. "As we both know."

"How's the Holiday Inn?" I said.

"Pretty busy. The flat track opens next week, so we'll be full. The high rollers all stay in Saratoga though. The ones we get give their money to the track and that's it."

"They don't have a budget for waitresses?" I said. "Mike would love to give you more shifts."

"I might," she said. "You could mention it to him if you felt like it. I hate to ask after telling him I wanted to cut back."

I said I would, though I hated to, knowing perfectly well why she wanted the hours. You didn't have to be able to see through wood to figure it out, either.

"So how is he?" she said finally.

"Dad? I just left him at Harry's trying to stare down a pork chop. He said he was going home."

She nodded unenthusiastically. "Greenie's is home. And Mike's. And The Glove. And . . ."

"I hate to tell you, but come September I think I'll be leaving."

The motorcycle started up again, then died again.

"I'm surprised," she said. "I heard you were in love."

"No, not really," I said. "At least I don't think so."

"You could do worse."

"I know," I said. "Especially around here."

I could tell she didn't care for the sound of that remark, and I had to admit, having said it, I didn't care for the sound of it all that much myself. "I don't know," I concluded, which was far closer to the truth.

"You're good for him, is the only thing," she said.

"Not really," I said. "I just get drunk with him. That's all."

She shook her head. "You're a good influence, believe it or not. He won't embarrass himself when you're around, or if he thinks you might show up."

"You're exaggerating," I said. "Sam Hall does as he pleases. He always has."

"Not anymore," she said with such conviction that I almost believed her. "You just can't see the change. I'll tell you something else, too, since he won't. He loves you."

"You too," I said.

"Not enough," she said, shoving her hands in the back pockets of her cords. "I almost had him once. For a while there he'd get off work, come over, eat some dinner, play gin for fun. Sometimes just us. Sometimes Wussy. He got so he could walk by the pool hall and Untemeyer and the gin mills and all of it. Sometimes he'd mention you, and I'd say call, and he'd say what for, he's doing fine."

"He'll be back," I said.

She nodded the way people do to indicate that they've heard

you, without necessarily buying into your point of view. "You think so."

"Yup," I said.

"Well . . . lucky me."

On his back beneath the new bike, Drew Littler reminded me of the boy he'd been back when I spotted for him in the garage. Much of the former muscle had gone soft now, but when he lay on his back he flattened out and his blondish hair hung straight back, just as it had when we were boys. I wondered if it was strictly necessary for him to lie on his back that way. After all, it wasn't a car he was underneath. "A one-owner," he said, looking up at the big Harley critically, then at me, my shadow having fallen across him.

"Who only used it to go back and forth to church," I said.

"That and haul his boat up to the lake," he agreed. "Still do a hundred and twenty."

"Who'd want to go a hundred and twenty on a motorcycle?" It was a dumb question.

"Let's," he said seriously. "Hop on."

He stood.

When I said thanks anyway, he swung a big thigh over the saddle and the Harley roared to life so loud I took an involuntary step back. I had to wait for him to throttle down, and even then I had to shout.

"I heard about a job."

He gunned the engine again, listened critically, then shut it down.

"Out at The Bachelors," I said, a little too loud, now that it was quiet again. I realized then that I had been wrong to come. The sound of my own voice was enough to convince me. "You know where that is?"

"Tending bar?" he said.

"Crowd control."

He grinned. "Bouncing. You think I'd be good at that."

"Yes," I said. "I know I'd think twice before starting trouble."

"You be smart, no bigger than you are." He stood straight and faced me with this observation, sucking in his gut. It pissed me off a little, but I was thinking twice.

"I should mention they kicked the shit out of the last one and stuffed him in a dumpster."

"What's the pay?"

"How would I know?"

"You know about the job."

"I just heard about the guy in the dumpster."

"And you thought of me."

"Right away," I said.

He nodded. "You sure you don't want to go for a ride?"

"Positive," I told him, wondering if he was considering strapping me on against my will. To change the subject, I said, "Guess who I saw the other night."

He waited.

"Roy Heinz," I told him. "You remember Willie?"

"What of it?" he said, his face a mask.

"Nothing. I wondered if you ever heard from him is all."

"Why would I hear from Willie Heinz?"

Somehow, it occurred to me, we were on the verge of hostilities again. His desire to provoke them seemed to have rhythmic peaks and troughs independent of the conversation itself. "No reason," I said. "He looked up to you."

"Listen," nodding vaguely in the general direction of the Ward house, miles away across the park and highway. "You can have it all, okay?"

The weird part was that I understood him. No reference had ever been more oblique or sudden, but I had the feeling that this was what we'd been talking about all along, or what he imagined we'd been talking about.

"Have what?" I said, trying to submerge the powerful feeling I'd had about him ever since the evening my father had beat him at arm wrestling and he'd threatened to break the arm he was suspended from. Drew Littler was insane.

But his eyes went vague again and he offered me a big paw to shake. "Thanks for the tip on the job."

"Sure," I said, accepting his offer, whatever it might mean. Then he kicked the Harley to life, did a circuit around the dirt yard, one booted foot dragging until the bike straightened and roared down the drive, narrowly missing my father's convertible.

Eileen's white face was in the only window that looked out on the backyard and our eyes met across it as the Harley burned through gears and stop signs all the way to the distant highway.

39

That night at the Wards' was the first of a new working arrangement. Tria's mother met me at the door and explained that her daughter was not at home. The pages I had worked on the previous Friday had been typed up and added to the others in the plastic tray. Over three hundred pages worth now. About half the manuscript, I guessed.

Nor was Tria in evidence the rest of the week, though when I arrived in the evenings the air was often rich with her perfume. The previous night's work was always typed neatly and added face-down in the stack. Even more disturbing than her absence from the proceedings was her mother's renewed presence. I began to feel as though I'd been the victim of some cruel slight of hand. I'd started out wooing the pretty daughter and ended up with the old hag, the basic plot of countless bedroom farces, only in my case the switch had been made not in the dark but rather in broad daylight as I looked on. Among the many reasons I wished ardently for Tria's return was the grotesque possibility that someone would tumble to the fact that Mrs. Ward and I were alone in the house every evening and draw an unnatural conclusion.

I didn't have to search the house to know that Tria was not there. Her yellow Chevette was always gone when I arrived, her lingering perfume strong at first, then dissipating as the evening wore on. I probably would have worked late and waited for the sound of her car pulling into the garage were it not for the fact that Mrs. Ward no longer retired at nine, the way she had when Tria and I were working together. Now it was clearly her intention to remain up until I finished each night, as if she didn't trust me to lock up on my way out. When she yawned, I suggested she go to bed, but she wouldn't hear of it, no matter how her eyelids drooped. She fed us strong dark coffee that wired me good, but hadn't the slightest effect upon herself.

The main reason I wished she'd go to bed was so that I could stay up late and be done with the whole project as soon as possible. I no longer really wanted to go out there. Drew Littler's remark that I could have it all, as far as he was concerned, rang in my ears, and the small library seemed more claustrophobic each night. As I paced around its perimeter to stretch my legs, clear my head, search for oxygen, I began to feel about it the way I suspected Jack Ward himself must have felt—that there was nothing I valued there, nothing of myself, nothing I wanted.

Why then did I make the journey up that hill through the dark corridor of trees each evening? Part of it may have been, as Drew Littler suggested, the rather satisfying notion that I was permitted to drive my father's convertible between the stone pillars that had once been a barrier to Drew Littler and me. Perhaps the fact that I had a standing invitation to visit continued to mean something long after the spell of the white jewel house itself had been broken. Maybe, in the end, that's what such spells and such houses are about.

And, too, part of the reason I continued to haunt the Ward House that August was guilt. I wanted to square things with Tria—though I wasn't sure whether this was possible or even what it might entail. She had taken me into her bed, and I had betrayed her in the classic way that Mohawk men betrayed their women, perhaps the way most men betray most women. I planned a rather elaborate confession on the subject, an admission that I was unworthy of her, that she could do far better, that I was and always had been both selfish and corrupt. Moreover I had been treating her the way my father had treated my mother, the way *her* father had treated *her* mother. I was perpetuating . . . well, I wasn't sure what, but I was perpetuating something. All of this was supposed to make her feel better. I know it made me feel better (I was twenty-four) as I rehearsed these observations.

But the real reason I kept pushing my father's convertible up the hill each evening was that in working over Tria's grandfather's history, I had rediscovered something of the strange, almost mystical delight I had felt in the Mohawk Free Library those years I had lived with my father. There in my cool little corner of the stacks, surrounded by books and periodicals I but dimly understood, I had felt connected to something as large and wondrous as the planet itself. With no teacher to direct my reading or to tell me in advance what to make of it, there was the off chance that I would go in a new direction. I often chose books by smell and was often rewarded. Sometimes I would look inside the back cover, where I would find a borrowers' history, due dates stamped in purple ink. Volumes that had not been checked out in twenty or thirty years held a special interest for me. I felt like I was in direct communication with the book's lonely author, that I would not have to raise my voice to be heard above the clamor of recent due dates.

I now felt a similar intimacy with Tria's grandfather, whose various relics made him a palpable presence in that icon-riddled room. I liked the idea that a man, many years ago, had labored over writings that I now labored over, that I could look inside his mind, see what occupied his thoughts, or at least those thoughts he chose to share with the world. And I wondered what he would have thought of me, a young man he couldn't have imagined or predicted, who entered his house, and twisted his sentences around until they suited himself. At the time I imagined that the author must be terribly grateful.

And I did love twisting those sentences around. It's a pleasure that I fear very few people can comprehend, much less share. Surgeons who perform intricate operations that allow twisted, maimed, hulking cripples to walk upright may know something of the editor's delight. I can only say that I discovered that summer in working over—and brother did I ever work it over—*The History of Mohawk County*, the joy of probing the opaque sentence until it surrendered something akin to meaning (*this* is what the son of a bitch meant!), making flexible (sometimes loosey-goosey, I fear) that which had been soldered stiff in a grimace of contorted syntax, giving energy and momentum to sentences stalled and flooded, like a carburetor, by leaden words. I was having a ball, and I do not regret in the least the many hours I labored over *The History of Mohawk County*. In fact, I didn't even regret it years later when I saw a display of the book in the small front window of Ford's Stationers, the closest Mohawk ever came to a bookstore. Having been rejected by dozens of commercial and university publishers, Mrs. Ward had somehow managed to convince a local press to do a limited edition. The editor, perhaps on his own initiative or, more likely, on the advice of the good Mrs. Ward herself, restored to the original every one of the thousand or so editorial changes I made, offering to the book-reading public of Mohawk County, her father's vision, complete, unmolested, faithful, and, trust me, utterly unreadable.

Seeing the modest edition, every copy of which was displayed in Ford's window, unless there was a carton or two in the den of the Ward house, made me feel sad for Tria's mother, because her plan for her father's work was nothing less than grandiose. I learned of it gradually that summer when she became the com-panion of my evenings. Meeting me at the front door, she would insist that I have "something cool, you know" before I sat down to work. Then she would tell me about her father, who seemed to me, even as Mrs. Ward described him, nearly as frozen as his syntax. That she worshiped him beyond measure was evident. That his ghost had intruded into her and her husband's bedroom seemed to me both then and now as the safest of inferences. That he had whispered counsel to her on long nights when Jack Ward did not come home, perhaps even the odd "I-told-you-so," was also a good bet. I doubt Mrs. Ward ever looked at her husband without imagining her father standing there beside him for the purposes of comparison.

And when Jack Ward had died, the ultimate I-told-you-so, Mrs. Ward had meekly returned to her father and begun to formulate her plan to offer him to the community. He had helped her through a bad marriage, saved her life by providing such a stern model of upright behavior. She began to see that it was wrong to keep such a man for her own private use when the entire commu-nity was in such dire need of a paradigm, an example of rectitude beyond reproach. Mohawk, Mrs. Ward explained to me, was a town that had lost its pride, its sense of self-worth, its recollections of its own pioneer history. The hearty men and women who had driven the savage Iroquois north and west, built long roads through the dark forest, erected churches and established settle-ments, had not been drunkards and fornicators and welfare recipients. They had been strong, earnest, God-fearing men and women who knew adversity, self-sacrifice and hard times. And when they'd won their battle with the wilderness and the wild heathens who had roamed the forest, these men begat scholars— men of intellectual courage and wisdom like her father, who had bequeathed to subsequent generations the gift of memory, the knowledge of great times and deeds.

If Mohawk could just be introduced to her father, Mrs. Ward felt certain, then the whole community would rediscover the pride that had lain dormant for so long. In the beginning she had doubted she would be able to go through with it—sharing her father with the world, that is. But then she realized that he was large, that he contained multitudes. And again he whispered in her ear, confirmed the wisdom of the course she had chosen. Use me, he had bravely insisted, and so she would. Because it wasn't just Mohawk, after all. There were towns all over the nation that would benefit. Didn't most Americans, even those now living—if you could call it living—in the hateful big cities, didn't they have their roots in places like the young Mohawk? Wouldn't all Americans answer the call to remember if sufficiently motivated?

She was thinking best seller. And who could blame her? After all, she was broke. As stony as stony could be. It was Tria who confirmed this later, when my work on the history was done, after Wussy, whose travels were wide and contacts myriad, came into Mike's one afternoon and wanted to know what the hell Jack Ward's daughter wanted with working as a cocktail waitress in Amsterdam. I said I was sure I didn't know. He'd probably heard wrong. But I knew he hadn't. Unlike just about everybody in Mohawk, Wussy's information was usually correct. Besides, as Tria herself had observed, some things were too terrible to be anything but true.

The night I drove to Amsterdam I passed the fairgrounds and saw the first tent going up. Summer had flown. Fourth of July, Mohawk Fair, Eat the Bird, and Winter. I thought of my own grandfather and felt a degree of sympathy for Mrs. Ward's warped nostalgic view of things. Indeed, a great deal of territory had been surrendered since our ancestors had stolen the land and erected white churches with felled trees. Up and down the Mohawk valley the green world had gone brown and gray, and the people who lived beneath the smokestacks and in the shadows of the tanneries were scared that even the brown and gray might not last. They didn't know what came after brown and gray, and neither did I. One thing was for sure. Each Mohawk Fair was sadder and grayer than the last. And winter followed. With a capital W.

Tria's boss at the T-Pee Lounge let her take five minutes. She looked like she'd been expecting me, sure I'd tumble to the truth eventually. The house, she explained, was paid for, but the money my father had once told me was impossible to spend was gone. And as more and more of the county was added to the welfare rolls, property taxes had increased proportionally. Jack Ward's army pension covered taxes, but not much else.

There in the dim light of the T-Pee Lounge I fell in love with Tria Ward all over again, and she let me hold her hand as we spoke. "It's a monster," I said. "Why doesn't she just sell it? Get an apartment, live off the sale?"

"Sell Grandfather's house?"

"Yes. Sell it. It's not a national shrine."

"She has this idea that it will be."

After a minute, I said, "You can *make* her do the right thing."

But she looked at me as if she couldn't think what I might mean. Maybe I didn't know myself.

"I'm going to leave in a week or so," I said finally. Our five minutes had stretched to fifteen, and Tria was getting looks. "Come with me. We'll go someplace where the sun shines. And play house." When the attempt at humor fell flat, I added, "We never gave it much of a chance, you know."

"It never *had* much of a chance, Ned."

Maybe she was right, but on the drive back to Mohawk I thought of all the arguments I should have used. Tria's mother, who rambled on about pioneer spirit, certainly didn't possess much. She didn't drive, you know. She didn't type, you know. She freely admitted that when skills were parceled out, you know, she had somehow been passed over. Her talent, you see, was simply as a witness. She had been called to witness her father's greatness, and she accepted her calling, you see. I don't know what she imagined her daughter's role might be. To witness the witness, perhaps. To chauffeur the witness up and down the tree-lined drive, to the market, the drugstore, the grave. Before this last, people would mistake them for sisters.

I looked everywhere for my father and finally found him, of all places, at home. Stretched out on the sofa, he snorted awake when I came in. Locking doors was foreign to his nature.

"Nice place you got here," I said.

He looked around to see if this could be true. "You haven't been up here before?" he said, and it was clear he honestly couldn't remember.

"Twice," I admitted. "How about you?"

He switched off the television, which had been keeping him company while he slept. "Not enough. From now on I'm gonna have to stay here a little more."

"Why's that," I said, rearranging some of the dirty work clothes he'd draped over the chair so I could sit down.

"You want a beer?" he said.

"Not really."

"Good," he said. "We'd have to go to the store. Coffee?"

He was rummaging through the tiny kitchen cabinets like an explorer.

I told him no thanks.

"Got some of that, someplace," he said. "I'm never here except at night, and I don't drink it then or I'd have to get up ten times."

He found a full jar of instant and held it up so I could see. I shook my head, said I was fine.

"I bought it the last time I said I was going to start staying home. Then I went out and forgot about it."

"I had one in Tucson just like it," I told him.

"Think you'll go back there?"

I shook my head.

"How come?"

"Nothing there for me," I admitted.

"What's here for you? You want to tend bar the rest of your life?"

This seemed to me a rhetorical question, but I should have known better.

"Do you?" he said. "Or work in some mill?"

I said no.

"Pretty much takes care of Mohawk, doesn't it?"

All true. And I *had* decided to leave, after all. I wasn't even sure why I was in my father's apartment discussing it. What was I hoping for? To be talked out of it? To be reassured that it was the only sensible course? To be given the opportunity to explain?

"Don't worry about me," he said. "Time I slowed down a step anyhow."

"Or two steps," I said. "I don't know how you do it every night."

He shrugged, as if it were a mystery to him too. "To hell with it. For a while, anyhow."

Neither of us said anything for a minute.

"I'd like to go out right now," he admitted, "but to hell with it.

I was meaning to ask . . . was it Eileen that called you back in the spring?"

I told him yes. I couldn't think of any reason not to now. Even Sam Hall couldn't get pissed off over a six-month-old indiscretion.

"She's a good girl," he said.

I said I thought so too. "In fact, you should make things up, if you don't mind my saying so."

"I know it," he said. "I think I'll wait till Numb Nuts goes back to jail though. How long can that be?"

I didn't say anything.

"How long?"

Maybe too long, I thought, remembering Eileen's remark that she was just about over my father. But I said, "Not too long."

"You're damn right."

"Anyway," I said. "I came over to cheer you up. Remember how you used to tell me Jack Ward was trying like hell to spend all the money he married?"

"He couldn't do it, either."

"Well, as it turns out, he did. Anyway, there's nothing left now but the house and what's in it."

"Don't you believe it," he said. "There's some wells that don't have bottoms. That's one of them."

I told him what Tria'd told me, leaving out that she was working as a cocktail waitress, which wasn't anybody's business. But he wouldn't buy a word of it. "Take my advice," he said. "Wait till the old lady kicks off and then start digging in the flower beds. Keep digging till you find it. She's probably got it buried all the way down to the highway.

"It would be nice if you were right."

"I am," he said, so confidently that I realized that I had challenged some article of his faith. "Some people are born lucky. You can't do a thing to change it."

I didn't say anything.

"You don't believe that, do you?"

"No," I said. "I guess I don't."

"Well, it's true whether you believe it or not."

"If you say so."

"Funny thing happened this morning," he said seriously. "I'm over in the drugstore . . ." he nodded out the unshaded window and across the street. "I gotta get a couple a things. Some razor blades in case I want to shave again. A tube of toothpaste. Suddenly there's this girl in a wheelchair. I don't know her. Never saw her before. Pretty little thing. Cute. Said she was seventeen, but I can't believe that. I step out of the way to let her through, but she just sits there looking at me. You'd never guess what she said."

Actually, I had a pretty terrible guess, but I kept it to myself.

"She says, 'Mr. Hall, I'm sorry. It wasn't your fault. I told my parents all along, but they wanted to sue. And the lawyer, he wanted to. We was all drinking and racing and none of this is your fault. I knew you'd be worrying about it, so I just wanted you to know.'"

"Pretty nice," I said.

He nodded. "Looked about fifteen, not seventeen," he said, as if the question of her age were important somehow. "Cute, too."

He sank back down into the dilapidated sofa, ran his hands through his hair. "And the funny part is that I don't think I'd given her two thoughts until right then. That's the funny part."

It was a terrible story, and I could tell it was giving him a terrible time. As it should have, probably. What I couldn't figure out was the introductory moral he'd prefaced it with—that some people were born lucky. I thought about it all the way home and couldn't decide whether I'd ever met anybody who was truly lucky. The person who came closest, the more I thought about it, was me.

40

And so I prepared to leave Mohawk again.

Mike took it hardest. It was tough to find a bartender who didn't either steal or give it away. My mother, on the other hand, seemed almost grateful. The fiction of my anthropological research was wearing thin. She wanted to believe me, but sometime during the summer the nature of our relationship had changed, and I'd cut back on the number of lies I told her. In spite of ourselves we'd had an honest moment or two, and they'd managed to spoil our former innocence. Often I'd catch her looking at me strangely, with equal shares disappointment and sympathy. Like most parents, it had been her goal to spare me, and like most children, I'd been determined not to be spared. Life, in these matters, almost always sides with youth. And so my mother and I had for the first time in our lives arrived at a quiet understanding.

The timing was just right, too. Because the evening I got off my last shift at Mike's Place, I met F. William Peterson, who'd been out of town all week on mysterious personal business, on the back stairs that led down from my mother's flat. He was consulting his watch as his heavy legs churned downward, and he reminded me of the rabbit in Alice. He didn't notice me until we nearly collided on the landing.

"Ned!" he said. "Wish me luck!"

"Good luck, Will," I said.

"Thanks." And then he was gone.

Upstairs, my mother sat on the sofa, surrounded by brochures. "San Diego!" one said. "Port O' The Sun!" proclaimed another. She was bent forward, staring at them, as if unsure she was permitted to touch. The glossy brochure that pictured Balboa Island was the one that occupied her direct attention. It was all blue sky and sea and orderly rows of small, well-kept cottages, their window sills decorated with bright plant boxes. F. William Peterson, it turned out, had just inherited one of them.

I could see in my mother's eyes that she considered this outrageous fortune another of life's cruelties. As a young telephone operator she had dreamed of places where winter wasn't capitalized. Phoenix, Arizona. Santa Fe, New Mexico. San Diego, California. Here was a wish from another lifetime, granted twenty-five years too late, as if God were in a place so distant that it took almost forever for wishes to travel there, like pale starlight from a distant galaxy, eons old and all worn out even as we look at it.

I did not see Tria again. I called once to say goodbye, but her mother answered and said she wasn't there in a tone of voice that reminded me of the one she'd used a decade earlier when, on Jack

Ward's advice, I'd called his lovely daughter from the Mohawk Grill. I didn't blame the old woman. For all I knew, she was acting on Tria's instructions. Either that or she'd finally read what I'd done to her father's book.

The day before I planned to leave, I drove around the block that contained the post office until Claude came out. What I had in mind was a staged chance meeting and a quick goodbye. It was a crummy way to handle things, but I wasn't up to another pizza in the steamy Schwartz flat. I thought I'd seen his wife Lisa once on the street, but I wasn't sure, since half the hopeless pregnant girls in Mohawk looked just like her.

When Claude finally lumbered down the marble steps at ten after five, I was just about to toot the horn when he looked up. I waved, thinking he'd seen me, but what had caught his attention was an old rusted-out Thunderbird that had passed just as I pulled over to the curb. Claude stood there on the steps, the stream of people leaving the building parting around him, like a rock in the middle of a stream. The T-Bird had stopped at the traffic light that dangled from a cable at the Four Corners intersection, and Claude watched until green released the line of cars. Only then was the spell broken.

He walked right past my father's convertible then, and I never did toot. In fact, I looked the other way, until it was safe to pull back into traffic. Out in the stream, I checked my rear view, but Claude had disappeared.

"Your mother all bent out of shape?" my father wanted to know when I'd tossed my duffel bag into the trunk and we were headed out of town. She and I had said our goodbyes upstairs in the kitchen. When the convertible pulled into the drive, she decided against coming down.

"No," I told him, settling deep into the convertible's front seat. "She thinks you're taking me directly to the airport though, so don't say anything if you see her."

"Why would *I* see her?" He crushed out what remained of his cigarette with what remained of his thumb, the stub crusted over and blackened just like the tip had been. He deposited the lifeless butt in the full ashtray. "I haven't seen her three times in the last ten years. I'm gonna see her tomorrow, right?"

It was true. They wouldn't run into each other soon. And in a

few months she and F. William Peterson would be gone from
Mohawk for good. I'd promised both of them I wouldn't say anything to my father, a promise I now considered breaking. He
seemed in the midst of an uncharacteristically reasonable phase.
There was no telling how much longer that would last, and it
would have been nice to elicit from him a promise not to torment
them, as he might decide to do if he found out from Wussy or
somebody else that they were planning on slipping out of town.
I decided to keep mum though. Benevolent intentions could
backfire. Especially around Sam Hall, who didn't always recognize them.

"You got everything you need?" he said, looking over at me.

"Probably not," I admitted. "I've got everything I own though.
Mike slipped me an extra two hundred bucks."

"Irma, you mean."

"Could be," I admitted. It was Mike who'd put the money in
my hand, but when I'd tried to say no, he'd nodded in the direction of the kitchen as if to suggest that his life wouldn't be worth
much if he returned with the money. The funny part was that
Irma wasn't even *in* the kitchen, having gone home early, out the
back way, which meant I hadn't had a chance to say goodbye.

"Count on it," my father said. "They don't come any tougher
than Irma, but once she decides you're all right . . ."

I looked out the back and saw we were trailing blue smoke. The
car smelled as if it were about to detonate.

"We'll put some oil in in a minute," he said.

What we'd planned was to catch the last afternoon of the
Saratoga flat track and, depending on how that worked out,
maybe the harness races in the evening. I'd get on a bus the next
morning. I had about six hundred I'd saved from working at
Mike's, plus a certified check for a thousand from F. William
Peterson, who didn't mind calling it a loan if that would get me
to take the money. He said my mother didn't know anything
about it, and I think he was telling the truth.

"We get lucky at the track, I want you to take the money," my
father said. "I owe you, anyhow."

This I recognized as a reference to the money he'd borrowed
over a dozen years ago, and I couldn't help smiling. "Whatever
you say," I told him. We could fight about it later if we had to. I
doubted we would.

For some reason we were not heading toward Saratoga, and

when he turned down a dirt road that couldn't possibly lead anywhere, I figured we were going to pick up Wussy. "Just as long as we don't end up at the Big Bend Hunting Lodge," I said.

"You don't want to say goodbye to what's-her-name?"

"Nor hello," I said, though that was unkind. There were worse people than Marion.

When we pulled into Wussy's drive, my father cut the engine and let the car roll to a stop about six inches from the end of the trailer, which was sunk into a hole so the doors would be at ground level. Then my father laid on the horn and the trailer shivered visibly. A few seconds later Wussy appeared in nothing but his shorts. He had changed very little since that morning so long ago when he had come out of the cabin in the woods. His needs hadn't changed either, because he came right over and peed on the front fender of the convertible before my father could start the engine and back up. "There," he said, putting himself back in his shorts.

"No class," my father said. "And plenty of it."

Wussy stretched, apparently unconcerned about standing there in his skivvies.

"Come on," my father said. "We'll go to the track."

"Mind if I put some pants on first?"

"We insist," I said.

Wussy and my father exchanged glances. I don't think I had ever before intruded on one of their verbal sparring sessions.

"Wise ass, all of a sudden," Wussy said. "Right before he's leaving."

My father shrugged, as if it were too late to do anything to improve me. In a minute Wussy returned, carrying his shoes and socks, but otherwise dressed. I offered to sit in the back, but Wussy said he knew how the front passenger seat was and thanks anyhow. Then he stretched out in the backseat.

Before backing out, my father studied him with mock seriousness. Finally he nudged me. "He'll be good to have along," my father said. "Otherwise we might be tempted to go someplace fancy for dinner."

There was something obligatory about that last day my father and Wussy and I spent together. Timing had always been at the heart of such outings, and all that day we never did manage to hit our stride. It wasn't just me out of synch either. We could have sur-

vived that. After all, it was only recently that I'd become tuned
in to the rhythms of their drinking and wandering and peeing and
pool shooting. The important thing had always been that my
father and Wussy were in step.

Today though, even they were messed up, somehow. At the
track, Wussy saw a guy he knew and stopped to talk and we
missed the first race as a result. My father refused to accept that
the accidental meeting was fortuitous, that the first race, at least,
was one we wouldn't lose. He preferred to think of it as the only
sure thing on the whole day's card. He said only a blind man could
have missed it. The rest, the ones that hadn't been run yet, were
tougher to figure. I managed to break even by ignoring my father's tips, but both he and Wussy took a bath.

Wussy kept on disappearing, sometimes for a half hour at a clip.
I think he may have been feeling a little odd sharing that last day
with my father and me. Either that or he thought maybe we had
things to talk about before I left. But we must not have, because
we didn't, and we both felt relieved each time Wussy reappeared.
I'd gotten over, long ago, my father's need to have third parties
around when we faced the prospect of a long period of time in
each other's company. I hadn't figured out what it meant and
didn't want to, though I think I'd always known that we were both
afraid. If we had too much time and too little to do, we'd be
tempted to talk to each other. Say things. About then, and now,
and why, and why not. It was Wussy's job to prevent that.

On the way home from the track we argued about the function
of the orange balls on the telephone cables that snaked along the
edge of the trees that formed a green tunnel along the Saratoga
road. My father said they were to keep animals off the lines.
Squirrels would jump out of trees and onto the cables and scoot
along them. When they came to one of those slick orange balls
they'd have to turn around and go back. I couldn't tell if he was
serious. Wussy said that as usual he was full of shit. All right, you
explain them, my father told him. Wussy tried. Somebody'd told
him once that the orange balls showed up good from above, that
the pilots of small planes could see them and stay clear of the
power lines they were attached to. Out by the Albany airport he
reminded us, there were orange balls everywhere. He had to
admit he couldn't say exactly what these particular orange balls
were doing way the fuck out in the middle of the woods, the tops
of the trees extending thirty feet above the cables and the nearest

airport thirty miles away, but he knew they didn't have a good goddamn thing to do with squirrels. Many years later I heard what I believe to be the explanation, though I may be mistaken— that in remote places where the winters were long and wet and cold, where ice would accumulate on the lines and make them heavy, the orange balls were used to keep the lines from crashing into one another and rupturing in the wind. But that day I had no explanation at all, and when the two of them wanted to know what the fuck I thought was so funny, I couldn't explain.

We ate at a bar halfway between Saratoga and Mohawk, getting back to town around dusk. Wussy insisted my father drop him off at the trailer. When my father intimated that going home for the night so early was unnatural and perverse, he admitted that he'd been with a woman that morning when we blasted the horn. Since she hadn't had any way to get back to town, he assumed she was still there.

"She'll be madder than a wet hen," my father said. "Where'd you tell her you were going?"

"Out for cigarettes," he admitted. "You got a spare pack by any chance?"

When we pulled in, his pickup was gone.

"Looks like she got tired of waiting," my father said.

"Must've hot-wired it," Wussy said, his voice full of admiration. "I got the keys right here."

I got out, pulled the front seat forward so he could too.

"Take it easy, Sam's Kid," he said. "Drop back by some day."

I said I would. I thought we were going to shake, but we didn't. When he turned toward the trailer, I asked him if it was the same one he'd had so many years ago when we'd gone fishing.

"Nope," he said. "This here's a new one. Dead ringer though, ain't it?"

At Greenie's, my father and I drank a slow beer. It was Sunday night and slow and there was no reason to get involved, to buy a round or get one bought. We were there only because we didn't want to go home and face the silent evening. So we shot the shit with Woody the bartender until a couple other guys came in and he went down to the other end of the bar to talk to them. Then Roy Heinz came in and asked my father if he could take twenty. When my father said he didn't have it, Roy looked like he would cry. Then he saw me and remembered we'd been introduced. My father told him not even to consider it, that I was leaving Mohawk in the morning and that there would be no way to pay me back.

"I could just mail it to him, Sammy," Roy Heinz said. "What's a stamp cost? Hell, I could do it. You know Roy Heinz is good for it."

"I *do* know you, Roy," my father said. "And we both know you aren't good for it."

Surprisingly, Roy Heinz did not take this as an insult. "You're lucky, Sammy," he said. "You got your boy here. I lost mine—"

"I know that, Roy," my father interrupted. "But I don't want to hear about it this once, if it's all the same to you. We aren't going to even get started with that shit tonight. I'll spring for one beer if you'll take it someplace else and drink it."

Roy Heinz looked at him, then at me again. "Your old man, he's the nuts. I just wisht I'd been the right kind of father to my boy—"

"What'd I just say, Roy," my father said.

Roy's eyes had gone liquid. "Hell, Sammy, I just—"

"What'd I say?"

"Sammy. I'm gone."

He wasn't though, for another minute. First he had to look at us both lovingly and make sure we had a chance to reconsider and give him the twenty. Then he wanted to shake. But finally he couldn't take the way my father was glaring at him and he turned on his heel.

"What a fuckin' pain in the ass," my father said when he was finally out of earshot. "I get like that you have permission to shoot me."

I said Roy Heinz was a pretty sad case all right.

"Pathetic is more like it. Most of the time I can take it, but the son of a bitch hasn't got any other speed. You can only milk a dead kid so long."

When I laughed out loud, he said what.

"It's just a funny image," I said.

My father got Woody's attention and bought Roy Heinz a beer. Then he handed me his car keys. "I want you to take it when you go in the morning."

"What," I said. "How will you get back and forth to work?"

"Walk. Mike's is just up the street. He'll pay me under the table and maybe I'll be okay if I can stay on the side of the bar where there aren't any stools. Try, anyway."

I said it sounded like a good idea. If things didn't work out, he could always go back on the road come spring. I didn't want the convertible, but taking it would probably be doing him a favor. It would certainly be a good deed to other motorists.

"Can't go on like this," my father said, examining his bad hand, the black stub of his shortened thumb. "The next dumb son of a bitch that drops a pipe might drop it on my cojones, and then where would I be."

"Right where you are now."

He grinned at me. "Grown up to be a regular smart-ass, haven't you."

When I took a swig of beer, he cuffed me hard on the back of the head, the way he always did when I was a kid. This time I rattled my teeth on the bottleneck and soaked the front of my shirt.

"I can still kick your ass, you know. Old and tired as I am."

We played Liars on the bar for a while, got nowhere. Finally, he said to hell with it, it must be Dummy Day, and we walked back to the apartment. He'd borrowed a folding cot from somebody, and we went right to bed. My watch said ten o'clock.

By ten-thirty he was snoring loudly and I was wide awake. The street below was noisy. Several times drivers honked and stopped, their conversations rising up from the street like mist and in our open window. I kept thinking about Roy Heinz and my father's remark about how you could only milk a dead kid so long, grinning to myself in his dark flat, his peculiar smell permeating everything, even the borrowed cot. Then I thought about Willie Heinz and how useless he'd been standing watch when I dove in the country club pond for golf balls, and how when we all fled from the victims of our senseless vandalism, he'd been incapable of running more than two blocks or so without doubling back toward home. He had to be dead, I thought, or he'd have doubled back by now. And I thought about Drew Littler and how he'd reacted to my mentioning our old friend.

I must have fallen asleep thinking about him, because when I awoke it was first light and the street below was quiet and I knew something I hadn't known before. And I realized I had one last stop to make before leaving.

The screen door was just slamming shut behind him when I pulled my father's convertible up into the drive behind the big Harley. Eileen's car was gone, for which I was grateful. When I turned off the convertible's ignition, hot blue smoke belched from the tailpipe, then floated in a lazy cloud up the drive. Drew Littler waved the air with one big hand.

"What an ugly piece of shit that car is," he said. "Your old man always owns piece-of-shit rust buckets."

"This one's mine," I said, not getting out. "He just gave it to me."

He chuckled without the slightest trace of good humor. "Must've got tired waiting for somebody dumb enough to steal it."

I shrugged.

"I heard you'd left."

"Now, actually," I said. "I just came over to say goodbye."

"She's over at work."

"To you. You had any luck looking for work?"

"I'm not looking for work."

"You ever check out that job at The Bachelors?"

"I'm not looking for work."

"All right," I said. "Forget it. I'll see you around sometime."

"It must be true then," he said. He was fiddling with the convertible's door lock, up and down. "She told me they were broke, but I didn't believe it."

I took a deep breath and almost got out of the car. It would have been suicide, of course. Besides, I didn't really want to fight Drew Littler, wouldn't have wanted to even if I'd had a chance of winning. In a way, I had him good, though he didn't know it, and it occurred to me then, as I sat there bristling under the force of his insinuation, that perhaps that was why I'd driven out there. To finish Drew Littler off. There he stood, big as a house, smirking at me, imagining that his bulk counted for something, that he could by sheer size and strength and intimidation crash through life's barriers. It was what he'd imagined when we were boys and he'd pumped iron, the vein in his big forehead wriggling angrily. At some level, he still believed it, his experience of life notwithstanding. Believed it, though he'd been to jail, been behind iron bars that would not be budged.

He must have guessed that he was wrong about things that first time he went to jail after battering the Negro boys outside the pool hall, must have seen the significance of finally getting out as a result of judicial discretion, not force of will. In his cell he'd have had plenty of time to think about the iron that neither bent nor moved. He had little else to think about in that cell. In there he would not have heard of Jack Ward's death and would not have known that it was a dead man's car he and Willie Heinz were stealing the minute he got out of jail. He must have found that out only when he got back to town, and by then everything in the world had changed. He'd still been damp from the river when we'd found him braced up in the entryway to my father's flat, raving and belligerent, the two deaths merging in what was left of his rationality. It must have taken Jack Ward's Lincoln a while to sink, and depending on where he had driven it into the river, the car may have made it a fair distance out into the current. Even in the dark he must have seen its black silhouette drifting downstream toward Amsterdam. They had barrel-assed down to the water's edge, no doubt, whooping all the way, and then something had gone wrong. Willie Heinz, who couldn't swim, had remained in the drifting car, trapped, probably afraid to open the door. Or perhaps they'd been drinking all during that long afternoon joyride and Willie Heinz had passed out or been drunk enough to imagine he wouldn't be afraid, until it was too late. I'd thought of a dozen or so variations on this basic scenario, and one of them had to be the truth.

There was now very little of the young Drew Littler it had taken three men and a needle-wielding physician to subdue that night. And I couldn't think of much to be gained from the truth. Maybe truth wasn't a concept I'd ever been all that devoted to. For the sake of the human race, it wouldn't be wise to execute all the liars.

"Actually," I told Drew Littler. "I dropped by to ask a favor."

"Yeah?"

"Yeah. I'd like to ask you not to let my father pick a fight with you."

"Tell *him.*"

"Nobody can tell him anything," I smiled. "You know that."

"Then I'm not responsible, am I."

"Nope," I said. "That's why it's a favor. Say it's for an old friend."

He studied me then and what he said surprised me, though it probably shouldn't have. "We was never friends," Drew said. "I'd've known."

The simple truth of his statement shamed me. He was right. I had no business asking him for a favor. I had always blackly hated him, even worse than my father hated him, perhaps. He was almost as dumb as my father thought, and twice as dangerous, but he wasn't the sort of man you could flatter into thinking you'd once been friends.

On the other hand, he wouldn't hold it against you that you hadn't been, and a second after he'd said his piece, he held out a hand. "We could shake anyhow," he said.

I took the hand. We shook.

"Don't worry about Sammy," he said.

I waited, but that was all he had to say on the subject. "All right," I said. "I won't."

I turned the key in the ignition and the car's exhaust spit very nearly solid matter. When I started to back down the drive, Drew Littler rapped on the hood. "You know what happened back then, don't you," he said.

"Know what?" I said.

I'd become a far better liar since that day twenty years ago when I'd told my first-grade classmates how come my father wasn't around. Drew Littler couldn't have told from my face. I've been over it and over it, and that's the conclusion I've come to.

I put in a quart of oil before leaving town, but my father's convertible gave a dreadful shudder and died right on the county line about ten miles out of Mohawk. The good news was I was at the crest of a long gradual hill that wound all the way down to the river, so I put the car in neutral and let it coast the last mile right into a gas station at the foot of the hill. The convertible came to rest right next to a phone booth, but I didn't use it. I'd delayed my getaway too long already. I signed the title back over to my father, stuffed it in the glove box, and locked the car. A southbound Trailways bus was parked a block and a half down the street and I got on. That night I called Mike's Place from New York and left a message.

It was almost three months later, a couple days after Thanksgiving, when the telephone rang and I recognized my father's voice.

"Well?" he said.

"Well hello," I said.

"How come you're never home when I call?"

I told him I was working every minute to pay for the dark,

dreadful apartment I'd rented and the few sticks of ratty furniture I had to keep me company.

"You're all straightened around though?"

I said I was all straightened around.

"Want to run up for a day or two?"

"Sure," I said. "Christmas is coming . . ."

"Have to be tomorrow to do any good," he said. Then he explained why. "Eileen will understand if you can't."

Drew Littler's funeral was going to be in the afternoon. They'd been trying to reach me and my father had gone over to my mother's, hoping she'd know my number. "How the hell did I know she's gone to San Diego of all fucking places?" he said. And for the next ten minutes he regaled me with the difficulties he'd had tracking me down through F. William Peterson's old law firm, how they wouldn't give him the California number, how he'd had to have Wussy find out, how somebody ought to have his ass kicked for keeping secrets, how my mother hadn't wanted to give him my number, how F. William Peterson had had to call back and leave it at Mike's Place. "He knew he better had," my father said, his voice rich with the memory of having shown F. William Peterson, on numerous occasions, where the bear shit in the buckwheat. "I never heard of this Balboa Island, but I bet I could find it, and I got just about enough money to get there, too."

A dreamy distant feeling had come over me as I listened to him talk, thoroughly sidetracked, imagining, as had always been his habit, that other people's stories were his own, that you couldn't understand their complete meaning unless they got filtered through his point of view. Eventually, he got back to Drew Littler. He'd been going so fast that when he hit the side of the Chevy van the impact had knocked the vehicle clear off the highway and onto its side in the ditch. Drew himself had ruptured the van's side paneling and ended up inside. "Most of him, anyhow," my father said. The driver of the van had had a green light and never saw the Harley enter the intersection. Eyewitnesses guessed Drew Littler had to be going a hundred. They said the Harley neither slowed nor swerved before impact.

"So," my father said. "You still there."

"I'm here," I said.

"Where's your apartment?"

I told him.

"I had one a couple blocks from there," he said.

"When?"

"A long time ago. Right after I left your mother. And you."

We left it that I'd try to get home around Christmas. "Send Eileen a card if you can find one," he said.

I said I would.

"She's a good girl," he reminded me. "Now she's got one less headache."

"Jesus, Dad," I said.

"Well?"

"It's an awful thing to say."

"Not really," he said. "Be honest."

"It really is. Honestly."

"If you say so," he said. "Anyway, remember. The streets go one way, the avenues the other."

"Thanks," I said. Words to live by.

"Is Balboa Island really an island?"

"I don't know," I told him. "She says the sun shines every day."

"Good," he said. "Good for her."

PART 4

WINTER

41

During the next decade I saw my father no more than a dozen times, this despite the fact that the buses ran from the Port Authority in Manhattan right to the cigar store on the Four Corners in downtown Mohawk in just under five hours. Twice during this period he called me from the Bronx with tickets to Yankee ball games that had come to him via a route so circuitous that it took him the first couple innings to explain. There was this guy who got them at work and who gave them to a guy who couldn't go, who gave them to his cousin, who discovered that morning that his car wouldn't start and who gave them to a guy my father hadn't seen since Christ was a corporal and who he just happened to run into outside the OTB. Over the years, my father had become increasingly fascinated with the workings of chance, and was every day more convinced that luck ruled the universe and kept him *un*lucky. Even when things like the odd fortuitous pair of Yankee tickets dropped into his lap, he liked examining the odds of such a thing happening, and when he was all finished studying the ins and outs of this particular good fortune, he'd go back to his original thesis about being unlucky, noting that real luck would have brought him Mets tickets. When the game was over he always insisted on heading back to Mohawk. He knew how to get from the stadium to the Thruway and was convinced that if I ever got him all the way downtown where I lived, he'd never find his way back.

"You can't get lost," I told him. "Just remember. The streets go one way, the avenues the other."

"Thanks anyhow," he said. "My luck, I'd be just as liable to get going wrong and end up in California, where I don't know anybody but your mother."

This was a hint for me to fill him in on how she was doing, whether she and F. William Peterson were still married.

"I never liked this town, even when I lived here," he said each time he came to the city. "It's full of people who don't know any better."

He did come all the way downtown once, about a year after the last of our meetings at Yankee Stadium. It was the week before Christmas, windy and wet and not quite cold enough to snow. I'd gotten home late and still had my overcoat on when the buzzer went off. On my way to see who it was, I ticked off half a dozen people who might be buzzing me at 7:30 on a Friday evening, and Sam Hall didn't even make the list. There he was though, the top of his head recognizable three stories down.

He'd been drinking at Mickey's across the street and waiting for me to turn up. "It's a wonder anybody ever gets drunk in this town," he said, even before hello, when I met him on the stairs half way up. "I ordered a bottle of beer and the bartender says two-fifty. I tell him I don't want the whole six-pack, just the one. That's good, he says, 'cause for two-fifty you just get the one."

We shook hands.

"What on earth are you doing here?" I said.

"Visiting my son, if that's all right."

"It's fine," I said. "It's great. You took the bus?"

"Drove."

"Where did you park?"

"Right out front."

We were back in the apartment by then, so I looked down into the street. "Right there," he pointed to the roof of a Plymouth Valiant.

"Amazing," I said. "Whatever you do, don't move it."

"This is all right," he said, looking around my place. It was, in fact, the first decent apartment I'd had since coming to New York. "What's it set you back?"

I told him.

He raised his eyebrows, but offered no comment. It figured, given the price of beer.

He'd planned to stay the weekend but by lunchtime the next day he was clearly itchy to get back to Mohawk. It depressed him that Manhattan barmaids didn't like to be teased. He didn't think there was much point in *being* a waitress if you couldn't let yourself have a little fun at least. The bartenders were just as bad. They looked at him strangely when he slid onto a bar stool and staked his claim to it with a twenty-dollar bill. His was always the only bill of any denomination on the entire length of the bar, which had been specially grooved to accommodate the tabs which were rung after each order and then arched before the patrons.

"Not me," my father said. "If I'm tending this bar, I gotta see green before I go near the tap. Otherwise, you got guys drinking till closing and coming up light."

He was sure of it, too. He'd be damned if there wasn't at least one deadbeat at the bar even as we spoke.

"I come in, I drink a couple of beers, I get up to go to the john, I go in, I come back, I drink another beer, I gotta go again, right? Except this time I keep right on going out the door. There's another spot around the block does things the same dumb way. Tomorrow night I go to a different part of town. By the time I run out of bars it's 1990 and I can start all over again."

He couldn't wait to tell Roy Heinz about it when he got back home. Could I imagine that son of a bitch down here? He'd drink five hundred dollars worth of free booze in a week. A thousand probably.

My father took his time about it, but eventually the reason for his visit came out. Eileen had married during the summer, and for six months he'd been flirting with the idea of regret.

"Who'd she marry?" I said.

"That's the worst part," he said. "She had to go and find the laziest Polack in Mohawk County, as if all she needed was another mouth to feed. I told her so, too."

"I'll bet she appreciated it."

"You never could tell her anything," he admitted, "so why try?"

I shrugged.

"So why try?" he repeated.

I said I didn't know. "Maybe she loves him," I ventured. "Maybe she's tired of being lonely."

In fact, he looked pretty lonely and confused himself, sitting there in a strange bar full of strange people and strange local customs that weren't worth trying to understand. It had finally occurred to him, I think, what he never suspected when he left my mother so many years ago. That he could end up alone.

My visits to Mohawk during this period were no more successful than my father's visits to New York, and far less frequent. If memory serves, I made the journey upstate only twice during the decade after I left Mohawk. The timing was all wrong for the first, my father having been out of work for a while and pretty broke. I wasn't all that flush myself, though I was working two jobs. I'd been in the city about two years then and was trying to save some money. I'd enrolled in a program in publishing at one of the city colleges for the fall, which would mean the end of one of my jobs. Something—some fucking thing, as my father would have put it—was going to have to give. I was going to have to find a cheaper, dirtier, less safe apartment, or take out a loan, or get a roommate, or something. I think that in the back of my mind I hoped that during my visit, the subject of money would come up, that I'd tell my father my plans, that he'd have some money for once and float me a loan. I'm ashamed to admit that I also remembered the loan I'd unknowingly floated him so many years before. That, I've concluded, is one of the worst things about not having money; it causes you to recall what people owe you, or what you imagine they owe you.

But the subject of money never came up. We went out to dinner at The Elms the night I arrived in Mohawk. Mike had bought the place back the year before and it looked just the same as it had when my father had taken me there as a boy. I half expected a young Jack Ward to swagger in wearing a cream-colored suit, his lovely dark-haired little daughter in tow. Mike's wife Irma was back in her old role as hostess, escorting couples into the dining room with an expression that suggested her indifference to whether the entire party dropped dead. She appeared genuinely pleased to see me though, and my father and I got the best table in the place. It had had a reserved sign on it, but she discreetly removed this and tucked it under her arm.

"How come I don't get this kind of treatment when I come here alone?" my father wanted to know.

"You just answered your own question, didn't you." Irma glowered at him.

"You better marry me pretty soon," my father said. "Otherwise I'm going to stop asking and then you'll be stuck with Mike for the rest of your life."

"I'm stuck with the both of you either way."

We ate a good dinner, and when we finished, I said, "Let me, for once."

No check had come and I was beginning to suspect that my

father had called Mike sometime that afternoon to see if he could take care of the bill later.

We went into the bar afterward and had a drink, which my father let me pay for. "You show the kid your elbow?" Mike asked my father.

"Big mouth," my father said.

I'd noticed him rubbing it during dinner and had been on the verge of asking about it, but gotten sidetracked.

"It's a beauty, huh?" my father said now, as he rolled up his sleeve. Mike set one of the red goblet bar candles next to the elbow, so we could see. The grotesqueness of the injury took my breath away. The skin covering the elbow was stretched tight over the hairless, tennis-ball-sized protuberance.

I said, "Jesus, Dad."

"Just water is all, the doctor says . . ."

"*Their* doctor says. What do you expect? You think they want to pay disability?"

It had happened in the spring. Up till then he'd been tending bar for Mike and things had been fine, except people in places like The Elms were always ordering drinks like banana daiquiris, which my father hated making, so when he had a chance to go back on the road he told Mike to hell with banana daiquiris and piña coladas and all the other asshole drinks. He'd fallen only a few feet off the form truck, but his elbow had taken the full impact. The surgeons had done what they could, pieced the shattered elbow back together, said that in a month or two, with a little luck and some physical therapy, he'd get back ninety percent use of the arm. For therapy he'd worked the other side of the bar, bending his elbow like he was told.

"It looks worse today than when you got out of the hospital," Mike said.

"I know it," my father conceded. "What do you want from me. They say I can work."

"Fuck 'em. Come back and work for me. I'll put Ned on too. Weekends you can work together."

"What good would I be? I can't straighten my arm past here." My father demonstrated.

"Right. You can't tend bar, but you can work construction," Mike said, shaking his head. "Your old man's got rocks upstairs."

"I just happen to be tough," my father told him. "Some guys are. Other guys are pussies. I'm not naming any names."

I was still working on the fact that my father had had a serious accident and an operation to boot, and hadn't called. "Thanks for telling me about all this," I said when Mike was gone.

"You're welcome," he said. "What would you have done? Come down here and held my hand while they operated?"

"If I had to have an operation, wouldn't you want to know?"

"That's different." He grinned. "I'd explain it if I thought you were smart enough to understand."

He rolled his sleeve back down, with some difficulty, because the elbow was still sore and there was much more of it than the shirt was designed to accommodate.

"We could try it . . . if you wanted to tend bar . . ."

"I was planning on taking some classes in the city this fall," I said.

"Good," he said. "Glad to hear it."

I couldn't be sure, but I thought I detected the slightest shade of disappointment in his voice, perhaps the result of my answering so quickly, as if the idea of returning to Mohawk and working with him had merited no serious consideration. But if he was disappointed, he covered it quickly, spinning around on his bar stool to offer his other hand and elbow on the bar. "Anyhow, this is the one I arm-wrestle with."

It was also the one that was missing part of a thumb from the earlier accident. It occurred to me then that my father was losing a subtle war of attrition.

My more recent visit to Mohawk was about three years after the one I just related. I'd flown in to Albany on the last commuter flight on Friday night. Our plan was to catch the Travers Stakes at Saratoga the next afternoon, spend the evening catching up (it had been nearly nine months since we'd spoken on the telephone, over a year since we'd seen each other), then I'd take the bus back to the city on Sunday.

I figured on an hour or so of quiet reading time in the airport before he arrived. My father always either lost track of the clock and left Mohawk about the same time the plane was landing, or left in plenty of time but got off at the wrong Albany exit and then claimed they moved the airport again. But this evening, to my surprise, he was right there at the gate when I got off my plane, looking as if he had secret doubts about being in the right place.

Also, he was wearing glasses. But even with them I spotted him long before he picked me out of the crowd.

"Well," he said, when we shook. "You *were* on there."

"I said I would be."

I couldn't help staring at his glasses, which were missing one arm. The other dutifully hooked one ear, providing an imperfect anchor for the lenses, which balanced precariously on the bridge of his nose.

"I'd about given up," he said.

"You expected me to be in first class?"

"Why not? You're getting to be such a big shot down there," he said, taking the small bag I was carrying.

"A little shot," I assured him. When I'd called to say I was coming I'd told him about the junior editorship I'd just been promoted to. "Just slightly bigger than a year ago when I was no shot at all."

"Well, that's all right," he said. "My son, the book editor. What do you think of my cheaters? I bought them so I could see the racing form."

"Most people like the kind that hook behind *both* ears."

"I like them that way myself," he admitted. "In fact, these were that way until I sat on 'em. I could probably fix them if I could see, but to fix them I have to take them off, and then I can't see anymore. They're just for night driving anyhow. Even the risk pool wouldn't insure me if I didn't get them."

"Don't they usually give you a spare set?"

"Yup. I lost those two days after I sat on these. If I could just lose this pair, I'd go back and order some more. But every time I walk off some asshole yells at me to take my glasses with me. You son of a bitch, I tell him. You couldn't yell at me when I walked off and left my *good* pair. Every time I try to lose these bastards you notice."

By this time we were outside the terminal on the ramp across from the short-term parking, which was only a quarter full. I started looking for a car that might be my father's.

"Where you going?" my father wanted to know. He'd stopped by a pale yellow Subaru compact parked squarely in the middle of a loading zone. He slipped a key into its trunk and turned. There was a reassuring thunk, but when he lifted up, the trunk stayed shut. "Bitch," he said. "It does this sometimes in wet weather."

I looked around. "It rained here today?"

He went around to the driver's side and slung my bag in the backseat, already piled high with miscellaneous junk. He shook his head no. "Why, did it rain in the city?"

I grinned at him across the Subaru's hood. "It's good to be home."

"Get in then," he said. "We aren't home yet, in case you didn't notice."

He was right, too.

Between the airport and the Thruway entrance he told me all about the Subaru, which somebody'd talked him into buying. That little shit? he wanted to know, but then he figured what the hell. We'd taught the Japs a thing or two. Maybe they'd learned how to make cars. People said they did, and the guy who'd owned it didn't want an arm and a leg, so . . .

What troubled me, but apparently not my father, was the way people kept honking and swerving around us. My father honked back, waved, and continued talking. People honked hellos at him all the time in Mohawk, where they knew him, and he saw no reason why they shouldn't in Albany, where they didn't.

"Do you have your lights on?" I said finally, noticing that the dash wasn't lit up.

He looked down over the rims of his glasses and had to let go of the wheel to catch them when they fell off. "Should be," he said.

The Thruway entrance was a hundred yards away. We pulled in. When the attendant at the gatehouse handed us our ticket, he said, "Your lights, Mac."

"Right," my father said, and he put the Subaru in gear. "Not this shit again," he said, flicking the light switch in and out. I tried the radio, windshield wipers, cigarette lighter. Nothing. My father tried the turn signals. Nothing. We merged onto the Thruway, regardless, a big sedan careening around us at the last second. I put on my seatbelt.

"I'll show you a little trick," my father said when a double-hitch Peterbilt roared by and tugged at us. Slipping into its wake, my father goosed the Subaru, which strained dutifully until be got right on the Peterbilt's big, well-lit ass end.

My father, pleased with himself, looked over at me from above the black rims of his cockeyed glasses. "You worry too much," he said. "You always did."

I checked the speedometer, which was vibrating between sixty-five and seventy. Mohawk was forty black miles away. I wondered if, when we hit the Peterbilt, I'd be able to get down quickly enough to avoid decapitation.

"I've always wanted a Subaru," I said, trying to sound more full of admiration than terror. "But there's not much point in owning a car in the city."

"I can't live without one," my father said, punching in the cigarette lighter, having already forgotten. After a few seconds he began to lean slightly toward the lighter in anticipation of its clicking out. His Camel dangled from his lips as he divided his attention between the big truck only a few feet in front of us and the recalcitrant lighter. Finally it dawned on him. "Argh!" he said, pulling the cold lighter out, examining it, putting it to his stubbled cheek to make sure. Then he tossed it out the window and turned to me. "So," he said. "Tell me about this editor shit."

"Editor*ship*," I corrected, and pointed at the Peterbilt. "Are those brake lights?"

I had only one other contact with Mohawk in the decade after I came to New York. It came in the form of a newspaper clipping, a month old by the time I received it. ELDERLY WOMAN VICTIM OF CARNIVAL RIDE, the headline said in bold black letters, though the account beneath was slender. Miss Rachael Agajanian, a resident of the Mohawk Valley Nursing Home, had been one of a party taken on an outing to the Mohawk Fair. According to witnesses, her wheelchair had rolled backward off the merry-go-round when the attendant had gone to the aid of another resident of the home who, seated on one of the stationary benches, had unaccountably begun to scream. Miss Agajanian's wheelchair had become entangled in the machinery and been dragged, with its occupant, several complete revolutions, before the ride, which had been left on automatic, could be stopped.

The clipping from the *Mohawk Republican* was inside a small envelope; there was no note. When my father called a month later I asked him about the incident and, predictably, he had a lot more information than the newspaper account, and some of it may even have been true. The mangled old woman had been rushed to the New Mohawk Medical Services Center, where the emergency room staff immediately began to attend to her. She had been quite a sight but the doctors and nurses did their best with her. Unfortunately, at some point, someone explained how the accident happened, that the old woman had been thrown from the merry-go-round, whereupon the entire team dissolved. Each time their hilarity was about to subside, someone else entered the room, looked at the patient and wanted to know what on earth had happened, setting everyone off again. This continued until the patient died.

"Hell of a way to go," my father said. "I bet she pissed in her pants that day."

"Listen," I said. "Do you ever see Claude Schwartz around?"

"That's funny," he said. "I heard something about him just the other day. The kid that hung himself, right? Worked at the post office?"

I said that was Claude Schwartz.

"He just took off one day about a month ago. Left his wife, kids, mother, all of them. Gave notice at the post office, cashed his last check and was gone. What kind of man does a thing like that?"

Foolishly, I took this to be a rhetorical question.

"Well?" my father said, his long distance voice full of genuine perplexity.

42

From the living room I heard the shower thunk off, the glass door open and close. Leigh usually took long showers, which made me wonder if she'd heard the phone in there. "The timing isn't so great, that's all," I told my father.

"So don't, then," he said. "Come in a couple weeks when you're straightened out. What's the difference. I'll be right here."

The bathroom door—the one off our bedroom—opened and I

caught a glimpse of her in the bedroom mirror, toweling her hair dry. Until Leigh, no woman had ever performed this womanly task in my presence. Had one done so, and looked the way Leigh did, her olive skin glistening, I think I'd have proposed marriage on the spot.

"Will you need help moving?" I said.

The sound of my voice caused her to pivot quickly and scoot behind the door until she could determine whether I was on the phone or we had company.

"Moving what?" my father wanted to know.

"Furniture."

"Haven't got any," he said. "I can carry my own suitcase, if I could find it."

"The new place is furnished?"

"Will be," he said. "That's all taken care of. The furniture store delivers, so all I gotta do is be there and point. I may get somebody else to do that. Putting things where they should go was one of the things I could never do to suit your mother."

"Aren't you glad you don't have to suit her anymore?"

"Yes, I am," he said, but there was a wistful quality to his answer that suggested he might like to try pleasing, if not my mother, then some woman, just one more time, to see if it could be done.

Leigh came out in her cotton robe and mouthed a "who?" at me.

I cupped my hand over the phone. "Your father-in-law-to-be." Then to him, "How's next weekend?"

"That's the only one that won't work," he said. I waited for him to elaborate, but he didn't, which was surprising. Usually such an opening produced a long, convoluted story, at the end of which you still wouldn't know why next weekend was out. "Your honey there?"

I told him she was and waved Leigh in from the kitchen like a third base coach. "The week after, then," I said before handing the phone over to Leigh.

"Whenever. There's a little something I want to tell you about, but it'll keep."

I handed the phone to Leigh, but stayed there, thinking about his last elliptical remark and wondering what it could mean. Coyness wasn't among my father's usual vices.

"Are you as sexy as your voice?" I heard him ask Leigh, who motioned for me to go away. Since she'd moved in with me ten months before, they always talked when he called. Frequently her conversations with my father were longer than my own. It had taken her a while to get the hang of him, but she thought she had his number now.

"Sexier," she said.

I went into the kitchen and made myself an iced tea.

"Right now?" I heard her say. "Nothing but a robe. I just got out of the shower . . . well . . . don't ask if you don't want to know. It's not my fault if you have a weak ticker."

She rolled her eyes at me. It was their usual contest to see who'd get embarrassed first.

"I don't know," she said. "Let me ask."

"What?" I said.

"He wants to know if you'll take some dirty pictures if he springs for the film?" Then, whispering urgently, "How do I get out of this?"

"My mother had to move to California."

She was listening again, though, and her expression had become serious before she turned her back to me. "No," she said, then, "I will."

I took a sip of tea, added another half teaspoon of sugar, watched Leigh wind strands of wet hair around her index finger. After a minute she turned around again and waved me back in. "He wants to talk to you again."

"Do you play golf?" he wanted to know.

"What?"

"Golf, dummy, golf."

"Yes," I said, then added. "Not really."

"You got clubs?"

I said I did, as if to prove that he could not so easily diagnose what was wrong with my game.

"Bring them when you come," he said.

"Don't tell me you've taken up golf?"

"Nah," he said. "Just some of these guys I'm hanging around with. Couple of them are your age. We ride around in carts, have a hell of a good time."

I tried to envision this. "Really?"

"Just if you want to," he said. "That's all."

"Incredible," I said after we'd hung up.

Leigh came over and sat on my lap. "Share?"

"Yes. Everything I have." I gave her the iced tea, which she drained.

"Why don't you want to go see your father this weekend?" she said, handing me back the empty glass. "You've been busy saying no to parties all week. You've never had a freer weekend."

Her robe had gapped open at the throat, and I slipped my hand in. "I have every minute planned. By the end of the weekend you will have come to your senses. In short, reconsider the folly of your present position."

"Which position is that? The one where I'm sitting on the lumpy lap of a certifiable sicko, or my reluctance to marry said sicko?"

"The second," I said, working clumsily at the sash of her robe. "Who taught you how to tie a seaman's knot?"

"The other sicko. The one I was married to. He was an expert knot tier."

"He tied you up? You never told me things got kinky."

"Metaphorically kinky. Because he thought of me as bound, he concluded I couldn't get away."

"You sure showed him," finally succeeding with the knot and slipping the robe off her shoulders.

"If you're planning on taking any pictures for your father," she said, looking down at her abdomen, which was showing the first signs of swelling, "you better do it soon."

Between New York's Port Authority and the bus station in Pough-keepsie, I sat next to a pugnacious woman from Brooklyn who was visiting her grandchildren. When I made the mistake of telling her that I worked for a publishing house, she immediately tried to pick a fight. "I never read the new books," she said.

"It's a free country," I said, smiling as sweetly as I knew how and wishing I'd taken the plane. The only reason I hadn't was that my father would have had to pick me up in Albany. I didn't know if he still had the killer Subaru, but I wasn't taking any chances.

"Too free," said my companion. "There ought to be a law against these young ones writing about us. They think we were like they are now, jumping from one bed to another. World War Two. Imagine. Jumping from one bed to another." She waved her hand in disgust. "I just read the same books over and over. *From Here to Eternity.*"

I said I knew what she meant.

"Twenty-four, twenty-eight, thirty years old. And they think they know how we felt. Why do they pretend they understand us?"

"I don't know," I told her.

"Of course you don't. How could you? How old are you?"

"Thirty-four," I admitted.

"There," she said. "How could you write about the Second World War?"

"My father was part of the Normandy invasion, actually," I said, unsure whether this intelligence would mollify or further inflame her. Her proscription against my writing about what she considered her war was entirely unnecessary, but I wasn't sure she'd believe me if I told her. She'd suspect that I was secretly doing it anyway.

"You listen to him then," she said. "Maybe you'll learn."

"I'm sure of it," I told her. "He never talks about it though."

"Why should he?" the good woman wanted to know. "The ones who *saw*, the ones who *did*, they aren't talkers. It's the others who are the talkers."

Her implication was clear. I was a talker. She could tell. If I wrote a book, she wouldn't read it.

"Do you know what I do?" she said. "I look at copyright dates. If it's written after 1955. . . ." she waved goodbye to it.

When we pulled into the station in Poughkeepsie, she took my hand and squeezed, suddenly full of goodwill. "It's like Frank Sinatra says. To look at us, you couldn't always tell what was in our heads, but you always knew where our hearts were."

The woman's eyes had gone misty and I could tell that her heart was somewhere, all right, and it wasn't Poughkeepsie either. After her departure I had the two seats to myself, but I kept thinking about the woman. In some ways she reminded me of my mother and the other women I'd known whose lives were compromised by the war and who now felt an odd affection for its memory and guarded their loss against new assailants. My mother had more than once remarked that my father was one of the war's casualties, that the Sam Hall who came back wasn't the one who left, the one she'd fallen in love with. I didn't doubt that she believed this simple truth or even that it *was* true, after a fashion. But it was a nice way of ignoring another simple truth—that people changed, with or without wars, and that we sometimes don't know people as well as we think we do, that the worst errors in judgment often result from imagining we understand what has escaped us entirely. That was almost certainly true in my mother's case. The Sam Hall she'd fallen in love with was only narrowly based on a real person. The war, their separation, had encouraged a kind of poetic license where he was concerned. If he hadn't come home, he'd have remained the love of her life. It seemed probable to me that my companion on the bus had lost someone, and that the loss had changed everything, created a truth that could not be modified, only accepted, reread.

I didn't envy the woman her text etched in stone. No good editor would. And yet there was something to be said for permanence. At thirty-four, there was precious little in my own life. I'd succeeded in falling in love with and getting pregnant the girl with whom I had been living for nearly a year, who had permitted, even encouraged, every decent intimacy engaged in by consenting adults, who looked forward to bearing, delivering, and raising our child, but who steadfastly drew the line at the prospect of a lifetime of my company. I tried to think of a good way to explain all this to my father, but the trip between Poughkeepsie and Mohawk wasn't nearly long enough, and when we pulled up in front of the cigar store on the Four Corners, I'd made exactly no progress.

I had decided against phoning him back to say that I was coming for the weekend after all. I thought now about calling from the cigar store and having him come fetch me, since his new apartment was twenty or so blocks away, but the evening was cool and my bag was light, containing little more than two days' change of clothing. So I walked up Main past the Mohawk Grill, which had closed for the night, along with everything else but the gin mills. The biggest change on Main was that Klein's Department Store was closed and boarded up, three stories' worth of windows all black and lifeless. There was no more Accounting Department and no way for me to settle my long-standing account, to make an honest man of myself. Further up the street, whoever inherited Mike's Place apparently hadn't felt sufficiently motivated to change the name of the establishment. New signs weren't cheap, and when the old one had a decent reputation to trade on, you were better off leaving it where it was. It was one of the constants of Mohawk life that businesses were bought, sold, bartered, and won in poker games every day without significantly altering the establishments themselves. There wasn't even any perceived need to print up an "Under New Management" sign to stick in the front window, because everybody already knew before you could put it there. The fact that you couldn't get a decent plate of spaghetti at Mike's anymore was common knowledge before the new owner had opened for business that first Monday morning. That he would attempt to appease the old crowd with Buffalo chicken wings was already the subject of conversation and conjecture at the Mohawk Grill.

When I got to Third Avenue, I headed north up the gentle hill toward the house that had been my mother's and mine until her breakdown. The fact that the neighborhood had deteriorated was presaged by the cracked, heaving sidewalks that lined both sides of the narrow street. Every other house sported a sagging porch, railings with missing spindles, chipped and yellowed paint, rusted mailboxes. Our old house was one of the worst, and when I saw it I felt a deep sense of personal failure. Whoever owned the little house now had begun to paint it pale green, then run out of paint, or money, or energy. And this had happened at least one summer before, by the looks of it. There was a monster Buick Skylark up on blocks in the drive, and broken children's toys strewn throughout the yard. Something was missing, too, and it took me a moment to realize what it was.

"Ice storm," explained a woman who came out onto the back porch of the house next door when she saw me standing there outside her kitchen window, staring at the spot where my climbing tree had been. "Killed every tree on the block."

It was true. When my mother and I had lived there, the street had been lined with mature trees along the narrow terrace between sidewalk and road. Not one was left, though a few slender young trees had been replanted. For some reason, these didn't look like they'd ever grow to be much taller than the wire mesh that encircled and protected them.

"You can't get decent people to live on a street that don't have nice trees," the woman said ruefully. "Where do you live?"

"New York City," I admitted reluctantly, then added, "I used to live right here."

"I lived here all my life," the woman said. "In Mohawk, that is. This used to be my aunt's house. Maybe you knew my aunt."

She told me her aunt's name, and I said that of course I had.

"I wouldn't want to live anyplace else," she said. "It gets worse

here every year, but so does everyplace, is the way I look at it.
Harold and I tried to plant new trees, but they won't take because
of the roots. You got to dig up the old stumps and go way down.
It cost a lot and the roots go everywhere. Under the streets and
the lawns. We got them in our cellar. And you seen the sidewalks."

I said I had.

"You'd like to plant a tree or two, but where?"

"The roots will die eventually," I said, trying to be optimistic,
since she really wanted to plant trees.

"That's what I said. Harold says no. He says they just petrify
there in the ground, make it impossible for anything alive to find
a space and grab ahold. 'Course Harold is a sourpuss. I think
sometimes he just says things like that so he won't have to go out
and try. Some people would rather do without trees than dig a
little hole."

I had written my father's new address on a note card and put it
in my wallet. When I got there, I took the note card out to double-
check, then set my bag down on the sidewalk and laughed out
loud. "McKinley Luxury Apartments" the new sign said. Above
the arched entrance, graven in stone, you could still see the old
one: "McKinley School." My father, it occurred to me now, had
been just about my present age when he sat out front of the school
in his white convertible, waiting for my young first grade teacher
to bring me out, so I could explain why I was telling everybody
he was dead.

There was nothing to do but walk up that long sloping terrace,
just as I had done every morning, grades one through six, so I did,
half expecting the old bell to sound. Beneath the stone arch was
a row of mailboxes and buzzers, and above the first of these was
a label that said: S. Hall, resident manager. I pushed the buzzer
and waited. Then I wandered around back where there was a big
metal dumpster and a parking lot that was empty except for half
a dozen cars, one of which was a yellow Subaru. It was unlocked,
so I tossed my bag inside, checked to make sure he hadn't left the
keys in the ignition, and locked it up. Across the street, where a
corner market had been when I was a kid, there was now an
establishment called Trip's, and Trip's had a big green, triangular

cocktail glass tilted over the front door. It looked like a good place to begin.

And there he was, swung around on his bar stool so he could follow the action at the shufflebowl machine. His head was cocked strangely, as if he were trying to see out from under his glasses and along the bridge of his nose. When I sat down next to him, he rotated around to see who it was. "Hey!" he said. "You're in New York!"

"No," I said. "I'm right here."

"I can see that. How come?"

"I thought you invited me. What's wrong with your neck?" He was tilted back, almost off the stool so he could look me over.

"Stiff as a bitch," he said. "Hurts, too. You bring your golf clubs?"

"No."

"How come?"

"I'll rent some."

"Can you do that?"

"Sure," I said. "Even in Mohawk."

One of the shufflebowl players, a guy about forty, dressed in a pale blue summer cardigan and breezy, lightweight slacks came over. "The resident manager is up," he said.

"Say hello to Smooth," my father said. "He owns this joint, along with those overpriced apartments across the street."

We shook hands, Smooth grinning at my father as we did. "What do I get from Sam Hall? Heartache. He gets his apartment for free, I buy the bar across the street so my legitimate tenants will know where to find the resident manager, and what do I get for my trouble? Heartache." He was grinning at me now. "It's worth it though, because I won the bet."

"Your ass," my father said.

"I bet him a hundred bucks two months ago that before the year was out, Sam Hall'd go back to school."

"You got room for one more tomorrow?" my father said.

"You don't have to ask. You're the resident manager. You got privileges," Smooth said, then to me, "You play golf?"

"Not well," I admitted.

"Can he rent clubs?" my father said.

"I got an extra set," Smooth said. "They wouldn't shoot straight for me, but they might for him. The only trouble is, they're home."

"Uh-oh," my father said.

"How pissed off can she be?" Smooth said. "It was a week ago. You can't keep a man out of his own house forever. There's a law."

My father got down off the stool, rather gingerly, it seemed to me, and headed for the shufflebowl. "His mother kept me out of mine for about twenty years," he said.

"Who can blame her?" Smooth said. Then, when my father was out of earshot, he said, "I'm glad you decided to come up. He said you weren't going to."

We watched my father hunch over the bowling machine, peering over the top of his glasses now at the still quivering pins. His first frame was a strike, but in the second he hit the head pin straight on and left a seven-ten split.

"He's all set up over there. They delivered the furniture yesterday," Smooth said, but there was something in his tone I didn't understand, as if there might be an irony about the arrangement. "Don't say I said anything, but he talks about you all the time. My son the publisher."

When the game was finished and my father came back over, Smooth said, "How'd you get such a smart kid?"

"I let his mother raise him."

"Good strategy," Smooth said. "Remind me of it if I ever start talking about going home."

"You never listened to anything I told you yet," my father said.

"It's the secret of my success," Smooth said. "You're like a compass that points due south. I look where you're headed and go the other way. Speaking of which, I better go bail for Uncle Willie before they get him settled in for the night." He turned to me. "Can you believe the cops in this town? Popping eighty-year-old bookies?"

"Don't forget about the golf clubs," my father said.

"I'll be back," Smooth said. "You'll be able to remind me half a dozen more times."

"I won't be here," my father said.

"Sure you won't," Smooth said.

When he was gone, my father looked me over. "Getting pretty fancy in your old age," he said.

I looked down at what I was wearing, trying to imagine what it was that struck him as fancy.

"You didn't bring anything with you?" he said.

"One bag."

He looked around. "What'd you do with it?"

I told him I'd locked it in the Subaru.

"Good," he said. "Only trouble is I sold it to a guy last week."

"Why is it out back of the apartment?"

"He said it wouldn't start. I've been meaning to try it myself, but I keep forgetting."

"You know his number?"

"No, why?"

"My stuff's locked up inside," I said.

"Don't worry, I kept a spare key, in case I needed to borrow it someday."

"What'd you buy?"

"Nothing. What do I need a car for?" he said. "Grocery store a block away. New place, new furniture, new TV . . ."

"Sounds good," I said.

"Most of the time I sit around. Something breaks over there, I fix it. If I can't fix it, I call somebody who can. Smooth always has a dozen things going on. Buys old buildings for taxes and fixes them up. If he needs somebody to sleep in one, make sure nobody walks off with the sheetrock, I do it. For that I get the apartment and a couple bucks under the table that nobody's gotta know about. Company truck if I need it."

"Sounds perfect," I said.

"It *is* perfect," he said, swinging halfway around to look at me. "There isn't a goddamn thing in the world wrong with it. Except I got cancer."

The next day I played in a foursome that contained a rather dour-spirited lawyer named Henderson Boyle; an insane high school English teacher named Alan Taggart who, by conservative estimate, did hundreds of dollars worth of damage to the course, taking monstrous divots with every swing, the clods of moist earth traveling, in most instances, considerably farther than his pristine ball; and Smooth himself, who seemed in the same extraordinarily good spirits as the night before. It took us fifteen minutes to get off the first tee because every time Smooth got into the middle of his backswing, he'd remember a funny story he wanted to share with us, the best being the one about Untemeyer, who had gone meekly to jail after being arrested, said nothing to nobody until

Smooth appeared with bail, whom he proceeded to bawl out for taking so long.

The other three players were making complex wagers from hole to hole. I think they would have liked me to get in on the betting, but after they saw my swing they were too kind to insist. Actually, I might have been able to break more or less even by beating Alan Taggart, but I was just as happy to be out of it altogether. The real contest was between Smooth and Boyle, who watched each other carefully without seeming to. We all ignored Alan Taggart's woes. The only time Smooth spoke to him was when he stepped up to address his own ball, and he continued to talk right through his swing, finishing his sentence at the precise moment of impact. "The ball, Tag, the goddamn ball! Hit the ball! The ball's the key to the whole thing, Tag! Hit the goddamn ball! Don't fuck with the ground!" And then, whack—Smooth's Titleist would jump off the tee, climbing an invisible ladder until it reached a tall plateau before dropping, as if off the end of a table into the middle of the smooth fairway.

Immediately after which, Alan Taggart took an even more heroic divot and then flung his club in its pursuit.

"Great follow-through, you gotta admit," Smooth whispered, arm around my shoulder. "Your old man fess up last night?"

I said he had.

"What'd you tell him to do?"

"You don't tell Sam Hall what to do," I said, though I had, last night. "I said I didn't see where he had much choice."

"That's what I told him," Smooth said. "When a doctor says you can either take the treatments or plan on being dead in two months, you take the goddamn treatments. Boyle says the same thing."

Actually, I wasn't so sure. According to what my father had told me, the tumor was large, advanced, positioned on the lung so as to be inoperable. He would have to take the most potent and dangerous chemotherapy there was, my father had said, six months of it, assuming you lasted six months. But if he could live through it, he might be able to buy another five years. Who knew? Maybe ten years. Who the hell knew?

"I told them I didn't want to trade two months for six months," he said. "They can shove the extra four, and I told 'em so."

But there was little heart behind this bravado, and when he was all through telling me about the conditions he'd laid down for the doctors, he'd sighed and said, "They got me by the balls, I'm afraid."

"Cancer doesn't always mean death anymore," I said. "Things have changed."

"That's what they said down at the VA." He nodded. "But death's what it's going to be in my case, so you better get used to the idea. The tumor's already the size of a golf ball. Bigger. They showed me on the X ray, just in case I didn't believe them."

Smooth shook his head as we waited for Boyle to hit from behind a tree. "Anybody else, there'd be no argument, but Sam Hall . . ."

"Is Sam Hall," I finished.

"He'll do what you tell him though," Smooth said. "If you say take the treatments, I think he will."

Actually, I suspected that the convincing was just a formality. My father wanted to make a show of saying the hell with it, but his mind was already made up. Over the phone he had told me that next week would be bad for a visit, and last night he'd told me that if he decided to do the treatments, they'd be admitting him on Tuesday to begin the first series and keeping him over the weekend for observation. "I may just tell them to fuck off," my father kept saying, but he wasn't going to.

"What the hell," he said before we left Trip's to see if we could find the key to the Subaru. "Try it once or twice, I guess. If they make me feel worse than I do now, then no more." He rubbed the back of his neck and blinked. "I don't see how I can feel much worse."

"You'll never guess what he was doing up till a week ago," Smooth said. "Ask Boyle. Boyle! Come here. Hit later. Let Tag have honors for once. Don't be a hog."

Boyle came over.

"Tell Ned what his old man was doing for his stiff neck before he went to the hospital. TAG! THE BALL! THE BALL'S THE KEY!"

We all watched Alan Taggart tee off.

"A goddamn *chiropractor* he was going to," Smooth said, having apparently forgotten that he'd brought Boyle over to impart this intelligence. "Too bad it wasn't a brain tumor, I told him. Then you could have gone to a proctologist. You're up, Boyle! Hit, for Christ's sake."

The strange part of all this was that Smooth was just what I

needed that day. His mouth went nonstop, reducing everything
to low comedy. Clearly, it took more than somebody else's cancer
to sober him or dampen his spirits. In fact, he gave the impression
that it would take more than his own cancer to dampen them. (I
would learn from my father that he had recently undergone tri-
ple bypass heart surgery.) The reality of the present situation
seemed to support his philosophy, which I took to mean that,
whatever else you said about it, life was entertaining as hell. After
all, here I was, playing golf for the first time in years, less than
twenty-four hours after learning of my father's malignant disease.

And where was Sam Hall? Where else but racing back and forth
among the foursomes Smooth had organized, two ice chests full
of beer strapped to the back of his motorized golf cart in the
compartment designated for clubs.

"No wonder you're in the risk pool," Boyle observed when my
father skidded to a halt on the cart path on number twelve after
we'd stopped for lunch. Smooth had won fifty dollars from him on
the front nine and it didn't look to me like his fortunes were going
to improve significantly on the back, even though Boyle was only
pretending to drink and Smooth was powering down one can of
beer after another. Alan Taggart, who had pulled a huge wad of
bills out of his canary-yellow slacks and handed several to Smooth,
drank viciously, draining each can in a few gulps, crushing them
as they were poised over his mouth, and then hooking them off
into the woods. After muffing his tee shot on ten, he examined his
driver maliciously and calmly wrapped it around the ball washer.
Boyle must have seen the look on my face, because he came over
and said that there was no reason to be alarmed. This sort of thing
had happened before. It was almost certainly Taggart's intention
to arrive back at the clubhouse with an empty bag. "Just be
prepared to say no if he asks you to borrow your putter."

My own game was not much better. I'd lost two balls to the
water, and wondered as I saw them rupture the serene surface of
the pond whether there might be an enterprising twelve-year-old
off in the trees, awaiting dusk and the chance to fish the murky
depths.

On the hole where Jack Ward had had his heart attack and died,
my father rolled up beside me in the beer cart.

"You ready for one?" he said.

"Sure," I said. "How's your neck?"

"Not too bad," he said, clearly surprised to have forgotten it for a while. "I put some of this stuff on it."

He held out a jar of liniment for me to inspect. It looked a like cold cream jar but the gel inside emitted a powerful odor I'd caught a whiff of earlier.

"You can't buy it," he said. "You gotta know somebody who has horses."

I blinked at this non sequitur. "Say again."

"Horse liniment."

I didn't know what to say. My father was treating lung cancer with horse liniment. "Who do you know that has horses?" I said.

"Smooth owns part interest in a couple trotters. Damn stuff works, too. The only trouble is you can taste it. Goes right through your neck and ends up on your tongue. I don't know how. I haven't been licking my neck, I know that."

He handed me a beer and popped one for himself, making a face at the way it tasted. The other three players were on the other side of the fairway, and we were all waiting for Alan Taggart, who was away as usual.

"You having a good time?" my father asked, as if it were important to him that I was.

"Sure," I said.

"I never thought I'd like golf," he said, "but it's all right."

I looked at him to see if this might be a joke.

"It's nice out here," he said, "and these are all good guys."

Alan Taggart swung and his orange ball burped and ran a few feet.

"Tag's an asshole, of course."

"English teachers must do pretty well in Mohawk County," I said, recalling the wad of bills he'd flashed.

"Not really," my father said. "His old man died and left him about half a million."

After the duff, Taggart was looking around for a tree, I could tell, and regretting there weren't any in the center of the fairway.

"I'm afraid I'm not going to have a fortune to leave you," my father said.

I managed a grin. "That's a shame," I said. "I was really counting on it."

"Whatever I got is yours. Boyle said he'd draw it up, so you'll be all set. It won't cost either one of us, so . . ."

Across the fairway they were waving for me to hit.

"Concentrate on getting better," I suggested, taking out an iron.

My father watched me address the ball, and together we watched its waffling flight. "What about this girl of yours?"

"What *about* her?"

"Is she it, or what?"

"She's trying to decide whether *I'm* it," I admitted. "She has her doubts."

"How come?"

I shrugged.

"Well," he said. "If she decides you are, be good to her. Don't end up old and stupid if you can help it."

What he hadn't added to old and stupid, was "alone," but it was hanging there in the air, understood, anyway.

From across the fairway a cry had gone up for the beer wagon, and my father, who was contemptuous of cart paths, sped directly across the fairway. Before he got to where the others were waiting, I saw him make a wide loop and retrace his path. I didn't understand what he was up to until I saw Boyle take off after him. On the second pass, my father had located the lawyer's golf ball on the moist fairway, the heavy front wheel of the cart driving it deep into the sod where it would take an Alan Taggart to dig it out. "Play it as it lays!" I heard Smooth hoot. "Play that sucker as it lays."

The rest of the weekend was an alcoholic haze, and when I got back to New York late Sunday night, my father having promised to check into the VA on Tuesday like he was supposed to, I told Leigh only that he had cancer. Had I been able to share any of the rest of it with her, I'd have told her about the ninth hole, a par three with an elevated tee that overlooked the clubhouse. Off to one side my father had set up a Weber kettle from which plumes of smoke rose. There were five foursomes in Smooth's entourage, of which we were the first. My father's job had been to throw a round of burgers and hot dogs on as each foursome reached the tee. The food would be about done when the golfers sank the last of their putts. My father, all alone down there with the grill, presented such an inviting target that Smooth had used his mulligan to shoot at him, and the ball had dropped softly a few feet from the kettle, after which Smooth, Boyle, and Alan Taggart all yelled, "Fore!" My father picked up the ball and chucked it into the trees and yelled back something that sounded like "Five."

I had hit second, with the kind of nice smooth three-quarter swing I can almost never manage when I'm actually concentrating on the game. The ball rose and rose until I thought I had chosen the wrong club, gone way too far. But the distance was all illusion, and my ball hit on the green like a pillow. It was the first shot I'd hit on the whole front nine that looked like a real golf shot, and I was surprised by the pleasure that hitting and watching the ball produced, the ease with which, for a moment in time, it replaced all considerations of love, obligation, regret.

I looked over to where my father was to see if he'd been watching, but he'd just raised the black lid of the Weber kettle and the smoke that billowed out obscured him entirely.

In the months that followed I tried to see him every other weekend or so, depending on his schedule with the Albany VA Hospital, which typically admitted him for treatments in the middle of the week, observed him for a day or two and released him until the next scheduled treatment with a list of specific dietary and behavioral instructions, which he wadded up and tossed in the receptacle outside the hospital's main entrance. On one occasion he saved the dietary list and presented it to Harry at the Mohawk Grill.

"I'd slice you a goddamn grapefruit, if you'd only do the rest," Harry said seriously. This, I later discovered, was in reference to the fact that my father continued not only to drink between chemotherapy treatments, but to smoke as well, at least occasionally. He never smoked around me, but both Smooth and Boyle reported seeing him. When I asked my father about it, he said he couldn't have smoked if he'd wanted to, that the chemicals reacted to the nicotine and made him sick. I think that this was true during the first week or so after his treatments, but then for a few days before he was due for the next one, he'd start feeling human again, in celebration of which the party would begin.

"As long as I have a few good days, I don't care," he told me. "When I start feeling bad all the while, they can all go fuck themselves. I told them so too, this last time."

I tried to plan my visits to coincide with his good days, just before he was due to be admitted back into the hospital. No doubt I'd have been more use to him during the bad days, but he didn't want me around, then, to see him. Only when he sensed that his cycle was again on the upswing, when he could eat and function, would he call and say to come on up if I felt like it, if I had the time, if I was caught up on my work, if Leigh could spare me, if I didn't have anything else going on. When I asked how the treatments had been going, he always said they were hell itself, but if they didn't get any worse, he'd make it.

On my father, the chemicals had the opposite of their predicted effect, binding him up so tight that for days he would yearn for the ecstasy of a bowel movement. During the first five or six days after his treatments, he remained in his dark apartment, getting out of bed only to try once more in the bathroom. If people came by wanting the services of the resident manager, he just ignored the knocking until they went away.

On one of my visits during this period I learned that my father and Wussy had had a falling out. I'd been wondering about Wussy's absence but when I asked, my father hadn't been at all forthcoming. From Smooth, I learned that Wussy had been seeing a white woman and that my father had had an opinion on that subject. I knew that Sam Hall was not above such opinions or above voicing them, but I suspected that there was more to it than even Smooth understood. They had argued before, my father claiming it'd be a long cold day before he'd have anything to do with "that black bastard" again, but the next time I'd see him (granted, a month or two might have elapsed), they'd be on adjacent bar stools. Now, the timing of the whole thing was suggestive. Perhaps they had fallen out before my father was diagnosed, but his stubbornness about not reconciling I took to be another instance of his wanting to do his most intense suffering in private. The current posture of anger and misunderstanding ensured that

Wussy would not be coming by when he wasn't wanted, offering assistance when my father wanted only to be left alone in his dark den.

I didn't realize how badly he needed to be alone during the worst of it until he miscalculated and had me come up before his personal pendulum had truly begun its upswing. He'd felt decent the day before, but by the time I arrived in Mohawk the next afternoon, he'd backslid into intense nausea, constipation, and their attendant depression. I found him in his dark, foul-smelling bedroom, almost unable to turn over, all the window shades drawn, as if to ensure that none of the pestilential atmosphere be allowed to dissipate. Despite his efforts to eat, he had by then begun to lose weight noticeably, and his skin had taken on a yellow tinge. His eyes were so wild and red that he resembled nothing so much as a rabid animal. "Perfect," he said when I appeared. He'd given me the spare key so I could come in and drop my stuff off before searching him out. "My son's here to watch me croak."

In fact, he looked like he would not live out the day, but when I sat down at the edge of the bed and tried to take his hand, he pulled it away with more strength than I imagined he possessed.

I took a room for the night in a sleazy motel on the highway and tried to think of what to do. I didn't want to go back to the city, leaving him in such a dreadful condition, but I made up my mind that I would, in the morning, if he showed no improvement. That evening I ate a hamburg steak in the Mohawk Grill where, except for Harry, I saw absolutely no one I knew. To kill some time I took a walk in the gathering dusk, ending up, for some reason, outside the chain-link fence that surrounded Our Lady of Sorrows. In the wide expanse between the church and the rectory, there was now nothing but lawn. All of Skinny Donovan's flowers had gone the way of Skinny Donovan. In their place the lawn had been resodded and the grass cared for meticulously, but it seemed to me, as I stood there in the gathering darkness, that the grass where the flowers had once been tended was a shade or two darker, and that, if you cared to see it, there was the old shape of the cross that Skinny and I had mowed around, still visible in the center of the broad lawn canvas.

Or maybe I just wanted to see it there. I changed my mind about the cross sometime during the night in my shabby motel room where I lay thinking of Leigh and myself and our unborn child. I must have been the only person in the ten-unit motel who was registered for the entire night. On both sides of me there were a great many comings and goings, and I was awakened once, long after midnight, when something crashed on the other side of the wall, and a young woman's voice rose from a low moan all the way up the musical scale to a high-pitched lament, then back down again and into silence.

At seven the next morning, when the phone rang, I expected to hear the voice of the old satyr of a desk clerk, with whom I had left a wake-up call before retiring the night before. Instead, it was my father, sounding chipper and none the worse for wear. "You gonna sleep all day or do you want to have some breakfast with me?"

I sat up in bed and shook my head to clear the cobwebs. The background racket put him at the Mohawk Grill, which explained how he knew where I was. I'd told Harry the night before. "How are you?" I said.

"Not so bad I need anybody to hold my hand."

"Good," I said.

"I got through one war with the Germans and another with your mother without needing any of that."

"I'm sorry," I said. "Pardon me for being concerned."

"You want me to come out there?"

"I can walk in," I told him. "I walked out."

"Stay there."

I went outside and waited. A minute later he pulled into the motel parking lot in a new Lincoln. I got in. "Who belongs to this?"

"Smooth," my father said. "He needs a big car. His wife makes him sleep in it half the time."

"He doesn't strike me as an easy guy to be married to."

"He's okay. Just young and loaded with money and full of vinegar."

The last couple times I'd been to Mohawk, we'd ended up drinking and playing the horses with Smooth and company in Trip's bar. Untemeyer was getting too old to make his usual rounds, so he set up shop permanently at Trip's after his noon hour at the Mohawk Grill. Most of his action came from Smooth's cronies and they set him up in a comfortable booth where he could write out his slips and complain about his bad back, which he blamed on having been incarcerated and left to rot for nearly three hours in the Mohawk jail by Smooth's inefficiency in getting him sprung.

It took a while, but it finally dawned on me that my father's association with this new younger crowd (Untemeyer excepted) signaled a significant change in him. From the time I was a boy, I had always been vaguely aware that there wasn't much that happened in Mohawk that my father didn't have a line on. If it was shady, he probably knew all about it, who was involved, what the risks were. As often as not, he'd been asked if he wanted in, or what he thought of the whole deal. Frequently he'd be drawn aside by somebody who slid into Harry's with an air of wished-for invisibility and engaged my father in an urgent, voices-lowered conversation. My sense of things was that my father seldom engaged in anything more serious than filling up at a closed gas station, or driving a car with a full trunk from one place to another, or engaging the fat cop on the corner in a conversation to keep him where he was instead of ambling up the street where somebody would just as soon he not be for another twenty minutes. But he was thought to be savvy by Mohawk's dumber petty criminals, and they consulted him the way one consults a stock broker. Often their conversations ended with my father saying, "Not if it was me, I wouldn't."

But the days when not much got past him were gone, as I discovered with respect to Alan Taggart, who was one of the semiregulars in Trip's and who was so obviously a dealer that I was astonished that my father hadn't tumbled to the fact. Unless of course he had, and simply wasn't sharing the knowledge with me. He'd always considered me a bit slow, permanently impaired by my mother's ethics and my early days as an altar boy. But I don't think this was the case, at least with regard to Alan Taggart, whose wealth my father had explained to me as having been inherited. The reason I'm so certain on this point is that one afternoon, after I'd walked in on a bathroom transaction, Smooth asked me not to mention it to my father. "He's death on recreational narcotics," Smooth explained conspiratorially, as if this were the one fault he could find with my father's otherwise sterling character.

What concerned me most about my father's new friends, though they may have been, as he said, "all good guys," according to the rather amorphous standards by which good guys are credentialed, was that I suspected that he was drawn to them not so much because they were mildly disreputable, which would have been in character, as because they were all successful. He had never buddied with lawyers, contractors, and real estate people before, and he seemed to be discovering, late in life, that he enjoyed the company of men whose manners and dress and wit would have made him feel awkward or even inadequate when he was younger. I remembered with some embarrassment the way he had behaved around Jack Ward, with whom he had served in the war, where social distinctions disappeared under the constant assault of threatened annihilation and the absolute need for competence. There was nothing like fear to make democracy real. But my father must have learned almost immediately after returning from Germany that the democracy he had fought to preserve was class-riddled. His attempts at jovial camaraderie with Jack Ward, as I now recalled them, had been closer to obsequious fawning.

Nor was this all. I often suspected that another motive in cultivating these new friends was myself. My father introduced each new person who came into Trip's according to his profession— pediatrician, insurance salesman, chiropractor (he held no grudge against the chiropractor who had failed to cure his lung cancer), dentist. His son was a professional and, therefore, must be provided with professional acquaintances during his visits. Five years earlier, such behavior would have been entirely out of character for my father, who went into his lawyer diatribe, the one he'd so often directed against F. William Peterson, at the slightest provocation. But no more. How could he, with Boyle seated two stools down, and Sam Hall the only working stiff in the joint.

When we got downtown, my father parked Smooth's Lincoln across from the Mohawk Grill (Smooth had his office two doors down, on Main) and we crossed the street. The diner was the only establishment the length of the street that was open, but for some reason a young woman was coming toward us from the direction of the Four Corners. She was pushing an unhappy infant in a tattered stroller and had two small grubby children in tow. At first I did not recognize Claude Schwartz's wife, though she had not changed significantly in either looks or expression.

When I stopped to say hello—I wouldn't have, except I feared she had recognized me too—my father went on into the diner, leaving the two of us in the street with the crying infant and the two quiet, staring, older children.

"You know what he done," the girl said, as if she meant to suggest that Claude, in abandoning them, had been acting on my explicit instructions.

I said I had heard and felt myself flush, perhaps because of the fact that if Claude *had* asked my opinion, I might very well have given this counsel.

"I knew he wasn't no good," she said. "His own mother says so. He caught me on the rebound or it never would have happened."

I resisted the impulse to ask her what she had been on the rebound from, for she was, I'm sorry to say, the most physically repulsive young woman I'd ever met, the kind any sensible man would flee from before he'd made any sad-eyed, hopeful kids to be drawn along in her awful wake.

"You ever see the weasel, do me a favor and give him a message for me," she began, but I held up my hand and said that I wasn't so great about remembering messages and that I doubted I'd be running into Claude.

Inside, my father had already ordered by the time I slid onto the stool next to him. "Who's she?" he wanted to know. When I told him, he nodded. "How'd you like to wake up next to that for the rest of your life?"

For some reason, despite my aversion to her, I felt an odd impulse to defend Lisa Schwartz, though I didn't know why or even how. And when Harry came over and asked me what I wanted, I didn't know the answer to that either.

During the long months of my father's chemotherapy, I made no mention to him of Leigh's pregnancy. If he thought it strange that she never came with me to Mohawk, he never said so. After all, he had just the small one-bedroom, and the couch I slept on in the living room was not a convertible sofa, like all the old Sam Hall couches had been. He may even have concluded that my visits were selfishly motivated. Most of the men he knew—indeed, most of the men he'd known all his life—had learned to prefer the company of men after they were married, and many of them had elevated to an art form the process of not going home until they were good and ready. Whenever the phone rang behind the bar in Mohawk gin mills, a motley chorus—"I'm not here," "I left ten minutes ago," "You ain't seen me in weeks"—went up along the bar. It's entirely possible that my father interpreted my always arriving alone as evidence that I was training Leigh right, the way he wished he'd trained my mother.

And, in fact, there *was* an element of selfishness to my frequent weekends in Mohawk. Leigh and I did fairly well during the week. She was still working and she headed uptown early in the morning, leaving the apartment quietly, so as not to wake me. I habitually read late into the night, rose late in the morning, arriving uptown in time for luncheon meetings with writers and marketing people and other editors. Then I typically worked at the office until nine or ten at night, when Leigh and I would share a late supper, the day's anecdotes and outrages, and, even now, frequently, our bed. The crowded day was what Leigh seemed to need, and I missed her far too much during that day to spend what little time we had in the evenings quarreling.

Weekends were different, though. I looked forward to them, but they almost never turned out well. With forty-eight uninterrupted hours before us, it always seemed to me that Leigh might be persuaded to change her mind by Monday morning. She must have feared the same thing, because come Friday evening she'd grow more distant, superficially affectionate, it seemed to me, without opening herself to the possibility of real passion. During the week, when she knew I wasn't foolish enough to think I could alter her resolve in an hour or two, she'd kiss me open-mouthed, drawing me eagerly toward our bed where she would receive and return my affections almost desperately, but Saturday night always found her more playful than loving, and her lips were then dry and cool. When I suggested we go someplace for the weekend, she always said, "Not a chance, pal. You think I don't know what you're up to?"

In fact, it was often Leigh who encouraged me to visit my father in Mohawk as an alternative to the certain unpleasantness of a weekend in the city, where every suggestion I made—a movie, dinner at one of our favorite restaurants, even some jazz on the stereo—was likely to be interpreted as my crossing over some invisible boundary she had staked out without telling me. "I don't see why you have to act this way," I told her. "You're behaving like a seventeen-year-old playing virgin the morning after. You've already given me all there is to give. This holding back, this pretending you don't love me when it suits your purpose is plain silly."

I shared exactly none of this with my father, of course. There were plenty of things in the world that he was pretty shrewd about, but he was even more helpless and confused around women than I. Neither my mother nor Eileen had been exactly complicated, but he'd shaken his head over the two of them as if comprehending what they wanted from him required a minute understanding of astrophysics. Perhaps Leigh was not so much more complex, but she seemed so to me, and I wasn't about to betray my confusion to a man who could only deepen it, not when he seemed to believe I had things pretty well in hand.

And so, every other weekend, or every third one, depending on his condition after the most recent treatments and how well he'd recovered from their debilitating effects, I went to Mohawk to see my father. Miraculously, throughout the strong chemotherapy, he kept most of his wiry hair, though he claimed his shower drain was full every day. The third or fourth day after his treatment he'd start eating again, even if it was only an apple at first, his appetite improving daily until it was time to go back to the hospital. Sometimes, in the middle of a meal, however, he would break out in a cold sweat and begin to shake. The cure for that was a cold beer. He couldn't stand the taste of the first one, but after that he'd be all right. He was under strict orders not to drink, of course, but he said that half the time he neither drank nor wanted to. Besides, beer wasn't really drinking anyway. According to his doctors, the tumor on his lung was shrinking, and that was the main thing. "You can't give up every damn thing and still call it living, right?" he said, nudging me. Then, when I didn't respond, "Right?"

"Whatever," I told him.

Then he'd put his thin arm on the bar, hand open. "Wanna arm-wrestle?"

"No."

"Good," he said. "This arm is about the only thing I got that still works, and it'd be just like you to break it."

"Your mouth still works," I said.

He decided to ignore me. "Besides," he went on, "if I ever beat you, it'd be pretty embarrassing, getting your ass kicked by a man with about two weeks to live."

The Christmas holidays found me in New York by myself. Leigh flew to Colorado to be with her mother, who was living alone in the large family house, Leigh's father having divorced her and remarried two years before, relocating in Seattle. I had known for some time that her father was part of what was not right between us. She'd been even more devastated than her mother to learn that for many years he had carried on a secret affair with a woman known to both her mother and herself, and who had often been a guest in their home. Leigh's own husband had been a good deal less discreet in his philandering, and I think she gave far less thought to him and what he'd done to her directly than to her father and his indirect breach of faith. The old man had not only fooled her but shaken her faith in her own judgment at a time when she could have used a little reinforcement. (The revelations of her husband's and her father's betrayals had virtually coincided.) New York was not the best place in which to search for lost faith.

I hated to see her go to Colorado for the holidays because I was very afraid she would not come back. She and her mother, who had never been close, were lately drawn together by the similarity of their misfortune—their status as victims—and I feared that the older woman's resignation and withdrawal, however understandable, would attract Leigh as a posture for coping. She had begun to talk of quitting her job instead of taking the maternity leave she was entitled to, and going someplace where you could breath the air. The morning I accompanied her to La Guardia I began to prepare myself for the phone call that seemed inevitable. Her voice would be more distant than Colorado when she assured me that I wouldn't have to do anything, that she'd already called the mover, that a date had been fixed for the van if I would just gather her things in some out-of-the-way place so they could be got at. I wouldn't even have to miss work.

This was the call I was expecting when the phone rang and my father's voice, much closer than Colorado, crackled on the line. "Merry Christmas," he said. "I didn't expect you to be home. How come you aren't visiting your mother?"

"Because she lives in California," I said. "That and about a hundred other reasons."

"I know a few of them," he said. "You want to run up for a day or two?"

I didn't, really. The cumulative effect of my recent weekends in Mohawk, as well as of leaving my mind there when I returned to the city, was that I was behind in my work. With the city shut down for the holidays, I had thought to get caught up. At least a little.

"I could," I told my father. "Maybe the week between Christmas and New Year's, if that's all right." I was already thinking of possible excuses to use later to put the visit off until after the first of the year.

"Doesn't matter now," he said. "I'm all done."

My chest knotted up like a fist. "What do you mean?"

"No more," he said, as if he imagined that this equally ambiguous phrase cleared matters up. When I didn't say anything, he finally added, "I'm cured. You don't have to act so surprised. I never promised to die. I just figured I would, that's all."

I still couldn't find words. The last time I'd spoken to him he had been discouraged. The size of the tumor had been reduced, but he had lost another five pounds, his blood count was off, his skin even more jaundiced. His doctor had balled him out too, told him to get serious, that he could only safely administer two more treatments without ensuring the destruction of all his healthy organs. He had to start eating whether he felt like it or not. Eat and exercise and nothing else, or it was all for nothing.

"The tumor's shrunk?" I finally managed.

"Not shrunk" he said. "Gone."

"That's astonishing."

"That's what I said. I said are you sure you got the right chart, Doc. I'm a sick man. He said not anymore. Showed me the X ray and everything. Last couple treatments did the trick, apparently. I'm clean as a whistle. He says go home and don't smoke and you might live to be a hundred."

Right then, I think I believed he would. Almost incredibly, it seemed he had beaten the odds again. If Sam Hall had a specialty, that was it. I remembered the rack of pool he'd shot against the skinny kid in the thin t-shirt, coaxing his far superior opponent into a scratch off the eight. Then there was the afternoon he had arm-wrestled Drew Littler on the kitchen table, putting all two hundred and fifty pounds of raw youth flat on his back. Not to mention Normandy, the survival of which was surely the greatest trick of all. What other name was there for it? Not luck. Not skill. Not even craft, exactly, because craft was something you could call upon routinely, whereas my father was able to summon whatever it was that he sometimes summoned only when the situation was seemingly hopeless. Only then could he be counted on to find the combination. I remembered his old promise to Eileen, that he'd outlive everybody and bury her under Nathan Littler's obelisk.

"You don't have to worry, though," he said. "I won't live to be a hundred."

"It's fine with me if you do," I told him. "Be two hundred."

"Your dolly there?"

"Yes," I said before I could think, responding to a reflex that did not want to admit to him that she was gone, maybe for good.

"Put her on a minute."

"She's out . . . Christmas shopping actually."

"Then why'd you say she was there?"

"I meant here in the city."

"Where the hell else would she be?"

"Right," I said. "I'm really glad about the news, Dad. I can't believe it."

"Me either," he said. "The only problem is the last treatment did something to my eyes. I suddenly can't see worth a shit."

"What's your doctor say?"

"New glasses. Thick ones. I'd get them except things are a little tight right now . . ."

"Listen," I said. "Would a couple hundred help?"

"You could if you wanted," he said. I could see him shrugging on the other end of the line. "I don't need them, really. There's nothing in this town worth looking at, and not a goddamn thing I haven't already seen a hundred times more than I wanted to."

So we left it that I'd send a check in the morning, not because he needed it, or because he wanted me to, but because I insisted. When we hung up, I discovered that instead of feeling elation, I was mildly, maybe even more than mildly, irritated with him. At first I thought it was because of the way he'd started out, saying he was "all done," a phrase even my father must have realized invited the wrong interpretation. Then I thought maybe it was the business about the glasses, his stubborn unwillingness to accept help, his insistence that everybody understand that any consideration or concern or affection shown him was done purely for the edification of the giver. But the annoyance went even deeper, and I knew it as I stared out the apartment window and up into the darkening New York sky. My reflection in the glass allowed me a brief, horrible glance at what lay at the heart of things. Strangely enough, I'd been thinking about it for days, ever since

I'd gone with Leigh to the airport and put her on the plane. What I'd been denying, even as I worried it like a scab, was the possibility that my father was the reason I was losing Leigh. I had made a terrible mistake, it occurred to me, in telling her all about him, of painting his portrait so vividly, of allowing her extended conversations with him on the phone. And I realized how grateful I was that circumstances had prevented their actual meeting. Had they done so, had Leigh been able to see my father and me standing shoulder to shoulder, she would at that moment have understood me, who I was, where I came from, all the things that—it now came home to me—I had been carefully concealing from her.

In his own way my father had both understood and expressed what I'd been feeling in that long moment of silence that had followed the news of his cure. I was afraid that he would live to be a hundred.

44

I didn't go to Mohawk the week between Christmas and New Year's, nor the week after that. To my surprise, Leigh called and said she was returning to the city the day before New Year's. On the phone she sounded depressed, but refused to talk about her stay in Colorado. At the time I concluded that her mother must have been lurking nearby. I didn't care, really. I was too happy to discover that Leigh was returning a week early—that she was returning at all—to press for details.

At La Guardia, she seemed happy to see me and she did not object when I told her I'd made reservations for a late dinner that night. I had in mind that we would see the new year in quietly, privately. She looked tired though, and I insisted she take a nap when we got back to the apartment. She slept the rest of the afternoon and well into the evening. I didn't go in until it was time to dress or miss our reservation, and I found her there in the semidark, awake and thoughtful, and again, it seemed, glad to see me. We walked to the restaurant through wet, slow-motion snow that fell straight down and melted on impact everywhere except along the cast iron fences and window gratings. On the way Leigh told me she'd been to see a gynecologist in Denver and that it was his opinion that we'd miscalculated—she was nearly a month farther along than we'd thought, which explained a lot. February now, not March. In fact, she was noticeably larger, and she was carrying our child right out in front now, though still high. Perhaps because I could tell that it mattered to Leigh, I said I didn't see what difference it made that we'd miscalculated, except that she was that much closer to the end of her discomfort. I knew her thinking though, and did not, for once, make matters worse by proposing again. That she had come back filled me with hope, and I didn't want to ruin New Year's Eve.

The quiet restaurant I'd chosen turned out to be anything but quiet, and the dark corner table I'd envisioned turned out to be in the center of the dining room. The place was still hopping at ten o'clock. People we didn't know stopped to congratulate us on Leigh's condition. We were sent a bottle of champagne by an elderly couple in the corner booth I'd hoped for, along with instructions that I was to drink most of it.

I was worried about Leigh, but I shouldn't have been, because she did fine, as if she'd discovered that the attentions she'd been trying to avoid were not to be feared after all. We had a good meal and everyone seemed to understand when we decided to leave ten minutes before the new year's arrival. We were escorted to the door by a dozen or so revelers and well-wishers, including the elderly couple who'd sent over the champagne. They offered to share a taxi with us, which we politely declined, explaining that we lived only a few blocks away. It had stopped snowing by then and as we walked slowly along the dusted sidewalks we listened to the mixed sounds of several parties cascading down from the apartments above.

And so the new year was ushered in without much help from Leigh and me. The clock above the refrigerator said five after midnight when we came in, and we undressed and climbed into bed without reference to the future and without making a single resolution, together or individually regarding it. When the lights were out, Leigh began to cry, and I let her until she felt better or, failing that, felt like stopping. "She's a horrible woman," Leigh said finally. "Small and mean-spirited and self-centered. I don't blame Daddy a bit."

"Well . . ." I began.

"Don't," she said. "I don't want to be comforted. I just want you to know that I'm just like her. If you marry me, I'll probably end up driving you to somebody else, and then I'll blame you for it and so will everybody. You'll even blame yourself."

"What do you want?" I said. "Do you want me to promise not to blame myself?"

She thought about it. "I don't want to be my mother. I want to be who I want to be."

"Fine," I said, stroking her hair. "Your wish is granted."

I heard the first ring as I stepped into the shower, but Leigh was there to answer it, so I climbed in anyway. She had started her maternity leave the last week in January to wait out the final few weeks in our warm apartment. It was now the first week of February and we were in the middle of the longest stretch of subzero weather since they'd started keeping records. It was the kind of demoralizing cold that I imagined had caused my grandfather to capitalize "Winter."

Leigh slid the shower door open partway and peeked in. "Hello there."

"Hello," I said.

"You know anybody named Norm? Sounds like long distance."

I started to say no, then realized who it was and got out of the shower.

"You know where the Albany VA is?" Wussy's voice crackled in the receiver.

I said I did.

"Then you better get on up there."

I sat down. "Not again?"

"Everywhere, this time. Or so I hear. Sorry, Sam's Kid. I figured you'd want to know."

The oxygen mask that covered my father's nose and mouth clouded, then cleared, then clouded again, tracking his sleeping respiration. His face was gaunt and yellow and rich with graying stubble. Even now he had most of his hair, though it had become patchy in the month or so since he'd called to tell me he was cured. The most dramatic change was in his body, which now occasioned little more than a ripple beneath the covers of the hospital bed. The arm that was connected to the I.V. was thin and dry and jaundiced. According to the nurse, he would be waking up soon when the pain killer he'd been given that morning began to wear off.

On the wall opposite his bed was a print that depicted a New England winter. In the foreground a horse-drawn wagon was emerging from a covered bridge, below which stick figures were skating on the frozen river. I don't know how long I'd been studying it when my father said, "That's some goddamn picture, isn't it?"

He'd removed the oxygen mask so he could speak, but he immediately replaced it when he finished. He was looking at the painting as if it genuinely consumed his interest.

"See how it's on . . . the left side of the road?" he said. "The wagon? In a few . . . minutes it'll be over there . . . on the right side . . . wait . . . you'll see."

He could only get out a few words before breaking off, gulping oxygen. After catching his breath though, he inched like a crab toward a sitting position. When I saw what he was trying to do, I stood to help, but he waved me off and finally accomplished the design himself. The effort cost him his breath again and it was a while before he spoke. Finally, he said, "Who blabbed?"

"Smooth called," I said, lying instinctively to protect Wussy, realizing even as I spoke that there was no reason to protect anybody from Sam Hall's wrath. Not anymore.

"Figures," he said, then thought about it. "How'd he get your number?"

I said I was in the book, and that seemed to satisfy him.

"Well," he said. "This is about it, I'm afraid."

"They lied to you, didn't they," I said.

He shrugged, closed his eyes sluggishly, opened them again. "That's all right . . . I never believed them . . . anyway . . . when you still got it . . . you know."

"You might have told me."

He looked at me. "What for?"

"Because I'm your son," I said, almost adding, "because I love you."

"So . . . you had a month without . . . any headaches . . . my treat."

"I shouldn't have believed you. I should have guessed."

"You never . . . could tell when I was lying," he said, grinning weakly, in reference to our old game. "How's your dolly?"

"Good," I said.

"You figure you'll marry her."

"Yes," I said.

"Good," he said. "You need somebody to . . . look after you . . . I never did, myself."

"She's a good girl," I said.

"Seems like it," he said. "Don't bring her . . . here . . . I'd like to meet her but . . ." He looked away, in the general direction of the hall, which was brightly lit, in contrast to the perpetual dusk of the room.

"See my new cheaters?" he said, spying them on the bedstand and handing them to me.

I tried them on, made a face, handed them back to him.

"New apartment . . . new glasses . . . new television . . . new furniture . . . old everything else. Smooth asks you . . . to pay for anything . . . tell him where to get off."

"I will."

Neither of us said anything for a minute, but I could tell he was worried about the way he was leaving things.

"Do me a favor," he said finally, taking off the oxygen mask and tossing it on the bed.

"Sure," I said, figuring that he was going to ask me to adjust the bed or something.

"Take me home," he said. "To hell with this place."

I blinked.

But he'd swung his thin legs over the side of the bed and was pointing to the small closet where his clothes hung.

I stood, but made no move to get them. "Dad," I said. "You can't. You'd never make it. *We'd* never make it."

"Just . . . do like I say for once," he said.

And then he stood up.

Seeing him do it filled me with awe. There was absolutely nothing left of him, you see. The nurses would tell me later that he had not eaten in days. For a week he'd politely pushed the tray away when it was set in front of him, unless there was ice cream, which tasted good to him, for some reason. Then one night he'd seen they were serving something he remembered liking and was for some reason half hungry. He thought he'd try a little, provided they'd hold the gravy, which he never could eat even when he was healthy. But despite his plea it had come smothered with gravy, and he'd picked up the dish and tossed it out into the hall. When the tough head nurse came in and read him the riot act, he'd told her from now on they could serve the food any goddamn way they liked, because he wasn't going to eat it anyway.

"Have you ever been force-fed, Mr. Hall?" the nurse had asked him.

"Have you ever had a spoon shoved up your ass?" he'd replied. "Sideways?"

And the next night when he didn't eat dinner he had the spoon in his hand when the nurse came in. She'd taken one look, shaken her head, and retreated, returning for the tray and the spoon after he'd fallen asleep. He hadn't eaten since.

So when he stood up and made clear to me that it was his intention to get dressed, with my help or without it, I did what I have never regretted doing. I got him his clothes and helped him into them. There weren't enough holes in his belt, so we had to tie it in a knot to keep his pants up. He swam in everything else, too, and by the time we were finished, he looked like nothing so much as a pile of discarded clothing awaiting a Salvation Army truck.

"Now," he said. "Go steal me a wheelchair . . . strap that mask on before you leave."

And so I did, suddenly right in the spirit of things, as if by sneaking out of the hospital, we could sneak away from the disease. It was an ability he had right to the end, to involve me in any lunacy, by the sheer force of his will. So off I went in search of a wheelchair, as instructed, delighted to be of service, wondering only vaguely if I was doing something I could be prosecuted for later. It took me about five minutes to locate a wheelchair on an adjacent ward. By the time I returned with it, he had leaned back against the wall to rest, his booted feet up on the bed in front of him.

He was fast asleep, the only visible sign of life the clouding, then clearing of his oxygen mask. He slept peacefully there until a nurse, the same one he'd asked about the spoon, came in, stopped dead in her tracks, assessed the situation at a glance and began undressing him. She was nearly finished when he woke up.

"You again," he said.

"Me again," she admitted.

"This is my son," he said. "He's all right . . . not like his old man."

"He looks just like you," she said.

When she was gone, my father pointed toward the painting on the wall. "See?" he said. "Now the wagon's on the left."

"Yes," I said. "It is."

"How'd he do that?" my father wanted to know, as if he'd die a happy man if I could explain it to him. I couldn't tell whether he meant the artist or the man driving the wagon, and I hadn't the heart to tell him that the wagon had been on the left side of the road all along, that it hadn't moved since the last time we'd looked at it, that the picture was just a cheap print, unworthy of his attention when there were so many things to say, things that wouldn't get said if we didn't say them soon.

But we sat there, my father and I, and stared at the wagon and the old covered bridge and the snow and the ice skaters and the frozen river, as if these were at the very heart of things, and had been forever.

EPILOGUE

At the airport I rented a car and took it onto the Thruway to avoid Albany, a gray city on the best of days, and this was not the best of days.

The VA was on the other side of town at the end of a long treeless drive, a tall building, stark and massive and undeniable as death. I parked the rental at the base of a recently plowed mountain of dingy snow and went inside. I'd been told I would have trouble locating room 135, but it was right where it should have been. A woman with a name plate that corresponded to what I had jotted down the morning before when the call came telling me of Sam Hall's death was standing in the office doorway, carrying on a conversation with another woman in full retreat down the corridor. "Did you get through to North Carolina?"

The woman slowed, as if on an invisible leash, but continued to strain in the direction she was heading. "I got the sister-in-law. The brother is supposed to call when he gets home from work. I have my doubts."

"Get some ice on the eyes just in case," said my woman, who became aware of me in midsentence.

"Nice job you've got," I said.

"It's not as bad as it sounds," she said, risking a half smile.

"Couldn't be," I said, introducing myself.

"Oh," she said seriously. "Mr. Hall."

For some reason I remembered a gag used by good ole boys and politicians. "No, Mr. Hall's my father. My name's Ned." I almost used it.

The woman's office was little more than a carrel with a small metal desk along one wall and several hundred brown packages, all one size, stacked all the way to the ceiling in one corner. "I'm afraid I'm going to have to ask you to sign a release," she said. "We still can't find the anatomical gift form."

I read the first sentence of the release and signed.

"According to your father, there was another copy. Do you think you could locate it?" she said, as if she suspected, now that she thought about it, that my signature wasn't likely to hold up.

"I'll try."

"That's all any of us can do," she said, without a trace of humor. "Here's a list of the items you can pick up downstairs. And you get a flag, of course."

While I scanned the short itemized list—bathrobe, slippers, pajamas, wallet, button-down shirt, one pair of brown slacks, one pair of shorts, one pair of socks, one pair black shoes, one pair black overshoes, one overcoat, one wool cap—she stapled several onionskin documents to the inside of a manila folder, then got up and handed me one of the brown packages from the middle of the stack. It was surprisingly heavy.

"What about his glasses?" I said.

She looked at the list over my shoulder.

"I don't see any reference to eyeglasses."

"They were new. He'd just bought them."

"There's no reference here . . . I could call up to the ward . . ."

I said I didn't see any reason to.

She studied my signatures, the one on the itemized personal effects sheet, the other on the consent form, as if to make sure they matched. "This will make things go more smoothly. Your father was a generous man. You should know that he could be with us anywhere from three months to two years."

"I'll try not to think about it."

"The research is important . . ."

I said I didn't doubt that.

"We all thought a great deal of your father," she said.

I put the flag under my arm and stood up. "You knew him?"

"No," she said. "That is, not personally."

On the phone my mother had said it was a terrible, terrible shame. This was not in reference to Sam Hall's death, but rather its timing. Isn't it always the way, she wanted to know, her voice full of wonder, that at this time when we were all anticipating

LIFE, when life was expected any day, any MINUTE, for heaven's sake, that I'd be required to go to Mohawk and attend to the details of my father's departure. She was sure that there would be endless details, given the clutter of my father's existence: unplanned funeral arrangements, dealings with people he'd borrowed money from, tedious conversations with the sort of people he knew. Well, at least it wasn't like he and I had been inseparable, she went on, by which she didn't mean that I didn't love him or wouldn't feel his loss. Of course I would. After all, I was a dutiful son, but what she meant was, well, we were different and all those years when he wasn't around, when he chose not to be, well, ironically, maybe it was just as well. She would never forget the devastation she'd felt when her own father died, and Lord knew she wouldn't wish that on me. Did I want to say hello to Will? Wouldn't you think they'd been best friends? she wanted to know. I should see the look on his face.

From the VA I drove to Mohawk, the slender brown package of my father's possessions on the front seat of the rental car with me, trying not to think about my mother, her insistence that I keep things in perspective ("Let's talk about something cheerful! How's our girl Leigh? I think if that baby doesn't get here before the weekend, I'll *die,* honestly!").

I parked out back of the McKinley Luxury Apartments next to my father's pale yellow Subaru. It was still his, I would learn later. He hadn't had money for repairs and didn't want to admit to that. Didn't want me making offers.

When I went around front, I found Wussy sitting under the stone arch eating a sandwich. "Sam's Kid," he said, patting the stone step next to him.

"Well," I said, accepting his invitation to join him. The freakish February weather had gone from subzero to low fifties in a week, but the stone steps were still cold.

"Right," Wussy said. "Last week it was Untemeyer."

"No kidding," I said. I'd always considered the bookie to be immortal. Even more than Sam Hall.

"Died sitting up straight at the Mohawk Grill. Nobody noticed for a hell of a while. Fortunately, his stool was a little off balance and he eventually got turned around so he was staring out the

back door, which was unnatural for Meyer. He faced front for
about eighty-five years."

"You going over to Mike's?" I said.

"Not me, Sam's Kid. I'm staying home where it's safe."

I wished I didn't have to go myself. Mike was closing The Elms
at five, then holding there in the lounge what he referred to over
the phone as a "send-off" in Sam Hall's honor. I had an idea Irma
was behind this, but I could have been wrong. The gathering
would be by informal invitation. "Jesus Christ," Mike said. "We
gotta do something, even if it's wrong."

I knew how he felt. One of the last things my father had made
me promise was that there'd be no funeral, no mass, no priest
making up lies about him from a pulpit. I'd said sure, whatever
he wanted, not thinking I'd have any trouble keeping such a
promise. After all, who'd have expected Sam Hall to exit life by
way of the altar? He hadn't been inside a church in thirty years.
Besides, there wasn't even going to be a body—Albany Medical
had dibs on that for up to two years. But now, like Mike, I couldn't
help thinking that we should do something, whether my father
had wanted it or not. So I'd gone along with a "send-off" at The
Elms. At least that way there was something to tell people who
called wanting to know when and where the services were going
to be.

The only trouble was that now, having agreed, I didn't feel up
to it. I even gave passing consideration to the idea of just slipping
quietly out of town. It was doubtful I'd ever return to Mohawk
after today, doubtful too that I'd even be missed among my father's cronies, most of whom had to be reminded who I was when
we met on the street. The send-off looked to be the kind of obligation I could default on without meaningful consequence.

"I wish I could get out of going myself," I confessed to Wussy,
thinking again of the semilegitimate justifications I might marshal
in my own defense. Leigh had been having false labor pains for
over a week. I could easily pretend to have received an urgent
call. I could probably even talk Wussy into making my apologies
for me. Perhaps because it would have been so easy, I decided not
to act on the impulse.

Wussy finished his sandwich and wadded up the cellophane.
"You got here a couple minutes earlier I'd've shared that with
you," he said. "Now you'll have to get your own."

"I need to go inside," I told him. "The VA lost a form he signed.

He must have figured they would and kept a copy. They can't find his new glasses either."

"I happen to have a key," he said, taking it off his chain.

I started to ask why, then intuited the situation. They had not made up, Wussy and my father. If Wussy had a key, he had gotten it from Smooth, a master key, probably, that would get him into the other apartments, so he could do the work of the resident manager.

We went inside the foyer and I inserted the key into the door of my father's apartment, formerly the kindergarten of McKinley School. "I'll be outside here if you need anything," Wussy said, standing in the doorway as if he weren't sure he'd been invited to follow. In fact, I didn't think I could take any company. Not even his. I said I wouldn't be long.

"You been down to the bank yet?"

I said I hadn't. A week earlier my father had given me a check for just over two hundred dollars and made me promise to cash it before the bank froze his account. He was adamant that the electric company not get his last dime. Either Wussy knew about this too, or had guessed.

"There isn't much," I told him, taking the check out of my wallet. "I was going to leave it there."

"You must not believe in ghosts," Wussy said.

"I don't really want the money," I said. "I doubt I'm even entitled to it."

"It's up to you, Sam's Kid," Wussy said. "Give it to Eileen. Sam Hall was a prince compared to the little moron she ended up marrying. If women didn't always want to save people, they'd be perfect."

I handed him the check, which my father had predated and signed, but otherwise left blank. "I'll leave it to your discretion," I said. I almost suggested he keep it himself, since he'd no doubt earned it and a good deal besides during the last few weeks and down through the years, but I didn't want to risk insulting his friendship. We looked around at my father's apartment, Wussy still on the threshold.

It took me all of two seconds to locate the other copy of the anatomical gift. In a last-minute uncharacteristic fit of organization, he'd left everything important in his upper righthand dresser drawer. Wussy, or somebody, had piled his three weeks' worth of accumulated mail right there under the mirror, so I went through it to make sure there wasn't anything I'd need later. Most of it was junk. I opened an insurance company envelope marked IMPORTANT, which contained a letter stating that because my father had had no accidents or speeding tickets for the past five years, he was now eligible for insurance outside the risk pool, at considerably reduced rates.

By the time I was finished, Wussy had returned from the bank. "You sure you don't want this," he said.

"Very sure."

We shook hands there on the schoolhouse steps.

"He was my friend, Ned," Wussy said. And then he invited me to come up sometime so we could go fishing. "I don't know about anymore," he said. "But you used to be a good patient fisherman."

Before going over to The Elms, I drove to Fonda and onto the small bridge that spanned the Mohawk River. There was one other thing I had discovered in the righthand drawer of my father's dresser—a .38 caliber revolver purchased, no doubt, as a hedge against the final ravages of the disease. It was this, I now realized, that he had wanted me to take him home to that afternoon almost three weeks before. I've never been able to resolve in my own mind whether or not he would have done it, and I couldn't that February afternoon as I stood on the bridge above the Mohawk River. If he had been able to do it, he'd have spared himself two senseless operations during those final weeks, and God only knew how many indignities, the last of which was an heroic attempt to resuscitate him, in direct violation of the written instructions he'd placed on his bedstand and which, now, were neatly folded somewhere in the same unmarked envelope that contained the anatomical gift he'd made of his remains.

But I cannot fault the doctors. In my own way, I too was unable to execute his wishes. He'd begged me before I left that afternoon when he'd tried to go home to stay away from the hospital, now that it was just a matter of time. But I couldn't, and toward the end I saw in his eyes each time that I appeared beside his bed that he was glad to see me, and scared as hell of dying alone. Which he ended up doing anyway.

The quirky February warm spell had thawed patches near the center of the icebound river where black water could be seen rolling swiftly, even in the late afternoon dusk. Spring, it occurred to me, was the season my grandfather had left out of his scheme of things, his personal credo.

The river received the handgun without a splash and hurried it deep out of sight, like a terrible thought. I didn't worry about its surfacing somewhere and causing harm. The Mohawk never surrendered her dead.

I didn't hurry back from Fonda, though my errand there had made me late. It was nearly six, and I'd told Mike I'd be at The Elms around five to help welcome my father's friends. Still, I was not prepared for what I saw when I rounded the curve and the restaurant came into view. The parking lot was full, and cars lined both sides of the two-lane blacktop for a quarter of a mile. My first errant conclusion was that Mike's plan to close the restaurant had run amuck. He'd forgotten some local festivity, the aftermath of which was now being felt at the restaurant. There had been a rush, too many expectant diners to turn away. I tried to think what festivity it might be in the middle of February in Mohawk as I weaved my way through the sea of cars and parked Sam Hall fashion, one wheel up a stump. My headlights caught Tree with his baggy pants down around his ankles, peeing on the side of a car that I doubted, from its overall excellent condition, could be his. The expression on his face was one of pure relief. "The l-l-line's a f-f-fucking mile long in there," he said when I got out.

That explained why he was peeing in the parking lot, but much was still shrouded in mystery, like why he'd chosen to pee on the door of the car and not its tire, and even more interestingly, why he'd found it necessary to drop his trousers altogether instead of simply unzipping.

"Don't those have a fly?" I said when he bent down to pull them up.

"Of course," he said, as if I'd insulted him. He might not be rich, but at least he could afford pants with zippers. When he'd fastened them at the waist, he pulled a portion of colorful shirttail through the opening to show me, in case I doubted his word. I nodded.

Even the restaurant's entryway was crowded, though I didn't recognize anyone there. Tree took the lead and parted the throng by announcing, "I f-found him. M-make way for S-sammy's boy."

Inside, the first person we ran into was Wussy, who was wearing a sport coat for only the second time in our long association. "Sam's Kid," he said. "I thought you'd got lost."

I grinned at him. I was Sam's Kid again. Demoted after an incredibly brief tenure as my own person. "Have you ever done anything you said you were going to?" I asked him.

"Yup," he said. "I warned your old man I was going to outlive him, for instance. Of course I'm taking your word for the fact that he's dead. I never saw no evidence."

"Neither did I, now that you mention it," I told him.

"Be just like him to turn up," Wussy said.

"Everybody else did," I said, looking around. Both the lounge and the big dining room were packed and noisy, like the evening so many years ago when I'd thought my mother was dead, was so positive, in fact, that it had taken my father and Eileen and F. William Peterson to convince me I was wrong. That recollection, together with Wussy's remark that it would be just like Sam Hall to turn up, engendered an almost overpowering sense that if I turned around quickly I'd see him grinning at me from across the room. And not the Sam Hall from the hospital, reduced almost to nothing by the cancer, but rather the old Sam Hall, in perfect health, who'd sparred with Jack Ward and Mike, and who'd offered on half a dozen occasions to put F. William Peterson on the seat of his pants and occasionally proved that this was no idle threat. Wussy was right; it wasn't like my father to miss this kind of an opportunity for sport, and it took me a moment to shake off my father's almost material presence.

Across the room Mike was passing beer glasses beneath two open taps, then placing them on the bar. I didn't see any money changing hands, nor was the cash register ringing. "Mike's doing an open bar?" I said.

Wussy nodded. "So far. He better stop pretty soon. Roy Heinz just came in, and he can drink a keg all by himself."

"I don't see Eileen."

"She'll be here," Wussy said. "You wait."

I was watching Roy Heinz, who appeared to be searching for something. I couldn't imagine what, given that he'd just arrived. After he'd gone into the dining room, peeked into the kitchen, and checked behind the bar, he came over to where Wussy and I were standing. "Where the hell's Sammy?"

"He died, Roy," Wussy said. "Didn't you hear?"

"But where *is* he?" Roy insisted, looking first at Wussy, then at me.

"No one knows," Wussy said.

Roy Heinz accepted this. "Open bar?" he said.

We told him it was.

"Nice gesture," he said, shaking my hand, apparently having arrived at the erroneous conclusion that I was footing the bill. "Sammy would've liked that. Sammy would always buy a drink."

"You gonna live around here now?" he added hopefully, as if he suspected I might have inherited from my father some liberal, beer-buying gene.

I went over to say hello to Mike as soon as there was an opportunity. "You invite all these people?" I said.

"Twenty or so. The others invited theirselves."

"You've got the whole county here," I said. For the most part, these were not people who normally frequented The Elms. They'd all come to have a look at the place, as they had for Jack Ward's wake at the white jewel house. "I hope you'll let me help out."

Mike waved my offer away good-naturedly. "Sammy and I go way back. This town might as well give up, now." He looked and sounded genuinely pessimistic on the community's behalf.

"We can give him a send-off, anyway," he added.

As people began to come over and introduce themselves to me, I kept thinking about Mike's remark—that Mohawk might as well give up, now that Sam Hall was gone. Given my father's comprehensive lack of garden variety civic obligation, it was a pretty funny observation. But I knew what he meant just the same, and as I looked around the packed restaurant and greeted strangers who wanted to say they'd miss Sam Hall, I was suddenly scared. I wasn't sure I'd be able to make it without him. Here I was, thirty-five years old, having lived more or less independently since leaving Mohawk for the university, a child of my own knocking for admittance at birth's door. I had become, since the two years I'd lived with my father, if not a model of success, at least a model of self-reliance. And yet, right then, as I stood among my father's friends and acquaintances drinking Mike's free beer in Sam Hall's honor, waves of panic as physically tangible as abdominal nausea crashed over me. It wasn't that I needed Sam Hall for anything specific. I'd have been satisfied to know that his consciousness had somehow been saved, that his essence was being

kept alive in some jar on a shelf somewhere, that he continued to
be. Of such fears, I thought as I drank off the rest of my beer in
a gulp, are religions born.

Also alcoholics. Before long, I began to feel the effects of both
the beer and the forced joviality of the crowd. Everybody had a
Sam Hall story to tell me. I was even introduced to the fabled
Angelo, the cop whose favorite pastime had been lying in wait for
my father outside bars so he could ticket him for drunk driving
before he had a chance to get out of first gear. "Your old man was
aces," he told me from beneath heavy, hooded eyes. Then he
repeated the story my father had told me the night I returned to
Mohawk, about how he'd fled down a dark side street, pulled the
convertible over to the curb, slid into the passenger seat, and then
tried to convince Angelo that Untemeyer had been driving. I
gathered that I was supposed to laugh, though Angelo didn't, and
something about his manner suggested that he'd be watching *me*
now that Sam Hall was gone.

My father's favorite cop, little Andy Winkler, who'd been a
paragon of sympathy and understanding the morning he'd discovered us breaking into the Night Owl to retrieve my duffel bag,
was there also, though he informed me sadly that he wasn't a
policeman anymore. A year or two earlier he'd pulled a trucker
over and tried to write him a ticket for doing eighty in a forty-
five-mile zone. When the trucker couldn't talk Andy out of it, he'd
beaten the tiny policeman senseless and drove off leaving Andy
in a ditch. It was not this that discouraged him, however, nor was
it the months he spent in the hospital recuperating. What finally
sent him in search of another line of work was fate. His first week
back in uniform, a trucker who bore an unfortunate resemblance
to the one who had pummeled him was blowing down the highway on the outskirts of town past Andy Winkler's police car,
which was parked, as always, behind a billboard. Andy gave chase
and pulled the semi over. When the trucker got out and saw Andy
Winkler, he made the mistake of grinning, probably at Andy's
size, though Andy concluded, and not without justification, that
the trucker was smiling at the prospect of beating him up. Then
he remembered the advice my father had given him so long ago,
and he took his revolver out and shot the trucker in the thigh to
prevent history repeating itself. But as luck would have it, several
passersby saw the unprovoked attack and so Andy was now finishing up his associate's degree in refrigerator repair at the com-

munity college in Glens Falls. He hadn't been beaten up once since matriculating and he'd discovered an aptitude for ferreting out what was wrong with refrigerators. Plus, he fit in behind them better than anybody in his class. "You miss the excitement though," he confided to me. "Once you've been a cop . . ." he let the thought trail off.

I discovered that talking to Andy Winkler had cheered me up considerably. His good-natured optimism dispelled some of the panic I'd been feeling, and when I spied Eileen Littler across the room, I was glad, though I had been dreading seeing her all day. I had not come to Mohawk for her son's funeral, nor had I spoken to her since his death.

I don't know what I expected, but her appearance gave me a jolt. Always angular, she now looked caved in, somehow, as if she'd finally stopped fighting and agreed to pay some long-deferred judgment. She'd always possessed an admirable vitality, and I found myself wondering whether she'd lost it waiting around for my father, or by finally giving up on him. Or it may have died when her son did. I would never understand Eileen Littler well enough to know for sure, but seeing her now reminded me of her ancestor, the mythical Myrtle Littler, who lent her name to the park, and who died of heartbreak. When Eileen spotted me and came over, though, her hug still had plenty of resolve. Among other things she seemed resolved not to cry in front of her husband, who waited an obedient step behind her and who was not much bigger than Andy Winkler. He looked to be in his mid-fifties and sported a pretty amazing cowlick for a man of his years. For some reason the cowlick grew faster than the rest of his close-cropped hair. Either that or he asked his barber not to trim it. Wussy had intimated that the man was not considered gifted, even by local standards, and a first glance tended to confirm that impression.

"Have you seen the pictures outside?" Eileen said when we broke off our embrace.

"Pictures?"

"In the entry. Look when you get a chance."

She hadn't introduced her husband, and the little man was making exactly no headway angling himself into our immediate vicinity. Apparently Eileen was of the opinion that he wouldn't earn acknowledgment until he'd shown sufficient skill at angling to appear in her peripheral vision.

When I asked her how she was doing, making the question sound as casual as possible, she said so-so, and forced a smile, adding, "All things considered. It's good that I did what I did when I did it, if you know what I mean."

I glanced at the little man again, who had heard his wife's elliptical remark and stopped angling a moment to consider whether it might apply to him.

"I do," I told her.

Then she surprised me by saying, "I was in Albany one day last week and thought of you."

This too was apparently news to her husband, who now had another riddle to ascend before he'd even established a toehold on the first.

"I had a distant relative in the hospital," Eileen went on. "She didn't recognize me at first. I almost didn't recognize her either. I was glad I went anyway."

By now the little man had made it almost into our presence, and his brow was furrowed with perplexity. "How'd she turn out?" he said.

Eileen faced him now as she might have to confront a child who isn't trying. "She died!"

The man reacted as if to a stiff jab. "Well, it wasn't me who killed her," he said.

"Ben," Eileen said, "this is Ned. You can talk to him for five minutes. Then leave him alone."

"Sure, babe," Ben said, checking his watch.

"Mike looks like he could use a hand," Eileen said, and before I could say anything, she'd gathered half a dozen empty glasses and returned them to the bar. I couldn't help smiling to myself, remembering how she'd fallen to at Jack Ward's funeral. And wondering as I often had, what, if anything, Eileen had told her son about his father's identity. My own father, despite his "probablies," didn't seem to know for sure it was Jack Ward, and it seemed doubtful that Eileen would have told Drew. But had she, in a moment of lonely pride and need, told the boy that his father was not someone to be ashamed of, but rather a wealthy, important man? Had the boy picked up and catalogued a detail at a time from her offhanded remarks (It's his father he gets his good looks from, not me) ending up with a composite sketch that Jack Ward fit? Perhaps. But if it *was* Jack Ward, it now occurred to me, then in all probability Eileen had nothing to do with her son's terrible knowledge. It would have been his father, acting on an impulse at once redemptive and self-destructive, who was responsible. I suddenly saw Jack Ward behind the wheel of the first of his shiny new Lincolns pulling into Eileen's steep drive, and encountering there on the porch a boy of six or seven with dark, liquid eyes, a boy who at that age was already wondering. And when he saw this strange, handsome man at the wheel of the shiny car, the boy felt something undeniable tightening inside him. This is the one, they would both have thought at the same precise moment, and when Jack Ward lost his nerve and quickly backed the Lincoln out into the street before the boy's mother saw, he could never have suspected that those dark, liquid eyes had already etched him too deeply, that this boy would remember and follow, years later, just as the boy's mother, inside, could have had no way of knowing that she'd lost her son forever.

This was the way it must have happened, or so it seemed to me that afternoon of my own father's send-off. I watched Eileen as she gathered glasses efficiently, putting right the mess, and thought it a shame that a lifetime of falling to didn't get you more, though it had apparently gotten her Ben, who now, instead of facing me, had turned so as to stand shoulder to shoulder with me, flexing at the knees, as if to suggest that he'd decided in my favor. If a fight broke out, he'd be with me, I could count on it. "Ned . . ." he said thoughtfully. "And what kind of name would that be?"

"Portuguese," I told him, and he nodded, having apparently received precisely the sort of explanation he'd expected, no more bizarre than necessary to explain the facts.

By ten the party had gained considerable momentum. Nobody knew how long Mike was going to give away beer, and so everybody drank as if last call had been announced. Wussy had said goodbye twice and twice returned. Several in-town bars had closed when it became known that Mike was giving beer away, and the cars now lined both sides of the road all the way back into Mohawk, according to Wussy, who deeply regretted having given up his spot in the parking lot only to be relegated to East Jesus upon his return. The crowd had swelled sufficiently to jam not only the entryway and lounge and dining room, but also the large kitchen where Irma had been hiding out until even this inner sanctum was violated. I discovered her sitting puffy-eyed on a tall stool like the one she'd always perched on at the end of the bar in Mike's other place on Main Street. There were about thirty other people in the kitchen too, and one couple had gone into the walk-in cooler, the only place left where they could argue in private. Several others were going through the refrigerator and passing out to their friends whatever looked good. Prime rib bones seemed to be a favorite. "Assholes," Irma said, but made no move to prevent the looting. "What'd he have to go and die for," she asked me. "He's the only man I ever met I couldn't stay mad at." She had her own bottle of bourbon between her knees and she wasn't sharing it either. She looked as if she'd have liked to offer me a belt, but saw the danger of such precedent.

Outside in the bar, somebody had discovered a way to turn up the jukebox, which now pounded out bass guitar and drums maniacally, while leaving every note above middle C entirely to the imagination. A woman it took me a minute to recognize as Marion asked me to dance to Fleetwood Mac and her breasts had the same slow, hypnotic motion that had put me to sleep that night in the Big Bend Hunting Lodge.

"I guess your old boyfriend never tracked you down," I shouted above the music, remembering the reason she'd given me for coming to Mohawk in the first place.

"Nope," she said happily. "His trackin' days are done."

Then she added, by way of explanation, just in case I hadn't put two and two together, "They gave him the chair."

I nodded, as if to suggest that I had been hip to her meaning all along, though I hadn't.

"I guess you heard about Drew Littler," she said.

I said I had.

"He left me a present, the rat. Not that I should complain. A child's about the most meanin'ful thing there is in life. His mother, I swear she loves the little birdbrain even more than me. You know Drew's momma? She's around here someplace. I asked her to babysit so I could come, and tonight's the first time she's ever said no."

I said I knew Eileen.

"Sometimes she even gives me money to help out," she went on, studying me as she spoke, as if she was trying to remember whether I owed her from the night at the Big Bend.

I got away from Marion as soon as I decently could. By putting the best possible face on things, she had driven my spirits into another slough. I found Wussy behind the bar with Mike washing glasses. Mike stopped to survey the damages already sustained along with those projected, and looked surprisingly satisfied, as if he'd have been disappointed to get off easily. When no one was looking he pulled out a dusty bottle of Napoleon brandy from under the sink, and poured shots for Wussy and himself and me. We drank a silent toast.

"You better hit the road, Sam's Kid," Wussy said. "Last I heard Roy Heinz was looking for you. Him and Tree are rounding up a posse to go rescue your old man's remains out of the hospital. They'd like you to go along."

"Somebody ought to tell them that's not such a great idea," I said.

"They'll never make Albany," Wussy said. "I saw the crew they got signed on and I doubt a one of them's ever *been* to Albany."

Mike looked more worried. "Anybody can find Albany," he said.

Wussy shook his head. "Not in the dark."

Then he added, "What they need is Sammy. If he was here to lead the troops, they'd end up in Montreal. I don't know who'll lead us astray now."

On the way out I stopped to look at the snapshots that people had been putting up with thumbtacks on the bulletin board. About half of them I'd've liked to swipe, but I took only the one that had been published in the *Mohawk Republican* in 1960, that first winter I'd lived with my father, where I appeared to be holding the white convertible about a foot and a half off the snowy pavement with one finger. In the newspaper the photograph had been grainy, but here the original was clear and I saw in it now what hadn't been clear before. My father had instructed me to mug for the camera, which I did, but not Sam Hall. He had one hand on my shoulder and was looking down at me proudly, as if he believed me to be truly capable of wondrous things.

I had intended to stay the night in Mohawk, but decided against the idea, preferring to spend the night in the Albany Airport if I had to. But luck was with me. There was a red-eye flight to the city and I walked right on. A message in my wife's small hand awaited me on the refrigerator door when I arrived. I went directly to the hospital where I found Leigh, looking tired but beautiful, the kind of girl who could flat-out corner the pussy market. She had the baby on her breast, and she turned it over so I could see my son's little stem. It was a touching moment.

ABOUT THE AUTHOR

RICHARD RUSSO did his graduate studies at the University of Arizona and now teaches fiction writing at Southern Illinois University in Carbondale, where he lives with his wife, Barbara, and their two daughters. His first novel, *Mohawk*, was published in 1986. He is currently at work on a new novel.

V I N T A G E
CONTEMPORARIES

V I N T A G E
CONTEMPORARIES